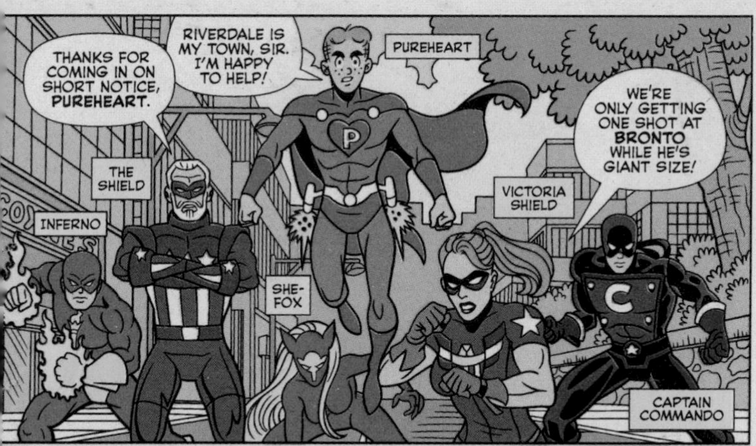
THANKS FOR COMING IN ON SHORT NOTICE, PUREHEART.
RIVERDALE IS MY TOWN, SIR. I'M HAPPY TO HELP!
PUREHEART
WE'RE ONLY GETTING ONE SHOT AT BRONTO WHILE HE'S GIANT SIZE!
THE SHIELD
INFERNO
VICTORIA SHIELD
SHE-FOX
CAPTAIN COMMANDO

THE CRUSADERS® in CHAIN of COMMAND

A TEAM OF UNLIKELY ALLIES BROUGHT TOGETHER BY THEIR HEROIC AMBITIONS! THEIR MULTI-GENERATIONAL CRUSADE: TO RID THE WORLD OF EVIL!

IAN FLYNN WRITER | STEVEN BUTLER PENCILS & LILY BUTLER INKS | GLENN WHITMORE COLORS | JACK MORELLI LETTERS

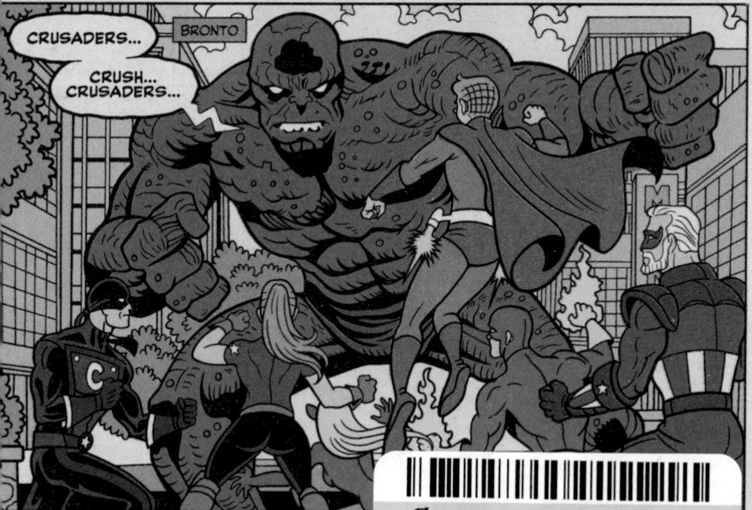
CRUSADERS...
BRONTO
CRUSH... CRUSADERS...

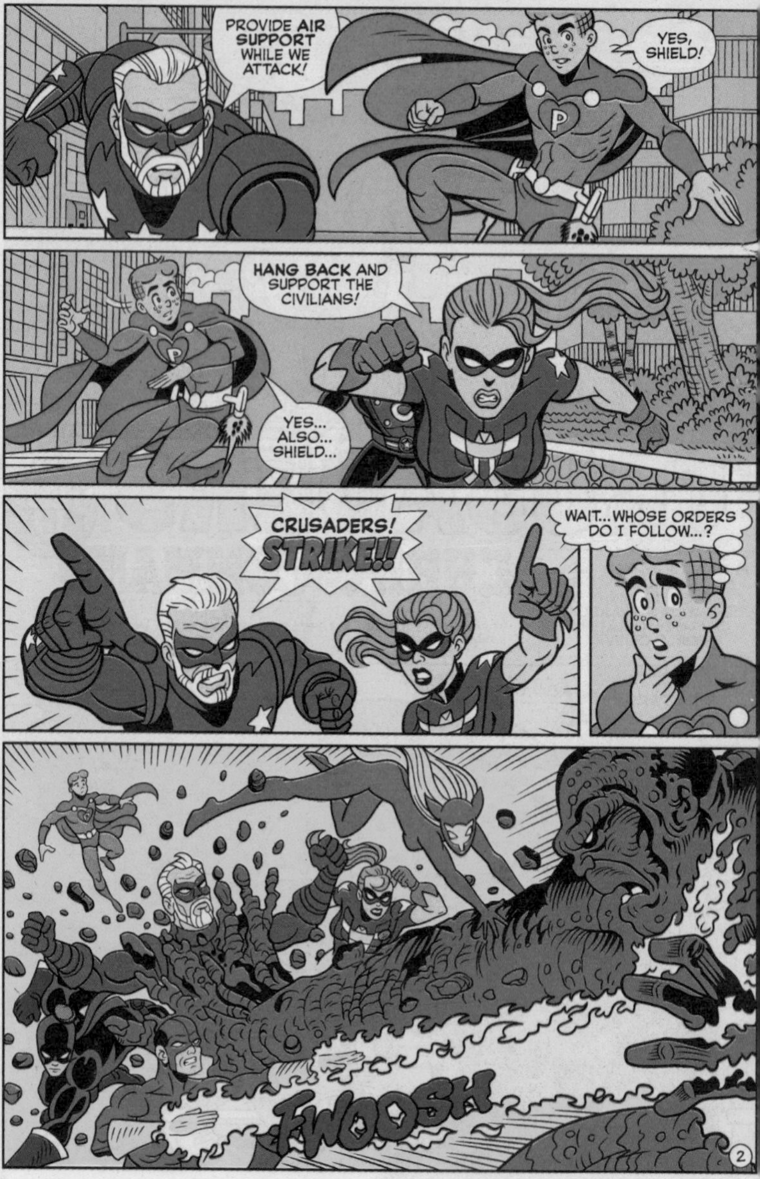
PROVIDE AIR SUPPORT WHILE WE ATTACK!
YES, SHIELD!
HANG BACK AND SUPPORT THE CIVILIANS!
YES... ALSO... SHIELD...
CRUSADERS! STRIKE!!
WAIT...WHOSE ORDERS DO I FOLLOW...?
FWOOSH
2

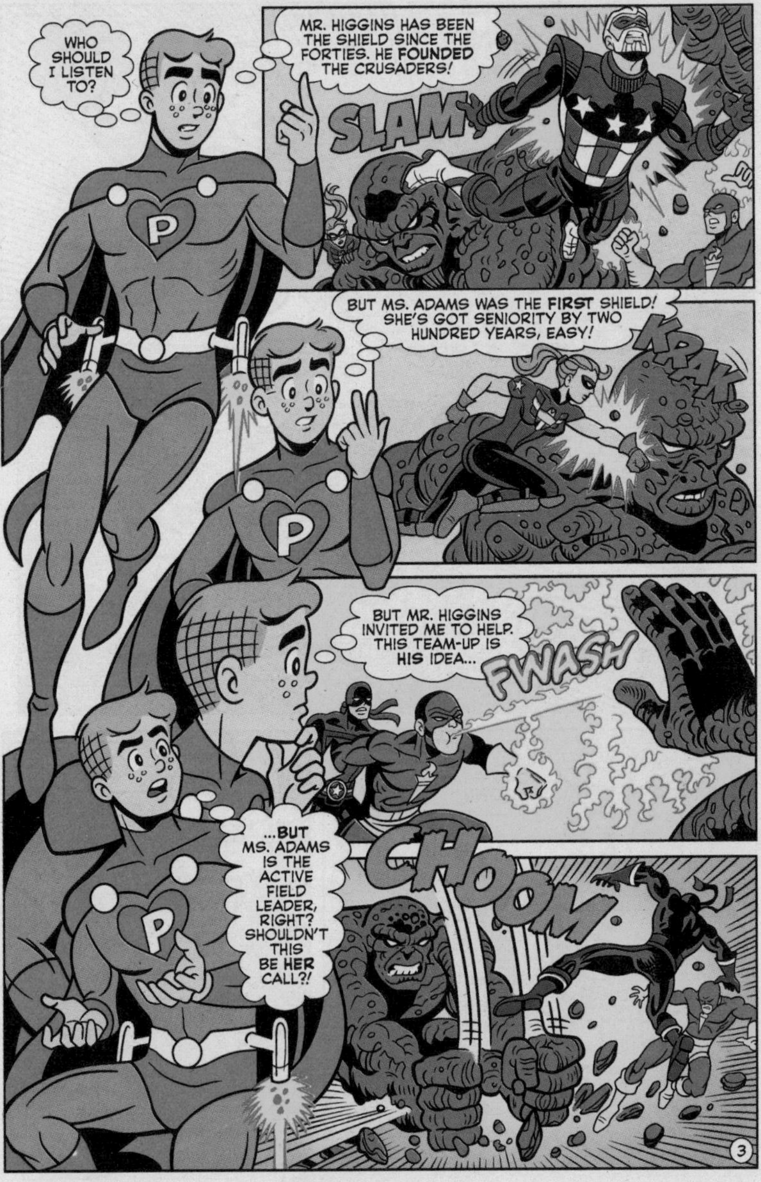
WHO SHOULD I LISTEN TO?
MR. HIGGINS HAS BEEN THE SHIELD SINCE THE FORTIES. HE FOUNDED THE CRUSADERS!
SLAM
BUT MS. ADAMS WAS THE FIRST SHIELD! SHE'S GOT SENIORITY BY TWO HUNDRED YEARS, EASY!
KRAK
BUT MR. HIGGINS INVITED ME TO HELP. THIS TEAM-UP IS HIS IDEA...
FWASH
...BUT MS. ADAMS IS THE ACTIVE FIELD LEADER, RIGHT? SHOULDN'T THIS BE HER CALL?!
CHOOOM
3

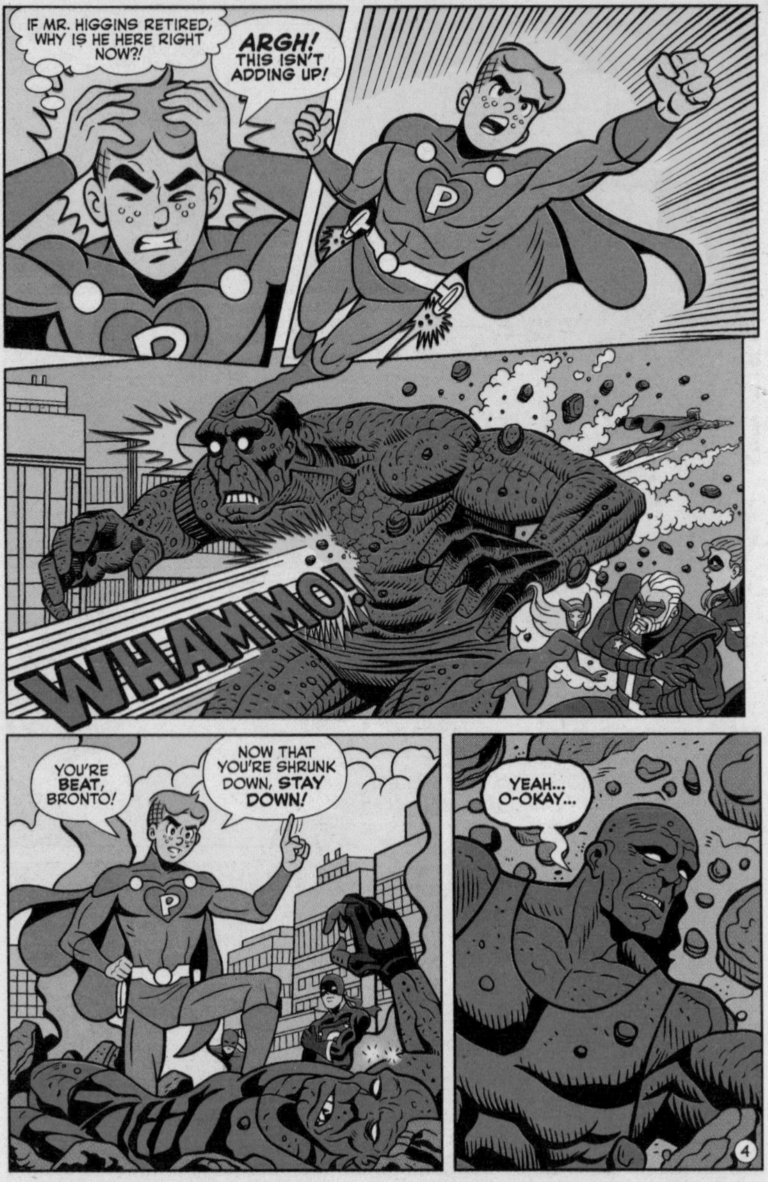
IF MR. HIGGINS RETIRED, WHY IS HE HERE RIGHT NOW?!
ARGH! THIS ISN'T ADDING UP!
WHAMMO!
YOU'RE BEAT, BRONTO!
NOW THAT YOU'RE SHRUNK DOWN, STAY DOWN!
YEAH... O-OKAY...

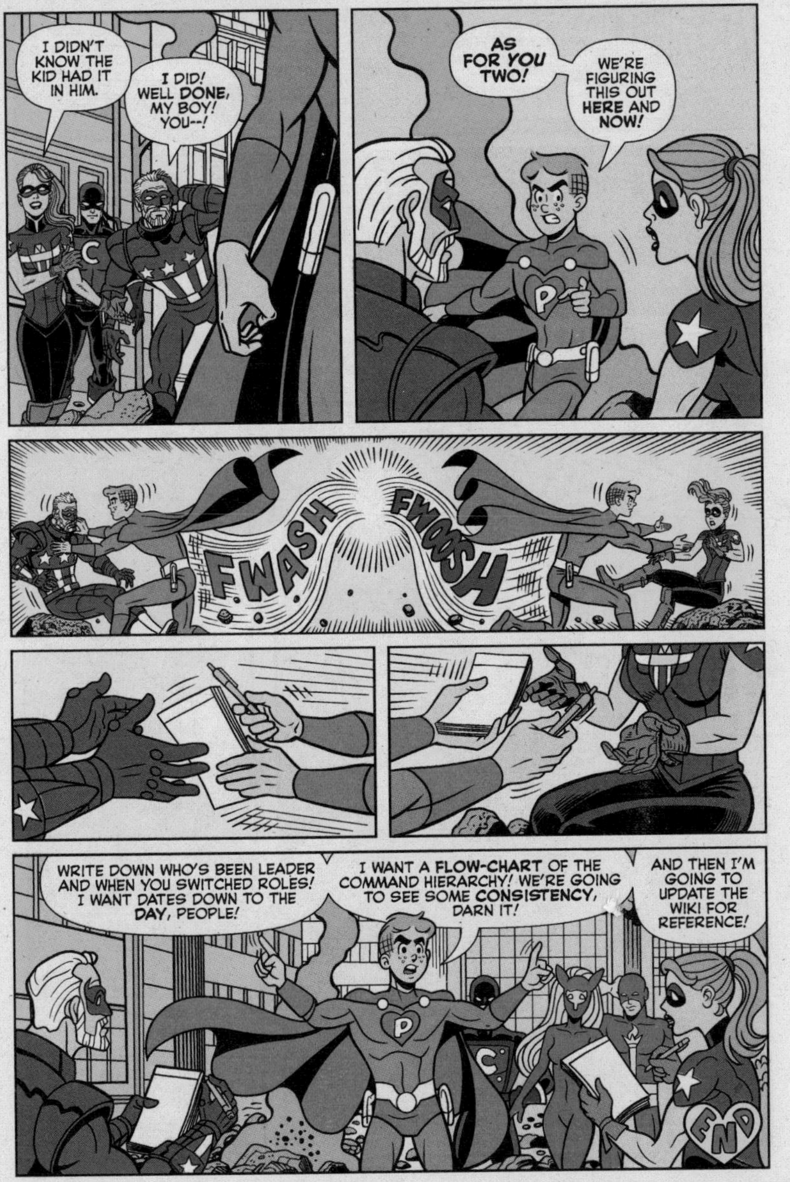
I DIDN'T KNOW THE KID HAD IT IN HIM.
I DID! WELL DONE, MY BOY! YOU--!
AS FOR YOU TWO!
WE'RE FIGURING THIS OUT HERE AND NOW!
FWASH
FWOOSH
WRITE DOWN WHO'S BEEN LEADER AND WHEN YOU SWITCHED ROLES! I WANT DATES DOWN TO THE DAY, PEOPLE!
I WANT A FLOW-CHART OF THE COMMAND HIERARCHY! WE'RE GOING TO SEE SOME CONSISTENCY, DARN IT!
AND THEN I'M GOING TO UPDATE THE WIKI FOR REFERENCE!
END

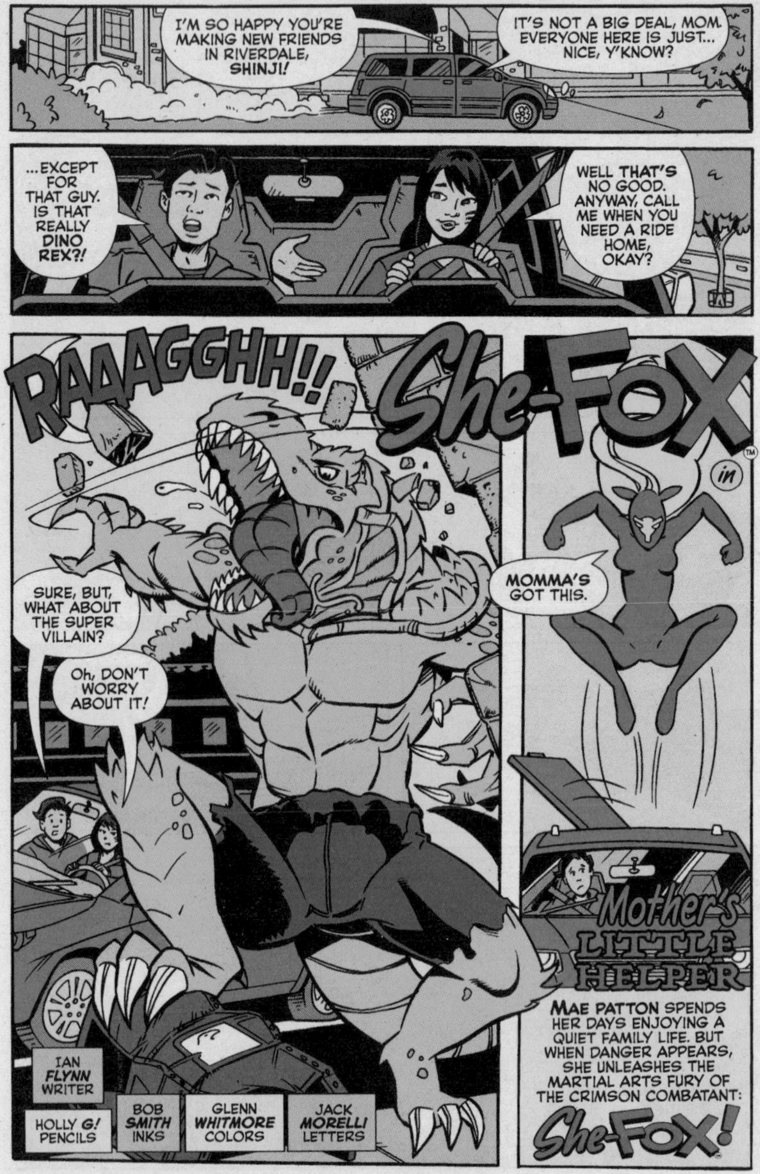
I'M SO HAPPY YOU'RE MAKING NEW FRIENDS IN RIVERDALE, SHINJI!
IT'S NOT A BIG DEAL, MOM. EVERYONE HERE IS JUST... NICE, Y'KNOW?
...EXCEPT FOR THAT GUY. IS THAT REALLY DINO REX?!
WELL THAT'S NO GOOD. ANYWAY, CALL ME WHEN YOU NEED A RIDE HOME, OKAY?
RAAAGGHH!!
She-FOX™ in
SURE, BUT, WHAT ABOUT THE SUPER VILLAIN?
Oh, DON'T WORRY ABOUT IT!
MOMMA'S GOT THIS.
Mother's LITTLE HELPER
MAE PATTON SPENDS HER DAYS ENJOYING A QUIET FAMILY LIFE. BUT WHEN DANGER APPEARS, SHE UNLEASHES THE MARTIAL ARTS FURY OF THE CRIMSON COMBATANT: She-FOX!™
IAN FLYNN WRITER
HOLLY G! PENCILS
BOB SMITH INKS
GLENN WHITMORE COLORS
JACK MORELLI LETTERS

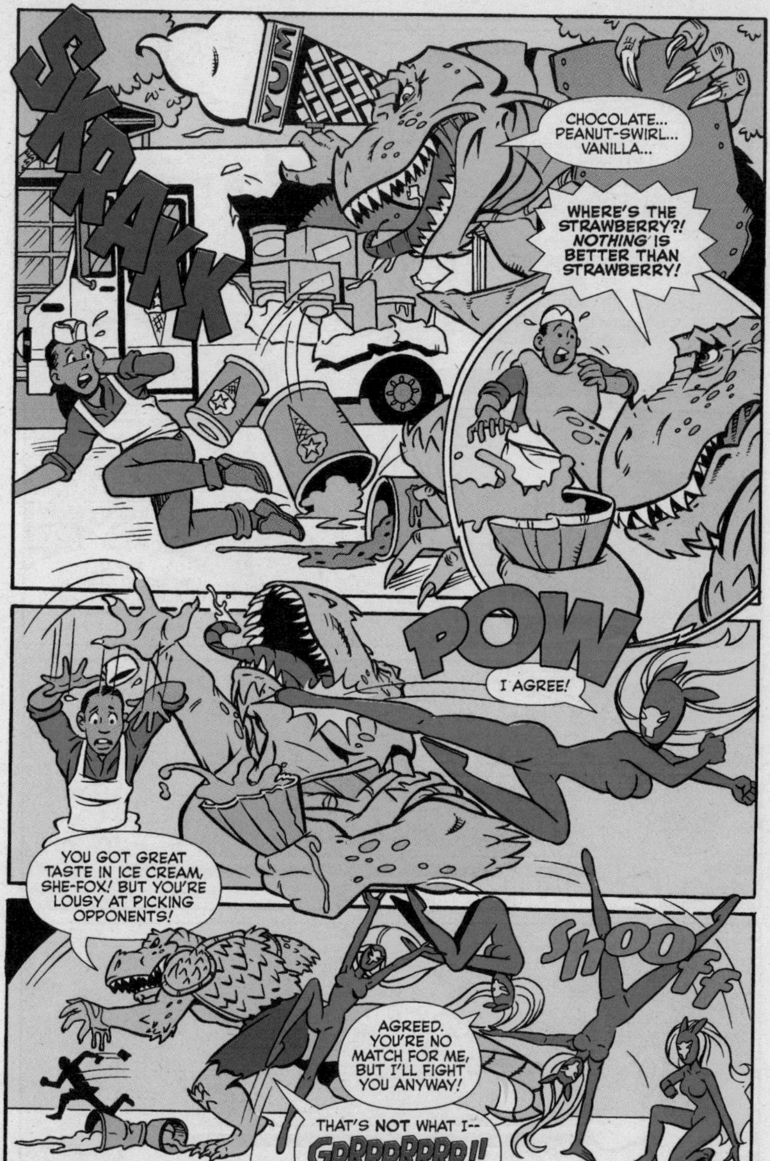
SKRAKK
YUM
CHOCOLATE... PEANUT-SWIRL... VANILLA...
WHERE'S THE STRAWBERRY?! *NOTHING* IS BETTER THAN STRAWBERRY!
POW
I AGREE!
YOU GOT GREAT TASTE IN ICE CREAM, SHE-FOX! BUT YOU'RE LOUSY AT PICKING OPPONENTS!
shooff
AGREED. YOU'RE NO MATCH FOR ME, BUT I'LL FIGHT YOU ANYWAY!
THAT'S **NOT** WHAT I-- GRRRRRRRR!!

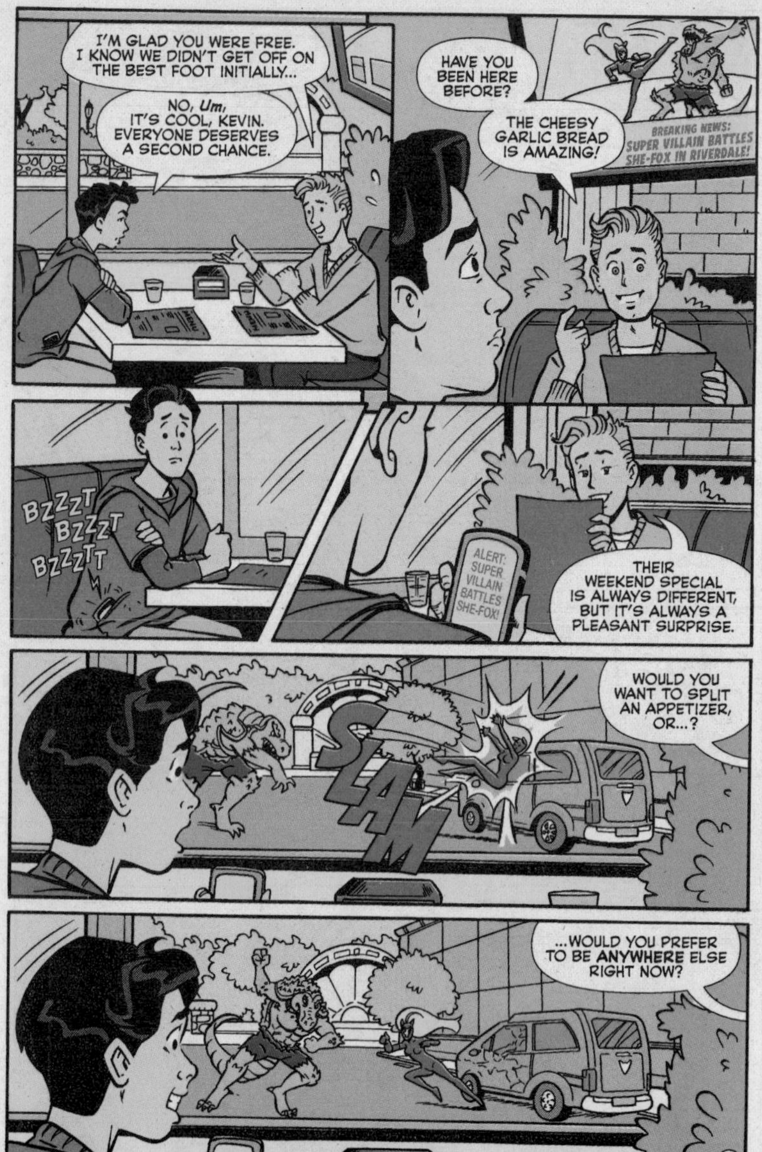

I'M GLAD YOU WERE FREE. I KNOW WE DIDN'T GET OFF ON THE BEST FOOT INITIALLY...
NO, *Um,* IT'S COOL, KEVIN. EVERYONE DESERVES A SECOND CHANCE.
MENU
MENU
BREAKING NEWS: SUPER VILLAIN BATTLES SHE-FOX IN RIVERDALE!
HAVE YOU BEEN HERE BEFORE?
THE CHEESY GARLIC BREAD IS AMAZING!
BZZZT BZZZT BZZZTT
ALERT: SUPER VILLAIN BATTLES SHE-FOX!
THEIR WEEKEND SPECIAL IS ALWAYS DIFFERENT, BUT IT'S ALWAYS A PLEASANT SURPRISE.
SLAM
WOULD YOU WANT TO SPLIT AN APPETIZER, OR...?
...WOULD YOU PREFER TO BE **ANYWHERE** ELSE RIGHT NOW?

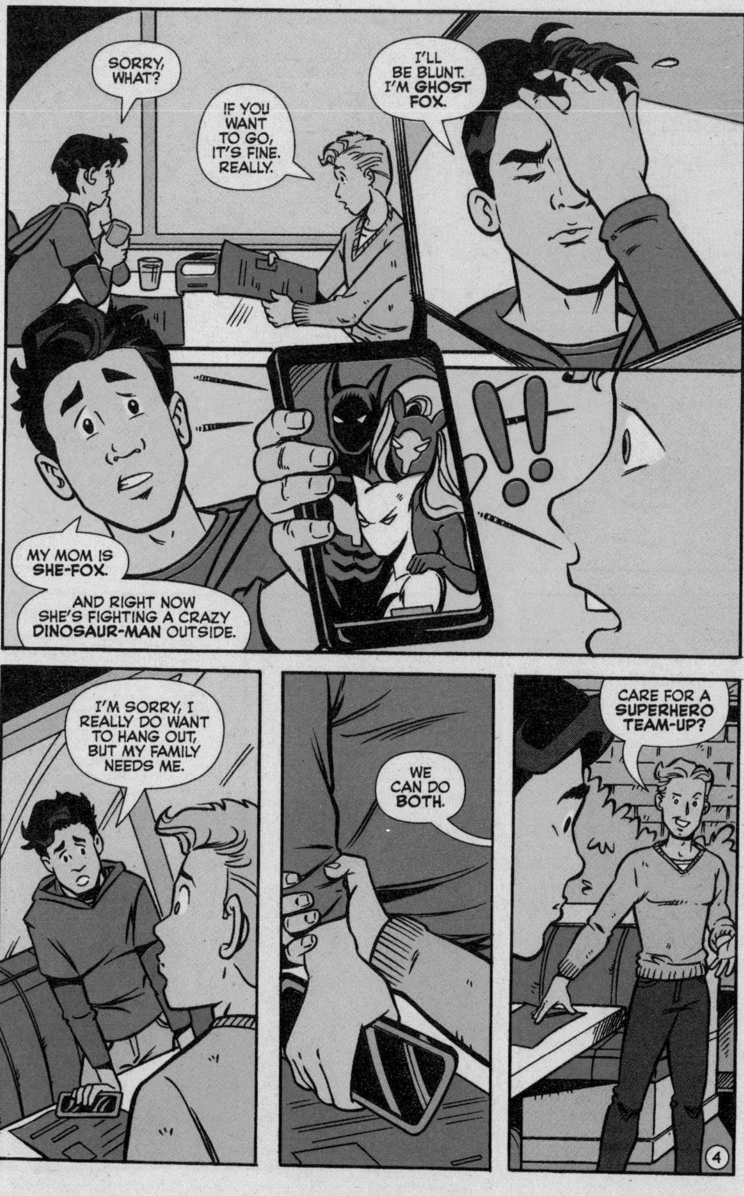
SORRY, WHAT?
IF YOU WANT TO GO, IT'S FINE. REALLY.
I'LL BE BLUNT. I'M GHOST FOX.
!!
MY MOM IS SHE-FOX.
AND RIGHT NOW SHE'S FIGHTING A CRAZY DINOSAUR-MAN OUTSIDE.
I'M SORRY, I REALLY DO WANT TO HANG OUT, BUT MY FAMILY NEEDS ME.
WE CAN DO BOTH.
CARE FOR A SUPERHERO TEAM-UP?

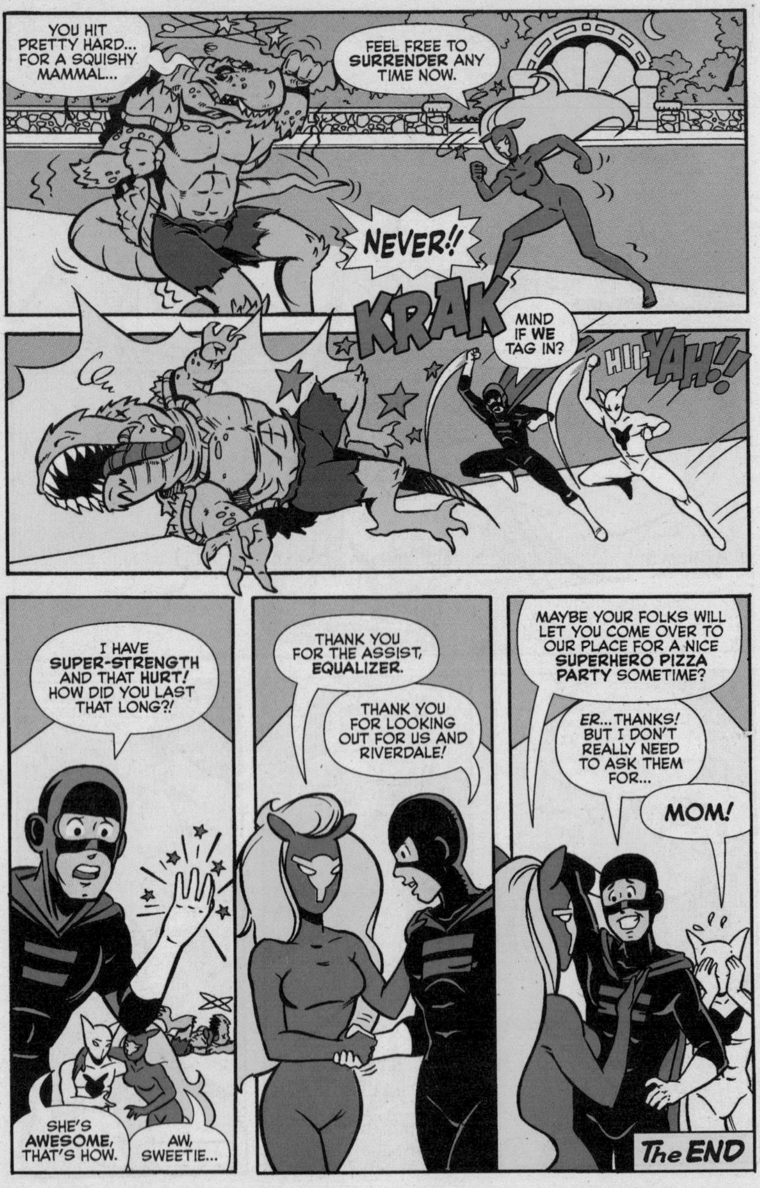

YOU HIT PRETTY HARD... FOR A SQUISHY MAMMAL...
FEEL FREE TO SURRENDER ANY TIME NOW.
NEVER!!
KRAK
MIND IF WE TAG IN?
HII-YAH!!
I HAVE SUPER-STRENGTH AND THAT HURT! HOW DID YOU LAST THAT LONG?!
SHE'S AWESOME, THAT'S HOW.
AW, SWEETIE...
THANK YOU FOR THE ASSIST, EQUALIZER.
THANK YOU FOR LOOKING OUT FOR US AND RIVERDALE!
MAYBE YOUR FOLKS WILL LET YOU COME OVER TO OUR PLACE FOR A NICE SUPERHERO PIZZA PARTY SOMETIME?
ER...THANKS! BUT I DON'T REALLY NEED TO ASK THEM FOR...
MOM!
The END

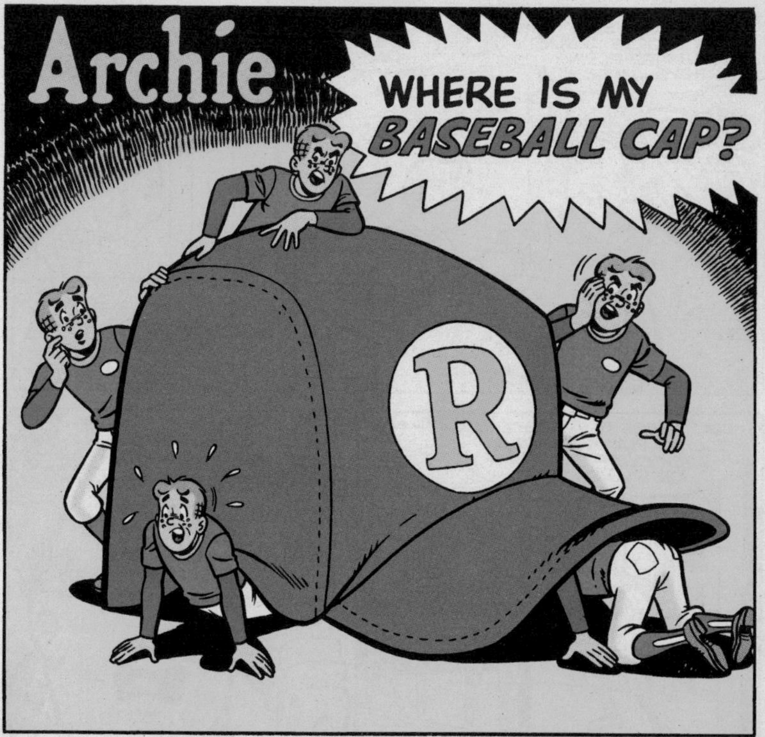
Archie
WHERE IS MY BASEBALL CAP?
R

Script & Pencils: Joe Edwards / Inks: Jon D'Agostino / Letters: Bill Yoshida

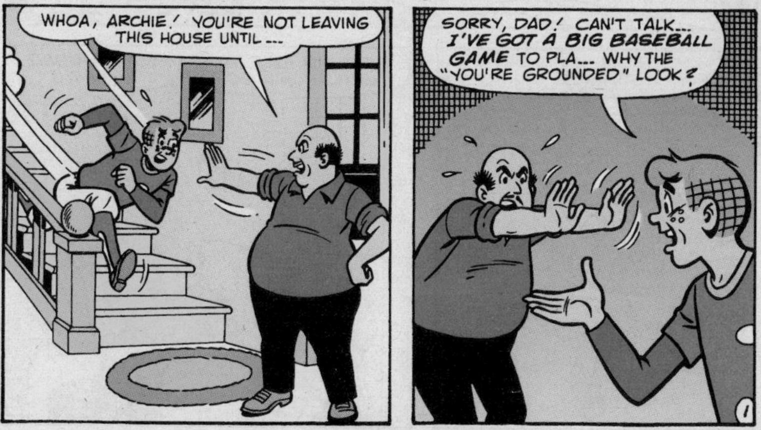
WHOA, ARCHIE! YOU'RE NOT LEAVING THIS HOUSE UNTIL ---
SORRY, DAD! CAN'T TALK... I'VE GOT A BIG BASEBALL GAME TO PLA... WHY THE "YOU'RE GROUNDED" LOOK?
1

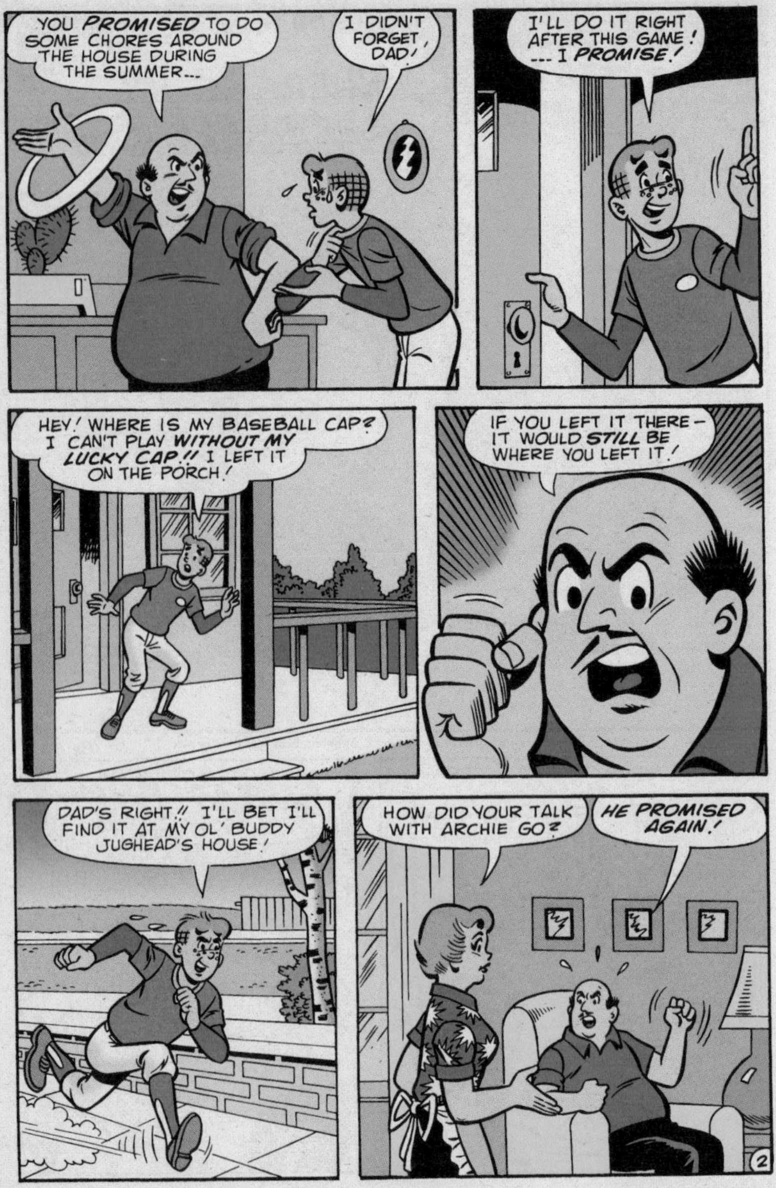
YOU PROMISED TO DO SOME CHORES AROUND THE HOUSE DURING THE SUMMER...
I DIDN'T FORGET, DAD!
I'LL DO IT RIGHT AFTER THIS GAME! --- I PROMISE!
HEY! WHERE IS MY BASEBALL CAP? I CAN'T PLAY WITHOUT MY LUCKY CAP!! I LEFT IT ON THE PORCH!
IF YOU LEFT IT THERE — IT WOULD STILL BE WHERE YOU LEFT IT!
DAD'S RIGHT!! I'LL BET I'LL FIND IT AT MY OL' BUDDY JUGHEAD'S HOUSE!
HOW DID YOUR TALK WITH ARCHIE GO?
HE PROMISED AGAIN!
2

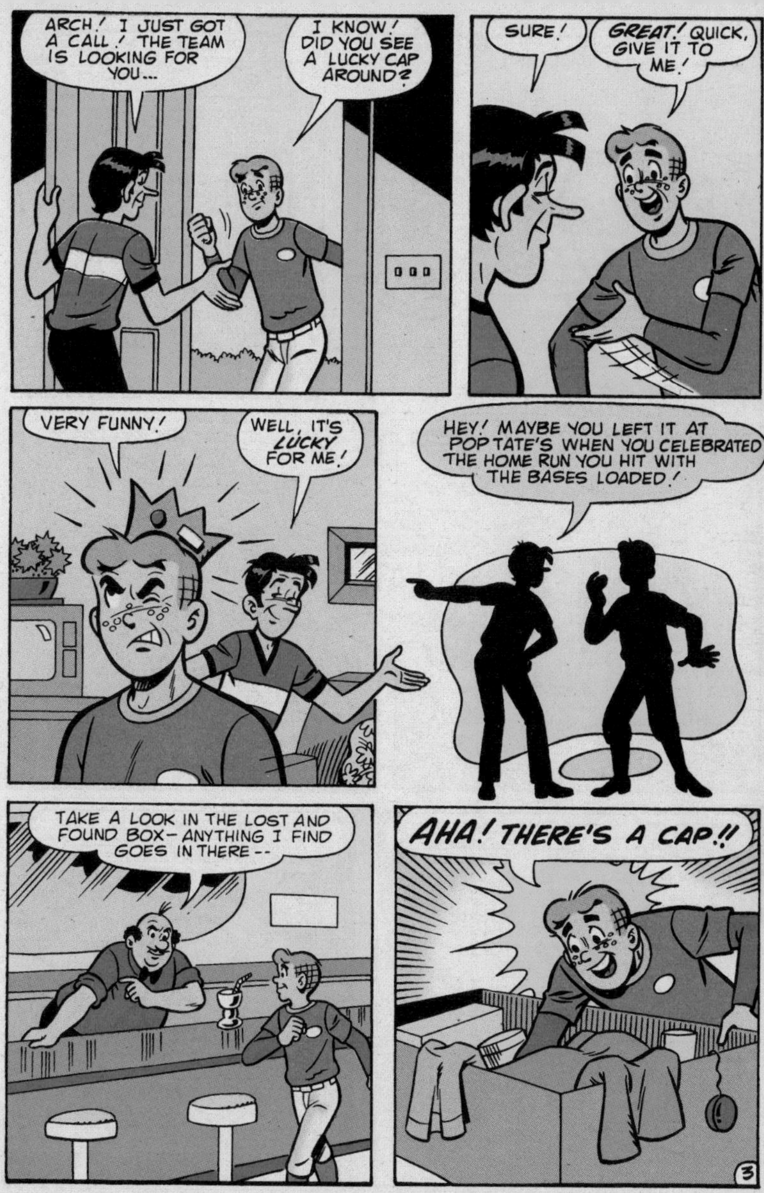
ARCH! I JUST GOT A CALL! THE TEAM IS LOOKING FOR YOU...
I KNOW! DID YOU SEE A LUCKY CAP AROUND?
SURE!
GREAT! QUICK, GIVE IT TO ME!
VERY FUNNY!
WELL, IT'S LUCKY FOR ME!
HEY! MAYBE YOU LEFT IT AT POP TATE'S WHEN YOU CELEBRATED THE HOME RUN YOU HIT WITH THE BASES LOADED!
TAKE A LOOK IN THE LOST AND FOUND BOX— ANYTHING I FIND GOES IN THERE--
AHA! THERE'S A CAP!!
3

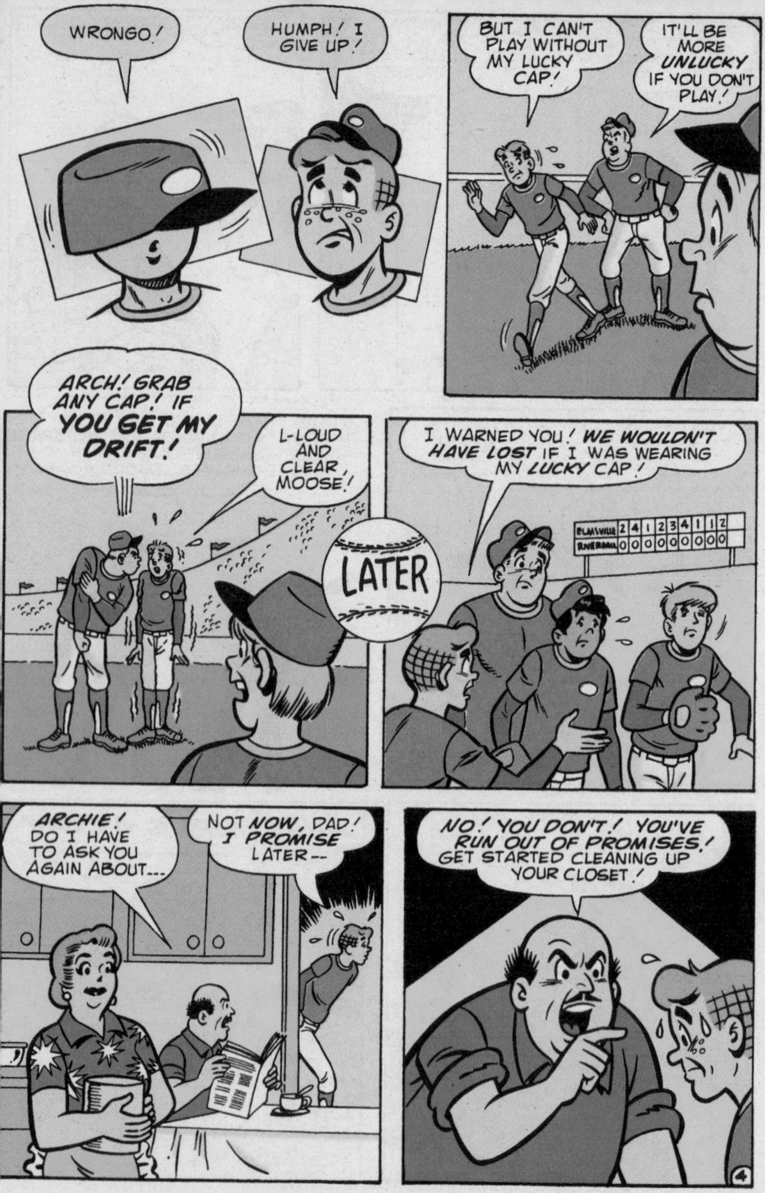
WRONGO!
HUMPH! I GIVE UP!
BUT I CAN'T PLAY WITHOUT MY LUCKY CAP!
IT'LL BE MORE UNLUCKY IF YOU DON'T PLAY!
ARCH! GRAB ANY CAP! IF YOU GET MY DRIFT!
L-LOUD AND CLEAR, MOOSE!
LATER
I WARNED YOU! WE WOULDN'T HAVE LOST IF I WAS WEARING MY LUCKY CAP!
ARCHIE! DO I HAVE TO ASK YOU AGAIN ABOUT...
NOT NOW, DAD! I PROMISE LATER--
NO! YOU DON'T! YOU'VE RUN OUT OF PROMISES! GET STARTED CLEANING UP YOUR CLOSET!

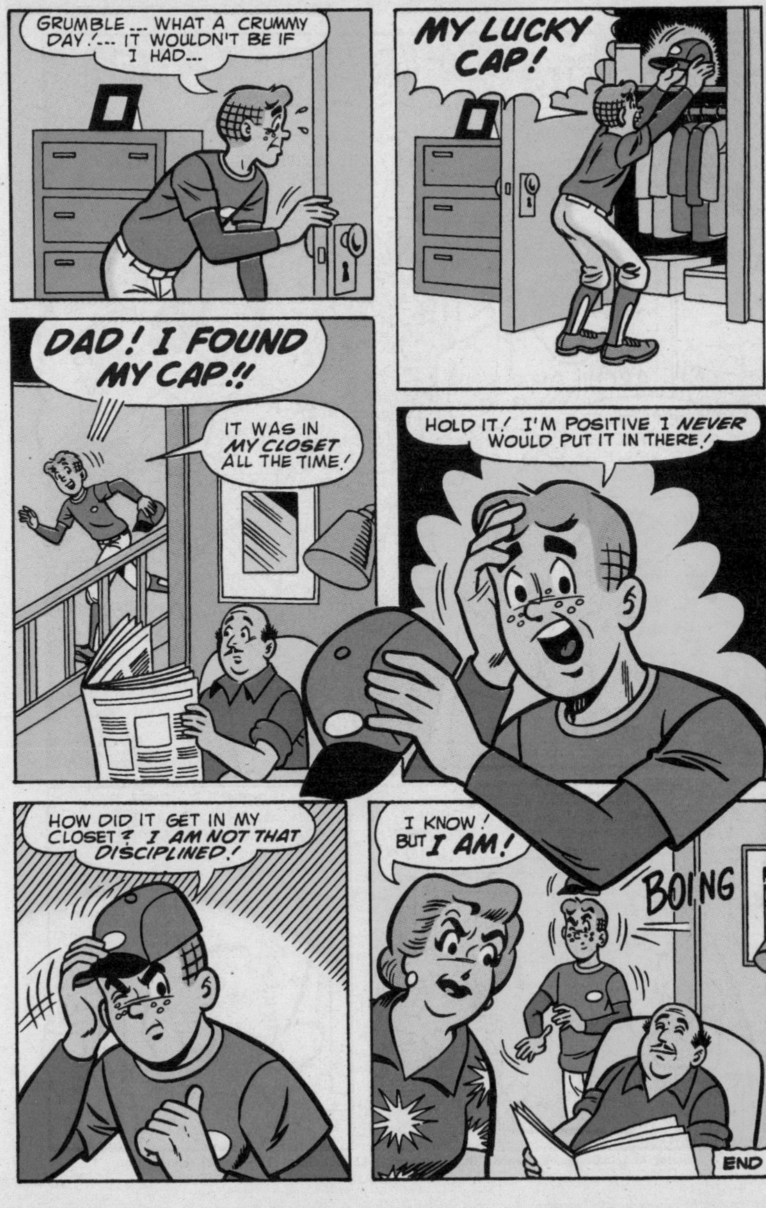
GRUMBLE... WHAT A CRUMMY DAY!... IT WOULDN'T BE IF I HAD...
MY LUCKY CAP!
DAD! I FOUND MY CAP!!
IT WAS IN MY CLOSET ALL THE TIME!
HOLD IT! I'M POSITIVE I NEVER WOULD PUT IT IN THERE!
HOW DID IT GET IN MY CLOSET? I AM NOT THAT DISCIPLINED!
I KNOW! BUT I AM!
BOING
END

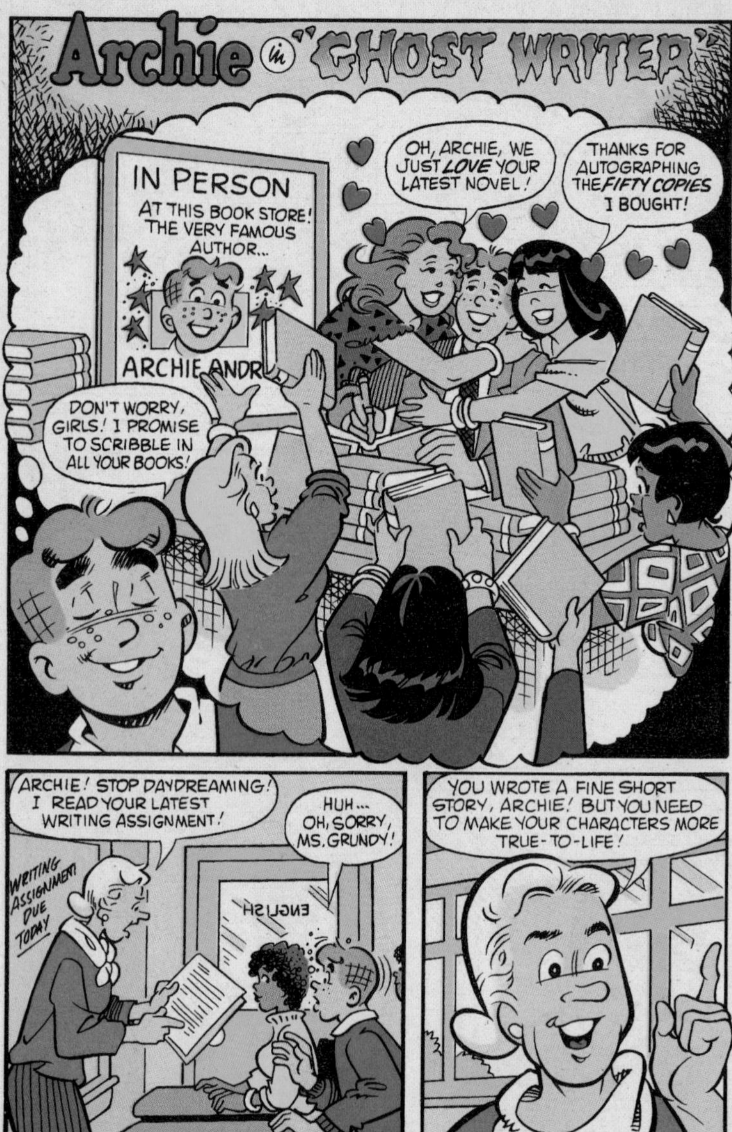
Archie in "GHOST WRITER"
IN PERSON
AT THIS BOOK STORE! THE VERY FAMOUS AUTHOR...
ARCHIE ANDR
OH, ARCHIE, WE JUST LOVE YOUR LATEST NOVEL!
THANKS FOR AUTOGRAPHING THE FIFTY COPIES I BOUGHT!
DON'T WORRY, GIRLS! I PROMISE TO SCRIBBLE IN ALL YOUR BOOKS!
ARCHIE! STOP DAYDREAMING! I READ YOUR LATEST WRITING ASSIGNMENT!
HUH... OH, SORRY, MS. GRUNDY!
WRITING ASSIGNMENT DUE TODAY
YOU WROTE A FINE SHORT STORY, ARCHIE! BUT YOU NEED TO MAKE YOUR CHARACTERS MORE TRUE-TO-LIFE!

Script: Angelo DeCesare / Pencils: Stan Goldberg / Inks: Bob Smith / Letters: Bill Yoshida

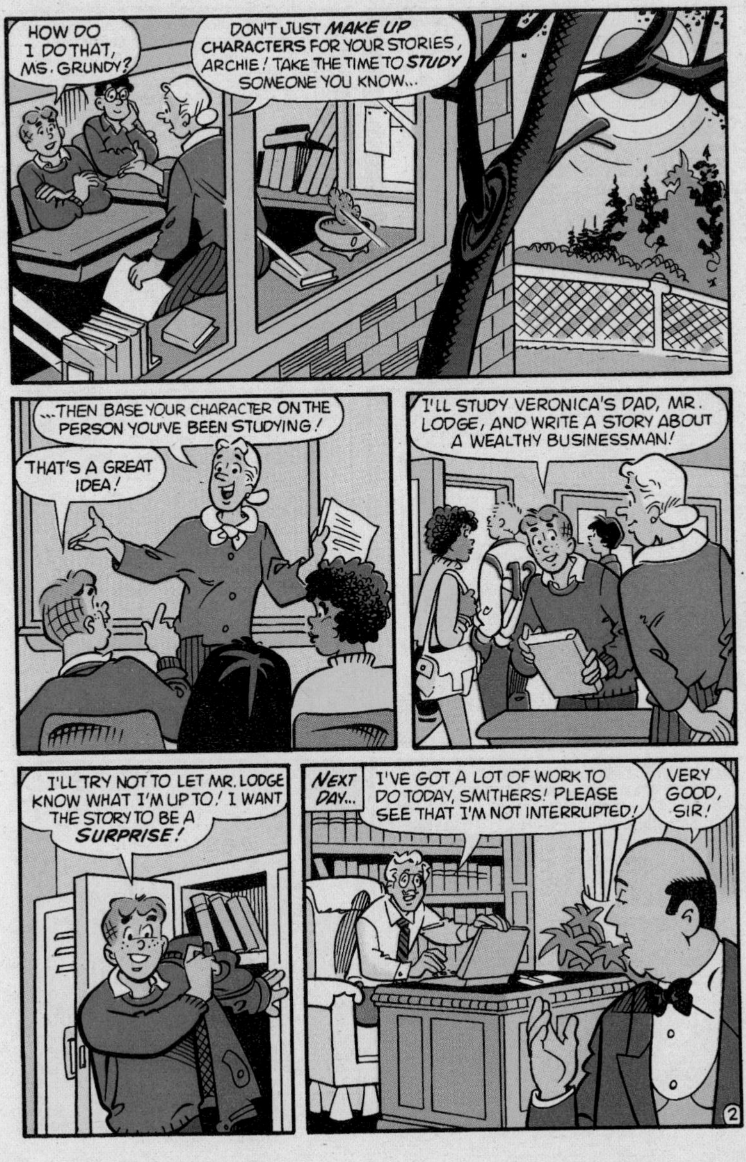
HOW DO I DO THAT, MS. GRUNDY?
DON'T JUST MAKE UP CHARACTERS FOR YOUR STORIES, ARCHIE! TAKE THE TIME TO STUDY SOMEONE YOU KNOW...
...THEN BASE YOUR CHARACTER ON THE PERSON YOU'VE BEEN STUDYING!
THAT'S A GREAT IDEA!
I'LL STUDY VERONICA'S DAD, MR. LODGE, AND WRITE A STORY ABOUT A WEALTHY BUSINESSMAN!
I'LL TRY NOT TO LET MR. LODGE KNOW WHAT I'M UP TO! I WANT THE STORY TO BE A SURPRISE!
NEXT DAY...
I'VE GOT A LOT OF WORK TO DO TODAY, SMITHERS! PLEASE SEE THAT I'M NOT INTERRUPTED!
VERY GOOD, SIR!
2

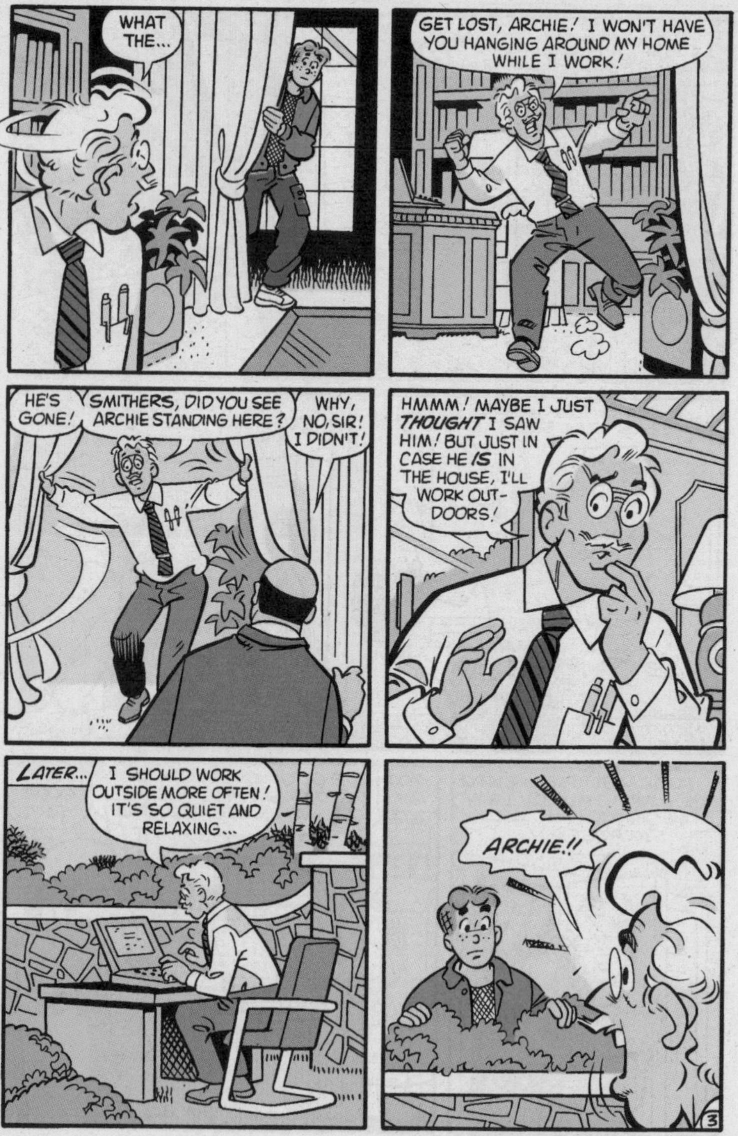
WHAT THE...
GET LOST, ARCHIE! I WON'T HAVE YOU HANGING AROUND MY HOME WHILE I WORK!
HE'S GONE!
SMITHERS, DID YOU SEE ARCHIE STANDING HERE?
WHY, NO, SIR! I DIDN'T!
HMMM! MAYBE I JUST THOUGHT I SAW HIM! BUT JUST IN CASE HE IS IN THE HOUSE, I'LL WORK OUT-DOORS!
LATER...
I SHOULD WORK OUTSIDE MORE OFTEN! IT'S SO QUIET AND RELAXING...
ARCHIE!!
3

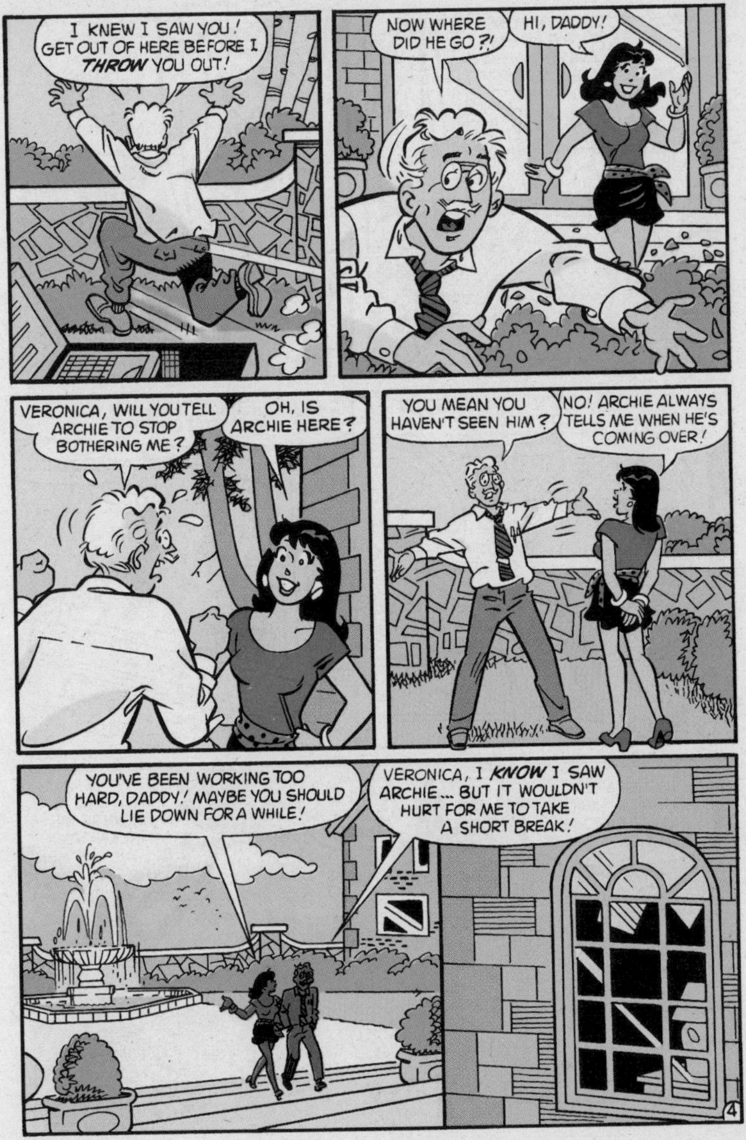

I KNEW I SAW YOU! GET OUT OF HERE BEFORE I *THROW* YOU OUT!
NOW WHERE DID HE GO?!
HI, DADDY!
VERONICA, WILL YOU TELL ARCHIE TO STOP BOTHERING ME?
OH, IS ARCHIE HERE?
YOU MEAN YOU HAVEN'T SEEN HIM?
NO! ARCHIE ALWAYS TELLS ME WHEN HE'S COMING OVER!
YOU'VE BEEN WORKING TOO HARD, DADDY! MAYBE YOU SHOULD LIE DOWN FOR A WHILE!
VERONICA, I *KNOW* I SAW ARCHIE... BUT IT WOULDN'T HURT FOR ME TO TAKE A SHORT BREAK!
4

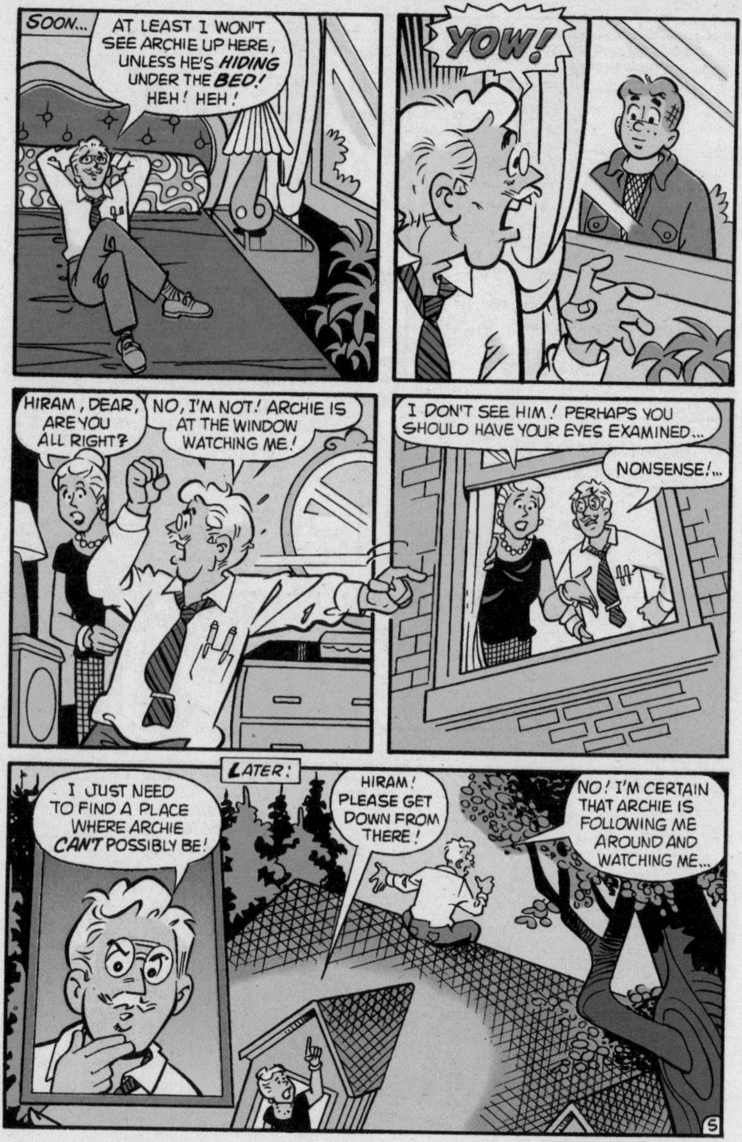
SOON...
AT LEAST I WON'T SEE ARCHIE UP HERE, UNLESS HE'S *HIDING* UNDER THE *BED!* HEH! HEH!
YOW!
HIRAM, DEAR, ARE YOU ALL RIGHT?
NO, I'M NOT! ARCHIE IS AT THE WINDOW WATCHING ME.!
I DON'T SEE HIM! PERHAPS YOU SHOULD HAVE YOUR EYES EXAMINED...
NONSENSE!...
LATER:
I JUST NEED TO FIND A PLACE WHERE ARCHIE *CAN'T* POSSIBLY BE!
HIRAM! PLEASE GET DOWN FROM THERE!
NO! I'M CERTAIN THAT ARCHIE IS FOLLOWING ME AROUND AND WATCHING ME...
5

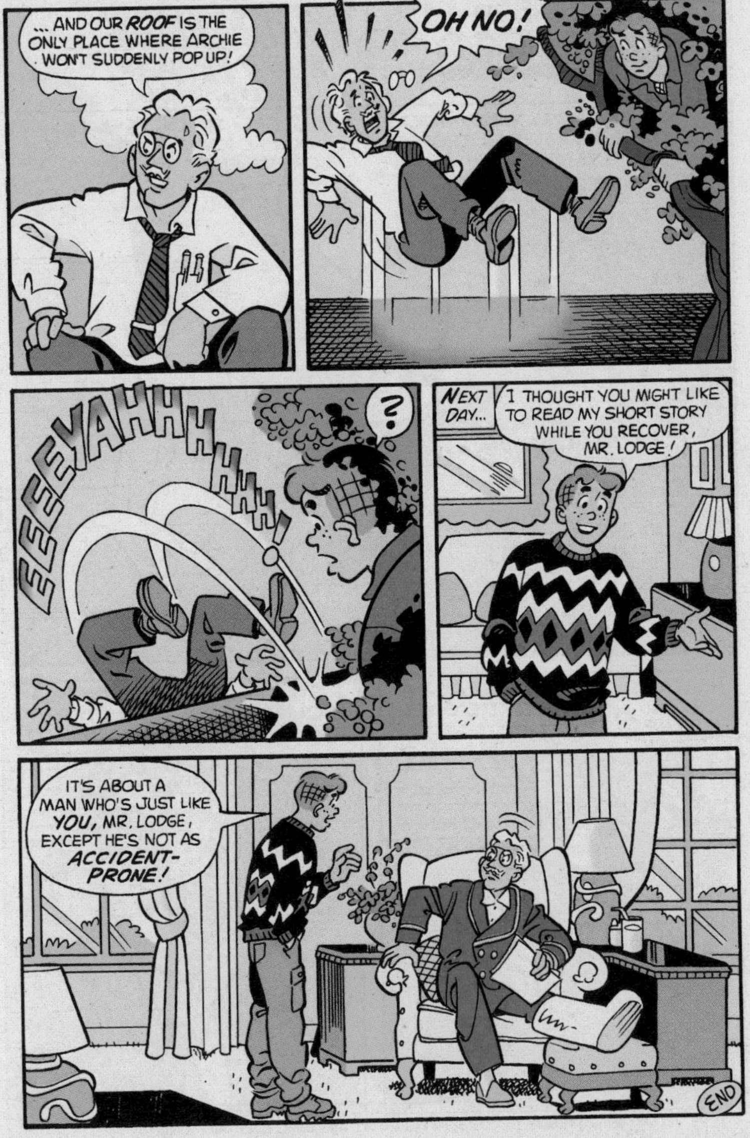
... AND OUR ROOF IS THE ONLY PLACE WHERE ARCHIE WON'T SUDDENLY POP UP!
OH NO!
EEEEYAHHHHHHH!
?
NEXT DAY...
I THOUGHT YOU MIGHT LIKE TO READ MY SHORT STORY WHILE YOU RECOVER, MR. LODGE!
IT'S ABOUT A MAN WHO'S JUST LIKE YOU, MR. LODGE, EXCEPT HE'S NOT AS ACCIDENT-PRONE!
END

Archie in "HIDDEN TALENT"

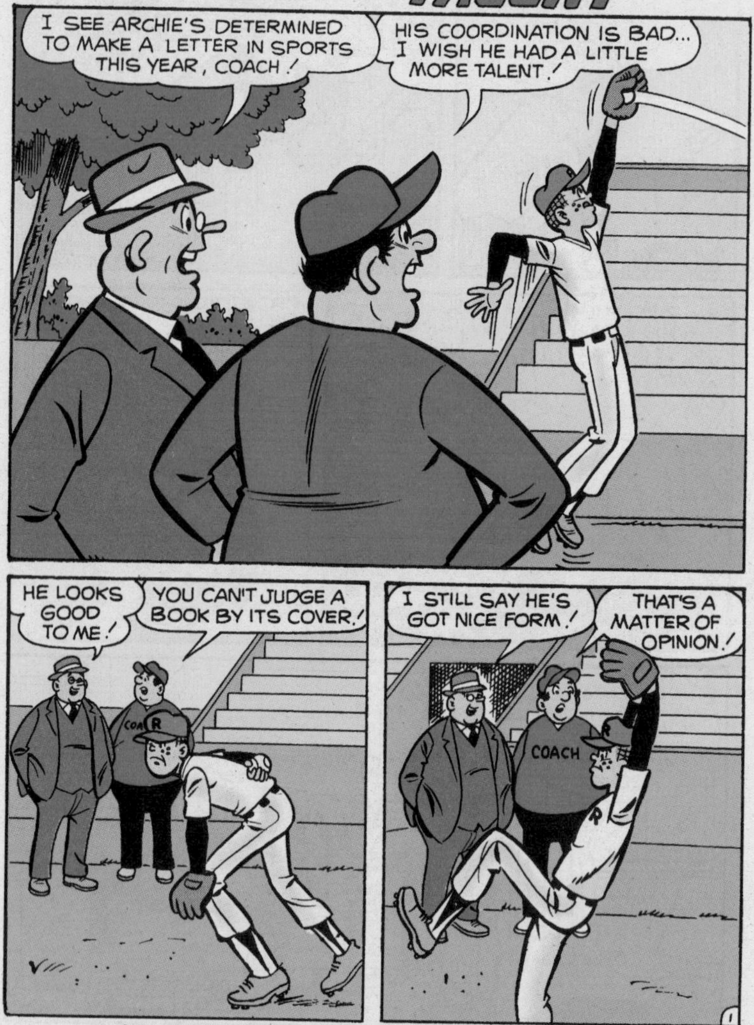
I SEE ARCHIE'S DETERMINED TO MAKE A LETTER IN SPORTS THIS YEAR, COACH!
HIS COORDINATION IS BAD... I WISH HE HAD A LITTLE MORE TALENT!
HE LOOKS GOOD TO ME!
YOU CAN'T JUDGE A BOOK BY ITS COVER!
I STILL SAY HE'S GOT NICE FORM!
THAT'S A MATTER OF OPINION!
COACH
1

Script & Pencils: Dick Malmgren / Inks: Jon D'Agostino / Letters: Bill Yoshida

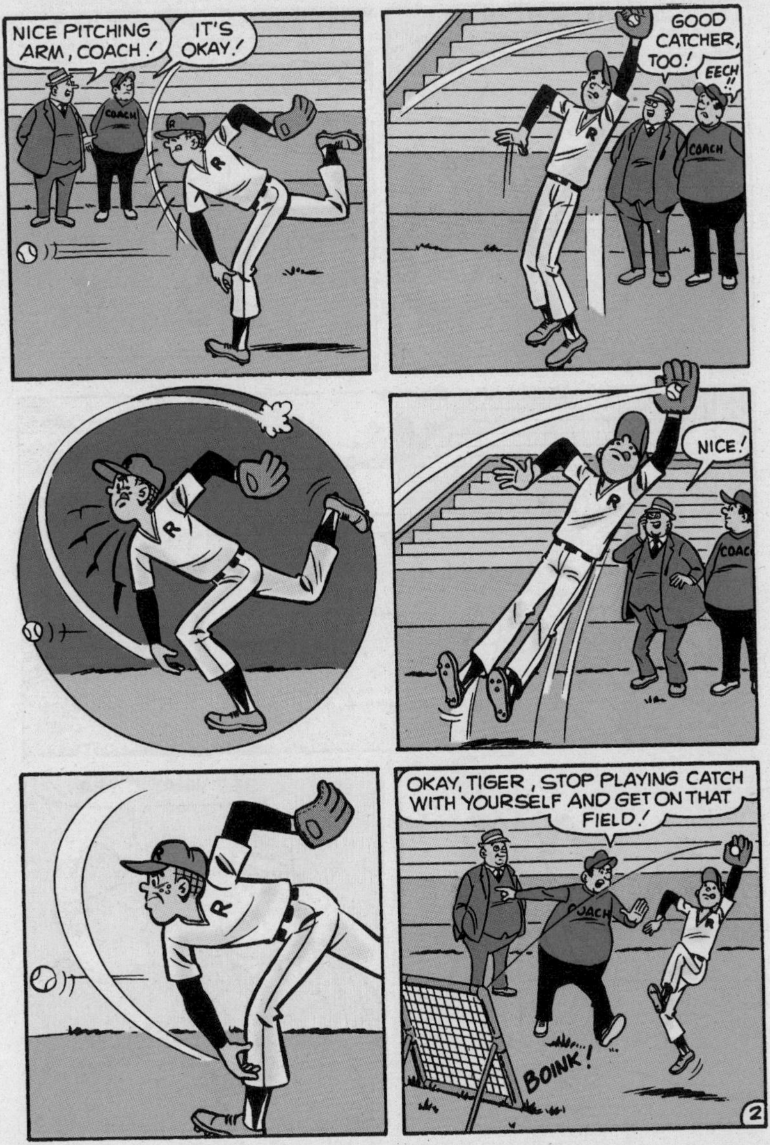
NICE PITCHING ARM, COACH!
IT'S OKAY!
GOOD CATCHER, TOO!
EECH!!
NICE!
OKAY, TIGER, STOP PLAYING CATCH WITH YOURSELF AND GET ON THAT FIELD!
BOINK!
2

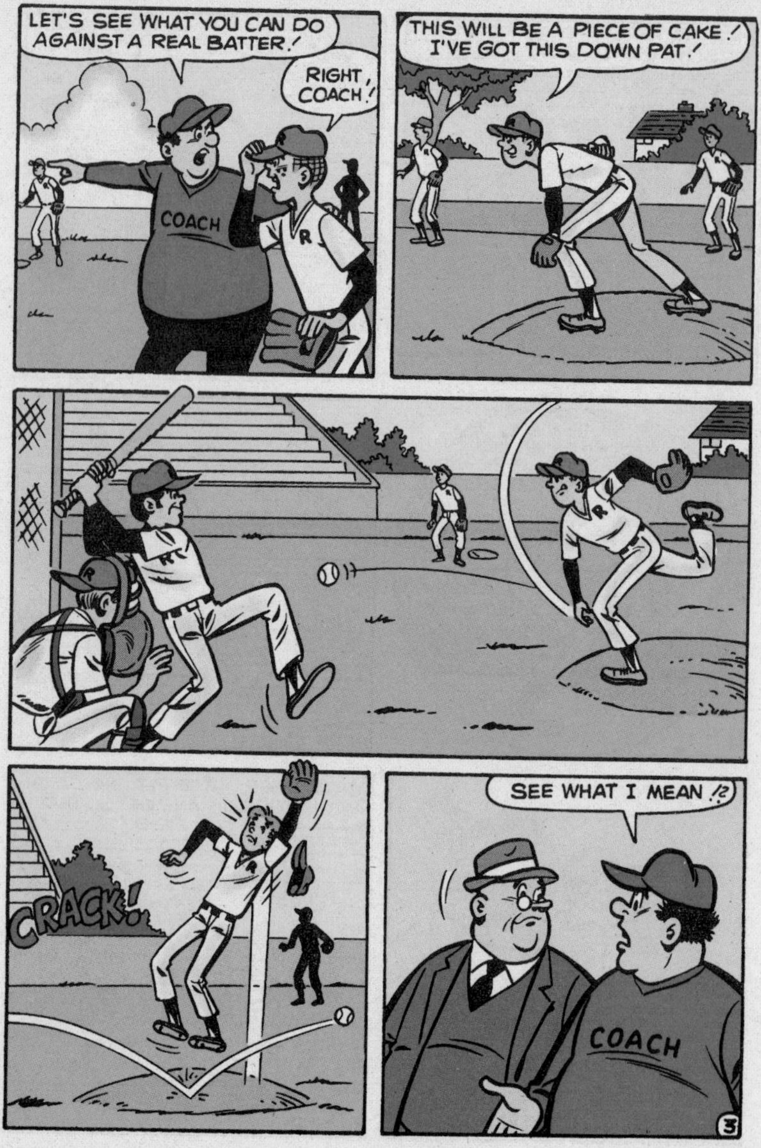
LET'S SEE WHAT YOU CAN DO AGAINST A REAL BATTER!
RIGHT, COACH!
COACH
THIS WILL BE A PIECE OF CAKE! I'VE GOT THIS DOWN PAT!
CRACK!
SEE WHAT I MEAN!?
COACH
3

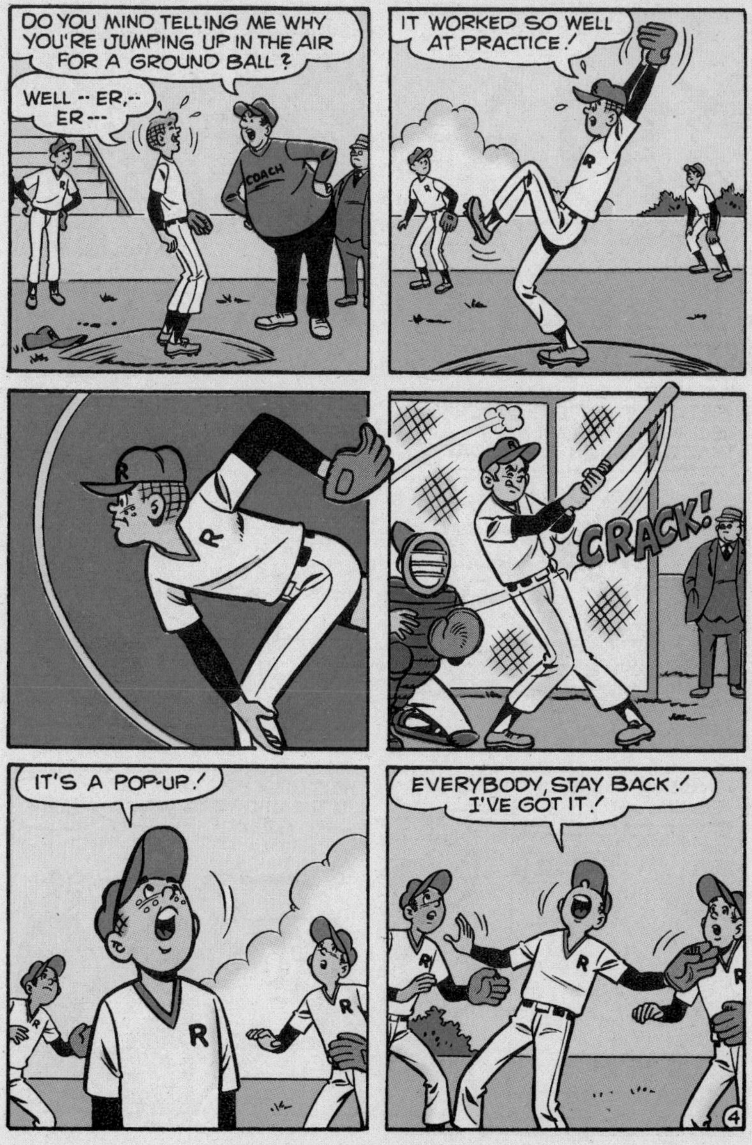
DO YOU MIND TELLING ME WHY YOU'RE JUMPING UP IN THE AIR FOR A GROUND BALL ?
WELL -- ER,-- ER ---
COACH
IT WORKED SO WELL AT PRACTICE !
CRACK!
IT'S A POP-UP !
EVERYBODY, STAY BACK ! I'VE GOT IT !
4

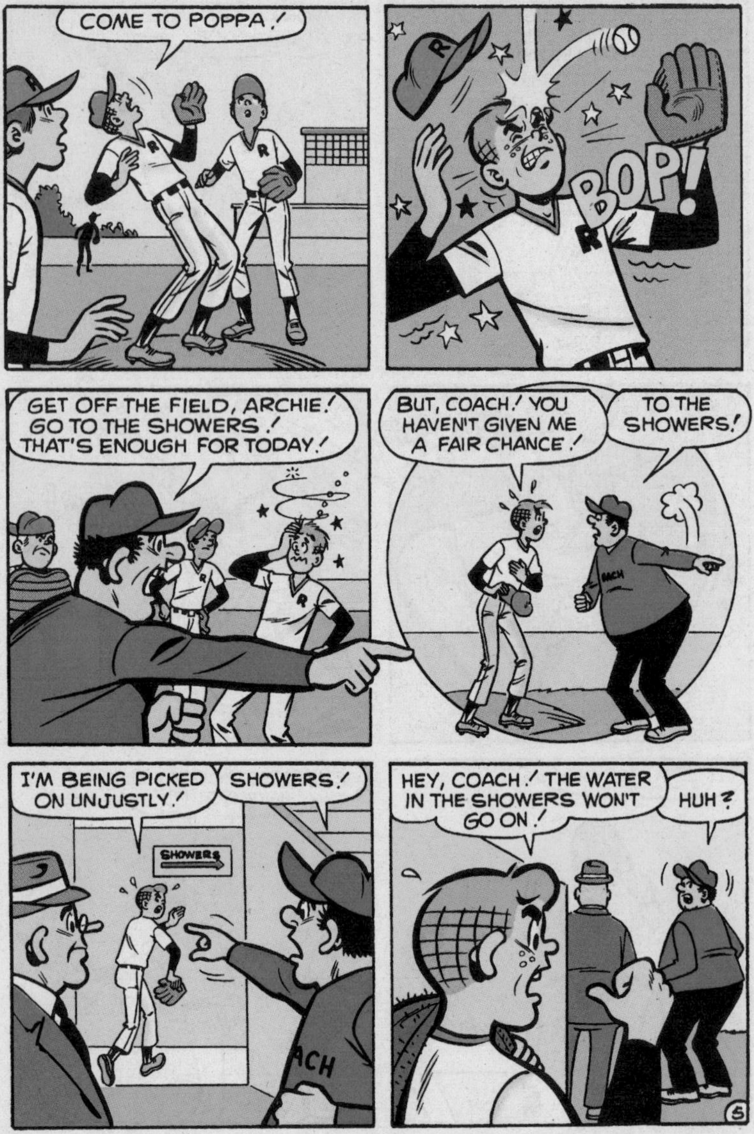
COME TO POPPA!
BOP!
GET OFF THE FIELD, ARCHIE! GO TO THE SHOWERS! THAT'S ENOUGH FOR TODAY!
BUT, COACH! YOU HAVEN'T GIVEN ME A FAIR CHANCE!
TO THE SHOWERS!
I'M BEING PICKED ON UNJUSTLY!
SHOWERS!
SHOWERS
HEY, COACH! THE WATER IN THE SHOWERS WON'T GO ON!
HUH?

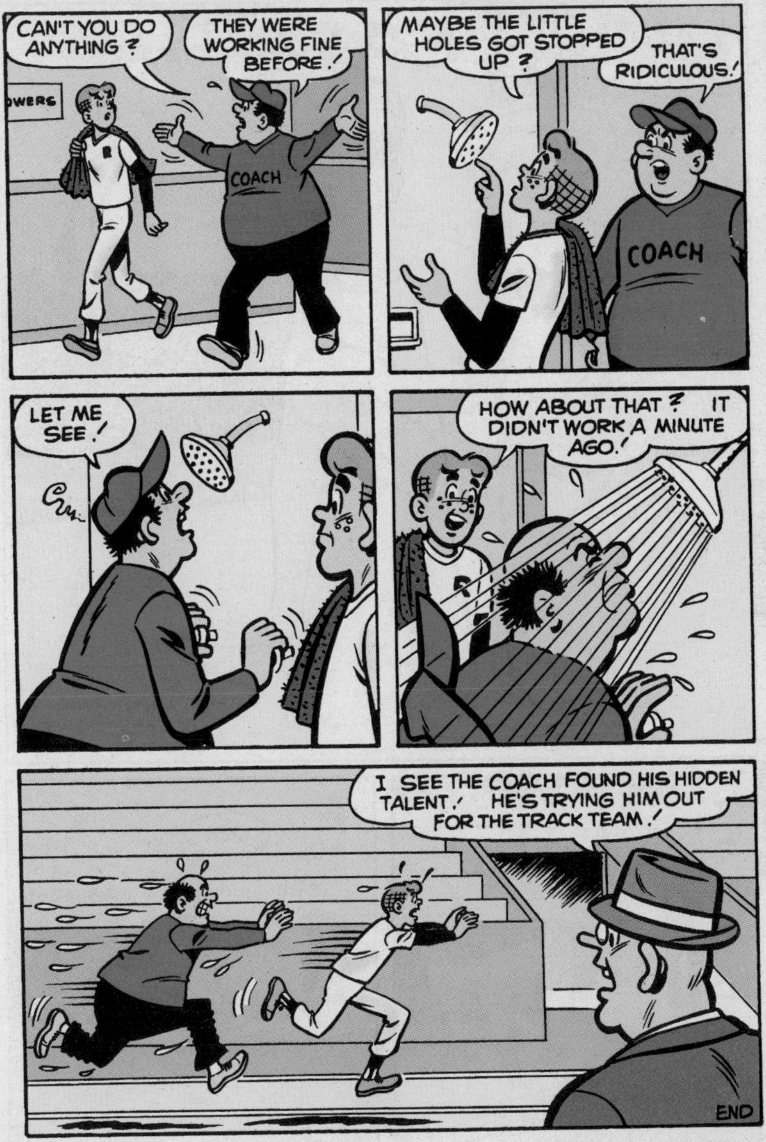

CAN'T YOU DO ANYTHING ?
THEY WERE WORKING FINE BEFORE !
OWERS
COACH
MAYBE THE LITTLE HOLES GOT STOPPED UP ?
THAT'S RIDICULOUS!
COACH
LET ME SEE!
HOW ABOUT THAT? IT DIDN'T WORK A MINUTE AGO!
I SEE THE COACH FOUND HIS HIDDEN TALENT! HE'S TRYING HIM OUT FOR THE TRACK TEAM!
END

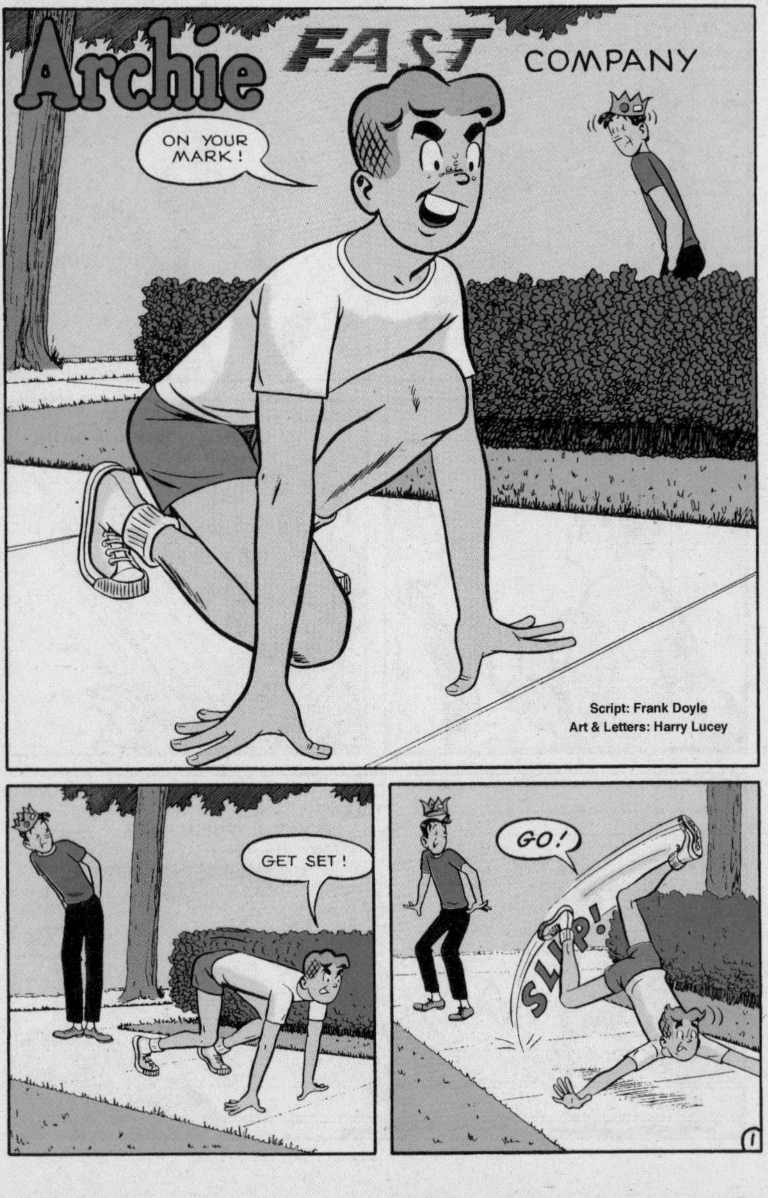
Archie
FAST COMPANY
ON YOUR MARK!
Script: Frank Doyle
Art & Letters: Harry Lucey
GET SET!
GO!
SLIP!
1

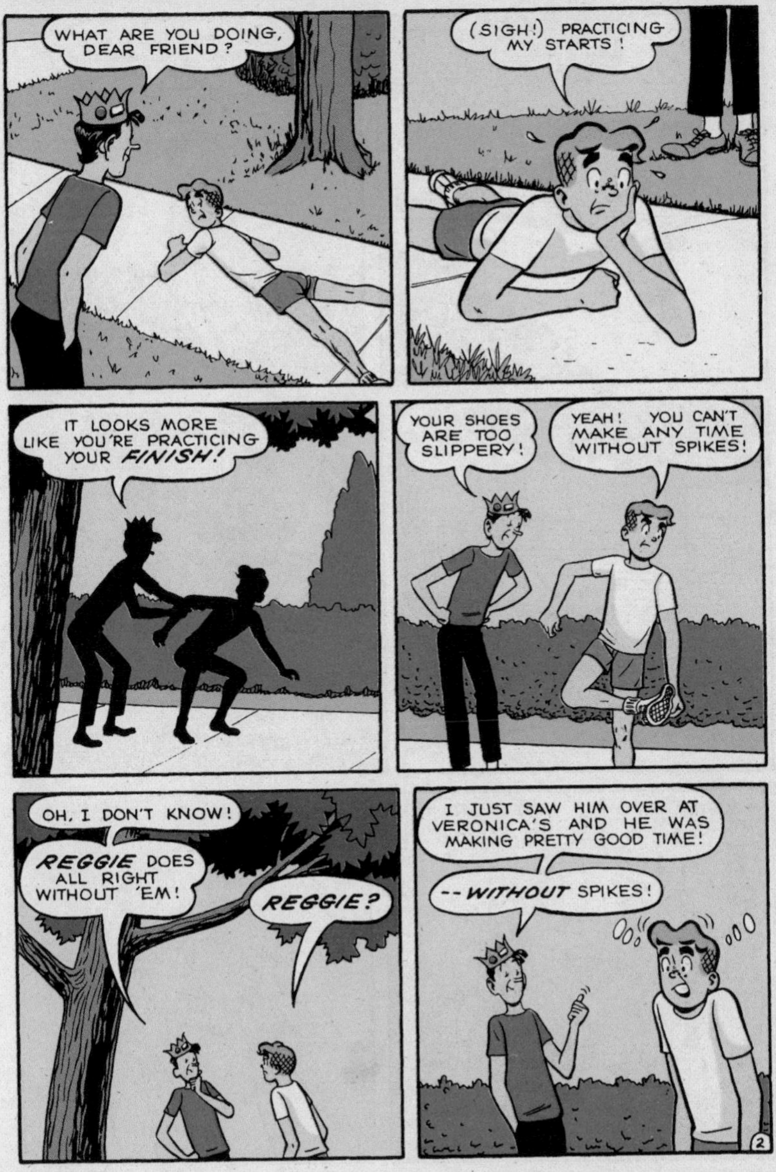
WHAT ARE YOU DOING, DEAR FRIEND?
(SIGH!) PRACTICING MY STARTS!
IT LOOKS MORE LIKE YOU'RE PRACTICING YOUR FINISH!
YOUR SHOES ARE TOO SLIPPERY!
YEAH! YOU CAN'T MAKE ANY TIME WITHOUT SPIKES!
OH, I DON'T KNOW!
REGGIE DOES ALL RIGHT WITHOUT 'EM!
REGGIE?
I JUST SAW HIM OVER AT VERONICA'S AND HE WAS MAKING PRETTY GOOD TIME!
--WITHOUT SPIKES!
2

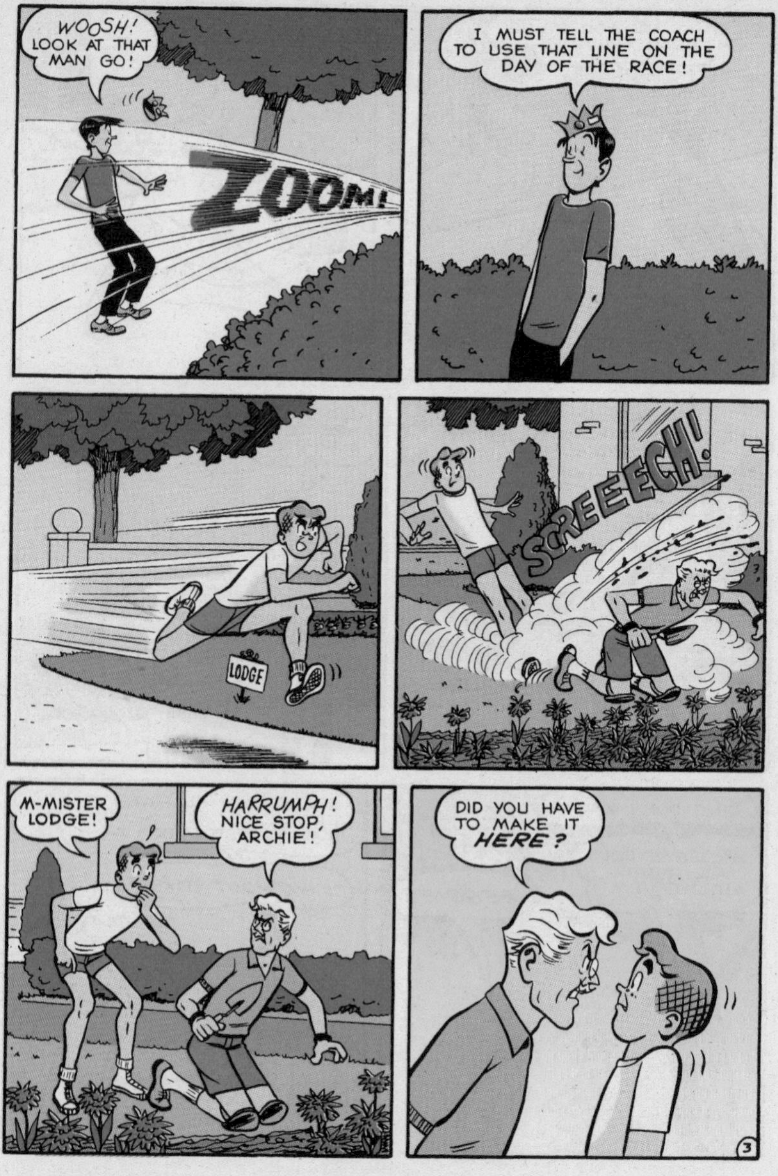
WOOSH! LOOK AT THAT MAN GO!
ZOOM!
I MUST TELL THE COACH TO USE THAT LINE ON THE DAY OF THE RACE!
LODGE
SCREEECH!
M-MISTER LODGE!
HARRUMPH! NICE STOP, ARCHIE!
DID YOU HAVE TO MAKE IT HERE?
3

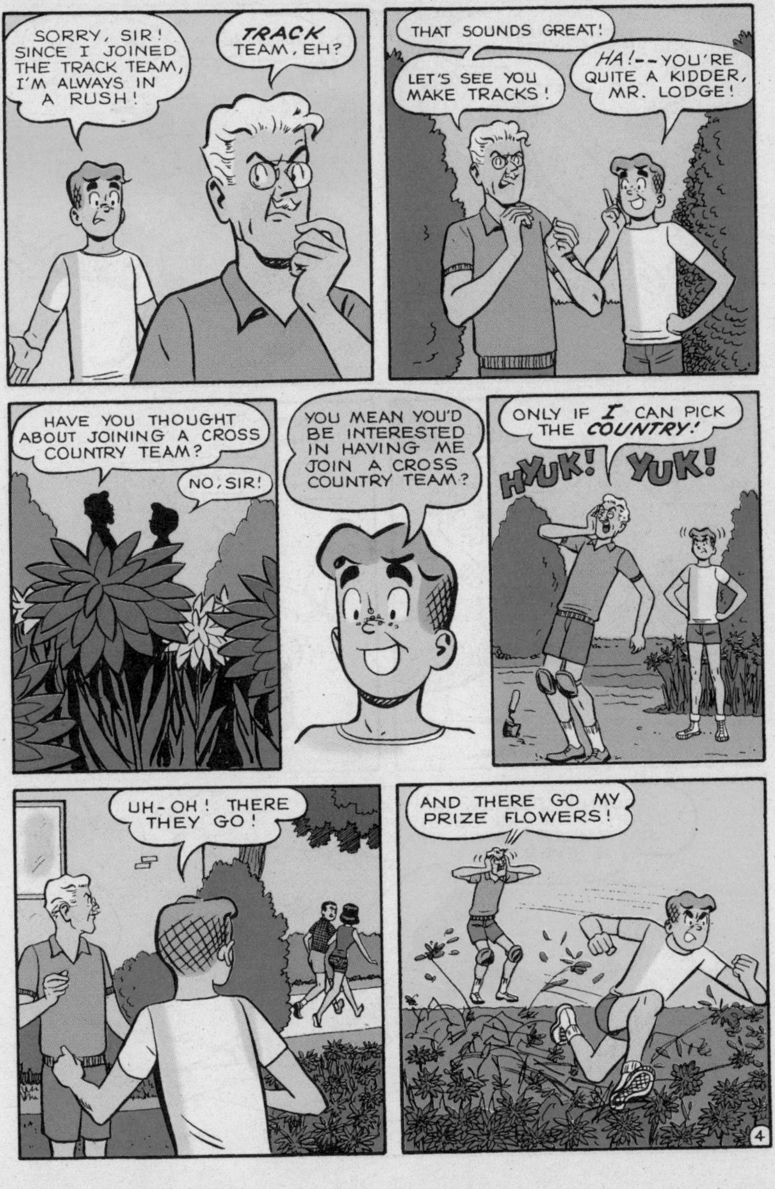
SORRY, SIR! SINCE I JOINED THE TRACK TEAM, I'M ALWAYS IN A RUSH!
TRACK TEAM, EH?
THAT SOUNDS GREAT!
LET'S SEE YOU MAKE TRACKS!
HA!--YOU'RE QUITE A KIDDER, MR. LODGE!
HAVE YOU THOUGHT ABOUT JOINING A CROSS COUNTRY TEAM?
NO, SIR!
YOU MEAN YOU'D BE INTERESTED IN HAVING ME JOIN A CROSS COUNTRY TEAM?
ONLY IF I CAN PICK THE COUNTRY!
HYUK! YUK!
UH-OH! THERE THEY GO!
AND THERE GO MY PRIZE FLOWERS!
4

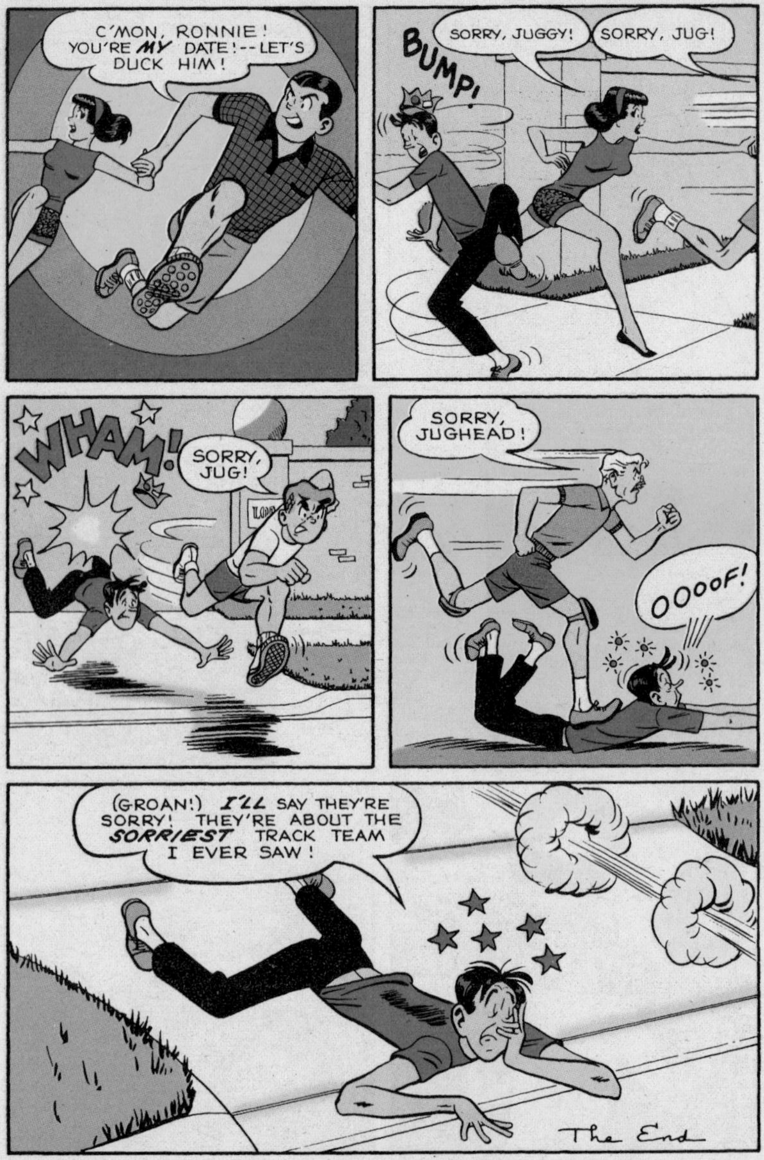
C'MON, RONNIE! YOU'RE *MY* DATE!--LET'S DUCK HIM!
BUMP!
SORRY, JUGGY!
SORRY, JUG!
WHAM!
SORRY, JUG!
SORRY, JUGHEAD!
OOOOF!
(GROAN!) *I'LL* SAY THEY'RE SORRY! THEY'RE ABOUT THE *SORRIEST* TRACK TEAM I EVER SAW!
The End

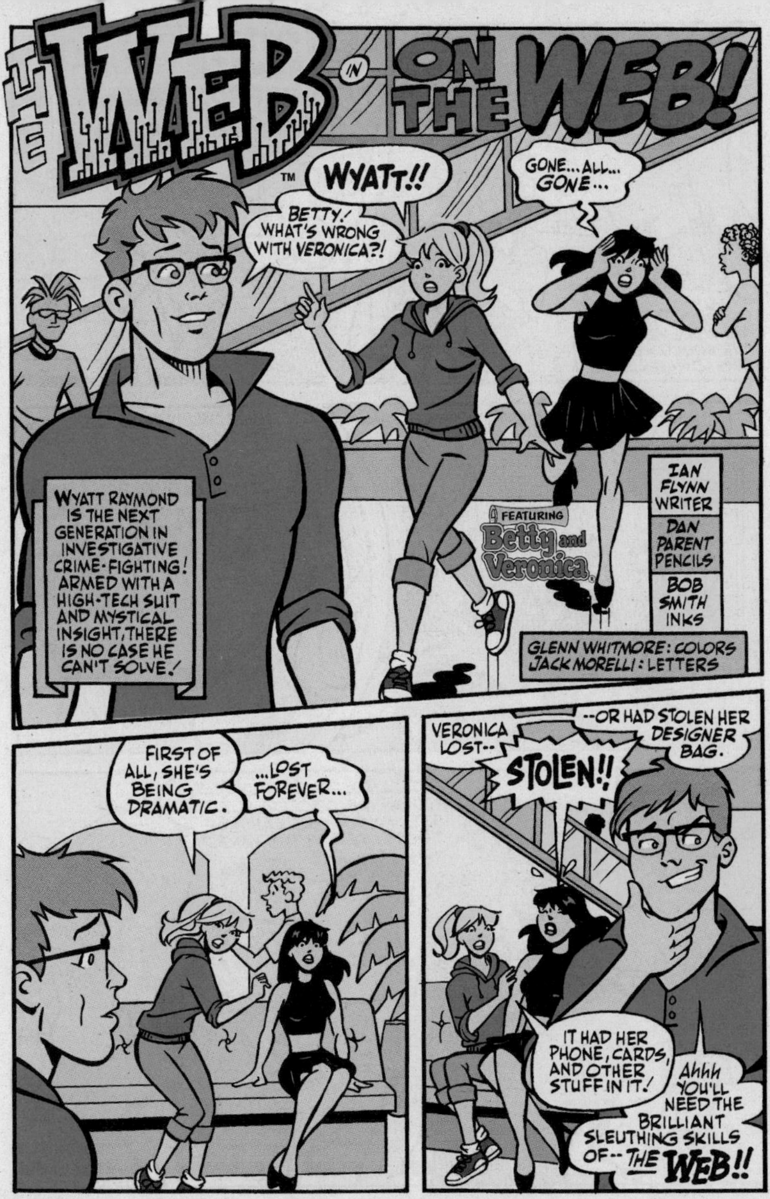
THE WEB IN ON THE WEB!
WYATT!!
BETTY! WHAT'S WRONG WITH VERONICA?!
GONE... ALL... GONE...
WYATT RAYMOND IS THE NEXT GENERATION IN INVESTIGATIVE CRIME-FIGHTING! ARMED WITH A HIGH-TECH SUIT AND MYSTICAL INSIGHT, THERE IS NO CASE HE CAN'T SOLVE!
FEATURING Betty and Veronica
IAN FLYNN WRITER
DAN PARENT PENCILS
BOB SMITH INKS
GLENN WHITMORE: COLORS
JACK MORELLI: LETTERS
FIRST OF ALL, SHE'S BEING DRAMATIC.
...LOST FOREVER...
VERONICA LOST--
STOLEN!!
--OR HAD STOLEN HER DESIGNER BAG.
IT HAD HER PHONE, CARDS, AND OTHER STUFF IN IT!
Ahhh YOU'LL NEED THE BRILLIANT SLEUTHING SKILLS OF-- THE WEB!!

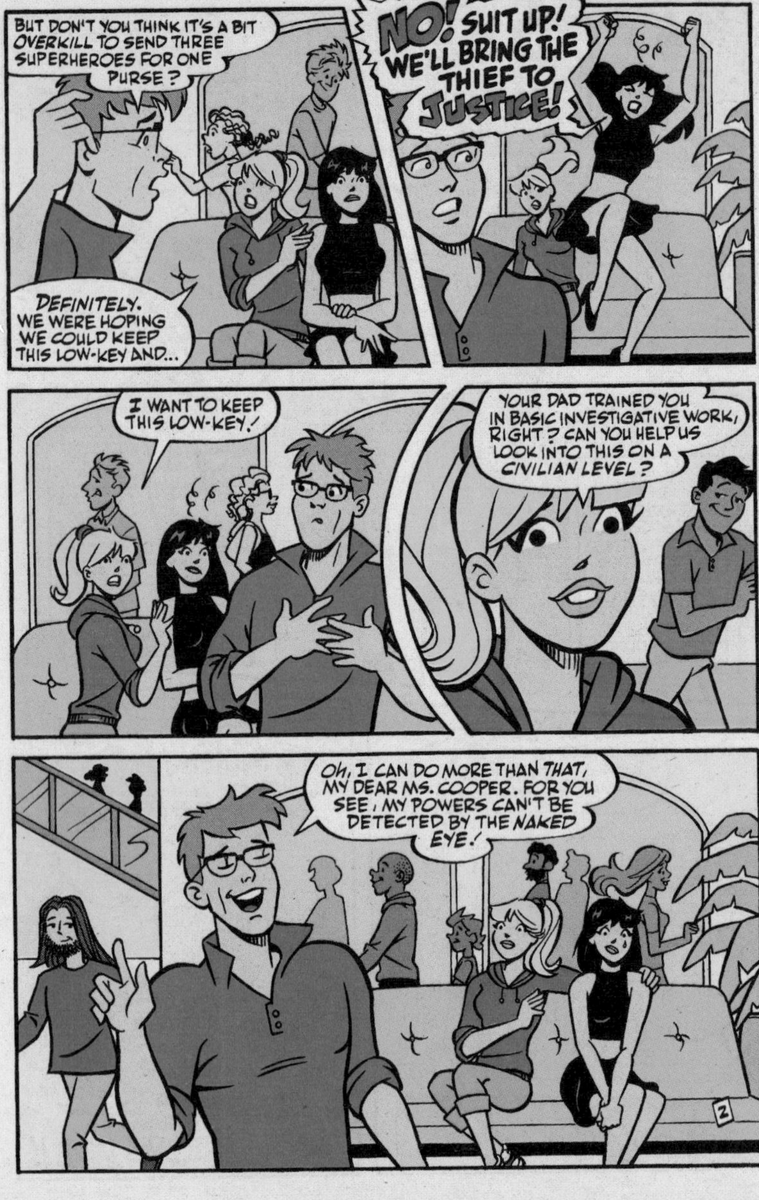
BUT DON'T YOU THINK IT'S A BIT OVERKILL TO SEND THREE SUPERHEROES FOR ONE PURSE?
DEFINITELY. WE WERE HOPING WE COULD KEEP THIS LOW-KEY AND...
NO! SUIT UP! WE'LL BRING THE THIEF TO JUSTICE!
I WANT TO KEEP THIS LOW-KEY!
YOUR DAD TRAINED YOU IN BASIC INVESTIGATIVE WORK, RIGHT? CAN YOU HELP US LOOK INTO THIS ON A CIVILIAN LEVEL?
Oh, I CAN DO MORE THAN THAT, MY DEAR MS. COOPER. FOR YOU SEE, MY POWERS CAN'T BE DETECTED BY THE NAKED EYE!
2

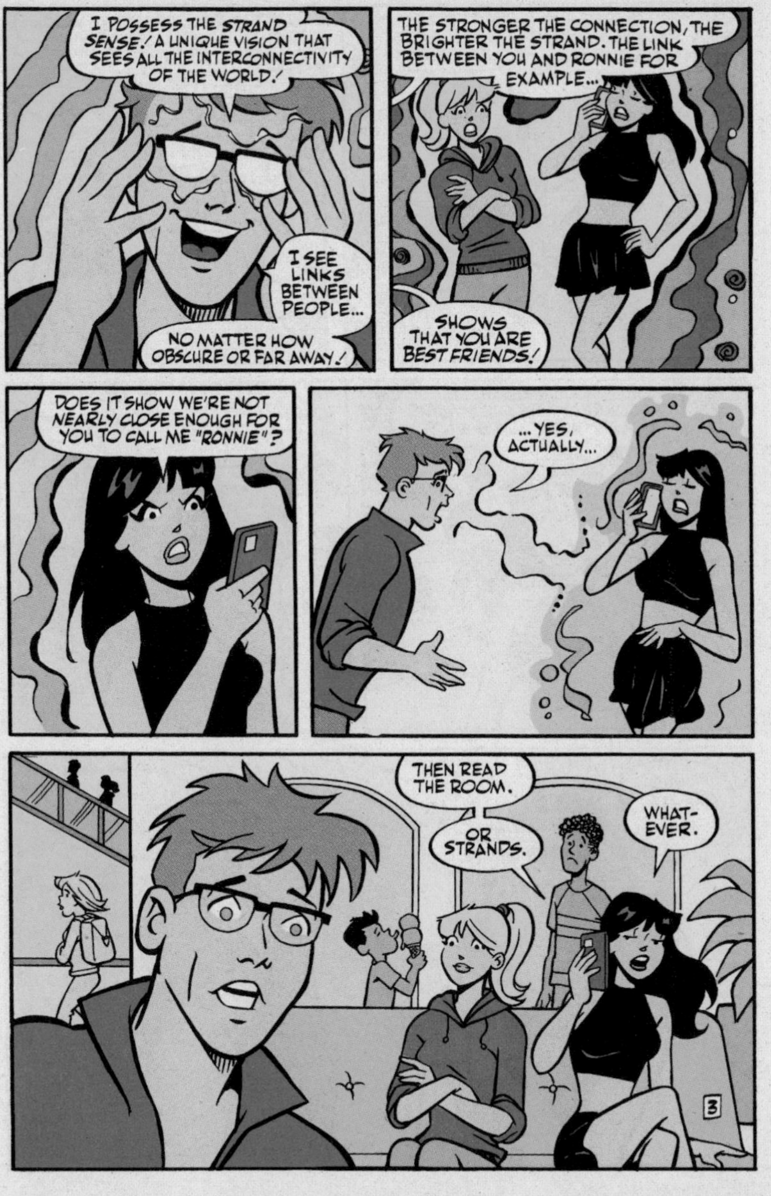
I POSSESS THE STRAND SENSE! A UNIQUE VISION THAT SEES ALL THE INTERCONNECTIVITY OF THE WORLD!
I SEE LINKS BETWEEN PEOPLE...
NO MATTER HOW OBSCURE OR FAR AWAY!
THE STRONGER THE CONNECTION, THE BRIGHTER THE STRAND. THE LINK BETWEEN YOU AND RONNIE FOR EXAMPLE...
SHOWS THAT YOU ARE BEST FRIENDS!
DOES IT SHOW WE'RE NOT NEARLY CLOSE ENOUGH FOR YOU TO CALL ME "RONNIE"?
...YES, ACTUALLY...
THEN READ THE ROOM.
OR STRANDS.
WHAT-EVER.
3

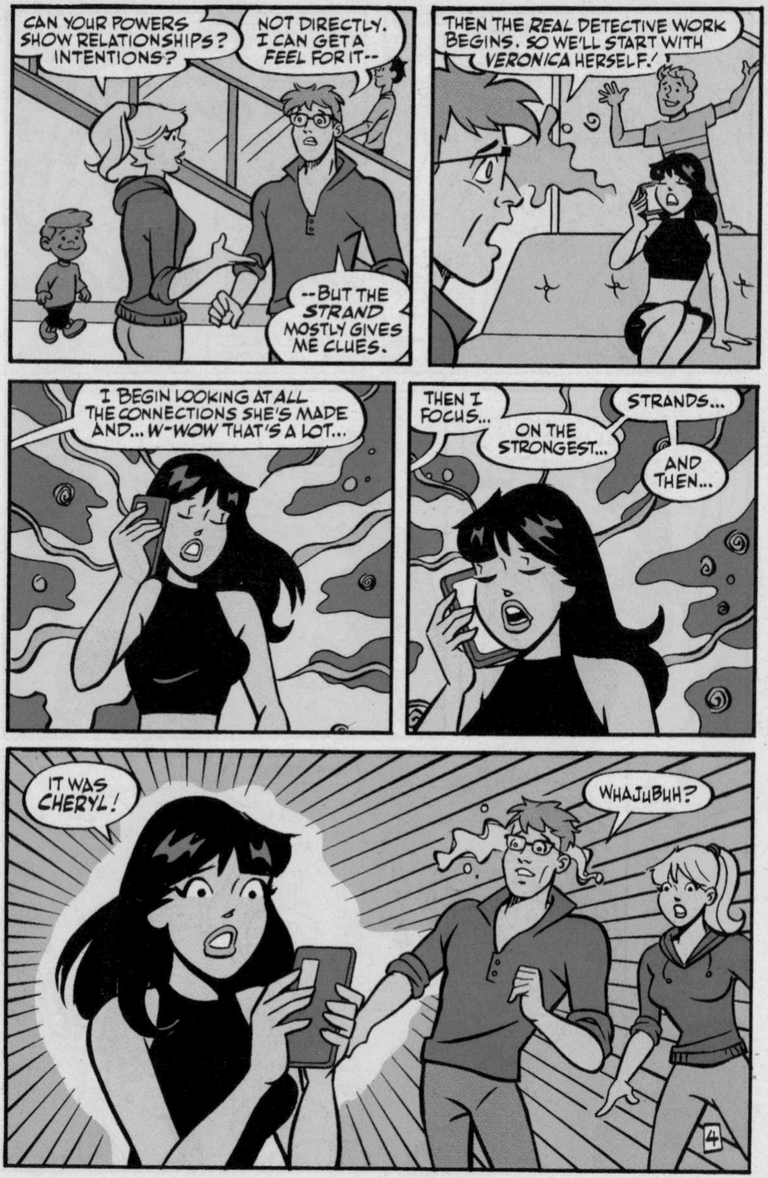
CAN YOUR POWERS SHOW RELATIONSHIPS? INTENTIONS?
NOT DIRECTLY. I CAN GET A FEEL FOR IT--
--BUT THE STRAND MOSTLY GIVES ME CLUES.
THEN THE REAL DETECTIVE WORK BEGINS. SO WE'LL START WITH VERONICA HERSELF!
I BEGIN LOOKING AT ALL THE CONNECTIONS SHE'S MADE AND... W-WOW THAT'S A LOT...
THEN I FOCUS...
ON THE STRONGEST...
STRANDS...
AND THEN...
IT WAS CHERYL!
WHAJUBUH?
4

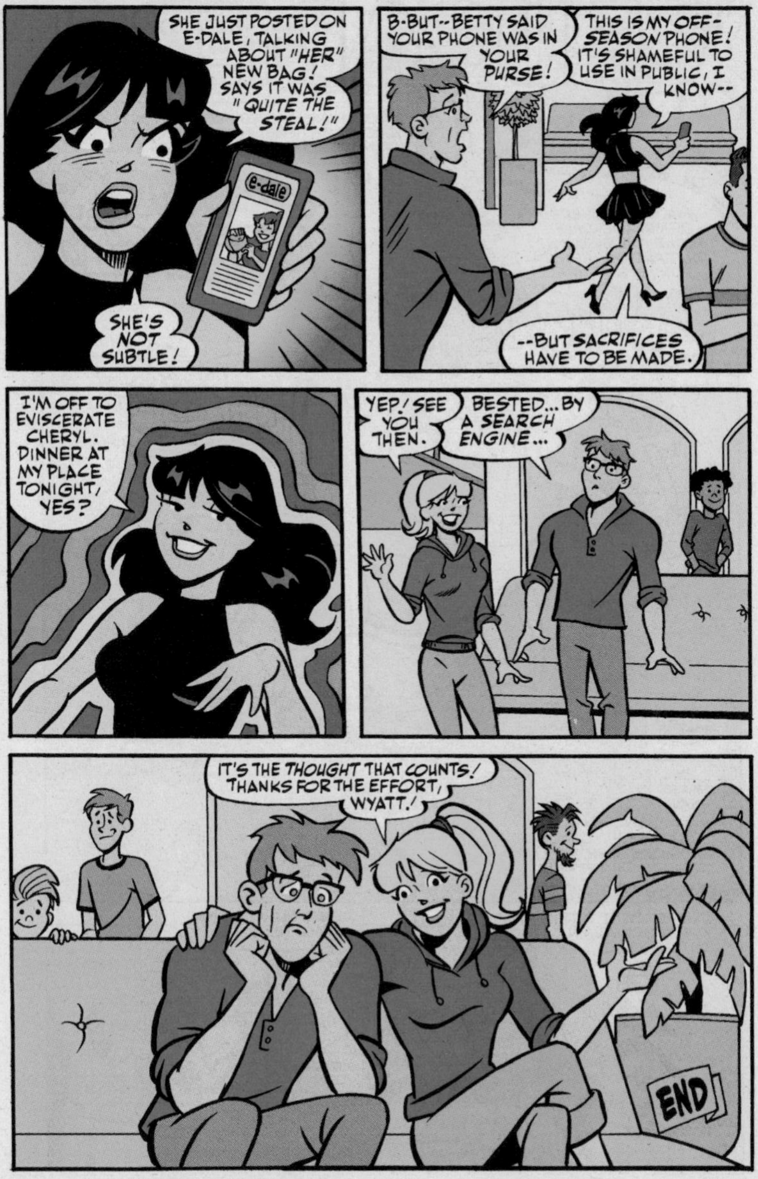
SHE JUST POSTED ON E-DALE, TALKING ABOUT "HER" NEW BAG! SAYS IT WAS "QUITE THE STEAL!"
e-dale
SHE'S NOT SUBTLE!
B-BUT--BETTY SAID YOUR PHONE WAS IN YOUR PURSE!
THIS IS MY OFF-SEASON PHONE! IT'S SHAMEFUL TO USE IN PUBLIC, I KNOW--
--BUT SACRIFICES HAVE TO BE MADE.
I'M OFF TO EVISCERATE CHERYL. DINNER AT MY PLACE TONIGHT, YES?
YEP! SEE YOU THEN.
BESTED... BY A SEARCH ENGINE...
IT'S THE THOUGHT THAT COUNTS! THANKS FOR THE EFFORT, WYATT.!
END

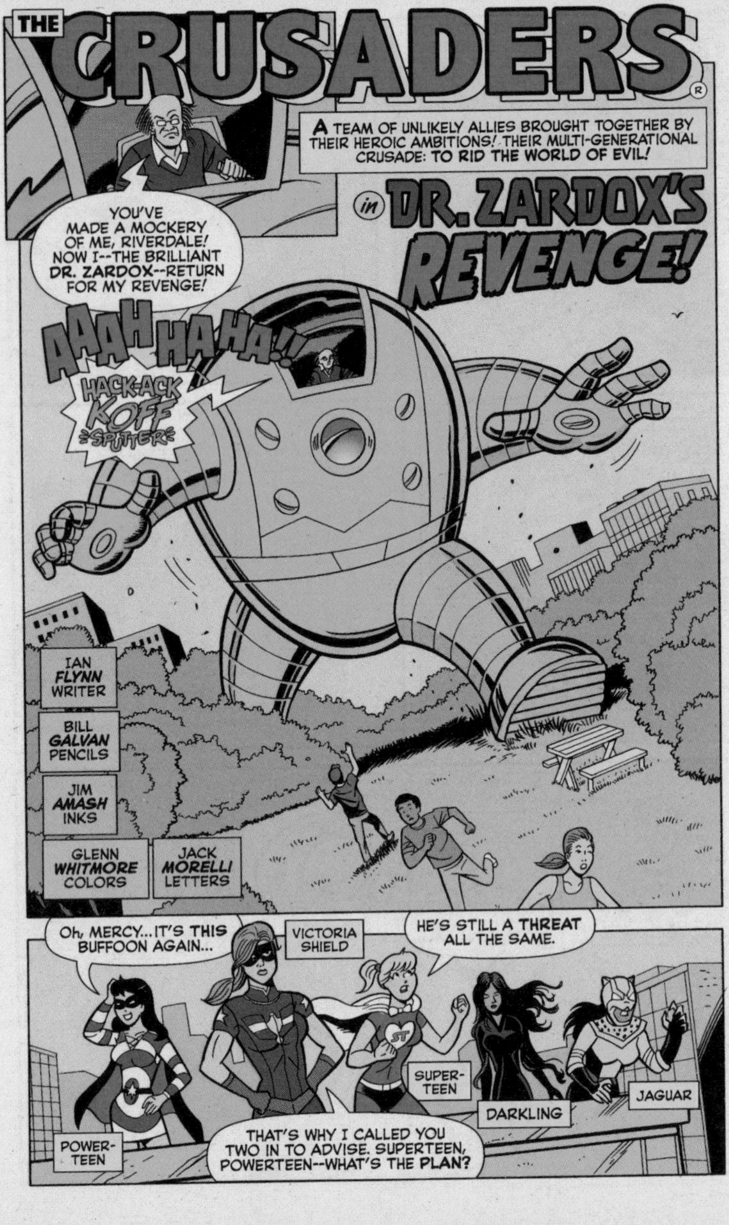
THE CRUSADERS®
A TEAM OF UNLIKELY ALLIES BROUGHT TOGETHER BY THEIR HEROIC AMBITIONS! THEIR MULTI-GENERATIONAL CRUSADE: TO RID THE WORLD OF EVIL!
in DR. ZARDOX'S REVENGE!
YOU'VE MADE A MOCKERY OF ME, RIVERDALE! NOW I--THE BRILLIANT DR. ZARDOX--RETURN FOR MY REVENGE!
AAAHHAHA!!!
HACK-ACK KOFF SPUTTER
IAN FLYNN WRITER
BILL GALVAN PENCILS
JIM AMASH INKS
GLENN WHITMORE COLORS
JACK MORELLI LETTERS
Oh, MERCY...IT'S THIS BUFFOON AGAIN...
VICTORIA SHIELD
HE'S STILL A THREAT ALL THE SAME.
POWER-TEEN
SUPER-TEEN
DARKLING
JAGUAR
THAT'S WHY I CALLED YOU TWO IN TO ADVISE. SUPERTEEN, POWERTEEN--WHAT'S THE PLAN?

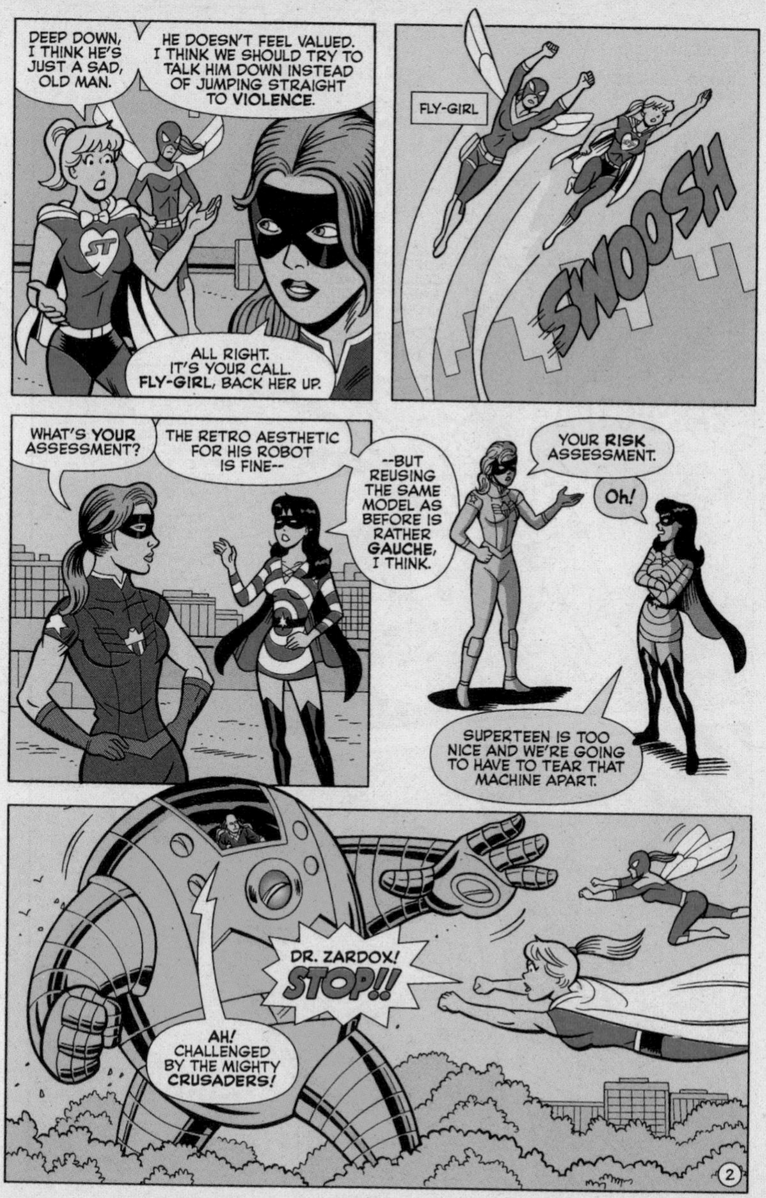
DEEP DOWN, I THINK HE'S JUST A SAD, OLD MAN.
HE DOESN'T FEEL VALUED. I THINK WE SHOULD TRY TO TALK HIM DOWN INSTEAD OF JUMPING STRAIGHT TO VIOLENCE.
ALL RIGHT. IT'S YOUR CALL. FLY-GIRL, BACK HER UP.
FLY-GIRL
SWOOSH
WHAT'S YOUR ASSESSMENT?
THE RETRO AESTHETIC FOR HIS ROBOT IS FINE--
--BUT REUSING THE SAME MODEL AS BEFORE IS RATHER GAUCHE, I THINK.
YOUR RISK ASSESSMENT.
Oh!
SUPERTEEN IS TOO NICE AND WE'RE GOING TO HAVE TO TEAR THAT MACHINE APART.
DR. ZARDOX! STOP!!
AH! CHALLENGED BY THE MIGHTY CRUSADERS!
2

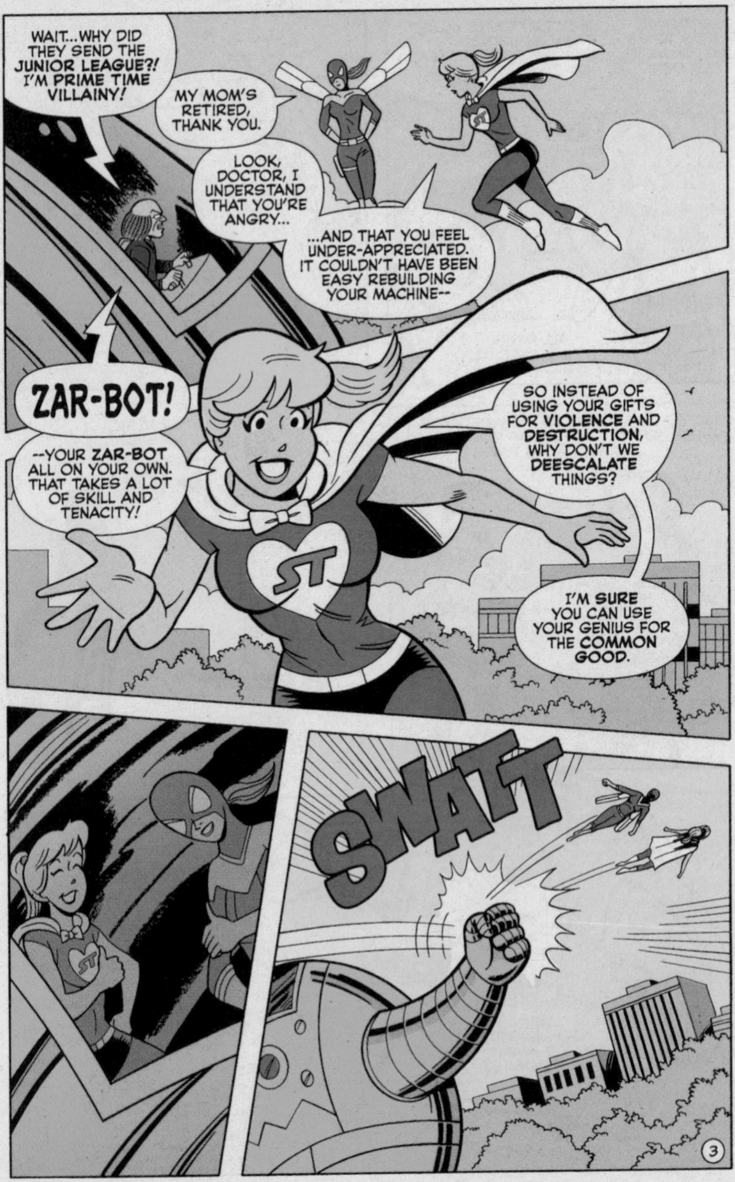
WAIT...WHY DID THEY SEND THE JUNIOR LEAGUE?! I'M PRIME TIME VILLAINY!
MY MOM'S RETIRED, THANK YOU.
LOOK, DOCTOR, I UNDERSTAND THAT YOU'RE ANGRY...
...AND THAT YOU FEEL UNDER-APPRECIATED. IT COULDN'T HAVE BEEN EASY REBUILDING YOUR MACHINE--
ZAR-BOT!
--YOUR ZAR-BOT ALL ON YOUR OWN. THAT TAKES A LOT OF SKILL AND TENACITY!
SO INSTEAD OF USING YOUR GIFTS FOR VIOLENCE AND DESTRUCTION, WHY DON'T WE DEESCALATE THINGS?
I'M SURE YOU CAN USE YOUR GENIUS FOR THE COMMON GOOD.
SWATT
3

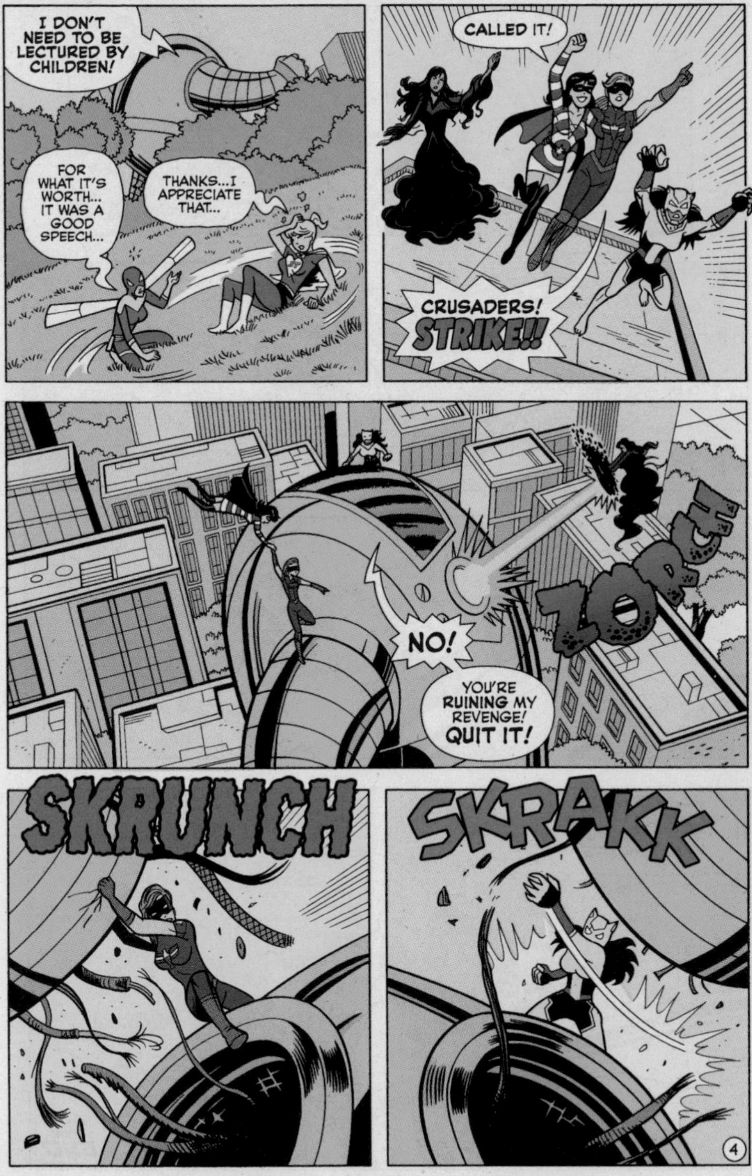
I DON'T NEED TO BE LECTURED BY CHILDREN!
FOR WHAT IT'S WORTH... IT WAS A GOOD SPEECH...
THANKS...I APPRECIATE THAT...
CALLED IT!
CRUSADERS! STRIKE!!
ZORCH
NO!
YOU'RE RUINING MY REVENGE! QUIT IT!
SKRUNCH
SKRAKK

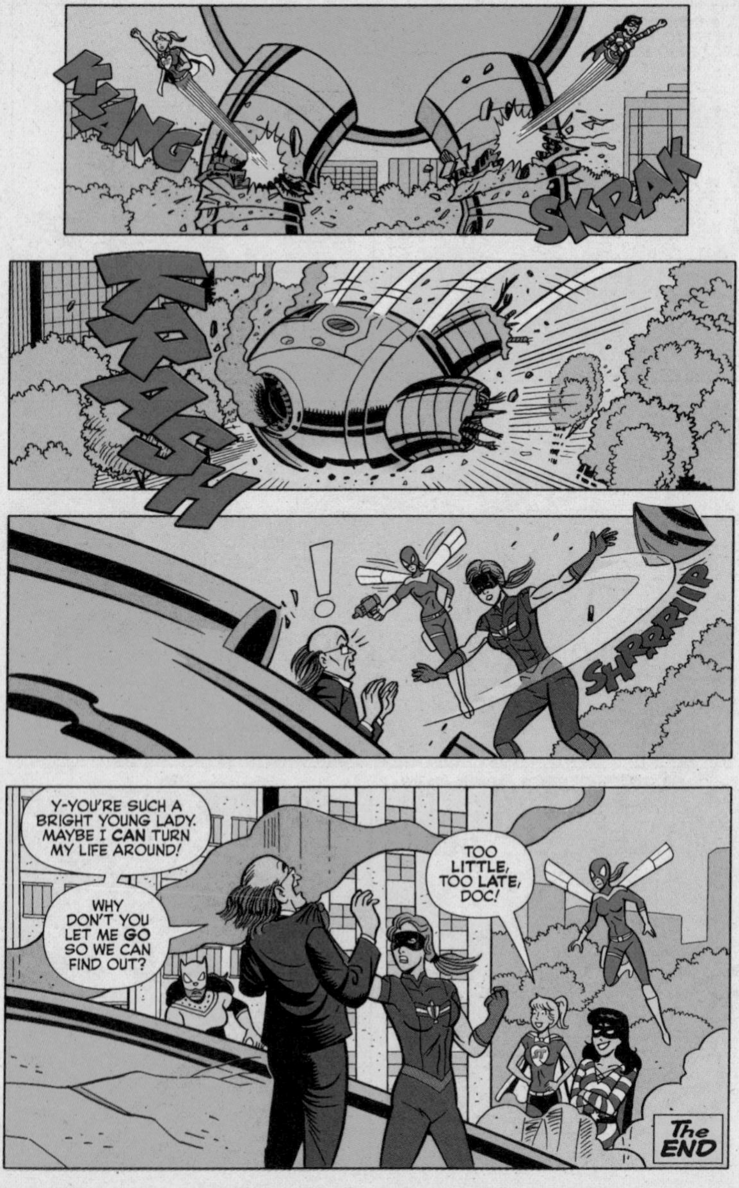
KLANG
SKRAK
KRASH
!
SHRRRIIP
Y-YOU'RE SUCH A BRIGHT YOUNG LADY. MAYBE I CAN TURN MY LIFE AROUND!
WHY DON'T YOU LET ME GO SO WE CAN FIND OUT?
TOO LITTLE, TOO LATE, DOC!
The END

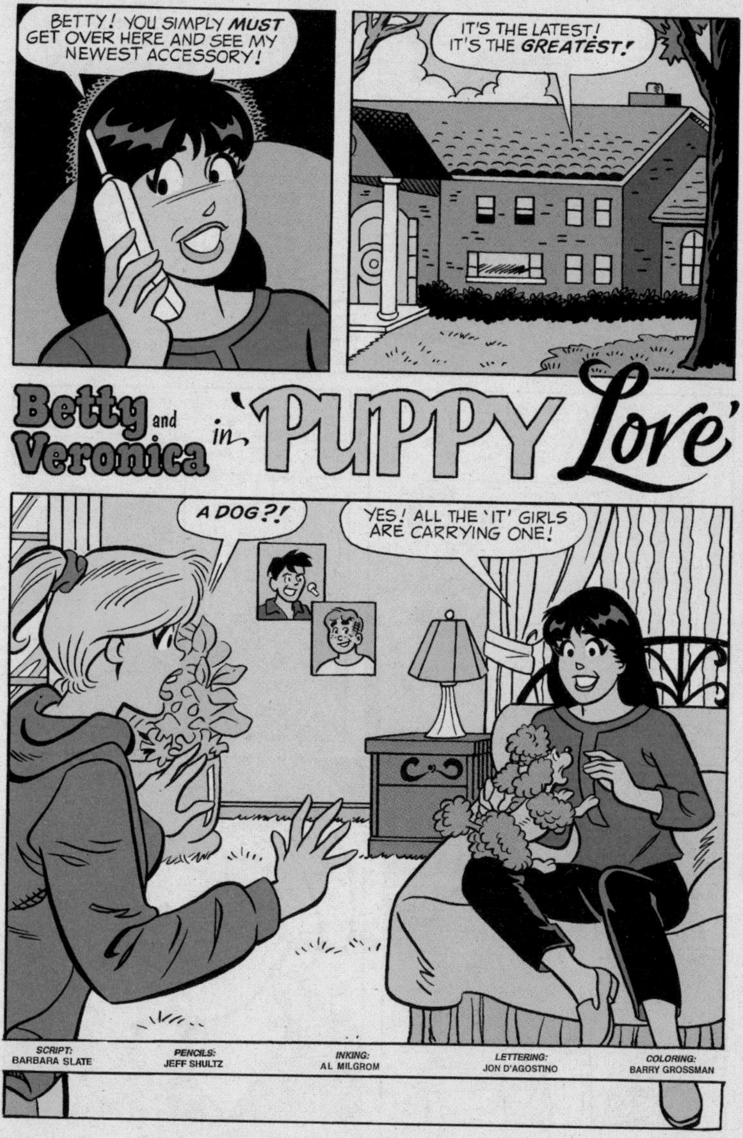
BETTY! YOU SIMPLY MUST GET OVER HERE AND SEE MY NEWEST ACCESSORY!
IT'S THE LATEST! IT'S THE GREATEST!
Betty and Veronica in 'PUPPY Love'
A DOG?!
YES! ALL THE 'IT' GIRLS ARE CARRYING ONE!
SCRIPT: BARBARA SLATE
PENCILS: JEFF SHULTZ
INKING: AL MILGROM
LETTERING: JON D'AGOSTINO
COLORING: BARRY GROSSMAN

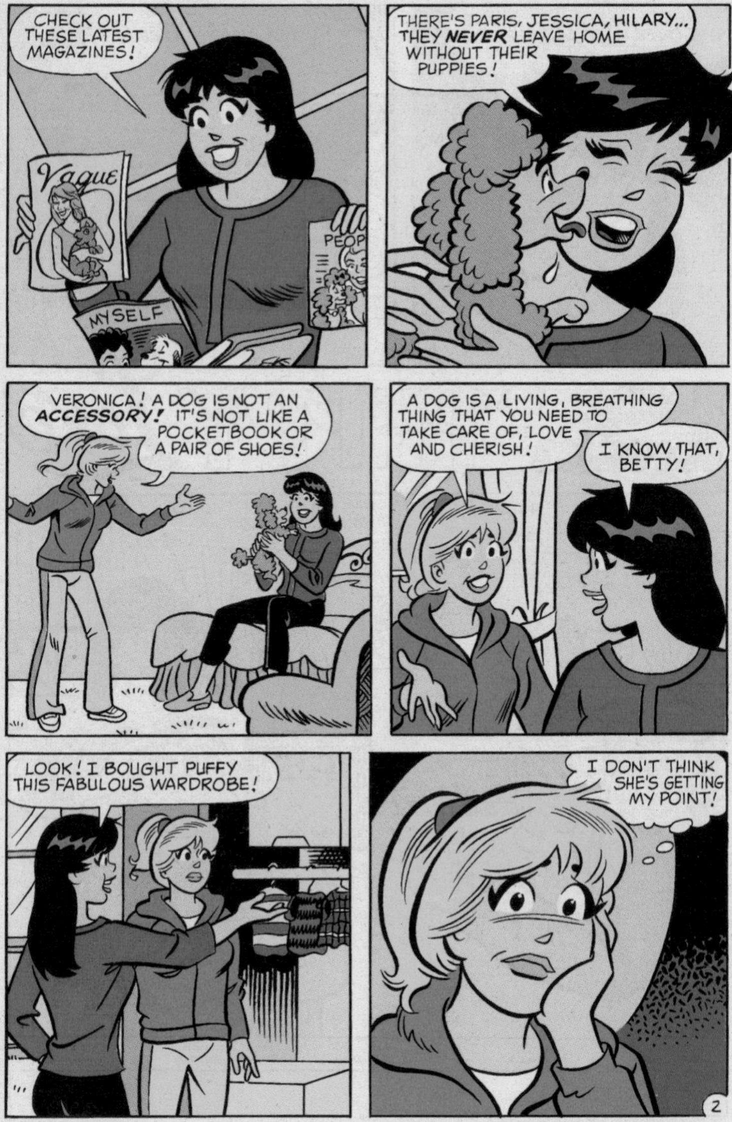
CHECK OUT THESE LATEST MAGAZINES!
Vague
PEOP
MYSELF
THERE'S PARIS, JESSICA, HILARY... THEY NEVER LEAVE HOME WITHOUT THEIR PUPPIES!
VERONICA! A DOG IS NOT AN ACCESSORY! IT'S NOT LIKE A POCKETBOOK OR A PAIR OF SHOES!
A DOG IS A LIVING, BREATHING THING THAT YOU NEED TO TAKE CARE OF, LOVE AND CHERISH!
I KNOW THAT, BETTY!
LOOK! I BOUGHT PUFFY THIS FABULOUS WARDROBE!
I DON'T THINK SHE'S GETTING MY POINT!

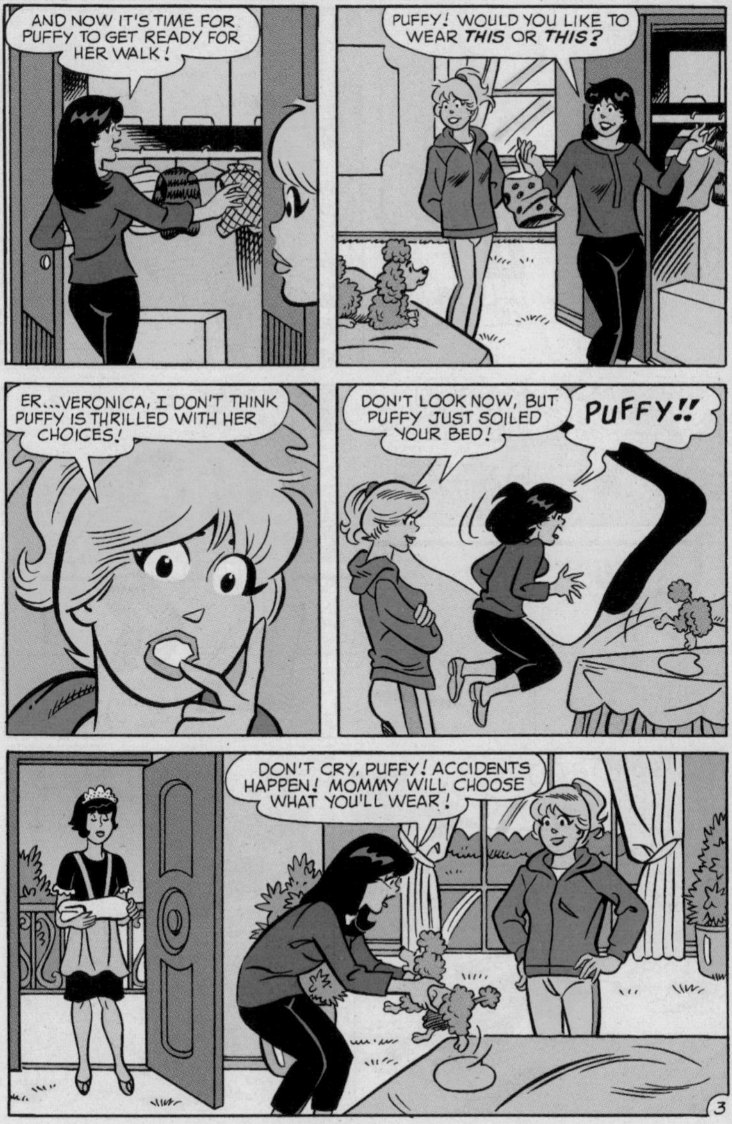
AND NOW IT'S TIME FOR PUFFY TO GET READY FOR HER WALK!
PUFFY! WOULD YOU LIKE TO WEAR *THIS* OR *THIS?*
ER...VERONICA, I DON'T THINK PUFFY IS THRILLED WITH HER CHOICES!
DON'T LOOK NOW, BUT PUFFY JUST SOILED YOUR BED!
PUFFY!!
DON'T CRY, PUFFY! ACCIDENTS HAPPEN! MOMMY WILL CHOOSE WHAT YOU'LL WEAR!
3

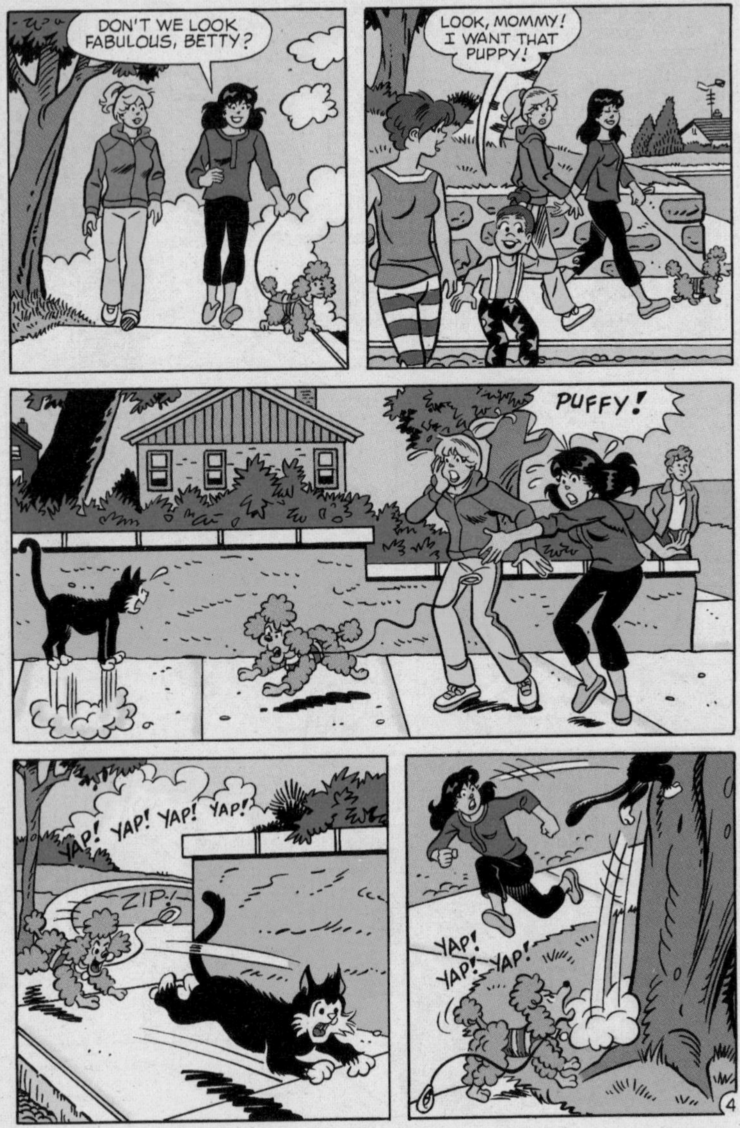
DON'T WE LOOK FABULOUS, BETTY?
LOOK, MOMMY! I WANT THAT PUPPY!
PUFFY!
YAP! YAP! YAP! YAP!
ZIP-!
YAP! YAP! YAP!

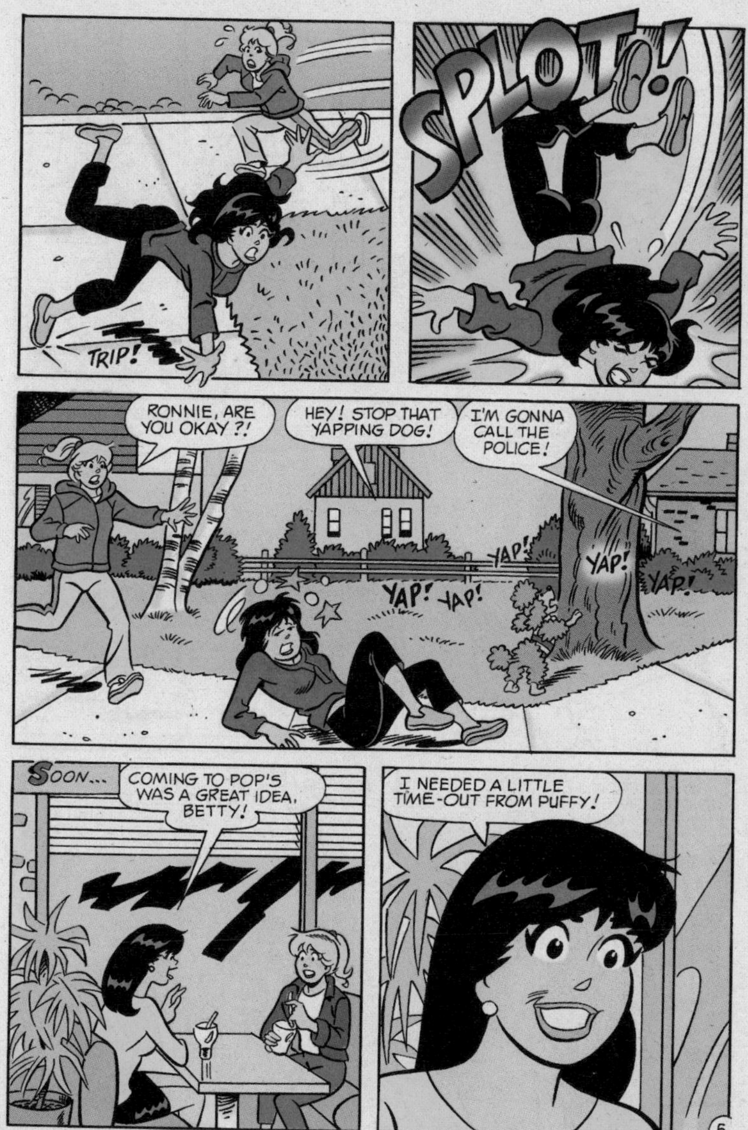
SPLOT!
TRIP!
RONNIE, ARE YOU OKAY ?!
HEY! STOP THAT YAPPING DOG!
I'M GONNA CALL THE POLICE!
YAP!
YAP!
YAP!
YAP!
YAP!
SOON...
COMING TO POP'S WAS A GREAT IDEA, BETTY!
I NEEDED A LITTLE TIME-OUT FROM PUFFY!

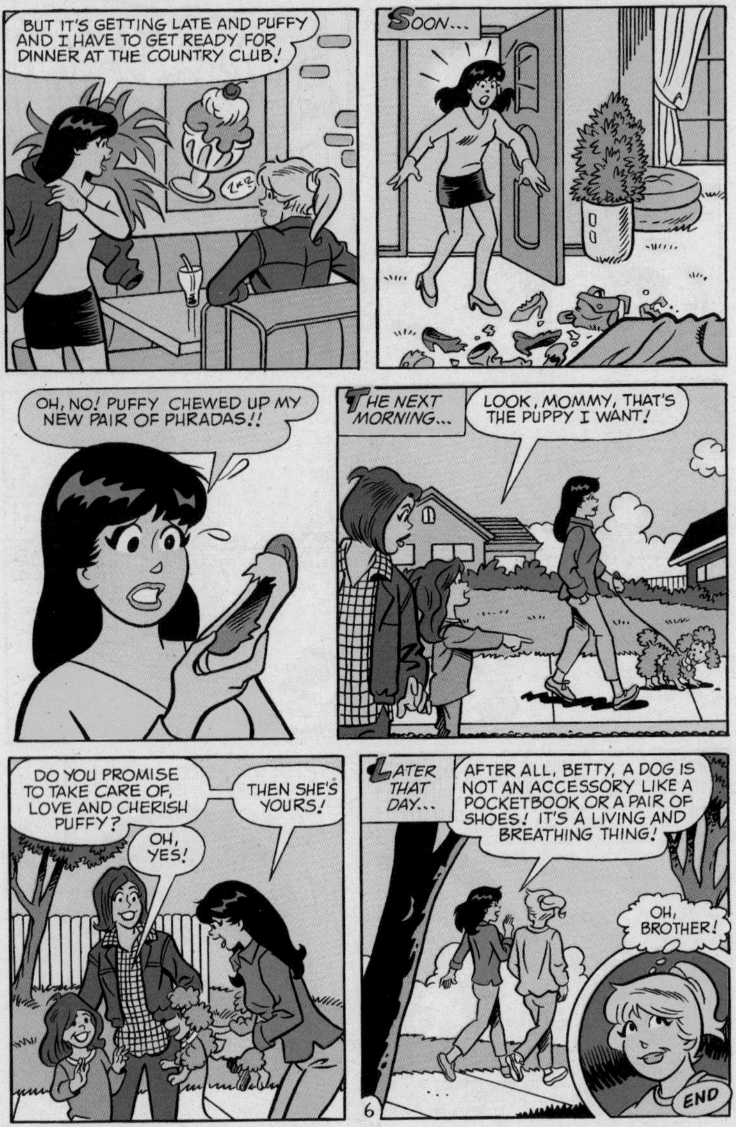
BUT IT'S GETTING LATE AND PUFFY AND I HAVE TO GET READY FOR DINNER AT THE COUNTRY CLUB!
SOON...
OH, NO! PUFFY CHEWED UP MY NEW PAIR OF PHRADAS!!
THE NEXT MORNING...
LOOK, MOMMY, THAT'S THE PUPPY I WANT!
DO YOU PROMISE TO TAKE CARE OF, LOVE AND CHERISH PUFFY?
OH, YES!
THEN SHE'S YOURS!
LATER THAT DAY...
AFTER ALL, BETTY, A DOG IS NOT AN ACCESSORY LIKE A POCKETBOOK OR A PAIR OF SHOES! IT'S A LIVING AND BREATHING THING!
OH, BROTHER!
END

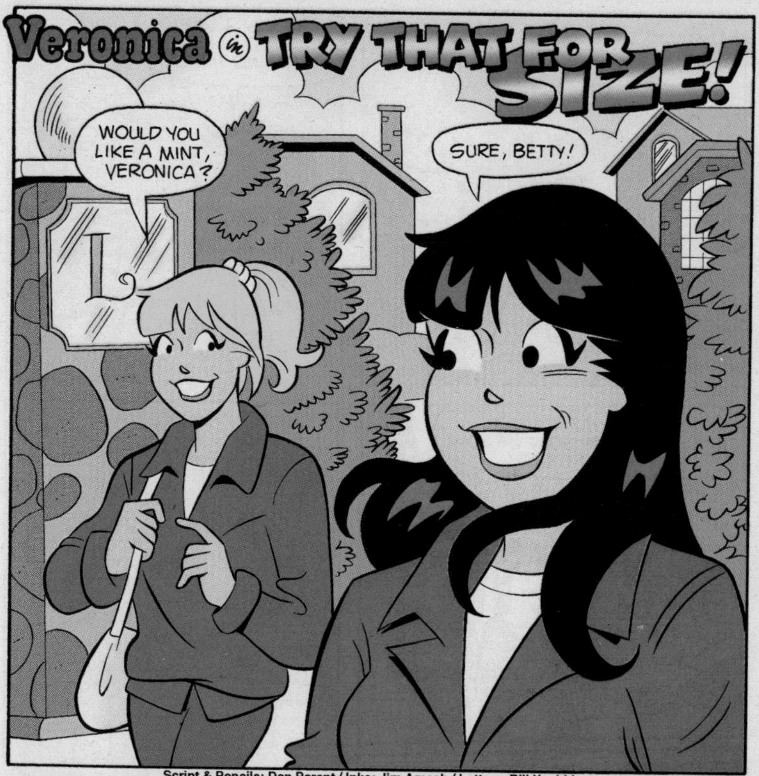
Veronica in TRY THAT FOR SIZE!
WOULD YOU LIKE A MINT, VERONICA?
SURE, BETTY!

Script & Pencils: Dan Parent / Inks: Jim Amash / Letters: Bill Yoshida

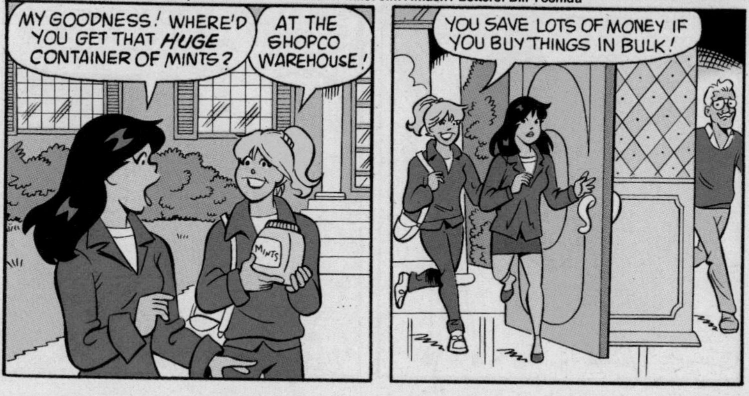
MY GOODNESS! WHERE'D YOU GET THAT *HUGE* CONTAINER OF MINTS?
AT THE SHOPCO WAREHOUSE!
MINTS
YOU SAVE LOTS OF MONEY IF YOU BUY THINGS IN BULK!

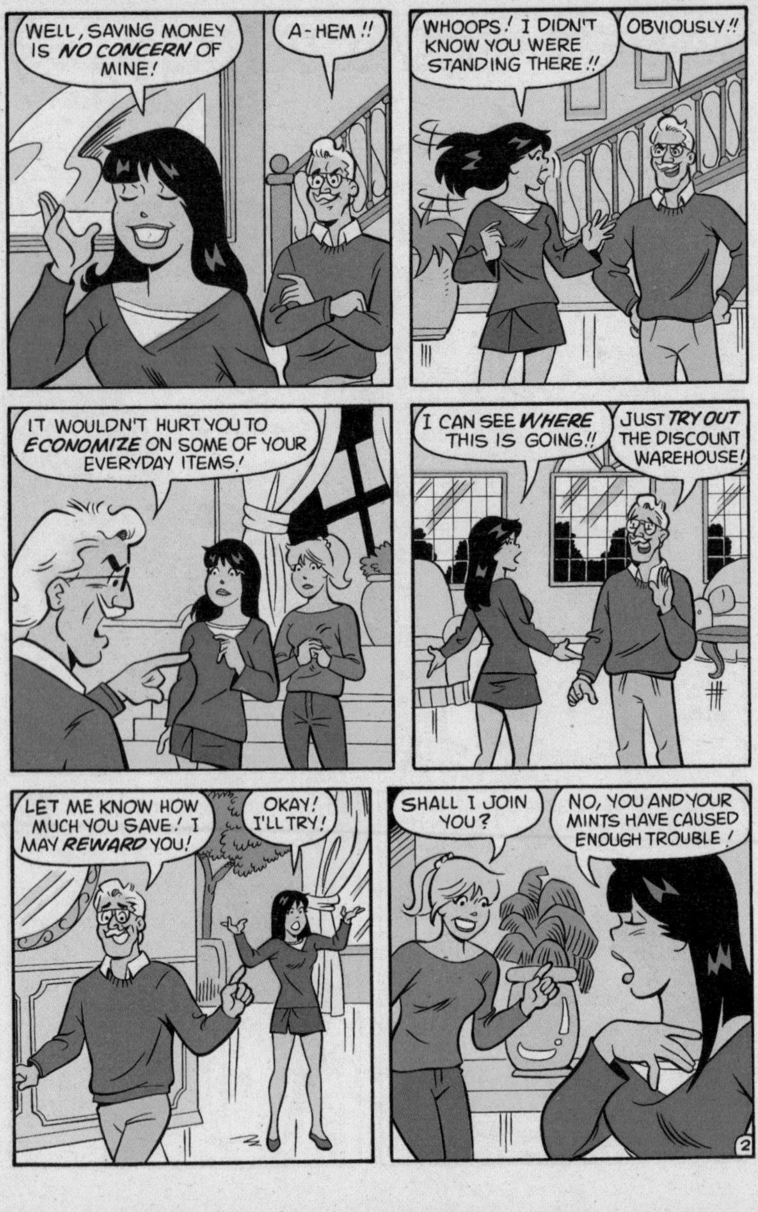
WELL, SAVING MONEY IS NO CONCERN OF MINE!
A-HEM!!
WHOOPS! I DIDN'T KNOW YOU WERE STANDING THERE!!
OBVIOUSLY!!
IT WOULDN'T HURT YOU TO ECONOMIZE ON SOME OF YOUR EVERYDAY ITEMS!
I CAN SEE WHERE THIS IS GOING!!
JUST TRY OUT THE DISCOUNT WAREHOUSE!
LET ME KNOW HOW MUCH YOU SAVE! I MAY REWARD YOU!
OKAY! I'LL TRY!
SHALL I JOIN YOU?
NO, YOU AND YOUR MINTS HAVE CAUSED ENOUGH TROUBLE!
2

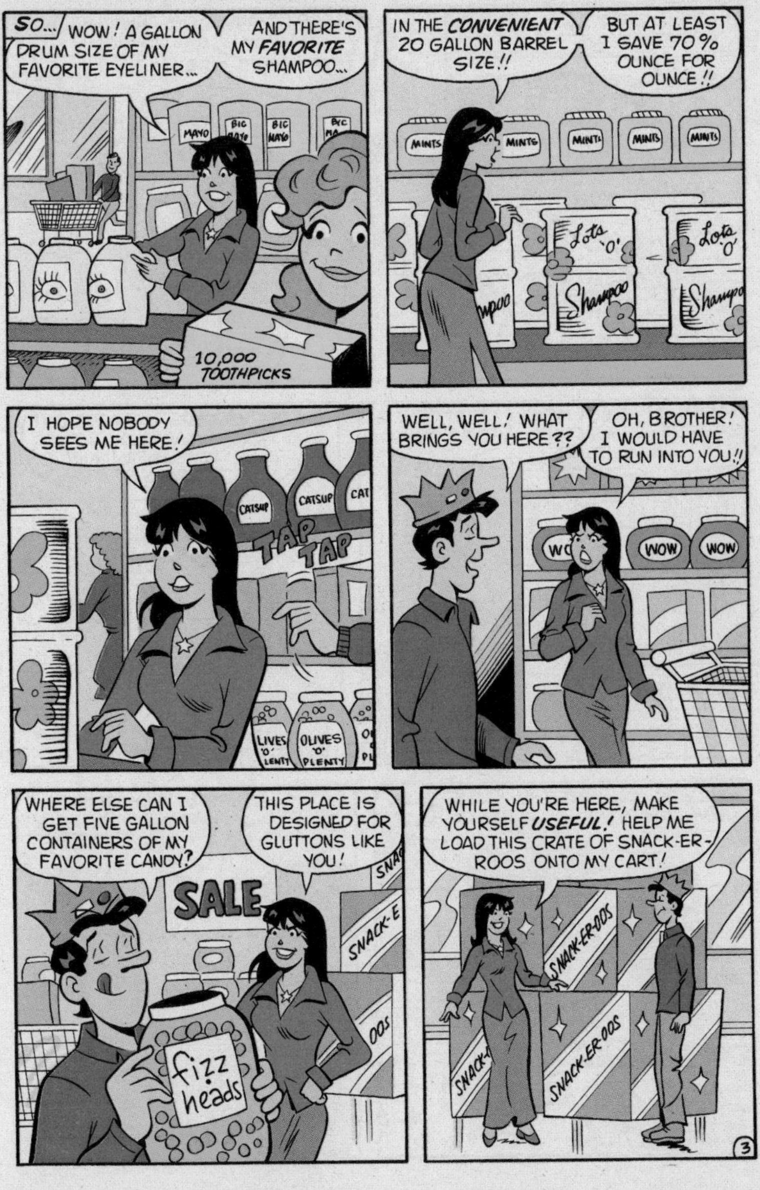
SO...
WOW! A GALLON DRUM SIZE OF MY FAVORITE EYELINER...
AND THERE'S MY FAVORITE SHAMPOO...
MAYO
BIG MAYO
BIG MAYO
10,000 TOOTHPICKS
IN THE CONVENIENT 20 GALLON BARREL SIZE!!
BUT AT LEAST I SAVE 70% OUNCE FOR OUNCE!!
MINTS
Lots 'O' Shampoo
I HOPE NOBODY SEES ME HERE!
CATSUP
TAP TAP
OLIVES 'O' PLENTY
WELL, WELL! WHAT BRINGS YOU HERE??
OH, BROTHER! I WOULD HAVE TO RUN INTO YOU!!
WOW
WHERE ELSE CAN I GET FIVE GALLON CONTAINERS OF MY FAVORITE CANDY?
THIS PLACE IS DESIGNED FOR GLUTTONS LIKE YOU!
SALE
fizz heads
WHILE YOU'RE HERE, MAKE YOURSELF USEFUL! HELP ME LOAD THIS CRATE OF SNACK-ER-ROOS ONTO MY CART!
SNACK-ER-OOS
3

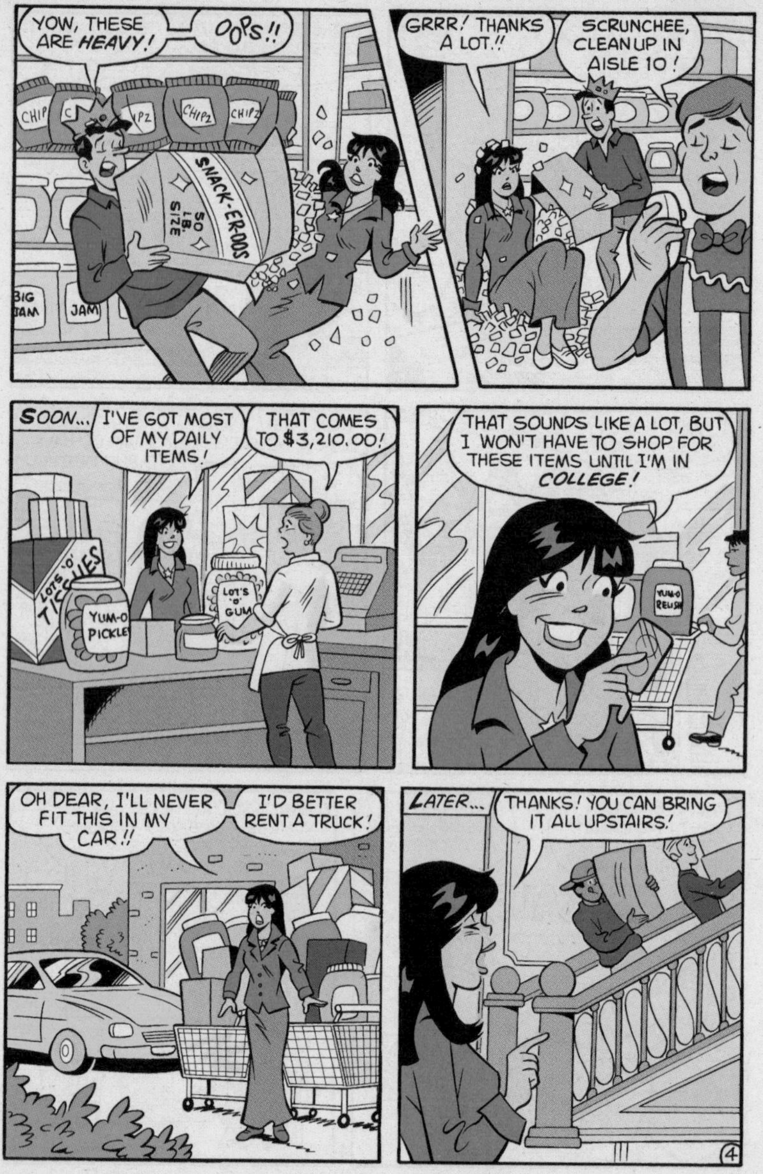
YOW, THESE ARE HEAVY!
OOPS!!
CHIPZ
SNACK-ER-OOS
50 LB. SIZE
BIG JAM
JAM
GRRR! THANKS A LOT!!
SCRUNCHEE, CLEANUP IN AISLE 10!
SOON...
I'VE GOT MOST OF MY DAILY ITEMS!
THAT COMES TO $3,210.00!
LOTS 'O' TISSUES
YUM-O PICKLES
LOT'S 'O' GUM
THAT SOUNDS LIKE A LOT, BUT I WON'T HAVE TO SHOP FOR THESE ITEMS UNTIL I'M IN COLLEGE!
YUM-O RELISH
OH DEAR, I'LL NEVER FIT THIS IN MY CAR!!
I'D BETTER RENT A TRUCK!
LATER...
THANKS! YOU CAN BRING IT ALL UPSTAIRS!
4

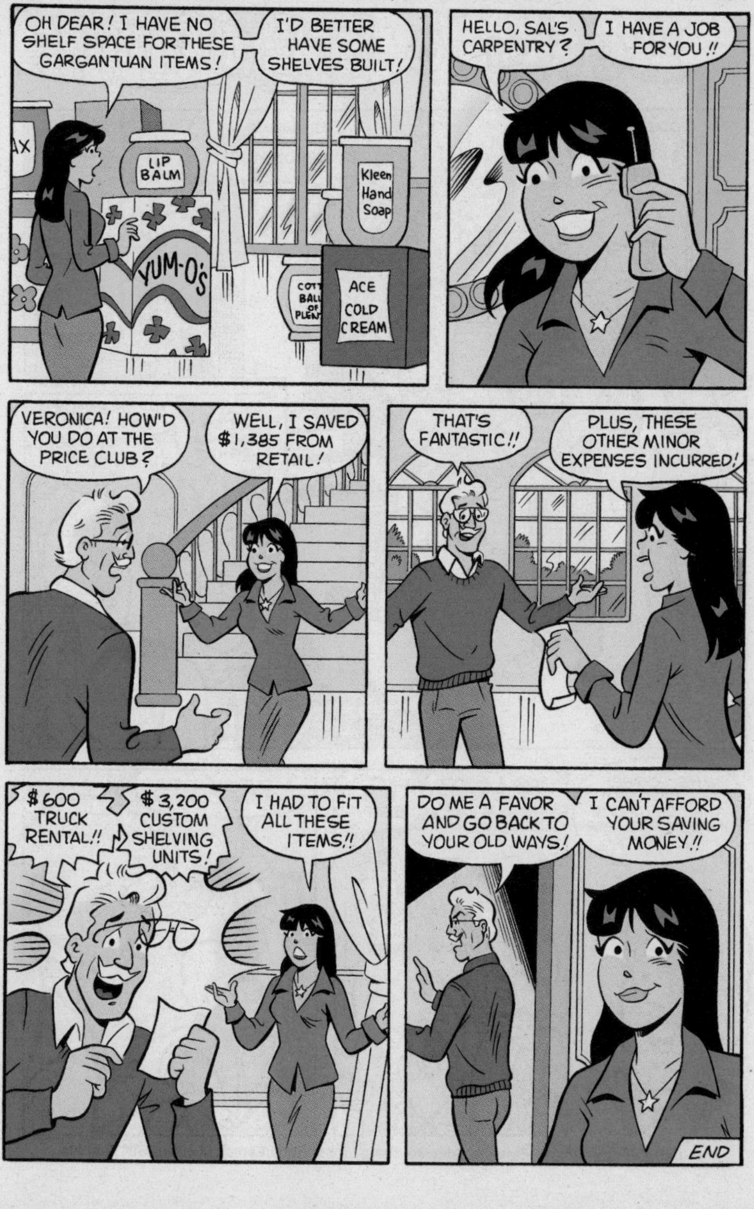
OH DEAR! I HAVE NO SHELF SPACE FOR THESE GARGANTUAN ITEMS!
I'D BETTER HAVE SOME SHELVES BUILT!
LIP BALM
Kleen Hand Soap
YUM-O's
ACE COLD CREAM
HELLO, SAL'S CARPENTRY?
I HAVE A JOB FOR YOU!!
VERONICA! HOW'D YOU DO AT THE PRICE CLUB?
WELL, I SAVED $1,385 FROM RETAIL!
THAT'S FANTASTIC!!
PLUS, THESE OTHER MINOR EXPENSES INCURRED!
$600 TRUCK RENTAL!!
$3,200 CUSTOM SHELVING UNITS!
I HAD TO FIT ALL THESE ITEMS!!
DO ME A FAVOR AND GO BACK TO YOUR OLD WAYS!
I CAN'T AFFORD YOUR SAVING MONEY!!
END

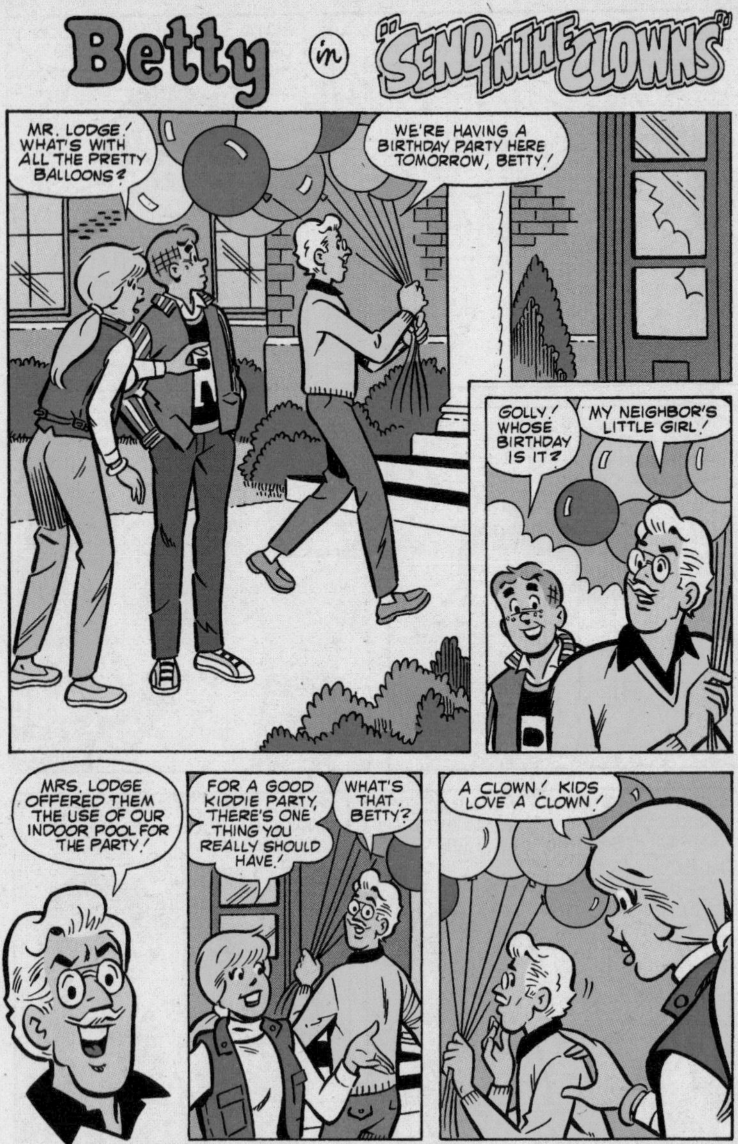
Betty in "SEND IN THE CLOWNS"
MR. LODGE! WHAT'S WITH ALL THE PRETTY BALLOONS?
WE'RE HAVING A BIRTHDAY PARTY HERE TOMORROW, BETTY!
GOLLY! WHOSE BIRTHDAY IS IT?
MY NEIGHBOR'S LITTLE GIRL!
MRS. LODGE OFFERED THEM THE USE OF OUR INDOOR POOL FOR THE PARTY!
FOR A GOOD KIDDIE PARTY, THERE'S ONE THING YOU REALLY SHOULD HAVE!
WHAT'S THAT, BETTY?
A CLOWN! KIDS LOVE A CLOWN!

Script: Frank Doyle / Pencils: Stan Goldberg / Inks: Rudy Lapick / Letters: Bill Yoshida

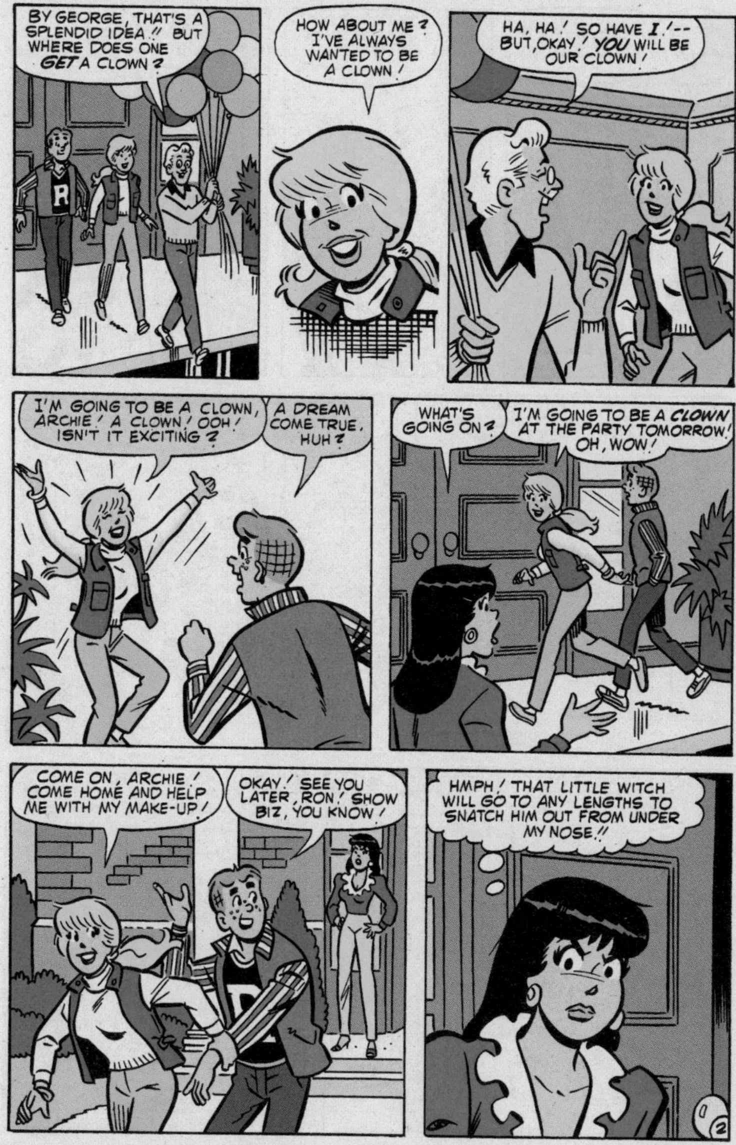

BY GEORGE, THAT'S A SPLENDID IDEA!! BUT WHERE DOES ONE GET A CLOWN?
HOW ABOUT ME? I'VE ALWAYS WANTED TO BE A CLOWN!
HA, HA! SO HAVE I!-- BUT, OKAY! YOU WILL BE OUR CLOWN!
I'M GOING TO BE A CLOWN, ARCHIE! A CLOWN! OOH! ISN'T IT EXCITING?
A DREAM COME TRUE, HUH?
WHAT'S GOING ON?
I'M GOING TO BE A CLOWN AT THE PARTY TOMORROW! OH, WOW!
COME ON, ARCHIE! COME HOME AND HELP ME WITH MY MAKE-UP!
OKAY! SEE YOU LATER, RON! SHOW BIZ, YOU KNOW!
HMPH! THAT LITTLE WITCH WILL GO TO ANY LENGTHS TO SNATCH HIM OUT FROM UNDER MY NOSE!!
2

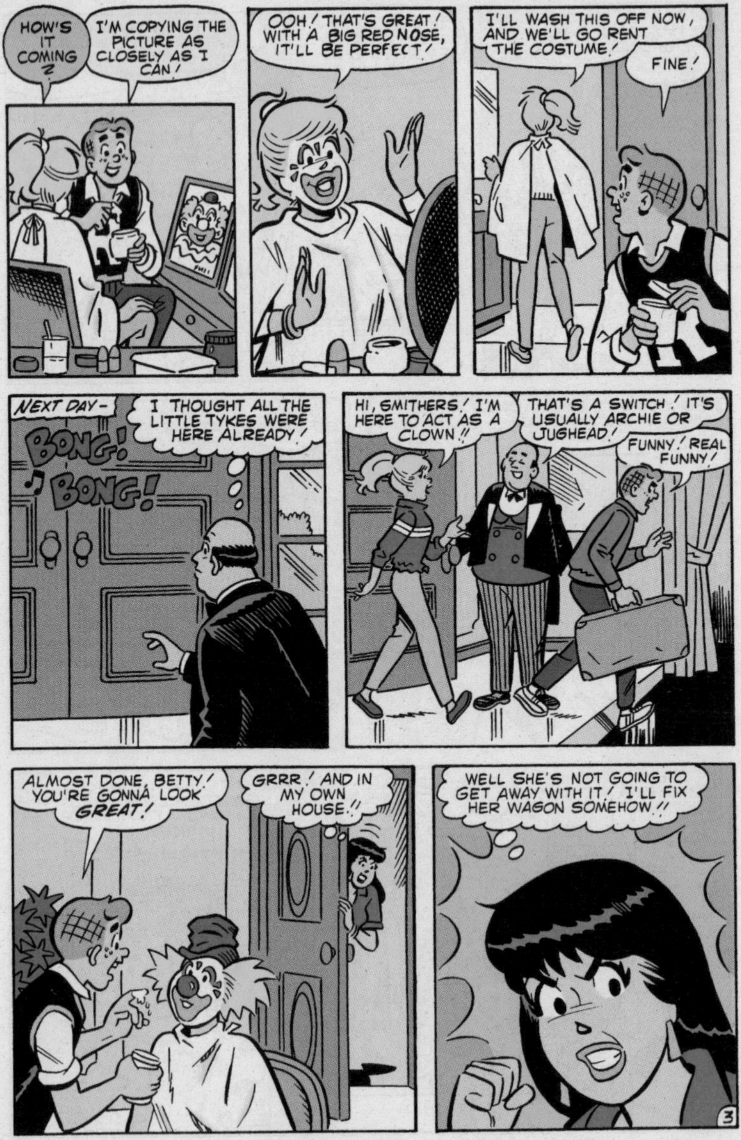

HOW'S IT COMING ?
I'M COPYING THE PICTURE AS CLOSELY AS I CAN!
OOH! THAT'S GREAT! WITH A BIG RED NOSE, IT'LL BE PERFECT!
I'LL WASH THIS OFF NOW, AND WE'LL GO RENT THE COSTUME!
FINE!
NEXT DAY-
I THOUGHT ALL THE LITTLE TYKES WERE HERE ALREADY!
BONG! BONG!
HI, SMITHERS! I'M HERE TO ACT AS A CLOWN!!
THAT'S A SWITCH! IT'S USUALLY ARCHIE OR JUGHEAD!
FUNNY! REAL FUNNY!
ALMOST DONE, BETTY! YOU'RE GONNA LOOK GREAT!
GRRR! AND IN MY OWN HOUSE!!
WELL SHE'S NOT GOING TO GET AWAY WITH IT! I'LL FIX HER WAGON SOMEHOW!!

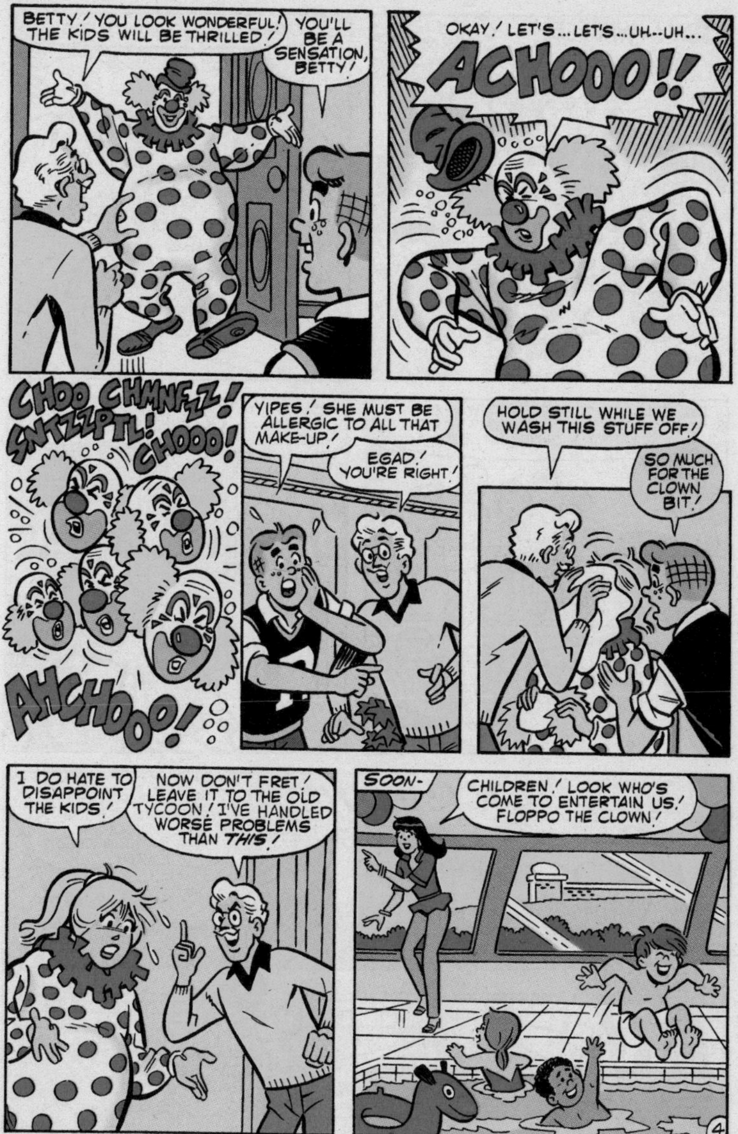
BETTY! YOU LOOK WONDERFUL! THE KIDS WILL BE THRILLED!
YOU'LL BE A SENSATION, BETTY!
OKAY! LET'S...LET'S...UH--UH...
ACHOOO!!
CHOO CHMNFZZZ! SNTZZZPTL! CHOOO!
AHCHOOOO!
YIPES! SHE MUST BE ALLERGIC TO ALL THAT MAKE-UP!
EGAD! YOU'RE RIGHT!
HOLD STILL WHILE WE WASH THIS STUFF OFF!
SO MUCH FOR THE CLOWN BIT!
I DO HATE TO DISAPPOINT THE KIDS!
NOW DON'T FRET! LEAVE IT TO THE OLD TYCOON! I'VE HANDLED WORSE PROBLEMS THAN THIS!
SOON-
CHILDREN! LOOK WHO'S COME TO ENTERTAIN US! FLOPPO THE CLOWN!
4

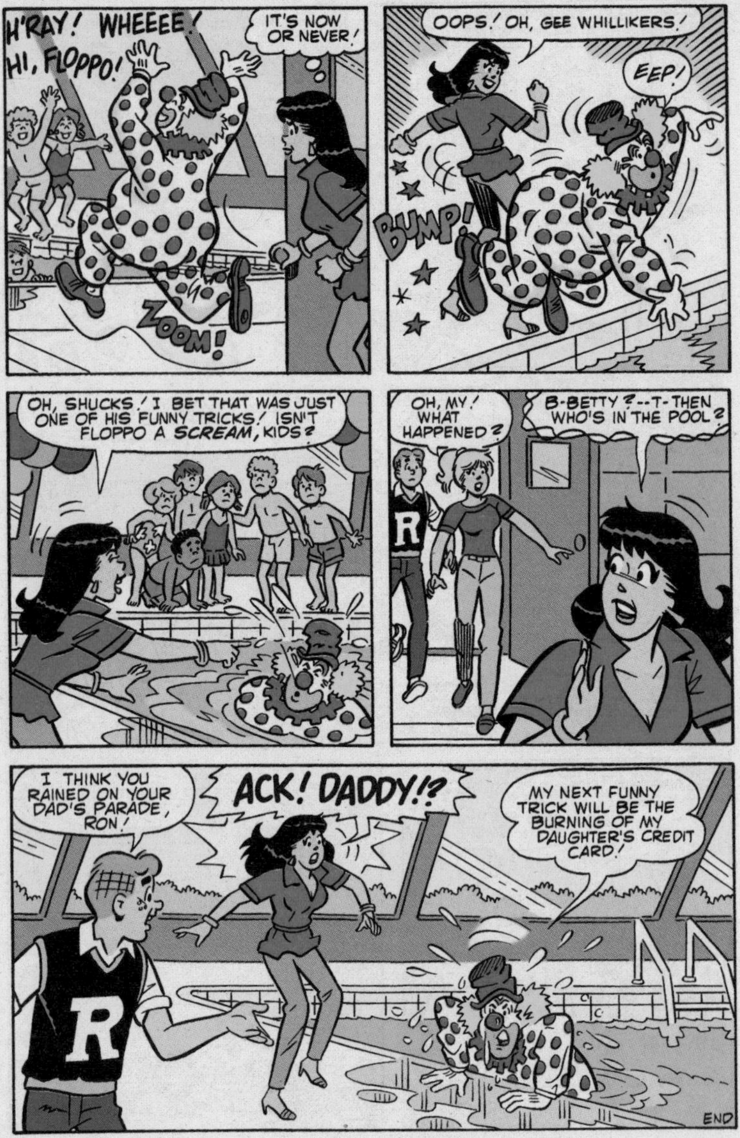
H'RAY! WHEEEE!
HI, FLOPPO!
IT'S NOW OR NEVER!
ZOOM!
OOPS! OH, GEE WHILLIKERS!
EEP!
BUMP!
OH, SHUCKS! I BET THAT WAS JUST ONE OF HIS FUNNY TRICKS! ISN'T FLOPPO A SCREAM, KIDS?
OH, MY! WHAT HAPPENED?
B-BETTY?--T-THEN WHO'S IN THE POOL?
I THINK YOU RAINED ON YOUR DAD'S PARADE, RON!
ACK! DADDY!?
MY NEXT FUNNY TRICK WILL BE THE BURNING OF MY DAUGHTER'S CREDIT CARD!
END

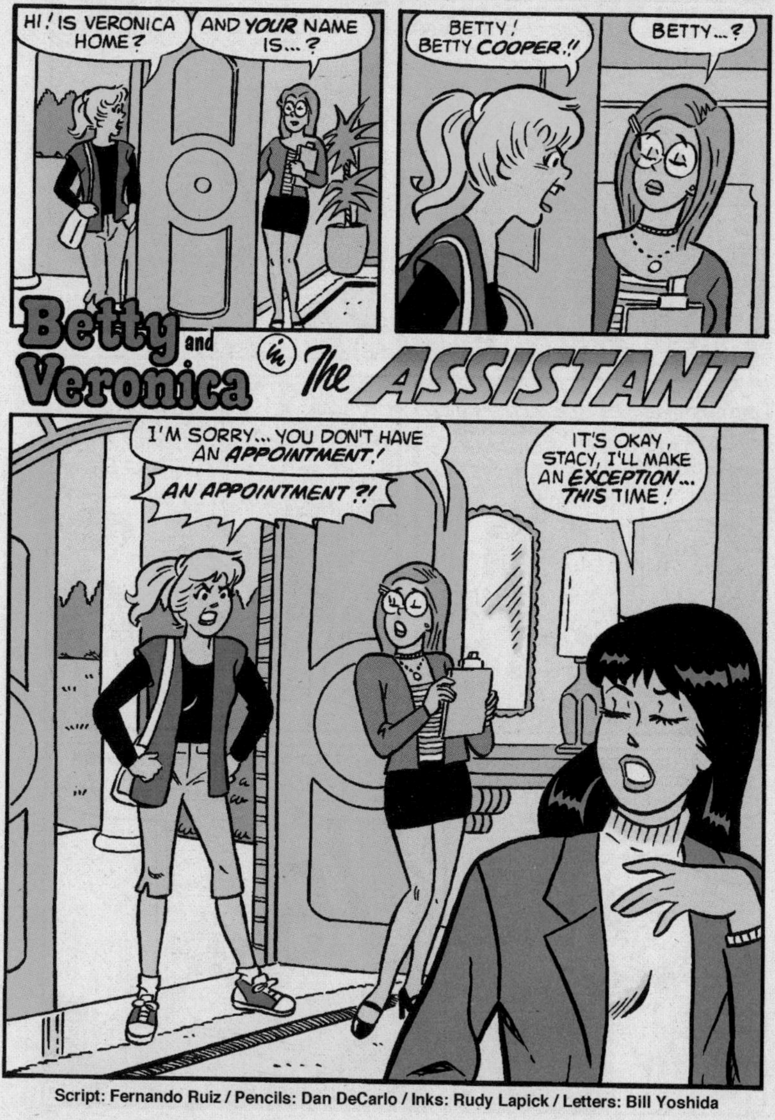
HI! IS VERONICA HOME?
AND YOUR NAME IS...?
BETTY! BETTY COOPER!!
BETTY...?
Betty and Veronica in The ASSISTANT
I'M SORRY... YOU DON'T HAVE AN APPOINTMENT!
AN APPOINTMENT?!
IT'S OKAY, STACY, I'LL MAKE AN EXCEPTION... THIS TIME!

Script: Fernando Ruiz / Pencils: Dan DeCarlo / Inks: Rudy Lapick / Letters: Bill Yoshida

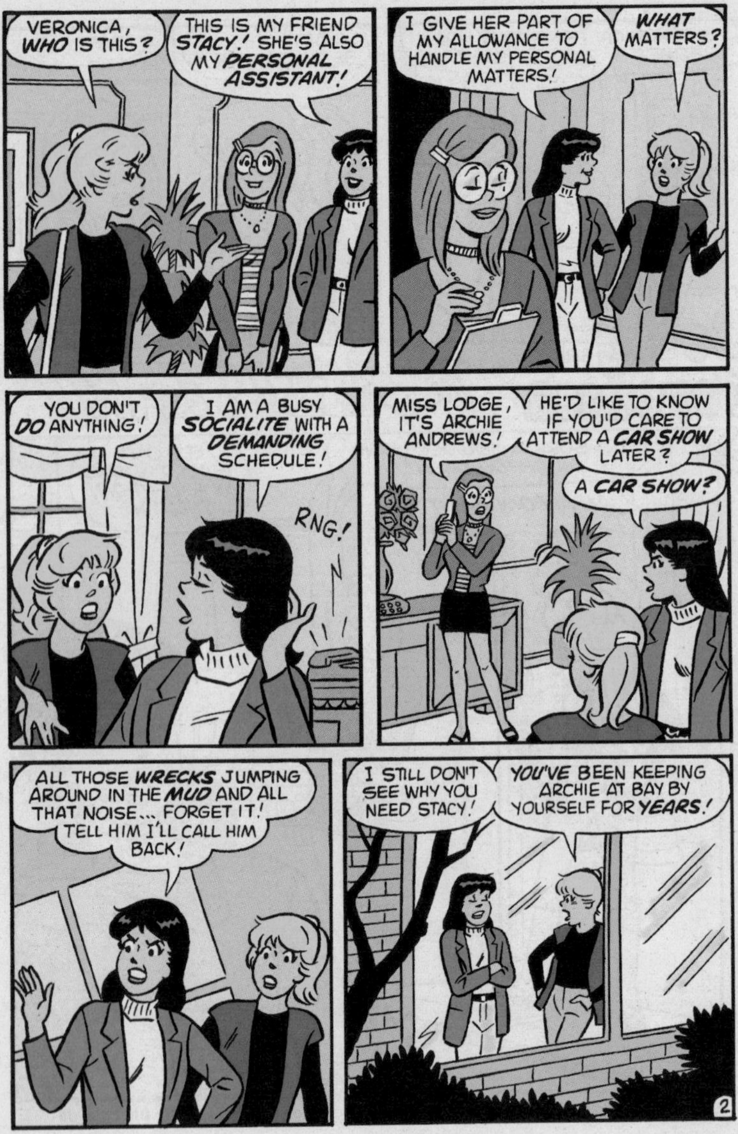

VERONICA, WHO IS THIS?
THIS IS MY FRIEND STACY! SHE'S ALSO MY PERSONAL ASSISTANT!
I GIVE HER PART OF MY ALLOWANCE TO HANDLE MY PERSONAL MATTERS!
WHAT MATTERS?
YOU DON'T DO ANYTHING!
I AM A BUSY SOCIALITE WITH A DEMANDING SCHEDULE!
RNG!
MISS LODGE, IT'S ARCHIE ANDREWS!
HE'D LIKE TO KNOW IF YOU'D CARE TO ATTEND A CAR SHOW LATER?
A CAR SHOW?
ALL THOSE WRECKS JUMPING AROUND IN THE MUD AND ALL THAT NOISE... FORGET IT!
TELL HIM I'LL CALL HIM BACK!
I STILL DON'T SEE WHY YOU NEED STACY!
YOU'VE BEEN KEEPING ARCHIE AT BAY BY YOURSELF FOR YEARS!
2

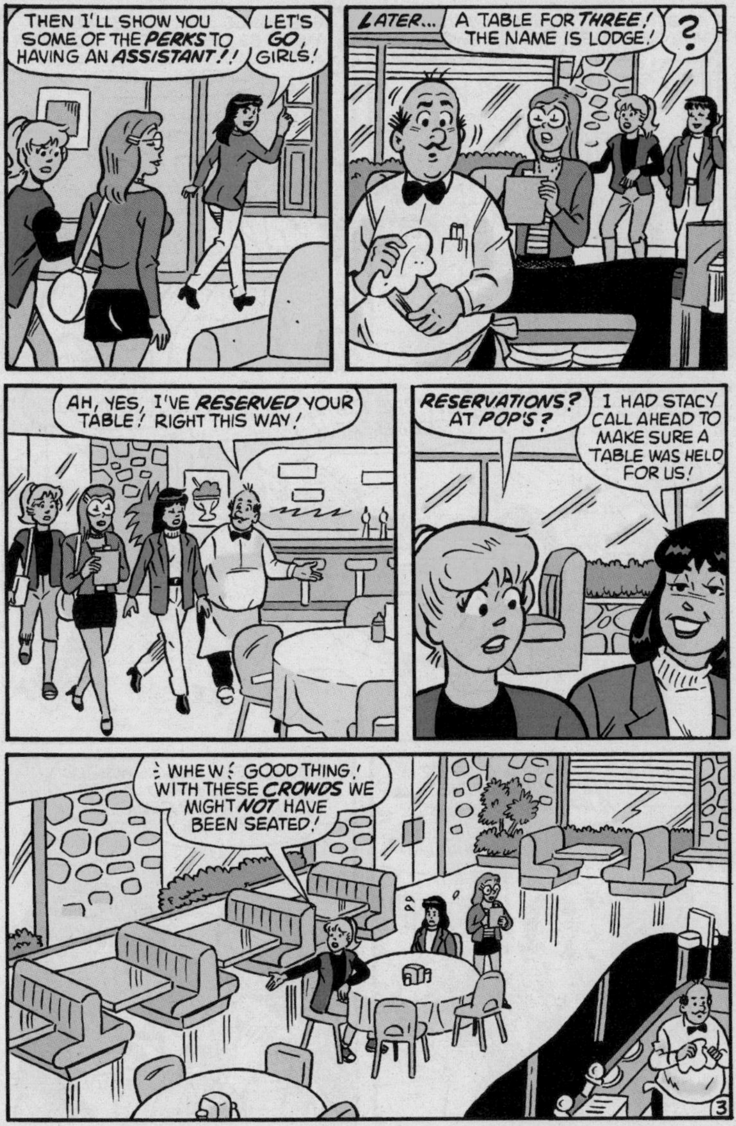
THEN I'LL SHOW YOU SOME OF THE PERKS TO HAVING AN ASSISTANT!!
LET'S GO, GIRLS!
LATER...
A TABLE FOR THREE! THE NAME IS LODGE!
?
AH, YES, I'VE RESERVED YOUR TABLE! RIGHT THIS WAY!
RESERVATIONS? AT POP'S?
I HAD STACY CALL AHEAD TO MAKE SURE A TABLE WAS HELD FOR US!
WHEW! GOOD THING! WITH THESE CROWDS WE MIGHT NOT HAVE BEEN SEATED!
3

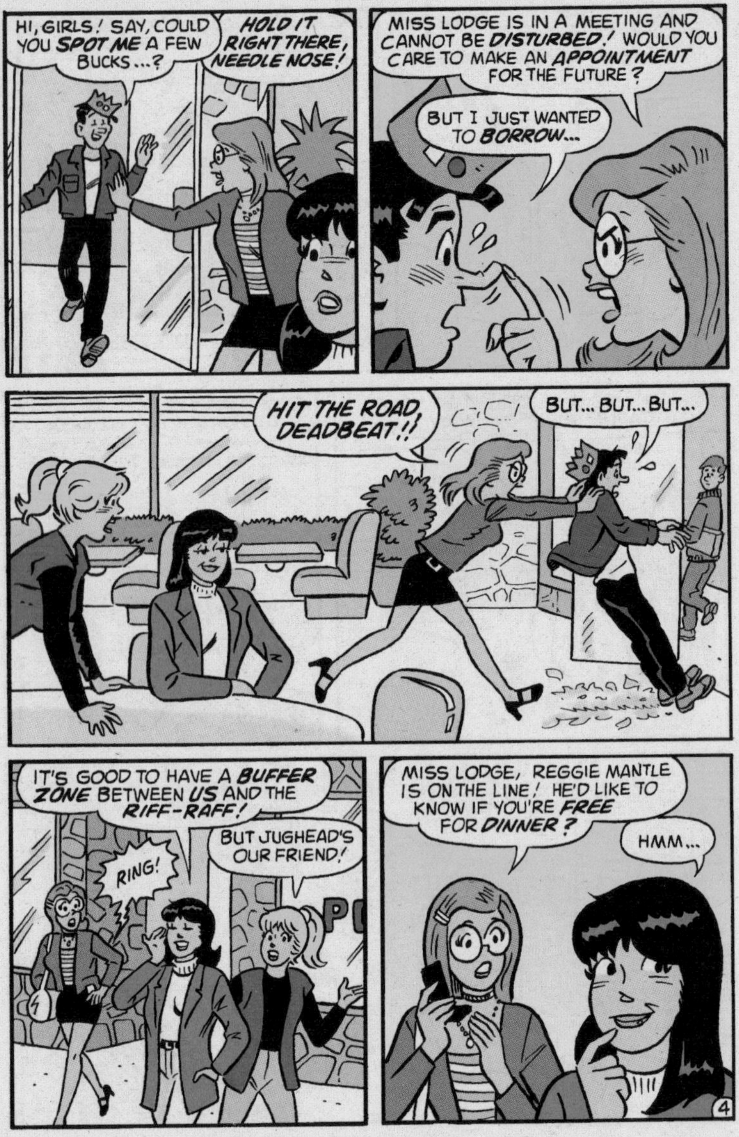
HI, GIRLS! SAY, COULD YOU SPOT ME A FEW BUCKS...?
HOLD IT RIGHT THERE, NEEDLE NOSE!
MISS LODGE IS IN A MEETING AND CANNOT BE DISTURBED! WOULD YOU CARE TO MAKE AN APPOINTMENT FOR THE FUTURE?
BUT I JUST WANTED TO BORROW...
HIT THE ROAD, DEADBEAT!!
BUT... BUT... BUT...
IT'S GOOD TO HAVE A BUFFER ZONE BETWEEN US AND THE RIFF-RAFF!
RING!
BUT JUGHEAD'S OUR FRIEND!
MISS LODGE, REGGIE MANTLE IS ON THE LINE! HE'D LIKE TO KNOW IF YOU'RE FREE FOR DINNER?
HMM...
4

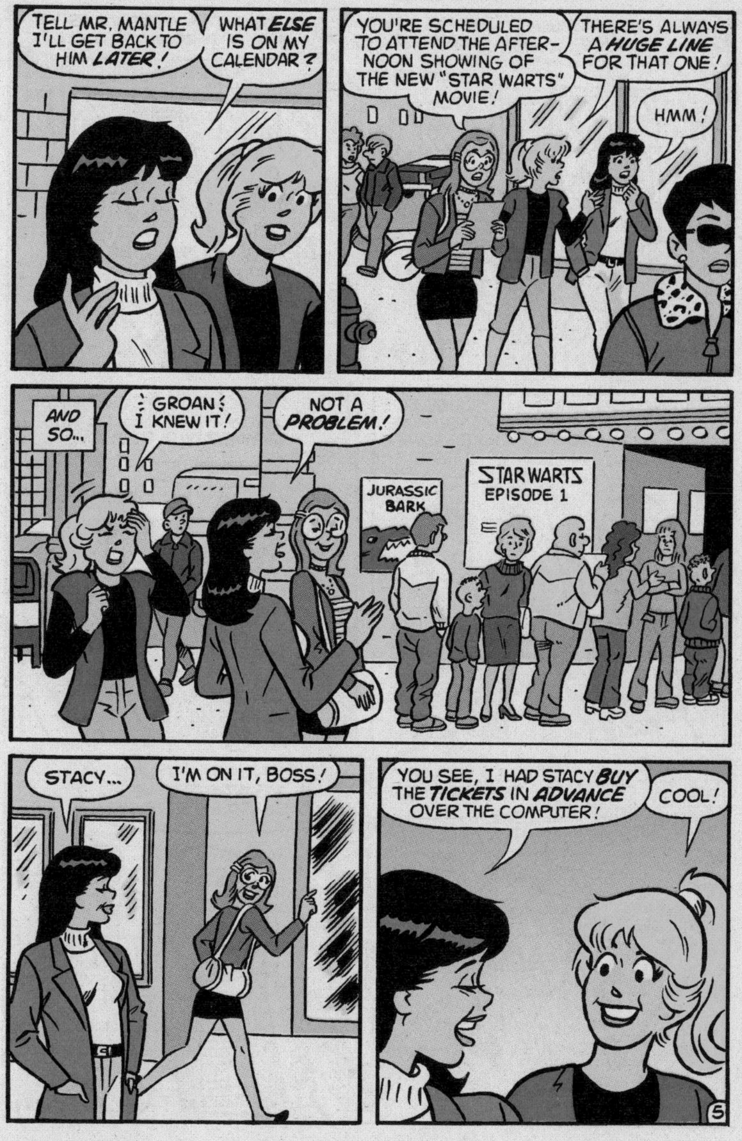
TELL MR. MANTLE I'LL GET BACK TO HIM LATER!
WHAT ELSE IS ON MY CALENDAR?
YOU'RE SCHEDULED TO ATTEND THE AFTER-NOON SHOWING OF THE NEW "STAR WARTS" MOVIE!
THERE'S ALWAYS A HUGE LINE FOR THAT ONE!
HMM!
AND SO...
GROAN! I KNEW IT!
NOT A PROBLEM!
JURASSIC BARK
STAR WARTS EPISODE 1
STACY...
I'M ON IT, BOSS!
YOU SEE, I HAD STACY BUY THE TICKETS IN ADVANCE OVER THE COMPUTER!
COOL!
5

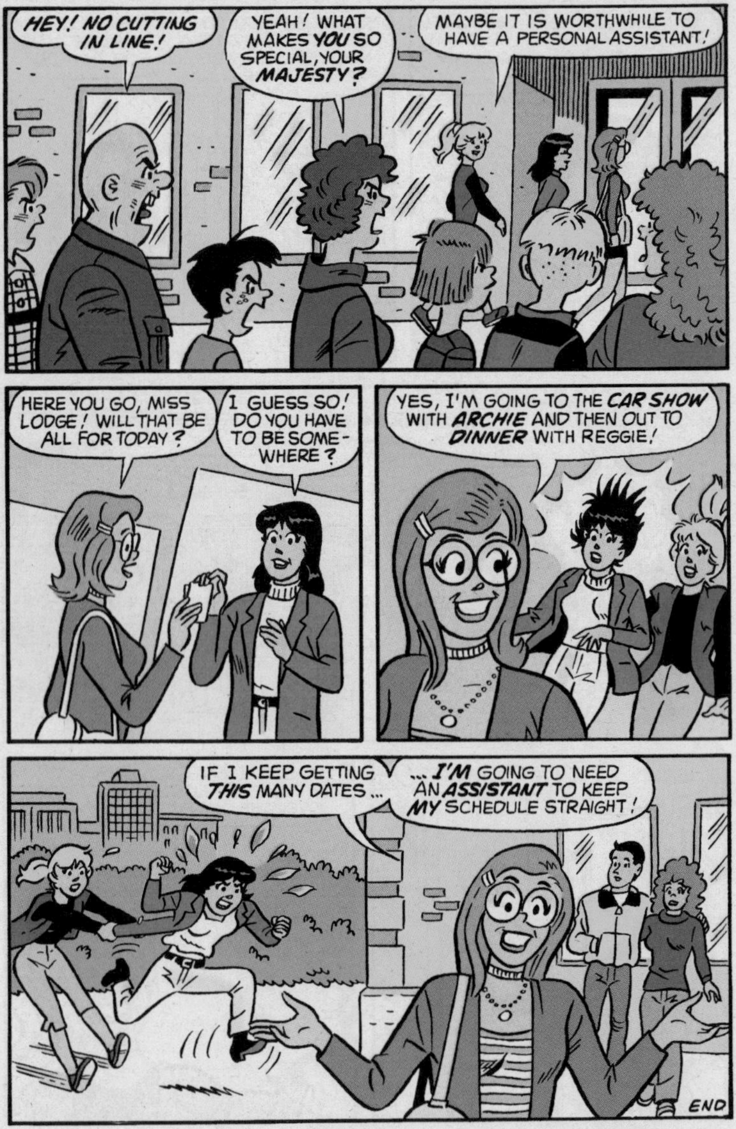

HEY! NO CUTTING IN LINE!
YEAH! WHAT MAKES YOU SO SPECIAL, YOUR MAJESTY?
MAYBE IT IS WORTHWHILE TO HAVE A PERSONAL ASSISTANT!
HERE YOU GO, MISS LODGE! WILL THAT BE ALL FOR TODAY?
I GUESS SO! DO YOU HAVE TO BE SOMEWHERE?
YES, I'M GOING TO THE CAR SHOW WITH ARCHIE AND THEN OUT TO DINNER WITH REGGIE!
IF I KEEP GETTING THIS MANY DATES...
...I'M GOING TO NEED AN ASSISTANT TO KEEP MY SCHEDULE STRAIGHT!
END

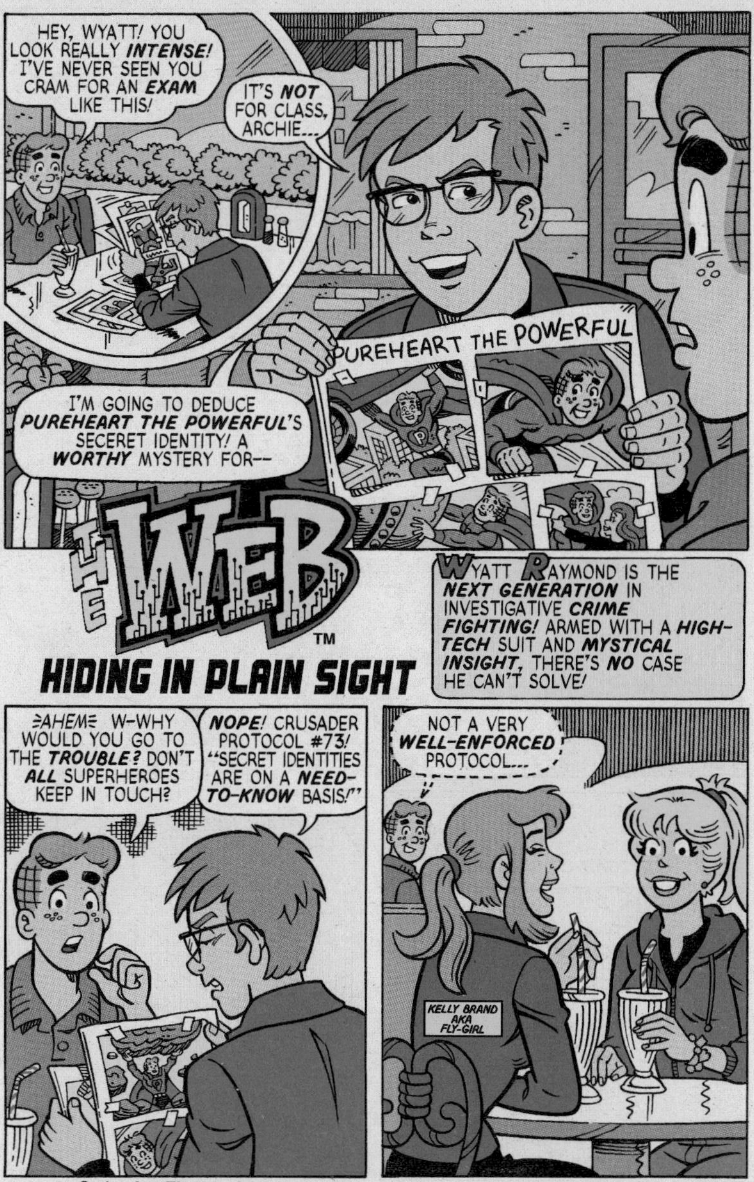
HEY, WYATT! YOU LOOK REALLY INTENSE! I'VE NEVER SEEN YOU CRAM FOR AN EXAM LIKE THIS!
IT'S NOT FOR CLASS, ARCHIE...
PUREHEART THE POWERFUL
I'M GOING TO DEDUCE PUREHEART THE POWERFUL'S SECERET IDENTITY! A WORTHY MYSTERY FOR--
THE WEB™
HIDING IN PLAIN SIGHT
WYATT RAYMOND IS THE NEXT GENERATION IN INVESTIGATIVE CRIME FIGHTING! ARMED WITH A HIGH-TECH SUIT AND MYSTICAL INSIGHT, THERE'S NO CASE HE CAN'T SOLVE!
=AHEM= W-WHY WOULD YOU GO TO THE TROUBLE? DON'T ALL SUPERHEROES KEEP IN TOUCH?
NOPE! CRUSADER PROTOCOL #73! "SECRET IDENTITIES ARE ON A NEED-TO-KNOW BASIS!"
NOT A VERY WELL-ENFORCED PROTOCOL...
KELLY BRAND AKA FLY-GIRL

Script: **Ian Flynn** Art & Letters: **Rex Lindsey** Colors: **Glenn Whitmore**

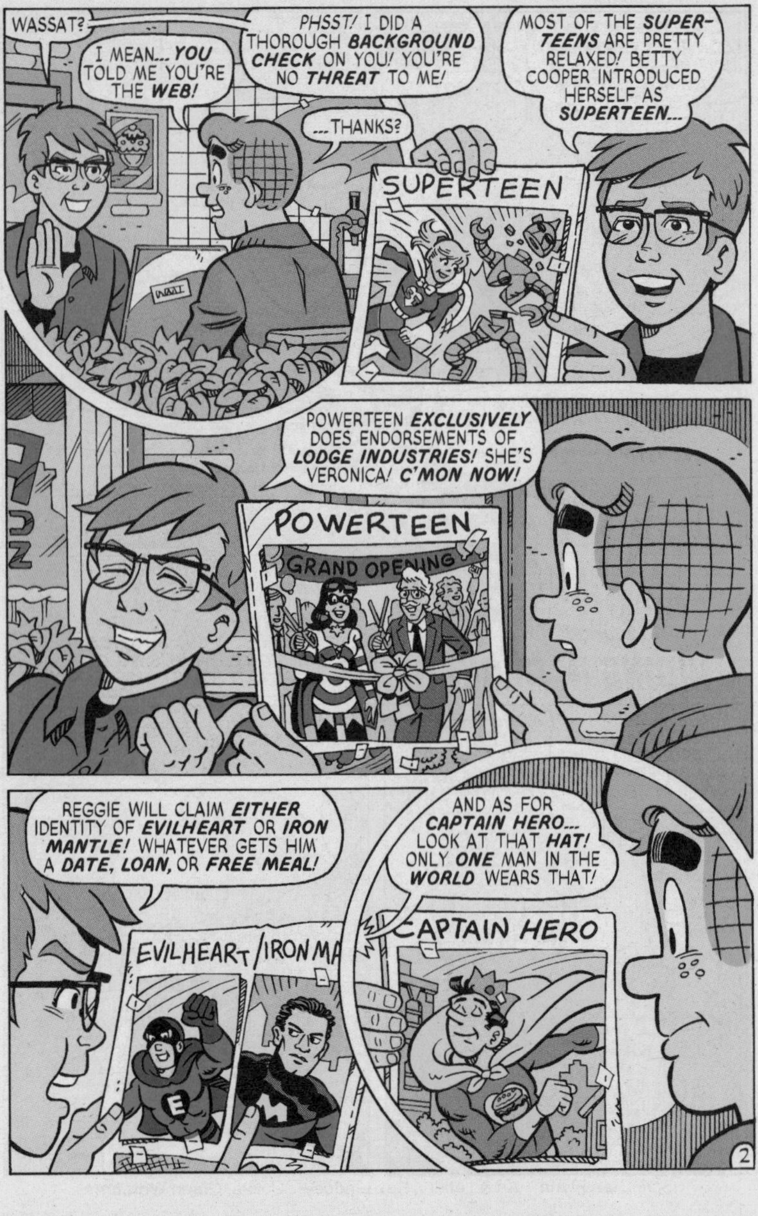

WASSAT?
I MEAN... YOU TOLD ME YOU'RE THE WEB!
PHSST! I DID A THOROUGH BACKGROUND CHECK ON YOU! YOU'RE NO THREAT TO ME!
...THANKS?
MOST OF THE SUPER-TEENS ARE PRETTY RELAXED! BETTY COOPER INTRODUCED HERSELF AS SUPERTEEN...
SUPERTEEN
POWERTEEN EXCLUSIVELY DOES ENDORSEMENTS OF LODGE INDUSTRIES! SHE'S VERONICA! C'MON NOW!
POWERTEEN
GRAND OPENING
REGGIE WILL CLAIM EITHER IDENTITY OF EVILHEART OR IRON MANTLE! WHATEVER GETS HIM A DATE, LOAN, OR FREE MEAL!
AND AS FOR CAPTAIN HERO... LOOK AT THAT HAT! ONLY ONE MAN IN THE WORLD WEARS THAT!
EVILHEART/IRON MA
CAPTAIN HERO

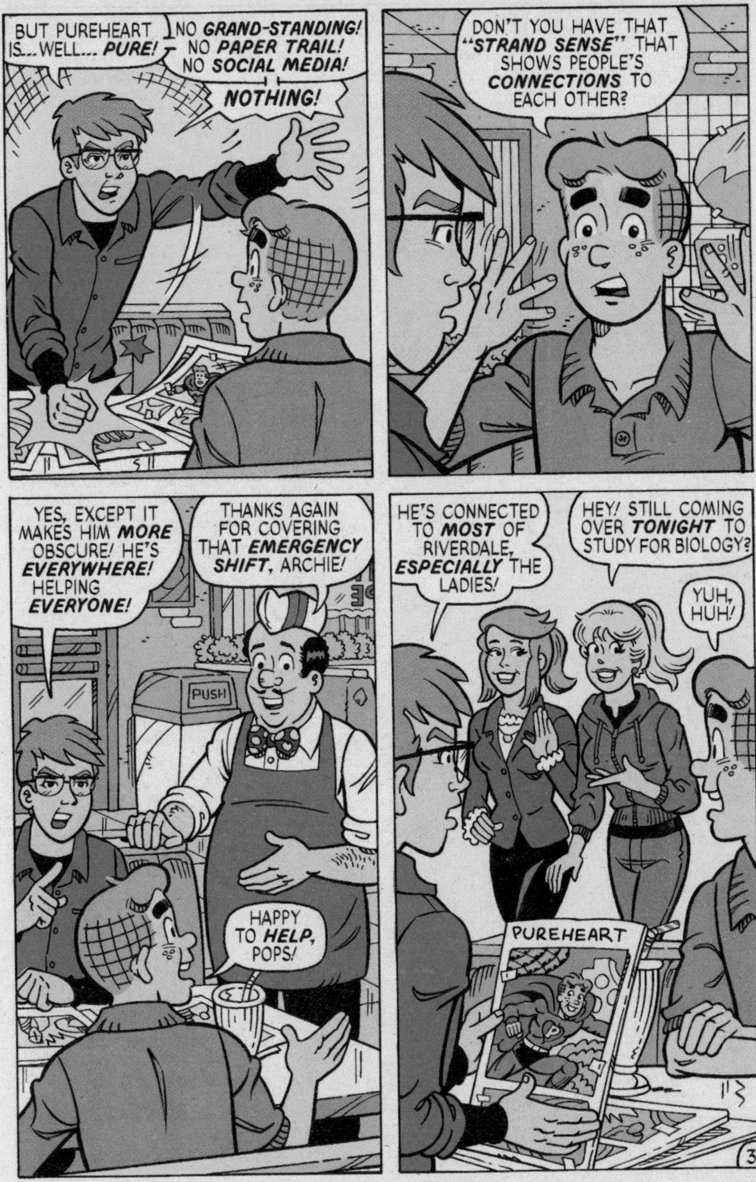
BUT PUREHEART IS... WELL... PURE!
NO GRAND-STANDING! NO PAPER TRAIL! NO SOCIAL MEDIA!
NOTHING!
DON'T YOU HAVE THAT "STRAND SENSE" THAT SHOWS PEOPLE'S CONNECTIONS TO EACH OTHER?
YES, EXCEPT IT MAKES HIM MORE OBSCURE! HE'S EVERYWHERE! HELPING EVERYONE!
THANKS AGAIN FOR COVERING THAT EMERGENCY SHIFT, ARCHIE!
PUSH
HAPPY TO HELP, POPS!
HE'S CONNECTED TO MOST OF RIVERDALE, ESPECIALLY THE LADIES!
HEY! STILL COMING OVER TONIGHT TO STUDY FOR BIOLOGY?
YUH, HUH!
PUREHEART

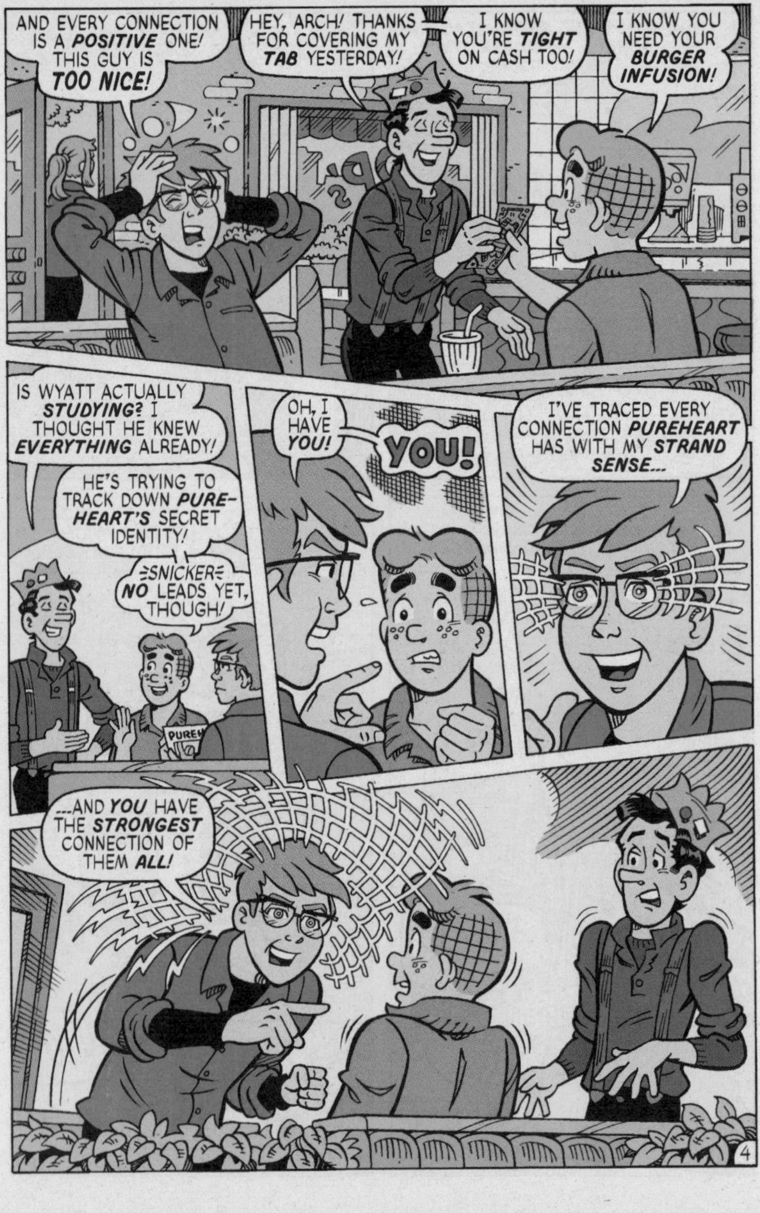

AND EVERY CONNECTION IS A POSITIVE ONE! THIS GUY IS TOO NICE!
HEY, ARCH! THANKS FOR COVERING MY TAB YESTERDAY!
I KNOW YOU'RE TIGHT ON CASH TOO!
I KNOW YOU NEED YOUR BURGER INFUSION!
IS WYATT ACTUALLY STUDYING? I THOUGHT HE KNEW EVERYTHING ALREADY!
HE'S TRYING TO TRACK DOWN PURE-HEART'S SECRET IDENTITY!
SNICKER NO LEADS YET, THOUGH!
PUREH
OH, I HAVE YOU!
YOU!
I'VE TRACED EVERY CONNECTION PUREHEART HAS WITH MY STRAND SENSE...
...AND YOU HAVE THE STRONGEST CONNECTION OF THEM ALL!

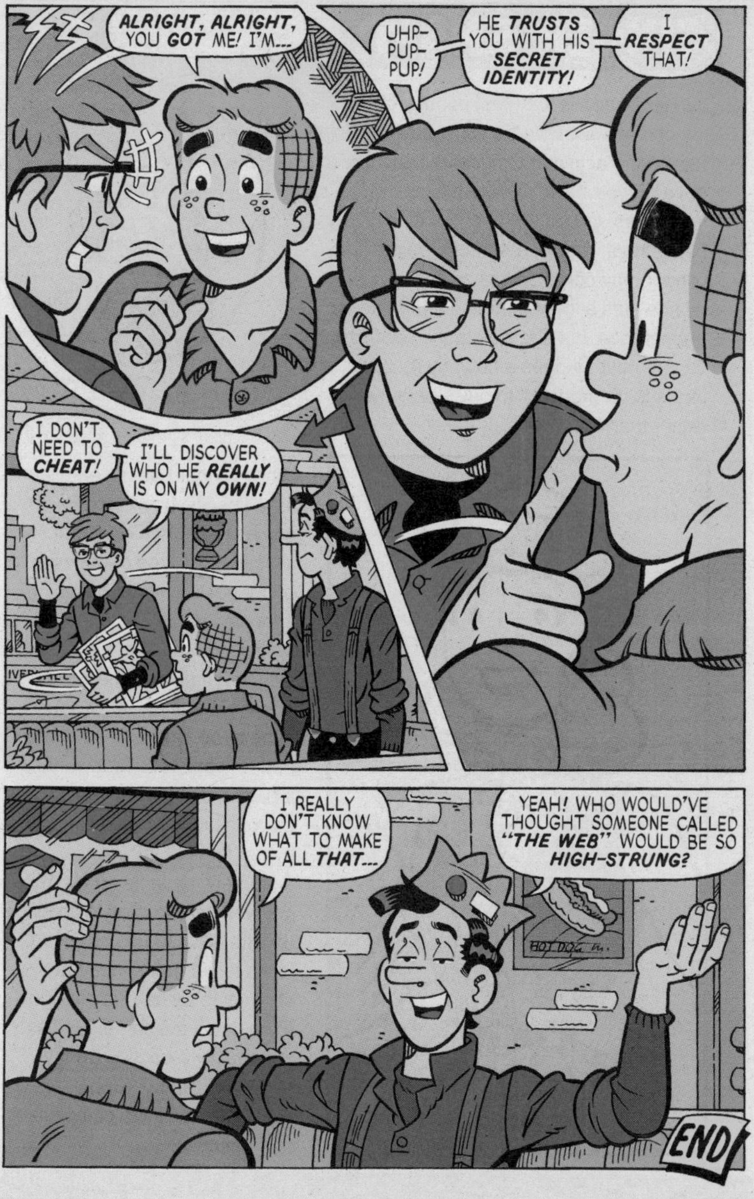
ALRIGHT, ALRIGHT, YOU GOT ME! I'M...
UHP-PUP-PUP!
HE TRUSTS YOU WITH HIS SECRET IDENTITY!
I RESPECT THAT!
I DON'T NEED TO CHEAT!
I'LL DISCOVER WHO HE REALLY IS ON MY OWN!
I REALLY DON'T KNOW WHAT TO MAKE OF ALL THAT...
YEAH! WHO WOULD'VE THOUGHT SOMEONE CALLED "THE WEB" WOULD BE SO HIGH-STRUNG?
HOT DOG
END

GINGER SNAPP

Ginger Snapp is the most popular girl in school! At least with the boys, that is! Ginger has a very active dating life, but she doesn't have "a type." She's dated all sorts of guys, from jocks, to straight-A students, shy boys, nerdy boys, rebels, etc. From the outside, Ginger may come across as superficial, as she puts a lot of time and effort into her appearance, but she's quite the opposite. Ginger never judges a book by its cover, and tends to be attracted to one's personality rather than their looks.

While Ginger has never fallen for a specific boy, there's something about Ickky that she likes, much to the bewilderment of her peers. Ginger has a shopping habit, and often spends too much of her father's income on new clothes. She doesn't like to wear the same outfit twice, and instead thinks of new ways to repeat wearing a piece with something new. Despite being raised primarily by her father, Ginger is extremely feminine and is quite crafty when it comes to coming up with ways to use her good looks to get dates, not that she has to try hard at all! She often dates the same guys as the equally attractive Bunny, but unlike Bunny, Ginger has a great personality to compliment her beauty.

DOTTIE

Dottie (later known as "Patsy") is Ginger's best friend and closest confidant. When Ginger has a crush, Dottie is the first to know, although she usually doesn't see what is so appealing to Ginger about these guys. Dottie is much pickier about her own dates, but for her that's a good thing. She'd rather wait for the right guy than date a bunch of boys she doesn't care much about.

ICKKY

His buddies are often confused how he can date a girl like Ginger, but Ickky's confidence might be his most attractive quality. However, their relationship isn't perfect, as Ickky takes Ginger for granted, before realizing how much he truly likes her. Ickky is thin and short for his age, and Ginger towers over him by quite a bit. But she is never embarrassed to be seen with him, and likes the attention he gives her. Ickky always feels the need to be right, and is awfully stubborn, which Ginger finds the most unappealing.

TOMMY TURNER

Tommy Turner is the only boy that Ginger is unable to "steal away" from Bunny, but when he sees how manipulative Bunny can be, he begins to like Ginger instead. Tommy is the complete opposite of Ickky, as he is tall, blonde, and muscular, which leads Ickky to see him as a rival for Ginger's affection.

SCAN ME

LEARN MORE ABOUT YOUR FAVORITE ARCHIE COMICS CHARACTERS IN THE ARCHIE ENCYCLOPEDIA! AVAILABLE NOW!

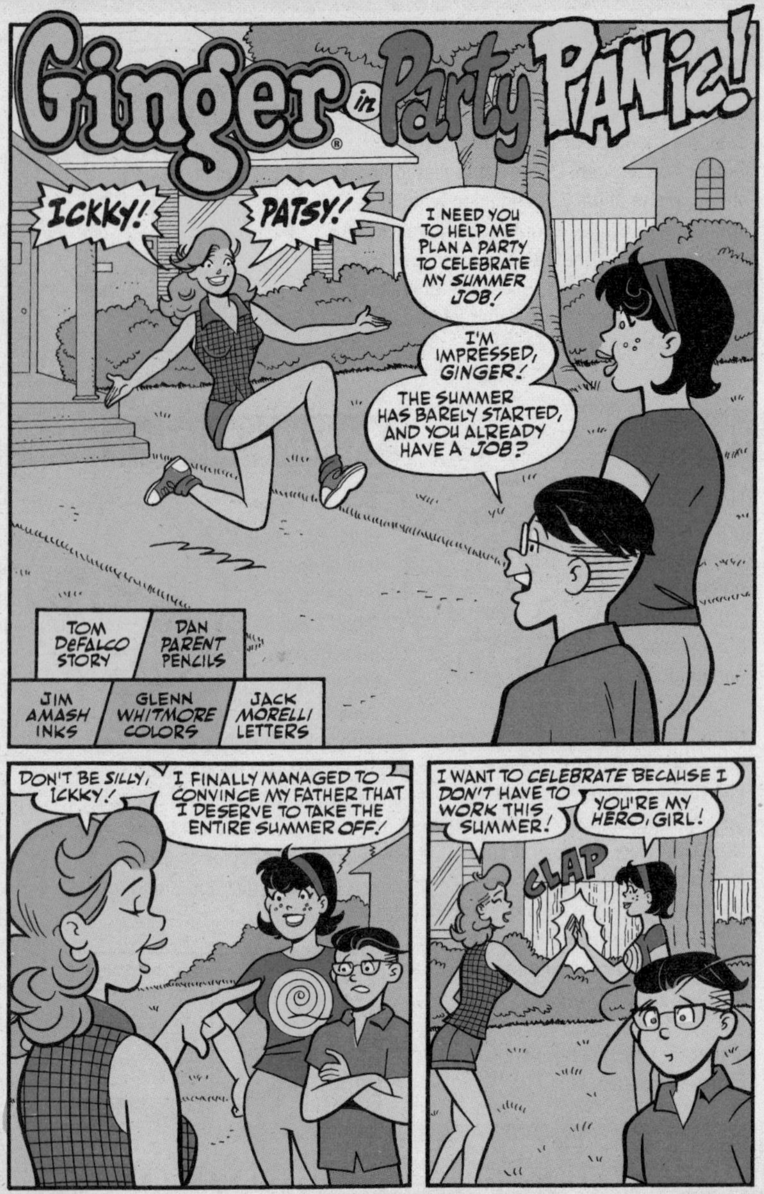
Ginger® in Party PANic!
ICKKY!
PATSY!
I NEED YOU TO HELP ME PLAN A PARTY TO CELEBRATE MY SUMMER JOB!
I'M IMPRESSED, GINGER!
THE SUMMER HAS BARELY STARTED, AND YOU ALREADY HAVE A JOB?
TOM DeFALCO STORY
DAN PARENT PENCILS
JIM AMASH INKS
GLENN WHITMORE COLORS
JACK MORELLI LETTERS
DON'T BE SILLY, ICKKY!
I FINALLY MANAGED TO CONVINCE MY FATHER THAT I DESERVE TO TAKE THE ENTIRE SUMMER OFF!
I WANT TO CELEBRATE BECAUSE I DON'T HAVE TO WORK THIS SUMMER!
YOU'RE MY HERO, GIRL!
CLAP

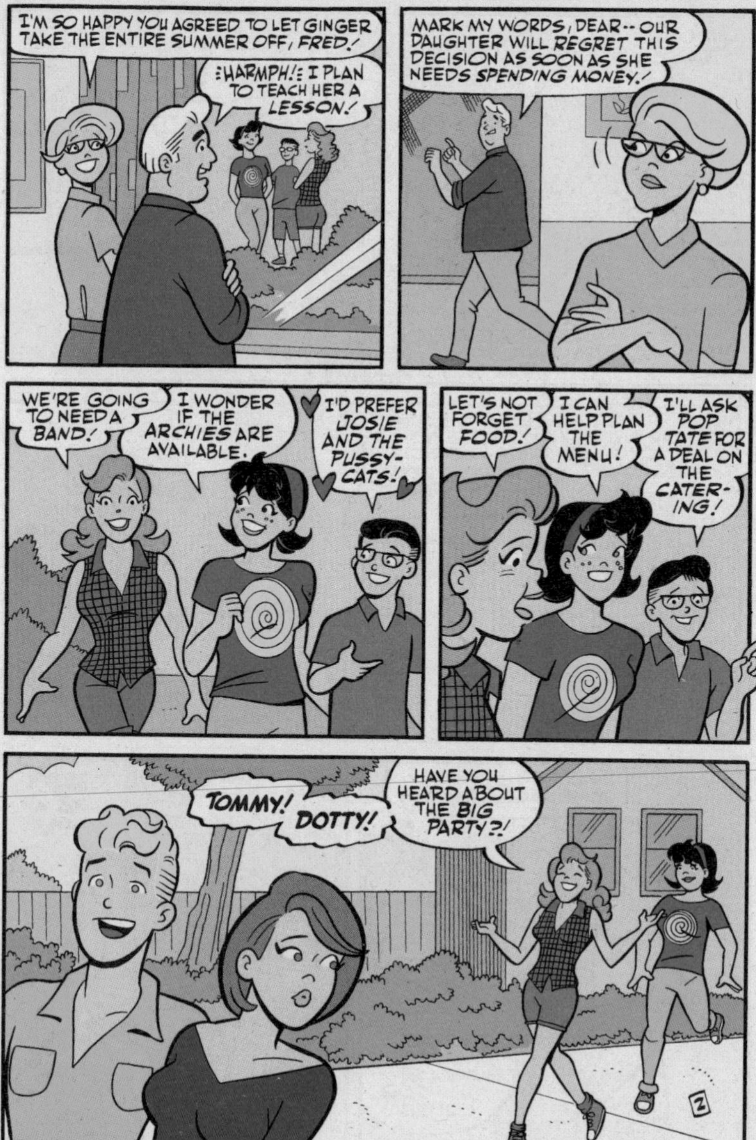
I'M SO HAPPY YOU AGREED TO LET GINGER TAKE THE ENTIRE SUMMER OFF, FRED!
:HARMPH!: I PLAN TO TEACH HER A LESSON!
MARK MY WORDS, DEAR-- OUR DAUGHTER WILL REGRET THIS DECISION AS SOON AS SHE NEEDS SPENDING MONEY!
WE'RE GOING TO NEED A BAND!
I WONDER IF THE ARCHIES ARE AVAILABLE.
I'D PREFER JOSIE AND THE PUSSY-CATS!
LET'S NOT FORGET FOOD!
I CAN HELP PLAN THE MENU!
I'LL ASK POP TATE FOR A DEAL ON THE CATER-ING!
TOMMY!
DOTTY!
HAVE YOU HEARD ABOUT THE BIG PARTY?!
2

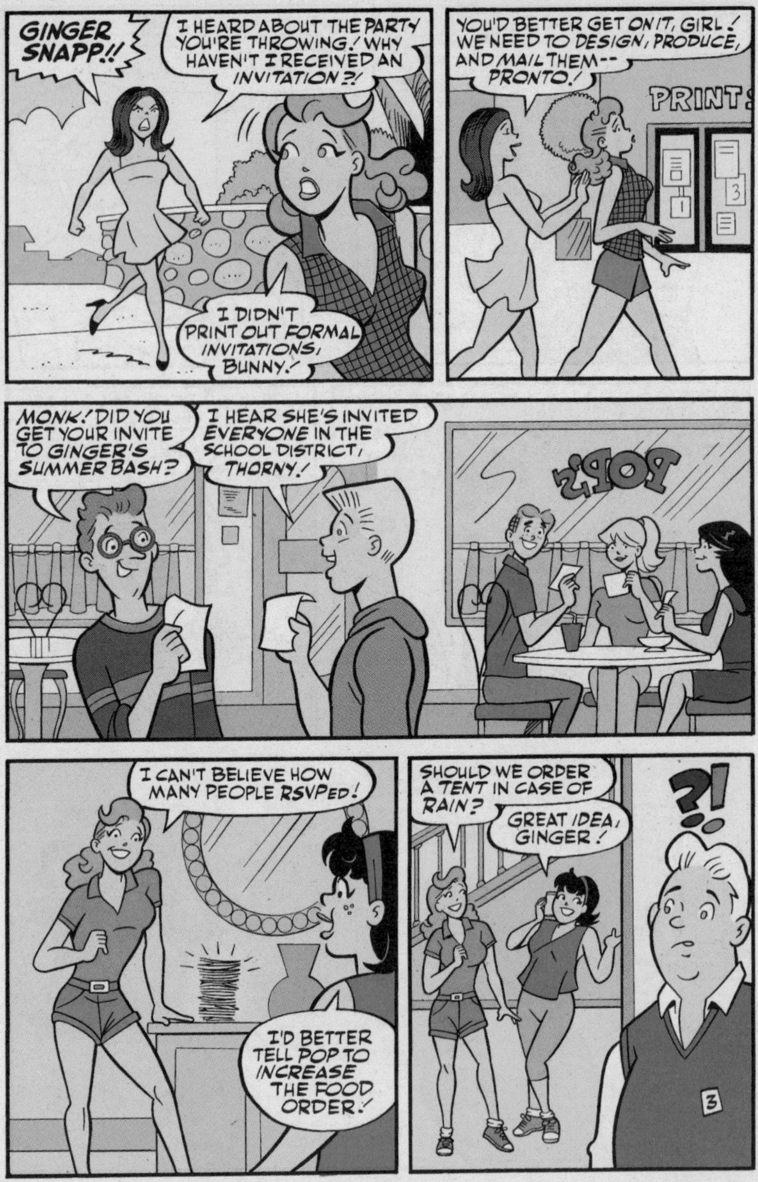
GINGER SNAPP!!
I HEARD ABOUT THE PARTY YOU'RE THROWING! WHY HAVEN'T I RECEIVED AN INVITATION?!
I DIDN'T PRINT OUT FORMAL INVITATIONS, BUNNY!
YOU'D BETTER GET ON IT, GIRL! WE NEED TO DESIGN, PRODUCE, AND MAIL THEM-- PRONTO!
PRINT
MONK! DID YOU GET YOUR INVITE TO GINGER'S SUMMER BASH?
I HEAR SHE'S INVITED EVERYONE IN THE SCHOOL DISTRICT, THORNY!
POP'S
I CAN'T BELIEVE HOW MANY PEOPLE RSVPED!
I'D BETTER TELL POP TO INCREASE THE FOOD ORDER!
SHOULD WE ORDER A TENT IN CASE OF RAIN?
GREAT IDEA, GINGER!
?!
3

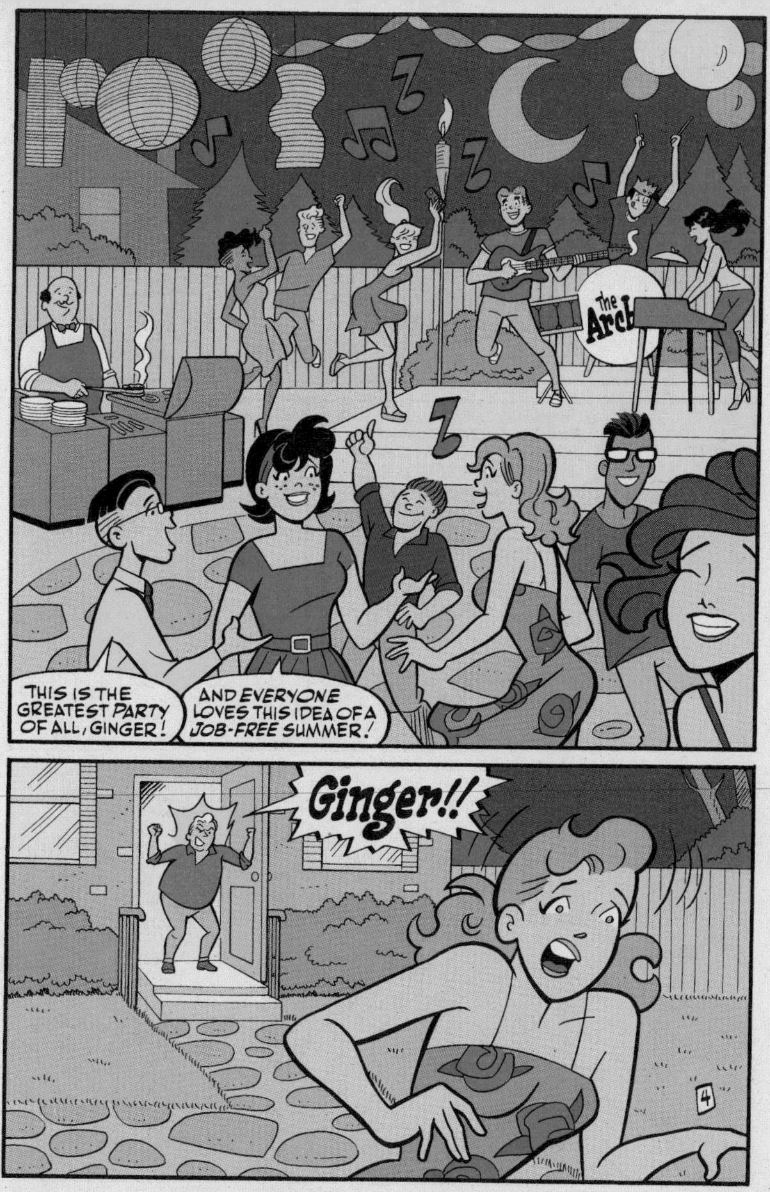

THE ARCH
THIS IS THE GREATEST PARTY OF ALL, GINGER!
AND EVERYONE LOVES THIS IDEA OF A JOB-FREE SUMMER!
Ginger!!
4

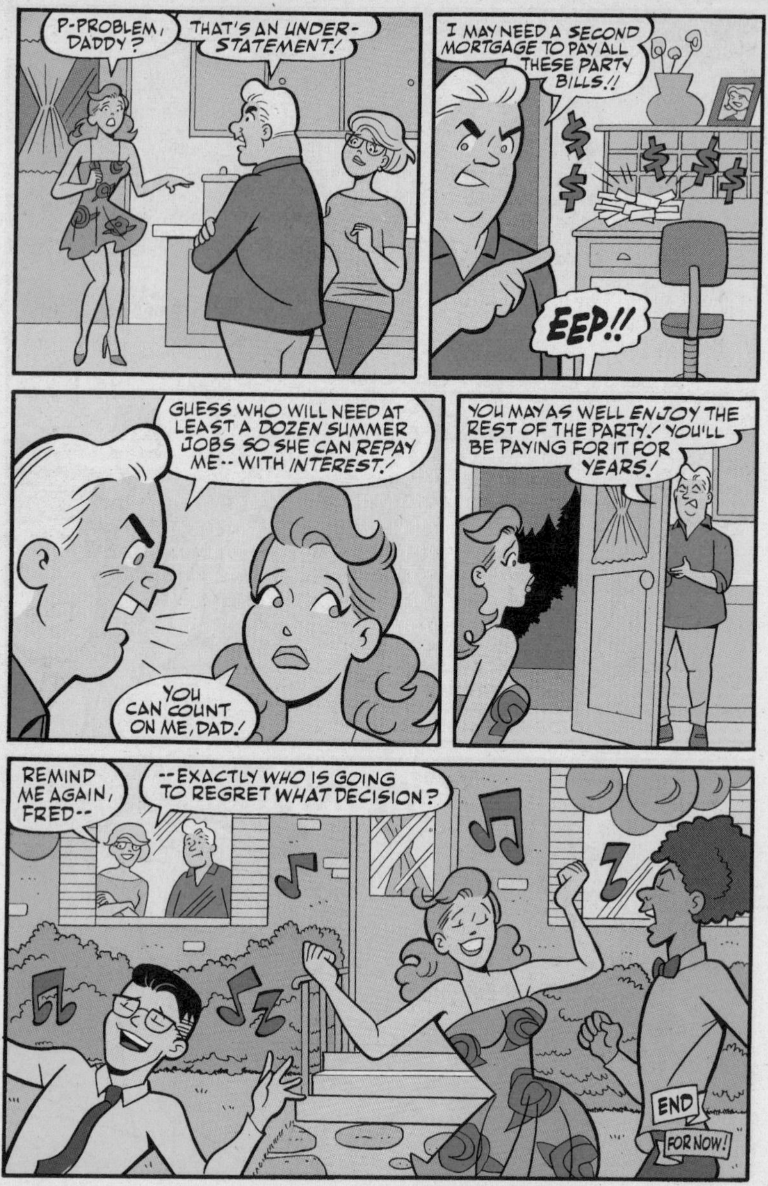
P-PROBLEM, DADDY?
THAT'S AN UNDER-STATEMENT!
I MAY NEED A SECOND MORTGAGE TO PAY ALL THESE PARTY BILLS!!
EEP!!
GUESS WHO WILL NEED AT LEAST A DOZEN SUMMER JOBS SO SHE CAN REPAY ME-- WITH INTEREST!
YOU CAN COUNT ON ME, DAD!
YOU MAY AS WELL ENJOY THE REST OF THE PARTY! YOU'LL BE PAYING FOR IT FOR YEARS!
REMIND ME AGAIN, FRED--
--EXACTLY WHO IS GOING TO REGRET WHAT DECISION?
END
FOR NOW!

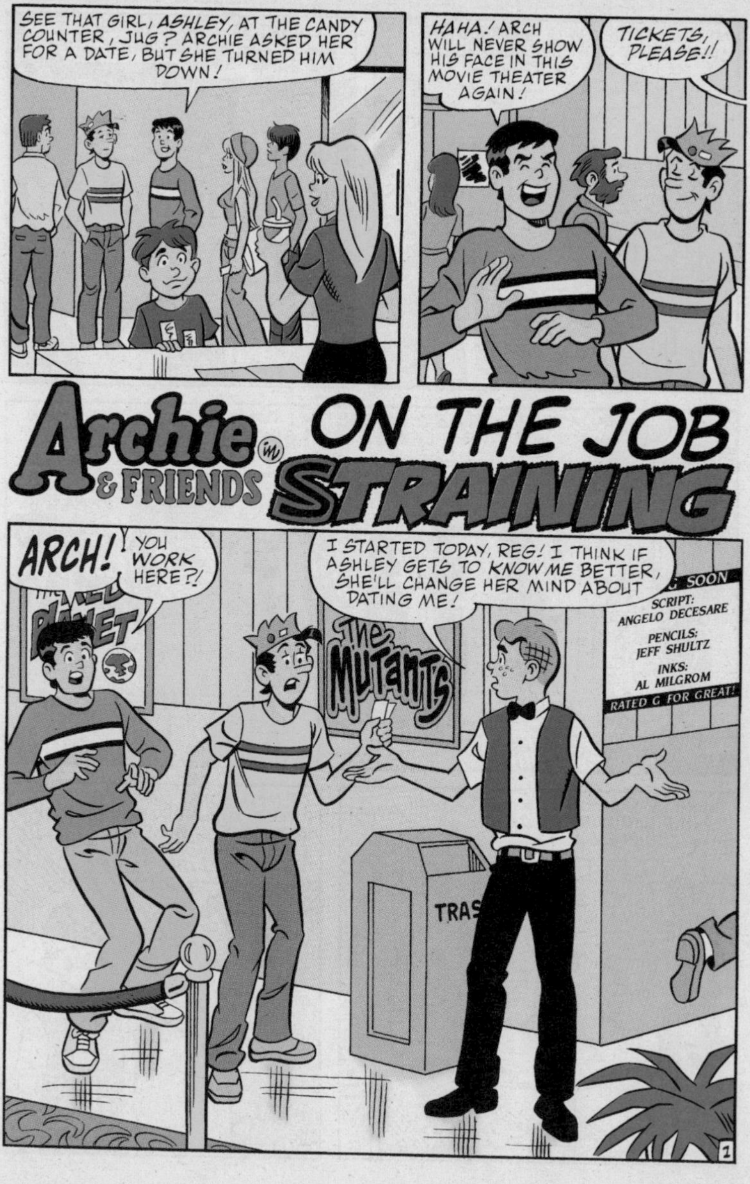

SEE THAT GIRL, ASHLEY, AT THE CANDY COUNTER, JUG? ARCHIE ASKED HER FOR A DATE, BUT SHE TURNED HIM DOWN!
HAHA! ARCH WILL NEVER SHOW HIS FACE IN THIS MOVIE THEATER AGAIN!
TICKETS, PLEASE!!
Archie & FRIENDS in ON THE JOB STRAINING
ARCH!
YOU WORK HERE?!
I STARTED TODAY, REG! I THINK IF ASHLEY GETS TO KNOW ME BETTER, SHE'LL CHANGE HER MIND ABOUT DATING ME!
The MUTANTS
SCRIPT: ANGELO DECESARE
PENCILS: JEFF SHULTZ
INKS: AL MILGROM
RATED G FOR GREAT!
TRAS

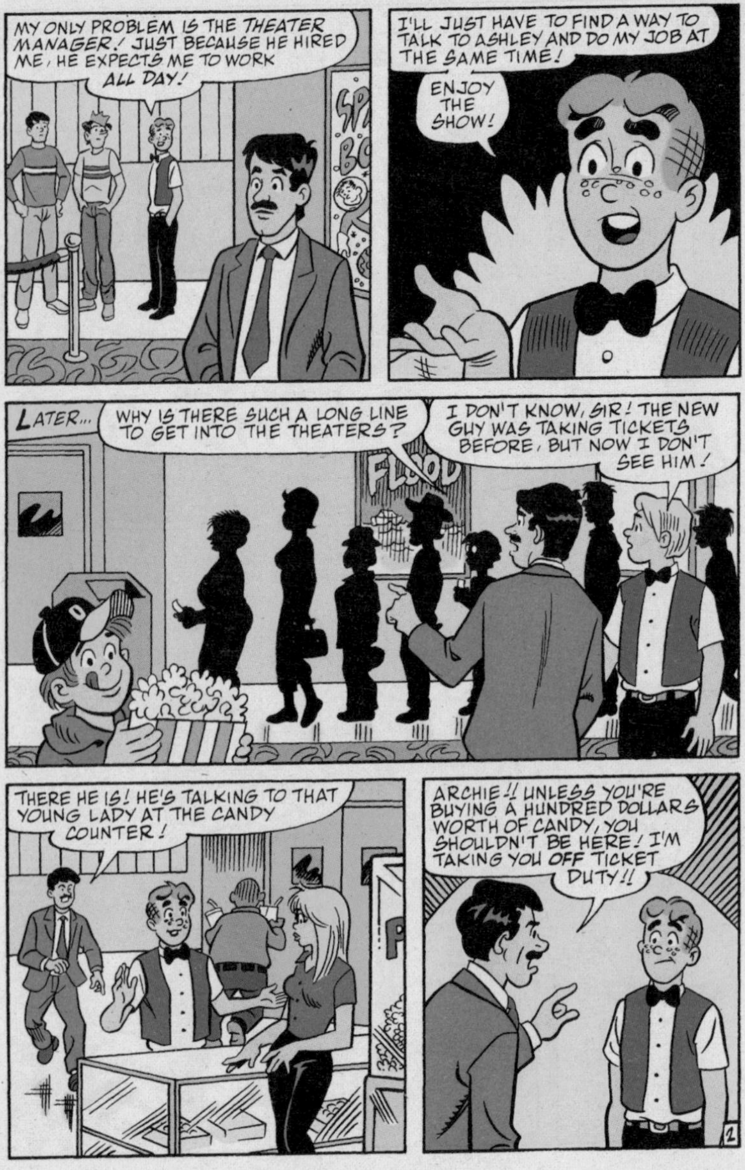
MY ONLY PROBLEM IS THE THEATER MANAGER! JUST BECAUSE HE HIRED ME, HE EXPECTS ME TO WORK ALL DAY!
I'LL JUST HAVE TO FIND A WAY TO TALK TO ASHLEY AND DO MY JOB AT THE SAME TIME!
ENJOY THE SHOW!
LATER...
WHY IS THERE SUCH A LONG LINE TO GET INTO THE THEATERS?
I DON'T KNOW, SIR! THE NEW GUY WAS TAKING TICKETS BEFORE, BUT NOW I DON'T SEE HIM!
FLOOD
THERE HE IS! HE'S TALKING TO THAT YOUNG LADY AT THE CANDY COUNTER!
ARCHIE!! UNLESS YOU'RE BUYING A HUNDRED DOLLARS WORTH OF CANDY, YOU SHOULDN'T BE HERE! I'M TAKING YOU OFF TICKET DUTY!!
2

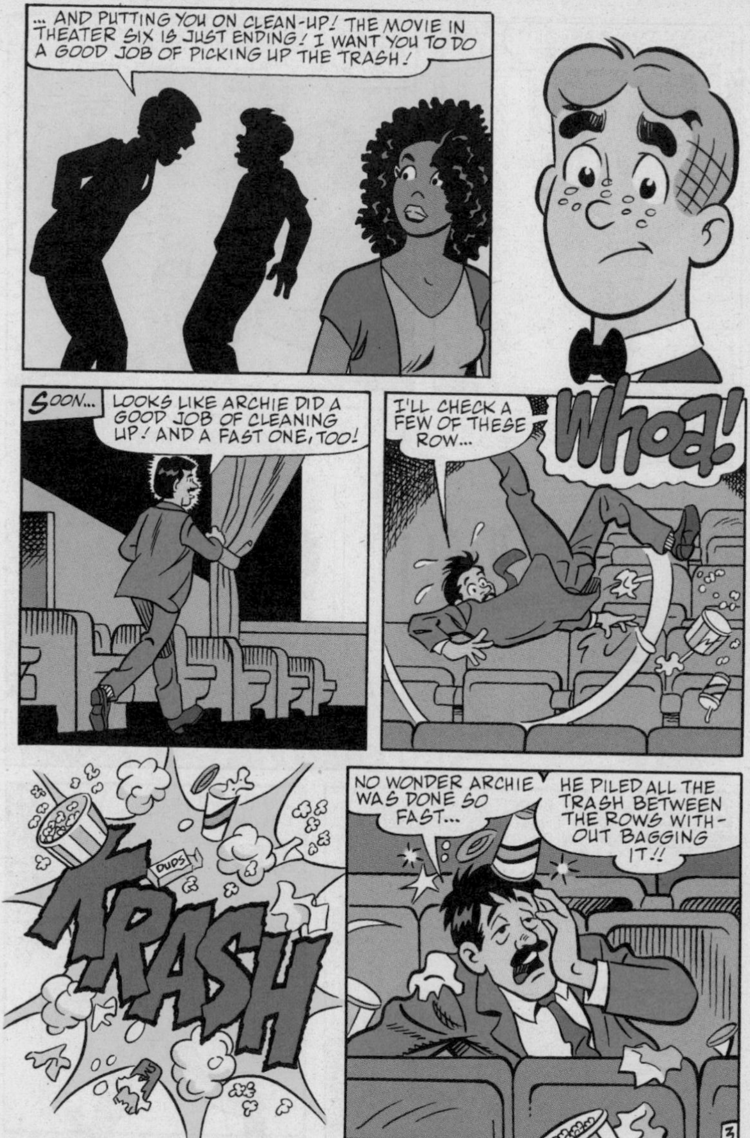
... AND PUTTING YOU ON CLEAN-UP! THE MOVIE IN THEATER SIX IS JUST ENDING! I WANT YOU TO DO A GOOD JOB OF PICKING UP THE TRASH!
SOON...
LOOKS LIKE ARCHIE DID A GOOD JOB OF CLEANING UP! AND A FAST ONE, TOO!
I'LL CHECK A FEW OF THESE ROW...
Whoa!
TRASH
DUDS
NO WONDER ARCHIE WAS DONE SO FAST...
HE PILED ALL THE TRASH BETWEEN THE ROWS WITHOUT BAGGING IT!!
3

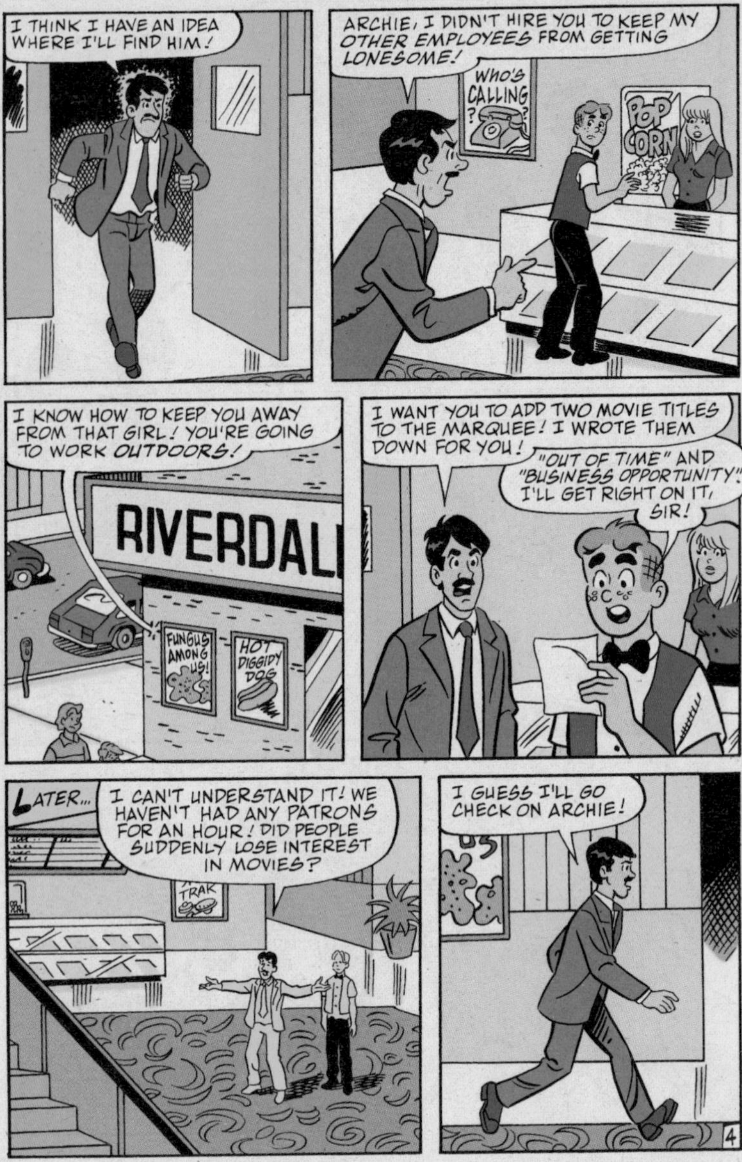
I THINK I HAVE AN IDEA WHERE I'LL FIND HIM!
ARCHIE, I DIDN'T HIRE YOU TO KEEP MY OTHER EMPLOYEES FROM GETTING LONESOME!
WHO'S CALLING ? ?
POP CORN
I KNOW HOW TO KEEP YOU AWAY FROM THAT GIRL! YOU'RE GOING TO WORK OUTDOORS!
RIVERDAL
FUNGUS AMONG US!
HOT DIGGIDY DOG
I WANT YOU TO ADD TWO MOVIE TITLES TO THE MARQUEE! I WROTE THEM DOWN FOR YOU!
"OUT OF TIME" AND "BUSINESS OPPORTUNITY"! I'LL GET RIGHT ON IT, SIR!
LATER...
I CAN'T UNDERSTAND IT! WE HAVEN'T HAD ANY PATRONS FOR AN HOUR! DID PEOPLE SUDDENLY LOSE INTEREST IN MOVIES?
I GUESS I'LL GO CHECK ON ARCHIE!
4

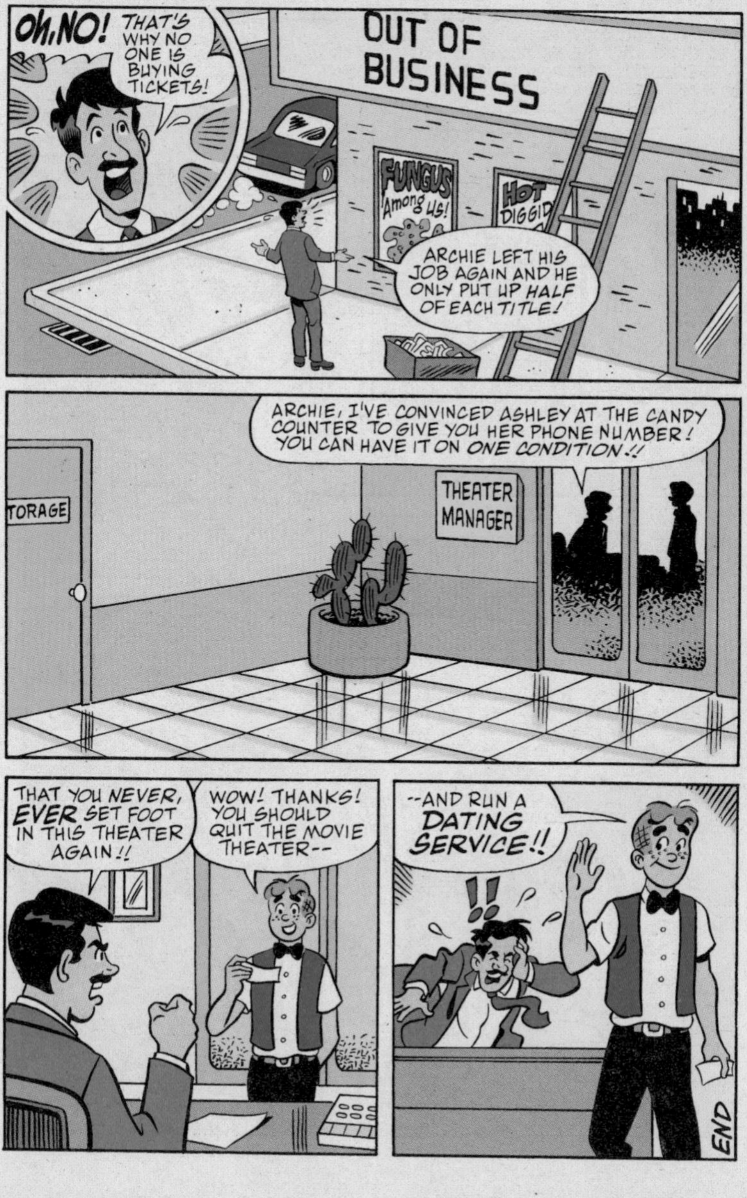
OH, NO! THAT'S WHY NO ONE IS BUYING TICKETS!
OUT OF BUSINESS
FUNGUS Among US!
HOT DIGGID
ARCHIE LEFT HIS JOB AGAIN AND HE ONLY PUT UP HALF OF EACH TITLE!
ARCHIE, I'VE CONVINCED ASHLEY AT THE CANDY COUNTER TO GIVE YOU HER PHONE NUMBER! YOU CAN HAVE IT ON ONE CONDITION!!
TORAGE
THEATER MANAGER
THAT YOU NEVER, EVER SET FOOT IN THIS THEATER AGAIN!!
WOW! THANKS! YOU SHOULD QUIT THE MOVIE THEATER--
--AND RUN A DATING SERVICE!!
END

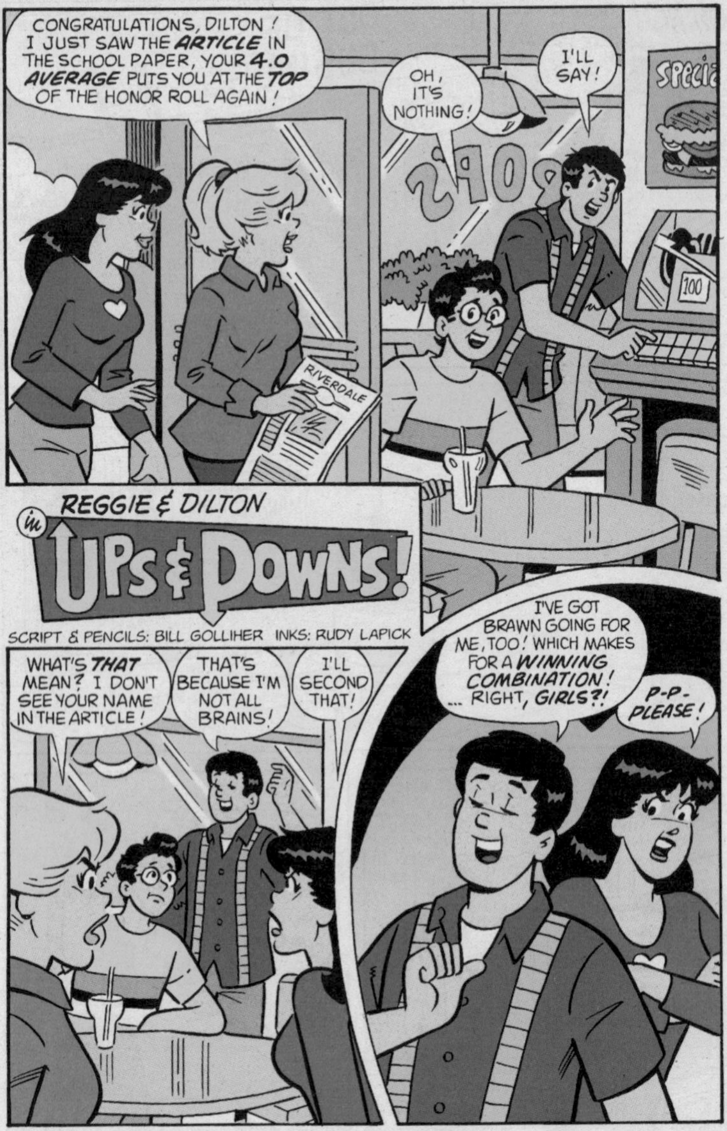
CONGRATULATIONS, DILTON! I JUST SAW THE ARTICLE IN THE SCHOOL PAPER, YOUR 4.0 AVERAGE PUTS YOU AT THE TOP OF THE HONOR ROLL AGAIN!
OH, IT'S NOTHING!
I'LL SAY!
POP'S
SPECIA
RIVERDALE
100
REGGIE & DILTON
in
UPs & DOWNS!
SCRIPT & PENCILS: BILL GOLLIHER INKS: RUDY LAPICK
WHAT'S THAT MEAN? I DON'T SEE YOUR NAME IN THE ARTICLE!
THAT'S BECAUSE I'M NOT ALL BRAINS!
I'LL SECOND THAT!
I'VE GOT BRAWN GOING FOR ME, TOO! WHICH MAKES FOR A WINNING COMBINATION! ... RIGHT, GIRLS?!
P-P-PLEASE!

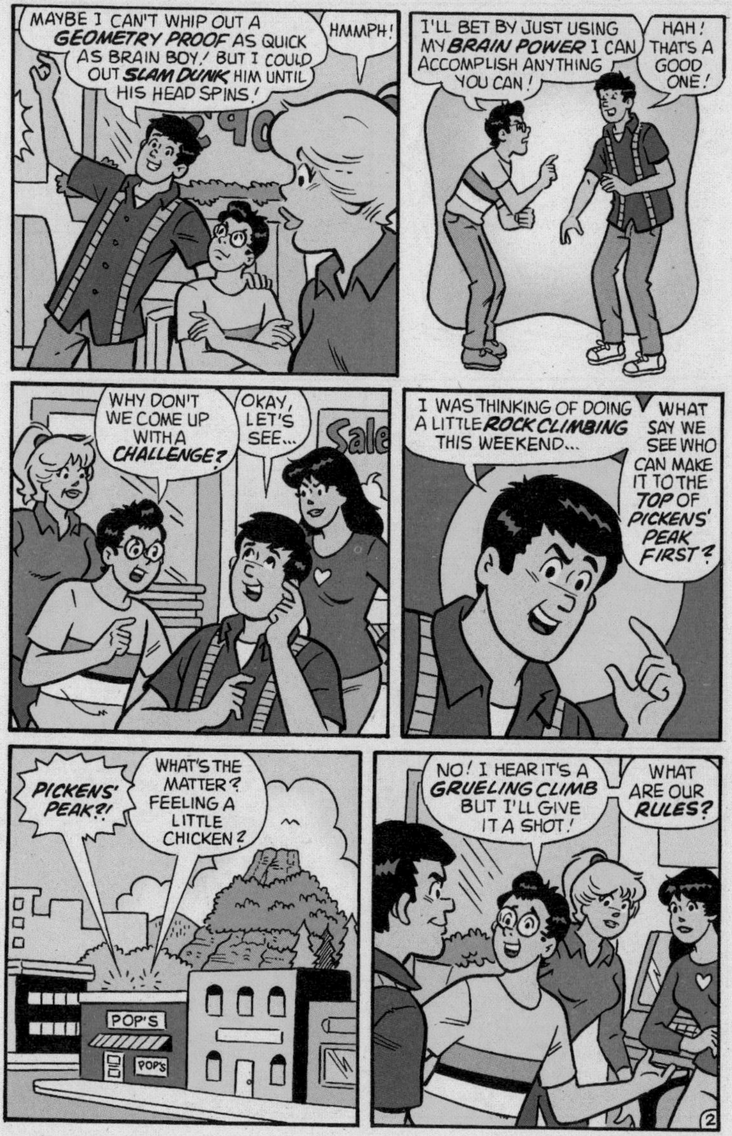
MAYBE I CAN'T WHIP OUT A GEOMETRY PROOF AS QUICK AS BRAIN BOY! BUT I COULD OUT SLAM DUNK HIM UNTIL HIS HEAD SPINS!
HMMPH!
I'LL BET BY JUST USING MY BRAIN POWER I CAN ACCOMPLISH ANYTHING YOU CAN!
HAH! THAT'S A GOOD ONE!
WHY DON'T WE COME UP WITH A CHALLENGE?
OKAY, LET'S SEE...
Sale
I WAS THINKING OF DOING A LITTLE ROCK CLIMBING THIS WEEKEND...
WHAT SAY WE SEE WHO CAN MAKE IT TO THE TOP OF PICKENS' PEAK FIRST?
PICKENS' PEAK?!
WHAT'S THE MATTER? FEELING A LITTLE CHICKEN?
POP'S
POP'S
NO! I HEAR IT'S A GRUELING CLIMB BUT I'LL GIVE IT A SHOT!
WHAT ARE OUR RULES?
2

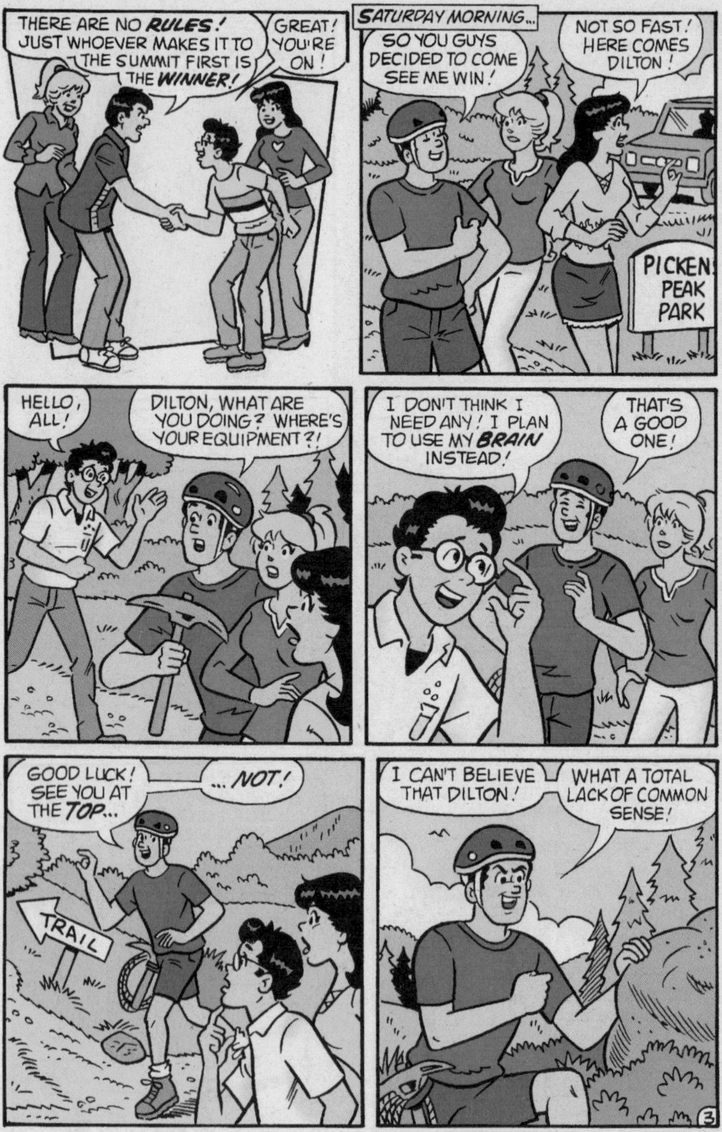
THERE ARE NO RULES! JUST WHOEVER MAKES IT TO THE SUMMIT FIRST IS THE WINNER!
GREAT! YOU'RE ON!
SATURDAY MORNING...
SO YOU GUYS DECIDED TO COME SEE ME WIN!
NOT SO FAST! HERE COMES DILTON!
PICKENS PEAK PARK
HELLO, ALL!
DILTON, WHAT ARE YOU DOING? WHERE'S YOUR EQUIPMENT?!
I DON'T THINK I NEED ANY! I PLAN TO USE MY BRAIN INSTEAD!
THAT'S A GOOD ONE!
GOOD LUCK! SEE YOU AT THE TOP...
...NOT!
TRAIL
I CAN'T BELIEVE THAT DILTON!
WHAT A TOTAL LACK OF COMMON SENSE!
3

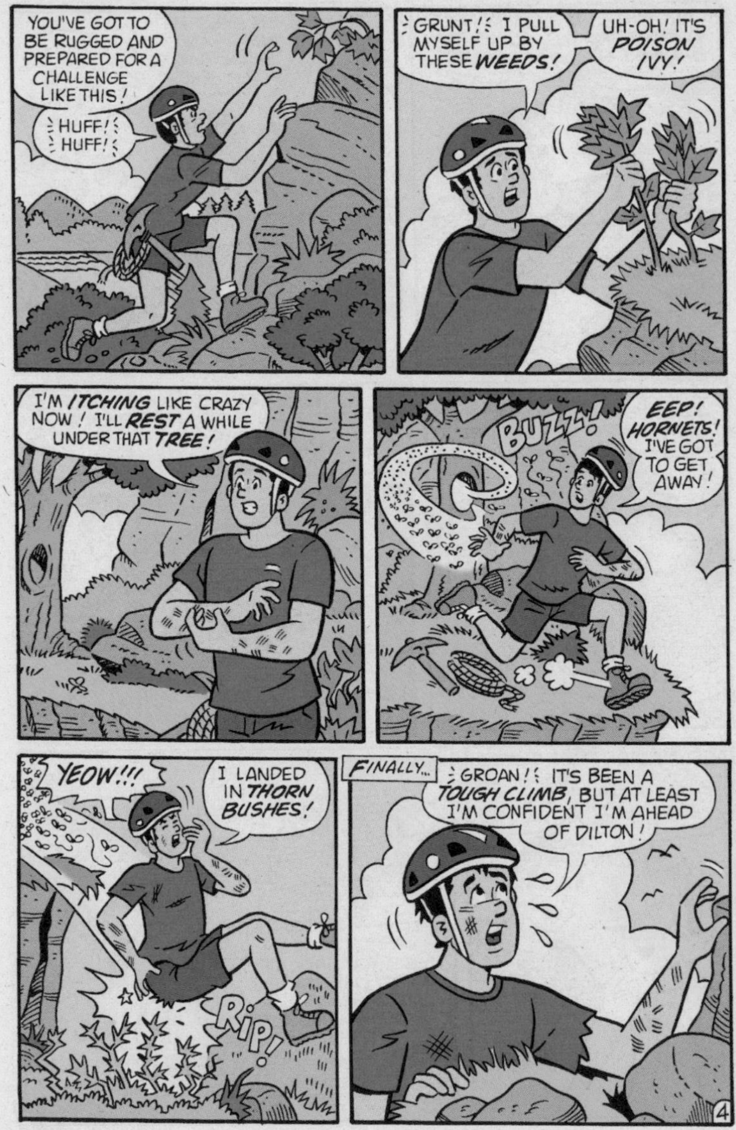
YOU'VE GOT TO BE RUGGED AND PREPARED FOR A CHALLENGE LIKE THIS!
HUFF! HUFF!
GRUNT! I PULL MYSELF UP BY THESE WEEDS!
UH-OH! IT'S POISON IVY!
I'M ITCHING LIKE CRAZY NOW! I'LL REST A WHILE UNDER THAT TREE!
BUZZZ!
EEP! HORNETS! I'VE GOT TO GET AWAY!
YEOW!!!
I LANDED IN THORN BUSHES!
RIP!
FINALLY...
GROAN! IT'S BEEN A TOUGH CLIMB, BUT AT LEAST I'M CONFIDENT I'M AHEAD OF DILTON!
4

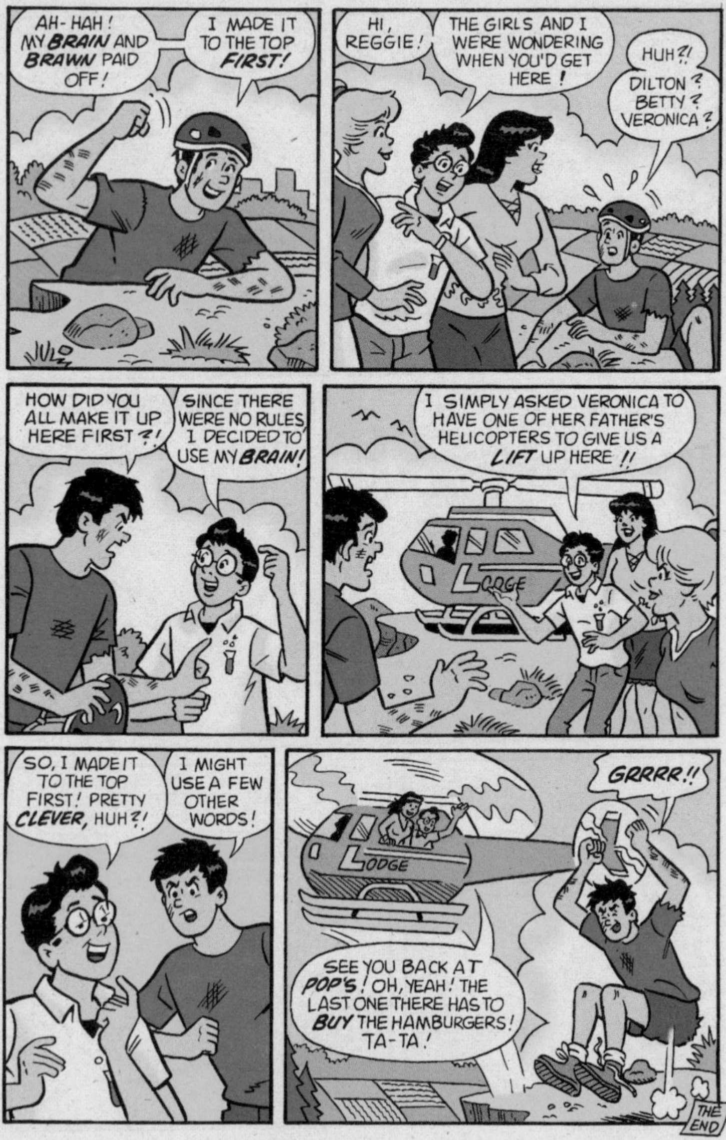
AH-HAH! MY BRAIN AND BRAWN PAID OFF!
I MADE IT TO THE TOP FIRST!
HI, REGGIE!
THE GIRLS AND I WERE WONDERING WHEN YOU'D GET HERE!
HUH?!
DILTON? BETTY? VERONICA?
HOW DID YOU ALL MAKE IT UP HERE FIRST?!
SINCE THERE WERE NO RULES, I DECIDED TO USE MY BRAIN!
I SIMPLY ASKED VERONICA TO HAVE ONE OF HER FATHER'S HELICOPTERS TO GIVE US A LIFT UP HERE!!
LODGE
SO, I MADE IT TO THE TOP FIRST! PRETTY CLEVER, HUH?!
I MIGHT USE A FEW OTHER WORDS!
GRRRR!!
LODGE
SEE YOU BACK AT POP'S! OH, YEAH! THE LAST ONE THERE HAS TO BUY THE HAMBURGERS! TA-TA!
THE END

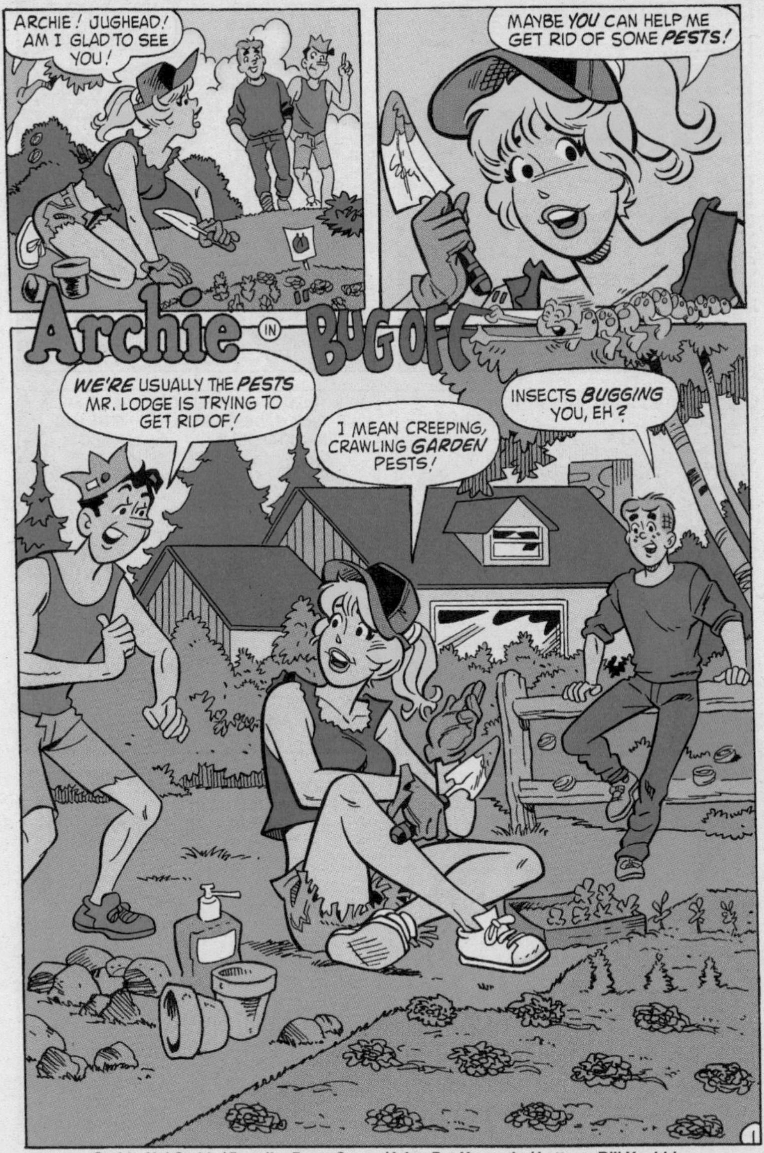
ARCHIE! JUGHEAD! AM I GLAD TO SEE YOU!
MAYBE YOU CAN HELP ME GET RID OF SOME PESTS!
Archie IN BUG OFF
WE'RE USUALLY THE PESTS MR. LODGE IS TRYING TO GET RID OF!
I MEAN CREEPING, CRAWLING GARDEN PESTS!
INSECTS BUGGING YOU, EH?
1

Script: Hal Smith / Pencils: Doug Crane / Inks: Pat Kennedy / Letters: Bill Yoshida

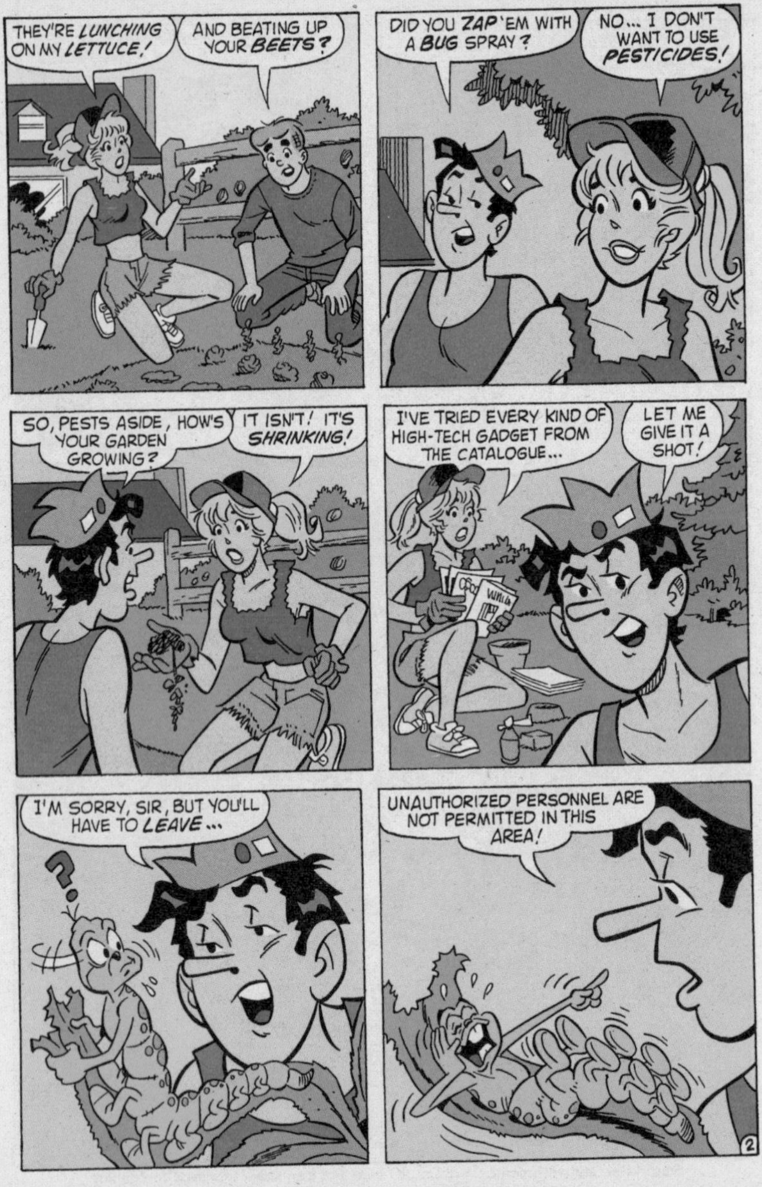
THEY'RE LUNCHING ON MY LETTUCE!
AND BEATING UP YOUR BEETS?
DID YOU ZAP 'EM WITH A BUG SPRAY?
NO... I DON'T WANT TO USE PESTICIDES!
SO, PESTS ASIDE, HOW'S YOUR GARDEN GROWING?
IT ISN'T! IT'S SHRINKING!
I'VE TRIED EVERY KIND OF HIGH-TECH GADGET FROM THE CATALOGUE...
LET ME GIVE IT A SHOT!
I'M SORRY, SIR, BUT YOU'LL HAVE TO LEAVE...
?
UNAUTHORIZED PERSONNEL ARE NOT PERMITTED IN THIS AREA!
2

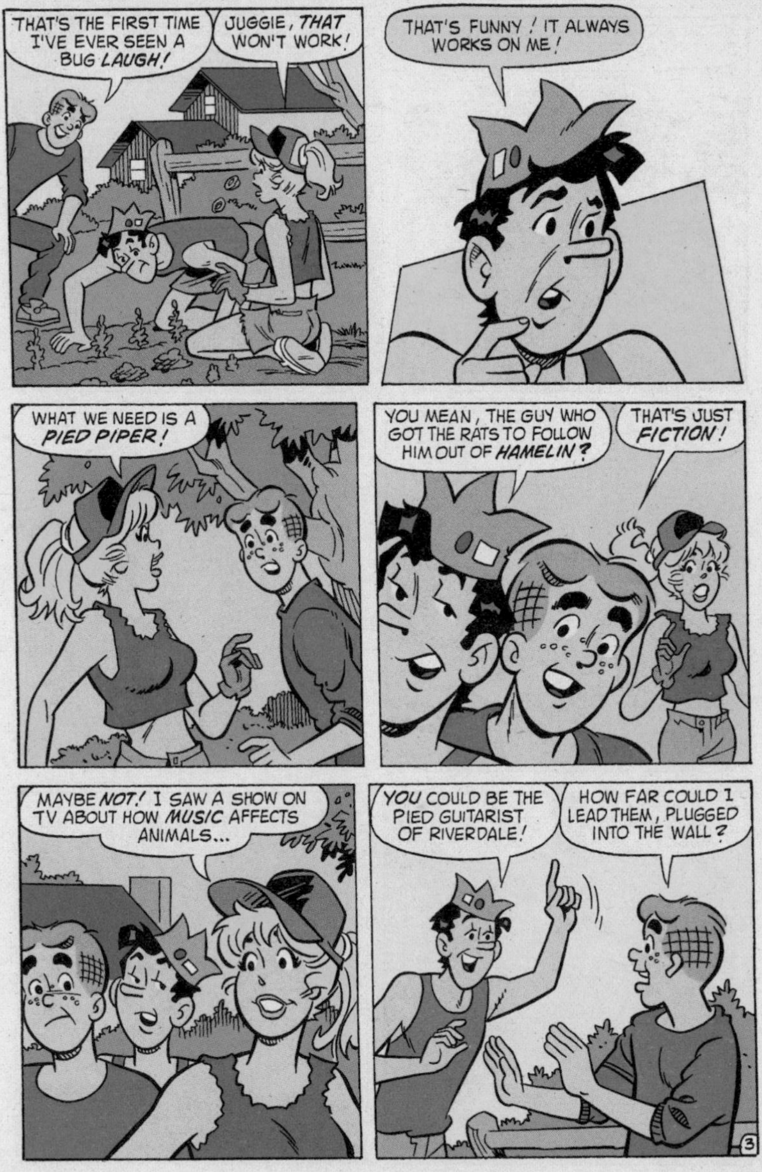
THAT'S THE FIRST TIME I'VE EVER SEEN A BUG LAUGH!
JUGGIE, THAT WON'T WORK!
THAT'S FUNNY! IT ALWAYS WORKS ON ME!
WHAT WE NEED IS A PIED PIPER!
YOU MEAN, THE GUY WHO GOT THE RATS TO FOLLOW HIM OUT OF HAMELIN?
THAT'S JUST FICTION!
MAYBE NOT! I SAW A SHOW ON TV ABOUT HOW MUSIC AFFECTS ANIMALS...
YOU COULD BE THE PIED GUITARIST OF RIVERDALE!
HOW FAR COULD I LEAD THEM, PLUGGED INTO THE WALL?
3

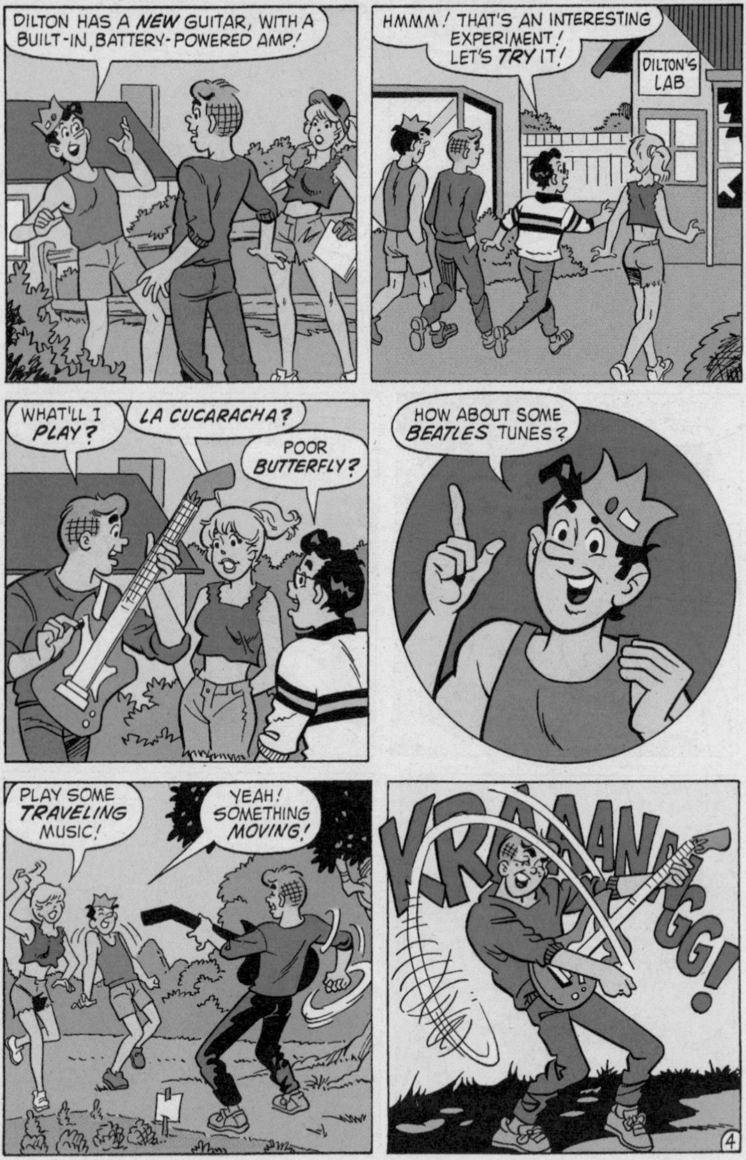
DILTON HAS A NEW GUITAR, WITH A BUILT-IN, BATTERY-POWERED AMP!
HMMM! THAT'S AN INTERESTING EXPERIMENT! LET'S TRY IT!
DILTON'S LAB
WHAT'LL I PLAY?
LA CUCARACHA?
POOR BUTTERFLY?
HOW ABOUT SOME BEATLES TUNES?
PLAY SOME TRAVELING MUSIC!
YEAH! SOMETHING MOVING!
KRAAAANNGG!
4

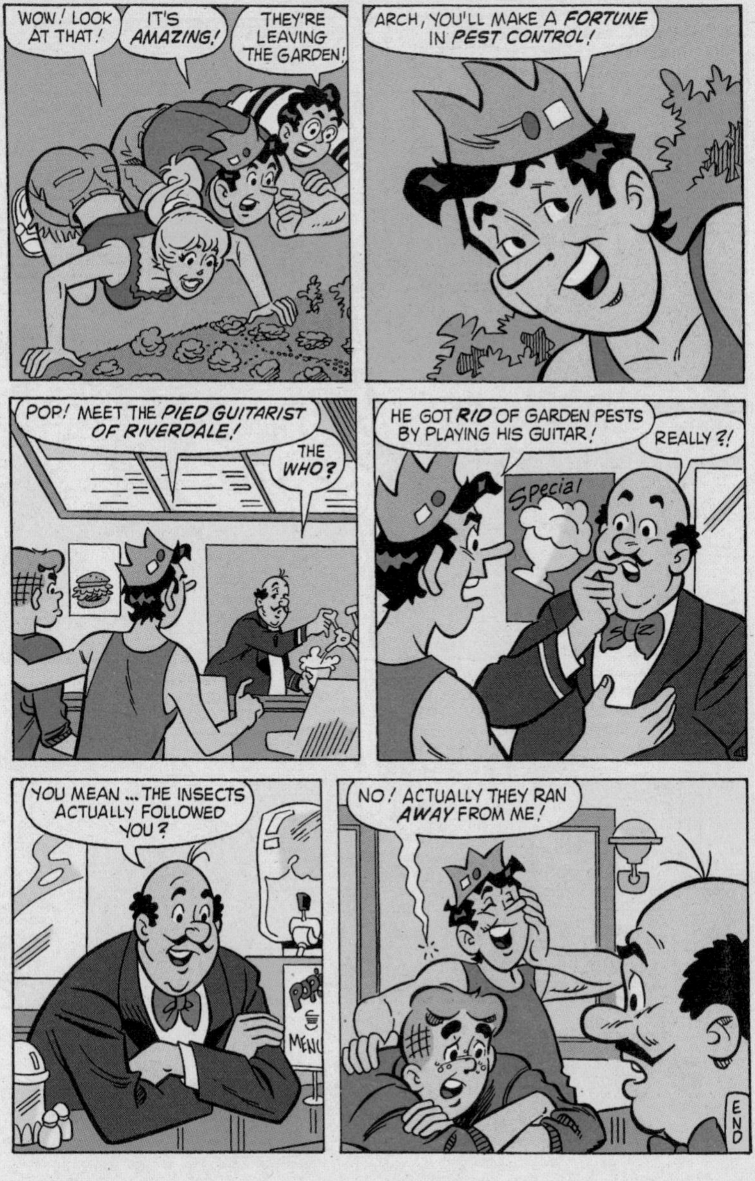
WOW! LOOK AT THAT!
IT'S AMAZING!
THEY'RE LEAVING THE GARDEN!
ARCH, YOU'LL MAKE A FORTUNE IN PEST CONTROL!
POP! MEET THE PIED GUITARIST OF RIVERDALE!
THE WHO?
HE GOT RID OF GARDEN PESTS BY PLAYING HIS GUITAR!
REALLY ?!
Special
YOU MEAN ... THE INSECTS ACTUALLY FOLLOWED YOU?
NO! ACTUALLY THEY RAN AWAY FROM ME!
END

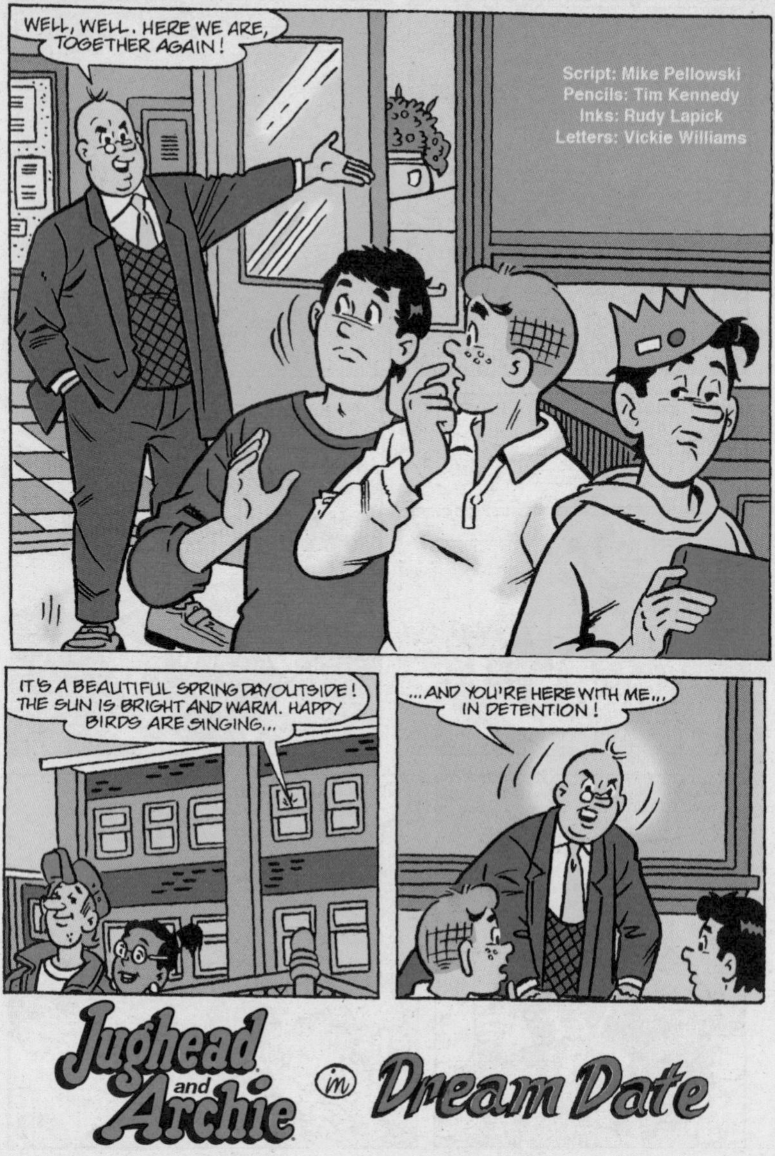
WELL, WELL. HERE WE ARE, TOGETHER AGAIN!
Script: Mike Pellowski
Pencils: Tim Kennedy
Inks: Rudy Lapick
Letters: Vickie Williams
IT'S A BEAUTIFUL SPRING DAY OUTSIDE! THE SUN IS BRIGHT AND WARM. HAPPY BIRDS ARE SINGING...
...AND YOU'RE HERE WITH ME... IN DETENTION!
Jughead and Archie in Dream Date

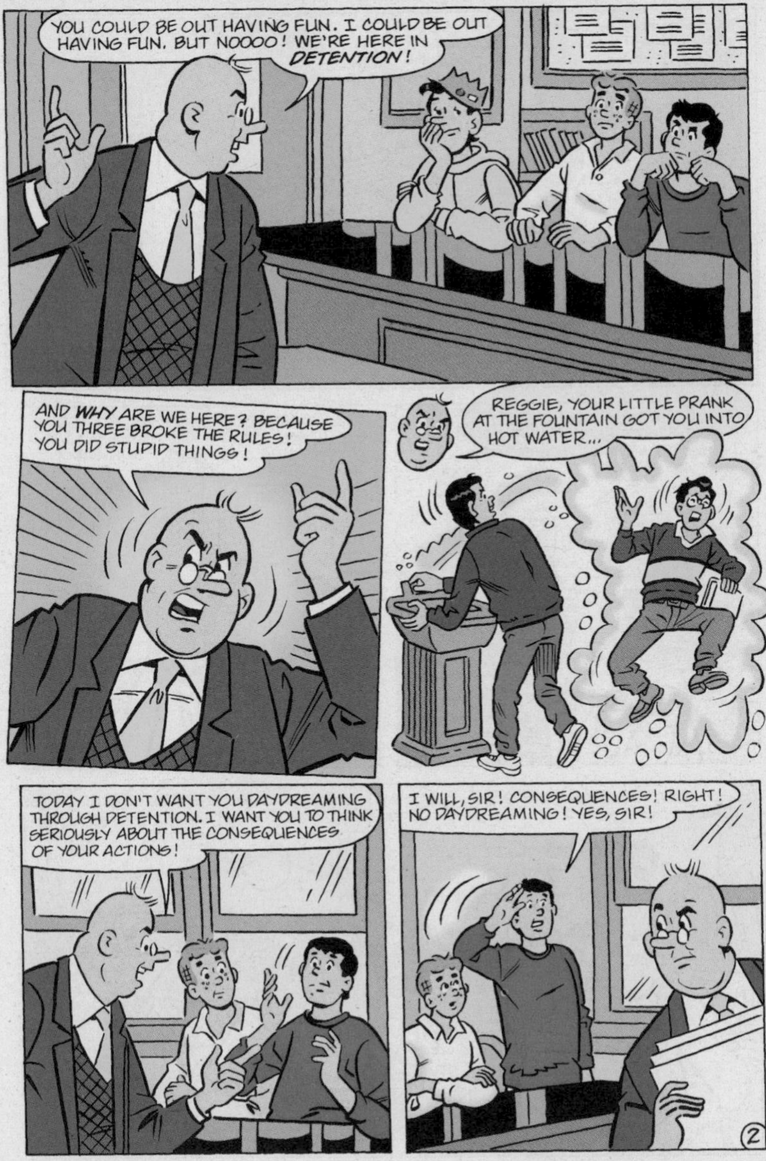
YOU COULD BE OUT HAVING FUN. I COULD BE OUT HAVING FUN. BUT NOOOO! WE'RE HERE IN DETENTION!
AND WHY ARE WE HERE? BECAUSE YOU THREE BROKE THE RULES! YOU DID STUPID THINGS!
REGGIE, YOUR LITTLE PRANK AT THE FOUNTAIN GOT YOU INTO HOT WATER...
TODAY I DON'T WANT YOU DAYDREAMING THROUGH DETENTION. I WANT YOU TO THINK SERIOUSLY ABOUT THE CONSEQUENCES OF YOUR ACTIONS!
I WILL, SIR! CONSEQUENCES! RIGHT! NO DAYDREAMING! YES, SIR!
2

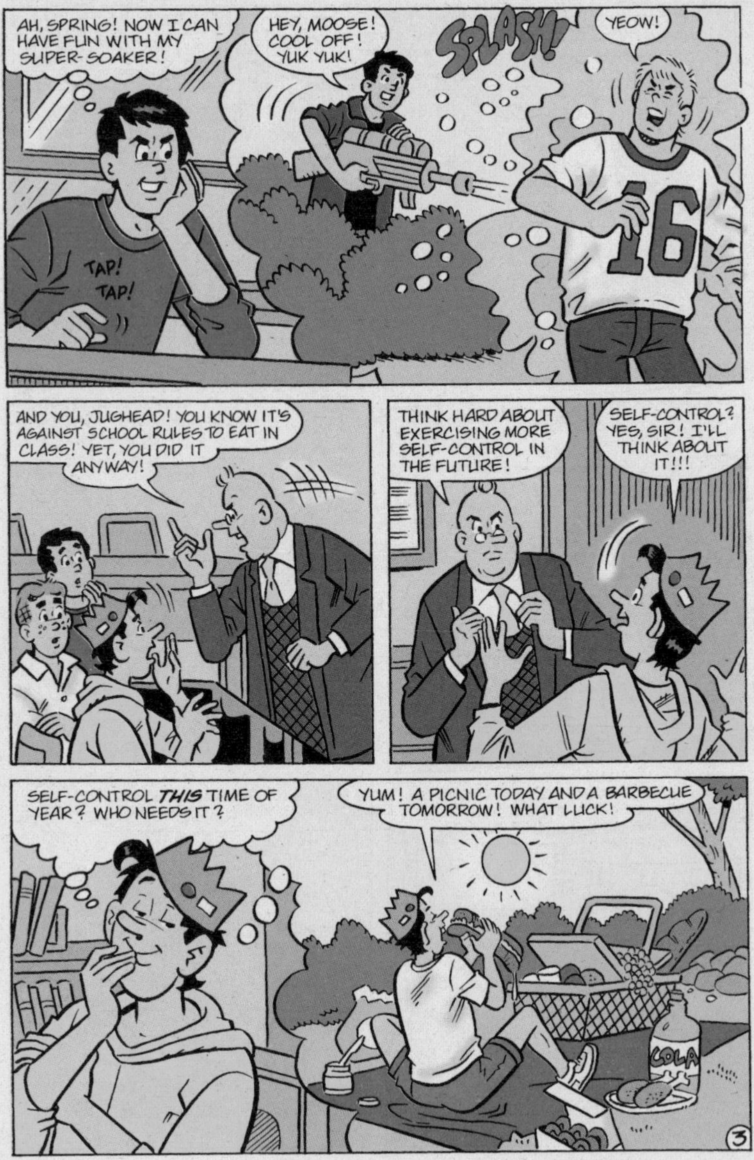
AH, SPRING! NOW I CAN HAVE FUN WITH MY SUPER-SOAKER!
HEY, MOOSE! COOL OFF! YUK YUK!
SPLASH!
YEOW!
TAP! TAP!
AND YOU, JUGHEAD! YOU KNOW IT'S AGAINST SCHOOL RULES TO EAT IN CLASS! YET, YOU DID IT ANYWAY!
THINK HARD ABOUT EXERCISING MORE SELF-CONTROL IN THE FUTURE!
SELF-CONTROL? YES, SIR! I'LL THINK ABOUT IT!!!
SELF-CONTROL THIS TIME OF YEAR? WHO NEEDS IT?
YUM! A PICNIC TODAY AND A BARBECUE TOMORROW! WHAT LUCK!
COLA
3

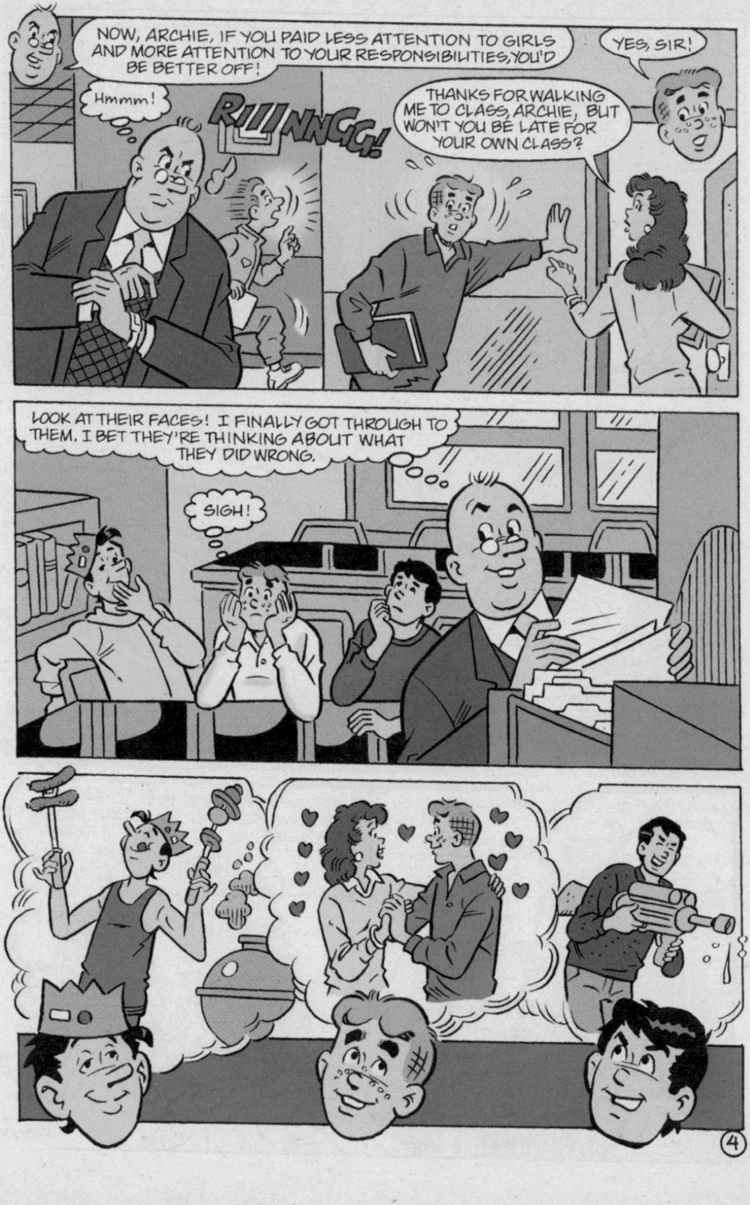
NOW, ARCHIE, IF YOU PAID LESS ATTENTION TO GIRLS AND MORE ATTENTION TO YOUR RESPONSIBILITIES, YOU'D BE BETTER OFF!
YES, SIR!
Hmmm!
RIIINNGG!
THANKS FOR WALKING ME TO CLASS, ARCHIE, BUT WON'T YOU BE LATE FOR YOUR OWN CLASS?
LOOK AT THEIR FACES! I FINALLY GOT THROUGH TO THEM. I BET THEY'RE THINKING ABOUT WHAT THEY DID WRONG.
SIGH!
4

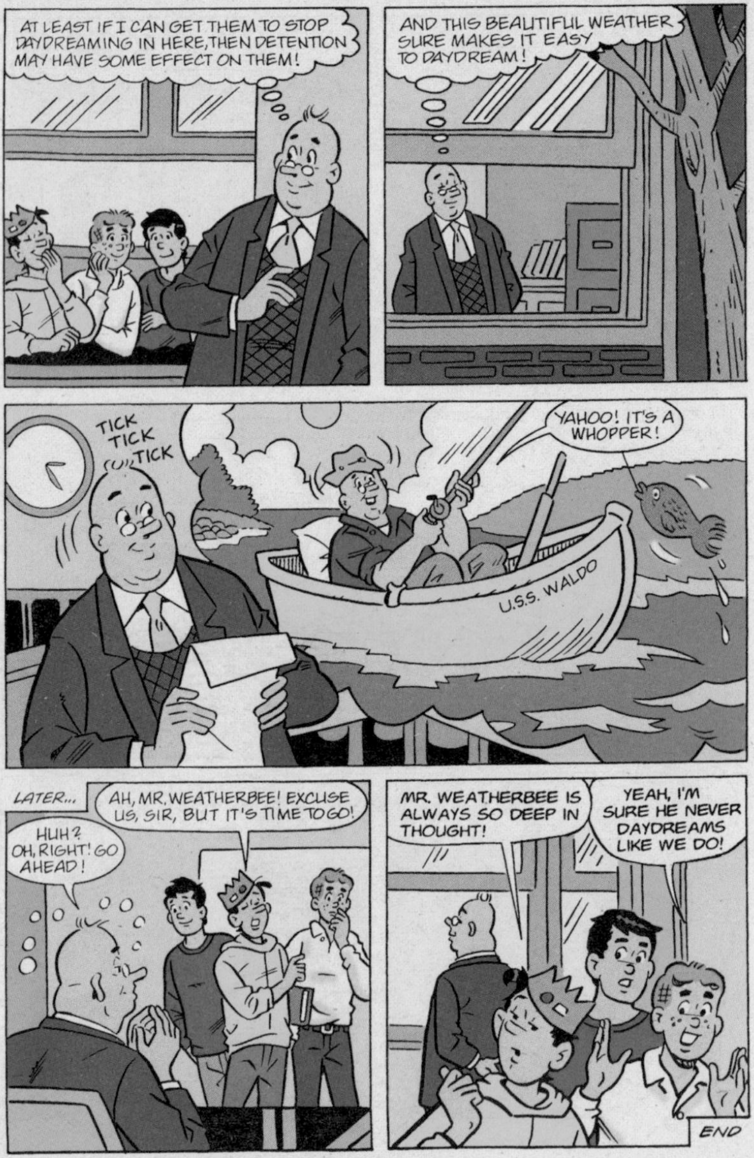
AT LEAST IF I CAN GET THEM TO STOP DAYDREAMING IN HERE, THEN DETENTION MAY HAVE SOME EFFECT ON THEM!
AND THIS BEAUTIFUL WEATHER SURE MAKES IT EASY TO DAYDREAM!
TICK TICK TICK
YAHOO! IT'S A WHOPPER!
U.S.S. WALDO
LATER...
AH, MR. WEATHERBEE! EXCUSE US, SIR, BUT IT'S TIME TO GO!
HUH? OH, RIGHT! GO AHEAD!
MR. WEATHERBEE IS ALWAYS SO DEEP IN THOUGHT!
YEAH, I'M SURE HE NEVER DAYDREAMS LIKE WE DO!
END

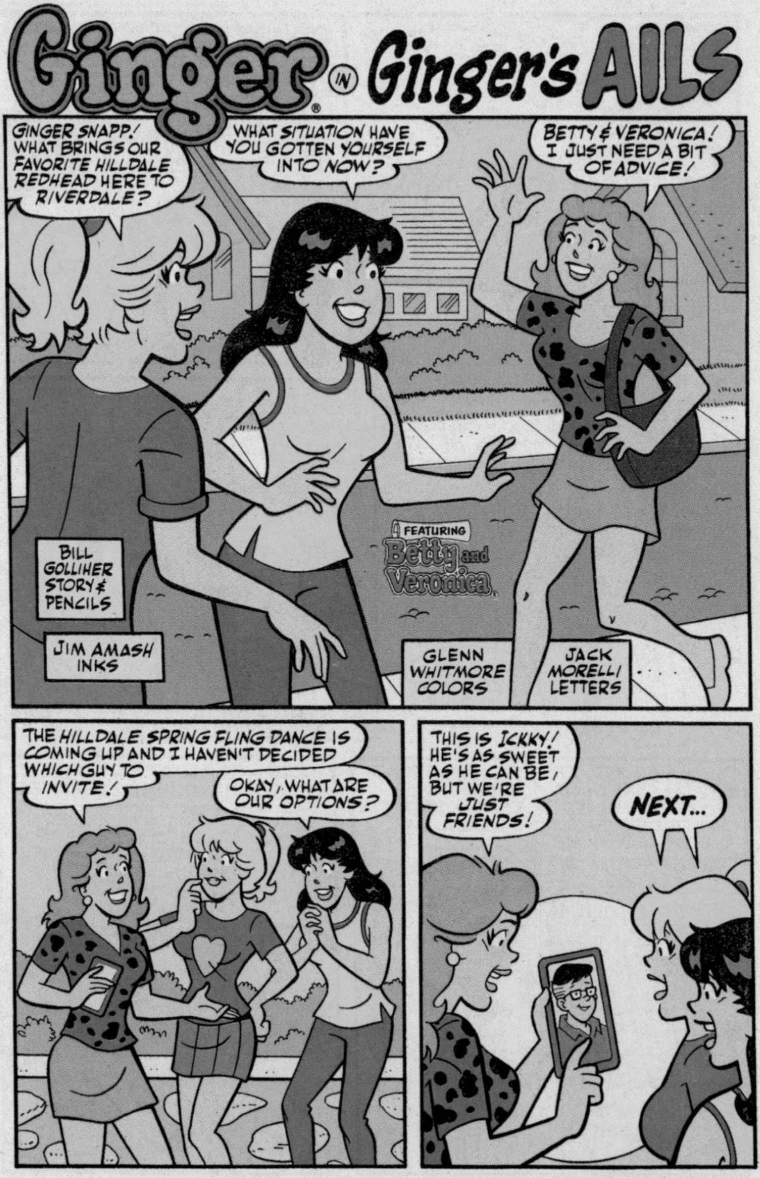

Ginger in Ginger's AILS
GINGER SNAPP! WHAT BRINGS OUR FAVORITE HILLDALE REDHEAD HERE TO RIVERDALE?
WHAT SITUATION HAVE YOU GOTTEN YOURSELF INTO NOW?
BETTY & VERONICA! I JUST NEED A BIT OF ADVICE!
FEATURING Betty and Veronica
BILL GOLLIHER STORY & PENCILS
JIM AMASH INKS
GLENN WHITMORE COLORS
JACK MORELLI LETTERS
THE HILLDALE SPRING FLING DANCE IS COMING UP AND I HAVEN'T DECIDED WHICH GUY TO INVITE!
OKAY, WHAT ARE OUR OPTIONS?
THIS IS ICKKY! HE'S AS SWEET AS HE CAN BE, BUT WE'RE JUST FRIENDS!
NEXT...

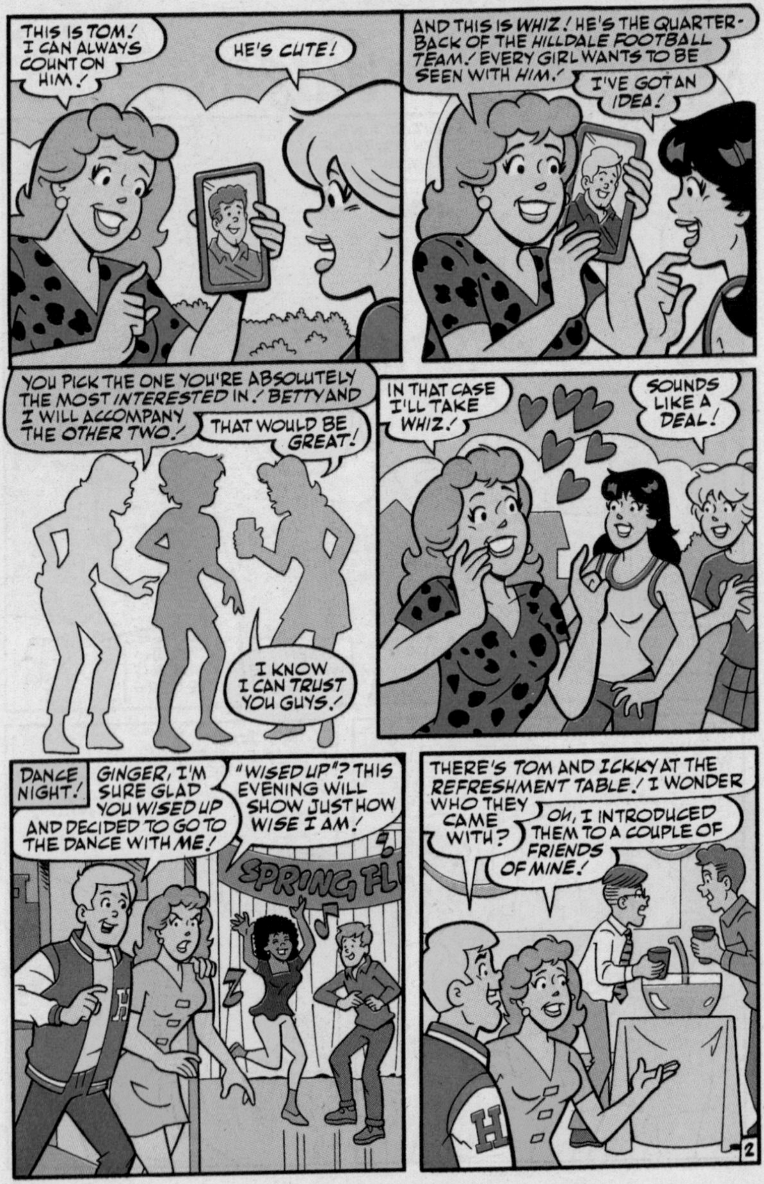
THIS IS TOM! I CAN ALWAYS COUNT ON HIM!
HE'S CUTE!
AND THIS IS WHIZ! HE'S THE QUARTER-BACK OF THE HILLDALE FOOTBALL TEAM! EVERY GIRL WANTS TO BE SEEN WITH HIM!
I'VE GOT AN IDEA!
YOU PICK THE ONE YOU'RE ABSOLUTELY THE MOST INTERESTED IN! BETTY AND I WILL ACCOMPANY THE OTHER TWO!
THAT WOULD BE GREAT!
I KNOW I CAN TRUST YOU GUYS!
IN THAT CASE I'LL TAKE WHIZ!
SOUNDS LIKE A DEAL!
DANCE NIGHT!
GINGER, I'M SURE GLAD YOU WISED UP AND DECIDED TO GO TO THE DANCE WITH ME!
"WISED UP"? THIS EVENING WILL SHOW JUST HOW WISE I AM!
SPRING FL
THERE'S TOM AND ICKKY AT THE REFRESHMENT TABLE! I WONDER WHO THEY CAME WITH?
OH, I INTRODUCED THEM TO A COUPLE OF FRIENDS OF MINE!
2

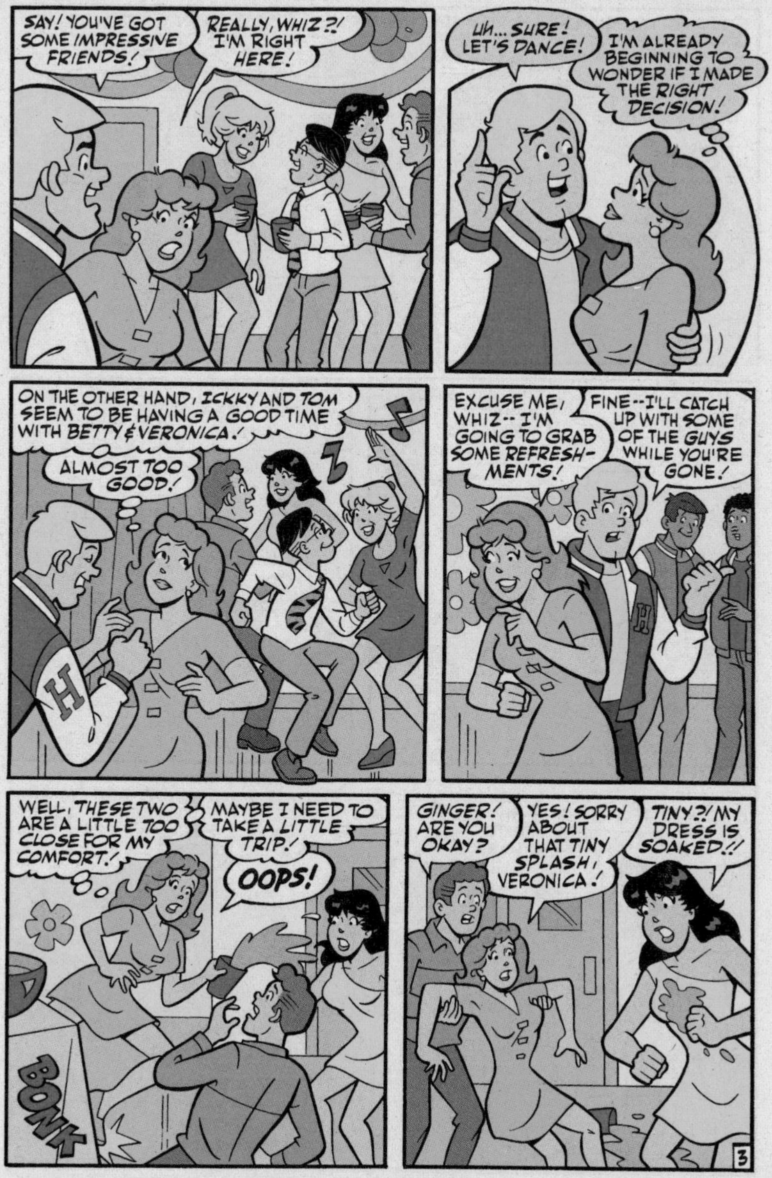
SAY! YOU'VE GOT SOME IMPRESSIVE FRIENDS!
REALLY, WHIZ?! I'M RIGHT HERE!
UH... SURE! LET'S DANCE!
I'M ALREADY BEGINNING TO WONDER IF I MADE THE RIGHT DECISION!
ON THE OTHER HAND, ICKKY AND TOM SEEM TO BE HAVING A GOOD TIME WITH BETTY & VERONICA!
ALMOST TOO GOOD!
EXCUSE ME, WHIZ-- I'M GOING TO GRAB SOME REFRESH-MENTS!
FINE--I'LL CATCH UP WITH SOME OF THE GUYS WHILE YOU'RE GONE!
WELL, THESE TWO ARE A LITTLE TOO CLOSE FOR MY COMFORT!
MAYBE I NEED TO TAKE A LITTLE TRIP!
OOPS!
BONK
GINGER! ARE YOU OKAY?
YES! SORRY ABOUT THAT TINY SPLASH, VERONICA!
TINY?! MY DRESS IS SOAKED!!
3

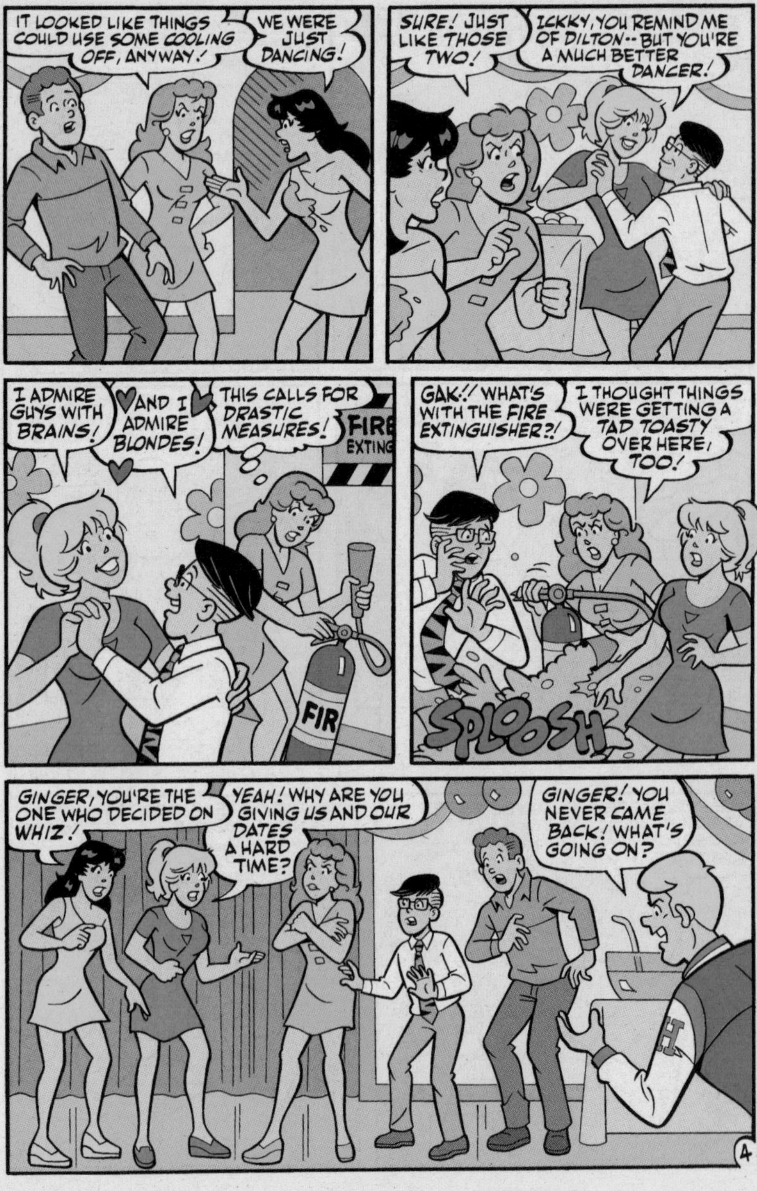
IT LOOKED LIKE THINGS COULD USE SOME COOLING OFF, ANYWAY!
WE WERE JUST DANCING!
SURE! JUST LIKE THOSE TWO!
ICKKY, YOU REMIND ME OF DILTON-- BUT YOU'RE A MUCH BETTER DANCER!
I ADMIRE GUYS WITH BRAINS!
AND I ADMIRE BLONDES!
THIS CALLS FOR DRASTIC MEASURES!
FIRE EXTING
FIR
GAK!! WHAT'S WITH THE FIRE EXTINGUISHER?!
I THOUGHT THINGS WERE GETTING A TAD TOASTY OVER HERE, TOO!
SPLOOSH
GINGER, YOU'RE THE ONE WHO DECIDED ON WHIZ!
YEAH! WHY ARE YOU GIVING US AND OUR DATES A HARD TIME?
GINGER! YOU NEVER CAME BACK! WHAT'S GOING ON?

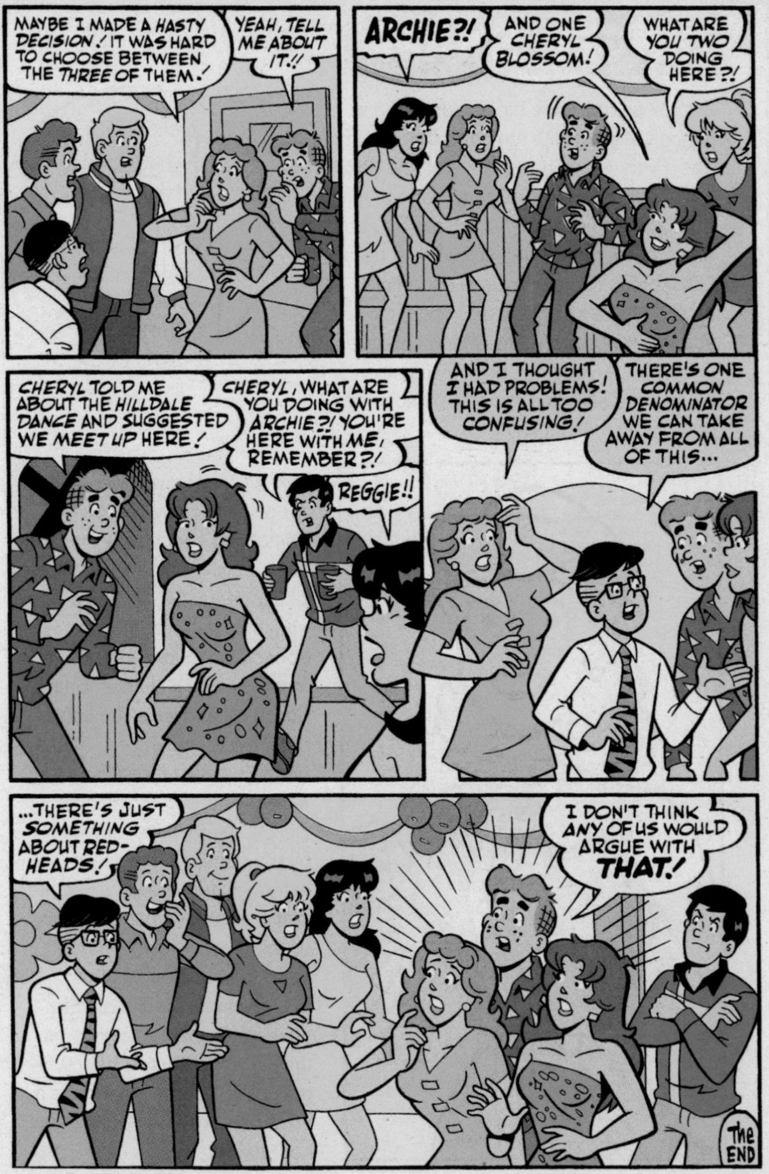
MAYBE I MADE A HASTY DECISION! IT WAS HARD TO CHOOSE BETWEEN THE THREE OF THEM!
YEAH, TELL ME ABOUT IT!!
ARCHIE?!
AND ONE CHERYL BLOSSOM!
WHAT ARE YOU TWO DOING HERE?!
CHERYL TOLD ME ABOUT THE HILLDALE DANCE AND SUGGESTED WE MEET UP HERE!
CHERYL, WHAT ARE YOU DOING WITH ARCHIE?! YOU'RE HERE WITH ME, REMEMBER?!
REGGIE!!
AND I THOUGHT I HAD PROBLEMS! THIS IS ALL TOO CONFUSING!
THERE'S ONE COMMON DENOMINATOR WE CAN TAKE AWAY FROM ALL OF THIS...
...THERE'S JUST SOMETHING ABOUT RED-HEADS!
I DON'T THINK ANY OF US WOULD ARGUE WITH THAT!
THE END

GINGER SNAPP

Ginger Snapp is the most popular girl in school! At least with the boys, that is! Ginger has a very active dating life, but she doesn't have "a type." She's dated all sorts of guys, from jocks, to straight-A students, shy boys, nerdy boys, rebels, etc. From the outside, Ginger may come across as superficial, as she puts a lot of time and effort into her appearance, but she's quite the opposite. Ginger never judges a book by its cover, and tends to be attracted to one's personality rather than their looks.

While Ginger has never fallen for a specific boy, there's something about Ickky that she likes, much to the bewilderment of her peers. Ginger has a shopping habit, and often spends too much of her father's income on new clothes. She doesn't like to wear the same outfit twice, and instead thinks of new ways to repeat wearing a piece with something new. Despite being raised primarily by her father, Ginger is extremely feminine and is quite crafty when it comes to coming up with ways to use her good looks to get dates, not that she has to try hard at all! She often dates the same guys as the equally attractive Bunny, but unlike Bunny, Ginger has a great personality to compliment her beauty.

DOTTIE

Dottie (later known as "Patsy") is Ginger's best friend and closest confidant. When Ginger has a crush, Dottie is the first to know, although she usually doesn't see what is so appealing to Ginger about these guys. Dottie is much pickier about her own dates, but for her that's a good thing. She'd rather wait for the right guy than date a bunch of boys she doesn't care much about.

ICKKY

His buddies are often confused how he can date a girl like Ginger, but Ickky's confidence might be his most attractive quality. However, their relationship isn't perfect, as Ickky takes Ginger for granted, before realizing how much he truly likes her. Ickky is thin and short for his age, and Ginger towers over him by quite a bit. But she is never embarrassed to be seen with him, and likes the attention he gives her. Ickky always feels the need to be right, and is awfully stubborn, which Ginger finds the most unappealing.

TOMMY TURNER

Tommy Turner is the only boy that Ginger is unable to "steal away" from Bunny, but when he sees how manipulative Bunny can be, he begins to like Ginger instead. Tommy is the complete opposite of Ickky, as he is tall, blonde, and muscular, which leads Ickky to see him as a rival for Ginger's affection.

SCAN ME

LEARN MORE ABOUT YOUR FAVORITE ARCHIE COMICS CHARACTERS IN THE ARCHIE ENCYCLOPEDIA! AVAILABLE NOW!

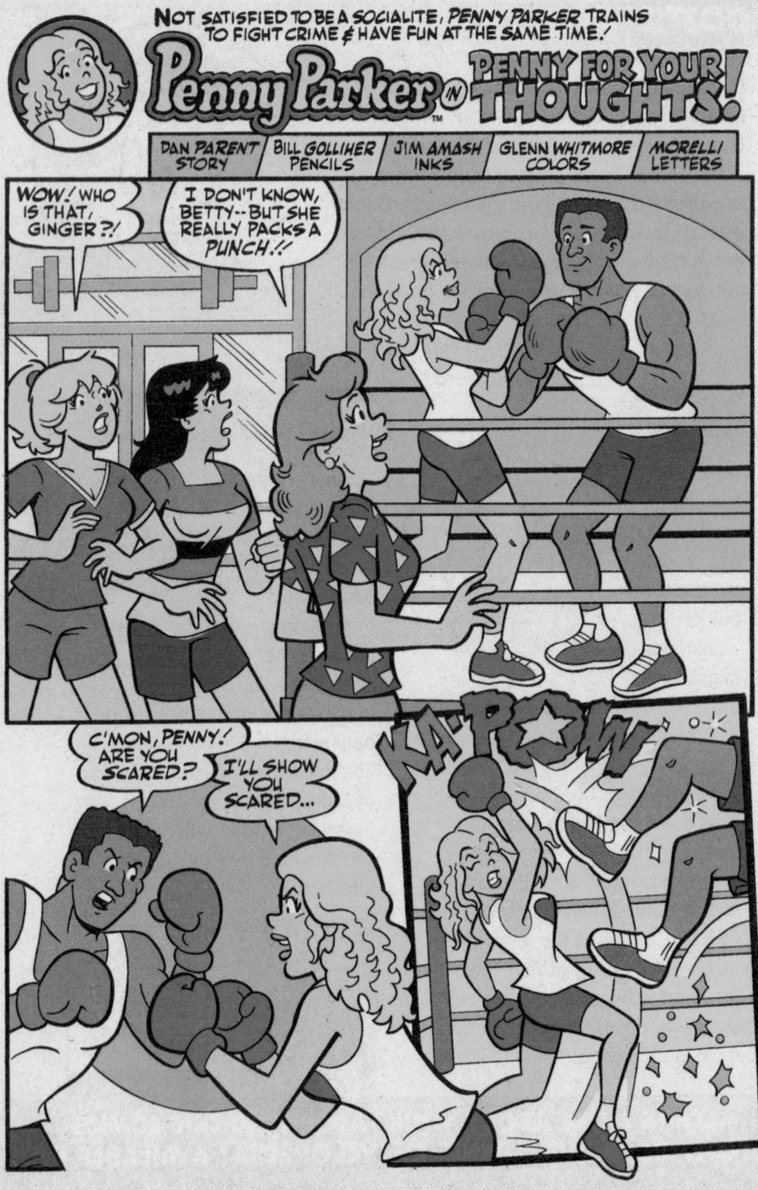
NOT SATISFIED TO BE A SOCIALITE, PENNY PARKER TRAINS TO FIGHT CRIME & HAVE FUN AT THE SAME TIME!
Penny Parker™ in PENNY FOR YOUR THOUGHTS!
DAN PARENT STORY
BILL GOLLIHER PENCILS
JIM AMASH INKS
GLENN WHITMORE COLORS
MORELLI LETTERS
WOW! WHO IS THAT, GINGER?!
I DON'T KNOW, BETTY-- BUT SHE REALLY PACKS A PUNCH!!
C'MON, PENNY! ARE YOU SCARED?
I'LL SHOW YOU SCARED...
KA-POW

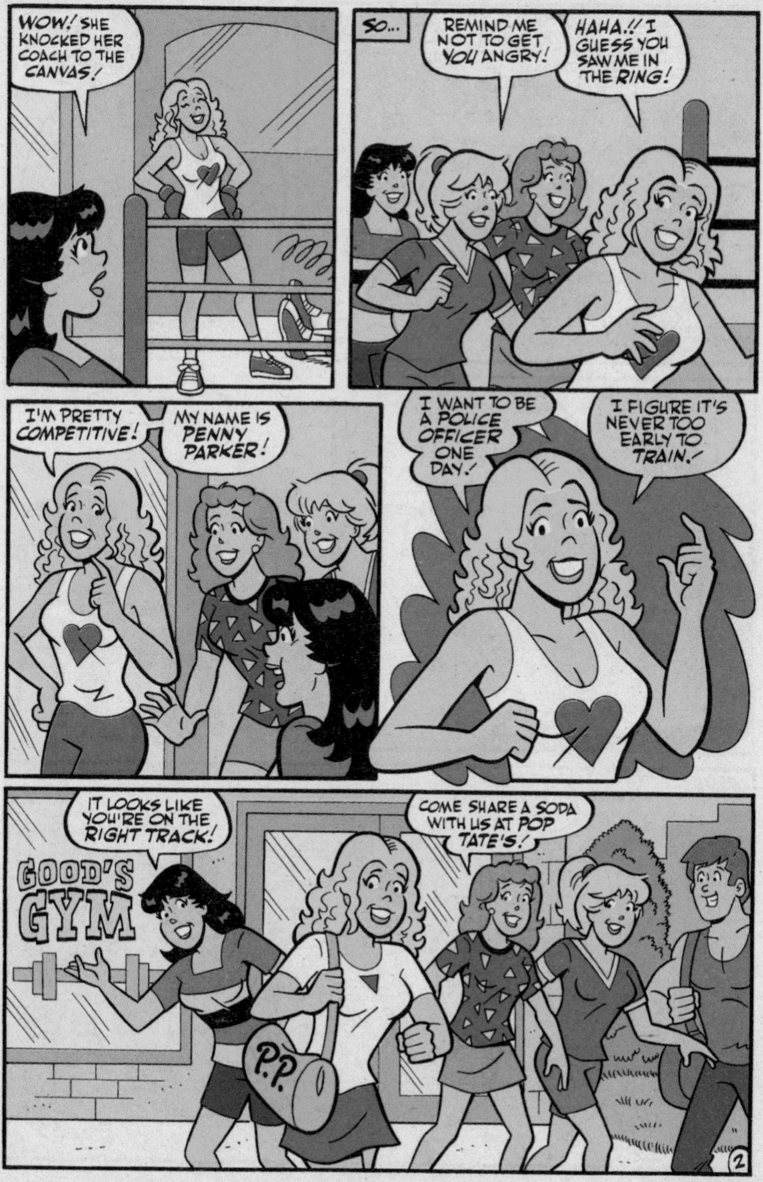
WOW! SHE KNOCKED HER COACH TO THE CANVAS!
SO...
REMIND ME NOT TO GET YOU ANGRY!
HAHA!! I GUESS YOU SAW ME IN THE RING!
I'M PRETTY COMPETITIVE!
MY NAME IS PENNY PARKER!
I WANT TO BE A POLICE OFFICER ONE DAY!
I FIGURE IT'S NEVER TOO EARLY TO TRAIN!
IT LOOKS LIKE YOU'RE ON THE RIGHT TRACK!
GOOD'S GYM
COME SHARE A SODA WITH US AT POP TATE'S!
P.P.
2

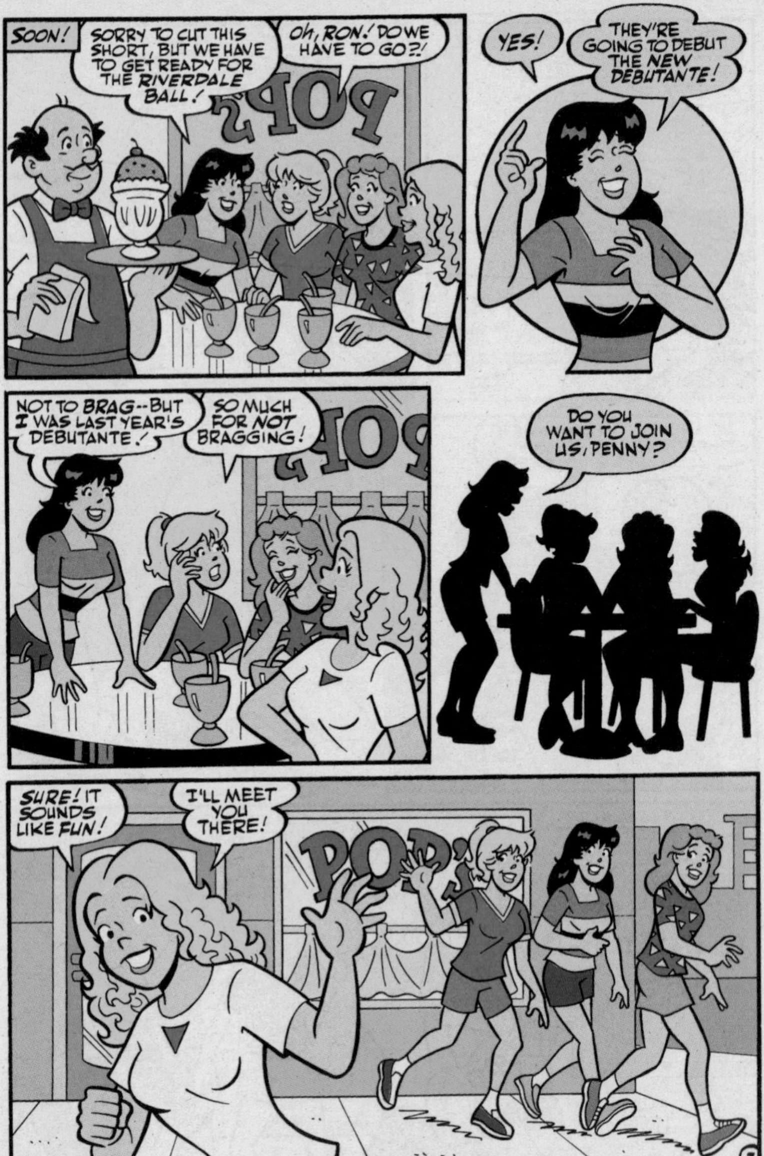
SOON!
SORRY TO CUT THIS SHORT, BUT WE HAVE TO GET READY FOR THE RIVERDALE BALL!
OH, RON! DO WE HAVE TO GO?!
POP'S
YES!
THEY'RE GOING TO DEBUT THE NEW DEBUTANTE!
NOT TO BRAG--BUT I WAS LAST YEAR'S DEBUTANTE!
SO MUCH FOR NOT BRAGGING!
DO YOU WANT TO JOIN US, PENNY?
SURE! IT SOUNDS LIKE FUN!
I'LL MEET YOU THERE!
POP'S
3

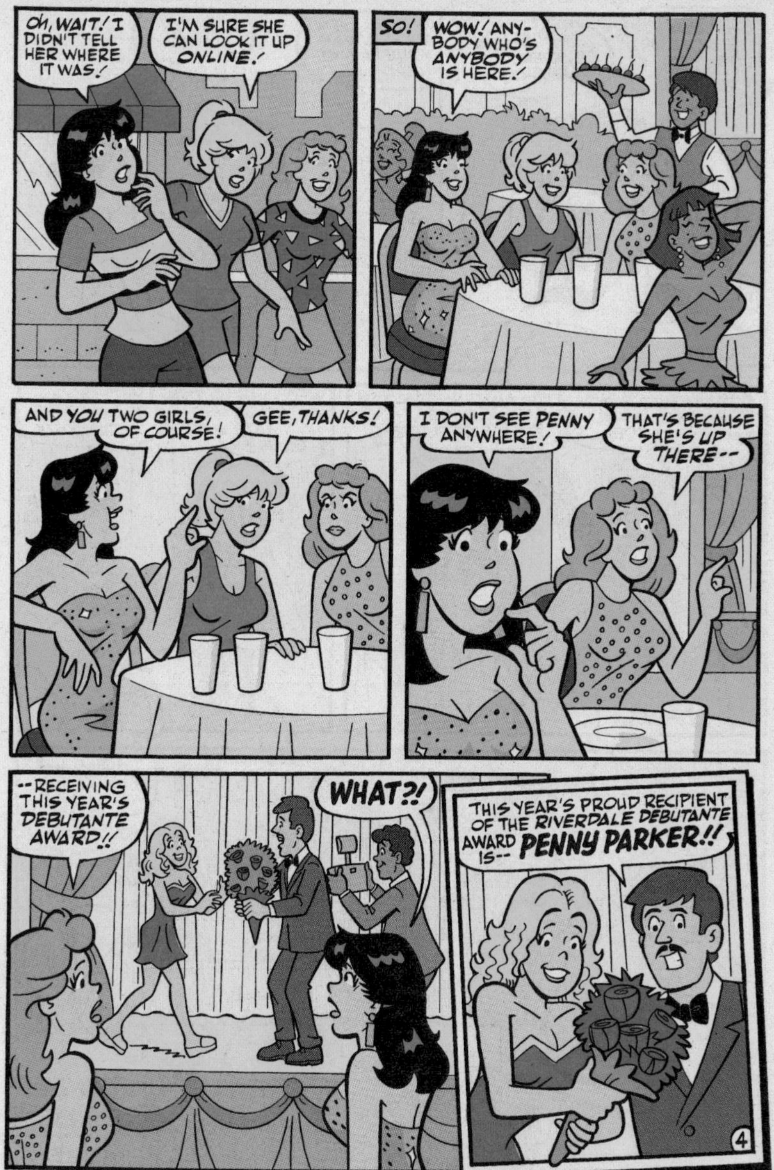

OH, WAIT! I DIDN'T TELL HER WHERE IT WAS!
I'M SURE SHE CAN LOOK IT UP ONLINE!
SO!
WOW! ANYBODY WHO'S ANYBODY IS HERE!
AND YOU TWO GIRLS, OF COURSE!
GEE, THANKS!
I DON'T SEE PENNY ANYWHERE!
THAT'S BECAUSE SHE'S UP THERE--
--RECEIVING THIS YEAR'S DEBUTANTE AWARD!!
WHAT?!
THIS YEAR'S PROUD RECIPIENT OF THE RIVERDALE DEBUTANTE AWARD IS-- PENNY PARKER!!
4

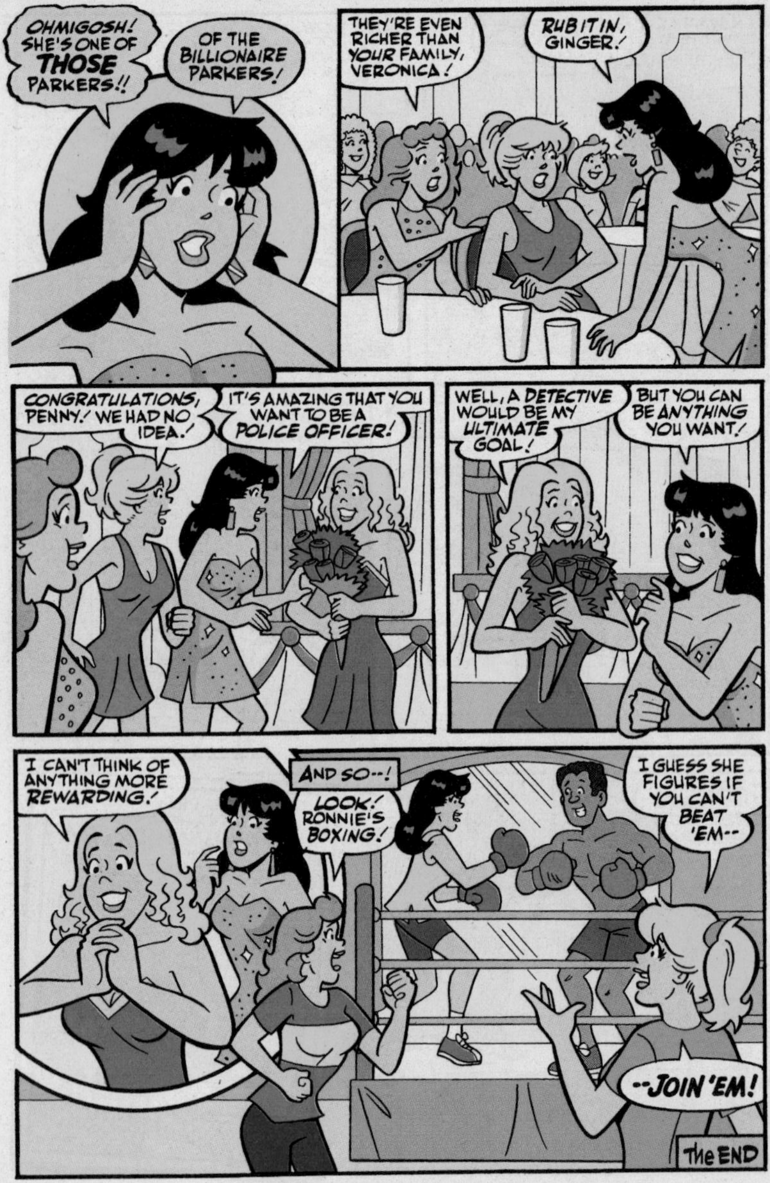
OHMIGOSH! SHE'S ONE OF THOSE PARKERS!!
OF THE BILLIONAIRE PARKERS!
THEY'RE EVEN RICHER THAN YOUR FAMILY, VERONICA!
RUB IT IN, GINGER!
CONGRATULATIONS, PENNY! WE HAD NO IDEA!
IT'S AMAZING THAT YOU WANT TO BE A POLICE OFFICER!
WELL, A DETECTIVE WOULD BE MY ULTIMATE GOAL!
BUT YOU CAN BE ANYTHING YOU WANT!
I CAN'T THINK OF ANYTHING MORE REWARDING!
AND SO--!
LOOK! RONNIE'S BOXING!
I GUESS SHE FIGURES IF YOU CAN'T BEAT 'EM--
--JOIN 'EM!
The END

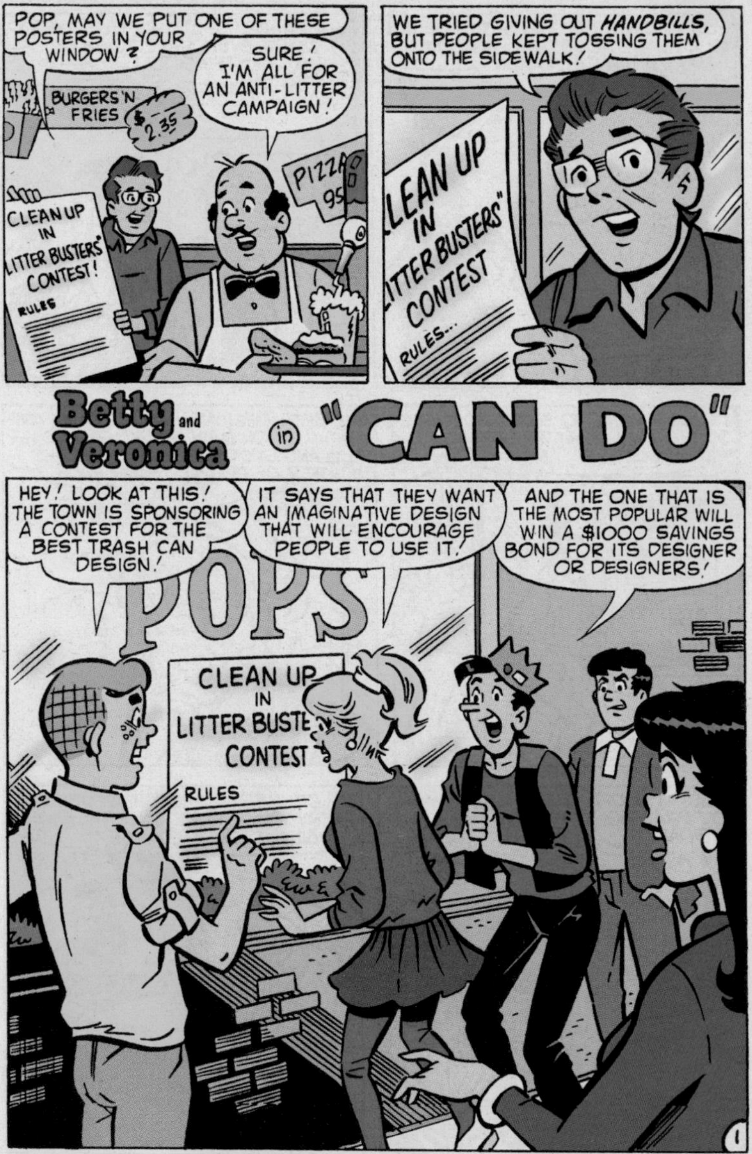
POP, MAY WE PUT ONE OF THESE POSTERS IN YOUR WINDOW?
SURE! I'M ALL FOR AN ANTI-LITTER CAMPAIGN!
BURGERS 'N FRIES
$2.35
PIZZA
CLEAN UP IN LITTER BUSTERS' CONTEST!
RULES
WE TRIED GIVING OUT HANDBILLS, BUT PEOPLE KEPT TOSSING THEM ONTO THE SIDEWALK!
CLEAN UP IN LITTER BUSTERS' CONTEST
RULES...
Betty and Veronica in "CAN DO"
HEY! LOOK AT THIS! THE TOWN IS SPONSORING A CONTEST FOR THE BEST TRASH CAN DESIGN!
IT SAYS THAT THEY WANT AN IMAGINATIVE DESIGN THAT WILL ENCOURAGE PEOPLE TO USE IT!
AND THE ONE THAT IS THE MOST POPULAR WILL WIN A $1000 SAVINGS BOND FOR ITS DESIGNER OR DESIGNERS!
POPS
CLEAN UP IN LITTER BUSTE
CONTEST
RULES
1

Script: Hal Smith / Pencils: Doug Crane / Inks: Rudy Lapick / Letters: Bill Yoshida

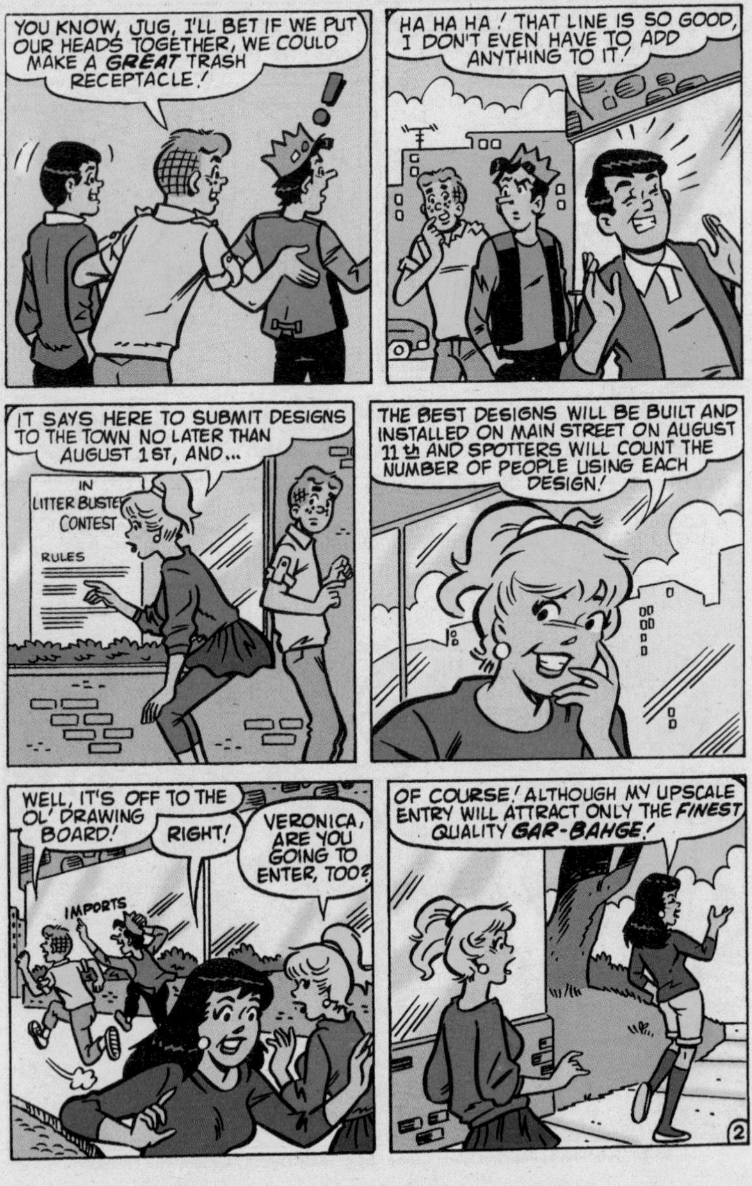
YOU KNOW, JUG, I'LL BET IF WE PUT OUR HEADS TOGETHER, WE COULD MAKE A GREAT TRASH RECEPTACLE!
HA HA HA! THAT LINE IS SO GOOD, I DON'T EVEN HAVE TO ADD ANYTHING TO IT!
IT SAYS HERE TO SUBMIT DESIGNS TO THE TOWN NO LATER THAN AUGUST 1ST, AND...
IN
LITTER BUSTE
CONTEST
RULES
THE BEST DESIGNS WILL BE BUILT AND INSTALLED ON MAIN STREET ON AUGUST 11th AND SPOTTERS WILL COUNT THE NUMBER OF PEOPLE USING EACH DESIGN!
WELL, IT'S OFF TO THE OL' DRAWING BOARD!
RIGHT!
IMPORTS
VERONICA, ARE YOU GOING TO ENTER, TOO?
OF COURSE! ALTHOUGH MY UPSCALE ENTRY WILL ATTRACT ONLY THE FINEST QUALITY GAR-BAHGE!
2

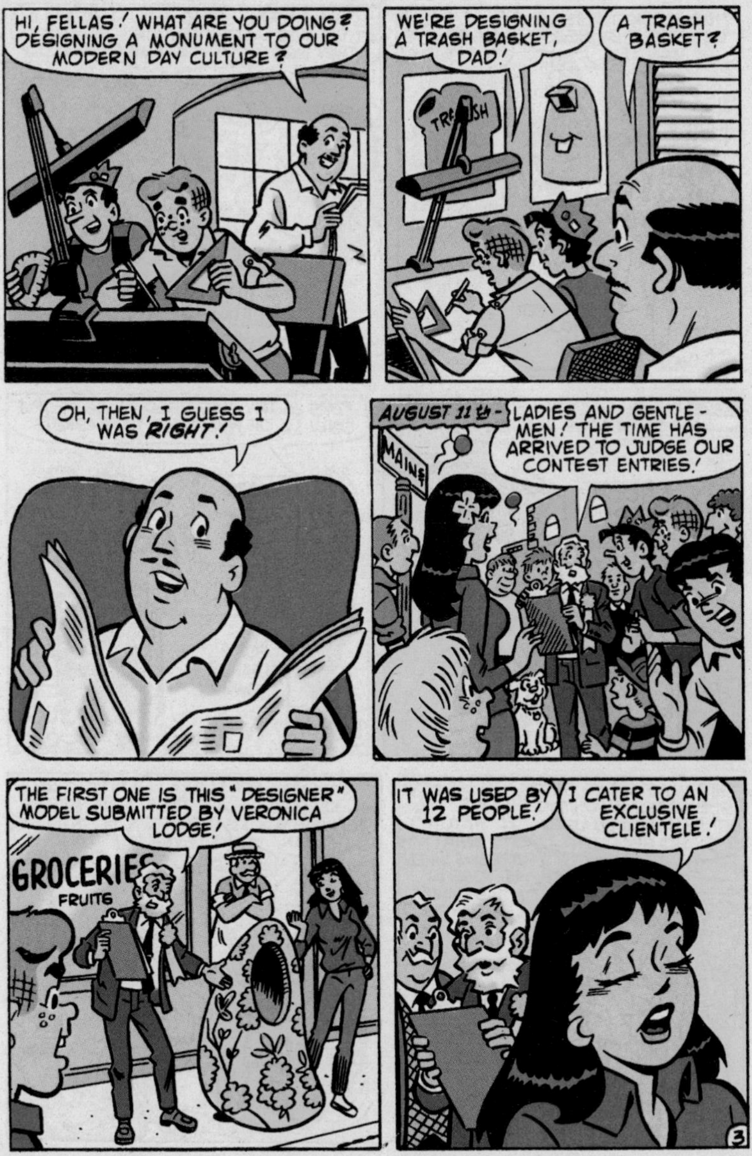
HI, FELLAS! WHAT ARE YOU DOING? DESIGNING A MONUMENT TO OUR MODERN DAY CULTURE?
WE'RE DESIGNING A TRASH BASKET, DAD!
A TRASH BASKET?
TRASH
OH, THEN, I GUESS I WAS RIGHT!
AUGUST 11th -
LADIES AND GENTLE-MEN! THE TIME HAS ARRIVED TO JUDGE OUR CONTEST ENTRIES!
MAIN ST
THE FIRST ONE IS THIS "DESIGNER" MODEL SUBMITTED BY VERONICA LODGE!
GROCERIES
FRUITS
IT WAS USED BY 12 PEOPLE!
I CATER TO AN EXCLUSIVE CLIENTELE!
3

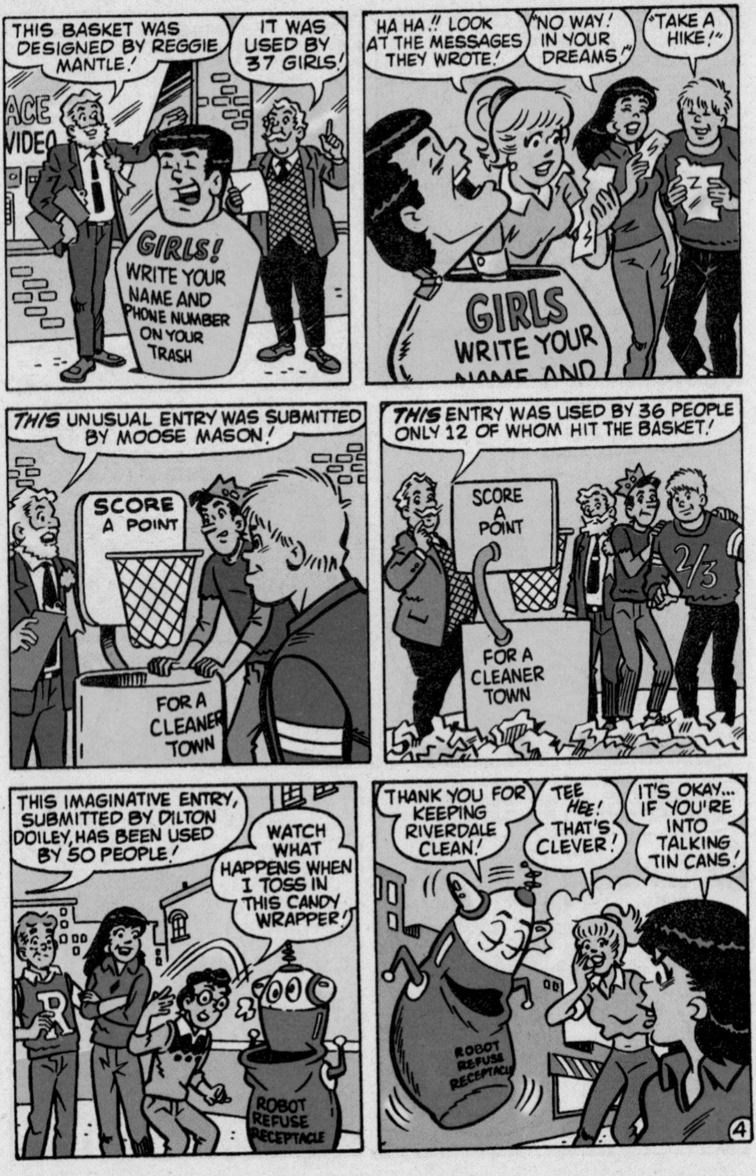
THIS BASKET WAS DESIGNED BY REGGIE MANTLE!
IT WAS USED BY 37 GIRLS!
ACE VIDEO
GIRLS! WRITE YOUR NAME AND PHONE NUMBER ON YOUR TRASH
HA HA!! LOOK AT THE MESSAGES THEY WROTE!
"NO WAY! IN YOUR DREAMS!"
"TAKE A HIKE!"
GIRLS WRITE YOUR
THIS UNUSUAL ENTRY WAS SUBMITTED BY MOOSE MASON!
SCORE A POINT
FOR A CLEANER TOWN
THIS ENTRY WAS USED BY 36 PEOPLE ONLY 12 OF WHOM HIT THE BASKET!
SCORE A POINT
FOR A CLEANER TOWN
2/3
THIS IMAGINATIVE ENTRY, SUBMITTED BY DILTON DOILEY, HAS BEEN USED BY 50 PEOPLE!
WATCH WHAT HAPPENS WHEN I TOSS IN THIS CANDY WRAPPER!
R
ROBOT REFUSE RECEPTACLE
THANK YOU FOR KEEPING RIVERDALE CLEAN!
TEE HEE! THAT'S CLEVER!
IT'S OKAY... IF YOU'RE INTO TALKING TIN CANS!
ROBOT REFUSE RECEPTACLE
4

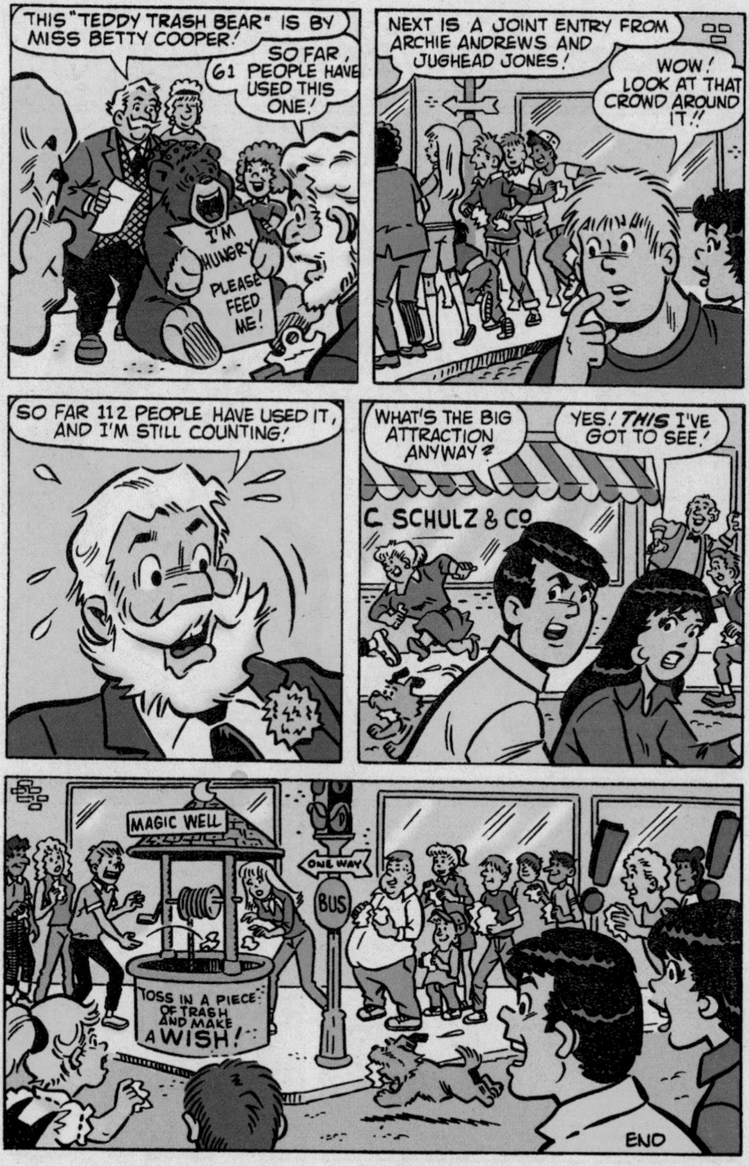
THIS "TEDDY TRASH BEAR" IS BY MISS BETTY COOPER!
SO FAR, 61 PEOPLE HAVE USED THIS ONE!
I'M HUNGRY PLEASE FEED ME!
NEXT IS A JOINT ENTRY FROM ARCHIE ANDREWS AND JUGHEAD JONES!
WOW! LOOK AT THAT CROWD AROUND IT!!
SO FAR 112 PEOPLE HAVE USED IT, AND I'M STILL COUNTING!
WHAT'S THE BIG ATTRACTION ANYWAY?
YES! THIS I'VE GOT TO SEE!
C. SCHULZ & CO
MAGIC WELL
ONE WAY
BUS
TOSS IN A PIECE OF TRASH AND MAKE A WISH!
END

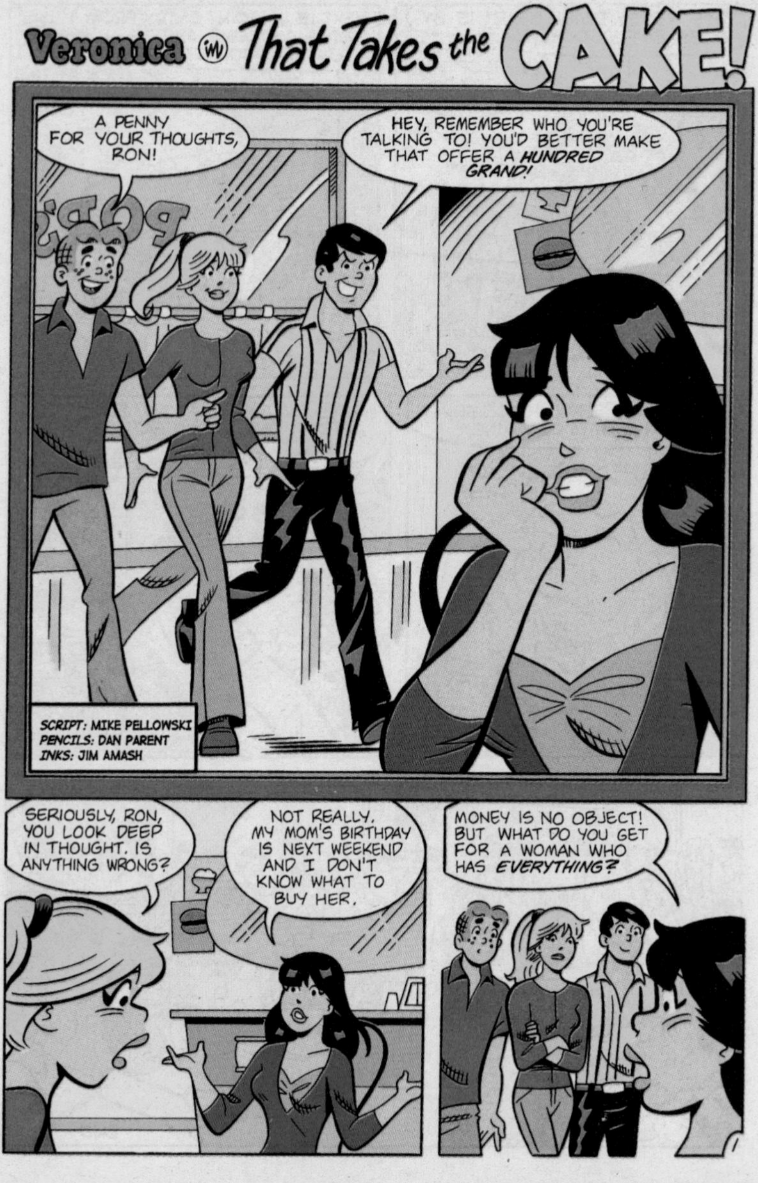
Veronica in That Takes the CAKE!
A PENNY FOR YOUR THOUGHTS, RON!
HEY, REMEMBER WHO YOU'RE TALKING TO! YOU'D BETTER MAKE THAT OFFER A *HUNDRED GRAND!*
SCRIPT: MIKE PELLOWSKI
PENCILS: DAN PARENT
INKS: JIM AMASH
SERIOUSLY, RON, YOU LOOK DEEP IN THOUGHT. IS ANYTHING WRONG?
NOT REALLY. MY MOM'S BIRTHDAY IS NEXT WEEKEND AND I DON'T KNOW WHAT TO BUY HER.
MONEY IS NO OBJECT! BUT WHAT DO YOU GET FOR A WOMAN WHO HAS *EVERYTHING?*
1

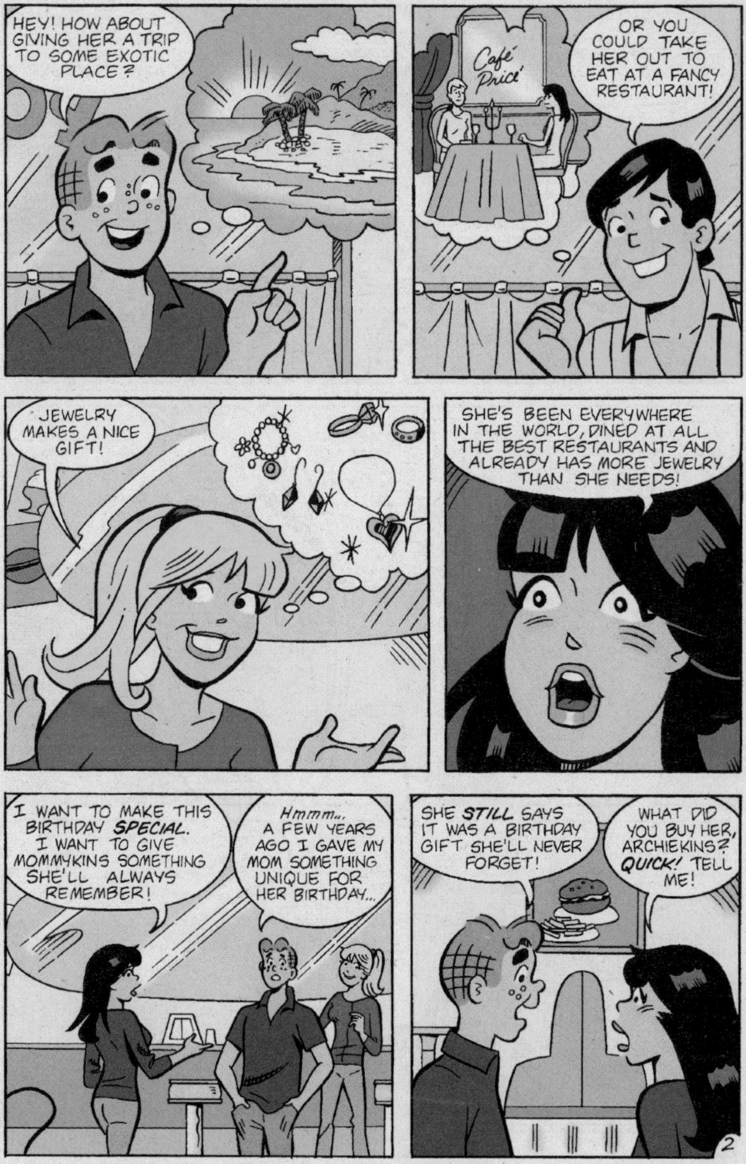
HEY! HOW ABOUT GIVING HER A TRIP TO SOME EXOTIC PLACE?
Café Price'
OR YOU COULD TAKE HER OUT TO EAT AT A FANCY RESTAURANT!
JEWELRY MAKES A NICE GIFT!
SHE'S BEEN EVERYWHERE IN THE WORLD, DINED AT ALL THE BEST RESTAURANTS AND ALREADY HAS MORE JEWELRY THAN SHE NEEDS!
I WANT TO MAKE THIS BIRTHDAY SPECIAL. I WANT TO GIVE MOMMYKINS SOMETHING SHE'LL ALWAYS REMEMBER!
Hmmm... A FEW YEARS AGO I GAVE MY MOM SOMETHING UNIQUE FOR HER BIRTHDAY...
SHE STILL SAYS IT WAS A BIRTHDAY GIFT SHE'LL NEVER FORGET!
WHAT DID YOU BUY HER, ARCHIEKINS? QUICK! TELL ME!
2

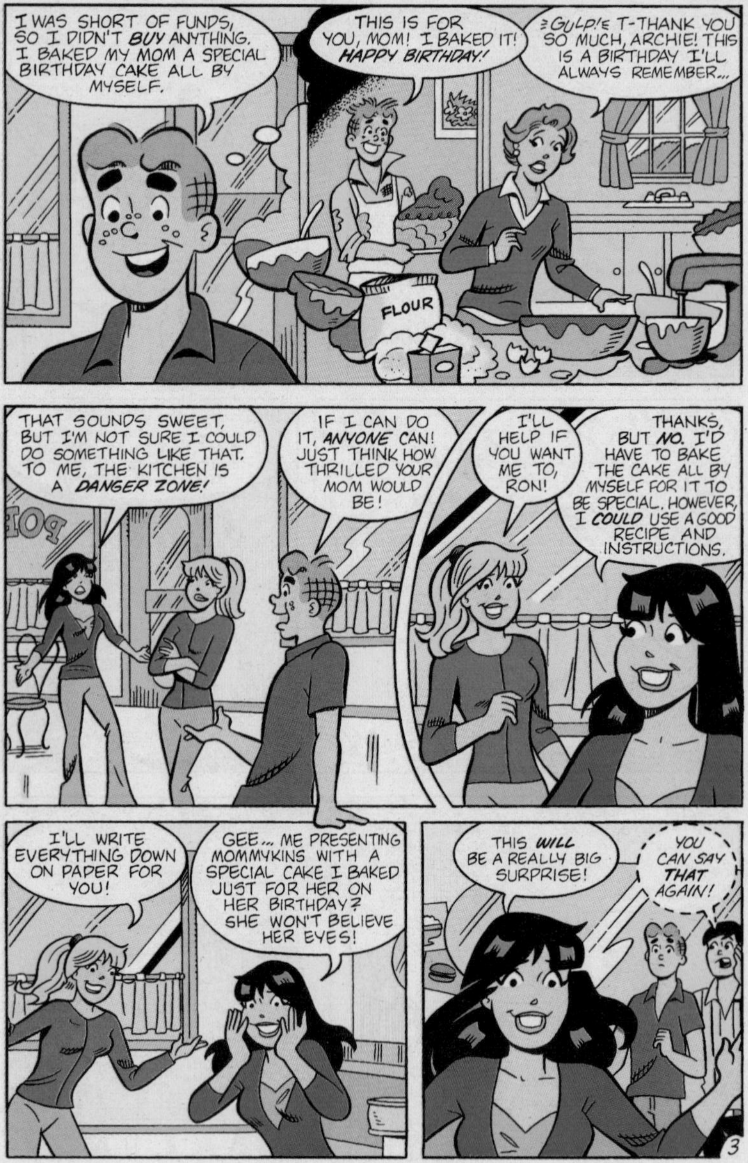
I WAS SHORT OF FUNDS, SO I DIDN'T **BUY** ANYTHING. I BAKED MY MOM A SPECIAL BIRTHDAY CAKE ALL BY MYSELF.
THIS IS FOR YOU, MOM! I BAKED IT! **HAPPY BIRTHDAY!**
GULP! T-THANK YOU SO MUCH, ARCHIE! THIS IS A BIRTHDAY I'LL ALWAYS REMEMBER...
FLOUR
THAT SOUNDS SWEET, BUT I'M NOT SURE I COULD DO SOMETHING LIKE THAT. TO ME, THE KITCHEN IS A **DANGER ZONE!**
IF I CAN DO IT, **ANYONE** CAN! JUST THINK HOW THRILLED YOUR MOM WOULD BE!
I'LL HELP IF YOU WANT ME TO, RON!
THANKS, BUT **NO.** I'D HAVE TO BAKE THE CAKE ALL BY MYSELF FOR IT TO BE SPECIAL. HOWEVER, I **COULD** USE A GOOD RECIPE AND INSTRUCTIONS.
I'LL WRITE EVERYTHING DOWN ON PAPER FOR YOU!
GEE... ME PRESENTING MOMMYKINS WITH A SPECIAL CAKE I BAKED JUST FOR HER ON HER BIRTHDAY? SHE WON'T BELIEVE HER EYES!
THIS **WILL** BE A REALLY BIG SURPRISE!
YOU CAN SAY **THAT** AGAIN!

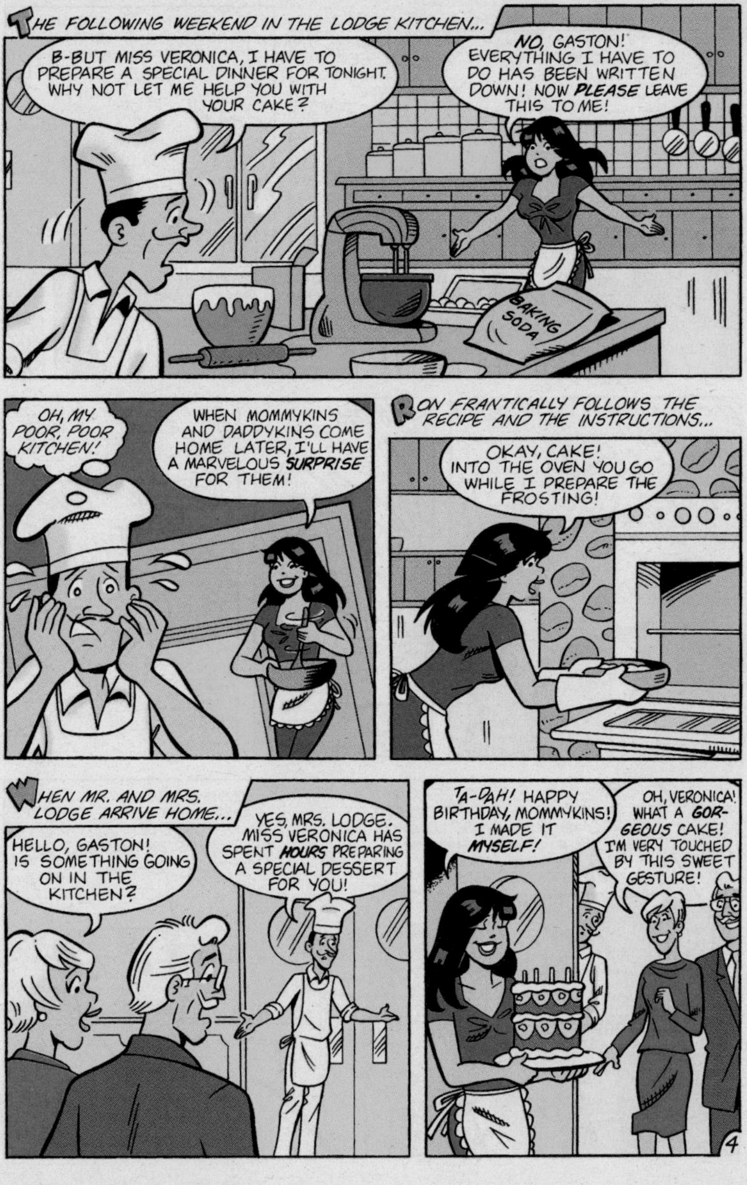
THE FOLLOWING WEEKEND IN THE LODGE KITCHEN...
B-BUT MISS VERONICA, I HAVE TO PREPARE A SPECIAL DINNER FOR TONIGHT. WHY NOT LET ME HELP YOU WITH YOUR CAKE?
NO, GASTON! EVERYTHING I HAVE TO DO HAS BEEN WRITTEN DOWN! NOW PLEASE LEAVE THIS TO ME!
BAKING SODA
OH, MY POOR, POOR KITCHEN!
WHEN MOMMYKINS AND DADDYKINS COME HOME LATER, I'LL HAVE A MARVELOUS SURPRISE FOR THEM!
RON FRANTICALLY FOLLOWS THE RECIPE AND THE INSTRUCTIONS...
OKAY, CAKE! INTO THE OVEN YOU GO WHILE I PREPARE THE FROSTING!
WHEN MR. AND MRS. LODGE ARRIVE HOME...
HELLO, GASTON! IS SOMETHING GOING ON IN THE KITCHEN?
YES, MRS. LODGE. MISS VERONICA HAS SPENT HOURS PREPARING A SPECIAL DESSERT FOR YOU!
TA-DAH! HAPPY BIRTHDAY, MOMMYKINS! I MADE IT MYSELF!
OH, VERONICA! WHAT A GORGEOUS CAKE! I'M VERY TOUCHED BY THIS SWEET GESTURE!
4

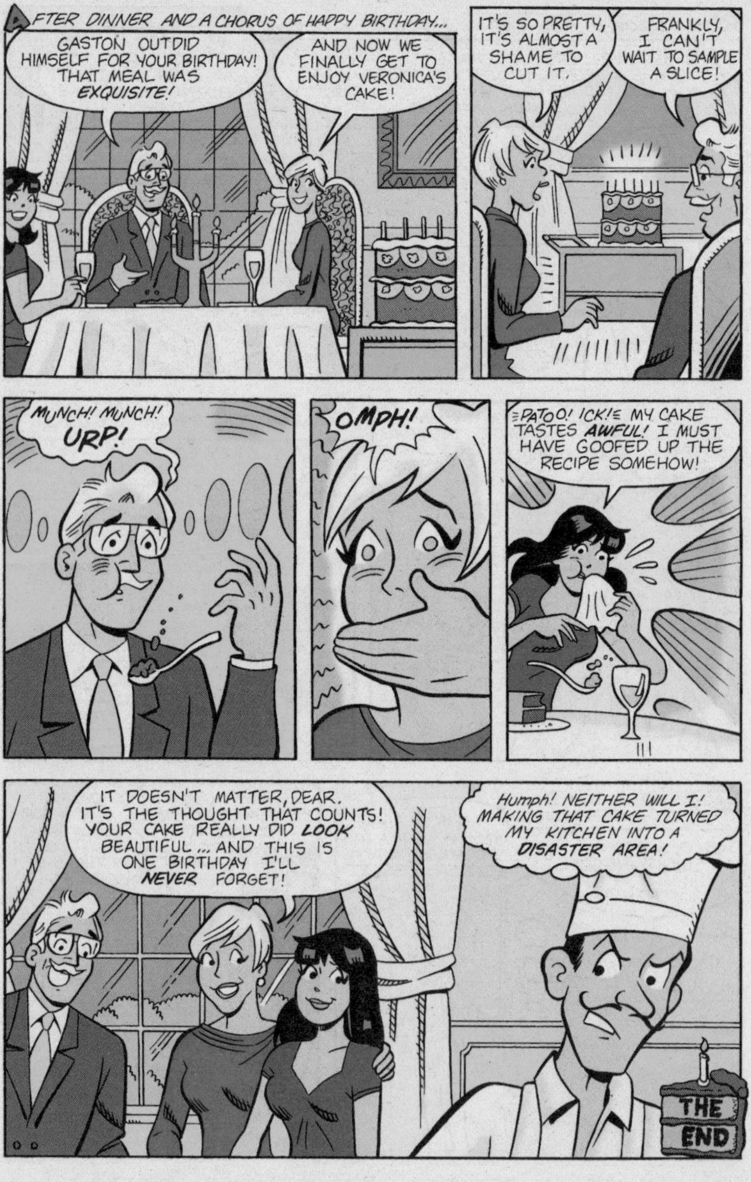
AFTER DINNER AND A CHORUS OF HAPPY BIRTHDAY...
GASTON OUTDID HIMSELF FOR YOUR BIRTHDAY! THAT MEAL WAS EXQUISITE!
AND NOW WE FINALLY GET TO ENJOY VERONICA'S CAKE!
IT'S SO PRETTY, IT'S ALMOST A SHAME TO CUT IT.
FRANKLY, I CAN'T WAIT TO SAMPLE A SLICE!
MUNCH! MUNCH! URP!
OMPH!
PATOO! ICK! MY CAKE TASTES AWFUL! I MUST HAVE GOOFED UP THE RECIPE SOMEHOW!
IT DOESN'T MATTER, DEAR. IT'S THE THOUGHT THAT COUNTS! YOUR CAKE REALLY DID LOOK BEAUTIFUL ... AND THIS IS ONE BIRTHDAY I'LL NEVER FORGET!
Humph! NEITHER WILL I! MAKING THAT CAKE TURNED MY KITCHEN INTO A DISASTER AREA!
THE END

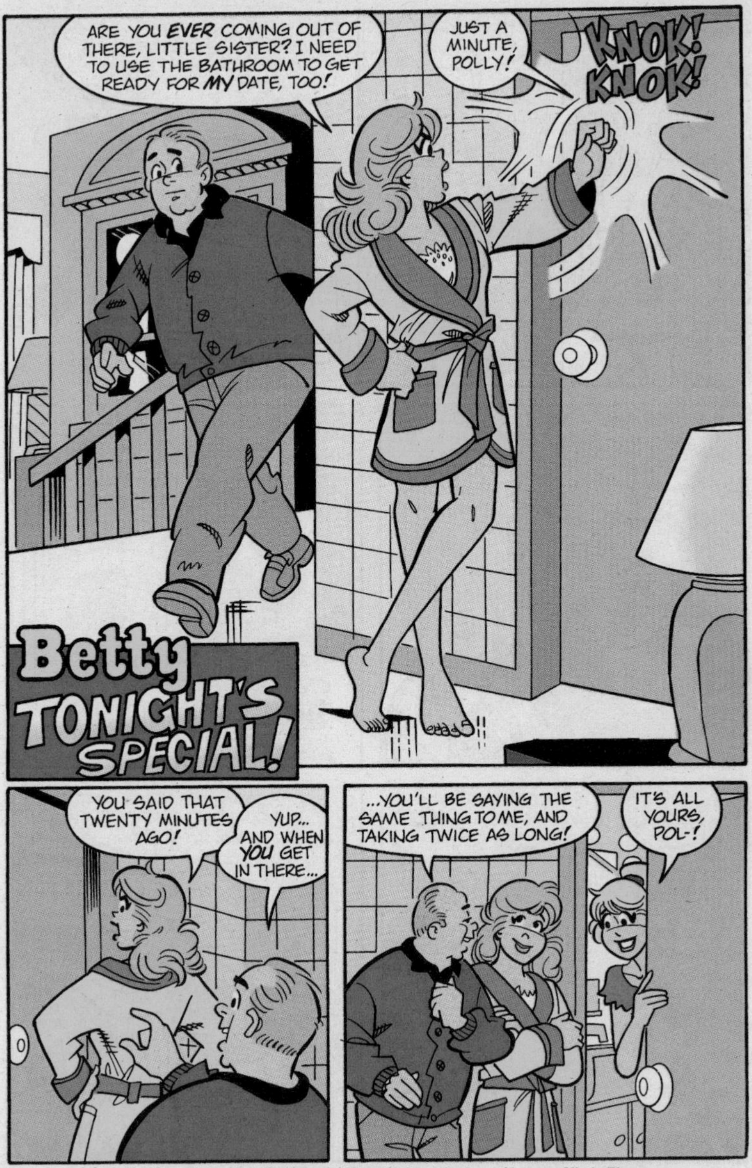
ARE YOU EVER COMING OUT OF THERE, LITTLE SISTER? I NEED TO USE THE BATHROOM TO GET READY FOR MY DATE, TOO!
JUST A MINUTE, POLLY!
KNOK! KNOK!
Betty
TONIGHT'S SPECIAL!
YOU SAID THAT TWENTY MINUTES AGO!
YUP... AND WHEN YOU GET IN THERE...
...YOU'LL BE SAYING THE SAME THING TO ME, AND TAKING TWICE AS LONG!
IT'S ALL YOURS, POL-!

Script: Kathleen Webb / Pencils: Stan Goldberg / Inks: John Lowe / Letters: Mindy Eisman

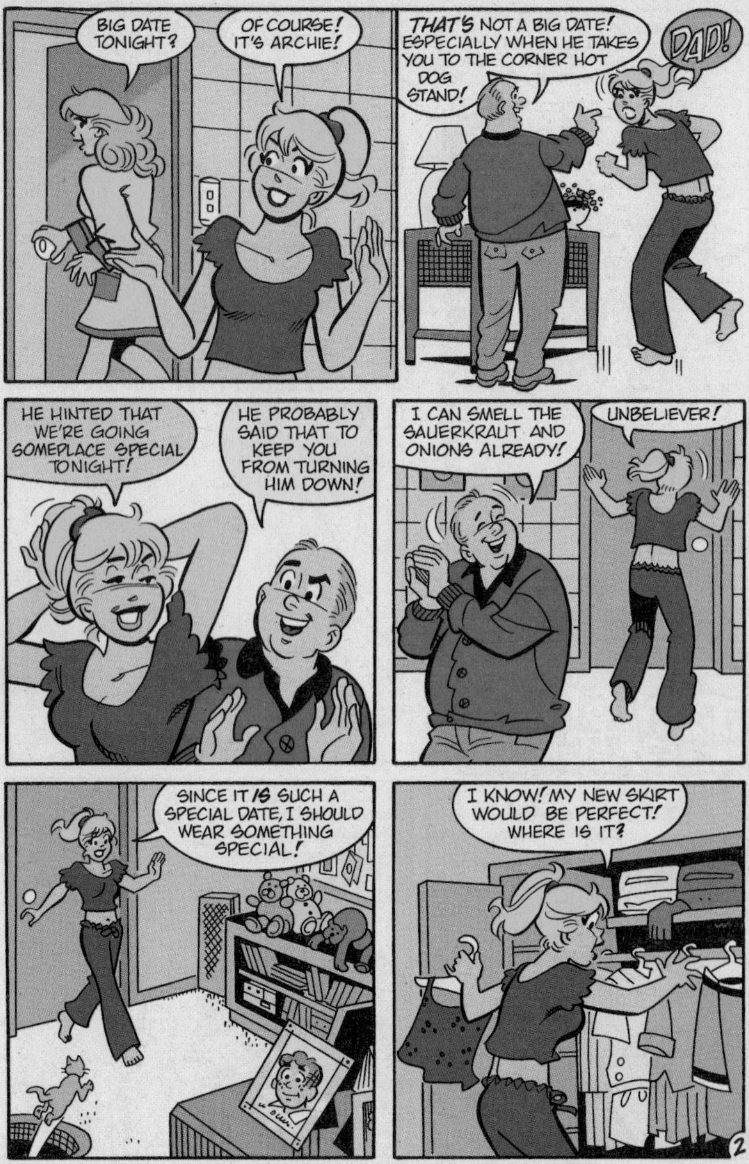
BIG DATE TONIGHT?
OF COURSE! IT'S ARCHIE!
THAT'S NOT A BIG DATE! ESPECIALLY WHEN HE TAKES YOU TO THE CORNER HOT DOG STAND!
DAD!
HE HINTED THAT WE'RE GOING SOMEPLACE SPECIAL TONIGHT!
HE PROBABLY SAID THAT TO KEEP YOU FROM TURNING HIM DOWN!
I CAN SMELL THE SAUERKRAUT AND ONIONS ALREADY!
UNBELIEVER!
SINCE IT IS SUCH A SPECIAL DATE, I SHOULD WEAR SOMETHING SPECIAL!
I KNOW! MY NEW SKIRT WOULD BE PERFECT! WHERE IS IT?

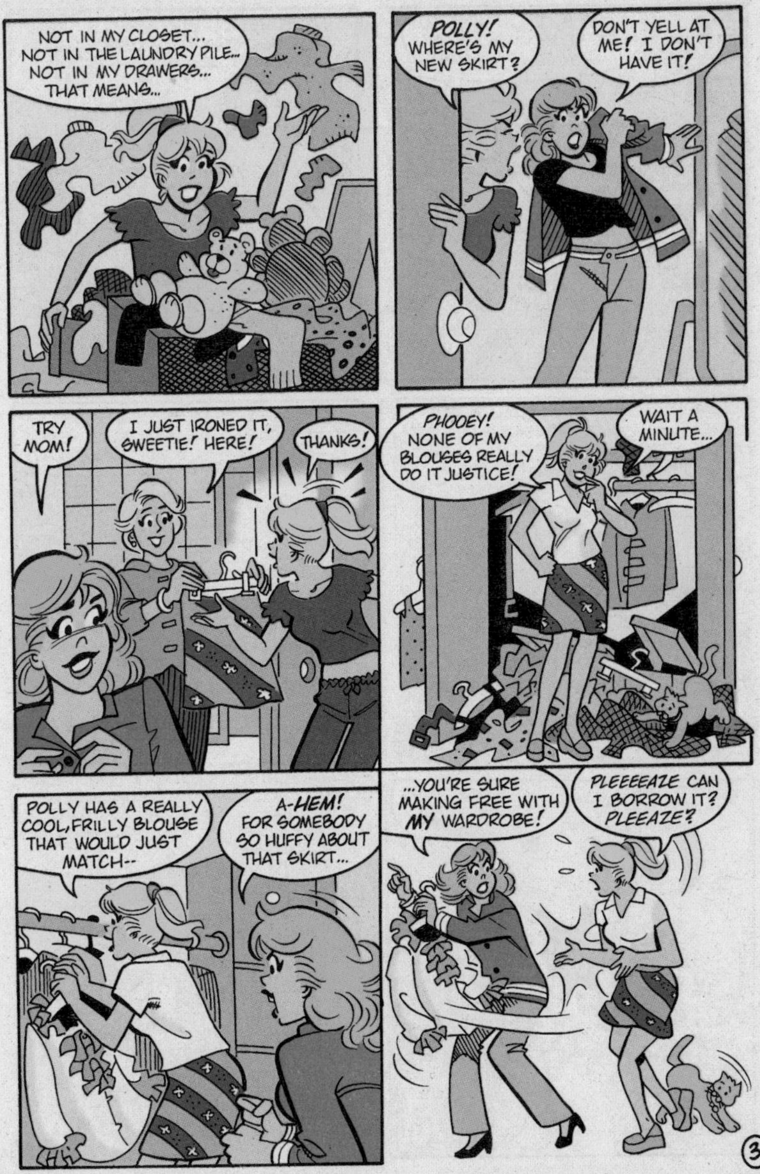
NOT IN MY CLOSET... NOT IN THE LAUNDRY PILE... NOT IN MY DRAWERS... THAT MEANS...
POLLY! WHERE'S MY NEW SKIRT?
DON'T YELL AT ME! I DON'T HAVE IT!
TRY MOM!
I JUST IRONED IT, SWEETIE! HERE!
THANKS!
PHOOEY! NONE OF MY BLOUSES REALLY DO IT JUSTICE!
WAIT A MINUTE...
POLLY HAS A REALLY COOL, FRILLY BLOUSE THAT WOULD JUST MATCH--
A-HEM! FOR SOMEBODY SO HUFFY ABOUT THAT SKIRT...
...YOU'RE SURE MAKING FREE WITH MY WARDROBE!
PLEEEEAZE CAN I BORROW IT? PLEEAZE?

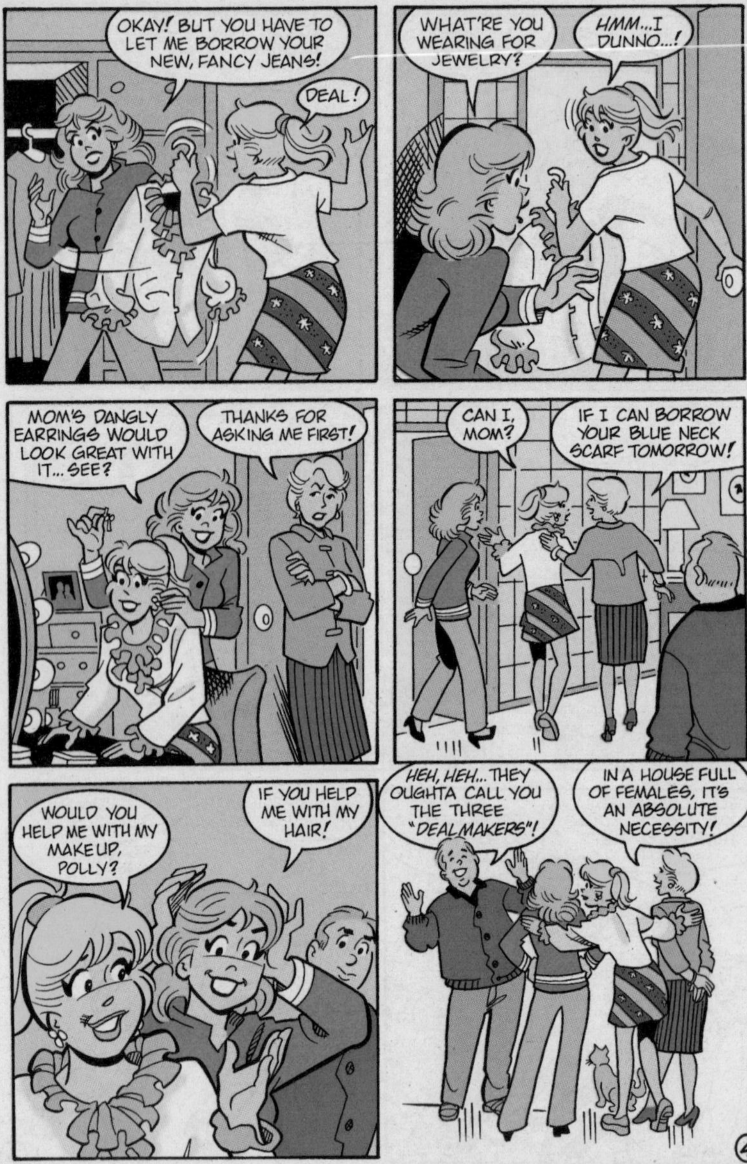
OKAY! BUT YOU HAVE TO LET ME BORROW YOUR NEW, FANCY JEANS!
DEAL!
WHAT'RE YOU WEARING FOR JEWELRY?
HMM...I DUNNO...!
MOM'S DANGLY EARRINGS WOULD LOOK GREAT WITH IT... SEE?
THANKS FOR ASKING ME FIRST!
CAN I, MOM?
IF I CAN BORROW YOUR BLUE NECK SCARF TOMORROW!
WOULD YOU HELP ME WITH MY MAKEUP, POLLY?
IF YOU HELP ME WITH MY HAIR!
HEH, HEH... THEY OUGHTA CALL YOU THE THREE "DEALMAKERS"!
IN A HOUSE FULL OF FEMALES, IT'S AN ABSOLUTE NECESSITY!

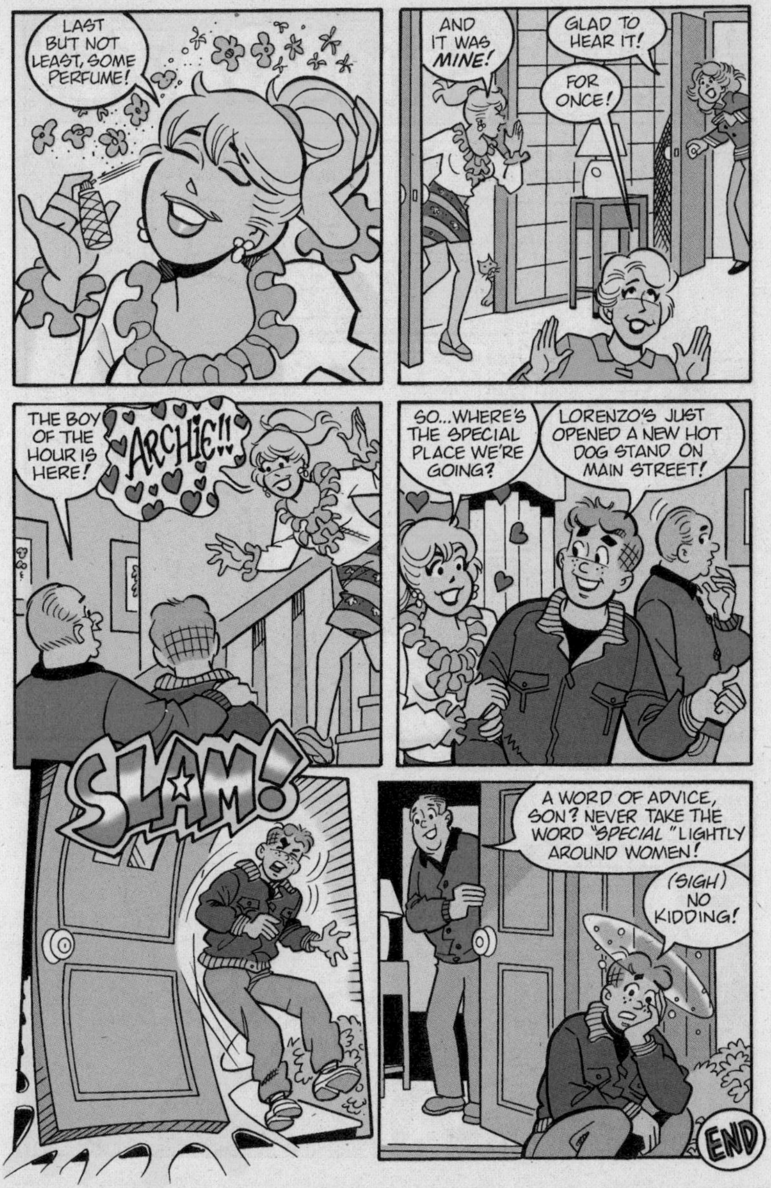
LAST BUT NOT LEAST, SOME PERFUME!
AND IT WAS MINE!
GLAD TO HEAR IT!
FOR ONCE!
THE BOY OF THE HOUR IS HERE!
ARCHIE!!
SO...WHERE'S THE SPECIAL PLACE WE'RE GOING?
LORENZO'S JUST OPENED A NEW HOT DOG STAND ON MAIN STREET!
SLAM!
A WORD OF ADVICE, SON? NEVER TAKE THE WORD "SPECIAL" LIGHTLY AROUND WOMEN!
(SIGH) NO KIDDING!
END

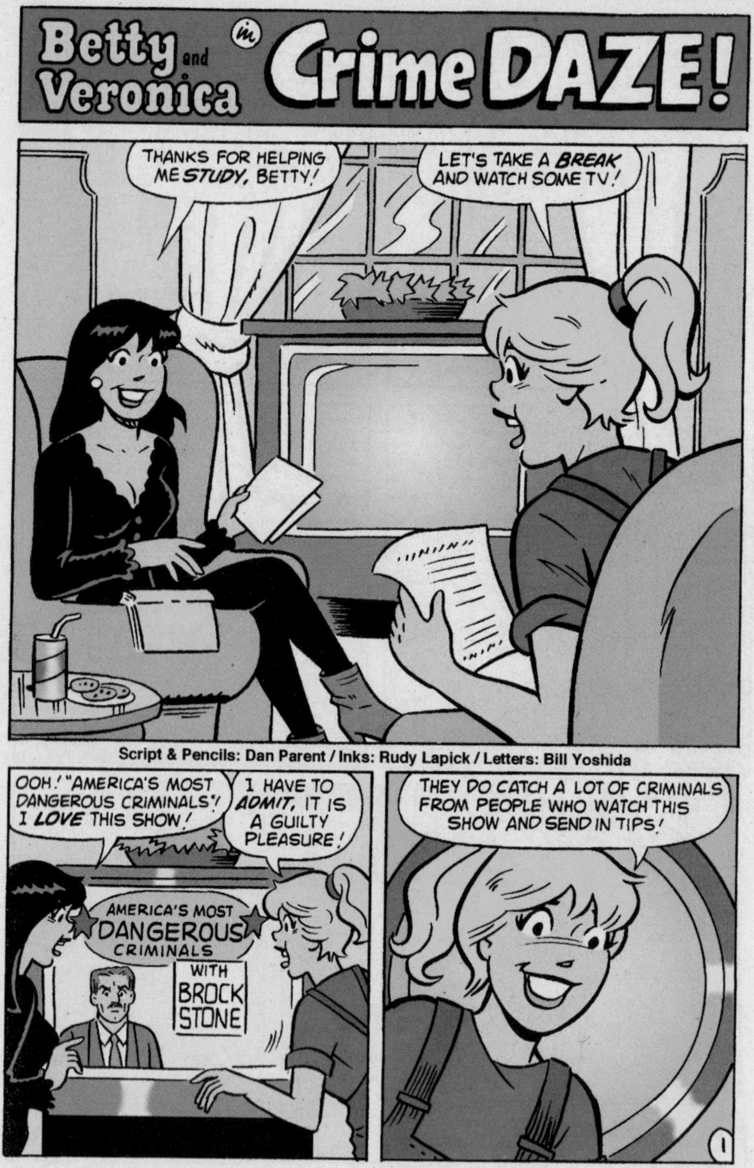
Betty and Veronica in Crime DAZE!
THANKS FOR HELPING ME STUDY, BETTY!
LET'S TAKE A BREAK AND WATCH SOME TV!
OOH! "AMERICA'S MOST DANGEROUS CRIMINALS"! I LOVE THIS SHOW!
I HAVE TO ADMIT, IT IS A GUILTY PLEASURE!
AMERICA'S MOST DANGEROUS CRIMINALS
WITH BROCK STONE
THEY DO CATCH A LOT OF CRIMINALS FROM PEOPLE WHO WATCH THIS SHOW AND SEND IN TIPS!
1

Script & Pencils: Dan Parent / Inks: Rudy Lapick / Letters: Bill Yoshida

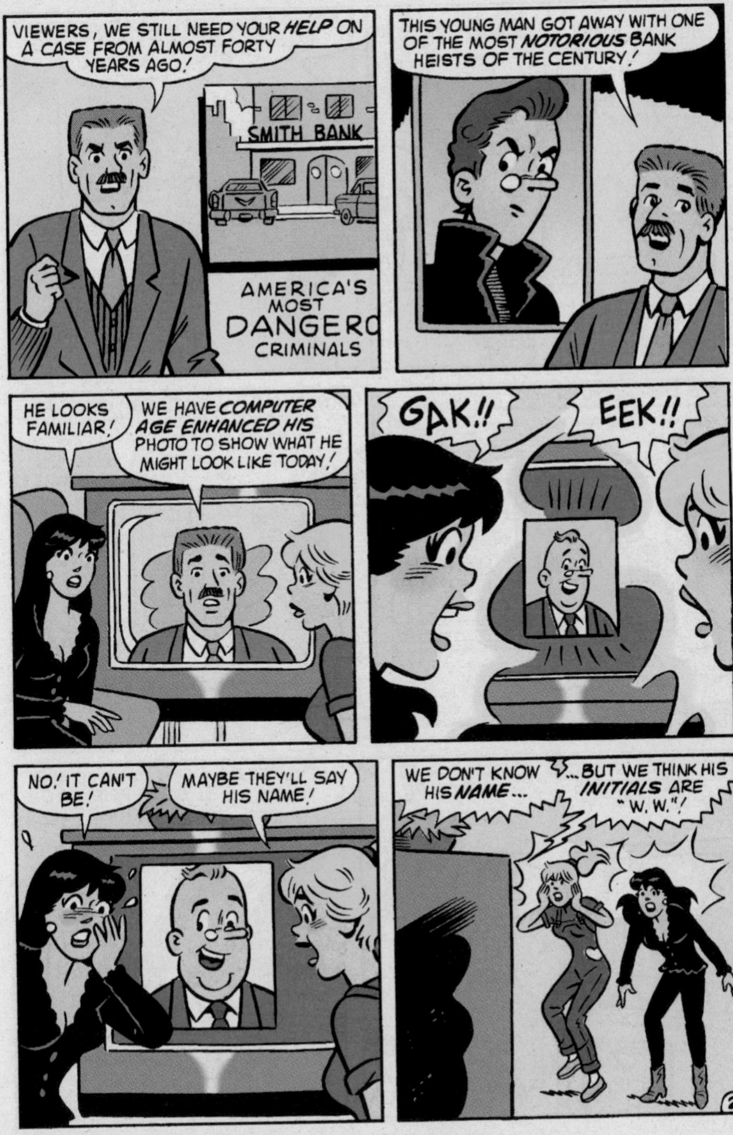

VIEWERS, WE STILL NEED YOUR HELP ON A CASE FROM ALMOST FORTY YEARS AGO!
SMITH BANK
AMERICA'S MOST DANGERO CRIMINALS
THIS YOUNG MAN GOT AWAY WITH ONE OF THE MOST NOTORIOUS BANK HEISTS OF THE CENTURY!
HE LOOKS FAMILIAR!
WE HAVE COMPUTER AGE ENHANCED HIS PHOTO TO SHOW WHAT HE MIGHT LOOK LIKE TODAY!
GAK!!
EEK!!
NO! IT CAN'T BE!
MAYBE THEY'LL SAY HIS NAME!
WE DON'T KNOW HIS NAME...
...BUT WE THINK HIS INITIALS ARE "W. W."!
2

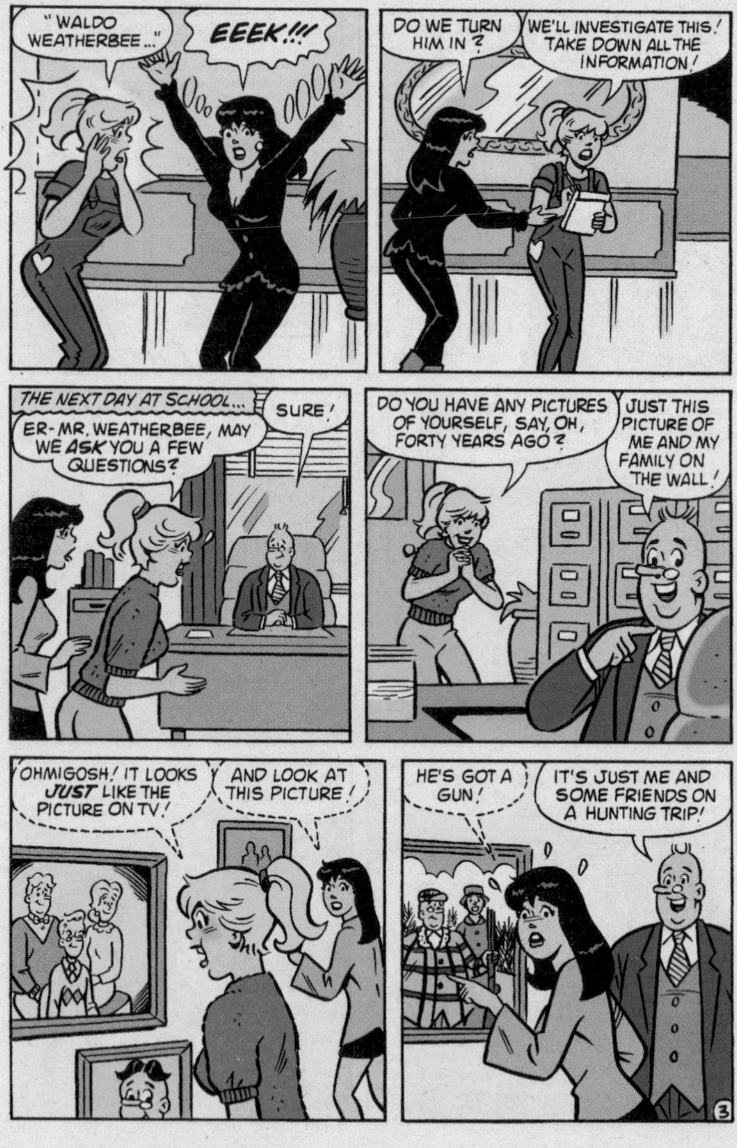
"WALDO WEATHERBEE..."
EEEK!!!
DO WE TURN HIM IN?
WE'LL INVESTIGATE THIS! TAKE DOWN ALL THE INFORMATION!
THE NEXT DAY AT SCHOOL...
ER- MR. WEATHERBEE, MAY WE ASK YOU A FEW QUESTIONS?
SURE!
DO YOU HAVE ANY PICTURES OF YOURSELF, SAY, OH, FORTY YEARS AGO?
JUST THIS PICTURE OF ME AND MY FAMILY ON THE WALL!
OHMIGOSH! IT LOOKS JUST LIKE THE PICTURE ON TV!
AND LOOK AT THIS PICTURE!
HE'S GOT A GUN!
IT'S JUST ME AND SOME FRIENDS ON A HUNTING TRIP!
3

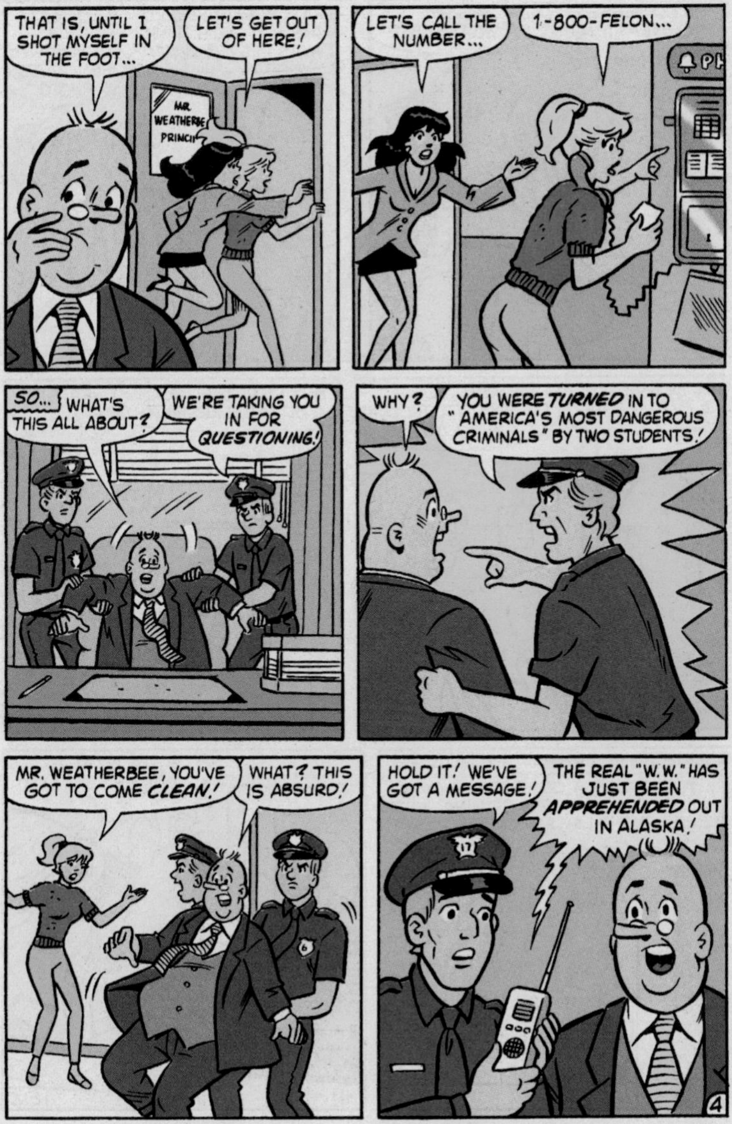
THAT IS, UNTIL I SHOT MYSELF IN THE FOOT...
LET'S GET OUT OF HERE!
MR. WEATHERBE PRINCI
LET'S CALL THE NUMBER...
1-800-FELON...
SO... WHAT'S THIS ALL ABOUT?
WE'RE TAKING YOU IN FOR QUESTIONING!
WHY?
YOU WERE TURNED IN TO "AMERICA'S MOST DANGEROUS CRIMINALS" BY TWO STUDENTS!
MR. WEATHERBEE, YOU'VE GOT TO COME CLEAN!
WHAT? THIS IS ABSURD!
HOLD IT! WE'VE GOT A MESSAGE!
THE REAL "W. W." HAS JUST BEEN APPREHENDED OUT IN ALASKA!
4

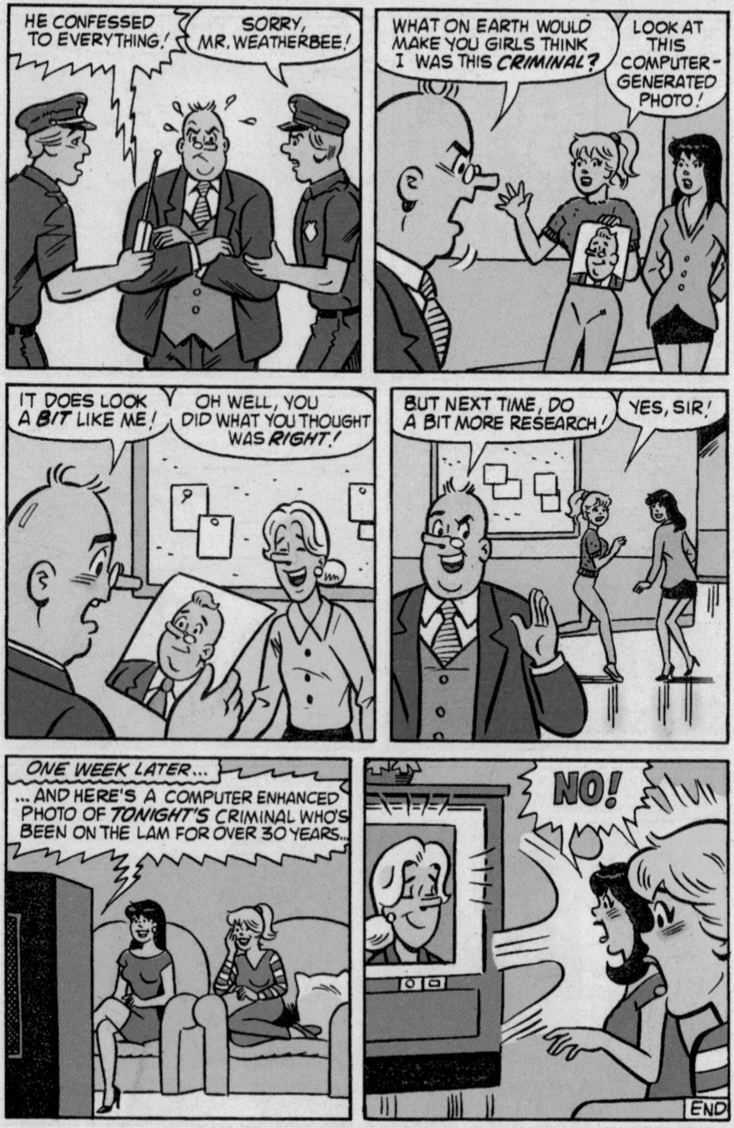
HE CONFESSED TO EVERYTHING!
SORRY, MR. WEATHERBEE!
WHAT ON EARTH WOULD MAKE YOU GIRLS THINK I WAS THIS CRIMINAL?
LOOK AT THIS COMPUTER-GENERATED PHOTO!
IT DOES LOOK A BIT LIKE ME!
OH WELL, YOU DID WHAT YOU THOUGHT WAS RIGHT!
BUT NEXT TIME, DO A BIT MORE RESEARCH!
YES, SIR!
ONE WEEK LATER...
...AND HERE'S A COMPUTER ENHANCED PHOTO OF TONIGHT'S CRIMINAL WHO'S BEEN ON THE LAM FOR OVER 30 YEARS...
NO!
END

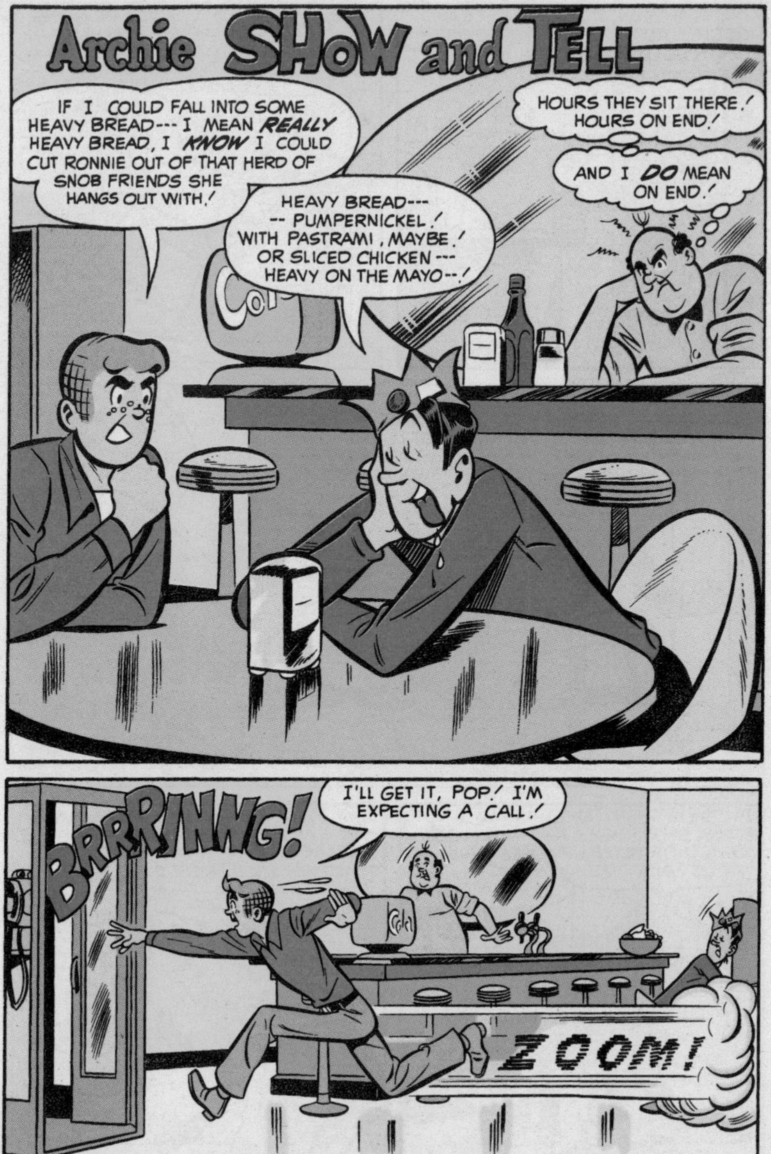
Archie SHOW and TELL
IF I COULD FALL INTO SOME HEAVY BREAD--- I MEAN REALLY HEAVY BREAD, I KNOW I COULD CUT RONNIE OUT OF THAT HERD OF SNOB FRIENDS SHE HANGS OUT WITH!
HEAVY BREAD--- -- PUMPERNICKEL! WITH PASTRAMI, MAYBE! OR SLICED CHICKEN --- HEAVY ON THE MAYO--!
HOURS THEY SIT THERE! HOURS ON END!
AND I DO MEAN ON END!
BRRRINNG!
I'LL GET IT, POP! I'M EXPECTING A CALL!
ZOOM!

Script: Frank Doyle / Pencils: Harry Lucey / Inks: Marty Epp / Letters: Bill Yoshida

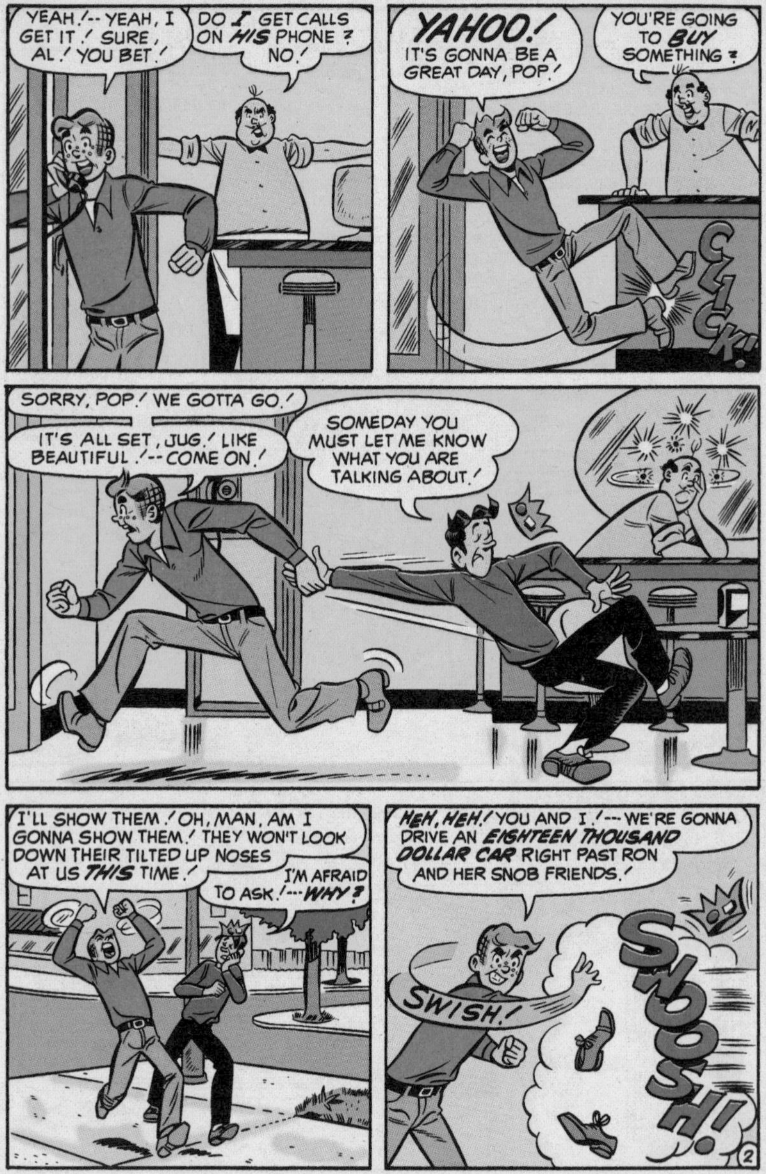
YEAH!-- YEAH, I GET IT! SURE, AL! YOU BET!
DO I GET CALLS ON HIS PHONE? NO!
YAHOO! IT'S GONNA BE A GREAT DAY, POP!
YOU'RE GOING TO BUY SOMETHING?
CLICK!
SORRY, POP! WE GOTTA GO!
IT'S ALL SET, JUG! LIKE BEAUTIFUL!-- COME ON!
SOMEDAY YOU MUST LET ME KNOW WHAT YOU ARE TALKING ABOUT!
I'LL SHOW THEM! OH, MAN, AM I GONNA SHOW THEM! THEY WON'T LOOK DOWN THEIR TILTED UP NOSES AT US THIS TIME!
I'M AFRAID TO ASK!--- WHY?
HEH, HEH! YOU AND I!--- WE'RE GONNA DRIVE AN EIGHTEEN THOUSAND DOLLAR CAR RIGHT PAST RON AND HER SNOB FRIENDS!
SWISH!
SWOOSH!
2

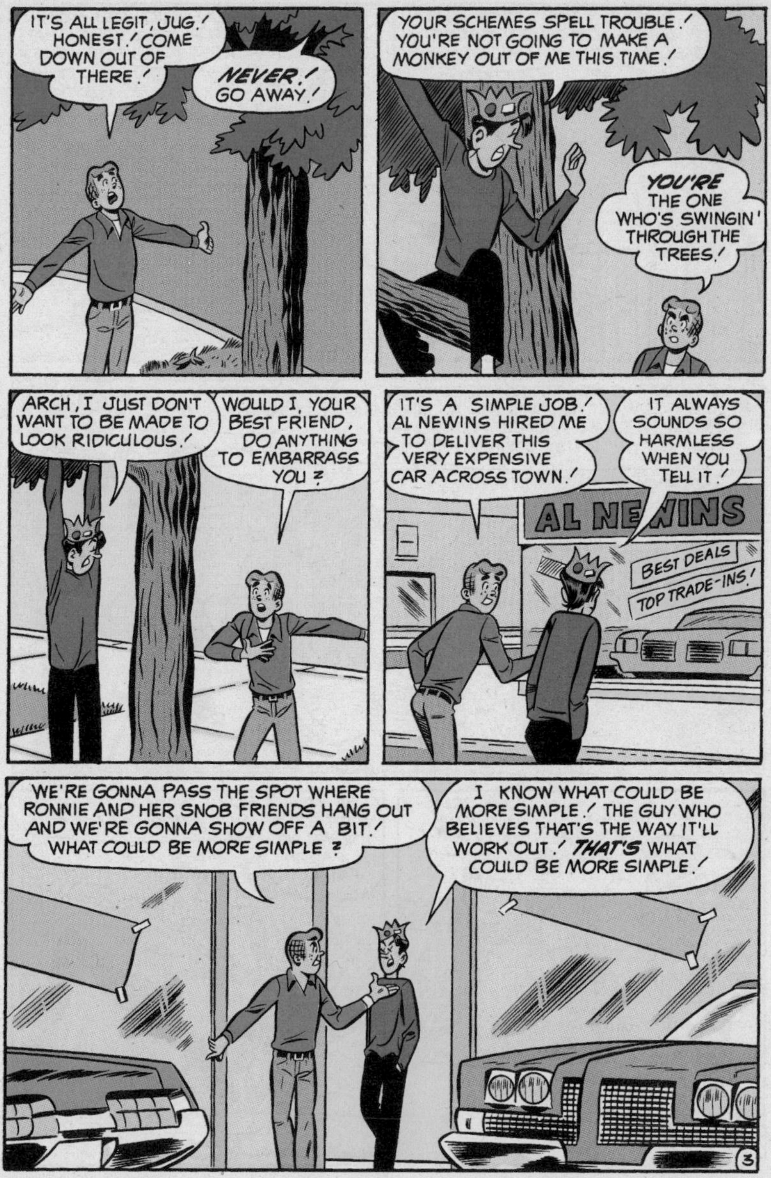
IT'S ALL LEGIT, JUG.! HONEST.! COME DOWN OUT OF THERE.!
NEVER.! GO AWAY.!
YOUR SCHEMES SPELL TROUBLE.! YOU'RE NOT GOING TO MAKE A MONKEY OUT OF ME THIS TIME.!
YOU'RE THE ONE WHO'S SWINGIN' THROUGH THE TREES.!
ARCH, I JUST DON'T WANT TO BE MADE TO LOOK RIDICULOUS.!
WOULD I, YOUR BEST FRIEND, DO ANYTHING TO EMBARRASS YOU?
IT'S A SIMPLE JOB.! AL NEWINS HIRED ME TO DELIVER THIS VERY EXPENSIVE CAR ACROSS TOWN.!
IT ALWAYS SOUNDS SO HARMLESS WHEN YOU TELL IT.!
AL NEWINS
BEST DEALS
TOP TRADE-INS.!
WE'RE GONNA PASS THE SPOT WHERE RONNIE AND HER SNOB FRIENDS HANG OUT AND WE'RE GONNA SHOW OFF A BIT.! WHAT COULD BE MORE SIMPLE?
I KNOW WHAT COULD BE MORE SIMPLE.! THE GUY WHO BELIEVES THAT'S THE WAY IT'LL WORK OUT.! THAT'S WHAT COULD BE MORE SIMPLE.!
3

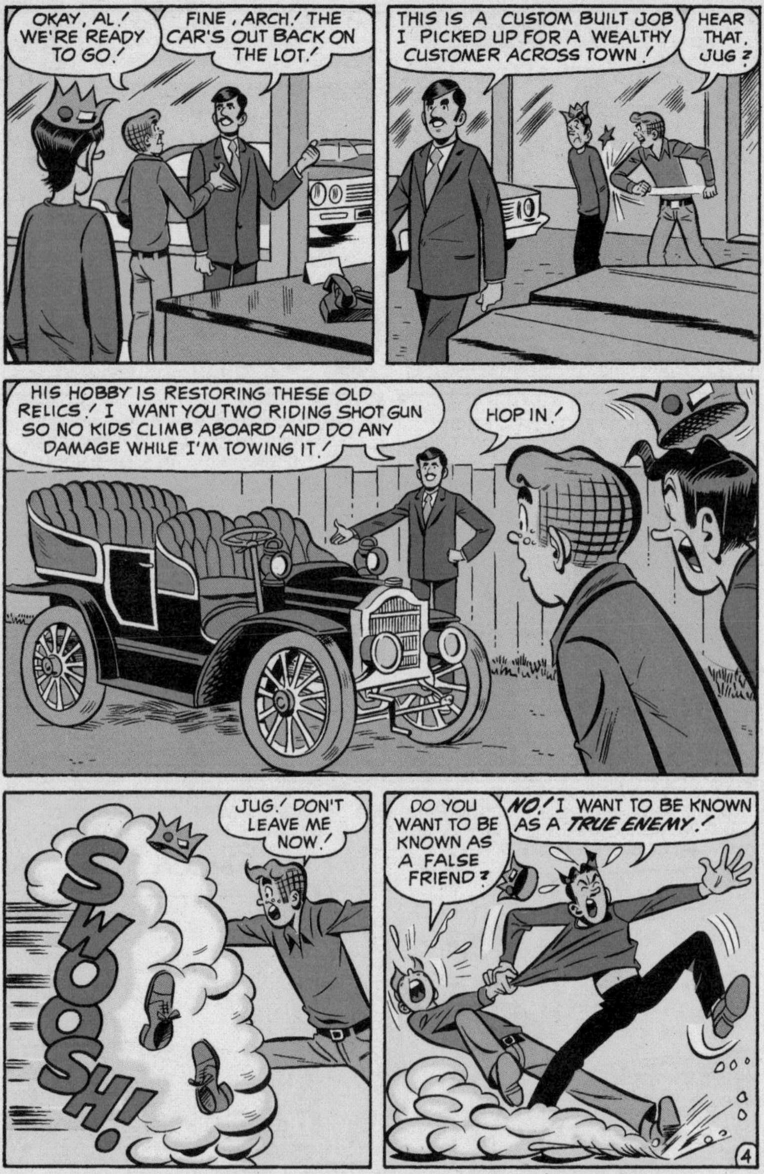
OKAY, AL! WE'RE READY TO GO!
FINE, ARCH! THE CAR'S OUT BACK ON THE LOT!
THIS IS A CUSTOM BUILT JOB I PICKED UP FOR A WEALTHY CUSTOMER ACROSS TOWN!
HEAR THAT, JUG?
HIS HOBBY IS RESTORING THESE OLD RELICS! I WANT YOU TWO RIDING SHOT GUN SO NO KIDS CLIMB ABOARD AND DO ANY DAMAGE WHILE I'M TOWING IT!
HOP IN!
JUG! DON'T LEAVE ME NOW!
SWOOSH!
DO YOU WANT TO BE KNOWN AS A FALSE FRIEND?
NO! I WANT TO BE KNOWN AS A TRUE ENEMY!
4

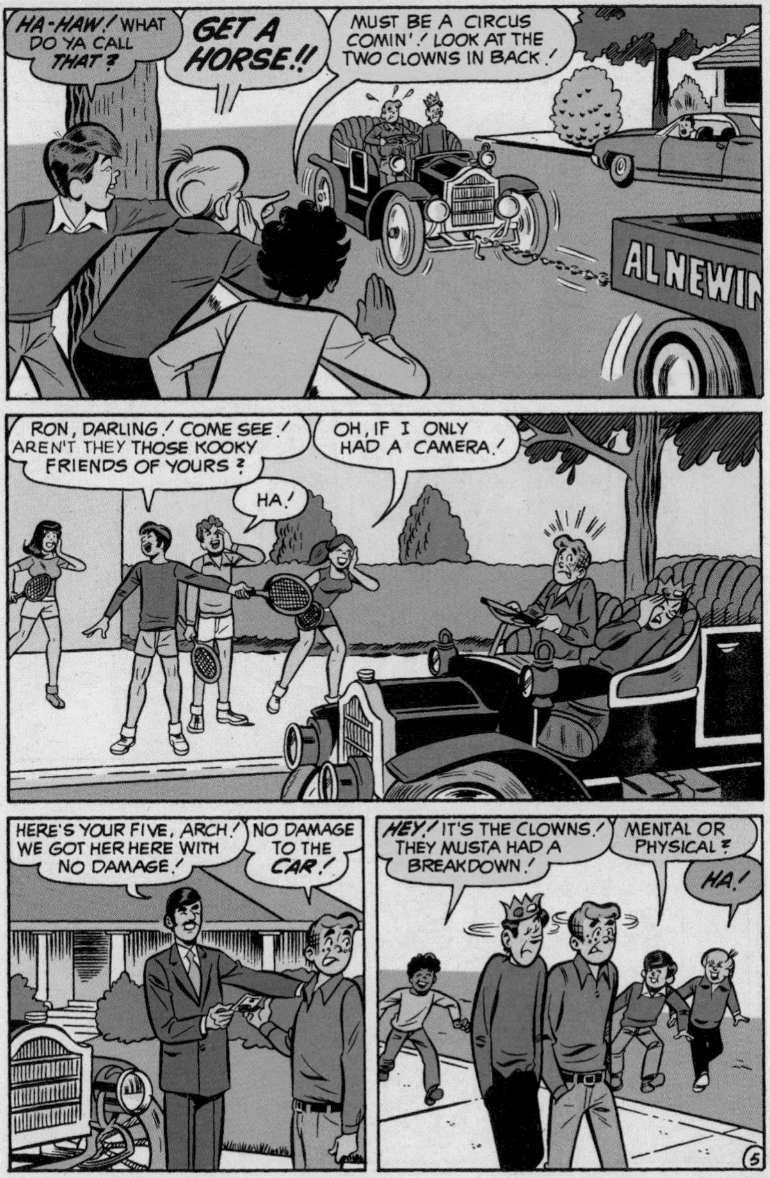
HA-HAW! WHAT DO YA CALL THAT?
GET A HORSE!!
MUST BE A CIRCUS COMIN'! LOOK AT THE TWO CLOWNS IN BACK!
AL NEWIN
RON, DARLING! COME SEE! AREN'T THEY THOSE KOOKY FRIENDS OF YOURS?
HA!
OH, IF I ONLY HAD A CAMERA!
HERE'S YOUR FIVE, ARCH! WE GOT HER HERE WITH NO DAMAGE!
NO DAMAGE TO THE CAR!
HEY! IT'S THE CLOWNS! THEY MUSTA HAD A BREAKDOWN!
MENTAL OR PHYSICAL?
HA!
5

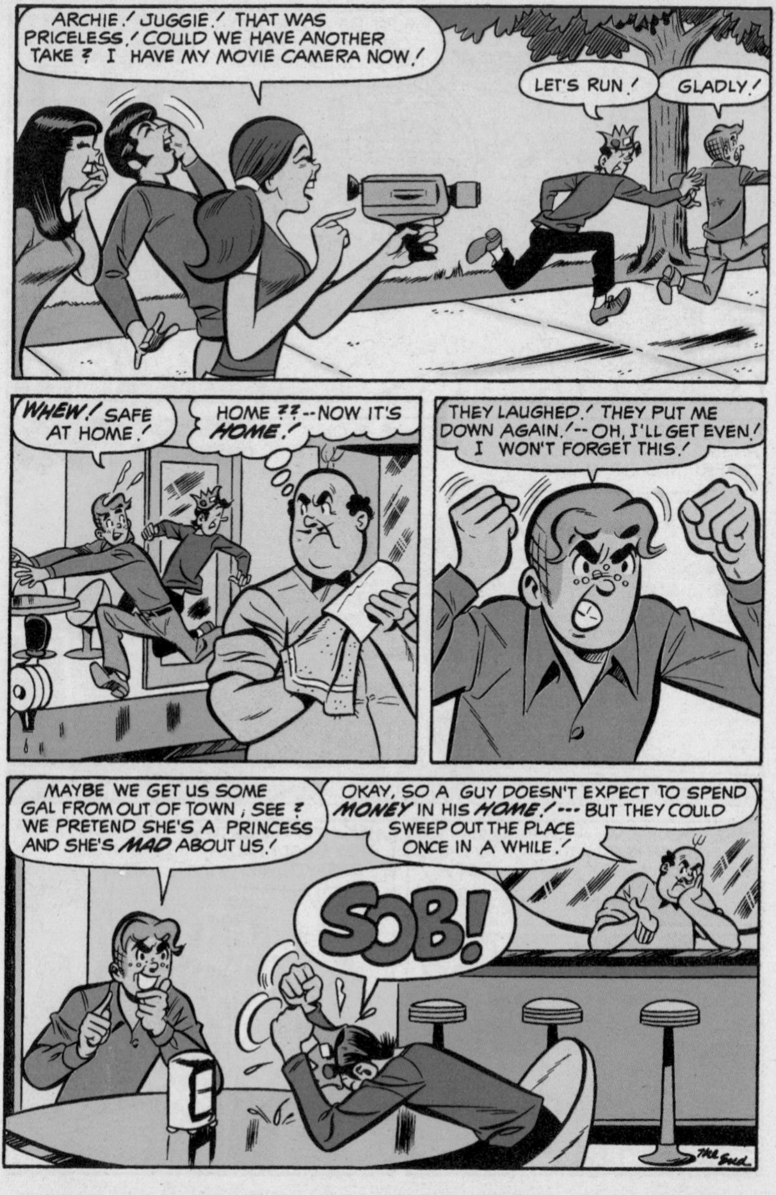
ARCHIE! JUGGIE! THAT WAS PRICELESS! COULD WE HAVE ANOTHER TAKE? I HAVE MY MOVIE CAMERA NOW!
LET'S RUN!
GLADLY!
WHEW! SAFE AT HOME!
HOME??--NOW IT'S HOME!
THEY LAUGHED! THEY PUT ME DOWN AGAIN!-- OH, I'LL GET EVEN! I WON'T FORGET THIS!
MAYBE WE GET US SOME GAL FROM OUT OF TOWN; SEE? WE PRETEND SHE'S A PRINCESS AND SHE'S MAD ABOUT US!
OKAY, SO A GUY DOESN'T EXPECT TO SPEND MONEY IN HIS HOME! --- BUT THEY COULD SWEEP OUT THE PLACE ONCE IN A WHILE!
SOB!
THE END

Archie -in- COMPULSION

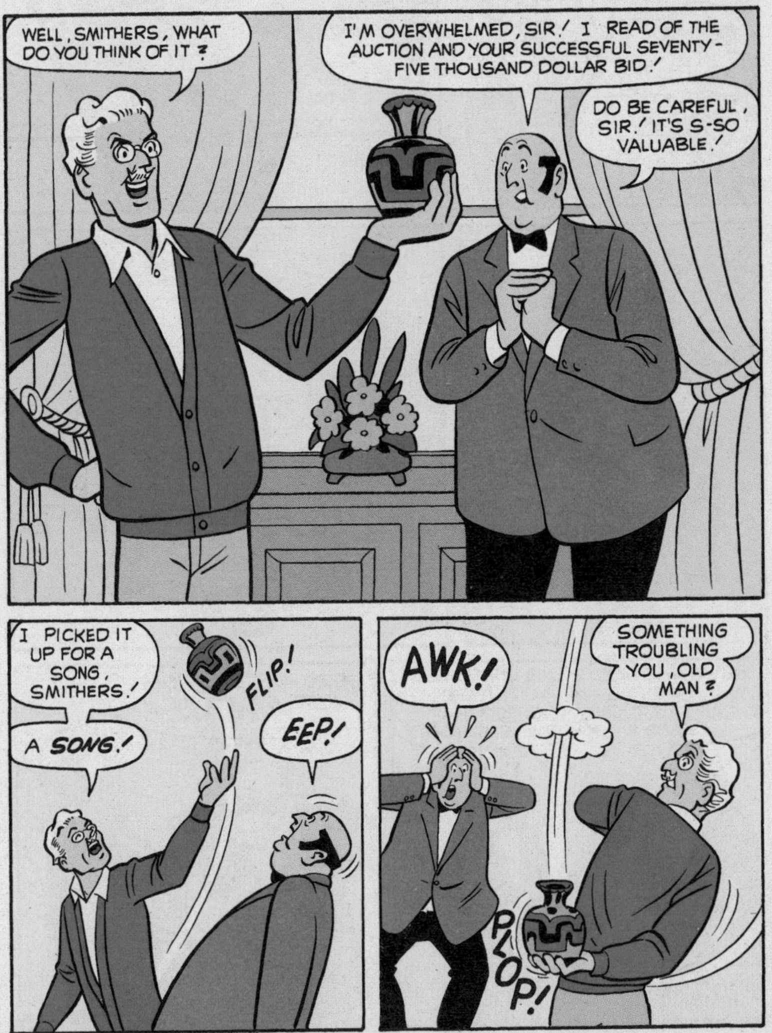

WELL, SMITHERS, WHAT DO YOU THINK OF IT ?
I'M OVERWHELMED, SIR! I READ OF THE AUCTION AND YOUR SUCCESSFUL SEVENTY-FIVE THOUSAND DOLLAR BID!
DO BE CAREFUL, SIR! IT'S S-SO VALUABLE!
I PICKED IT UP FOR A SONG, SMITHERS!
A SONG!
FLIP!
EEP!
AWK!
SOMETHING TROUBLING YOU, OLD MAN ?
PLOP!

Script: Frank Doyle / Pencils: Harry Lucey / Inks: Chic Stone / Letters: Bill Yoshida

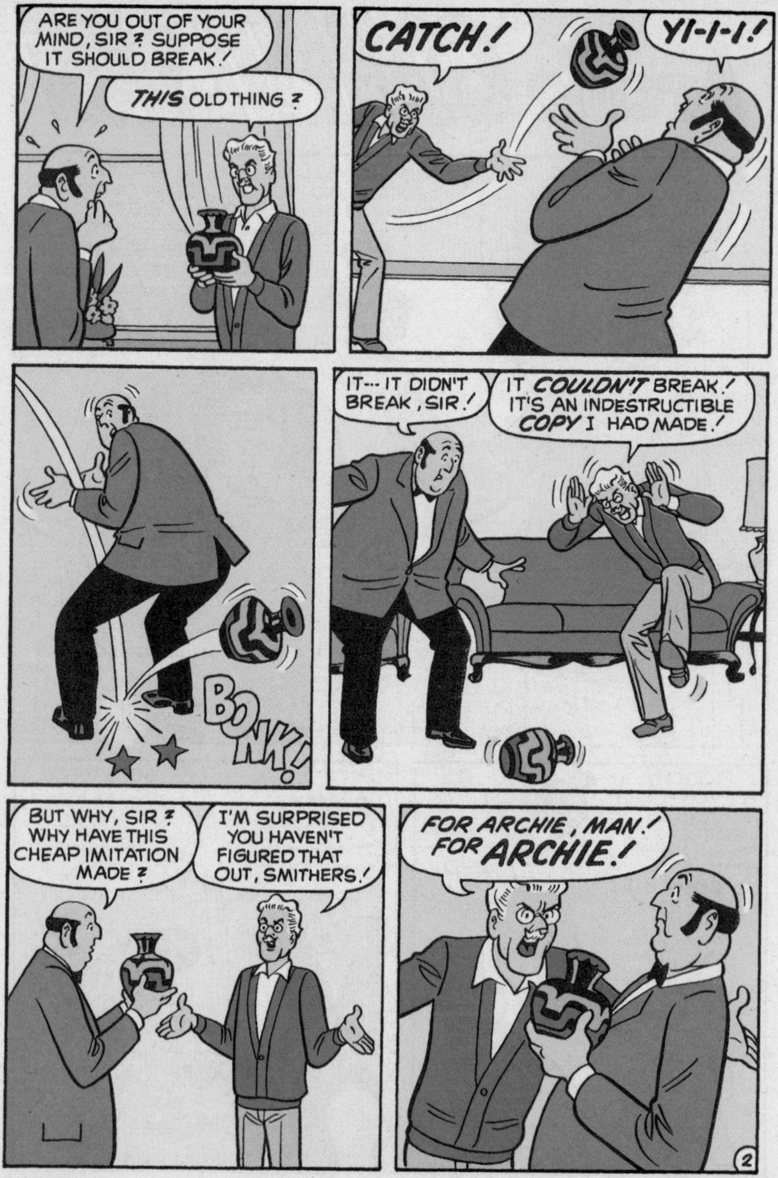
ARE YOU OUT OF YOUR MIND, SIR? SUPPOSE IT SHOULD BREAK!
THIS OLD THING?
CATCH!
YI-I-I!
BONK!
IT--- IT DIDN'T BREAK, SIR!
IT COULDN'T BREAK! IT'S AN INDESTRUCTIBLE COPY I HAD MADE!
BUT WHY, SIR? WHY HAVE THIS CHEAP IMITATION MADE?
I'M SURPRISED YOU HAVEN'T FIGURED THAT OUT, SMITHERS!
FOR ARCHIE, MAN! FOR ARCHIE!
2

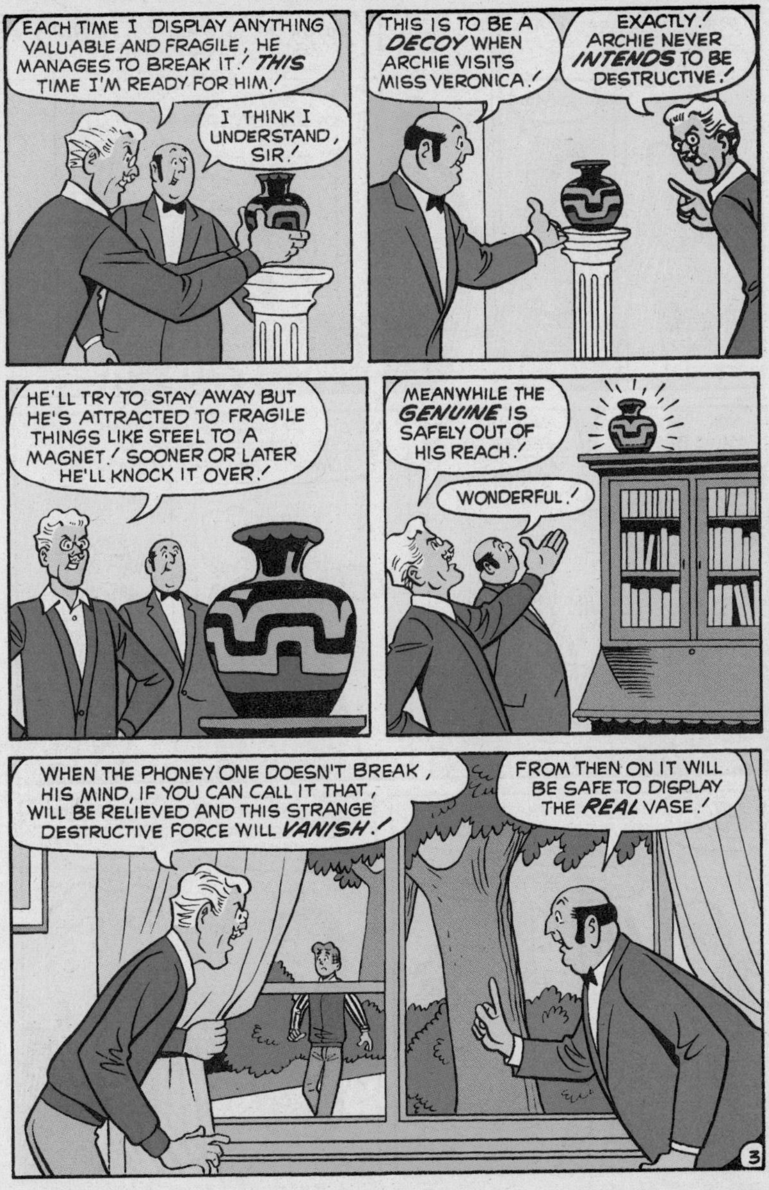
EACH TIME I DISPLAY ANYTHING VALUABLE AND FRAGILE, HE MANAGES TO BREAK IT! THIS TIME I'M READY FOR HIM!
I THINK I UNDERSTAND, SIR!
THIS IS TO BE A DECOY WHEN ARCHIE VISITS MISS VERONICA!
EXACTLY! ARCHIE NEVER INTENDS TO BE DESTRUCTIVE!
HE'LL TRY TO STAY AWAY BUT HE'S ATTRACTED TO FRAGILE THINGS LIKE STEEL TO A MAGNET! SOONER OR LATER HE'LL KNOCK IT OVER!
MEANWHILE THE GENUINE IS SAFELY OUT OF HIS REACH!
WONDERFUL!
WHEN THE PHONEY ONE DOESN'T BREAK, HIS MIND, IF YOU CAN CALL IT THAT, WILL BE RELIEVED AND THIS STRANGE DESTRUCTIVE FORCE WILL VANISH!
FROM THEN ON IT WILL BE SAFE TO DISPLAY THE REAL VASE!
3

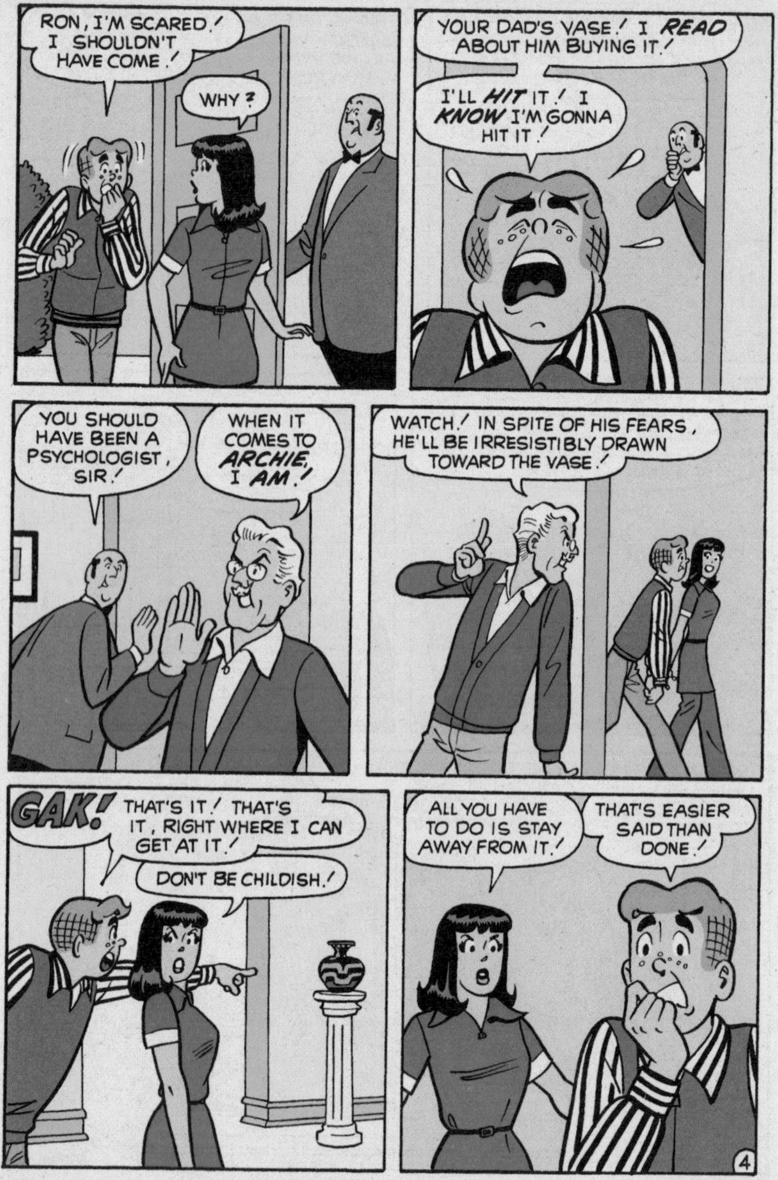
RON, I'M SCARED! I SHOULDN'T HAVE COME!
WHY?
YOUR DAD'S VASE! I READ ABOUT HIM BUYING IT!
I'LL HIT IT! I KNOW I'M GONNA HIT IT!
YOU SHOULD HAVE BEEN A PSYCHOLOGIST, SIR!
WHEN IT COMES TO ARCHIE, I AM!
WATCH! IN SPITE OF HIS FEARS, HE'LL BE IRRESISTIBLY DRAWN TOWARD THE VASE!
GAK!
THAT'S IT! THAT'S IT, RIGHT WHERE I CAN GET AT IT!
DON'T BE CHILDISH!
ALL YOU HAVE TO DO IS STAY AWAY FROM IT!
THAT'S EASIER SAID THAN DONE!
4

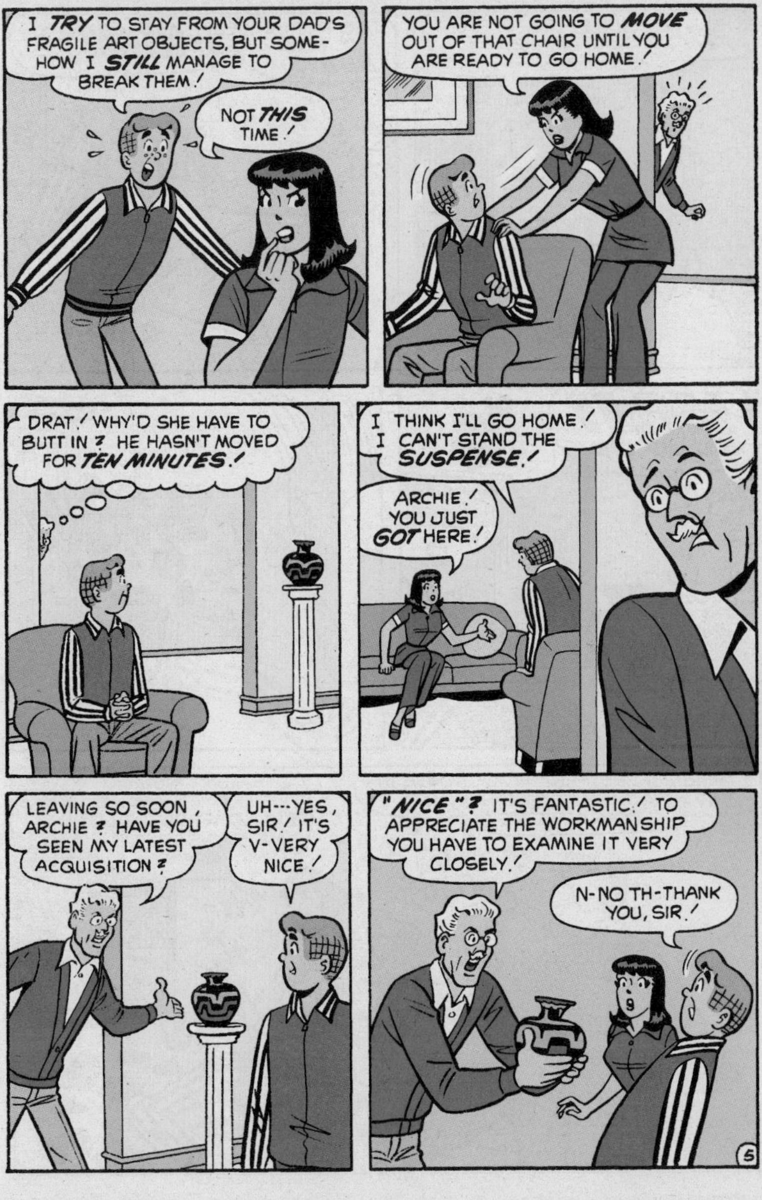
I TRY TO STAY FROM YOUR DAD'S FRAGILE ART OBJECTS, BUT SOME-HOW I STILL MANAGE TO BREAK THEM!
NOT THIS TIME!
YOU ARE NOT GOING TO MOVE OUT OF THAT CHAIR UNTIL YOU ARE READY TO GO HOME!
DRAT! WHY'D SHE HAVE TO BUTT IN? HE HASN'T MOVED FOR TEN MINUTES!
I THINK I'LL GO HOME! I CAN'T STAND THE SUSPENSE!
ARCHIE! YOU JUST GOT HERE!
LEAVING SO SOON, ARCHIE? HAVE YOU SEEN MY LATEST ACQUISITION?
UH---YES, SIR! IT'S V-VERY NICE!
"NICE"? IT'S FANTASTIC! TO APPRECIATE THE WORKMANSHIP YOU HAVE TO EXAMINE IT VERY CLOSELY!
N-NO TH-THANK YOU, SIR!
5

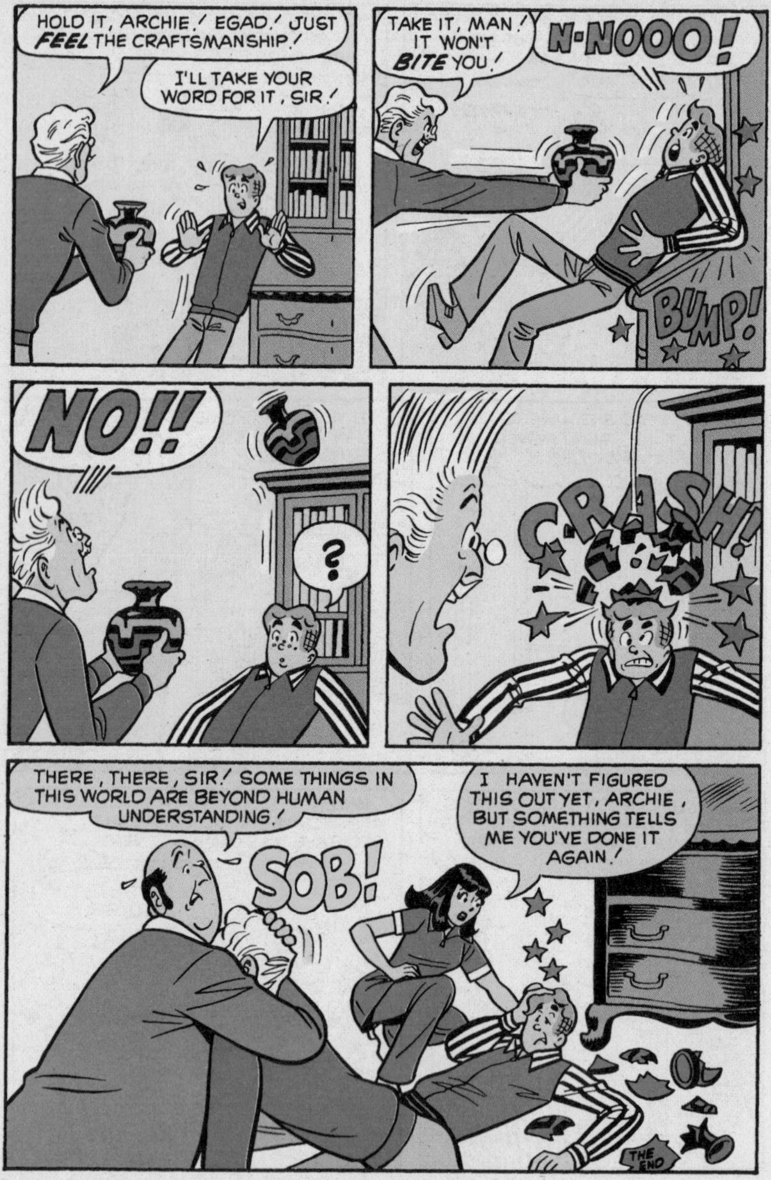
HOLD IT, ARCHIE! EGAD! JUST FEEL THE CRAFTSMANSHIP!
I'LL TAKE YOUR WORD FOR IT, SIR!
TAKE IT, MAN! IT WON'T BITE YOU!
N-NOOO!
BUMP!
NO!!
?
CRASH!
THERE, THERE, SIR! SOME THINGS IN THIS WORLD ARE BEYOND HUMAN UNDERSTANDING!
SOB!
I HAVEN'T FIGURED THIS OUT YET, ARCHIE, BUT SOMETHING TELLS ME YOU'VE DONE IT AGAIN!
THE END

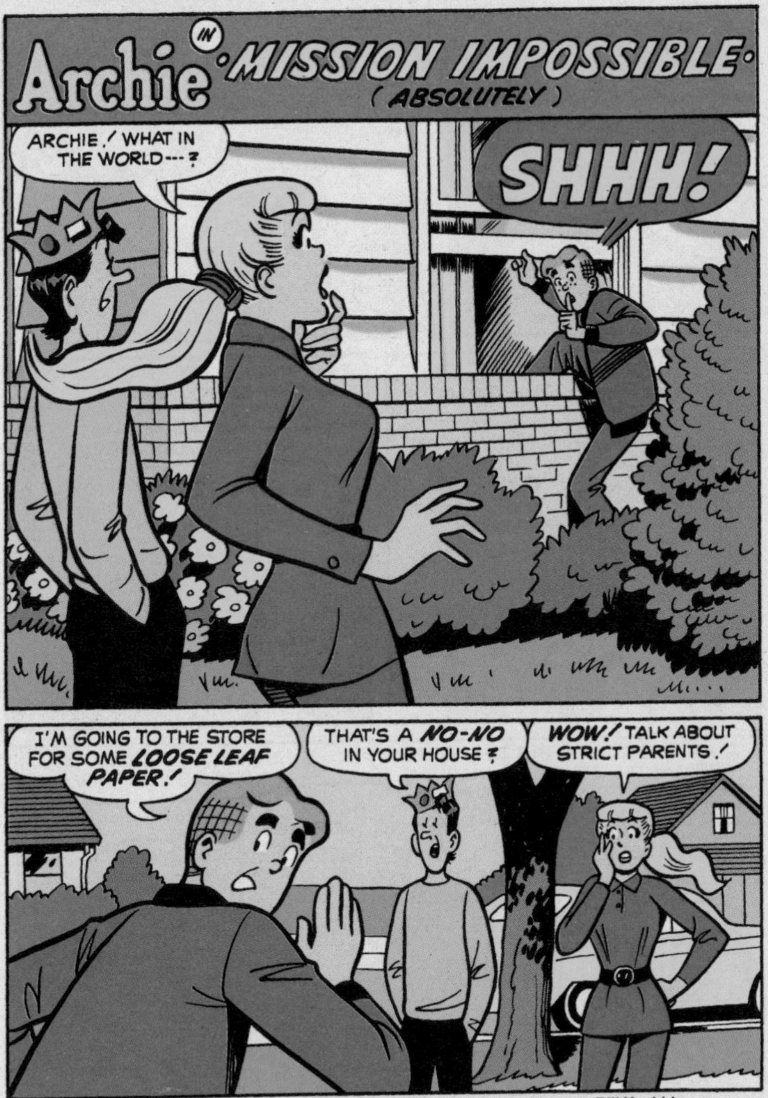
Archie
IN
MISSION IMPOSSIBLE
(ABSOLUTELY)
ARCHIE! WHAT IN THE WORLD---?
SHHH!
I'M GOING TO THE STORE FOR SOME LOOSE LEAF PAPER!
THAT'S A NO-NO IN YOUR HOUSE?
WOW! TALK ABOUT STRICT PARENTS!

Script: Frank Doyle / Pencils: Harry Lucey / Inks: Chic Stone / Letters: Bill Yoshida

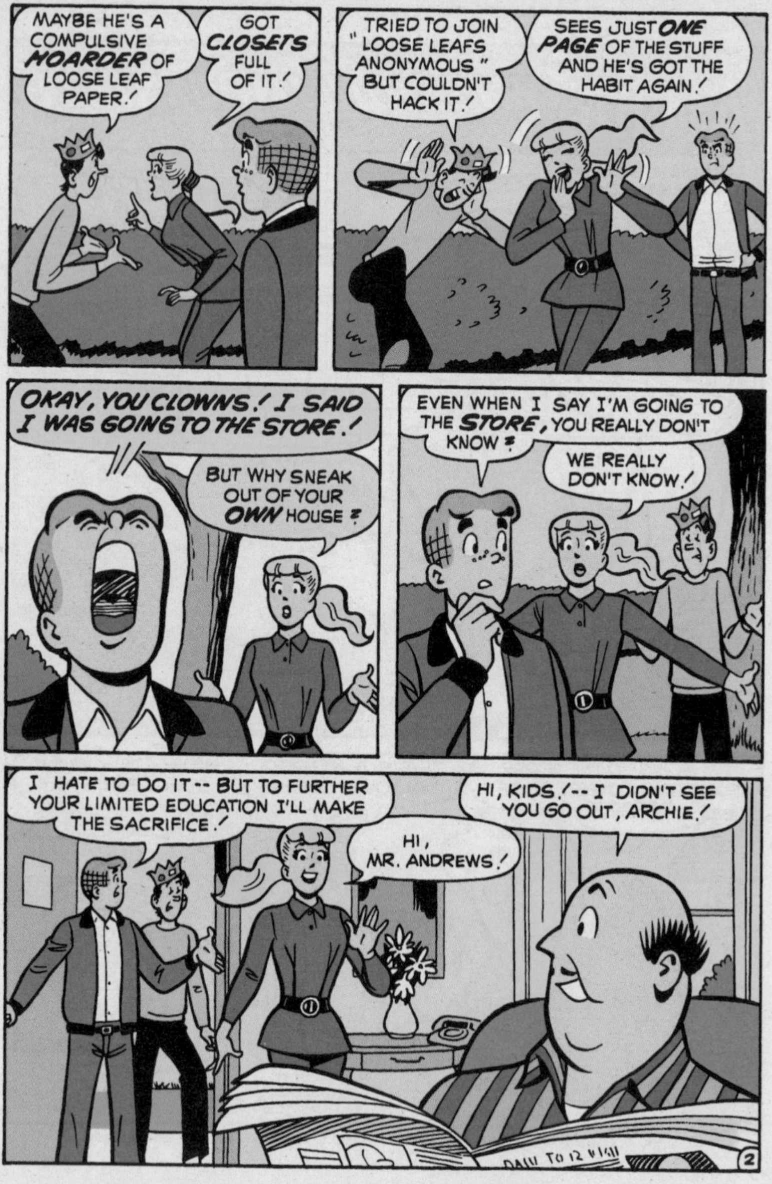
MAYBE HE'S A COMPULSIVE HOARDER OF LOOSE LEAF PAPER.!
GOT CLOSETS FULL OF IT.!
" TRIED TO JOIN LOOSE LEAFS ANONYMOUS " BUT COULDN'T HACK IT.!
SEES JUST ONE PAGE OF THE STUFF AND HE'S GOT THE HABIT AGAIN.!
OKAY, YOU CLOWNS.! I SAID I WAS GOING TO THE STORE.!
BUT WHY SNEAK OUT OF YOUR OWN HOUSE ?
EVEN WHEN I SAY I'M GOING TO THE STORE, YOU REALLY DON'T KNOW ?
WE REALLY DON'T KNOW.!
I HATE TO DO IT -- BUT TO FURTHER YOUR LIMITED EDUCATION I'LL MAKE THE SACRIFICE.!
HI, MR. ANDREWS.!
HI, KIDS.! -- I DIDN'T SEE YOU GO OUT, ARCHIE.!
2

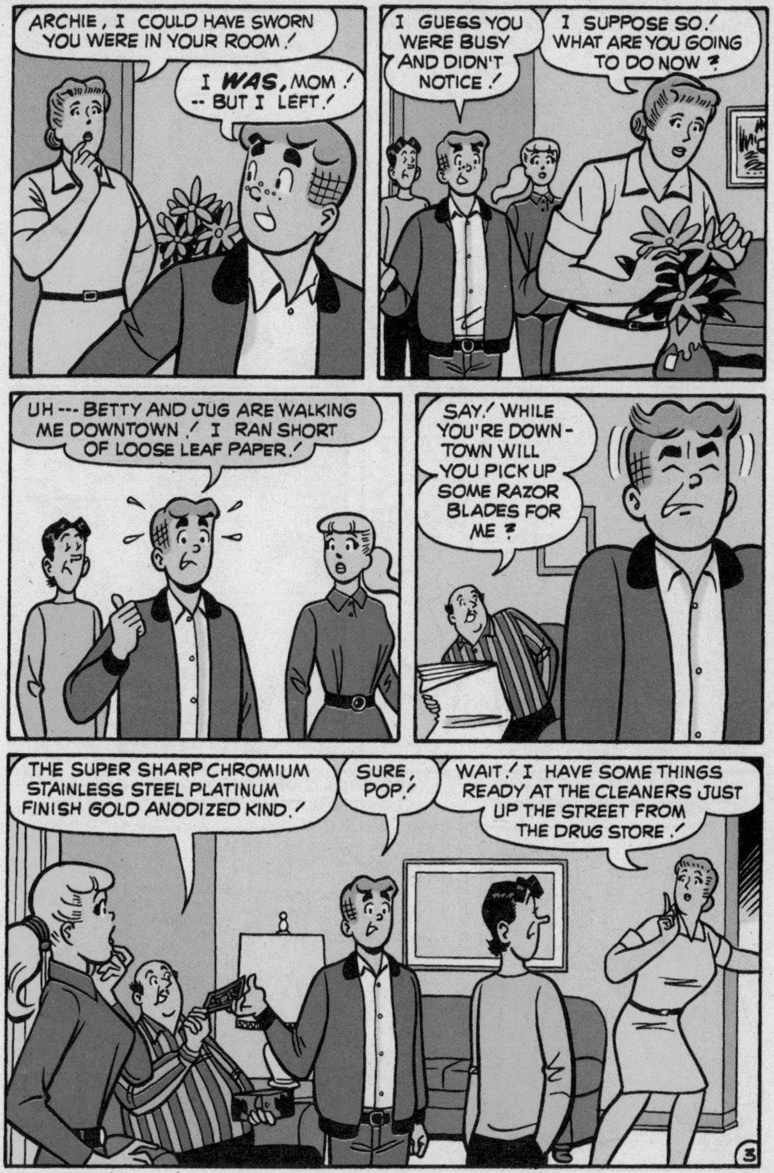
ARCHIE, I COULD HAVE SWORN YOU WERE IN YOUR ROOM!
I WAS, MOM! -- BUT I LEFT!
I GUESS YOU WERE BUSY AND DIDN'T NOTICE!
I SUPPOSE SO! WHAT ARE YOU GOING TO DO NOW?
UH --- BETTY AND JUG ARE WALKING ME DOWNTOWN! I RAN SHORT OF LOOSE LEAF PAPER!
SAY! WHILE YOU'RE DOWN-TOWN WILL YOU PICK UP SOME RAZOR BLADES FOR ME?
THE SUPER SHARP CHROMIUM STAINLESS STEEL PLATINUM FINISH GOLD ANODIZED KIND!
SURE, POP!
WAIT! I HAVE SOME THINGS READY AT THE CLEANERS JUST UP THE STREET FROM THE DRUG STORE!
3

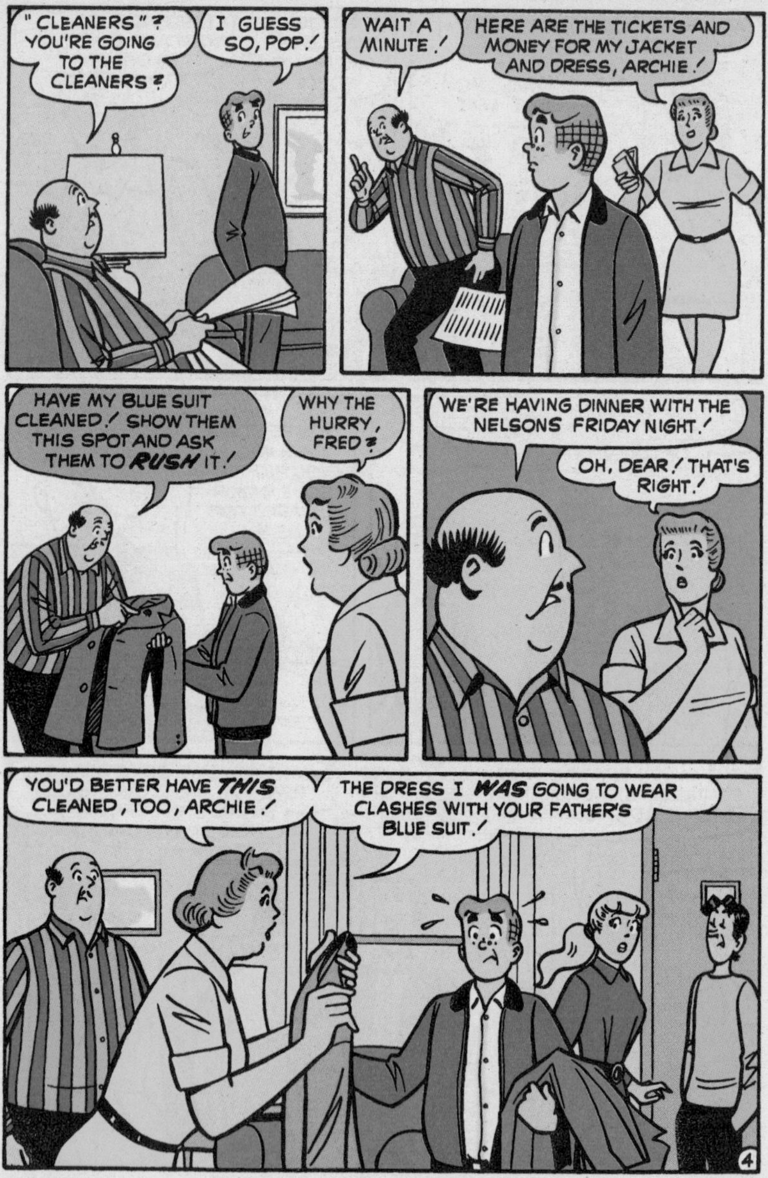
"CLEANERS"? YOU'RE GOING TO THE CLEANERS?
I GUESS SO, POP!
WAIT A MINUTE!
HERE ARE THE TICKETS AND MONEY FOR MY JACKET AND DRESS, ARCHIE!
HAVE MY BLUE SUIT CLEANED! SHOW THEM THIS SPOT AND ASK THEM TO RUSH IT!
WHY THE HURRY, FRED?
WE'RE HAVING DINNER WITH THE NELSONS FRIDAY NIGHT!
OH, DEAR! THAT'S RIGHT!
YOU'D BETTER HAVE THIS CLEANED, TOO, ARCHIE!
THE DRESS I WAS GOING TO WEAR CLASHES WITH YOUR FATHER'S BLUE SUIT!
4

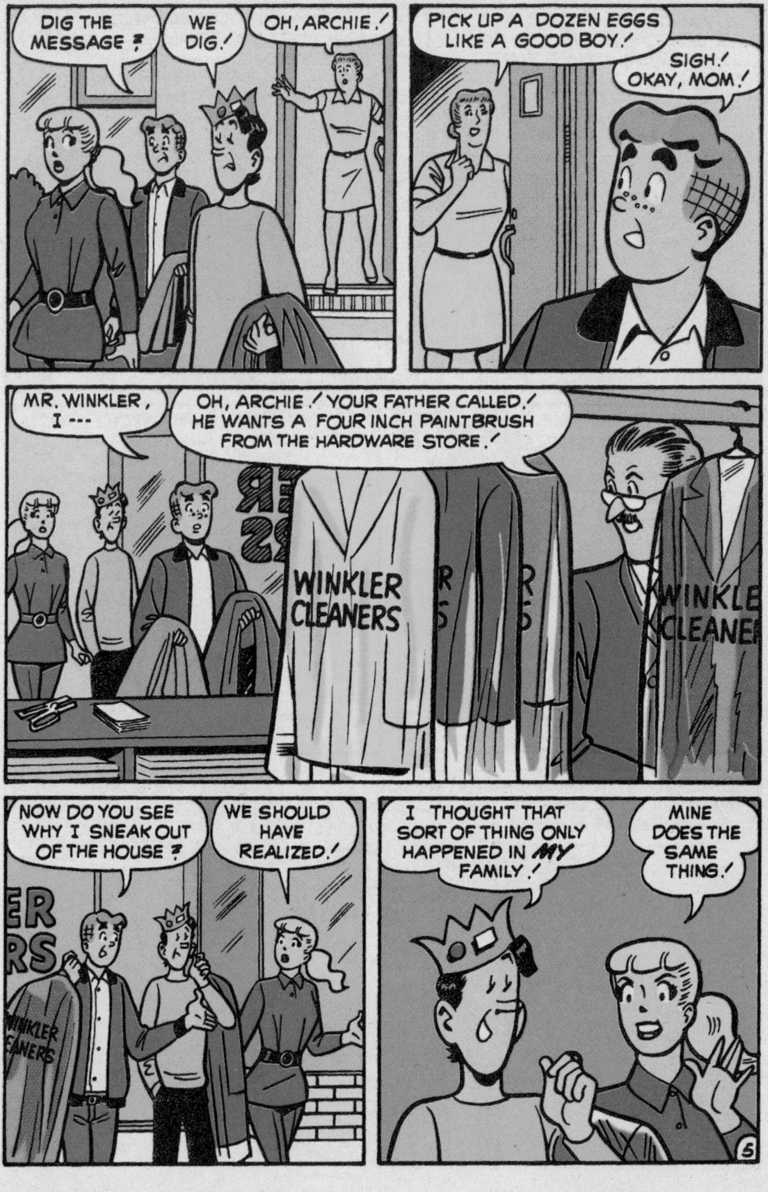

DIG THE MESSAGE ?
WE DIG!
OH, ARCHIE!
PICK UP A DOZEN EGGS LIKE A GOOD BOY!
SIGH! OKAY, MOM!
MR. WINKLER, I ---
OH, ARCHIE! YOUR FATHER CALLED! HE WANTS A FOUR INCH PAINTBRUSH FROM THE HARDWARE STORE!
WINKLER CLEANERS
NOW DO YOU SEE WHY I SNEAK OUT OF THE HOUSE ?
WE SHOULD HAVE REALIZED!
I THOUGHT THAT SORT OF THING ONLY HAPPENED IN MY FAMILY!
MINE DOES THE SAME THING!
5

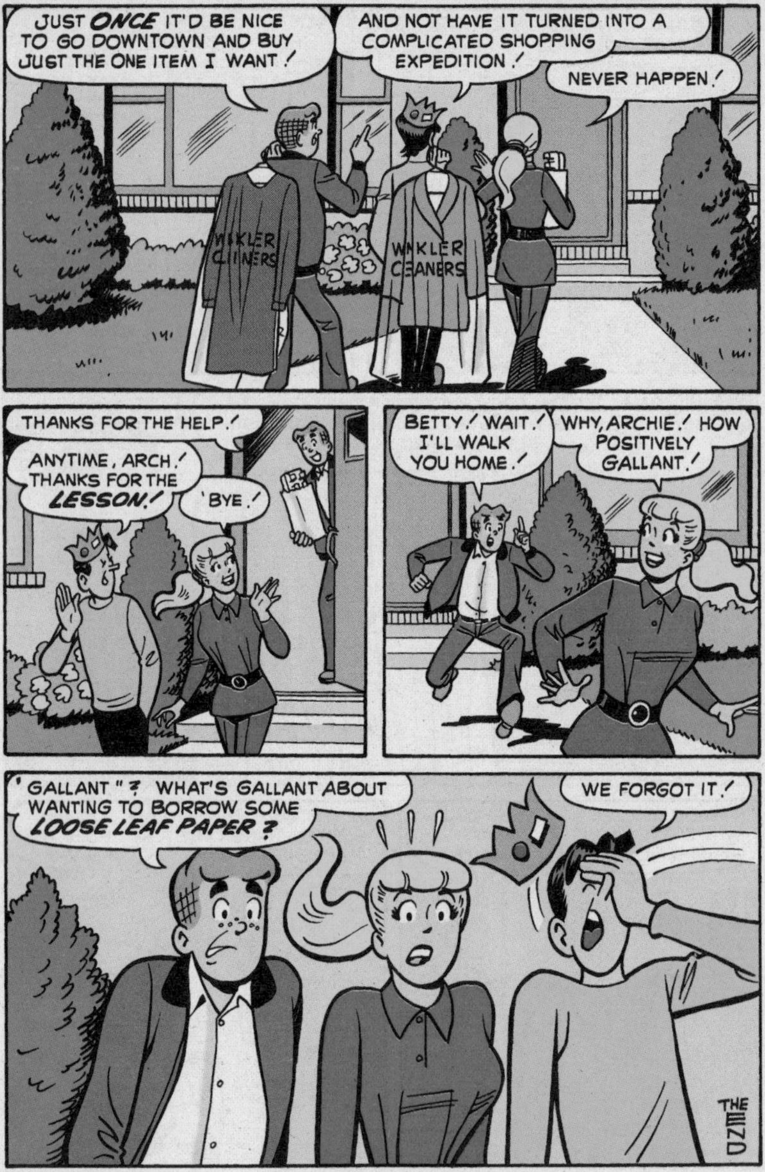
JUST ONCE IT'D BE NICE TO GO DOWNTOWN AND BUY JUST THE ONE ITEM I WANT!
AND NOT HAVE IT TURNED INTO A COMPLICATED SHOPPING EXPEDITION!
NEVER HAPPEN!
THANKS FOR THE HELP!
ANYTIME, ARCH! THANKS FOR THE LESSON!
'BYE!
BETTY! WAIT! I'LL WALK YOU HOME!
WHY, ARCHIE! HOW POSITIVELY GALLANT!
"GALLANT"? WHAT'S GALLANT ABOUT WANTING TO BORROW SOME LOOSE LEAF PAPER?
WE FORGOT IT!
THE END

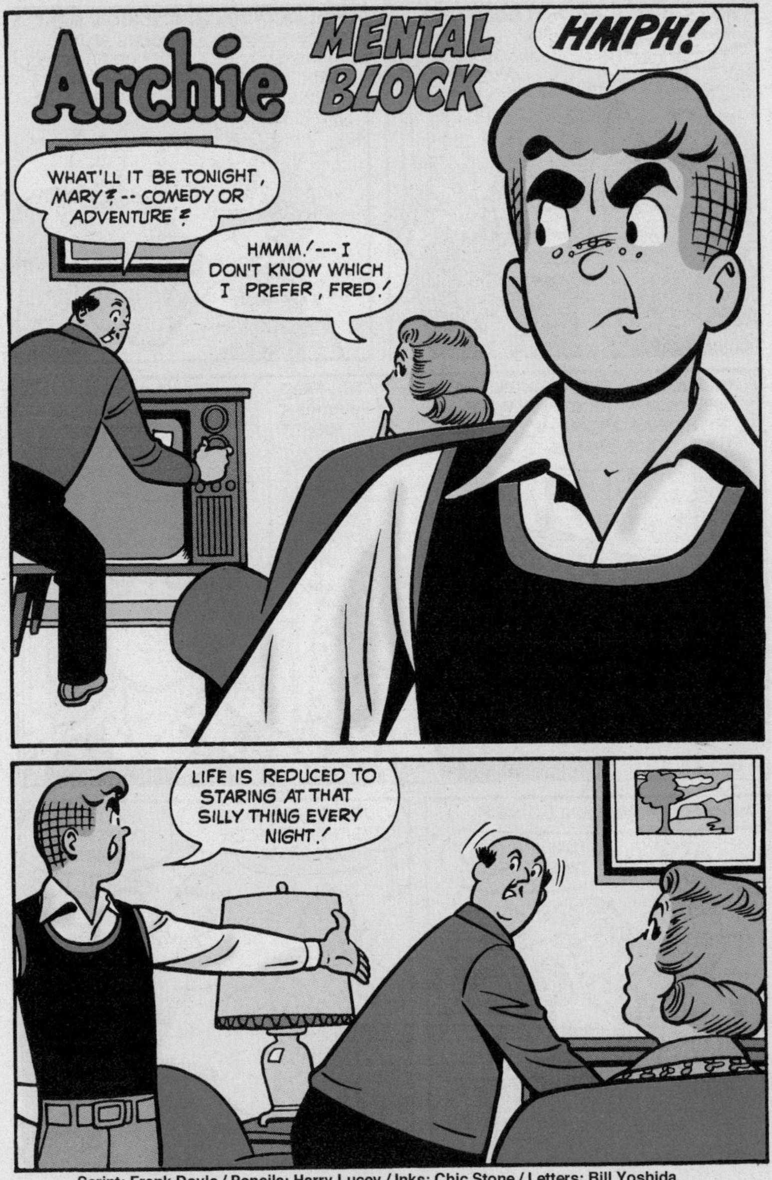
Archie
MENTAL BLOCK
HMPH!
WHAT'LL IT BE TONIGHT, MARY? -- COMEDY OR ADVENTURE?
HMMM! --- I DON'T KNOW WHICH I PREFER, FRED!
LIFE IS REDUCED TO STARING AT THAT SILLY THING EVERY NIGHT!

Script: Frank Doyle / Pencils: Harry Lucey / Inks: Chic Stone / Letters: Bill Yoshida

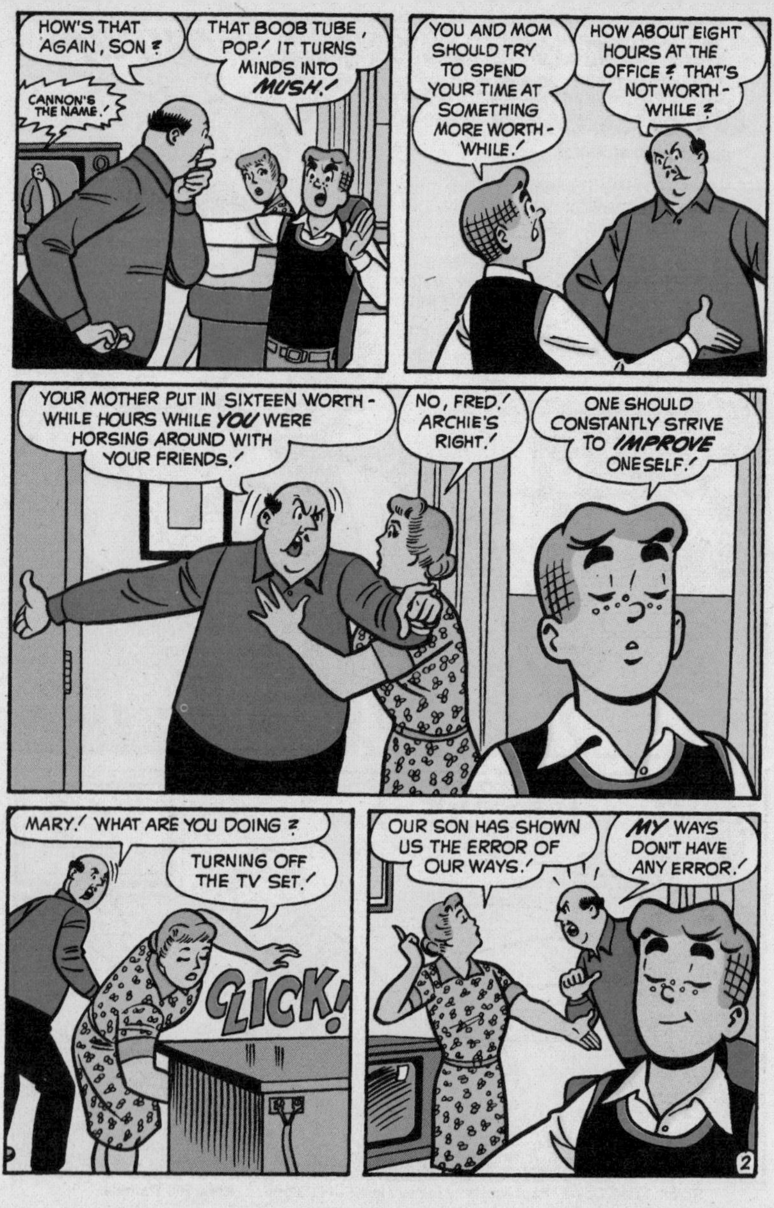
HOW'S THAT AGAIN, SON ?
THAT BOOB TUBE, POP! IT TURNS MINDS INTO MUSH!
CANNON'S THE NAME!
YOU AND MOM SHOULD TRY TO SPEND YOUR TIME AT SOMETHING MORE WORTH-WHILE!
HOW ABOUT EIGHT HOURS AT THE OFFICE ? THAT'S NOT WORTH-WHILE ?
YOUR MOTHER PUT IN SIXTEEN WORTH-WHILE HOURS WHILE YOU WERE HORSING AROUND WITH YOUR FRIENDS!
NO, FRED! ARCHIE'S RIGHT!
ONE SHOULD CONSTANTLY STRIVE TO IMPROVE ONESELF!
MARY! WHAT ARE YOU DOING ?
TURNING OFF THE TV SET!
CLICK!
OUR SON HAS SHOWN US THE ERROR OF OUR WAYS!
MY WAYS DON'T HAVE ANY ERROR!
2

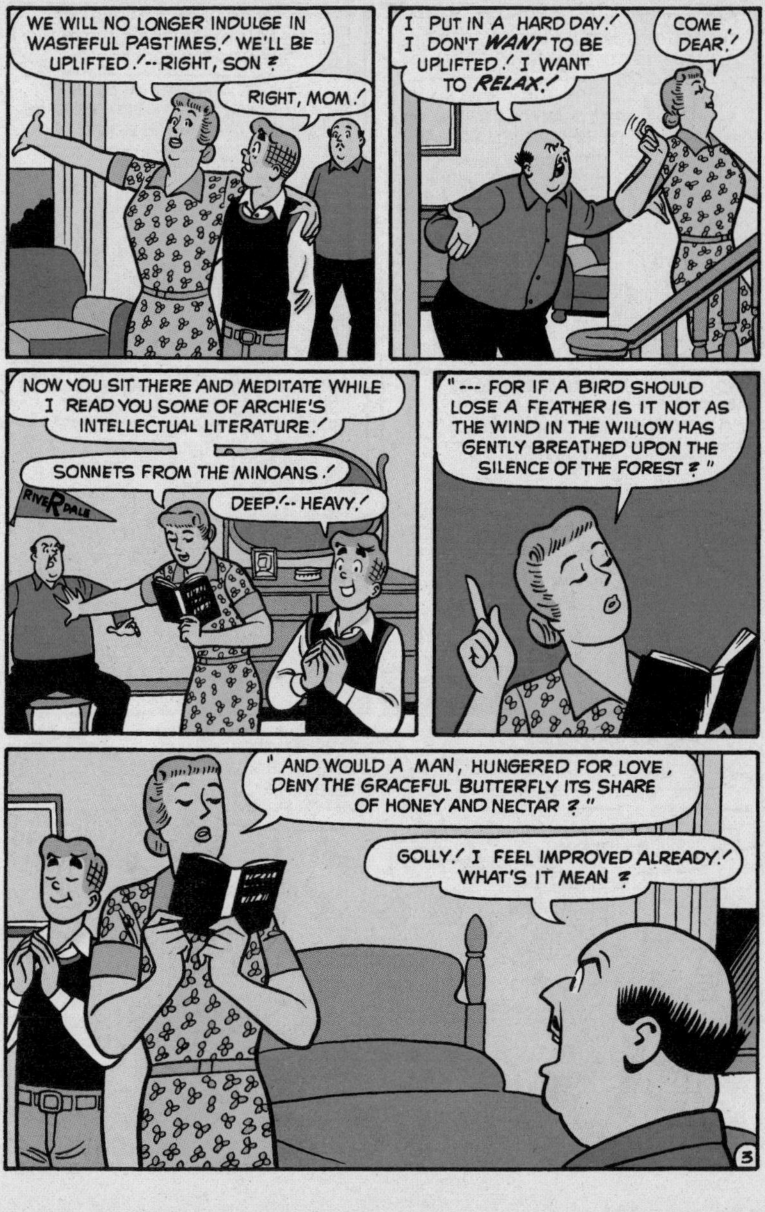
WE WILL NO LONGER INDULGE IN WASTEFUL PASTIMES.! WE'LL BE UPLIFTED.!-- RIGHT, SON ?
RIGHT, MOM.!
I PUT IN A HARD DAY.! I DON'T WANT TO BE UPLIFTED.! I WANT TO RELAX.!
COME, DEAR.!
NOW YOU SIT THERE AND MEDITATE WHILE I READ YOU SOME OF ARCHIE'S INTELLECTUAL LITERATURE.!
SONNETS FROM THE MINOANS.!
RIVERDALE
DEEP.!-- HEAVY.!
"--- FOR IF A BIRD SHOULD LOSE A FEATHER IS IT NOT AS THE WIND IN THE WILLOW HAS GENTLY BREATHED UPON THE SILENCE OF THE FOREST ?"
"AND WOULD A MAN, HUNGERED FOR LOVE, DENY THE GRACEFUL BUTTERFLY ITS SHARE OF HONEY AND NECTAR ?"
GOLLY.! I FEEL IMPROVED ALREADY.! WHAT'S IT MEAN ?
3

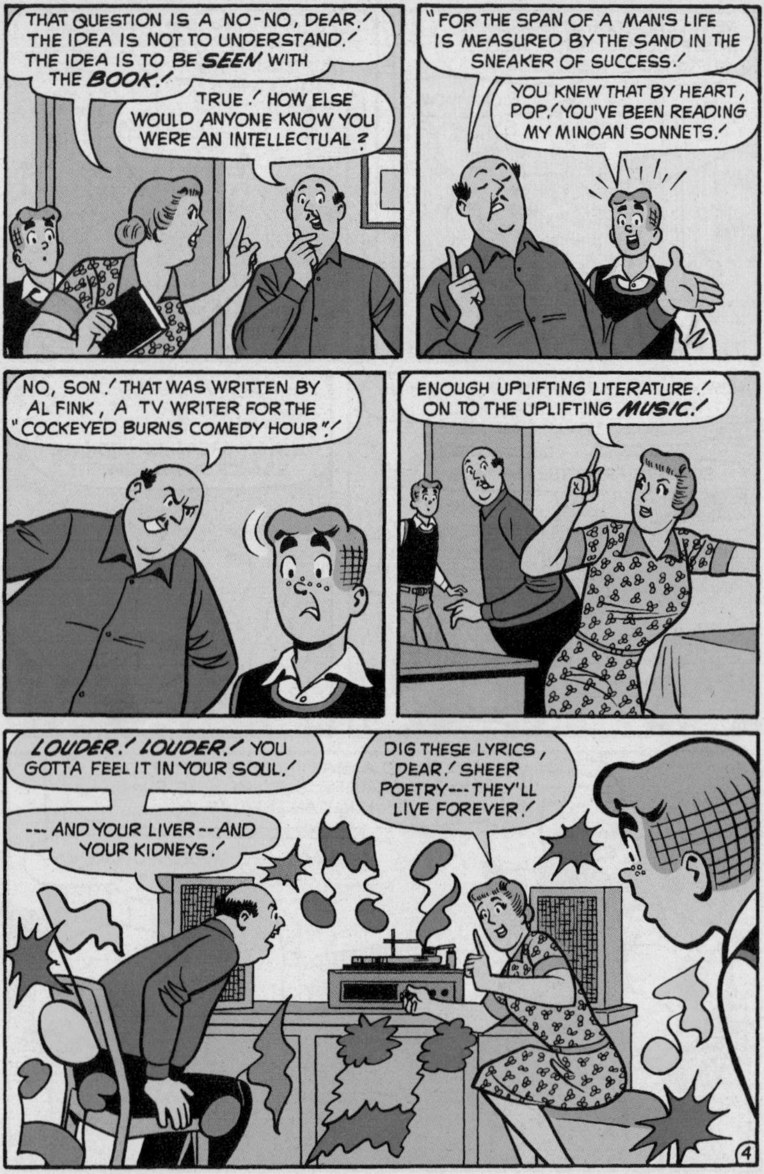
THAT QUESTION IS A NO-NO, DEAR! THE IDEA IS NOT TO UNDERSTAND! THE IDEA IS TO BE *SEEN* WITH THE *BOOK!*
TRUE! HOW ELSE WOULD ANYONE KNOW YOU WERE AN INTELLECTUAL?
"FOR THE SPAN OF A MAN'S LIFE IS MEASURED BY THE SAND IN THE SNEAKER OF SUCCESS!"
YOU KNEW THAT BY HEART, POP! YOU'VE BEEN READING MY MINOAN SONNETS!
NO, SON! THAT WAS WRITTEN BY AL FINK, A TV WRITER FOR THE "COCKEYED BURNS COMEDY HOUR"!
ENOUGH UPLIFTING LITERATURE! ON TO THE UPLIFTING *MUSIC!*
LOUDER! LOUDER! YOU GOTTA FEEL IT IN YOUR SOUL!
--- AND YOUR LIVER -- AND YOUR KIDNEYS!
DIG THESE LYRICS, DEAR! SHEER POETRY--- THEY'LL LIVE FOREVER!
4

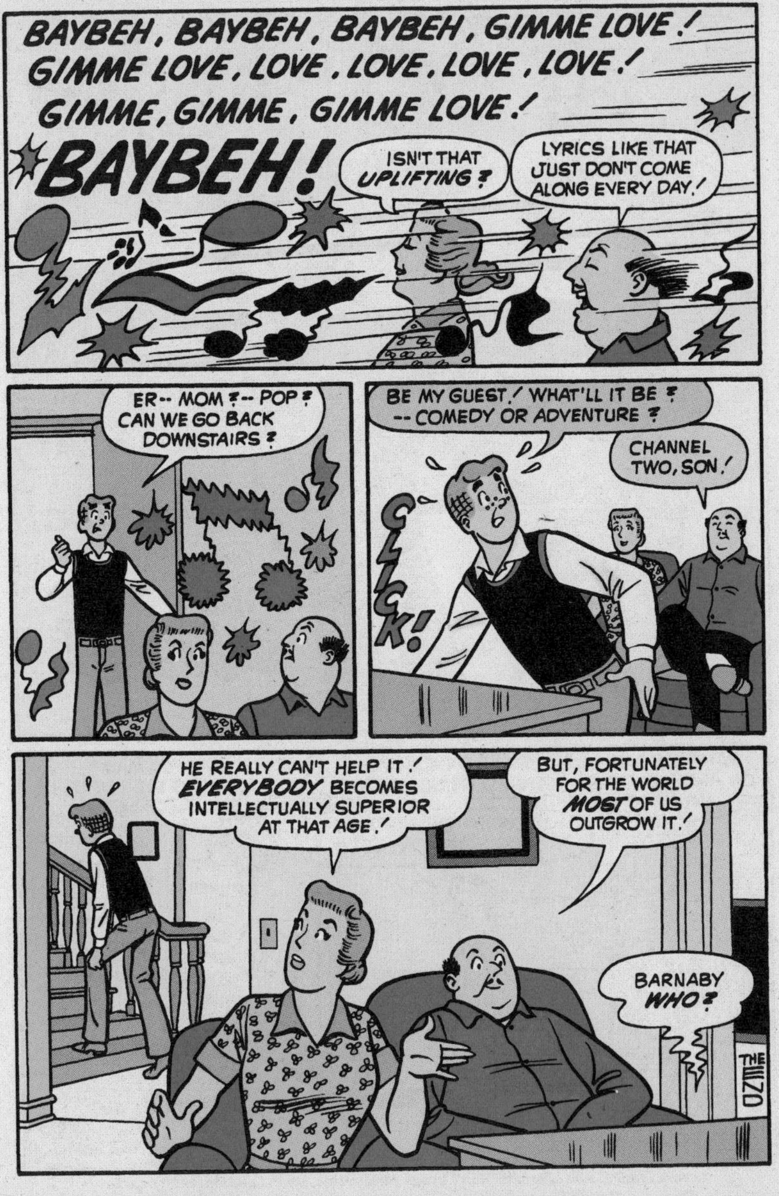
BAYBEH, BAYBEH, BAYBEH, GIMME LOVE!
GIMME LOVE, LOVE, LOVE, LOVE, LOVE!
GIMME, GIMME, GIMME LOVE!
BAYBEH!
ISN'T THAT UPLIFTING?
LYRICS LIKE THAT JUST DON'T COME ALONG EVERY DAY!
ER-- MOM?-- POP? CAN WE GO BACK DOWNSTAIRS?
BE MY GUEST! WHAT'LL IT BE? -- COMEDY OR ADVENTURE?
CLICK!
CHANNEL TWO, SON!
HE REALLY CAN'T HELP IT! EVERYBODY BECOMES INTELLECTUALLY SUPERIOR AT THAT AGE!
BUT, FORTUNATELY FOR THE WORLD MOST OF US OUTGROW IT!
BARNABY WHO?
THE END

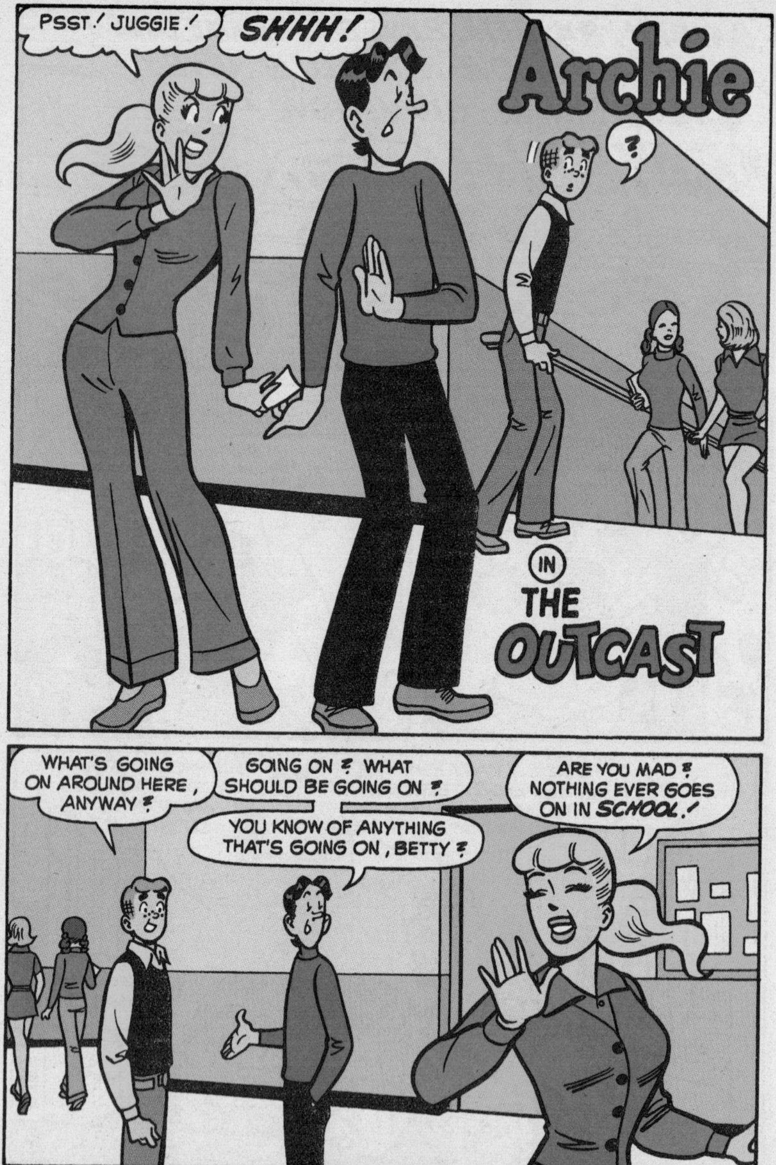
PSST! JUGGIE!
SHHH!
Archie
?
IN
THE
OUTCAST
WHAT'S GOING ON AROUND HERE, ANYWAY?
GOING ON? WHAT SHOULD BE GOING ON?
YOU KNOW OF ANYTHING THAT'S GOING ON, BETTY?
ARE YOU MAD? NOTHING EVER GOES ON IN SCHOOL!

Script: Frank Doyle / Pencils: Harry Lucey / Inks: Chic Stone / Letters: Bill Yoshida

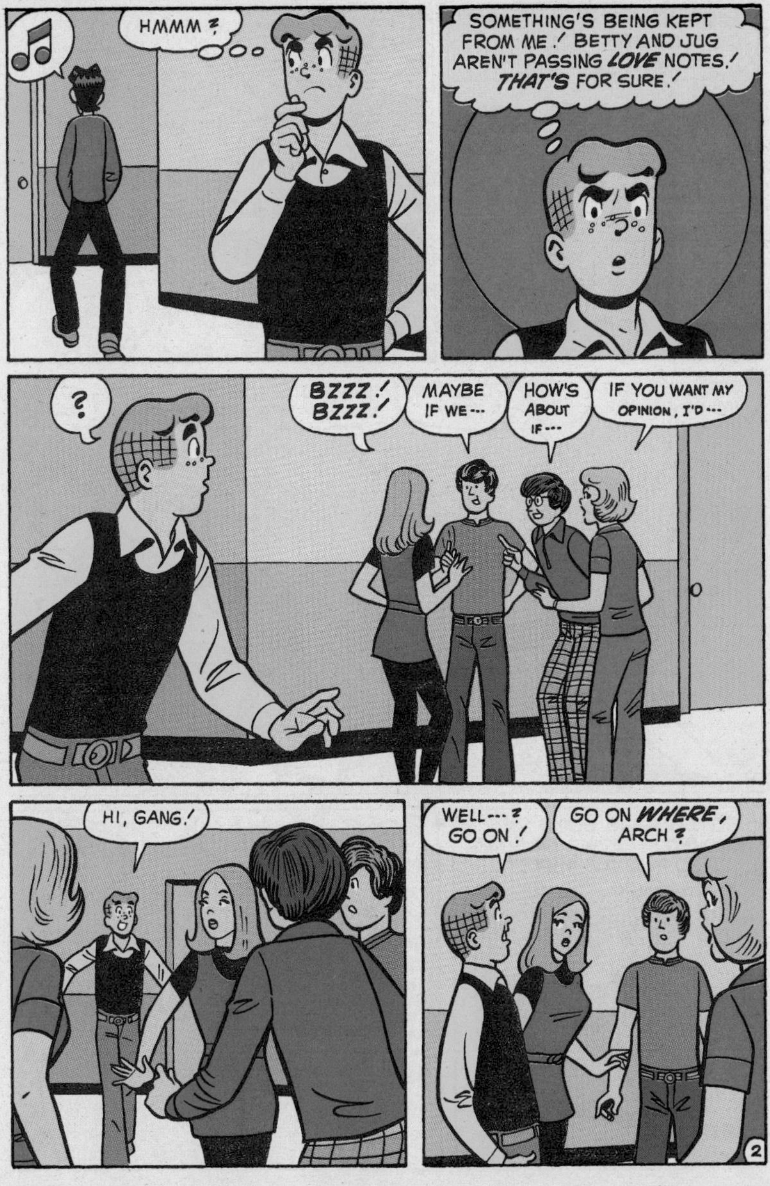
HMMM ?
SOMETHING'S BEING KEPT FROM ME! BETTY AND JUG AREN'T PASSING LOVE NOTES! THAT'S FOR SURE!
?
BZZZ! BZZZ!
MAYBE IF WE---
HOW'S ABOUT IF---
IF YOU WANT MY OPINION, I'D---
HI, GANG!
WELL---? GO ON!
GO ON WHERE, ARCH?
2

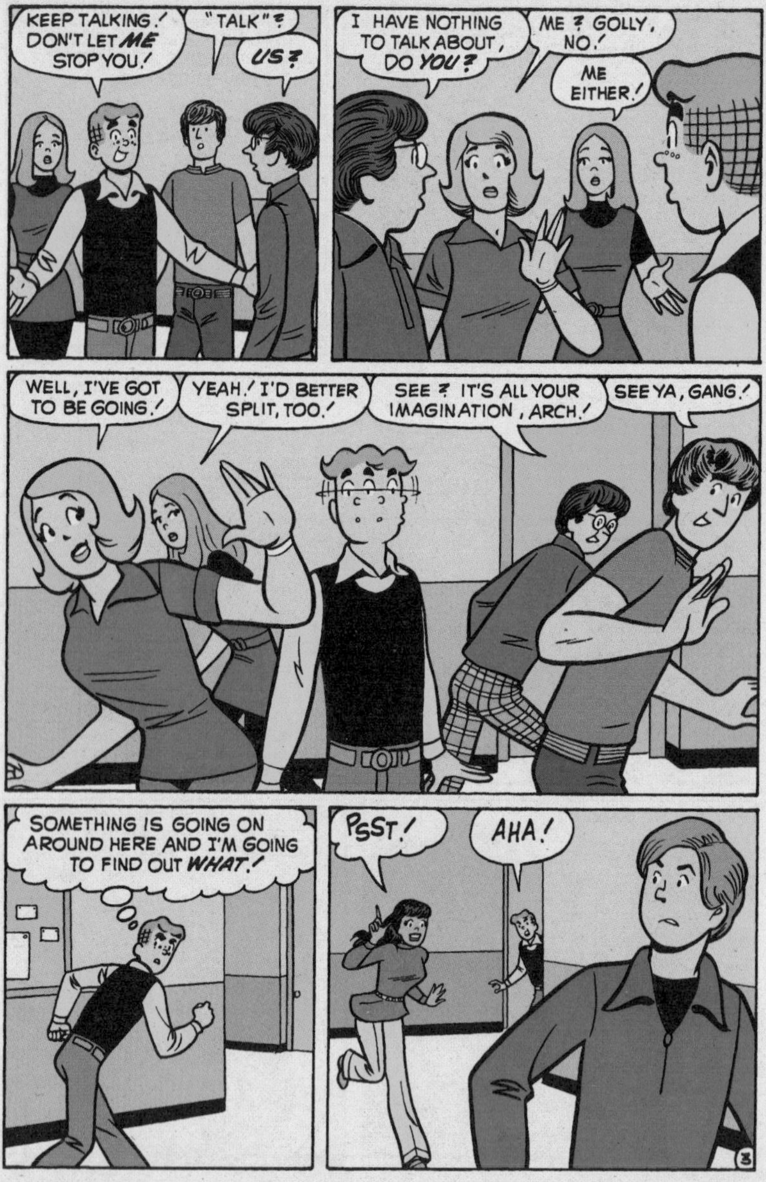

KEEP TALKING! DON'T LET ME STOP YOU!
"TALK"?
US?
I HAVE NOTHING TO TALK ABOUT, DO YOU?
ME? GOLLY, NO!
ME EITHER!
WELL, I'VE GOT TO BE GOING!
YEAH! I'D BETTER SPLIT, TOO!
SEE? IT'S ALL YOUR IMAGINATION, ARCH!
SEE YA, GANG!
SOMETHING IS GOING ON AROUND HERE AND I'M GOING TO FIND OUT WHAT!
PSST!
AHA!
3

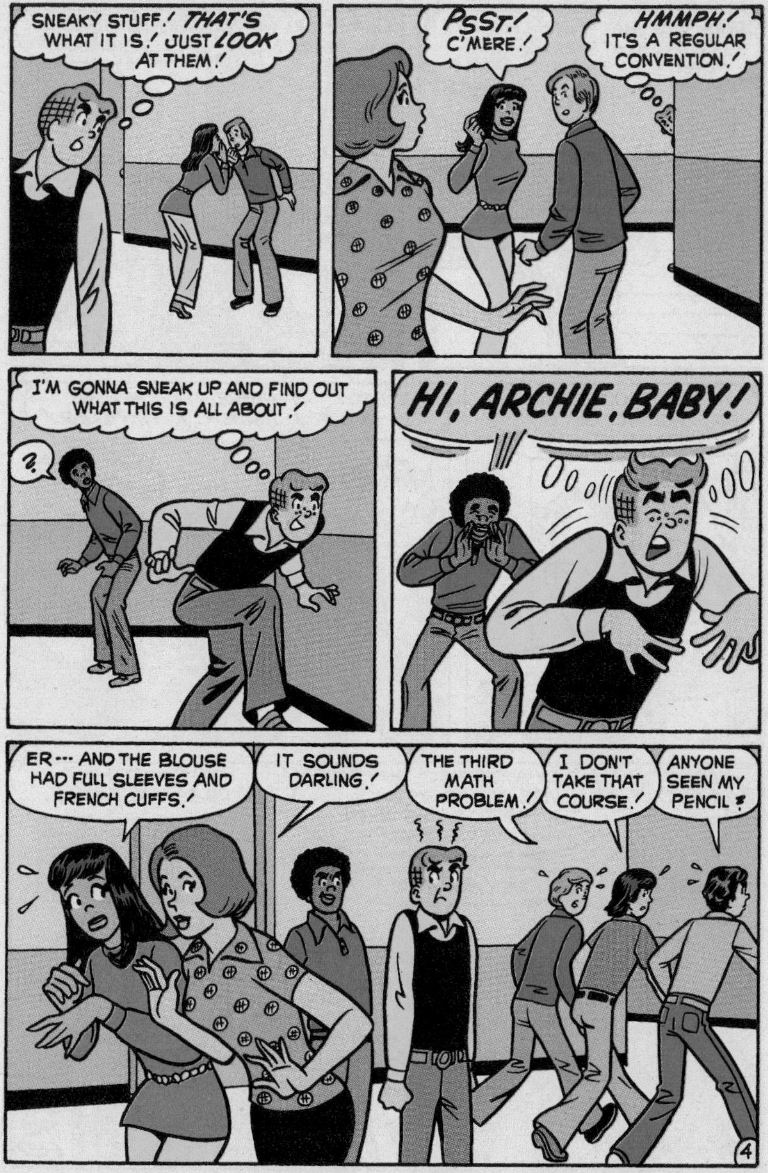
SNEAKY STUFF! THAT'S WHAT IT IS! JUST LOOK AT THEM!
PSST! C'MERE!
HMMPH! IT'S A REGULAR CONVENTION!
I'M GONNA SNEAK UP AND FIND OUT WHAT THIS IS ALL ABOUT!
?
HI, ARCHIE, BABY!
ER--- AND THE BLOUSE HAD FULL SLEEVES AND FRENCH CUFFS!
IT SOUNDS DARLING!
THE THIRD MATH PROBLEM!
I DON'T TAKE THAT COURSE!
ANYONE SEEN MY PENCIL?
4

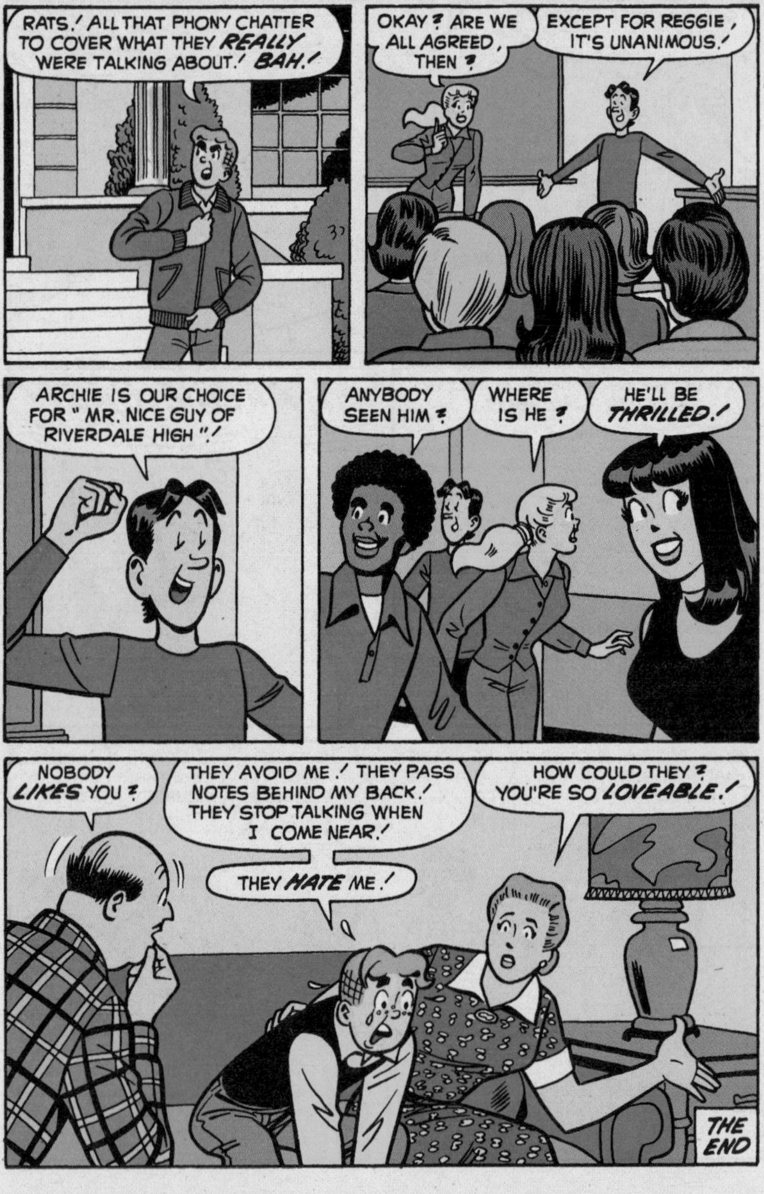
RATS! ALL THAT PHONY CHATTER TO COVER WHAT THEY REALLY WERE TALKING ABOUT! BAH!
OKAY? ARE WE ALL AGREED, THEN?
EXCEPT FOR REGGIE, IT'S UNANIMOUS!
ARCHIE IS OUR CHOICE FOR "MR. NICE GUY OF RIVERDALE HIGH"!
ANYBODY SEEN HIM?
WHERE IS HE?
HE'LL BE THRILLED!
NOBODY LIKES YOU?
THEY AVOID ME! THEY PASS NOTES BEHIND MY BACK! THEY STOP TALKING WHEN I COME NEAR!
THEY HATE ME!
HOW COULD THEY? YOU'RE SO LOVEABLE!
THE END

Archie in "FIRST COME FIRST SERVED"

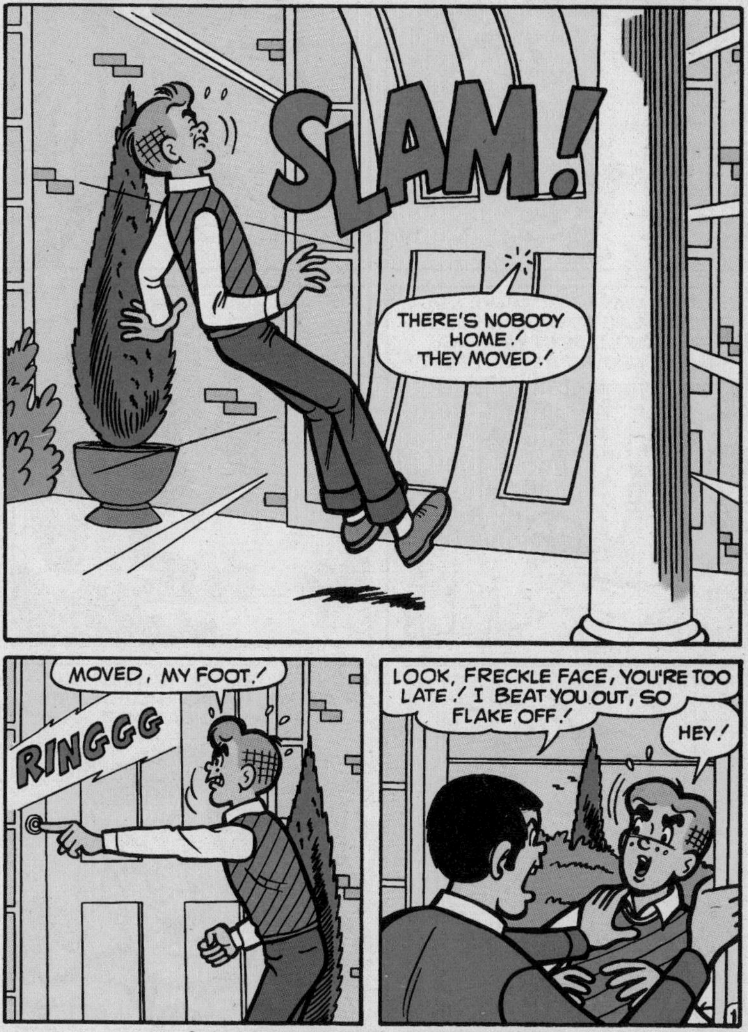
SLAM!
THERE'S NOBODY HOME! THEY MOVED!
MOVED, MY FOOT!
RINGGG
LOOK, FRECKLE FACE, YOU'RE TOO LATE! I BEAT YOU OUT, SO FLAKE OFF!
HEY!

Script & Art: Dick Malmgren / Letters: Bill Yoshida

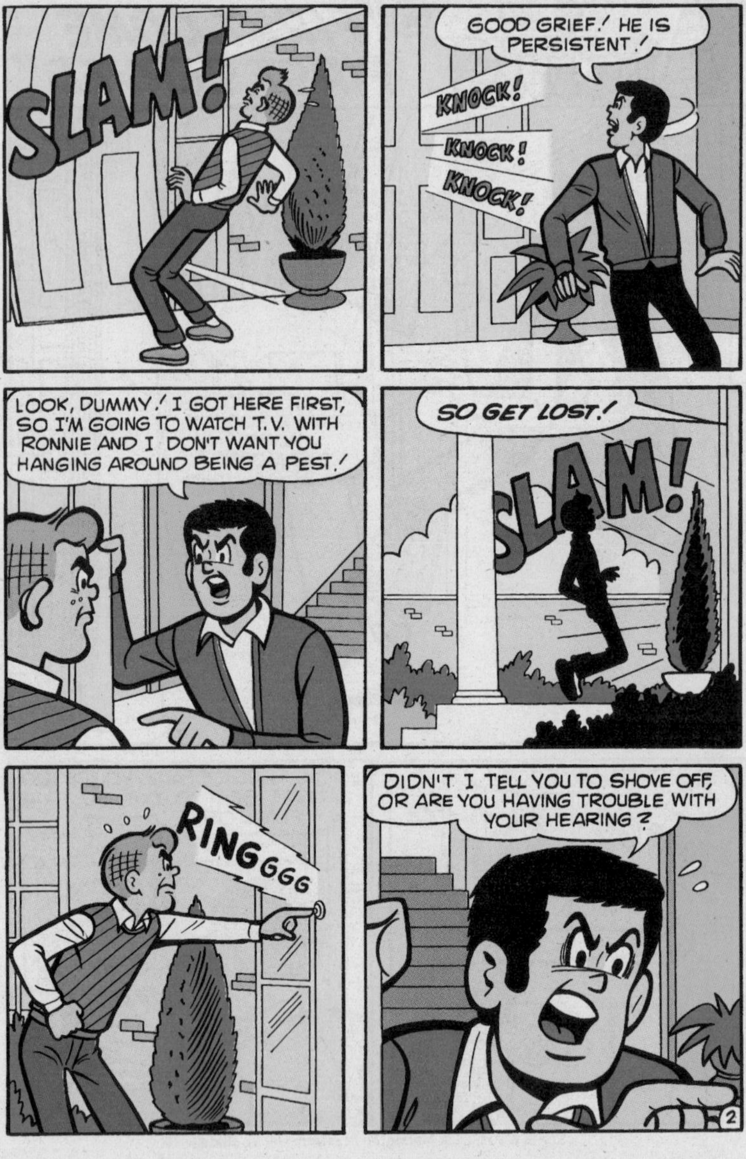
SLAM!
GOOD GRIEF! HE IS PERSISTENT!
KNOCK!
KNOCK!
KNOCK!
LOOK, DUMMY! I GOT HERE FIRST, SO I'M GOING TO WATCH T.V. WITH RONNIE AND I DON'T WANT YOU HANGING AROUND BEING A PEST!
SO GET LOST!
SLAM!
RINGGGG
DIDN'T I TELL YOU TO SHOVE OFF, OR ARE YOU HAVING TROUBLE WITH YOUR HEARING?
2

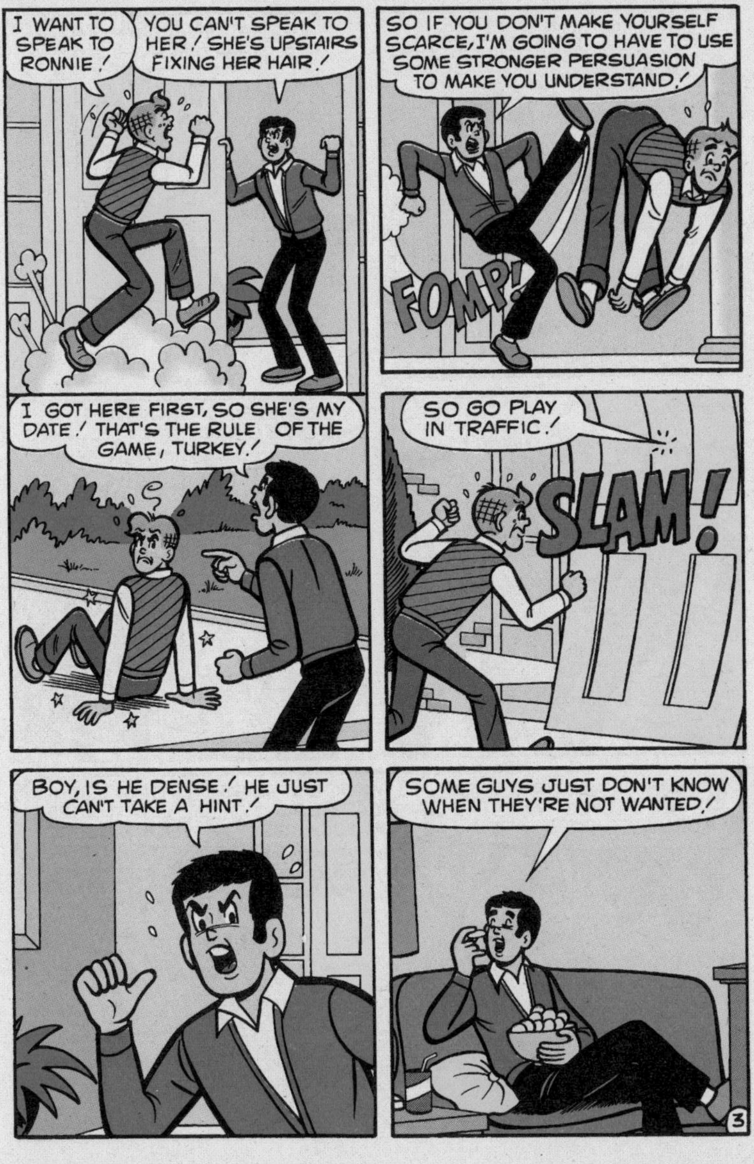
I WANT TO SPEAK TO RONNIE!
YOU CAN'T SPEAK TO HER! SHE'S UPSTAIRS FIXING HER HAIR!
SO IF YOU DON'T MAKE YOURSELF SCARCE, I'M GOING TO HAVE TO USE SOME STRONGER PERSUASION TO MAKE YOU UNDERSTAND!
FOMP!
I GOT HERE FIRST, SO SHE'S MY DATE! THAT'S THE RULE OF THE GAME, TURKEY!
SO GO PLAY IN TRAFFIC!
SLAM!
BOY, IS HE DENSE! HE JUST CAN'T TAKE A HINT!
SOME GUYS JUST DON'T KNOW WHEN THEY'RE NOT WANTED!
3

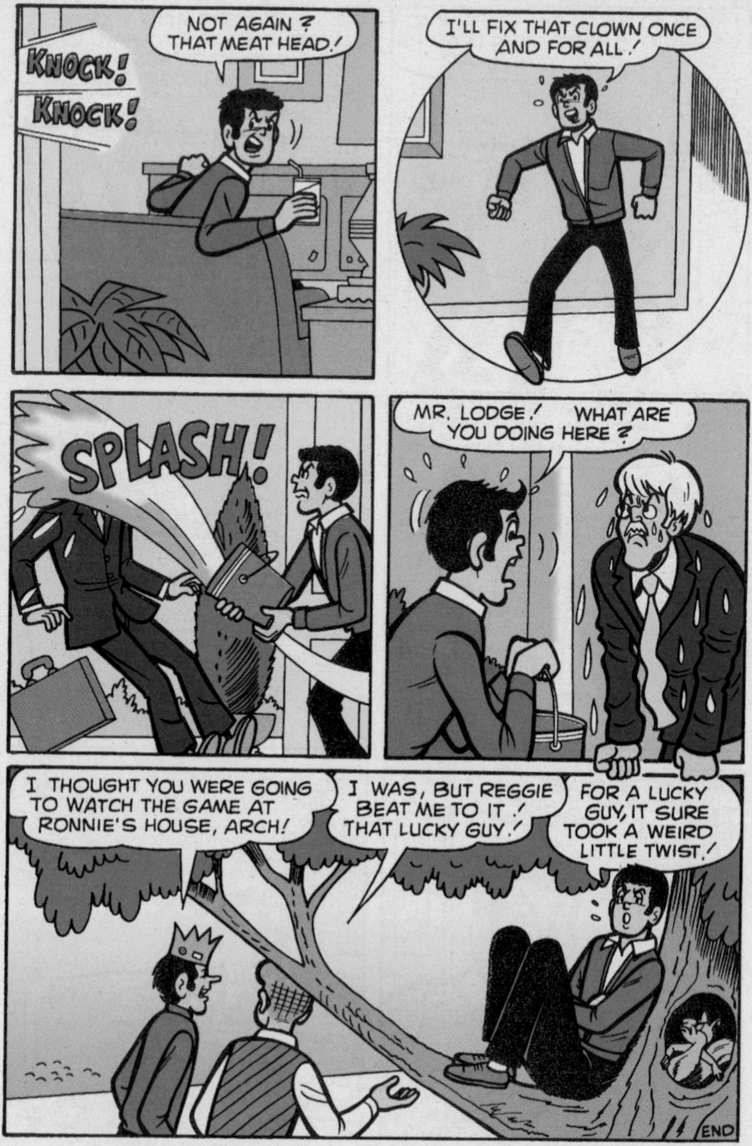
KNOCK! KNOCK!
NOT AGAIN? THAT MEAT HEAD!
I'LL FIX THAT CLOWN ONCE AND FOR ALL!
SPLASH!
MR. LODGE! WHAT ARE YOU DOING HERE?
I THOUGHT YOU WERE GOING TO WATCH THE GAME AT RONNIE'S HOUSE, ARCH!
I WAS, BUT REGGIE BEAT ME TO IT! THAT LUCKY GUY!
FOR A LUCKY GUY, IT SURE TOOK A WEIRD LITTLE TWIST!
END

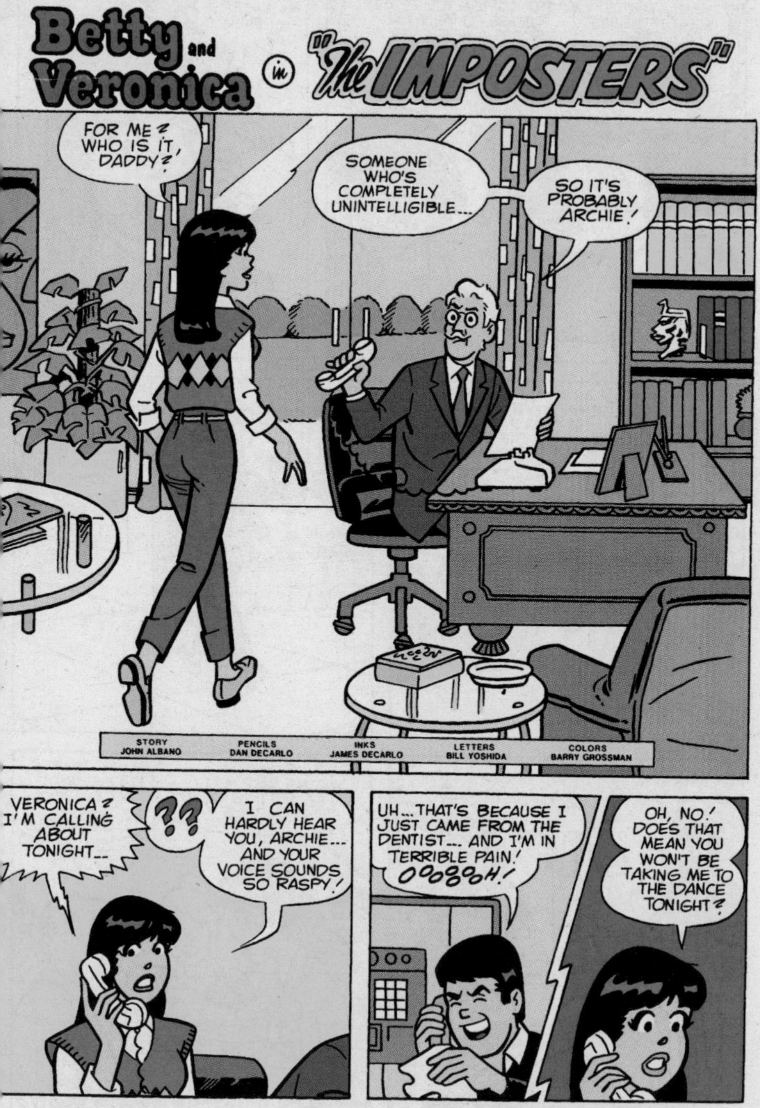

Betty and Veronica in "The IMPOSTERS"
FOR ME? WHO IS IT, DADDY?
SOMEONE WHO'S COMPLETELY UNINTELLIGIBLE...
SO IT'S PROBABLY ARCHIE!
STORY JOHN ALBANO
PENCILS DAN DECARLO
INKS JAMES DECARLO
LETTERS BILL YOSHIDA
COLORS BARRY GROSSMAN
VERONICA? I'M CALLING ABOUT TONIGHT...
??
I CAN HARDLY HEAR YOU, ARCHIE... AND YOUR VOICE SOUNDS SO RASPY!
UH... THAT'S BECAUSE I JUST CAME FROM THE DENTIST... AND I'M IN TERRIBLE PAIN! OOOOOOH!
OH, NO! DOES THAT MEAN YOU WON'T BE TAKING ME TO THE DANCE TONIGHT?

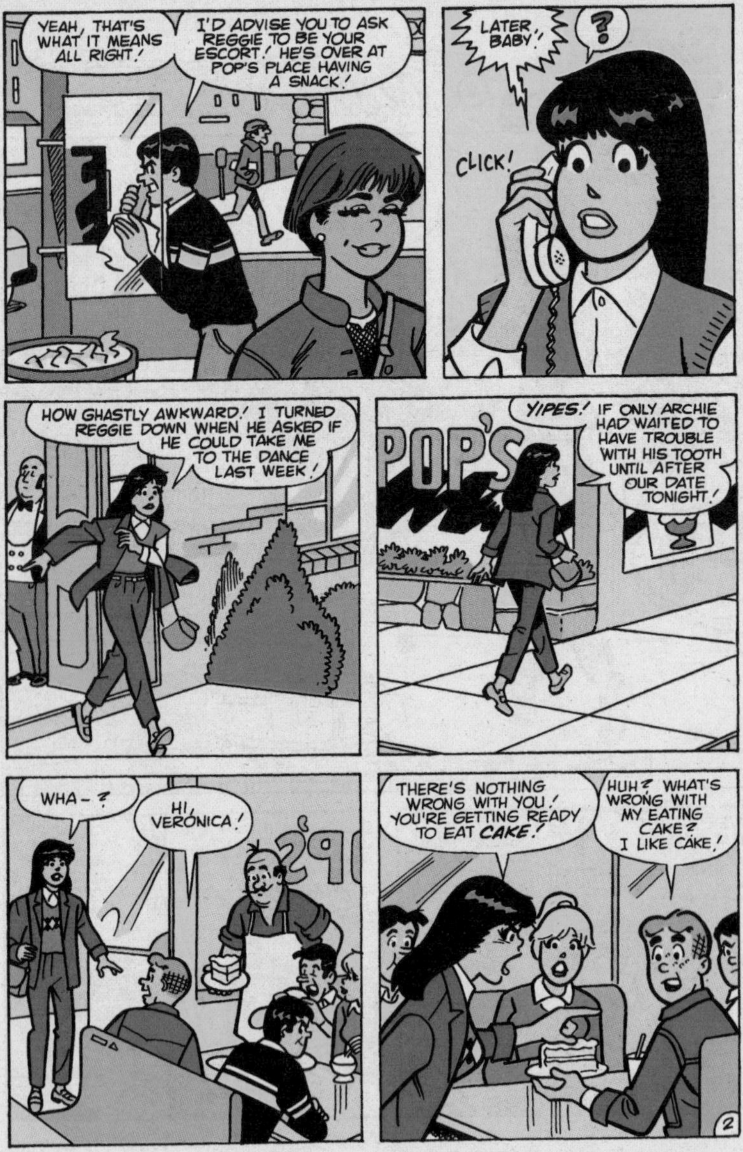
YEAH, THAT'S WHAT IT MEANS ALL RIGHT!
I'D ADVISE YOU TO ASK REGGIE TO BE YOUR ESCORT! HE'S OVER AT POP'S PLACE HAVING A SNACK!
LATER, BABY!
?
CLICK!
HOW GHASTLY AWKWARD! I TURNED REGGIE DOWN WHEN HE ASKED IF HE COULD TAKE ME TO THE DANCE LAST WEEK!
POP'S
YIPES! IF ONLY ARCHIE HAD WAITED TO HAVE TROUBLE WITH HIS TOOTH UNTIL AFTER OUR DATE TONIGHT!
WHA-?
HI, VERONICA!
THERE'S NOTHING WRONG WITH YOU! YOU'RE GETTING READY TO EAT CAKE!
HUH? WHAT'S WRONG WITH MY EATING CAKE? I LIKE CAKE!
2

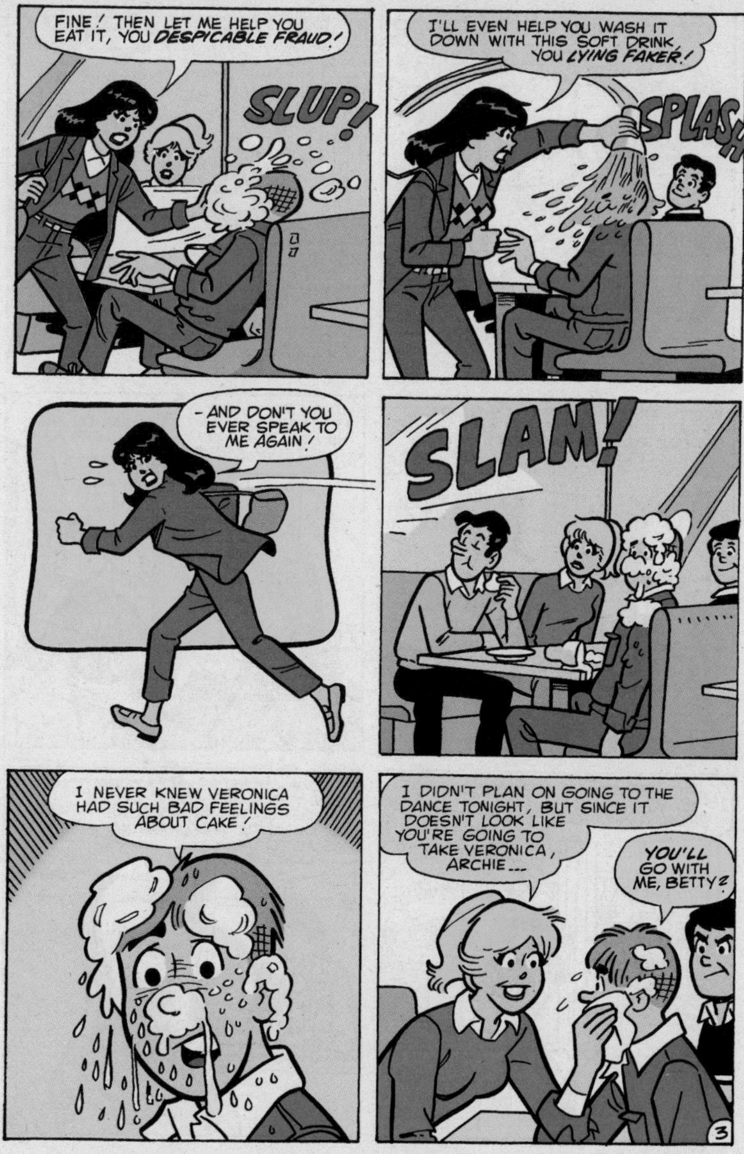
FINE! THEN LET ME HELP YOU EAT IT, YOU DESPICABLE FRAUD!
SLUP!
I'LL EVEN HELP YOU WASH IT DOWN WITH THIS SOFT DRINK, YOU LYING FAKER!
SPLASH
- AND DON'T YOU EVER SPEAK TO ME AGAIN!
SLAM!
I NEVER KNEW VERONICA HAD SUCH BAD FEELINGS ABOUT CAKE!
I DIDN'T PLAN ON GOING TO THE DANCE TONIGHT, BUT SINCE IT DOESN'T LOOK LIKE YOU'RE GOING TO TAKE VERONICA, ARCHIE...
YOU'LL GO WITH ME, BETTY?
3

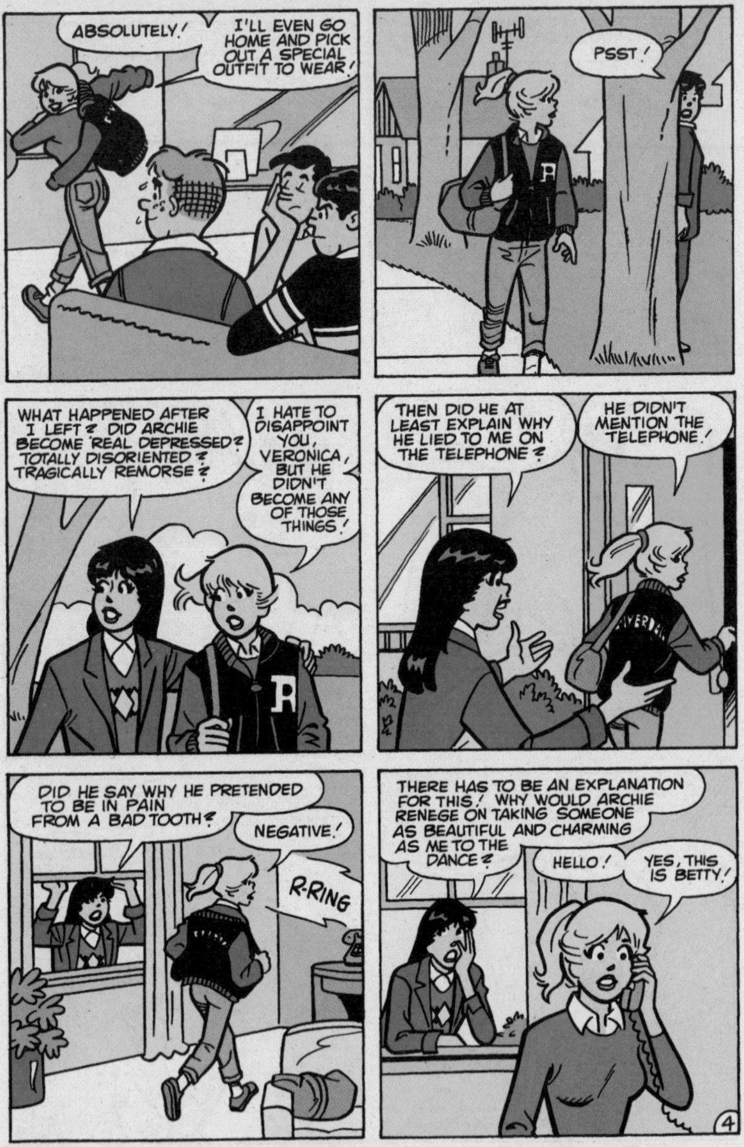
ABSOLUTELY!
I'LL EVEN GO HOME AND PICK OUT A SPECIAL OUTFIT TO WEAR!
PSST!
WHAT HAPPENED AFTER I LEFT? DID ARCHIE BECOME REAL DEPRESSED? TOTALLY DISORIENTED? TRAGICALLY REMORSE?
I HATE TO DISAPPOINT YOU, VERONICA, BUT HE DIDN'T BECOME ANY OF THOSE THINGS!
THEN DID HE AT LEAST EXPLAIN WHY HE LIED TO ME ON THE TELEPHONE?
HE DIDN'T MENTION THE TELEPHONE!
DID HE SAY WHY HE PRETENDED TO BE IN PAIN FROM A BAD TOOTH?
NEGATIVE!
R-RING
THERE HAS TO BE AN EXPLANATION FOR THIS! WHY WOULD ARCHIE RENEGE ON TAKING SOMEONE AS BEAUTIFUL AND CHARMING AS ME TO THE DANCE?
HELLO!
YES, THIS IS BETTY!
4

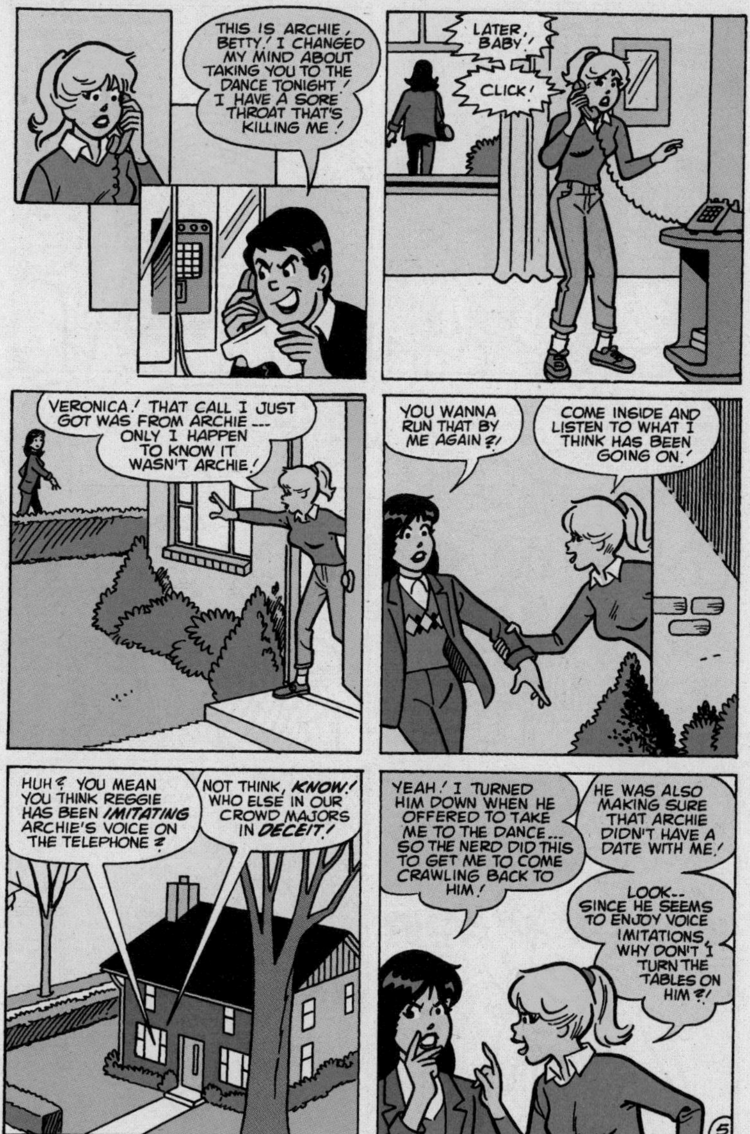
THIS IS ARCHIE, BETTY! I CHANGED MY MIND ABOUT TAKING YOU TO THE DANCE TONIGHT! I HAVE A SORE THROAT THAT'S KILLING ME!
LATER, BABY!
CLICK!
VERONICA! THAT CALL I JUST GOT WAS FROM ARCHIE --- ONLY I HAPPEN TO KNOW IT WASN'T ARCHIE!
YOU WANNA RUN THAT BY ME AGAIN?!
COME INSIDE AND LISTEN TO WHAT I THINK HAS BEEN GOING ON!
HUH? YOU MEAN YOU THINK REGGIE HAS BEEN IMITATING ARCHIE'S VOICE ON THE TELEPHONE?
NOT THINK, KNOW! WHO ELSE IN OUR CROWD MAJORS IN DECEIT!
YEAH! I TURNED HIM DOWN WHEN HE OFFERED TO TAKE ME TO THE DANCE... SO THE NERD DID THIS TO GET ME TO COME CRAWLING BACK TO HIM!
HE WAS ALSO MAKING SURE THAT ARCHIE DIDN'T HAVE A DATE WITH ME!
LOOK-- SINCE HE SEEMS TO ENJOY VOICE IMITATIONS, WHY DON'T I TURN THE TABLES ON HIM?!
5

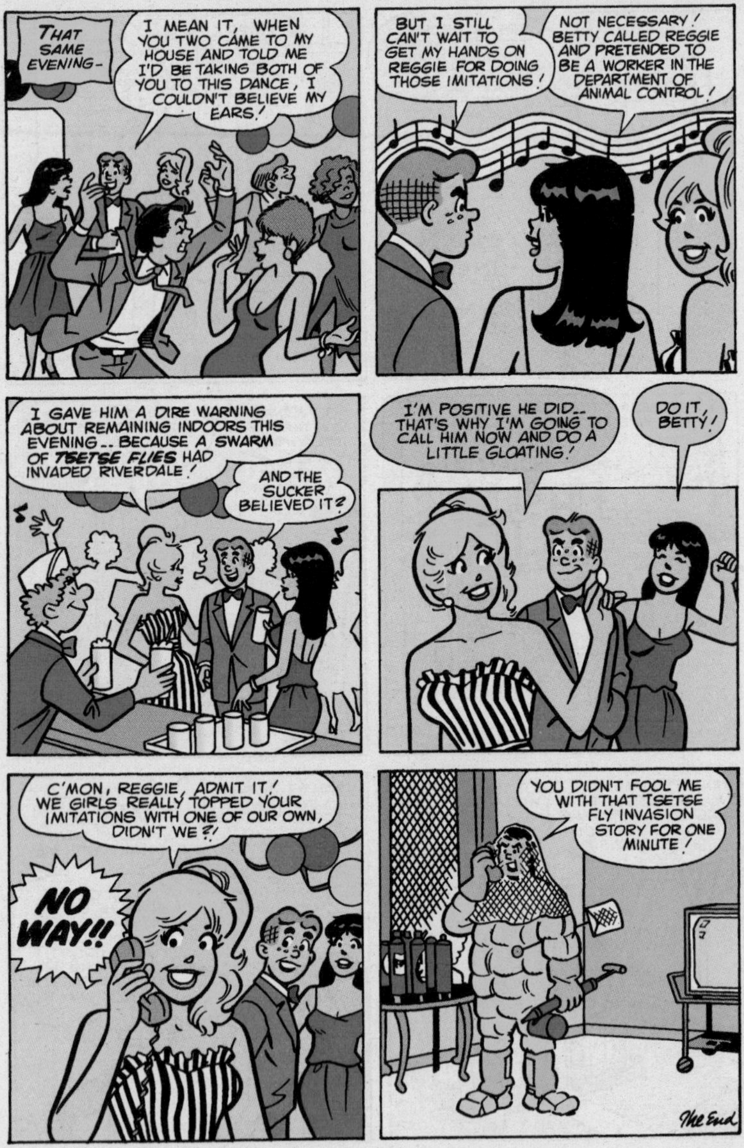
THAT SAME EVENING-
I MEAN IT, WHEN YOU TWO CAME TO MY HOUSE AND TOLD ME I'D BE TAKING BOTH OF YOU TO THIS DANCE, I COULDN'T BELIEVE MY EARS!
BUT I STILL CAN'T WAIT TO GET MY HANDS ON REGGIE FOR DOING THOSE IMITATIONS!
NOT NECESSARY! BETTY CALLED REGGIE AND PRETENDED TO BE A WORKER IN THE DEPARTMENT OF ANIMAL CONTROL!
I GAVE HIM A DIRE WARNING ABOUT REMAINING INDOORS THIS EVENING.. BECAUSE A SWARM OF TSETSE FLIES HAD INVADED RIVERDALE!
AND THE SUCKER BELIEVED IT?
I'M POSITIVE HE DID.. THAT'S WHY I'M GOING TO CALL HIM NOW AND DO A LITTLE GLOATING!
DO IT, BETTY!
C'MON, REGGIE, ADMIT IT! WE GIRLS REALLY TOPPED YOUR IMITATIONS WITH ONE OF OUR OWN, DIDN'T WE?!
NO WAY!!
YOU DIDN'T FOOL ME WITH THAT TSETSE FLY INVASION STORY FOR ONE MINUTE!
The End

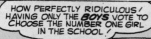 **Betty** and **Veronica** in **"NUMERO UNO"**

HOW PERFECTLY RIDICULOUS! HAVING ONLY THE *BOYS* VOTE TO CHOOSE THE NUMBER ONE GIRL IN THE SCHOOL!

WHAT'S SILLY ABOUT THAT? I THINK IT'S FUN! IT'S A VERY CUTE IDEA!

BOYS! WHO IS YOUR CHOICE FOR FINEST FEMALE! CAST YOUR VOTE!

WHO WILL WEAR THE SWEATER?

RIVERDALE HIGH TROPHY CASE

HAVE YOU VOTED?

DON'T BE NAIVE, CHILD! WITH ONLY *BOYS* VOTING, WHO COULD POSSIBLY WIN BUT ME?

BY DOYLE & DECARLO JR.

GOLLEE! HOW COULD I HAVE OVERLOOKED THAT OBVIOUS FACT?

WE'LL ASK ARCHIE WHAT *HE* THINKS!

THINKS? WHO THINKS?

WHEN I'M NEAR YOU, SWEET LIPS, MY MIND CEASES TO FUNCTION!

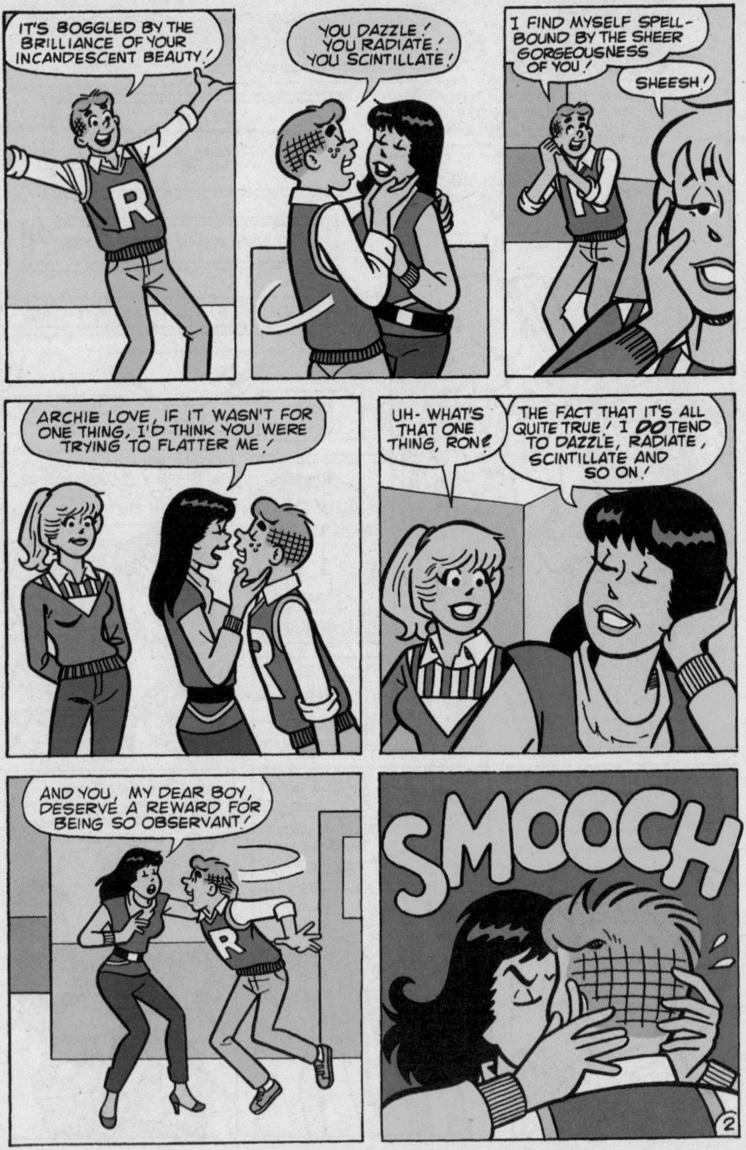
IT'S BOGGLED BY THE BRILLIANCE OF YOUR INCANDESCENT BEAUTY!
YOU DAZZLE! YOU RADIATE! YOU SCINTILLATE!
I FIND MYSELF SPELL-BOUND BY THE SHEER GORGEOUSNESS OF YOU!
SHEESH!
ARCHIE LOVE, IF IT WASN'T FOR ONE THING, I'D THINK YOU WERE TRYING TO FLATTER ME!
UH- WHAT'S THAT ONE THING, RON?
THE FACT THAT IT'S ALL QUITE TRUE! I DO TEND TO DAZZLE, RADIATE, SCINTILLATE AND SO ON!
AND YOU, MY DEAR BOY, DESERVE A REWARD FOR BEING SO OBSERVANT!
SMOOCH
2

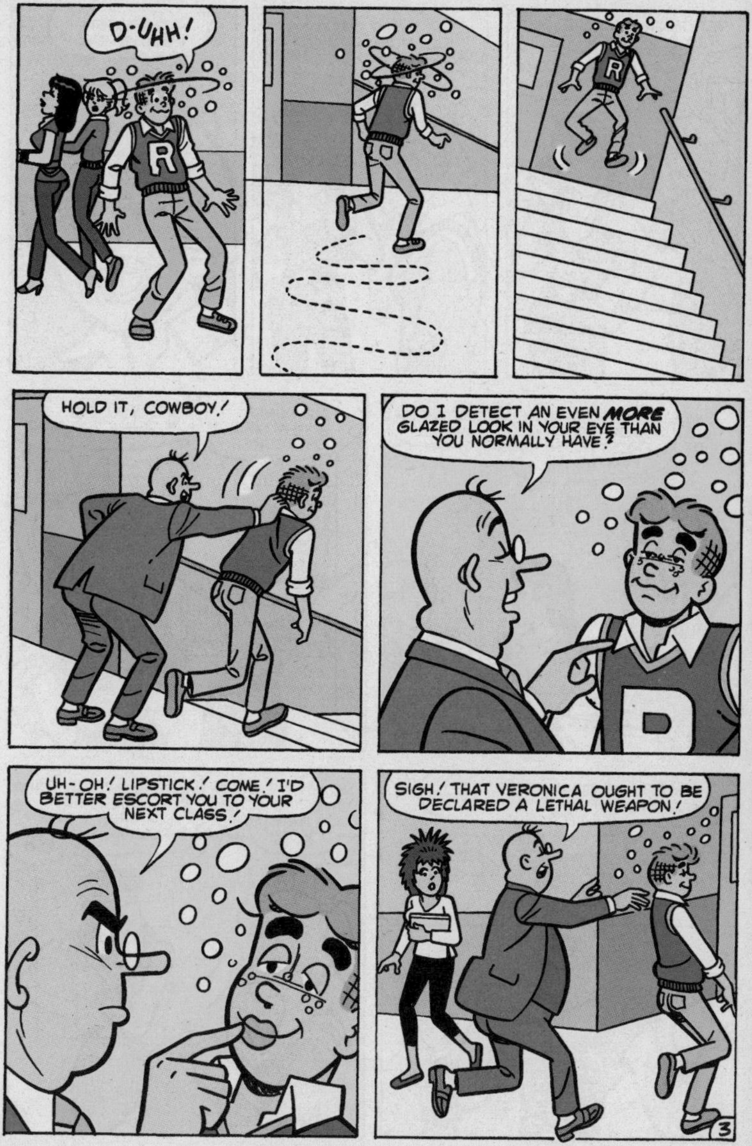

D-UHH!
HOLD IT, COWBOY!
DO I DETECT AN EVEN MORE GLAZED LOOK IN YOUR EYE THAN YOU NORMALLY HAVE?
UH-OH! LIPSTICK! COME! I'D BETTER ESCORT YOU TO YOUR NEXT CLASS!
SIGH! THAT VERONICA OUGHT TO BE DECLARED A LETHAL WEAPON!
3

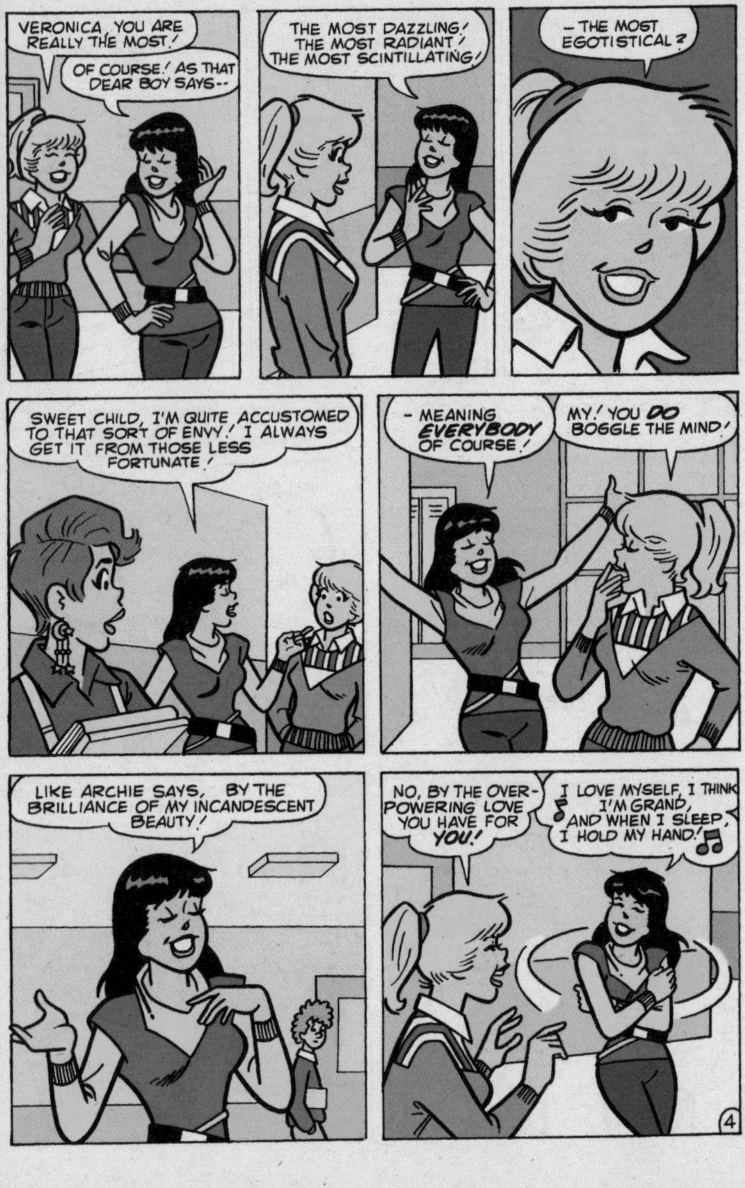
VERONICA, YOU ARE REALLY THE MOST!
OF COURSE! AS THAT DEAR BOY SAYS--
THE MOST DAZZLING! THE MOST RADIANT! THE MOST SCINTILLATING!
- THE MOST EGOTISTICAL?
SWEET CHILD, I'M QUITE ACCUSTOMED TO THAT SORT OF ENVY! I ALWAYS GET IT FROM THOSE LESS FORTUNATE!
- MEANING EVERYBODY OF COURSE!
MY! YOU DO BOGGLE THE MIND!
LIKE ARCHIE SAYS, BY THE BRILLIANCE OF MY INCANDESCENT BEAUTY!
NO, BY THE OVER-POWERING LOVE YOU HAVE FOR YOU!
I LOVE MYSELF, I THINK I'M GRAND, AND WHEN I SLEEP, I HOLD MY HAND!
4

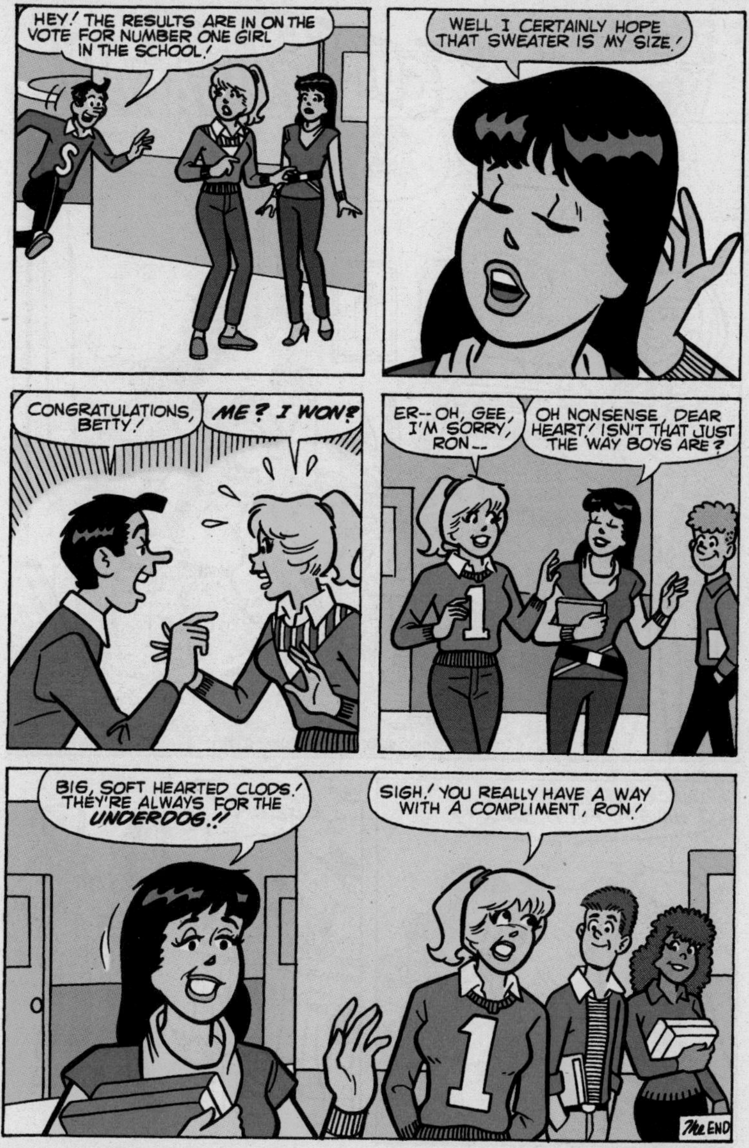
HEY! THE RESULTS ARE IN ON THE VOTE FOR NUMBER ONE GIRL IN THE SCHOOL!
WELL I CERTAINLY HOPE THAT SWEATER IS MY SIZE!
CONGRATULATIONS, BETTY!
ME? I WON?
ER-- OH, GEE, I'M SORRY, RON --
OH NONSENSE, DEAR HEART! ISN'T THAT JUST THE WAY BOYS ARE?
BIG, SOFT HEARTED CLODS! THEY'RE ALWAYS FOR THE UNDERDOG!!
SIGH! YOU REALLY HAVE A WAY WITH A COMPLIMENT, RON!
The END

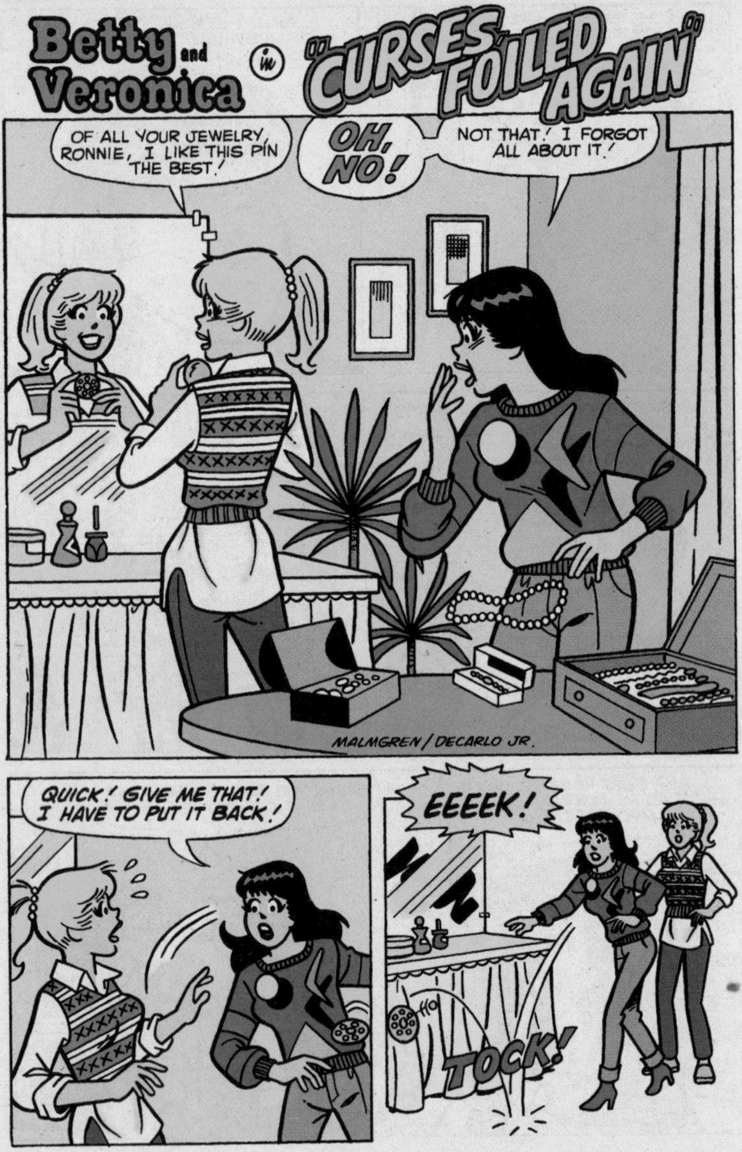
Betty and Veronica in "CURSES, FOILED AGAIN"
OF ALL YOUR JEWELRY, RONNIE, I LIKE THIS PIN THE BEST!
OH, NO!
NOT THAT! I FORGOT ALL ABOUT IT!
MALMGREN / DECARLO JR.
QUICK! GIVE ME THAT! I HAVE TO PUT IT BACK!
EEEEK!
TOCK!

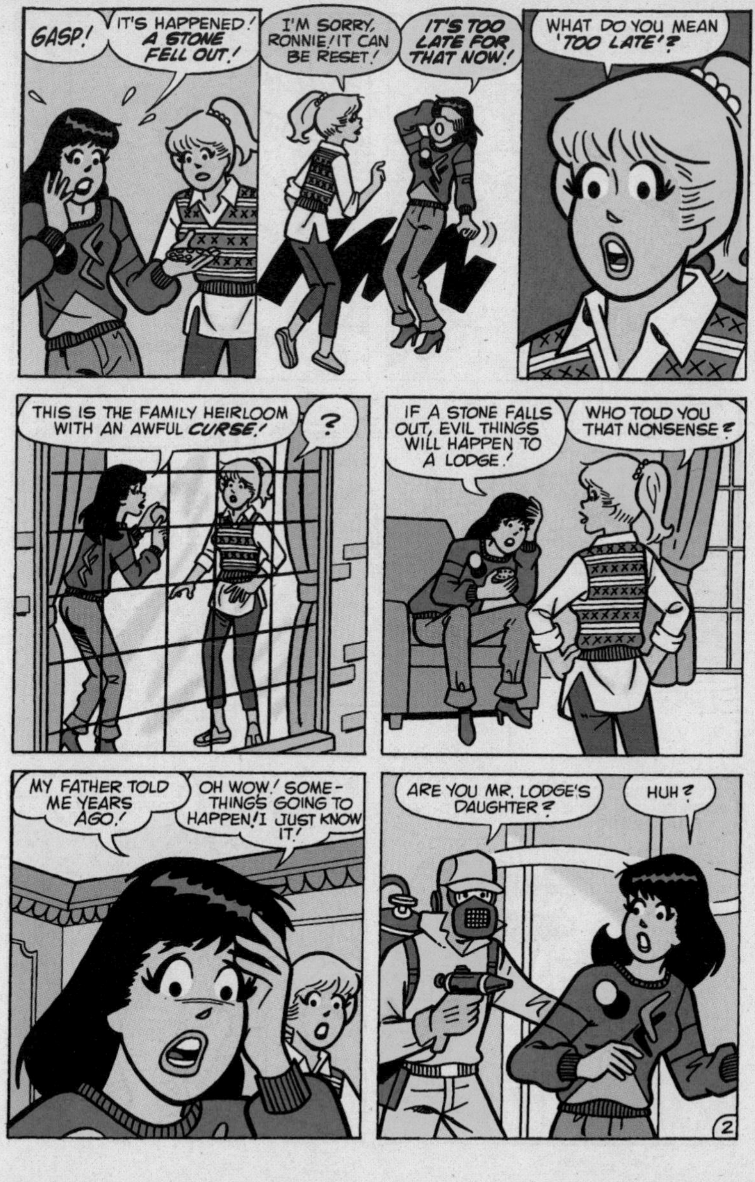

GASP!
IT'S HAPPENED! A STONE FELL OUT!
I'M SORRY, RONNIE! IT CAN BE RESET!
IT'S TOO LATE FOR THAT NOW!
WHAT DO YOU MEAN 'TOO LATE'?
THIS IS THE FAMILY HEIRLOOM WITH AN AWFUL CURSE!
?
IF A STONE FALLS OUT, EVIL THINGS WILL HAPPEN TO A LODGE!
WHO TOLD YOU THAT NONSENSE?
MY FATHER TOLD ME YEARS AGO!
OH WOW! SOMETHING'S GOING TO HAPPEN! I JUST KNOW IT!
ARE YOU MR. LODGE'S DAUGHTER?
HUH?
2

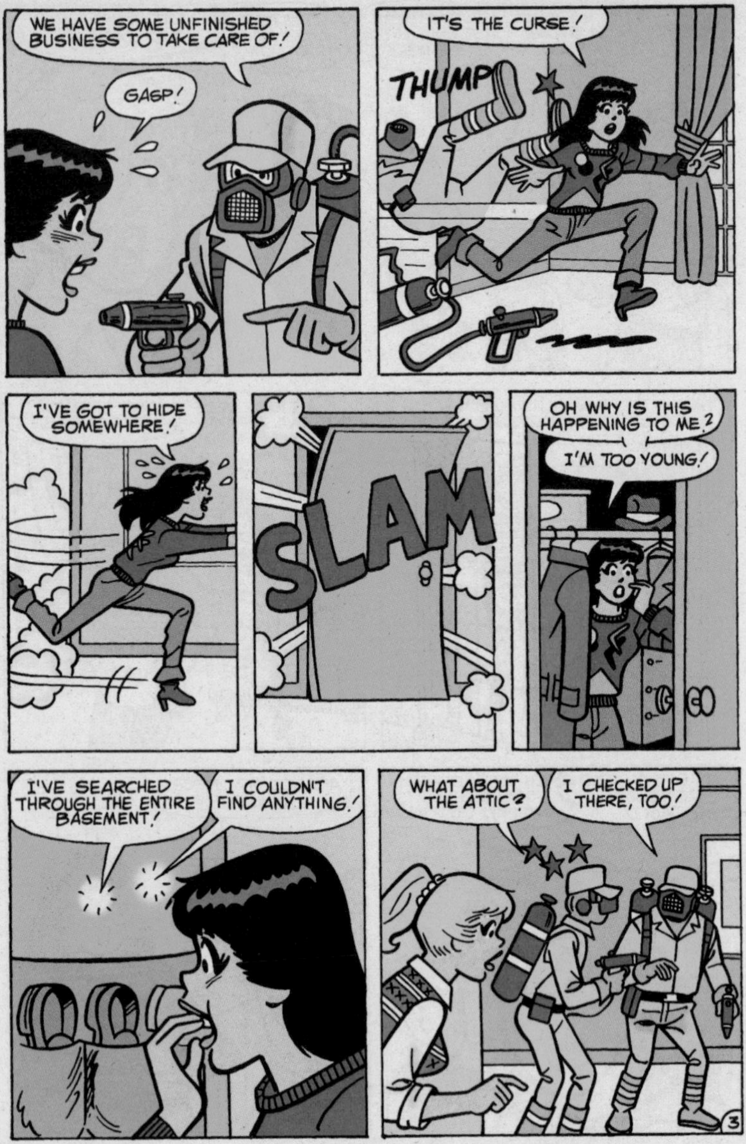
WE HAVE SOME UNFINISHED BUSINESS TO TAKE CARE OF!
GASP!
IT'S THE CURSE!
THUMP
I'VE GOT TO HIDE SOMEWHERE!
SLAM
OH WHY IS THIS HAPPENING TO ME?
I'M TOO YOUNG!
I'VE SEARCHED THROUGH THE ENTIRE BASEMENT!
I COULDN'T FIND ANYTHING!
WHAT ABOUT THE ATTIC?
I CHECKED UP THERE, TOO!
3

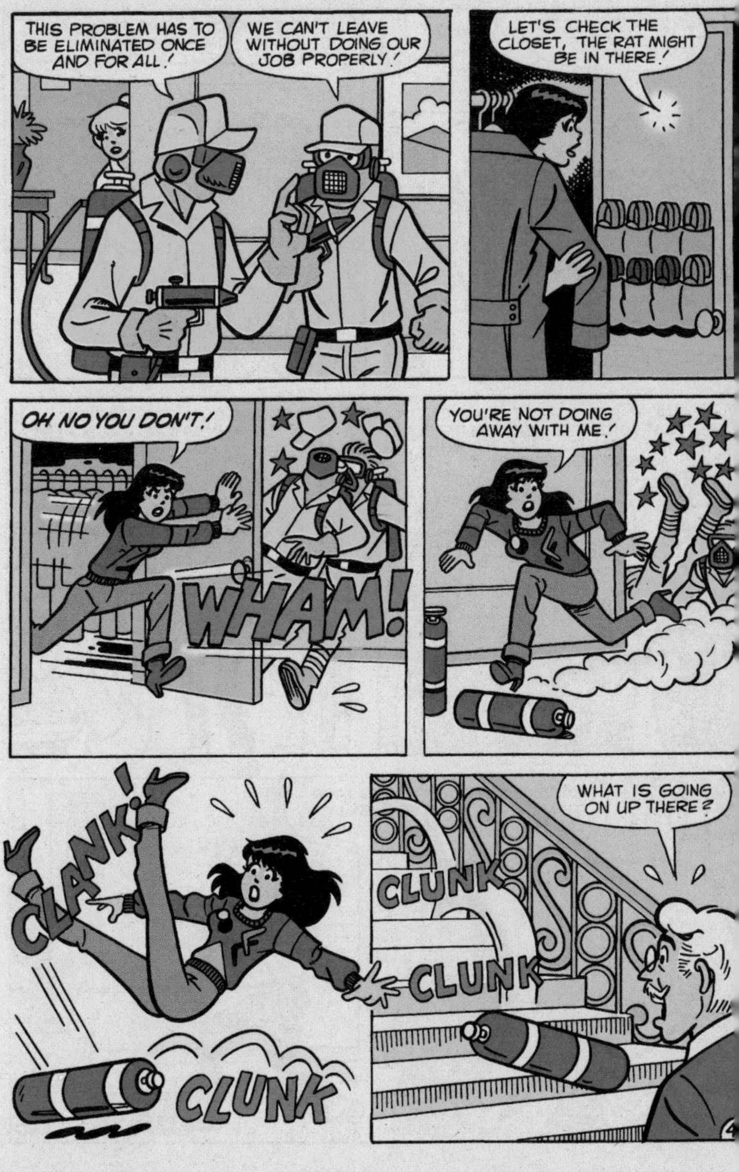
THIS PROBLEM HAS TO BE ELIMINATED ONCE AND FOR ALL!
WE CAN'T LEAVE WITHOUT DOING OUR JOB PROPERLY!
LET'S CHECK THE CLOSET, THE RAT MIGHT BE IN THERE!
OH NO YOU DON'T!
WHAM!
YOU'RE NOT DOING AWAY WITH ME!
CLANK!
CLUNK
CLUNK
CLUNK
WHAT IS GOING ON UP THERE?

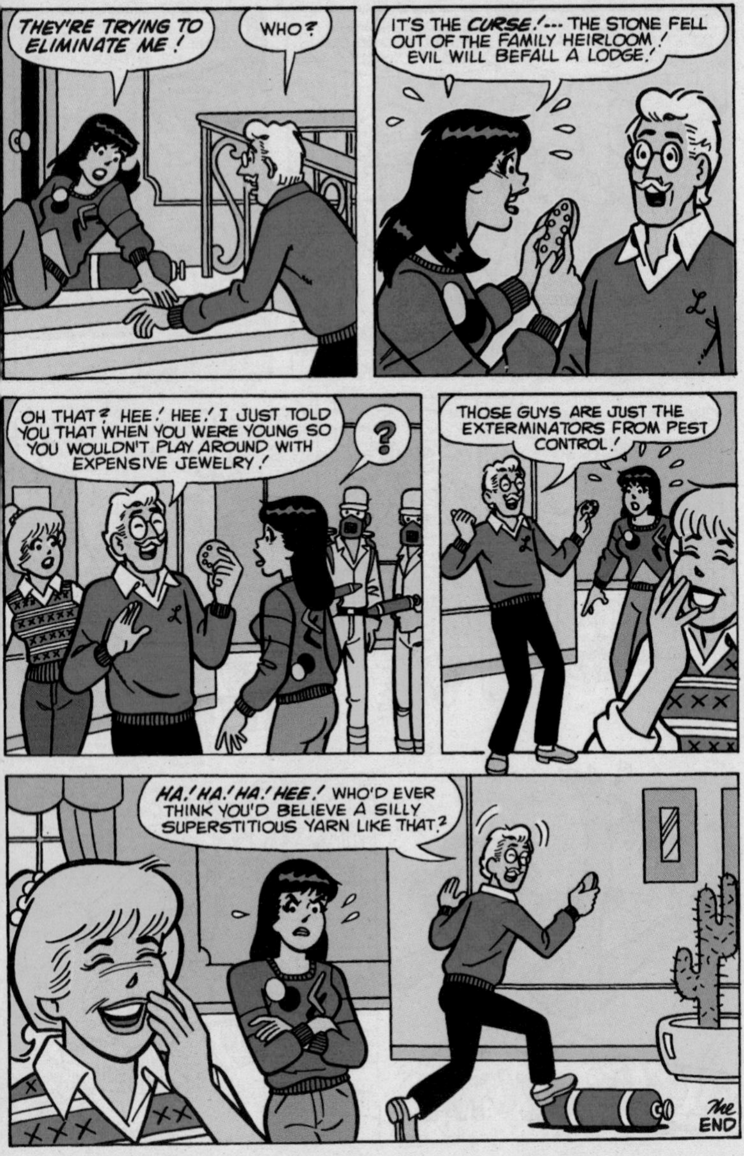
THEY'RE TRYING TO ELIMINATE ME!
WHO?
IT'S THE CURSE! --- THE STONE FELL OUT OF THE FAMILY HEIRLOOM! EVIL WILL BEFALL A LODGE!
OH THAT? HEE! HEE! I JUST TOLD YOU THAT WHEN YOU WERE YOUNG SO YOU WOULDN'T PLAY AROUND WITH EXPENSIVE JEWELRY!
?
THOSE GUYS ARE JUST THE EXTERMINATORS FROM PEST CONTROL!
HA! HA! HA! HEE! WHO'D EVER THINK YOU'D BELIEVE A SILLY SUPERSTITIOUS YARN LIKE THAT?
The END

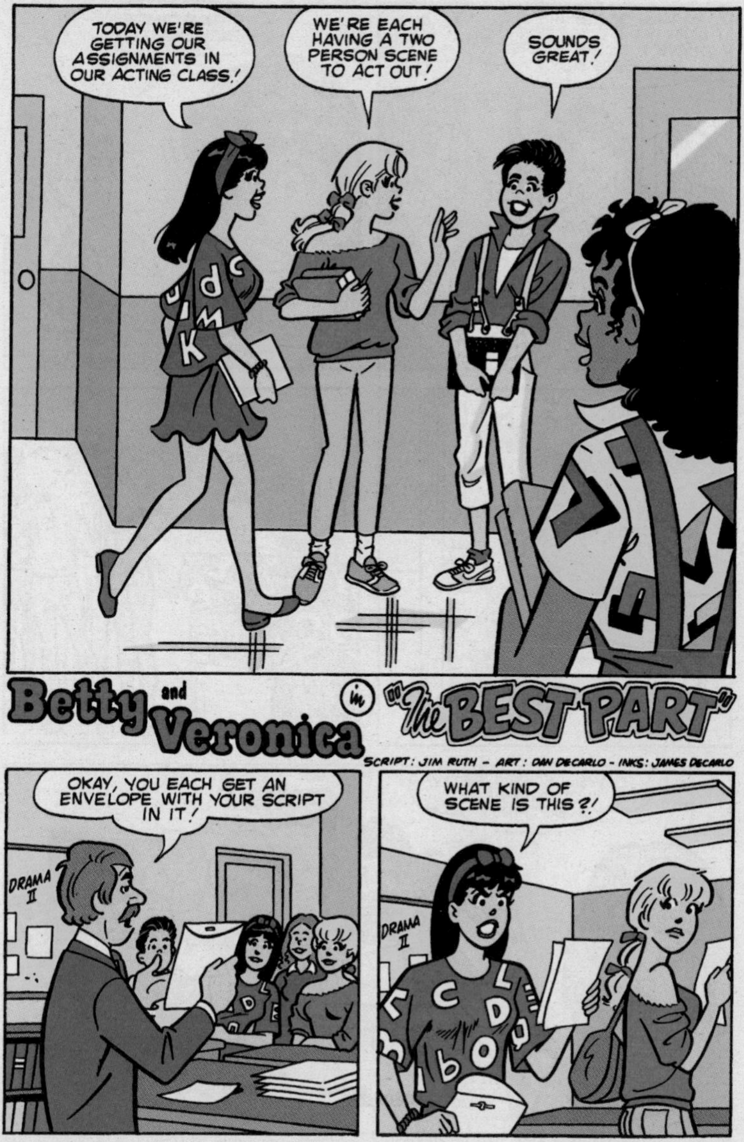
TODAY WE'RE GETTING OUR ASSIGNMENTS IN OUR ACTING CLASS!
WE'RE EACH HAVING A TWO PERSON SCENE TO ACT OUT!
SOUNDS GREAT!
Betty and Veronica in "The BEST PART"
SCRIPT: JIM RUTH - ART: DAN DECARLO - INKS: JAMES DECARLO
OKAY, YOU EACH GET AN ENVELOPE WITH YOUR SCRIPT IN IT!
DRAMA II
WHAT KIND OF SCENE IS THIS ?!
DRAMA II

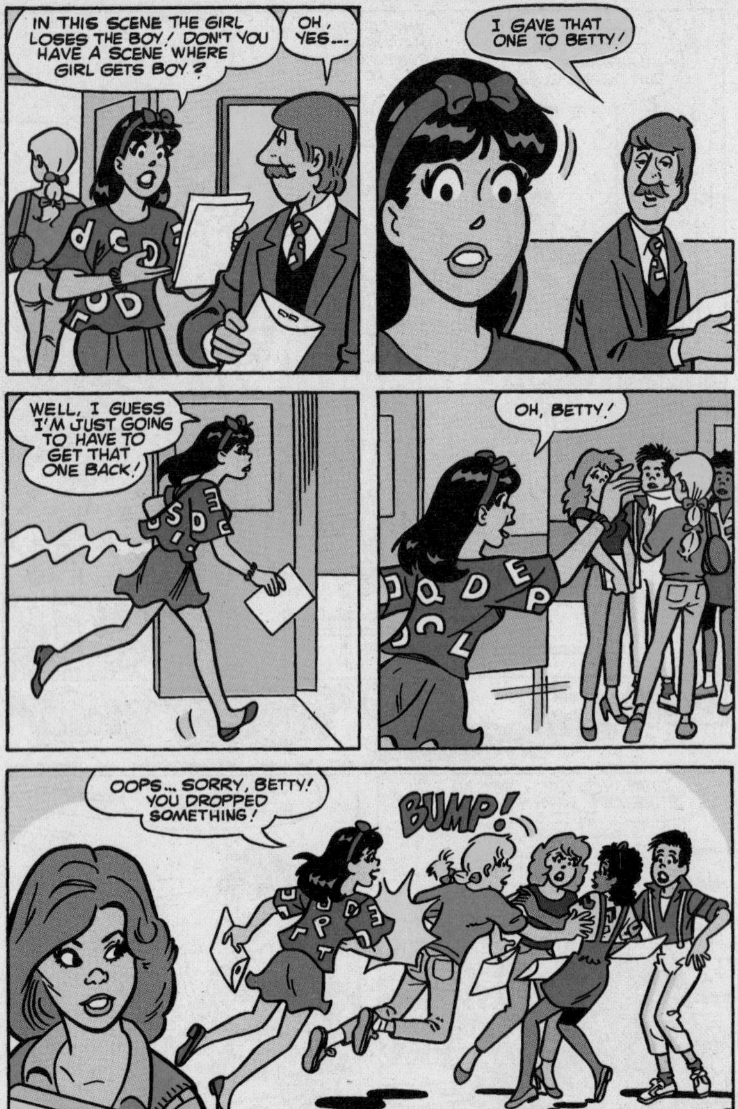
IN THIS SCENE THE GIRL LOSES THE BOY! DON'T YOU HAVE A SCENE WHERE GIRL GETS BOY?
OH, YES...
I GAVE THAT ONE TO BETTY!
WELL, I GUESS I'M JUST GOING TO HAVE TO GET THAT ONE BACK!
OH, BETTY!
OOPS... SORRY, BETTY! YOU DROPPED SOMETHING!
BUMP!
2

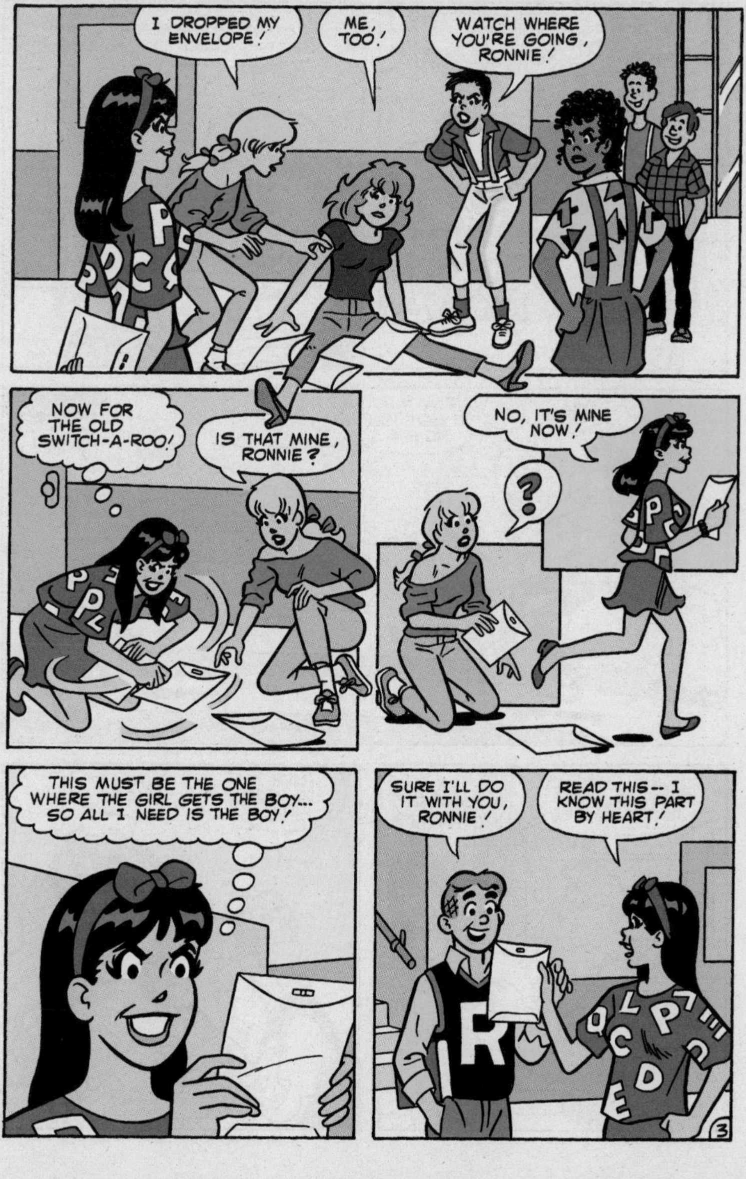
I DROPPED MY ENVELOPE!
ME, TOO!
WATCH WHERE YOU'RE GOING, RONNIE!
NOW FOR THE OLD SWITCH-A-ROO!
IS THAT MINE, RONNIE?
NO, IT'S MINE NOW!
?
THIS MUST BE THE ONE WHERE THE GIRL GETS THE BOY... SO ALL I NEED IS THE BOY!
SURE I'LL DO IT WITH YOU, RONNIE!
READ THIS-- I KNOW THIS PART BY HEART!
3

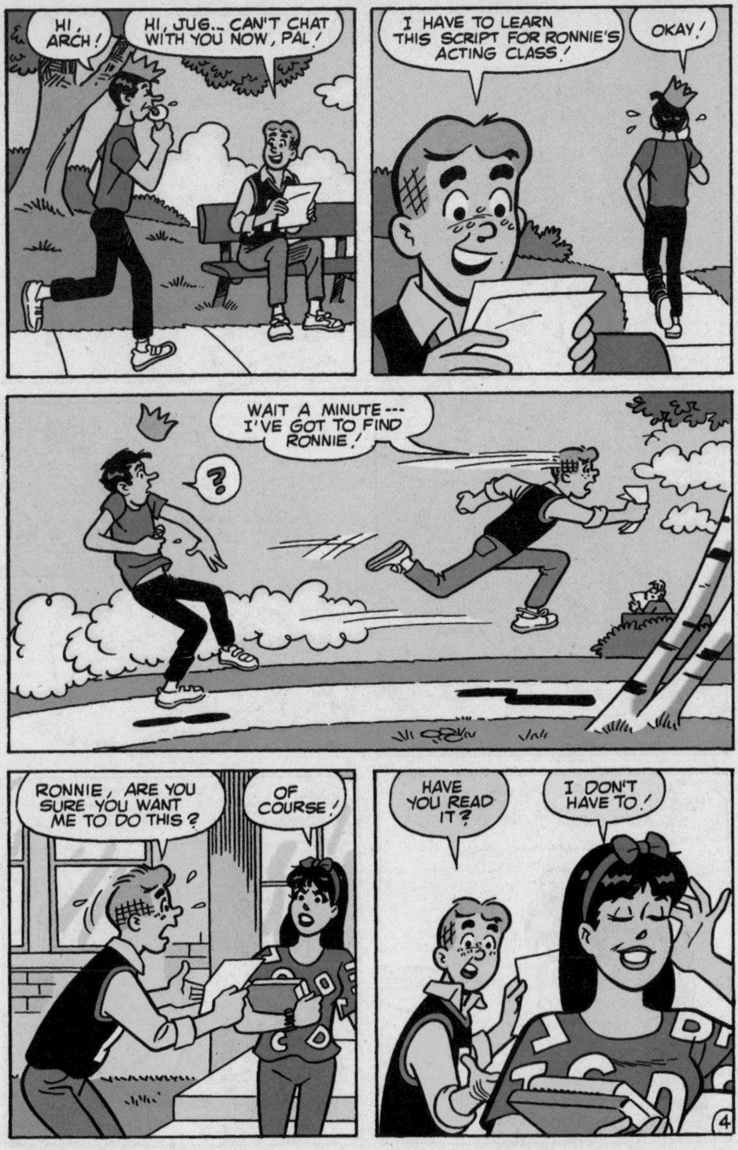
HI, ARCH!
HI, JUG... CAN'T CHAT WITH YOU NOW, PAL!
I HAVE TO LEARN THIS SCRIPT FOR RONNIE'S ACTING CLASS!
OKAY!
WAIT A MINUTE--- I'VE GOT TO FIND RONNIE!
?
RONNIE, ARE YOU SURE YOU WANT ME TO DO THIS?
OF COURSE!
HAVE YOU READ IT?
I DON'T HAVE TO!
4

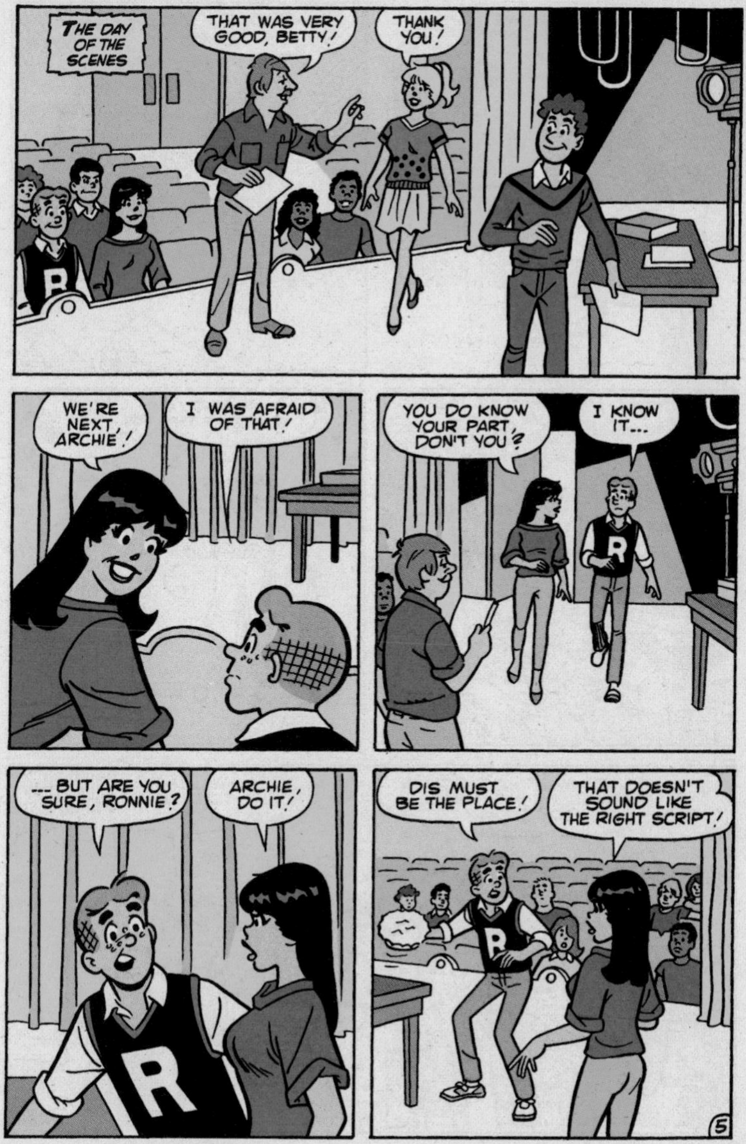
THE DAY OF THE SCENES
THAT WAS VERY GOOD, BETTY!
THANK YOU!
WE'RE NEXT, ARCHIE!
I WAS AFRAID OF THAT!
YOU DO KNOW YOUR PART, DON'T YOU?
I KNOW IT...
...BUT ARE YOU SURE, RONNIE?
ARCHIE, DO IT!
DIS MUST BE THE PLACE!
THAT DOESN'T SOUND LIKE THE RIGHT SCRIPT!
5

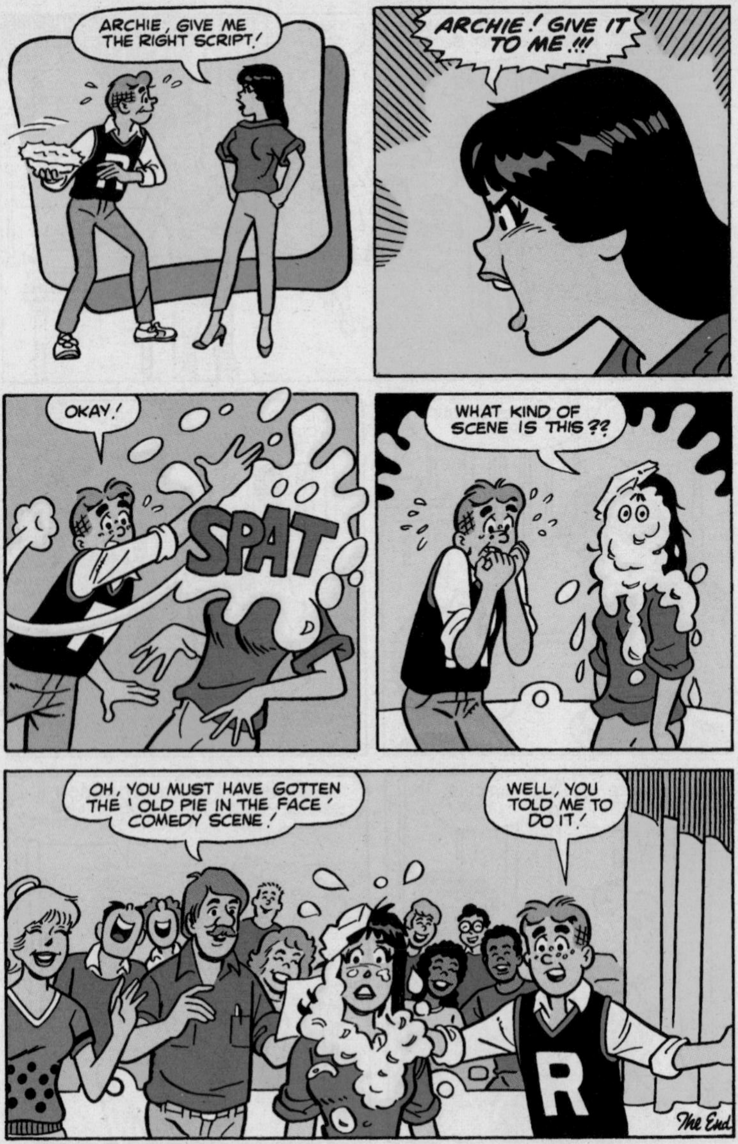
ARCHIE, GIVE ME THE RIGHT SCRIPT!
ARCHIE! GIVE IT TO ME!!!
OKAY!
SPAT
WHAT KIND OF SCENE IS THIS??
OH, YOU MUST HAVE GOTTEN THE 'OLD PIE IN THE FACE' COMEDY SCENE!
WELL, YOU TOLD ME TO DO IT!
The End

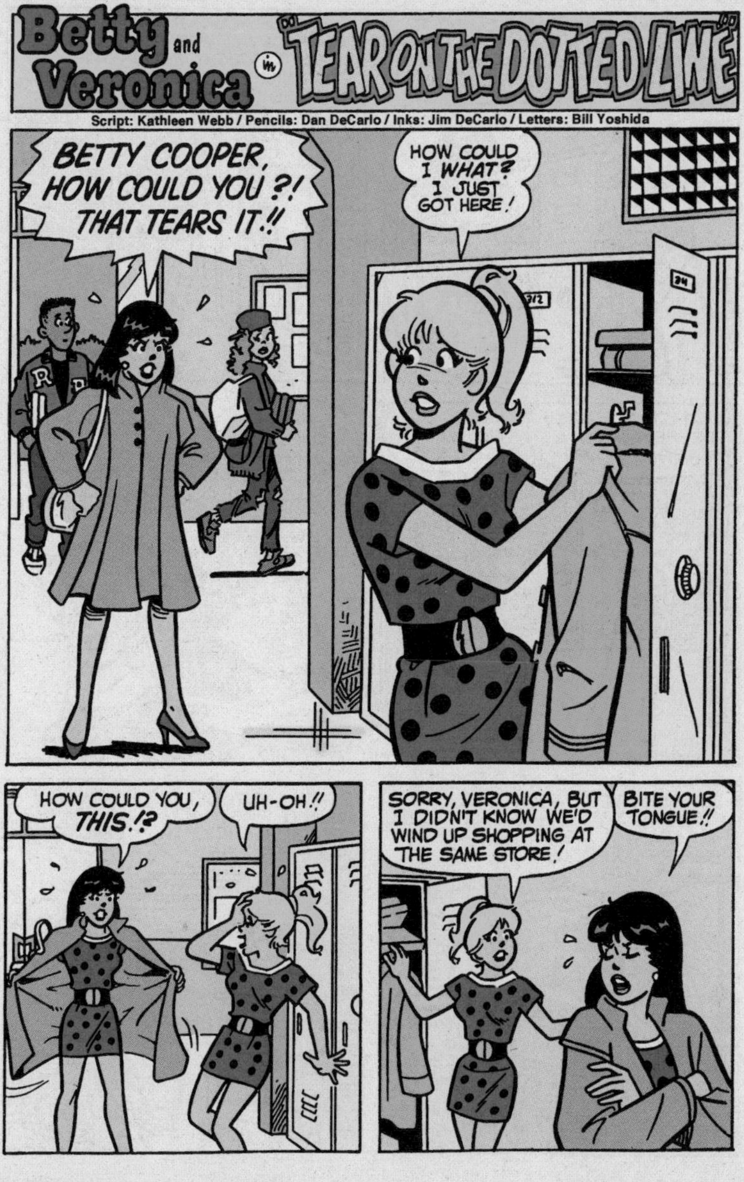
Betty and Veronica in
"TEAR ON THE DOTTED LINE"
Script: Kathleen Webb / Pencils: Dan DeCarlo / Inks: Jim DeCarlo / Letters: Bill Yoshida
BETTY COOPER, HOW COULD YOU ?! THAT TEARS IT.!!
HOW COULD I WHAT? I JUST GOT HERE!
HOW COULD YOU, THIS.!?
UH-OH.!!
SORRY, VERONICA, BUT I DIDN'T KNOW WE'D WIND UP SHOPPING AT THE SAME STORE!
BITE YOUR TONGUE.!!

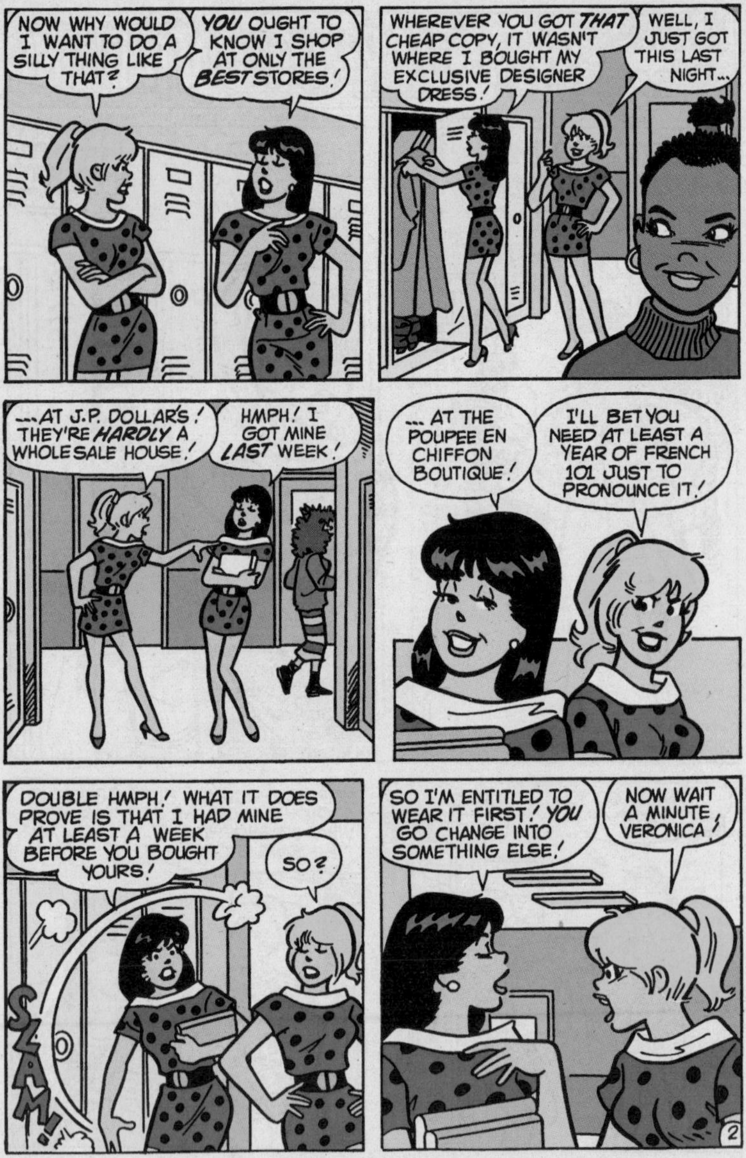
NOW WHY WOULD I WANT TO DO A SILLY THING LIKE THAT?
YOU OUGHT TO KNOW I SHOP AT ONLY THE BEST STORES!
WHEREVER YOU GOT THAT CHEAP COPY, IT WASN'T WHERE I BOUGHT MY EXCLUSIVE DESIGNER DRESS!
WELL, I JUST GOT THIS LAST NIGHT...
...AT J.P. DOLLAR'S! THEY'RE HARDLY A WHOLESALE HOUSE!
HMPH! I GOT MINE LAST WEEK!
... AT THE POUPEE EN CHIFFON BOUTIQUE!
I'LL BET YOU NEED AT LEAST A YEAR OF FRENCH 101 JUST TO PRONOUNCE IT!
DOUBLE HMPH! WHAT IT DOES PROVE IS THAT I HAD MINE AT LEAST A WEEK BEFORE YOU BOUGHT YOURS!
SO?
SLAM!
SO I'M ENTITLED TO WEAR IT FIRST! YOU GO CHANGE INTO SOMETHING ELSE!
NOW WAIT A MINUTE, VERONICA!
2

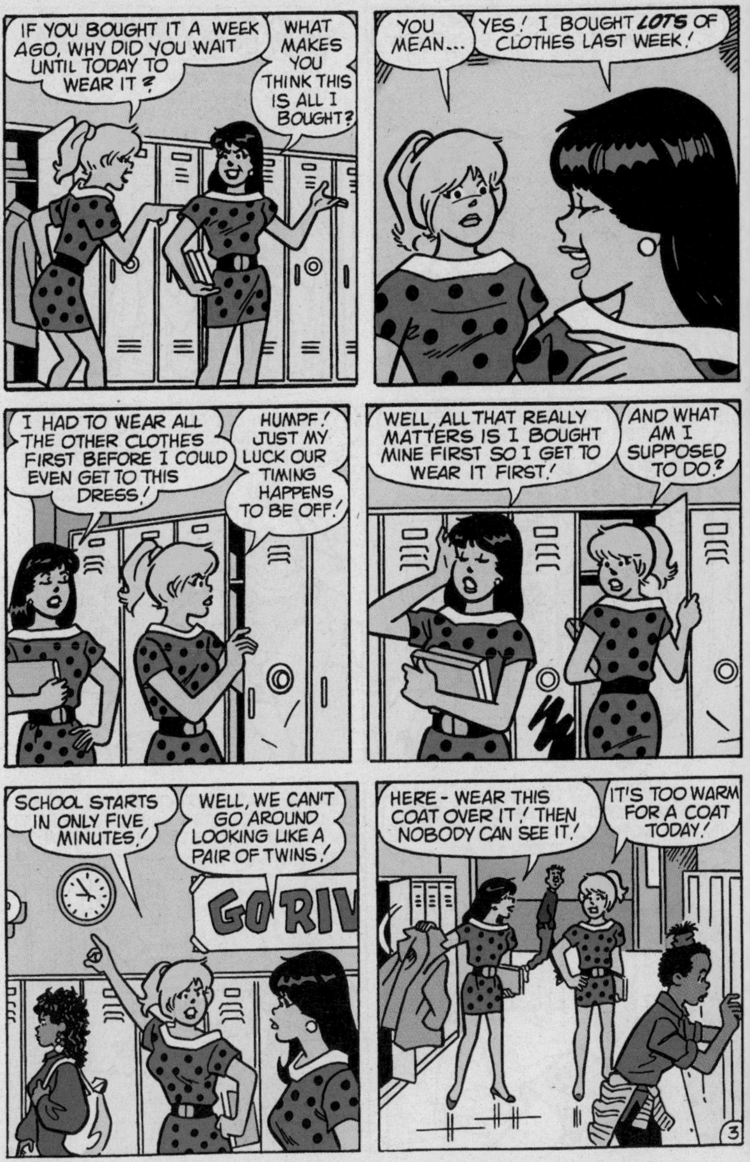
IF YOU BOUGHT IT A WEEK AGO, WHY DID YOU WAIT UNTIL TODAY TO WEAR IT?
WHAT MAKES YOU THINK THIS IS ALL I BOUGHT?
YOU MEAN...
YES! I BOUGHT LOTS OF CLOTHES LAST WEEK!
I HAD TO WEAR ALL THE OTHER CLOTHES FIRST BEFORE I COULD EVEN GET TO THIS DRESS!
HUMPF! JUST MY LUCK OUR TIMING HAPPENS TO BE OFF!
WELL, ALL THAT REALLY MATTERS IS I BOUGHT MINE FIRST SO I GET TO WEAR IT FIRST!
AND WHAT AM I SUPPOSED TO DO?
SCHOOL STARTS IN ONLY FIVE MINUTES!
WELL, WE CAN'T GO AROUND LOOKING LIKE A PAIR OF TWINS!
GO RIV
HERE - WEAR THIS COAT OVER IT! THEN NOBODY CAN SEE IT!
IT'S TOO WARM FOR A COAT TODAY!
3

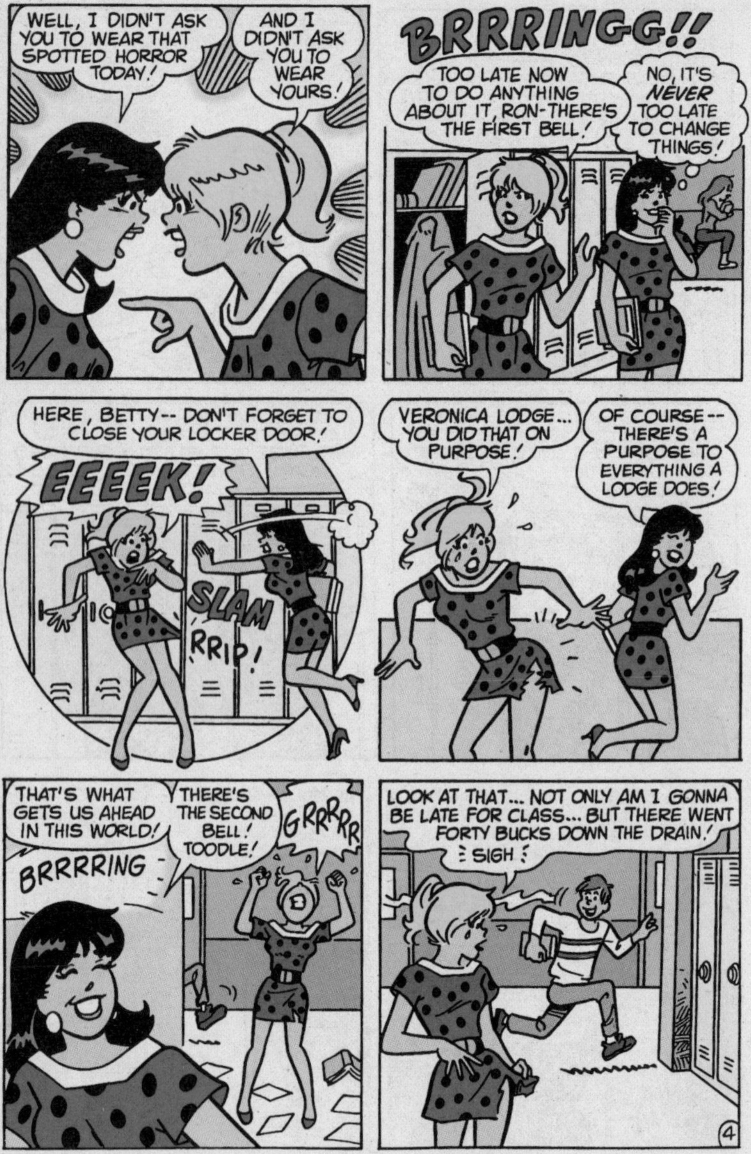
WELL, I DIDN'T ASK YOU TO WEAR THAT SPOTTED HORROR TODAY!
AND I DIDN'T ASK YOU TO WEAR YOURS!
BRRRINGG!!
TOO LATE NOW TO DO ANYTHING ABOUT IT, RON-THERE'S THE FIRST BELL!
NO, IT'S NEVER TOO LATE TO CHANGE THINGS!
HERE, BETTY-- DON'T FORGET TO CLOSE YOUR LOCKER DOOR!
EEEEK!
SLAM
RRIP!
VERONICA LODGE... YOU DID THAT ON PURPOSE!
OF COURSE -- THERE'S A PURPOSE TO EVERYTHING A LODGE DOES!
THAT'S WHAT GETS US AHEAD IN THIS WORLD!
BRRRRING
THERE'S THE SECOND BELL! TOODLE!
GRRRRR
LOOK AT THAT... NOT ONLY AM I GONNA BE LATE FOR CLASS... BUT THERE WENT FORTY BUCKS DOWN THE DRAIN!
SIGH
4

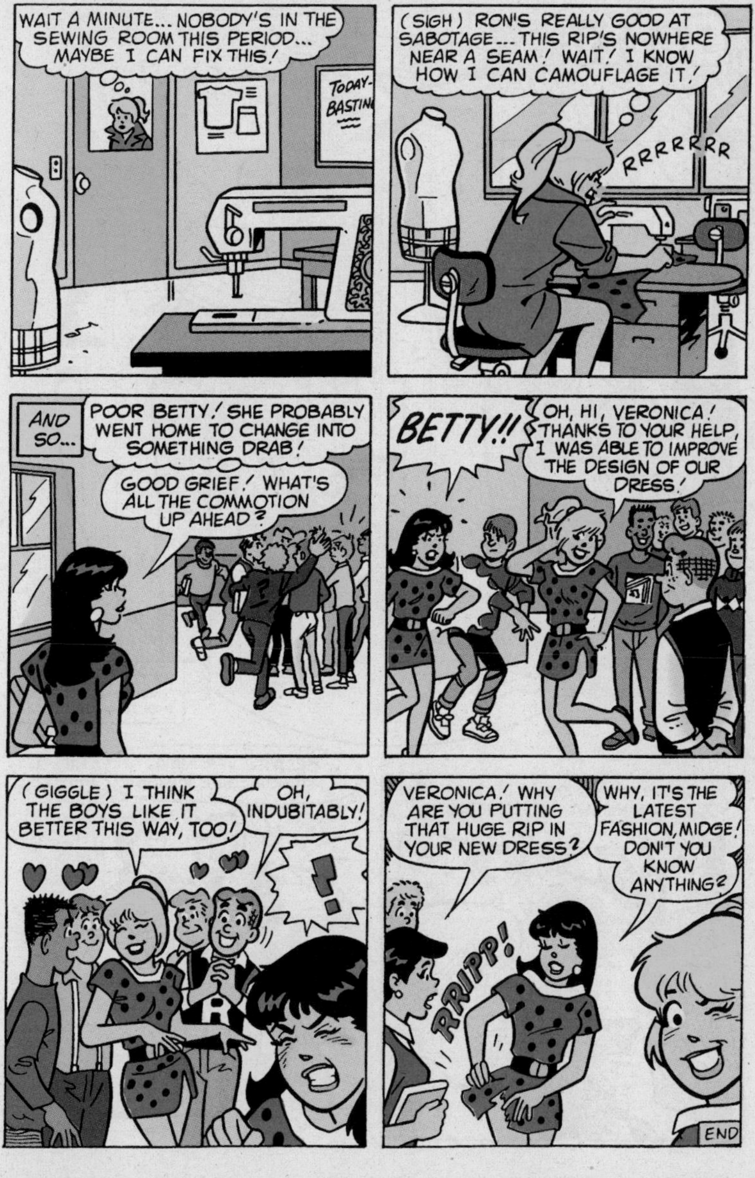
WAIT A MINUTE... NOBODY'S IN THE SEWING ROOM THIS PERIOD... MAYBE I CAN FIX THIS!
TODAY- BASTING
(SIGH) RON'S REALLY GOOD AT SABOTAGE... THIS RIP'S NOWHERE NEAR A SEAM! WAIT! I KNOW HOW I CAN CAMOUFLAGE IT!
RRRRRRR
AND SO...
POOR BETTY! SHE PROBABLY WENT HOME TO CHANGE INTO SOMETHING DRAB!
GOOD GRIEF! WHAT'S ALL THE COMMOTION UP AHEAD?
BETTY!!
OH, HI, VERONICA! THANKS TO YOUR HELP, I WAS ABLE TO IMPROVE THE DESIGN OF OUR DRESS!
(GIGGLE) I THINK THE BOYS LIKE IT BETTER THIS WAY, TOO!
OH, INDUBITABLY!
VERONICA! WHY ARE YOU PUTTING THAT HUGE RIP IN YOUR NEW DRESS?
RRIPP!
WHY, IT'S THE LATEST FASHION, MIDGE! DON'T YOU KNOW ANYTHING?
END

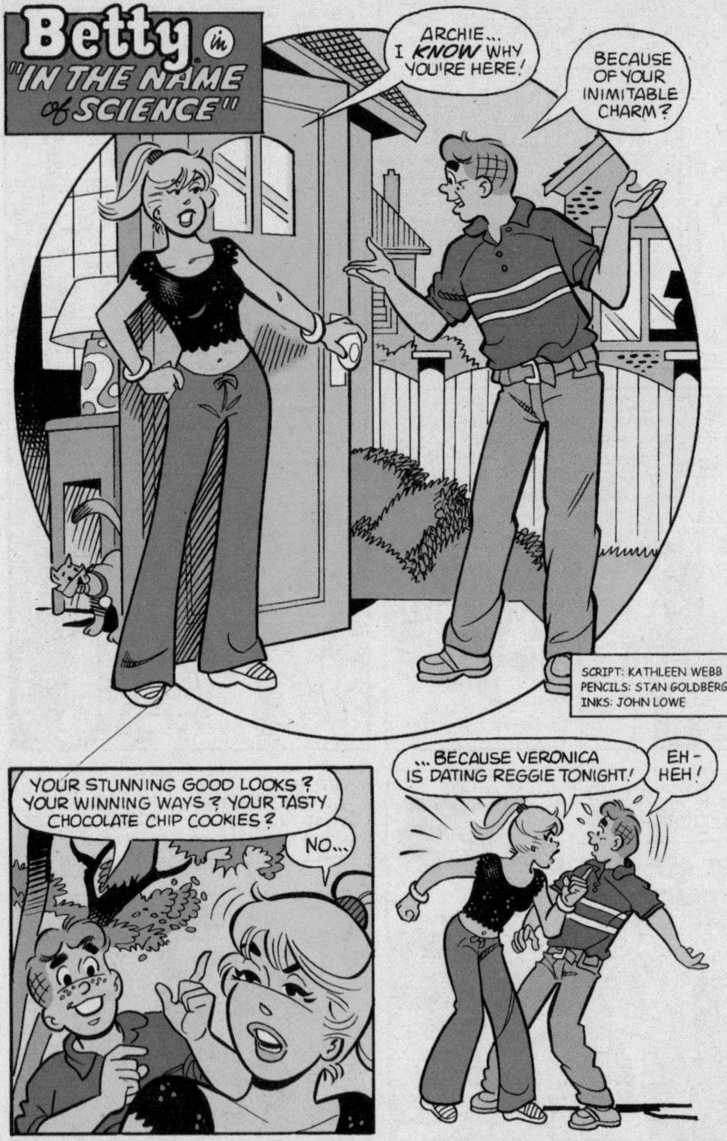
Betty in
"IN THE NAME of SCIENCE"
ARCHIE... I KNOW WHY YOU'RE HERE!
BECAUSE OF YOUR INIMITABLE CHARM?
SCRIPT: KATHLEEN WEBB
PENCILS: STAN GOLDBERG
INKS: JOHN LOWE
YOUR STUNNING GOOD LOOKS? YOUR WINNING WAYS? YOUR TASTY CHOCOLATE CHIP COOKIES?
NO...
...BECAUSE VERONICA IS DATING REGGIE TONIGHT!
EH-HEH!

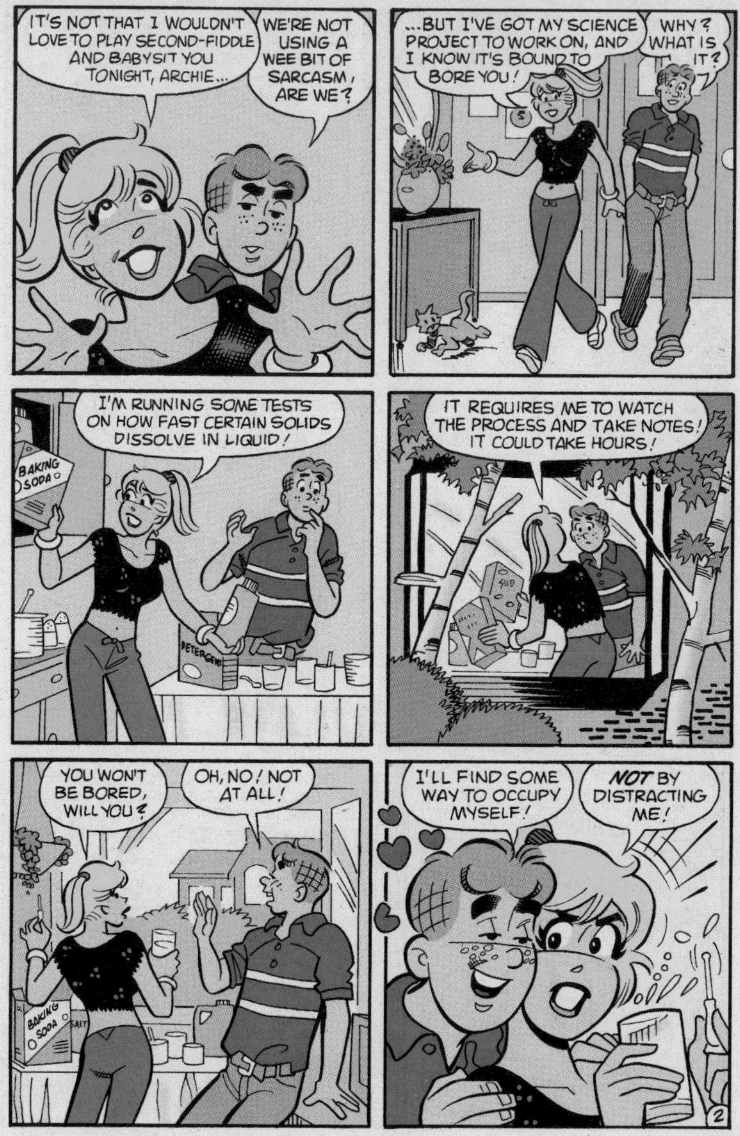
IT'S NOT THAT I WOULDN'T LOVE TO PLAY SECOND-FIDDLE AND BABYSIT YOU TONIGHT, ARCHIE...
WE'RE NOT USING A WEE BIT OF SARCASM, ARE WE?
...BUT I'VE GOT MY SCIENCE PROJECT TO WORK ON, AND I KNOW IT'S BOUND TO BORE YOU!
WHY? WHAT IS IT?
I'M RUNNING SOME TESTS ON HOW FAST CERTAIN SOLIDS DISSOLVE IN LIQUID!
BAKING SODA
DETERGENT
IT REQUIRES ME TO WATCH THE PROCESS AND TAKE NOTES! IT COULD TAKE HOURS!
YOU WON'T BE BORED, WILL YOU?
OH, NO! NOT AT ALL!
BAKING SODA
SALT
I'LL FIND SOME WAY TO OCCUPY MYSELF!
NOT BY DISTRACTING ME!
2

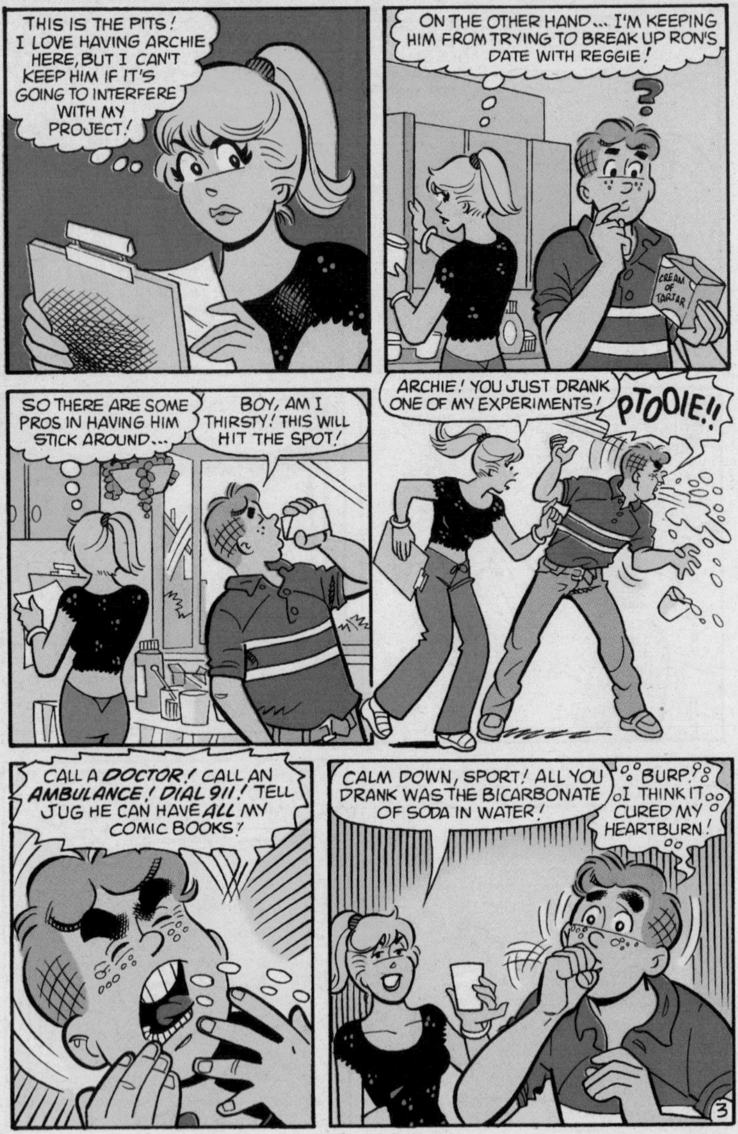

THIS IS THE PITS! I LOVE HAVING ARCHIE HERE, BUT I CAN'T KEEP HIM IF IT'S GOING TO INTERFERE WITH MY PROJECT!
ON THE OTHER HAND... I'M KEEPING HIM FROM TRYING TO BREAK UP RON'S DATE WITH REGGIE!
?
CREAM OF TARTAR
SO THERE ARE SOME PROS IN HAVING HIM STICK AROUND...
BOY, AM I THIRSTY! THIS WILL HIT THE SPOT!
ARCHIE! YOU JUST DRANK ONE OF MY EXPERIMENTS!
PTOOIE!!
CALL A *DOCTOR*! CALL AN *AMBULANCE*! *DIAL 911*! TELL JUG HE CAN HAVE *ALL* MY COMIC BOOKS!
CALM DOWN, SPORT! ALL YOU DRANK WAS THE BICARBONATE OF SODA IN WATER!
BURP! I THINK IT CURED MY HEARTBURN!
3

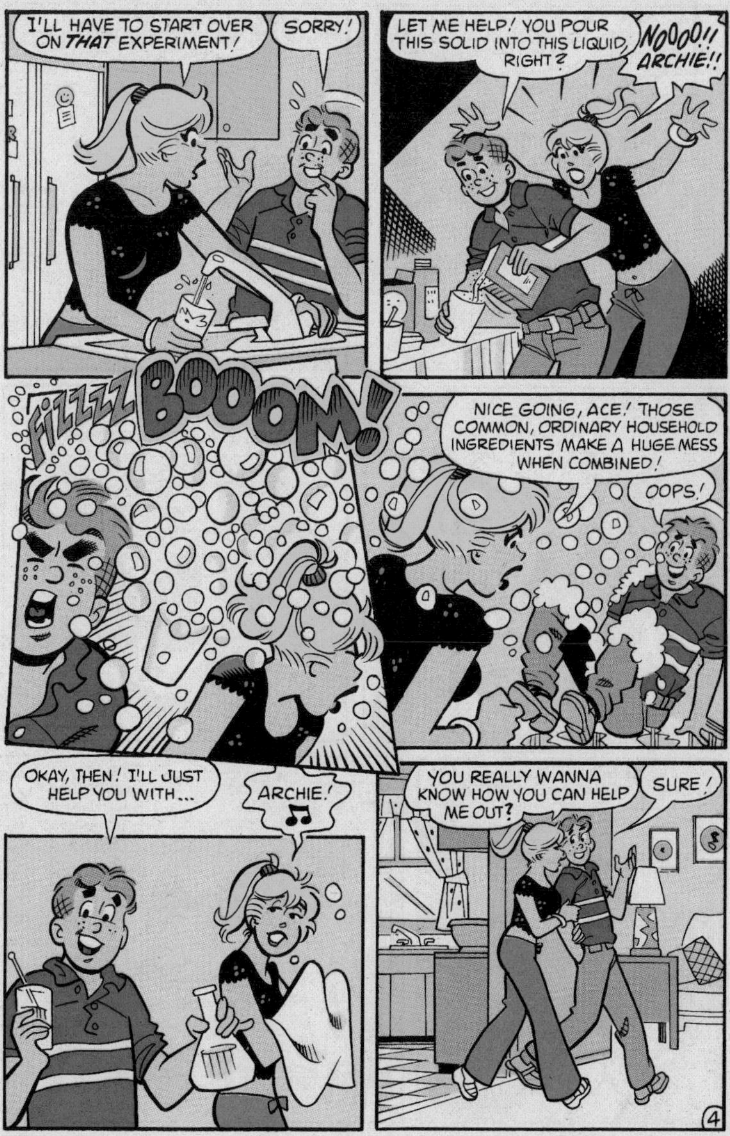

I'LL HAVE TO START OVER ON *THAT* EXPERIMENT!
SORRY!
LET ME HELP! YOU POUR THIS SOLID INTO THIS LIQUID, RIGHT?
NOOOO!! ARCHIE!!
FIZZZZ BOOOM!
NICE GOING, ACE! THOSE COMMON, ORDINARY HOUSEHOLD INGREDIENTS MAKE A HUGE MESS WHEN COMBINED!
OOPS!
OKAY, THEN! I'LL JUST HELP YOU WITH...
ARCHIE! ♫
YOU REALLY WANNA KNOW HOW YOU CAN HELP ME OUT?
SURE!
4

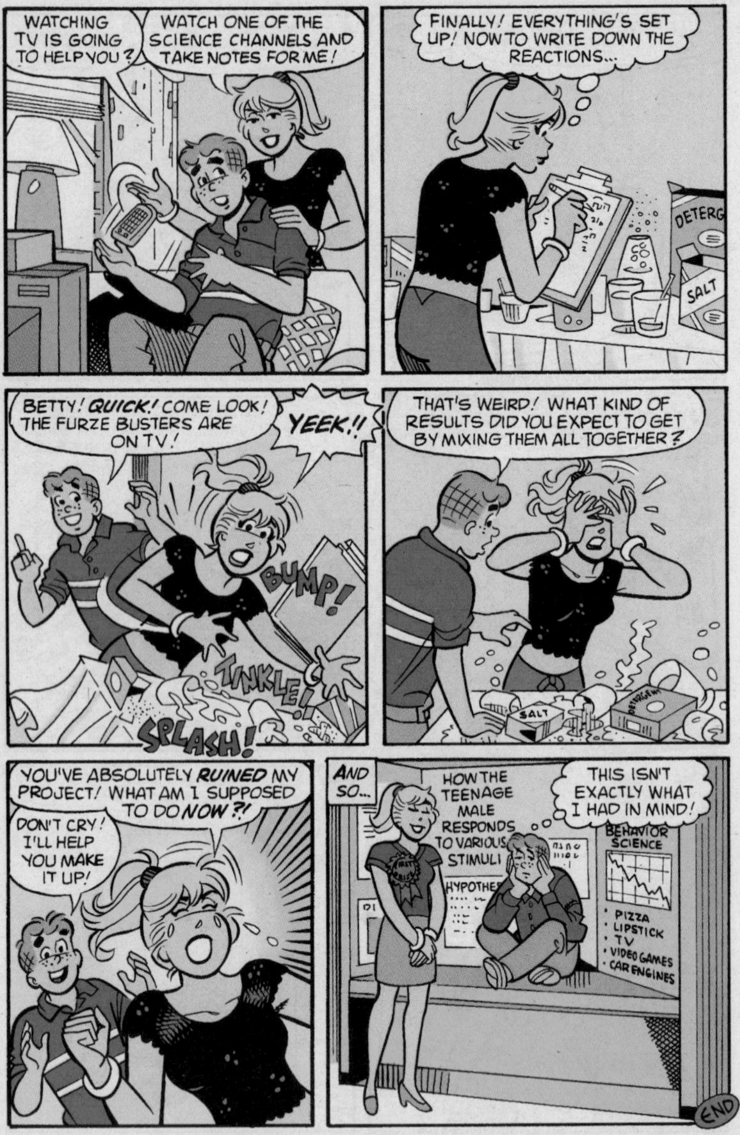
WATCHING TV IS GOING TO HELP YOU?
WATCH ONE OF THE SCIENCE CHANNELS AND TAKE NOTES FOR ME!
FINALLY! EVERYTHING'S SET UP! NOW TO WRITE DOWN THE REACTIONS...
DETERG
SALT
BETTY! QUICK! COME LOOK! THE FURZE BUSTERS ARE ON TV!
YEEK!!
BUMP!
TINKLE!
SPLASH!
THAT'S WEIRD! WHAT KIND OF RESULTS DID YOU EXPECT TO GET BY MIXING THEM ALL TOGETHER?
SALT
YOU'VE ABSOLUTELY RUINED MY PROJECT! WHAT AM I SUPPOSED TO DO NOW?!
DON'T CRY! I'LL HELP YOU MAKE IT UP!
AND SO...
HOW THE TEENAGE MALE RESPONDS TO VARIOUS STIMULI
THIS ISN'T EXACTLY WHAT I HAD IN MIND!
BEHAVIOR SCIENCE
HYPOTHE
• PIZZA
• LIPSTICK
• TV
• VIDEO GAMES
• CAR ENGINES
END

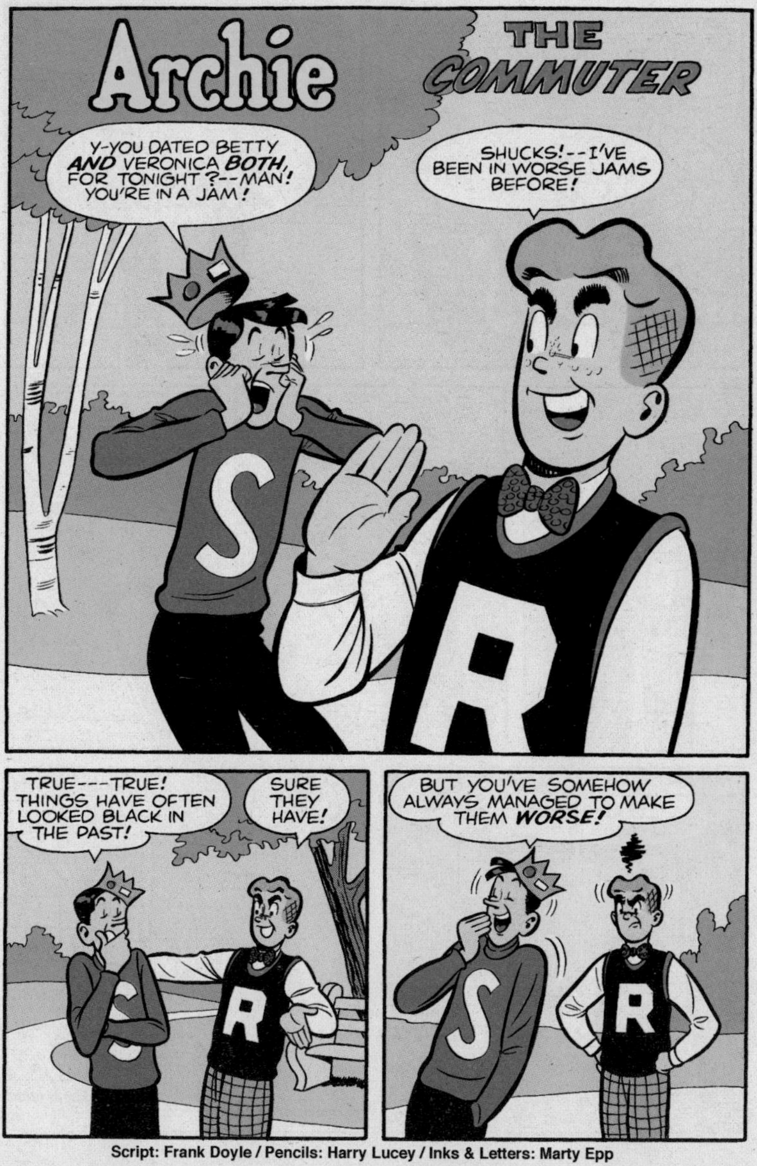
Archie
THE COMMUTER
Y-YOU DATED BETTY AND VERONICA BOTH, FOR TONIGHT ?--MAN! YOU'RE IN A JAM!
SHUCKS!--I'VE BEEN IN WORSE JAMS BEFORE!
TRUE---TRUE! THINGS HAVE OFTEN LOOKED BLACK IN THE PAST!
SURE THEY HAVE!
BUT YOU'VE SOMEHOW ALWAYS MANAGED TO MAKE THEM WORSE!

Script: Frank Doyle / Pencils: Harry Lucey / Inks & Letters: Marty Epp

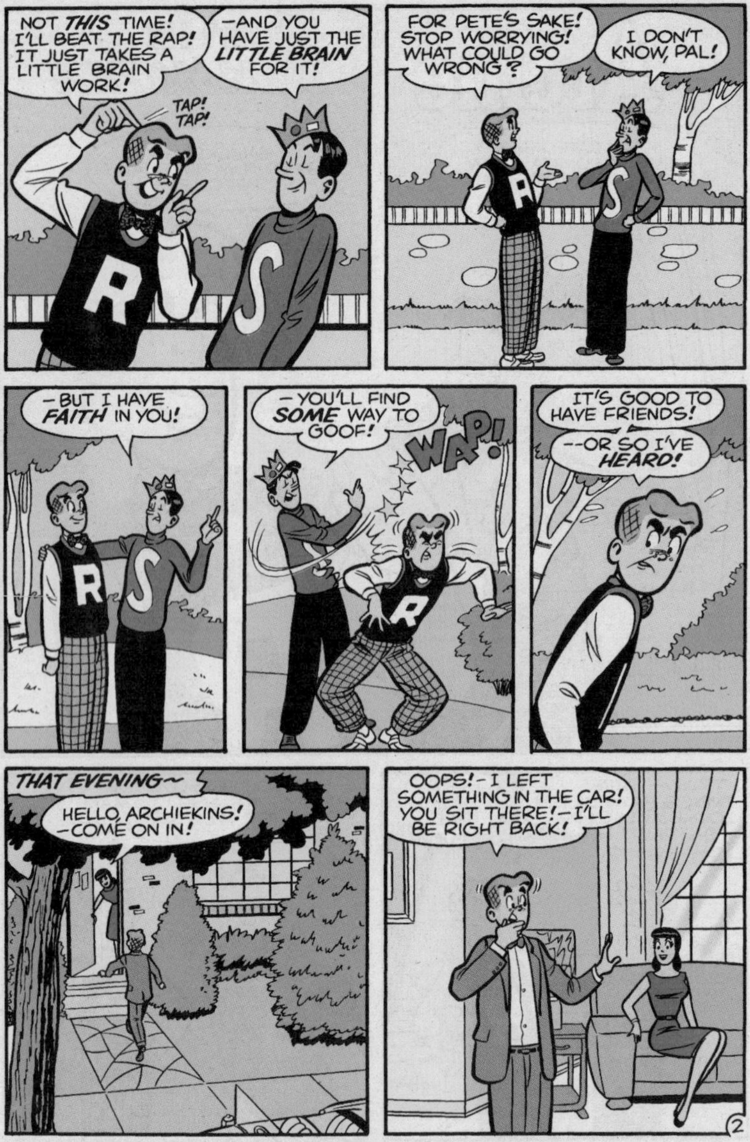
NOT THIS TIME! I'LL BEAT THE RAP! IT JUST TAKES A LITTLE BRAIN WORK!
TAP! TAP!
—AND YOU HAVE JUST THE LITTLE BRAIN FOR IT!
FOR PETE'S SAKE! STOP WORRYING! WHAT COULD GO WRONG?
I DON'T KNOW, PAL!
—BUT I HAVE FAITH IN YOU!
—YOU'LL FIND SOME WAY TO GOOF!
WAP!
IT'S GOOD TO HAVE FRIENDS!
--OR SO I'VE HEARD!
THAT EVENING~
HELLO, ARCHIEKINS! —COME ON IN!
OOPS!—I LEFT SOMETHING IN THE CAR! YOU SIT THERE!—I'LL BE RIGHT BACK!
2

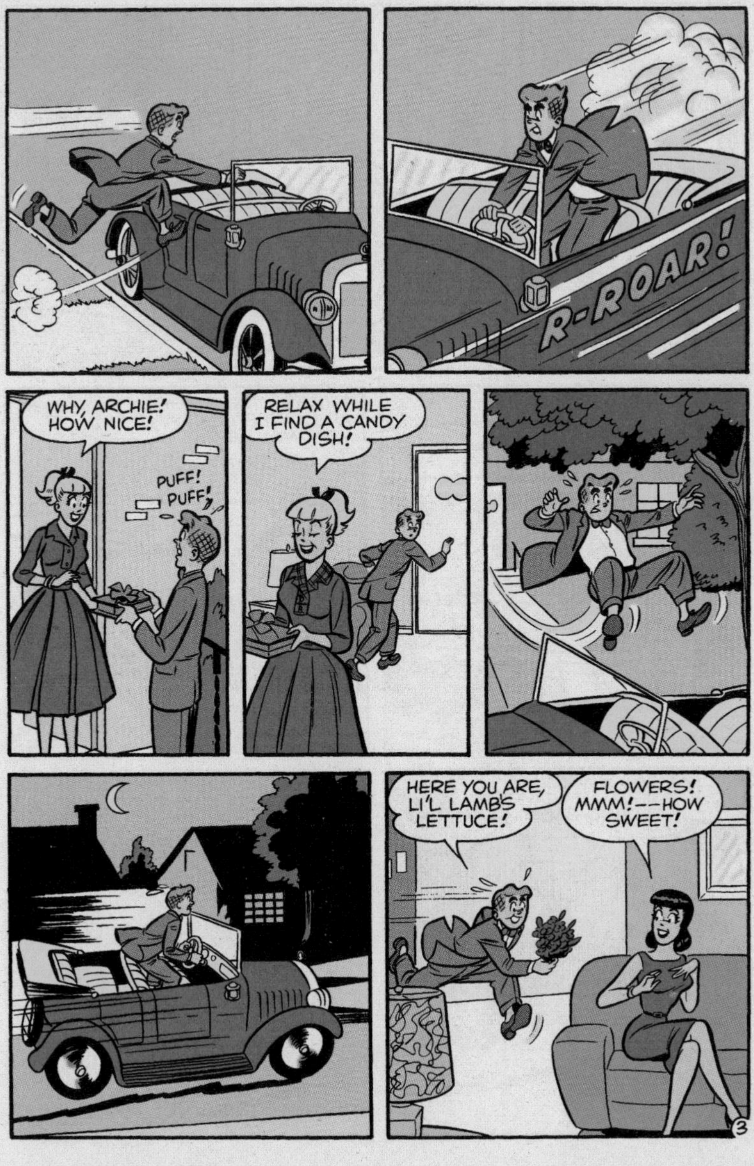
R-ROAR!
WHY, ARCHIE! HOW NICE!
PUFF! PUFF!
RELAX WHILE I FIND A CANDY DISH!
HERE YOU ARE, LI'L LAMB'S LETTUCE!
FLOWERS! MMM!--HOW SWEET!
3

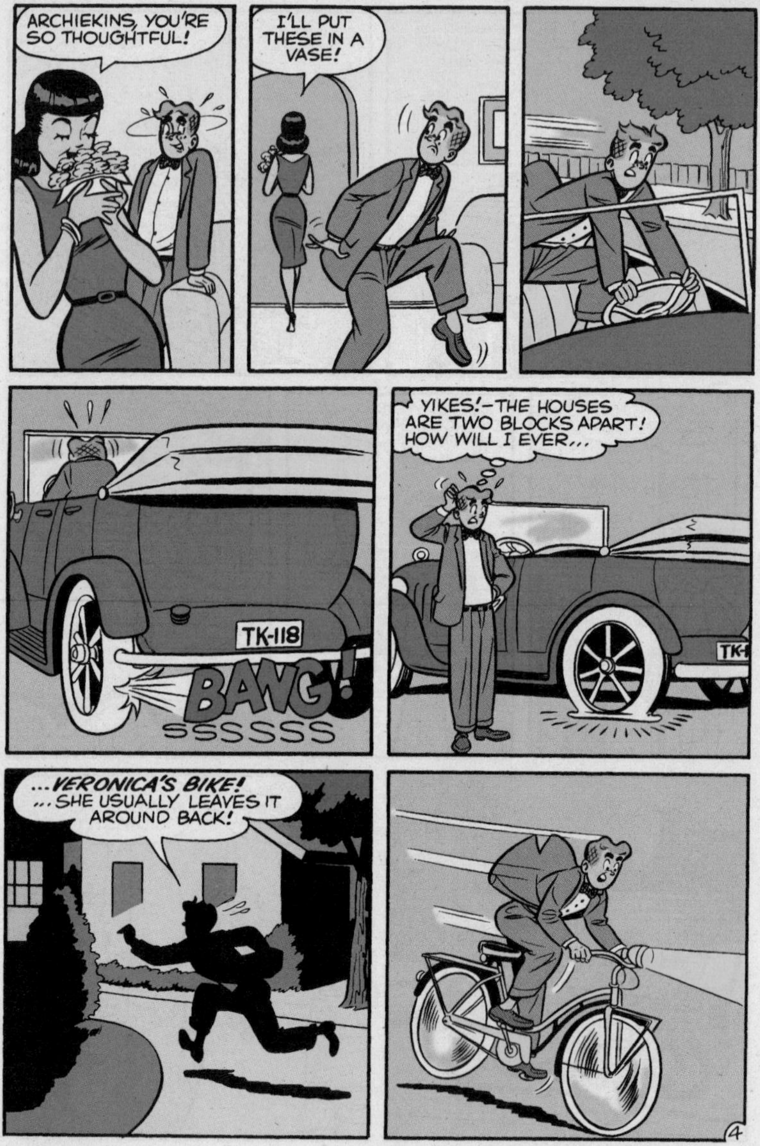
ARCHIEKINS, YOU'RE SO THOUGHTFUL!
I'LL PUT THESE IN A VASE!
TK-118
BANG!
SSSSSS
YIKES!—THE HOUSES ARE TWO BLOCKS APART! HOW WILL I EVER...
...VERONICA'S BIKE! ...SHE USUALLY LEAVES IT AROUND BACK!
4

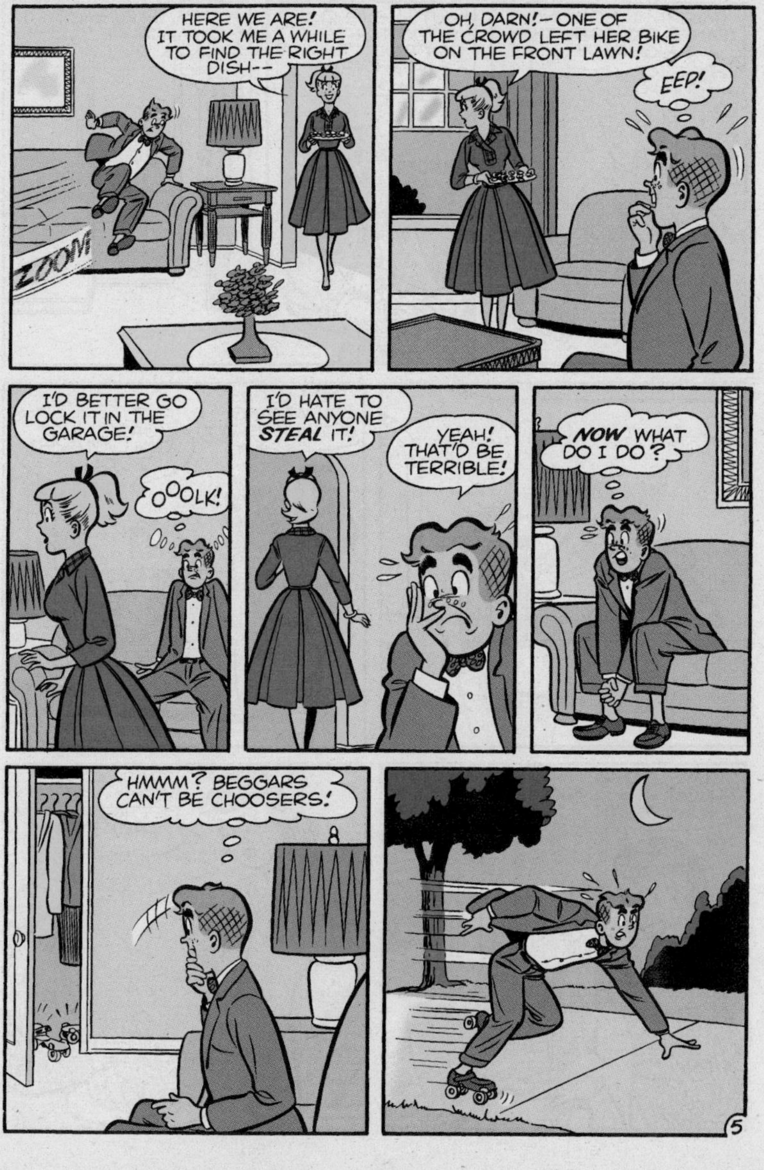
HERE WE ARE! IT TOOK ME A WHILE TO FIND THE RIGHT DISH--
ZOOM
OH, DARN!—ONE OF THE CROWD LEFT HER BIKE ON THE FRONT LAWN!
EEP!
I'D BETTER GO LOCK IT IN THE GARAGE!
OOOLK!
I'D HATE TO SEE ANYONE STEAL IT!
YEAH! THAT'D BE TERRIBLE!
NOW WHAT DO I DO?
HMMM? BEGGARS CAN'T BE CHOOSERS!
5

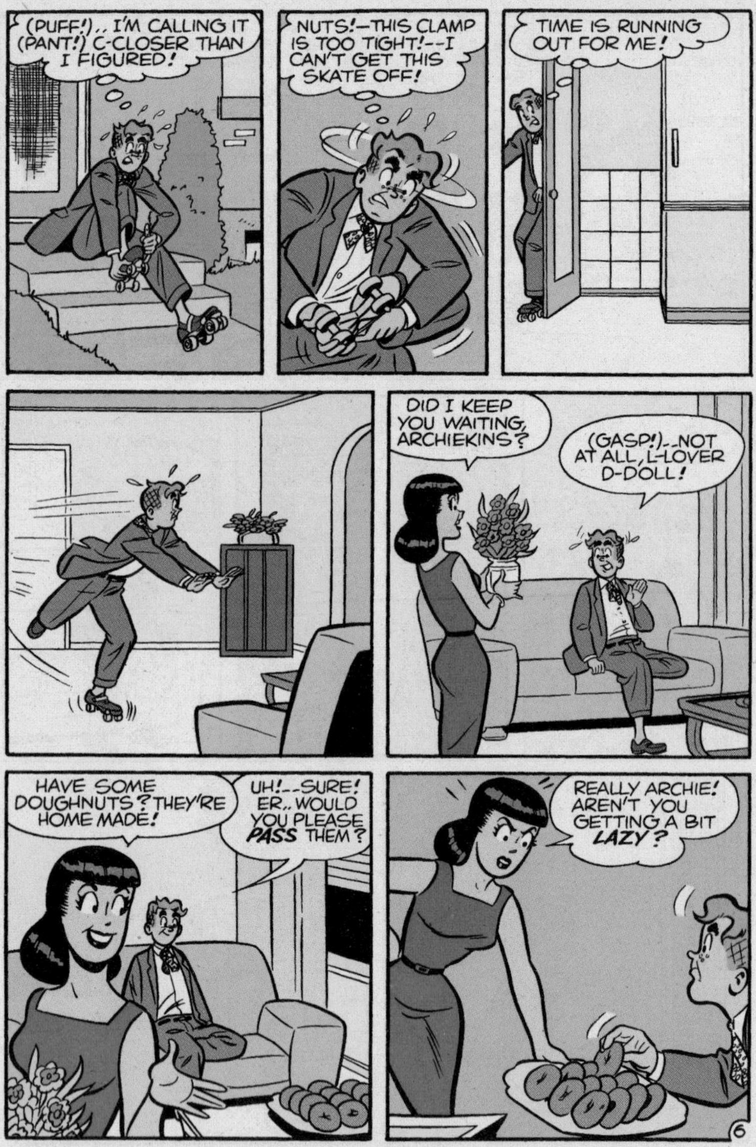
(PUFF!).. I'M CALLING IT (PANT!) C-CLOSER THAN I FIGURED!
NUTS!—THIS CLAMP IS TOO TIGHT!--I CAN'T GET THIS SKATE OFF!
TIME IS RUNNING OUT FOR ME!
DID I KEEP YOU WAITING, ARCHIEKINS?
(GASP!)--NOT AT ALL, L-LOVER D-DOLL!
HAVE SOME DOUGHNUTS? THEY'RE HOME MADE!
UH!--SURE! ER.. WOULD YOU PLEASE PASS THEM?
REALLY ARCHIE! AREN'T YOU GETTING A BIT LAZY?
6

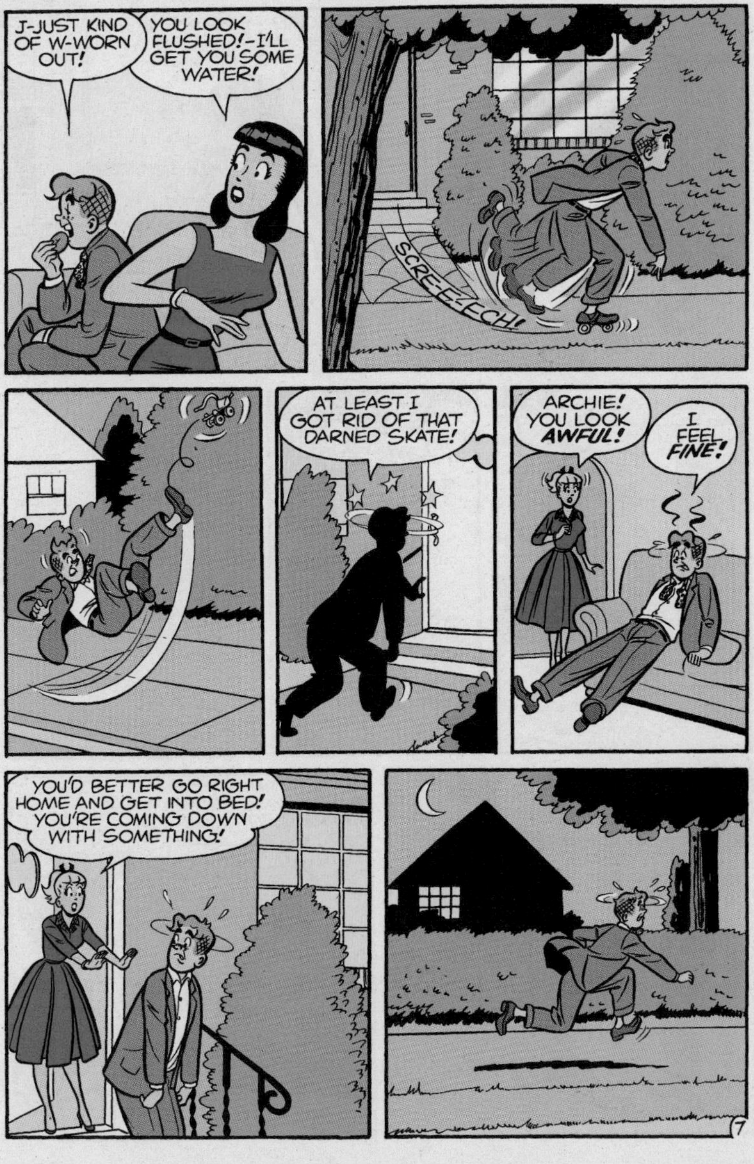
J-JUST KIND OF W-WORN OUT!
YOU LOOK FLUSHED!-I'LL GET YOU SOME WATER!
SCRE-E-ECH!
AT LEAST I GOT RID OF THAT DARNED SKATE!
ARCHIE! YOU LOOK **AWFUL!**
I FEEL **FINE!**
YOU'D BETTER GO RIGHT HOME AND GET INTO BED! YOU'RE COMING DOWN WITH SOMETHING!
7

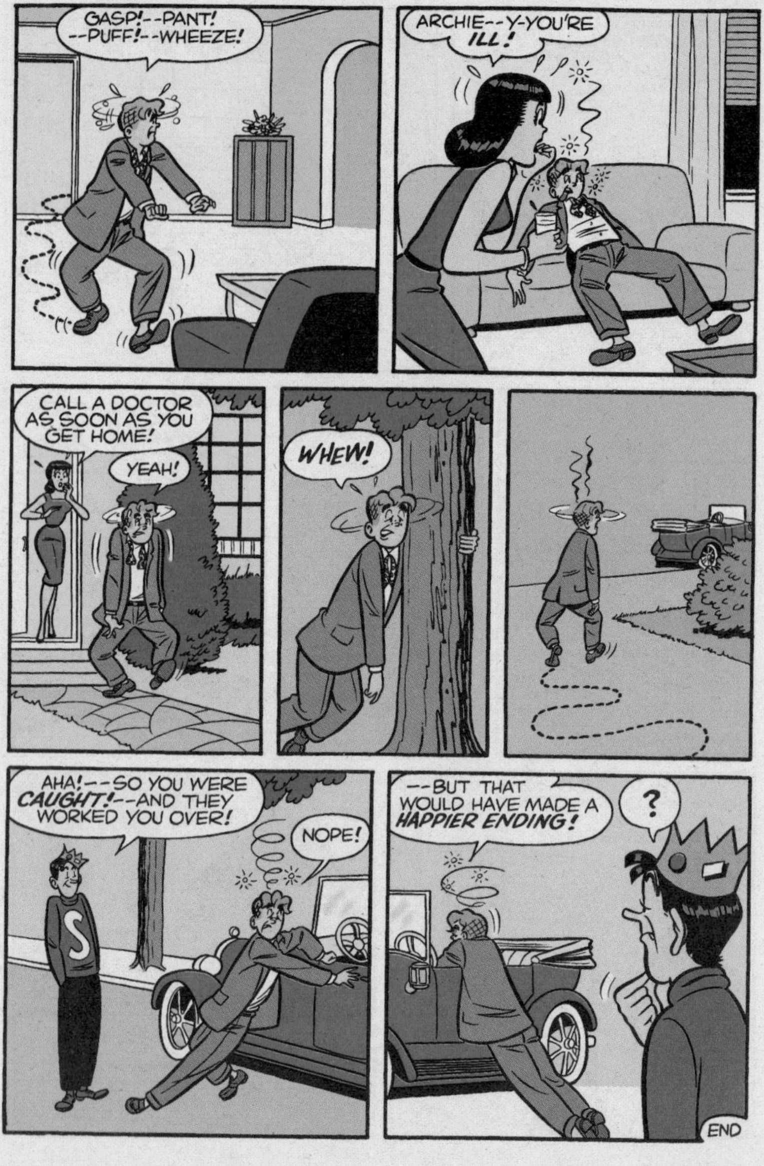
GASP!--PANT! --PUFF!--WHEEZE!
ARCHIE--Y-YOU'RE ILL!
CALL A DOCTOR AS SOON AS YOU GET HOME!
YEAH!
WHEW!
AHA!--SO YOU WERE CAUGHT!--AND THEY WORKED YOU OVER!
NOPE!
--BUT THAT WOULD HAVE MADE A HAPPIER ENDING!
?
END

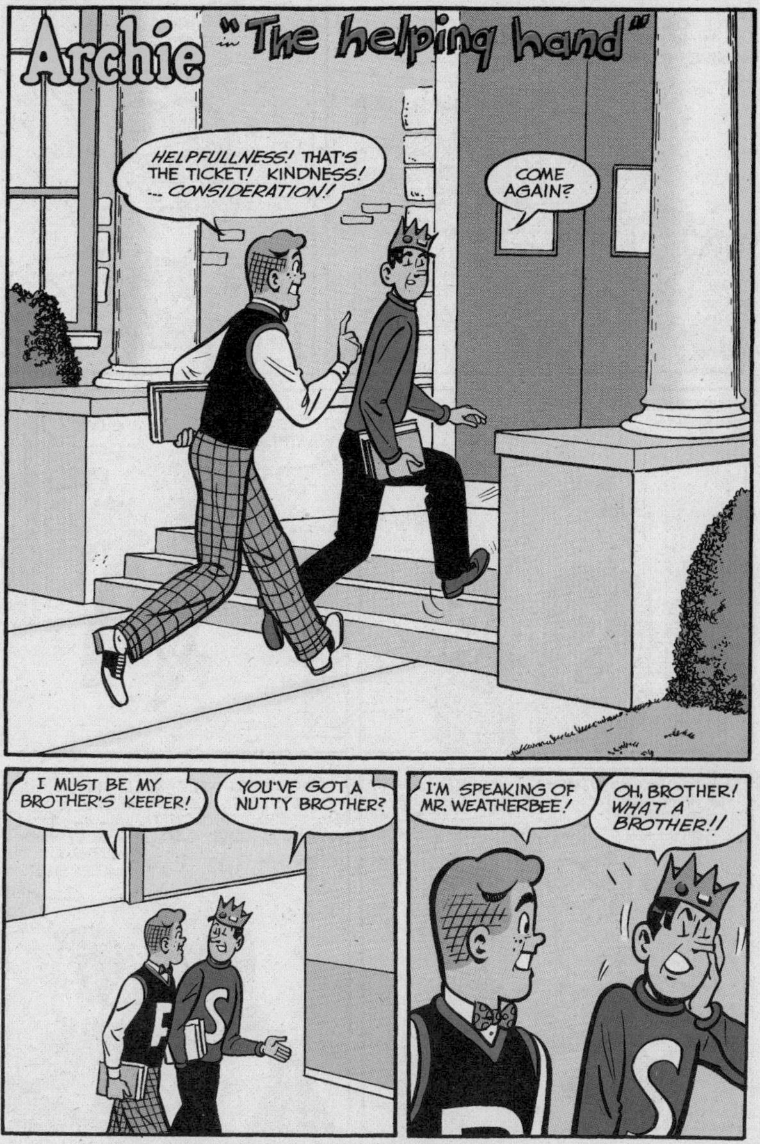
Archie
in "The helping hand"
HELPFULLNESS! THAT'S THE TICKET! KINDNESS! ... CONSIDERATION!
COME AGAIN?
I MUST BE MY BROTHER'S KEEPER!
YOU'VE GOT A NUTTY BROTHER?
I'M SPEAKING OF MR. WEATHERBEE!
OH, BROTHER! WHAT A BROTHER!!

Script: Frank Doyle / Pencils: Bill Vigoda

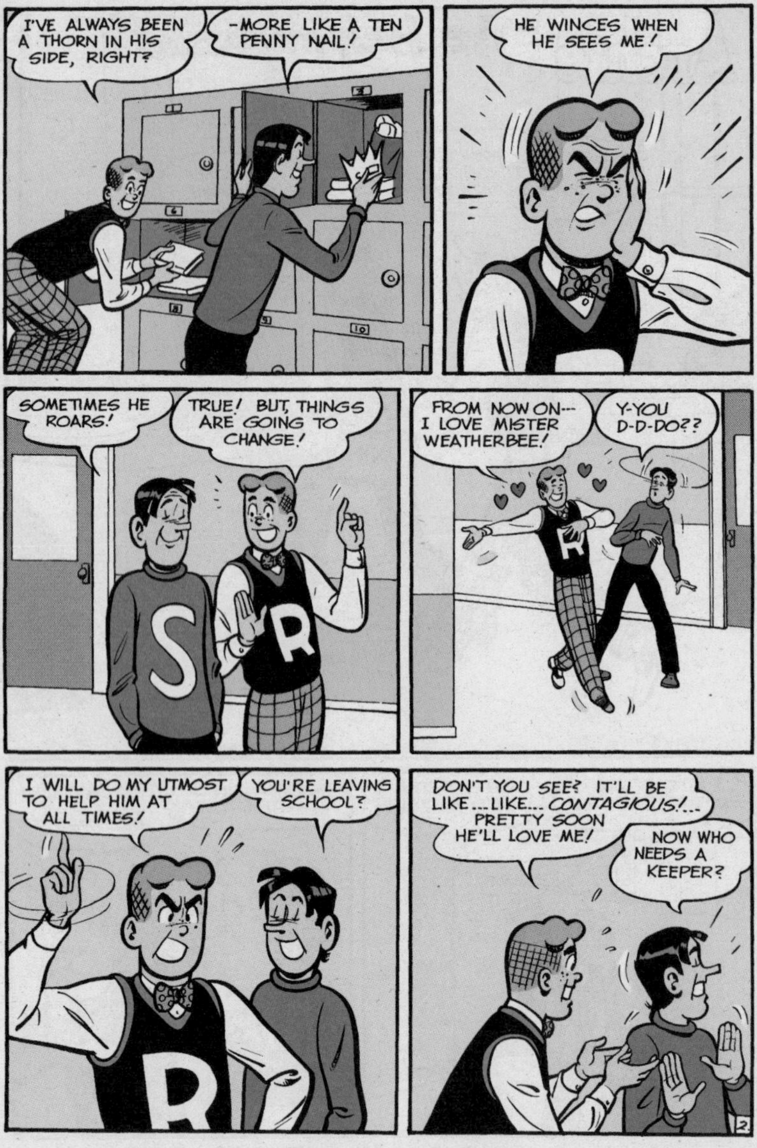
I'VE ALWAYS BEEN A THORN IN HIS SIDE, RIGHT?
-MORE LIKE A TEN PENNY NAIL!
HE WINCES WHEN HE SEES ME!
SOMETIMES HE ROARS!
TRUE! BUT, THINGS ARE GOING TO CHANGE!
FROM NOW ON--- I LOVE MISTER WEATHERBEE!
Y-YOU D-D-DO??
I WILL DO MY UTMOST TO HELP HIM AT ALL TIMES!
YOU'RE LEAVING SCHOOL?
DON'T YOU SEE? IT'LL BE LIKE...LIKE...CONTAGIOUS!... PRETTY SOON HE'LL LOVE ME!
NOW WHO NEEDS A KEEPER?
2

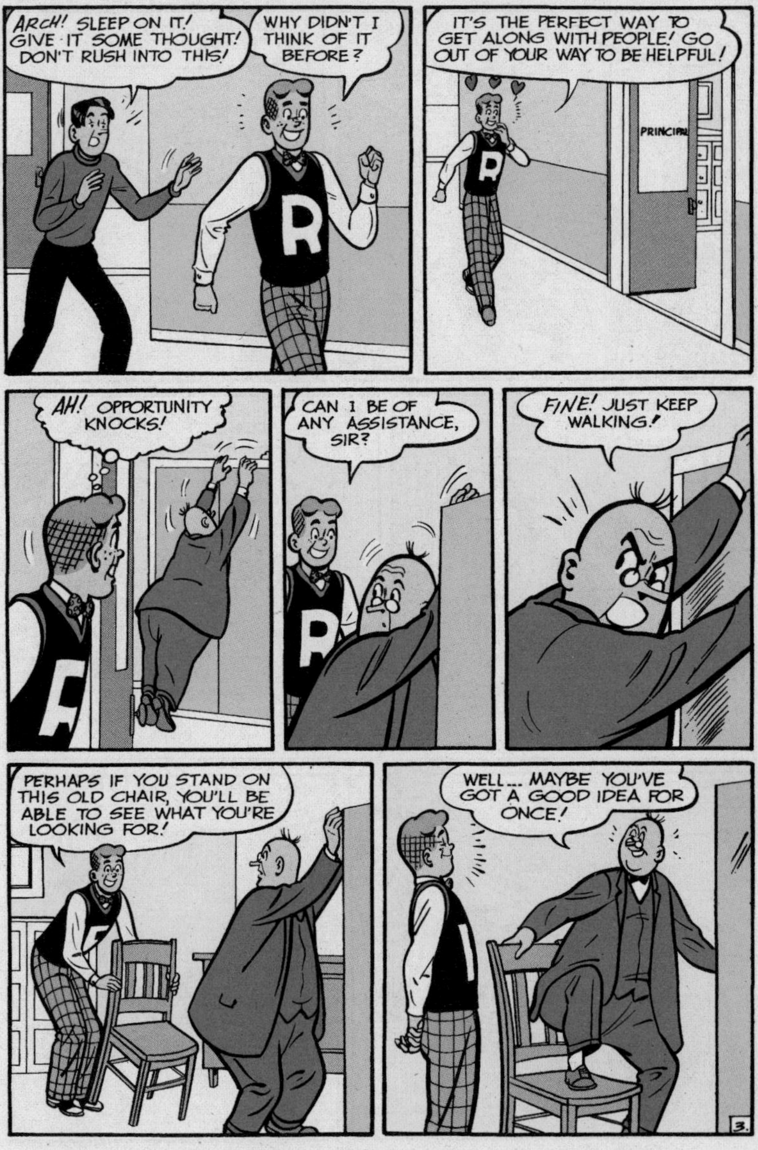
ARCH! SLEEP ON IT! GIVE IT SOME THOUGHT! DON'T RUSH INTO THIS!
WHY DIDN'T I THINK OF IT BEFORE?
IT'S THE PERFECT WAY TO GET ALONG WITH PEOPLE! GO OUT OF YOUR WAY TO BE HELPFUL!
PRINCIPAL
AH! OPPORTUNITY KNOCKS!
CAN I BE OF ANY ASSISTANCE, SIR?
FINE! JUST KEEP WALKING!
PERHAPS IF YOU STAND ON THIS OLD CHAIR, YOU'LL BE ABLE TO SEE WHAT YOU'RE LOOKING FOR!
WELL... MAYBE YOU'VE GOT A GOOD IDEA FOR ONCE!
3.

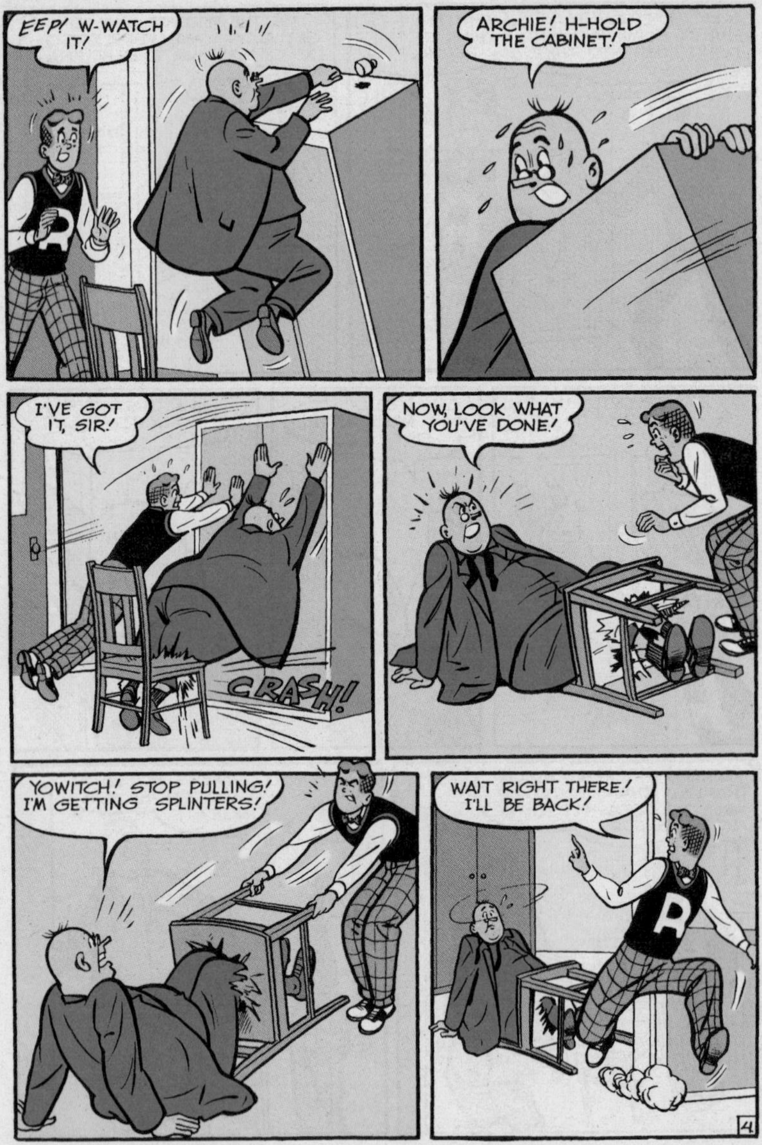
EEP! W-WATCH IT!
ARCHIE! H-HOLD THE CABINET!
I'VE GOT IT, SIR!
CRASH!
NOW, LOOK WHAT YOU'VE DONE!
YOWITCH! STOP PULLING! I'M GETTING SPLINTERS!
WAIT RIGHT THERE! I'LL BE BACK!
4

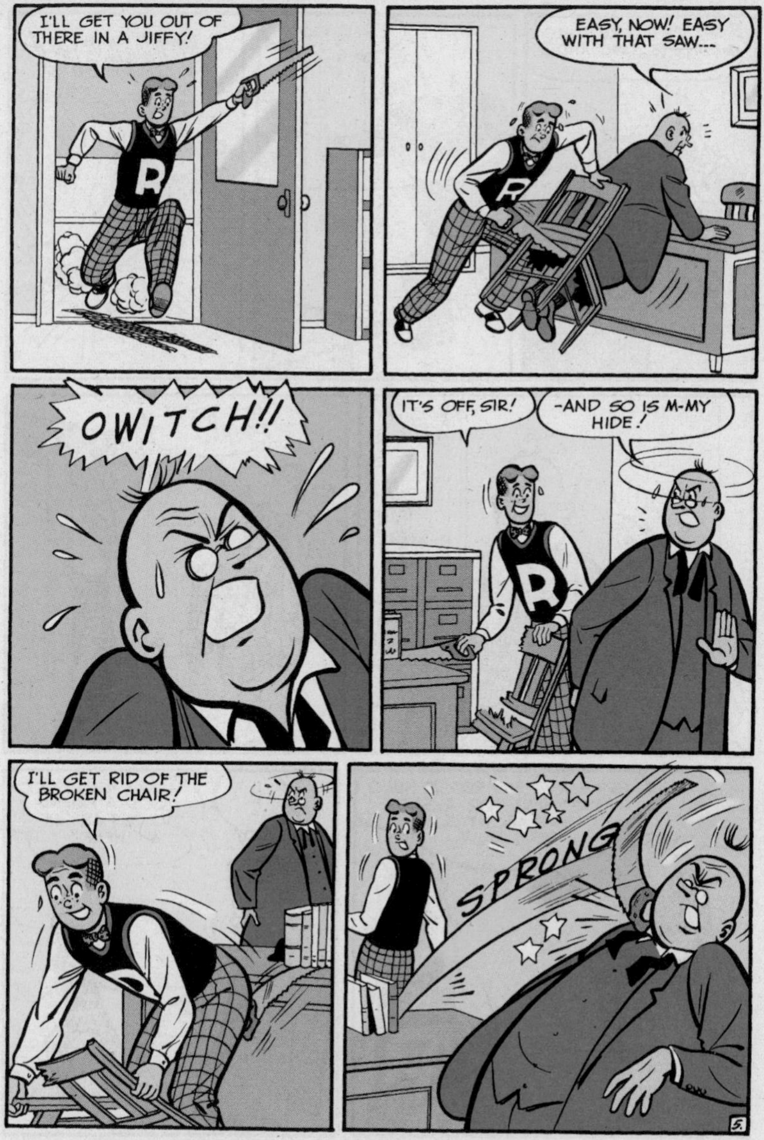
I'LL GET YOU OUT OF THERE IN A JIFFY!
EASY, NOW! EASY WITH THAT SAW...
OWITCH!!
IT'S OFF, SIR!
-AND SO IS M-MY HIDE!
I'LL GET RID OF THE BROKEN CHAIR!
SPRONG
5.

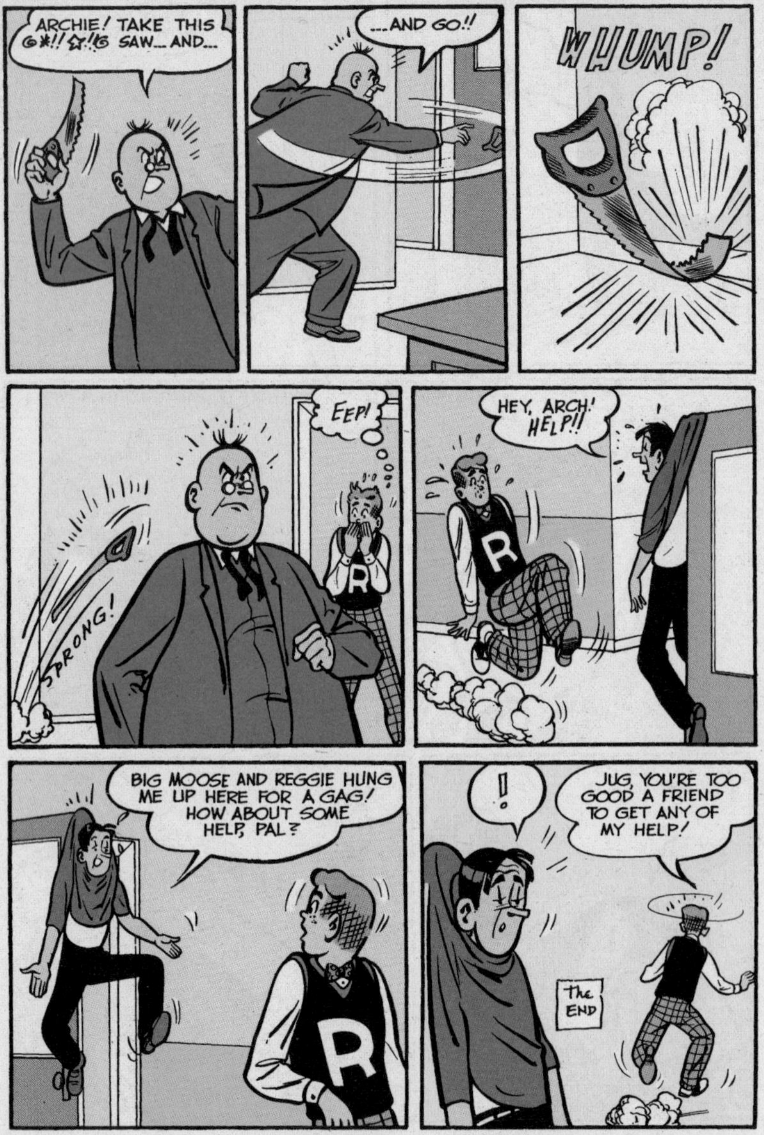
ARCHIE! TAKE THIS @*!!☆!!@ SAW... AND...
...AND GO!!
WHUMP!
EEP!
SPRONG!
HEY, ARCH! HELP!!
BIG MOOSE AND REGGIE HUNG ME UP HERE FOR A GAG! HOW ABOUT SOME HELP, PAL?
!
JUG, YOU'RE TOO GOOD A FRIEND TO GET ANY OF MY HELP!
The END

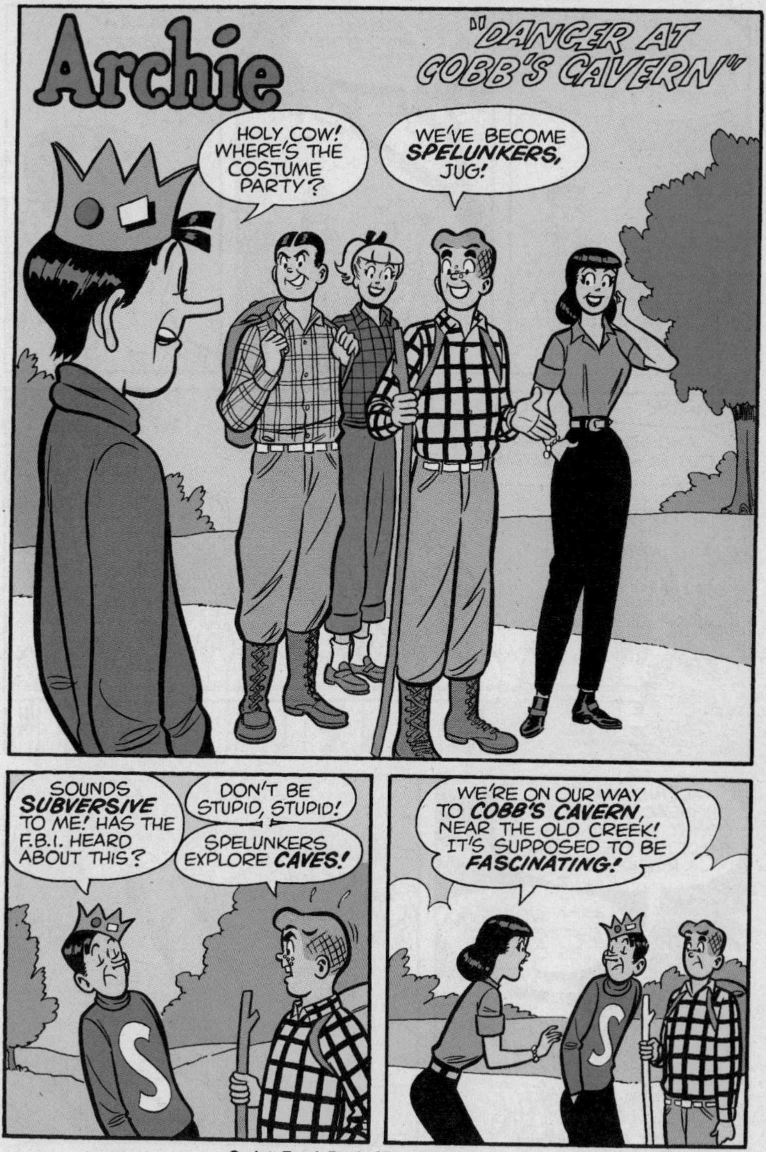
Archie
"DANGER AT COBB'S CAVERN"
HOLY COW! WHERE'S THE COSTUME PARTY?
WE'VE BECOME SPELUNKERS, JUG!
SOUNDS SUBVERSIVE TO ME! HAS THE F.B.I. HEARD ABOUT THIS?
DON'T BE STUPID, STUPID!
SPELUNKERS EXPLORE CAVES!
WE'RE ON OUR WAY TO COBB'S CAVERN, NEAR THE OLD CREEK! IT'S SUPPOSED TO BE FASCINATING!

Script: Frank Doyle / Pencils: Harry Lucey

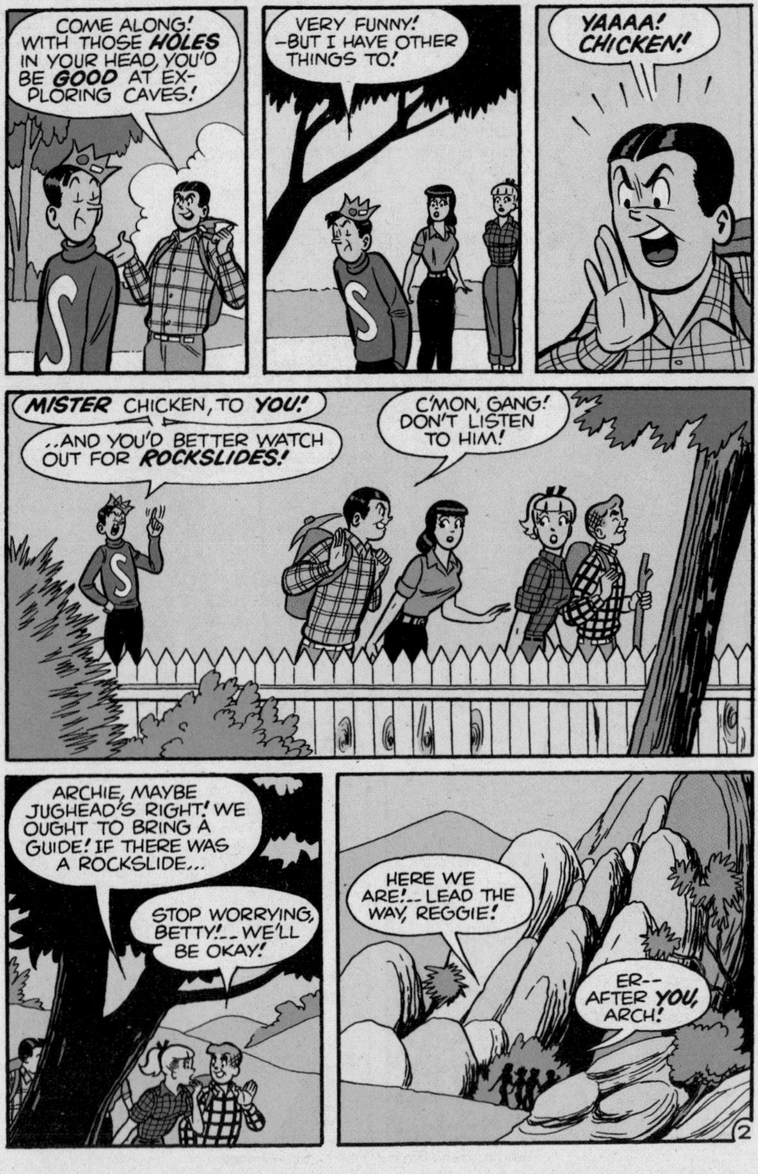
COME ALONG! WITH THOSE HOLES IN YOUR HEAD, YOU'D BE GOOD AT EXPLORING CAVES!
VERY FUNNY! —BUT I HAVE OTHER THINGS TO!
YAAAA! CHICKEN!
MISTER CHICKEN, TO YOU!
..AND YOU'D BETTER WATCH OUT FOR ROCKSLIDES!
C'MON, GANG! DON'T LISTEN TO HIM!
ARCHIE, MAYBE JUGHEAD'S RIGHT! WE OUGHT TO BRING A GUIDE! IF THERE WAS A ROCKSLIDE...
STOP WORRYING, BETTY!-- WE'LL BE OKAY!
HERE WE ARE!-- LEAD THE WAY, REGGIE!
ER-- AFTER YOU, ARCH!
2

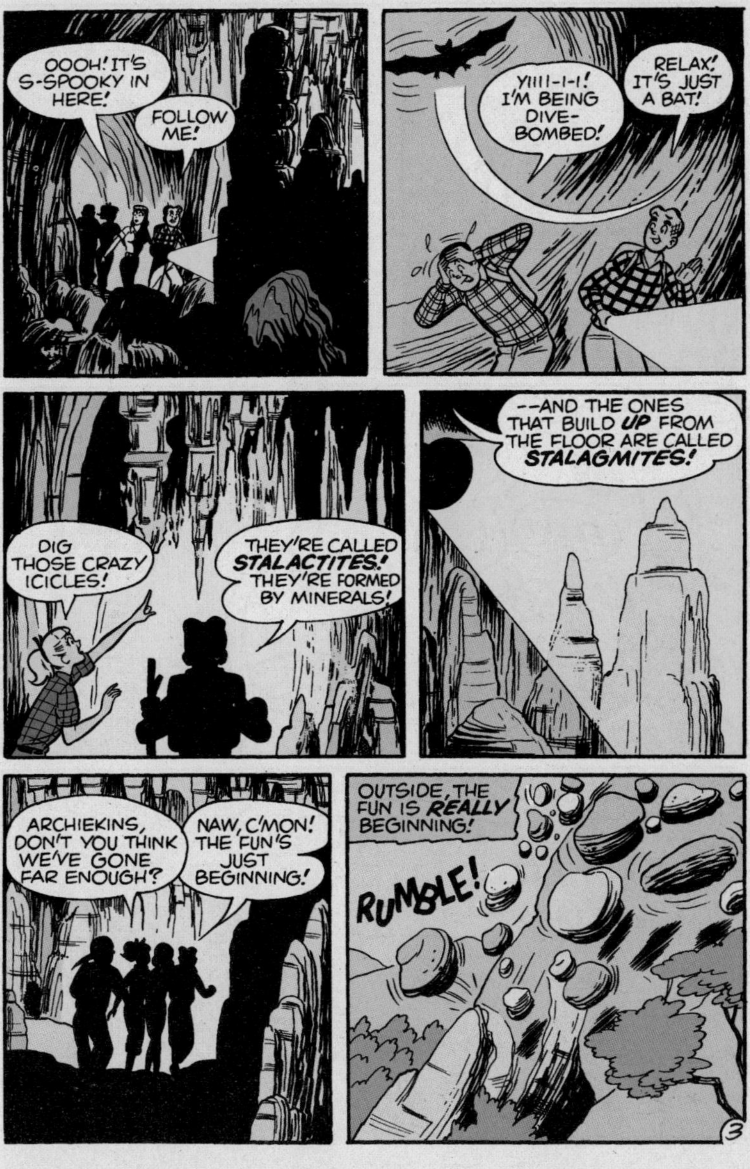
OOOH! IT'S S-SPOOKY IN HERE!
FOLLOW ME!
YIIII-I-I! I'M BEING DIVE-BOMBED!
RELAX! IT'S JUST A BAT!
DIG THOSE CRAZY ICICLES!
THEY'RE CALLED STALACTITES! THEY'RE FORMED BY MINERALS!
--AND THE ONES THAT BUILD UP FROM THE FLOOR ARE CALLED STALAGMITES!
ARCHIEKINS, DON'T YOU THINK WE'VE GONE FAR ENOUGH?
NAW, C'MON! THE FUN'S JUST BEGINNING!
OUTSIDE, THE FUN IS REALLY BEGINNING!
RUMBLE!
3

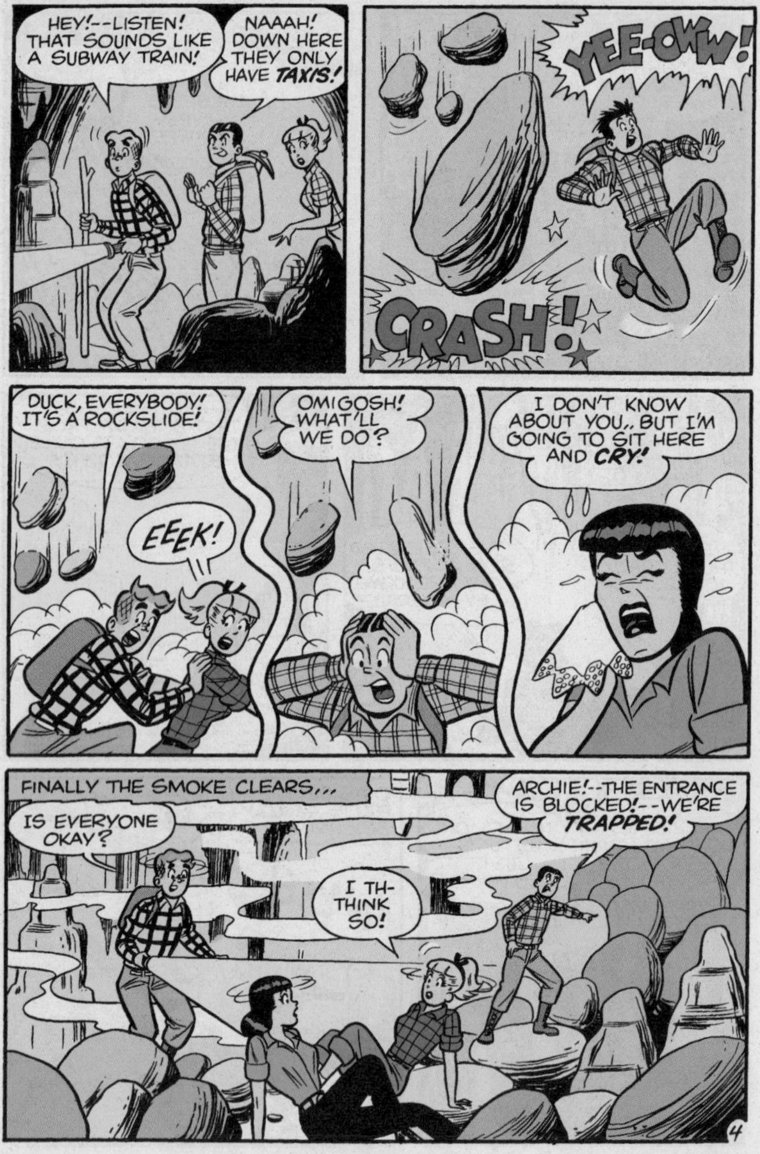

HEY!--LISTEN! THAT SOUNDS LIKE A SUBWAY TRAIN!
NAAAH! DOWN HERE THEY ONLY HAVE TAXIS!
YEE-OWW!
CRASH!
DUCK, EVERYBODY! IT'S A ROCKSLIDE!
EEEK!
OMIGOSH! WHAT'LL WE DO?
I DON'T KNOW ABOUT YOU,, BUT I'M GOING TO SIT HERE AND CRY!
FINALLY THE SMOKE CLEARS,,,
IS EVERYONE OKAY?
I TH-THINK SO!
ARCHIE!--THE ENTRANCE IS BLOCKED!--WE'RE TRAPPED!
4

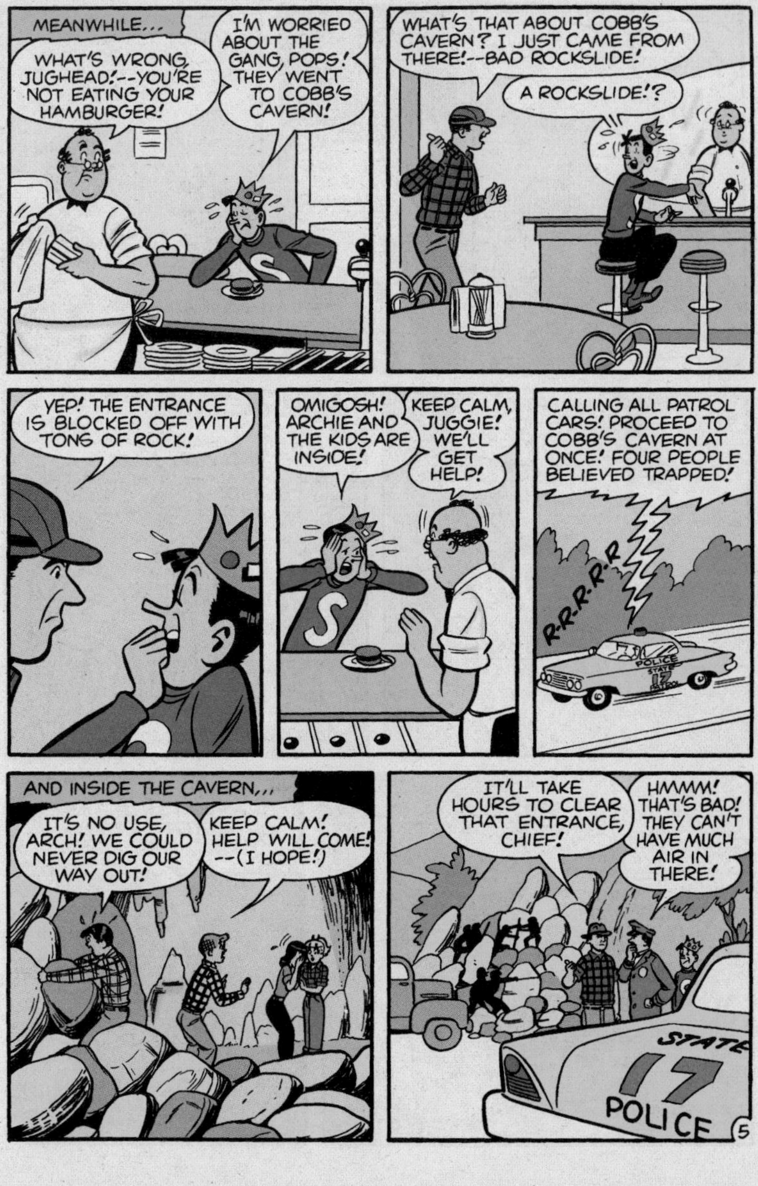
MEANWHILE...
WHAT'S WRONG, JUGHEAD!--YOU'RE NOT EATING YOUR HAMBURGER!
I'M WORRIED ABOUT THE GANG, POPS! THEY WENT TO COBB'S CAVERN!
WHAT'S THAT ABOUT COBB'S CAVERN? I JUST CAME FROM THERE!--BAD ROCKSLIDE!
A ROCKSLIDE!?
YEP! THE ENTRANCE IS BLOCKED OFF WITH TONS OF ROCK!
OMIGOSH! ARCHIE AND THE KIDS ARE INSIDE!
KEEP CALM, JUGGIE! WE'LL GET HELP!
CALLING ALL PATROL CARS! PROCEED TO COBB'S CAVERN AT ONCE! FOUR PEOPLE BELIEVED TRAPPED!
R-R-R-R-R
AND INSIDE THE CAVERN...
IT'S NO USE, ARCH! WE COULD NEVER DIG OUR WAY OUT!
KEEP CALM! HELP WILL COME! --(I HOPE!)
IT'LL TAKE HOURS TO CLEAR THAT ENTRANCE, CHIEF!
HMMM! THAT'S BAD! THEY CAN'T HAVE MUCH AIR IN THERE!
STATE
17
POLICE

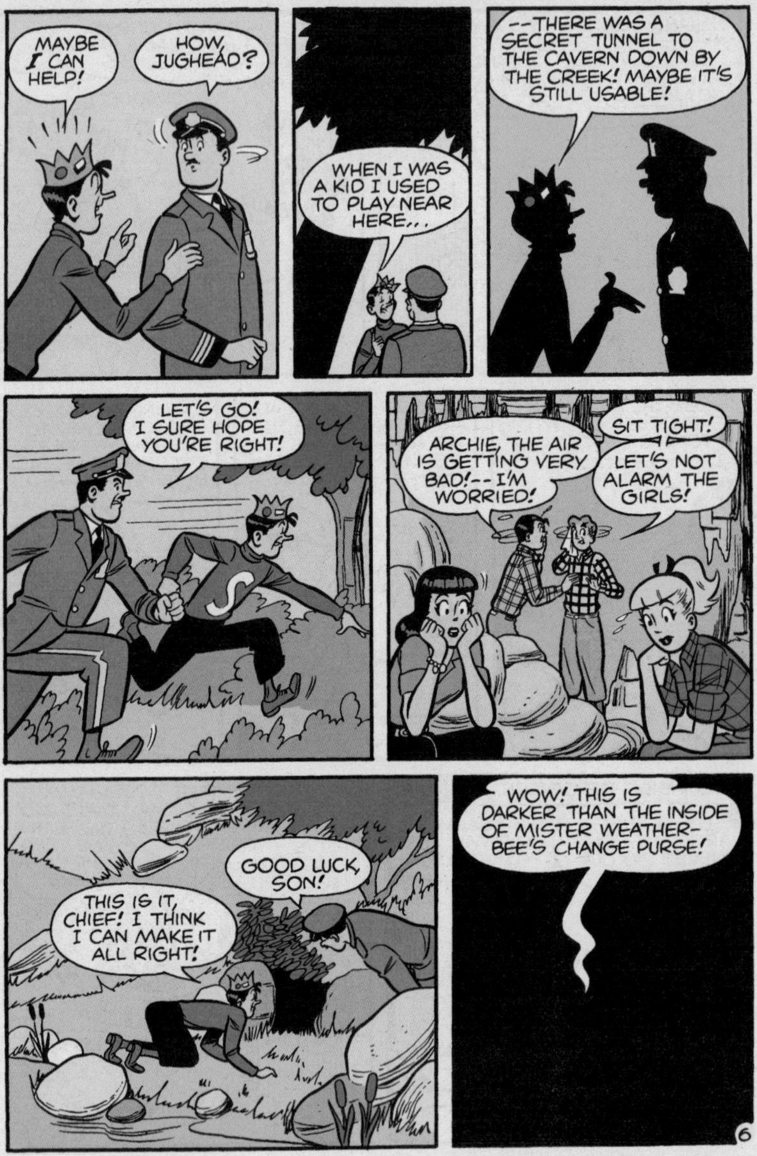
MAYBE I CAN HELP!
HOW, JUGHEAD?
WHEN I WAS A KID I USED TO PLAY NEAR HERE...
--THERE WAS A SECRET TUNNEL TO THE CAVERN DOWN BY THE CREEK! MAYBE IT'S STILL USABLE!
LET'S GO! I SURE HOPE YOU'RE RIGHT!
ARCHIE, THE AIR IS GETTING VERY BAD!--I'M WORRIED!
SIT TIGHT!
LET'S NOT ALARM THE GIRLS!
THIS IS IT, CHIEF! I THINK I CAN MAKE IT ALL RIGHT!
GOOD LUCK, SON!
WOW! THIS IS DARKER THAN THE INSIDE OF MISTER WEATHER-BEE'S CHANGE PURSE!

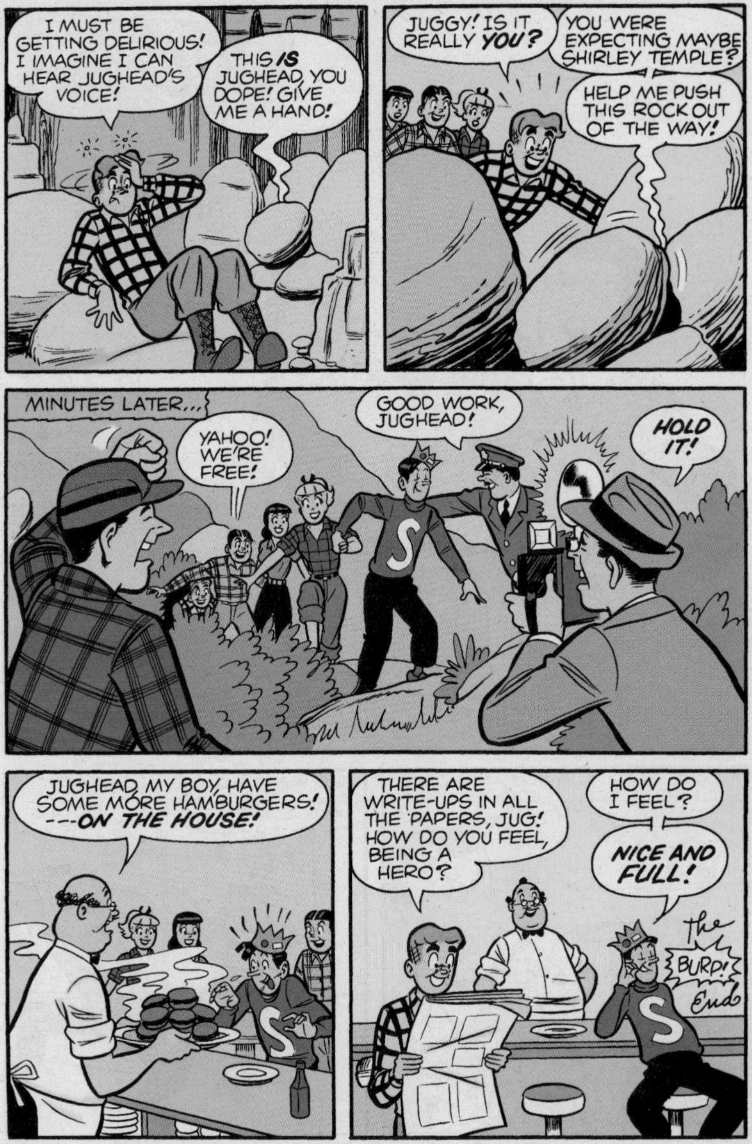
I MUST BE GETTING DELIRIOUS! I IMAGINE I CAN HEAR JUGHEAD'S VOICE!
THIS IS JUGHEAD, YOU DOPE! GIVE ME A HAND!
JUGGY! IS IT REALLY YOU?
YOU WERE EXPECTING MAYBE SHIRLEY TEMPLE?
HELP ME PUSH THIS ROCK OUT OF THE WAY!
MINUTES LATER...
YAHOO! WE'RE FREE!
GOOD WORK, JUGHEAD!
HOLD IT!
JUGHEAD, MY BOY, HAVE SOME MORE HAMBURGERS! ---ON THE HOUSE!
THERE ARE WRITE-UPS IN ALL THE PAPERS, JUG! HOW DO YOU FEEL, BEING A HERO?
HOW DO I FEEL?
NICE AND FULL!
BURP!
The End

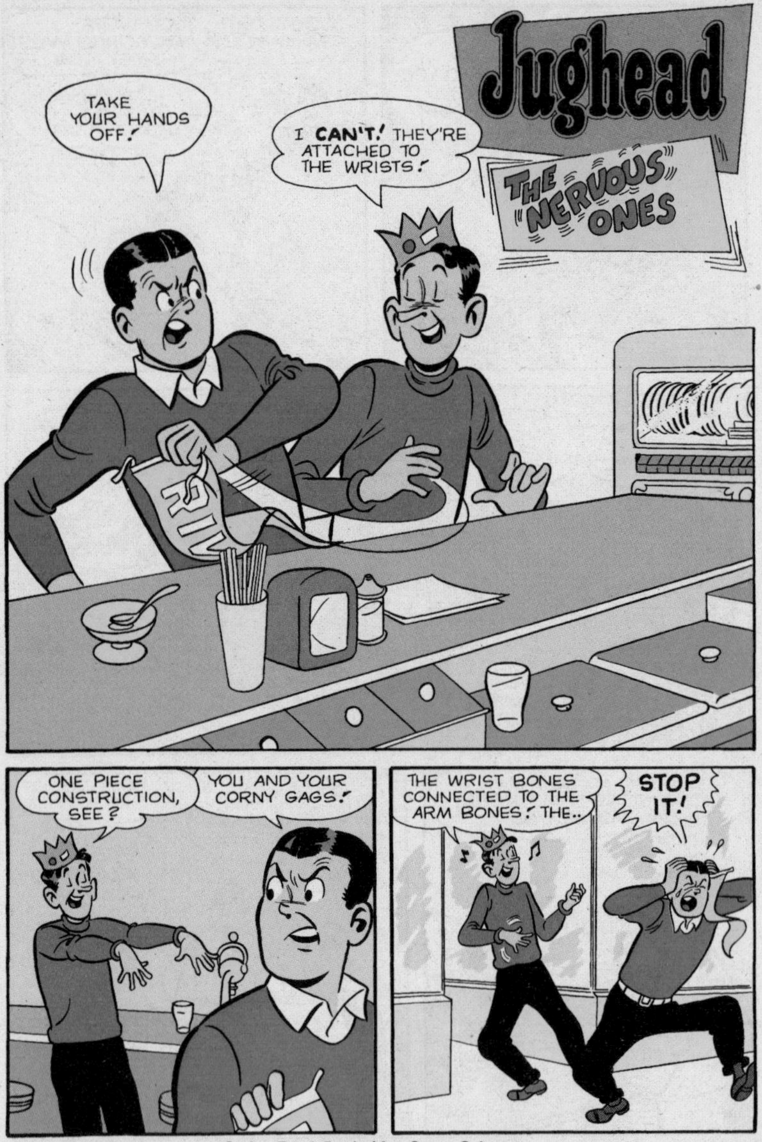
Jughead
THE NERVOUS ONES
TAKE YOUR HANDS OFF!
I CAN'T! THEY'RE ATTACHED TO THE WRISTS!
ONE PIECE CONSTRUCTION, SEE?
YOU AND YOUR CORNY GAGS!
THE WRIST BONES CONNECTED TO THE ARM BONES! THE..
STOP IT!

Script: Frank Doyle / Art: Samm Schwartz

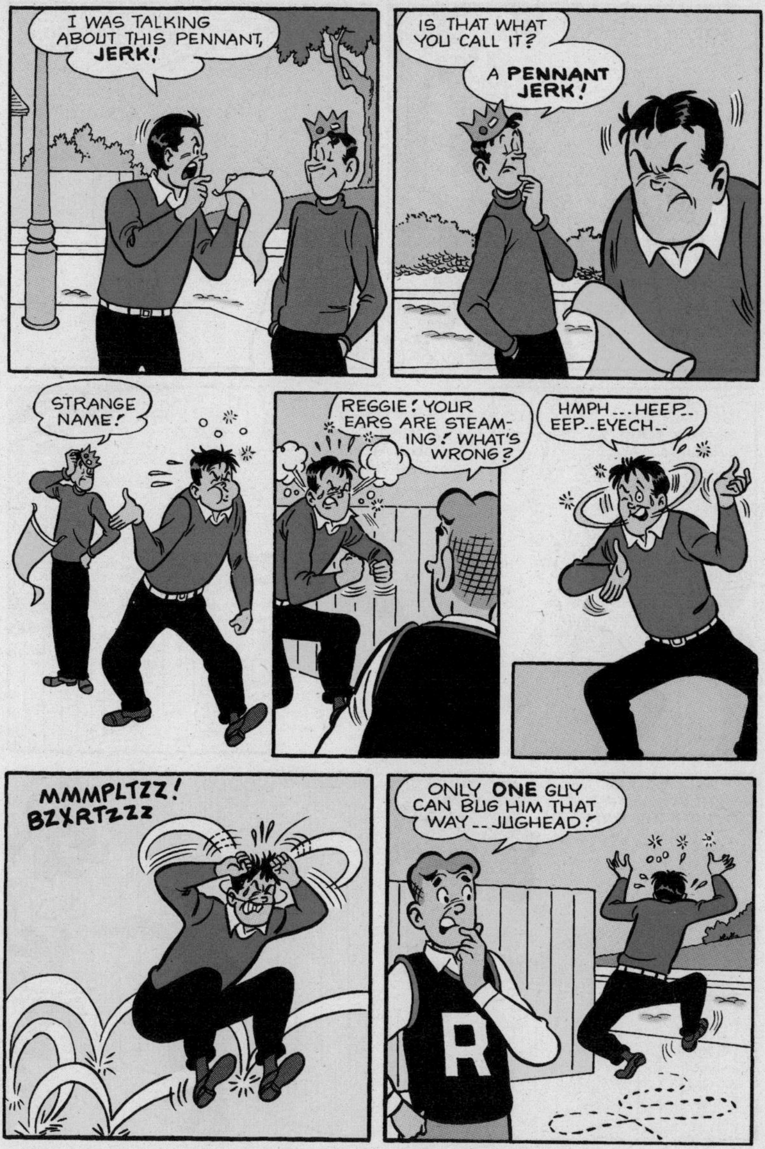
I WAS TALKING ABOUT THIS PENNANT, **JERK**!
IS THAT WHAT YOU CALL IT?
A **PENNANT JERK**!
STRANGE NAME!
REGGIE! YOUR EARS ARE STEAMING! WHAT'S WRONG?
HMPH... HEEP.. EEP.. EYECH..
MMMPLTZZ! BZXRTZZZ
ONLY **ONE** GUY CAN BUG HIM THAT WAY.. JUGHEAD!

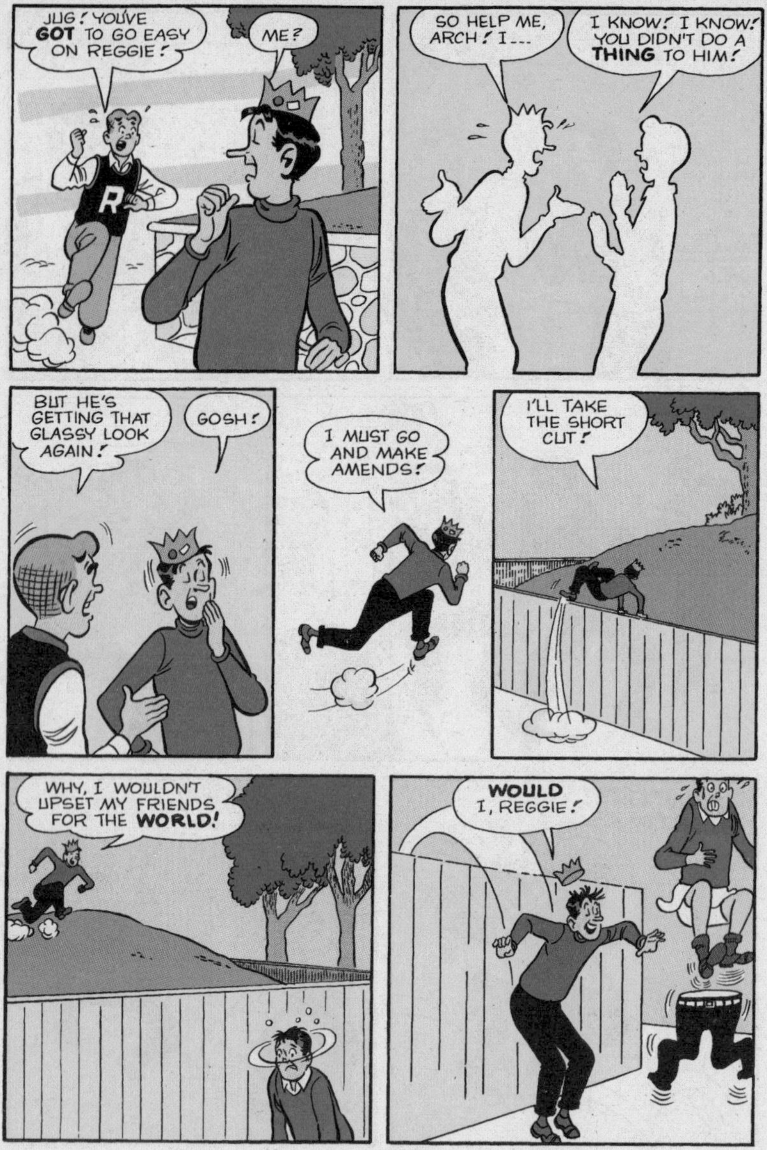

JUG! YOU'VE GOT TO GO EASY ON REGGIE!
ME?
SO HELP ME, ARCH! I...
I KNOW! I KNOW! YOU DIDN'T DO A THING TO HIM!
BUT HE'S GETTING THAT GLASSY LOOK AGAIN!
GOSH!
I MUST GO AND MAKE AMENDS!
I'LL TAKE THE SHORT CUT!
WHY, I WOULDN'T UPSET MY FRIENDS FOR THE WORLD!
WOULD I, REGGIE!

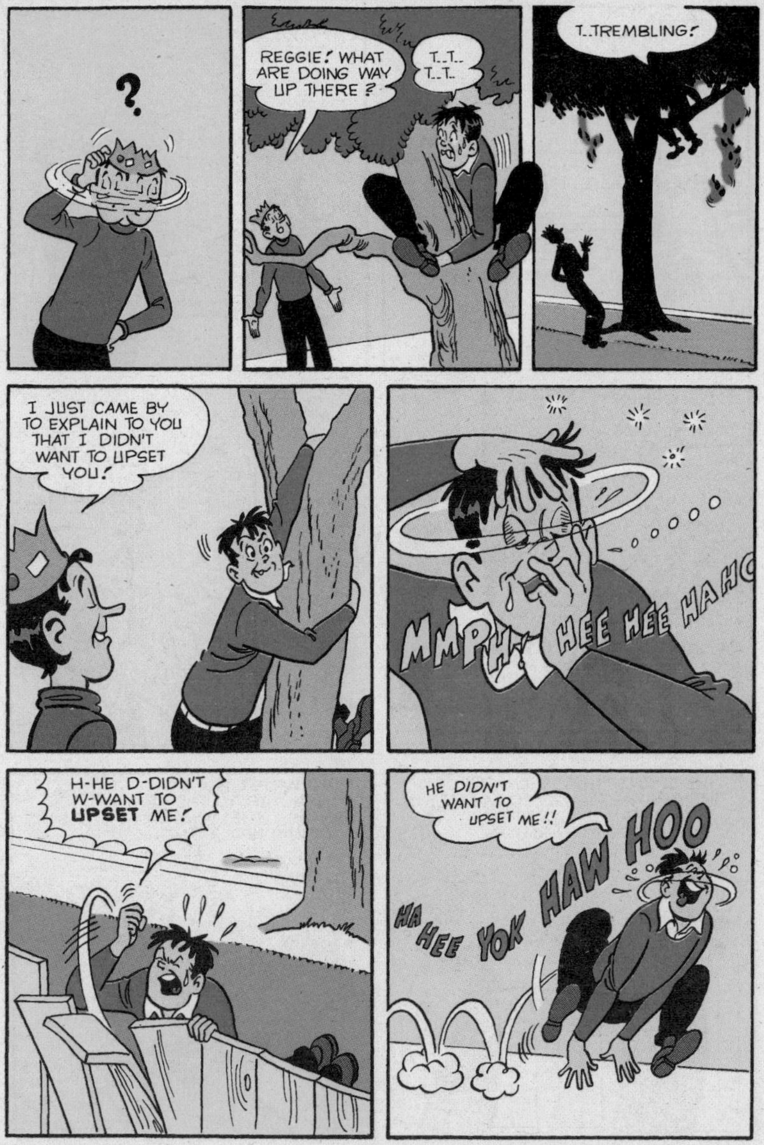
?
REGGIE! WHAT ARE DOING WAY UP THERE?
T..T.. T..T..
T..TREMBLING!
I JUST CAME BY TO EXPLAIN TO YOU THAT I DIDN'T WANT TO UPSET YOU!
MMPH! HEE HEE HAHO
H-HE D-DIDN'T W-WANT TO UPSET ME!
HE DIDN'T WANT TO UPSET ME!!
HA HEE YOK HAW HOO

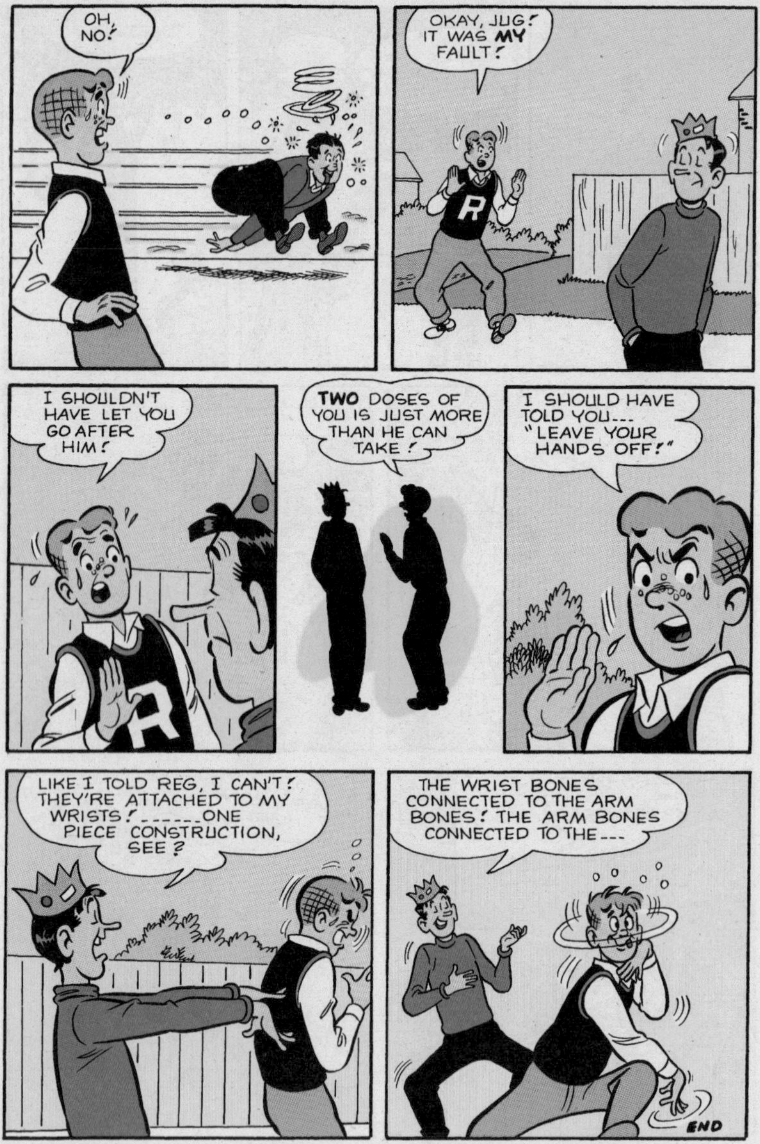
OH, NO!
OKAY, JUG! IT WAS MY FAULT!
I SHOULDN'T HAVE LET YOU GO AFTER HIM!
TWO DOSES OF YOU IS JUST MORE THAN HE CAN TAKE!
I SHOULD HAVE TOLD YOU--- "LEAVE YOUR HANDS OFF!"
LIKE I TOLD REG, I CAN'T! THEY'RE ATTACHED TO MY WRISTS! ------ONE PIECE CONSTRUCTION, SEE?
THE WRIST BONES CONNECTED TO THE ARM BONES! THE ARM BONES CONNECTED TO THE---
END

Dilton in "UNPOPULAR MECHANICS!"

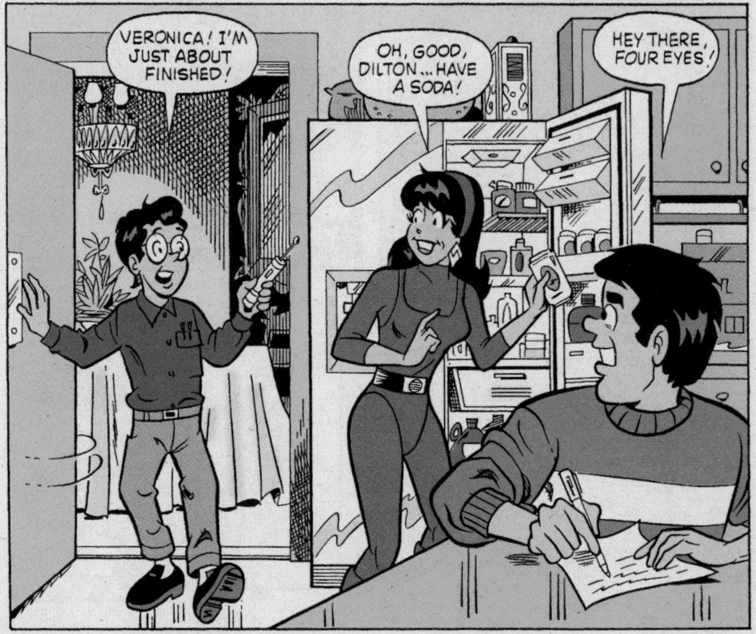
VERONICA! I'M JUST ABOUT FINISHED!
OH, GOOD, DILTON... HAVE A SODA!
HEY THERE, FOUR EYES!

Script: Mike Gallagher / Art: Dave Manak / Letters: Bill Yoshida

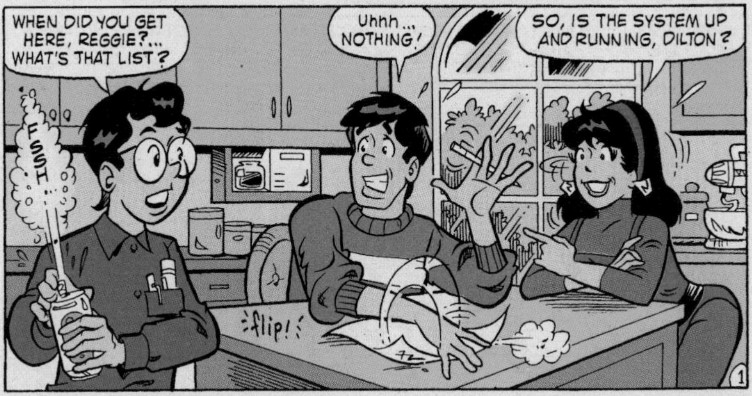
WHEN DID YOU GET HERE, REGGIE?... WHAT'S THAT LIST?
FSSH
Uhhh... NOTHING!
SO, IS THE SYSTEM UP AND RUNNING, DILTON?
flip!
1

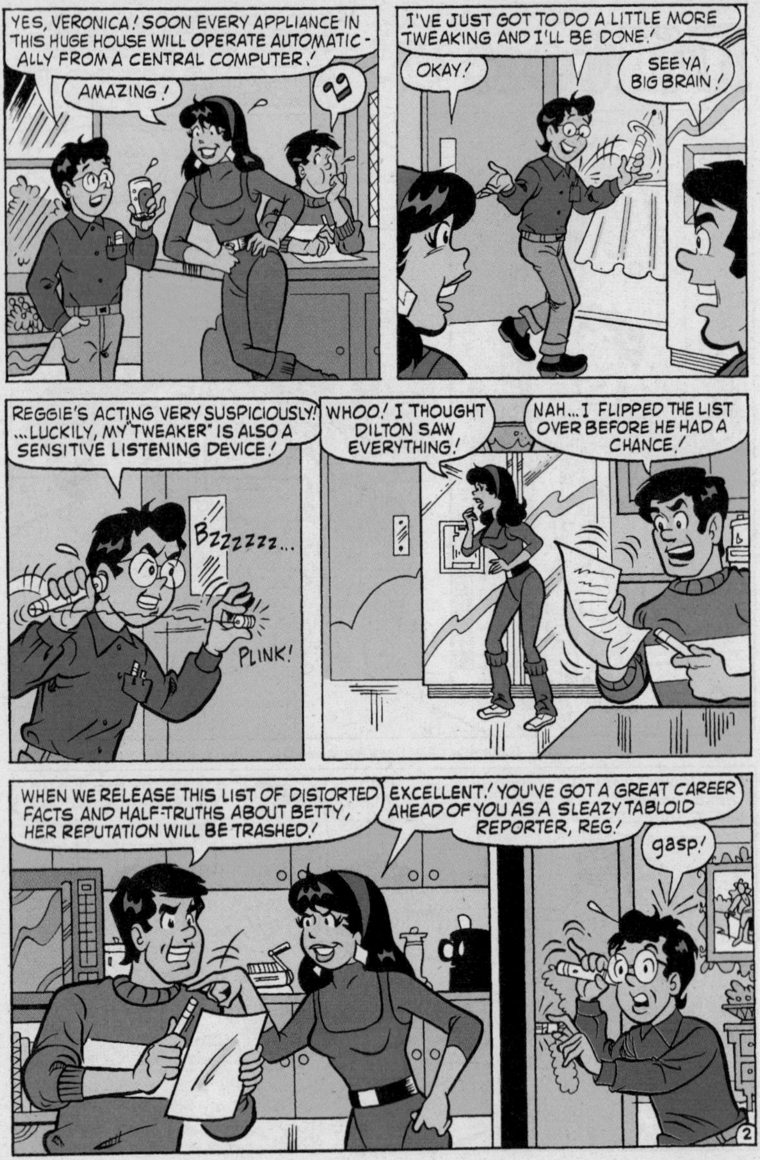
YES, VERONICA! SOON EVERY APPLIANCE IN THIS HUGE HOUSE WILL OPERATE AUTOMATIC-ALLY FROM A CENTRAL COMPUTER!
AMAZING!
I'VE JUST GOT TO DO A LITTLE MORE TWEAKING AND I'LL BE DONE!
OKAY!
SEE YA, BIG BRAIN!
REGGIE'S ACTING VERY SUSPICIOUSLY! ...LUCKILY, MY "TWEAKER" IS ALSO A SENSITIVE LISTENING DEVICE!
BZZZZZZ...
PLINK!
WHOO! I THOUGHT DILTON SAW EVERYTHING!
NAH... I FLIPPED THE LIST OVER BEFORE HE HAD A CHANCE!
WHEN WE RELEASE THIS LIST OF DISTORTED FACTS AND HALF-TRUTHS ABOUT BETTY, HER REPUTATION WILL BE TRASHED!
EXCELLENT! YOU'VE GOT A GREAT CAREER AHEAD OF YOU AS A SLEAZY TABLOID REPORTER, REG!
gasp!
2

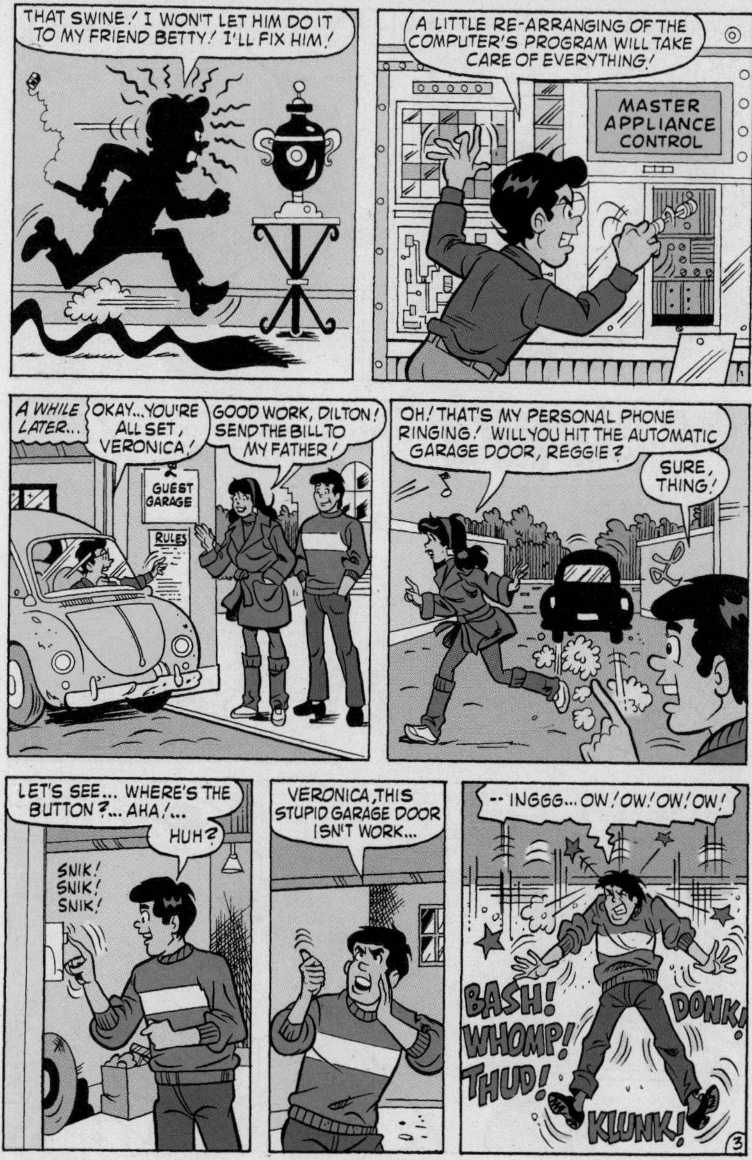
THAT SWINE! I WON'T LET HIM DO IT TO MY FRIEND BETTY! I'LL FIX HIM!
A LITTLE RE-ARRANGING OF THE COMPUTER'S PROGRAM WILL TAKE CARE OF EVERYTHING!
MASTER APPLIANCE CONTROL
A WHILE LATER...
OKAY...YOU'RE ALL SET, VERONICA!
GOOD WORK, DILTON! SEND THE BILL TO MY FATHER!
GUEST GARAGE
RULES
OH! THAT'S MY PERSONAL PHONE RINGING! WILL YOU HIT THE AUTOMATIC GARAGE DOOR, REGGIE?
SURE, THING!
LET'S SEE... WHERE'S THE BUTTON?... AHA!...
HUH?
SNIK! SNIK! SNIK!
VERONICA, THIS STUPID GARAGE DOOR ISN'T WORK...
-- INGGG... OW! OW! OW! OW!
BASH!
WHOMP!
THUD!
DONK!
KLUNK!
3

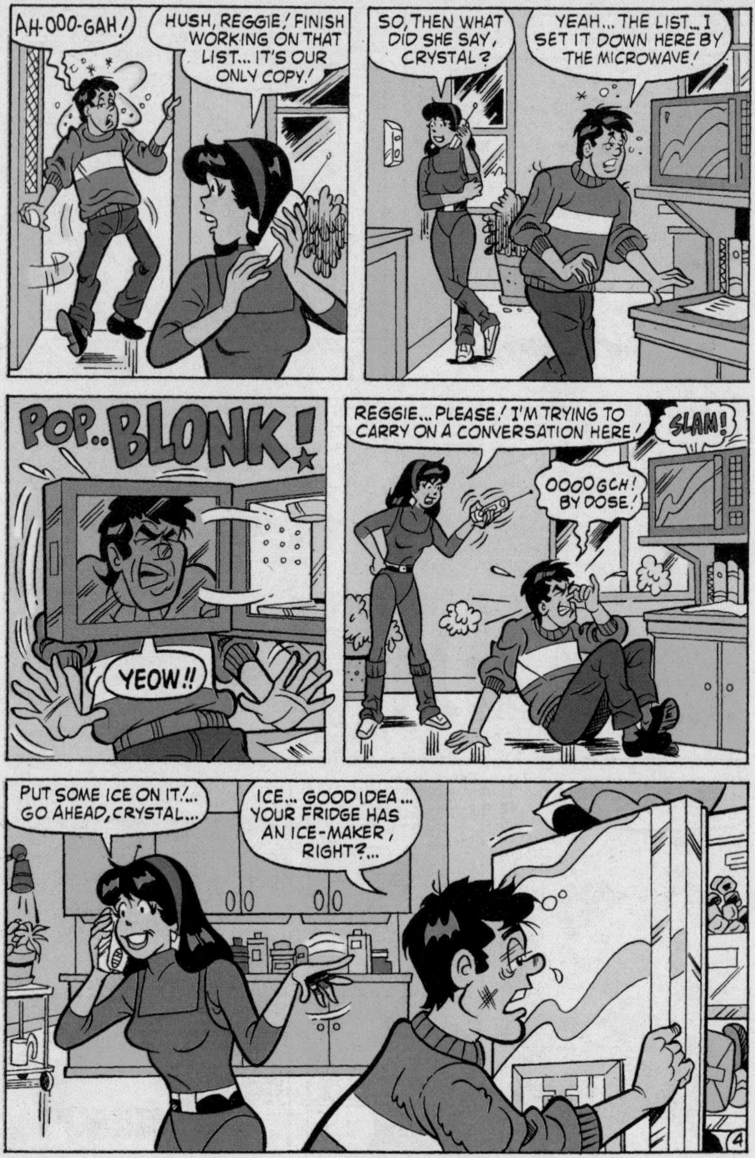

AH-OOO-GAH!
HUSH, REGGIE! FINISH WORKING ON THAT LIST... IT'S OUR ONLY COPY!
SO, THEN WHAT DID SHE SAY, CRYSTAL?
YEAH... THE LIST... I SET IT DOWN HERE BY THE MICROWAVE!
POP.. BLONK!
YEOW!!
REGGIE... PLEASE! I'M TRYING TO CARRY ON A CONVERSATION HERE!
SLAM!
OOOOGCH! BY DOSE!
PUT SOME ICE ON IT!... GO AHEAD, CRYSTAL...
ICE... GOOD IDEA... YOUR FRIDGE HAS AN ICE-MAKER, RIGHT?...
4

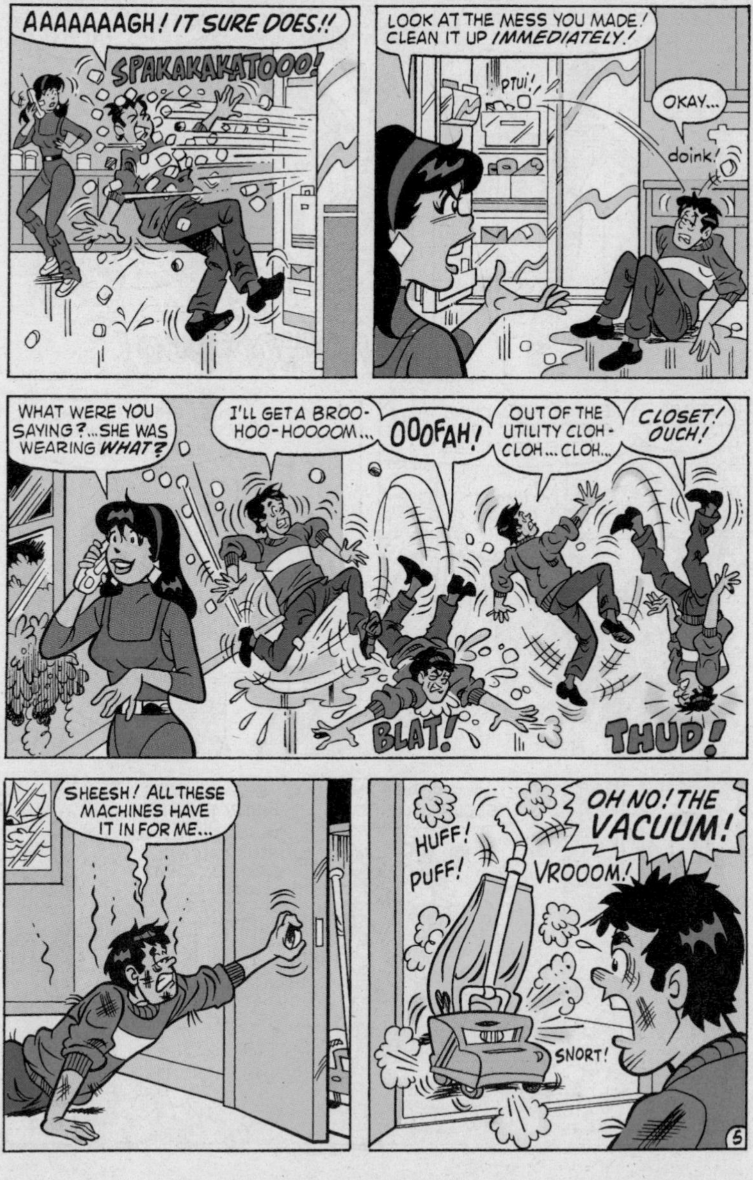
AAAAAAAGH! IT SURE DOES!!
SPAKAKAKATOOO!
LOOK AT THE MESS YOU MADE! CLEAN IT UP IMMEDIATELY!
PTUI!
OKAY...
doink!
WHAT WERE YOU SAYING?...SHE WAS WEARING WHAT?
I'LL GET A BROO-HOO-HOOOOM...
OOOFAH!
OUT OF THE UTILITY CLOH-CLOH... CLOH...
CLOSET! OUCH!
BLAT!
THUD!
SHEESH! ALL THESE MACHINES HAVE IT IN FOR ME...
HUFF!
PUFF!
VROOOM!
OH NO! THE VACUUM!
SNORT!
5

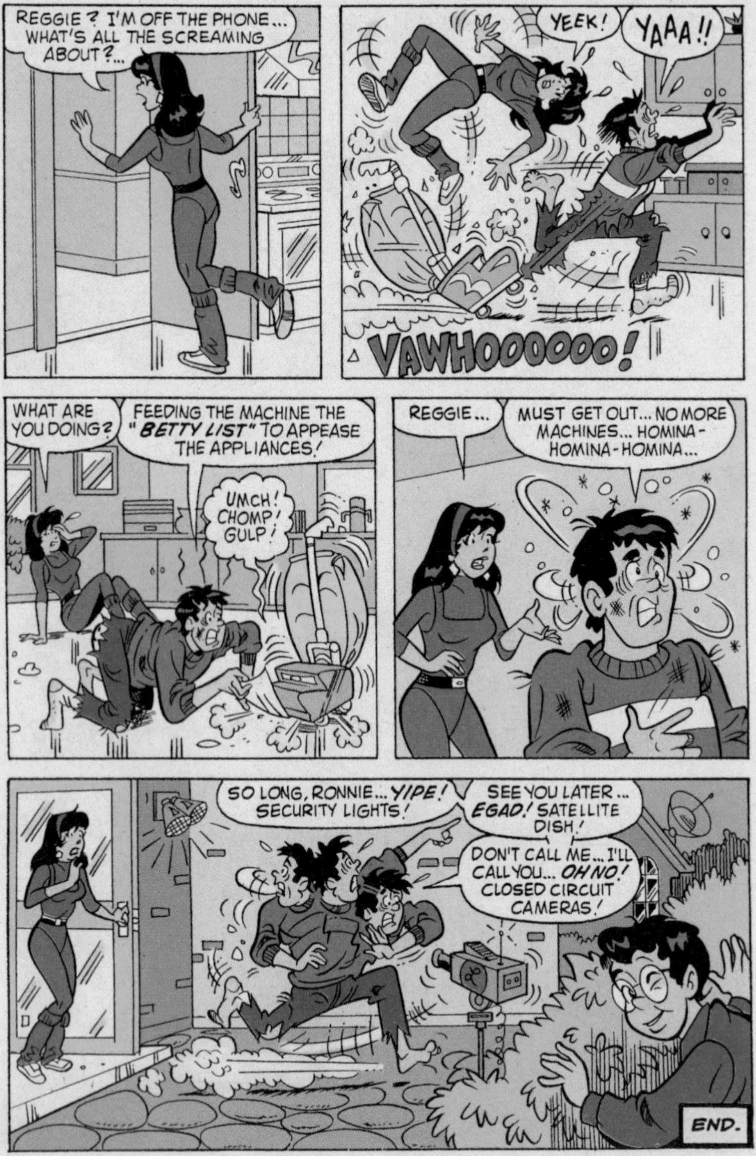
REGGIE? I'M OFF THE PHONE... WHAT'S ALL THE SCREAMING ABOUT?...
YEEK!
YAAA!!
VAWHOOOOOO!
WHAT ARE YOU DOING?
FEEDING THE MACHINE THE "BETTY LIST" TO APPEASE THE APPLIANCES!
UMCH! CHOMP! GULP!
REGGIE...
MUST GET OUT... NO MORE MACHINES... HOMINA-HOMINA-HOMINA...
SO LONG, RONNIE... YIPE! SECURITY LIGHTS!
SEE YOU LATER... EGAD! SATELLITE DISH!
DON'T CALL ME... I'LL CALL YOU... OH NO! CLOSED CIRCUIT CAMERAS!
END.

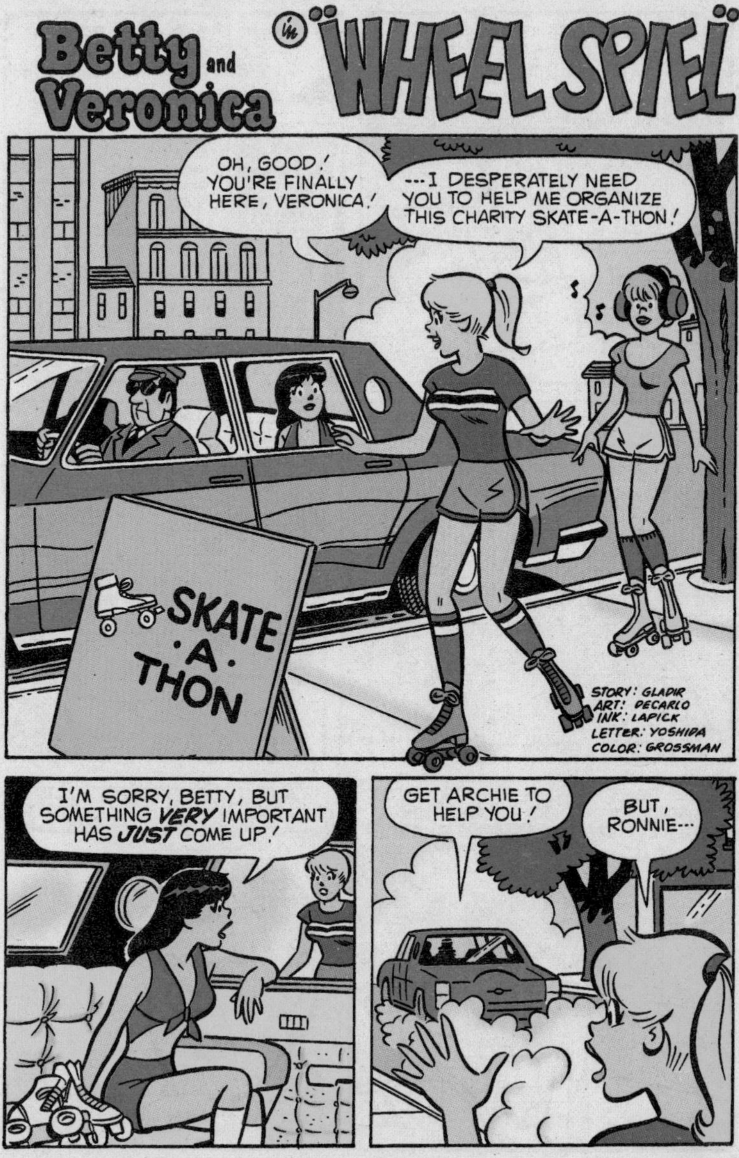
Betty and Veronica in "WHEEL SPIEL"
OH, GOOD! YOU'RE FINALLY HERE, VERONICA!
---I DESPERATELY NEED YOU TO HELP ME ORGANIZE THIS CHARITY SKATE-A-THON!
SKATE ·A· THON
STORY: GLADIR
ART: DECARLO
INK: LAPICK
LETTER: YOSHIDA
COLOR: GROSSMAN
I'M SORRY, BETTY, BUT SOMETHING VERY IMPORTANT HAS JUST COME UP!
GET ARCHIE TO HELP YOU!
BUT, RONNIE---

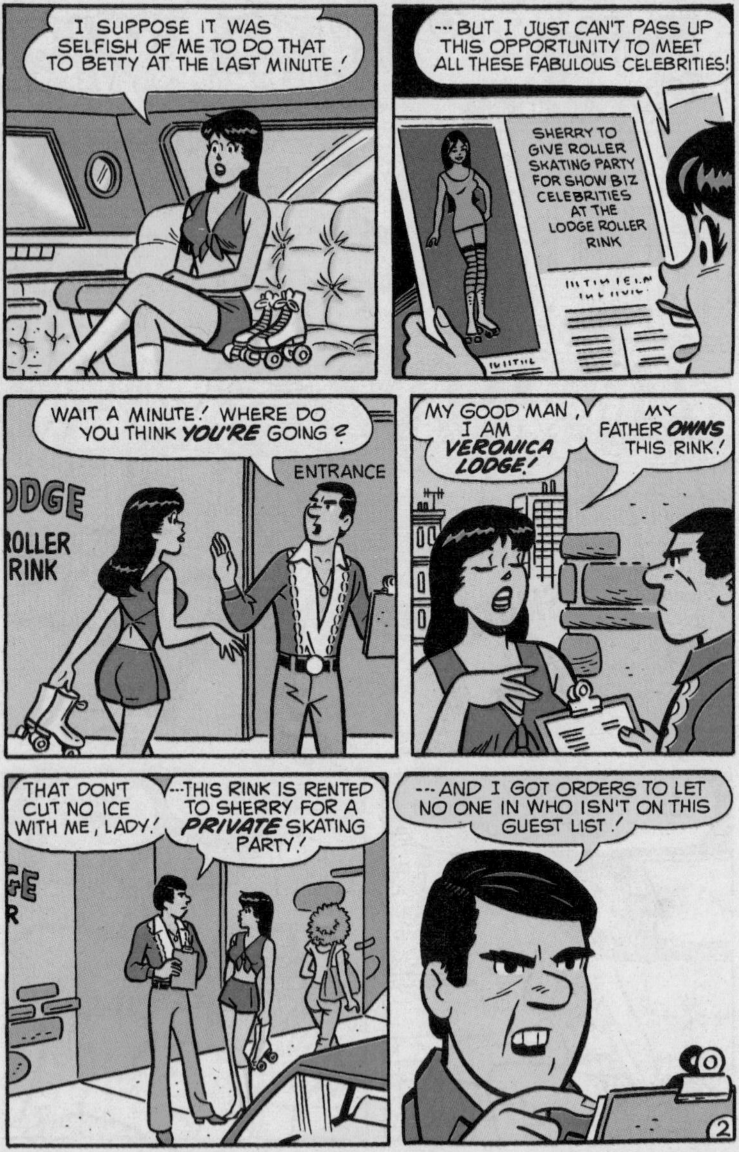
I SUPPOSE IT WAS SELFISH OF ME TO DO THAT TO BETTY AT THE LAST MINUTE!
---BUT I JUST CAN'T PASS UP THIS OPPORTUNITY TO MEET ALL THESE FABULOUS CELEBRITIES!
SHERRY TO GIVE ROLLER SKATING PARTY FOR SHOW BIZ CELEBRITIES AT THE LODGE ROLLER RINK
WAIT A MINUTE! WHERE DO YOU THINK *YOU'RE* GOING?
ENTRANCE
ROLLER RINK
MY GOOD MAN, I AM *VERONICA LODGE!*
MY FATHER *OWNS* THIS RINK!
THAT DON'T CUT NO ICE WITH ME, LADY!
---THIS RINK IS RENTED TO SHERRY FOR A *PRIVATE* SKATING PARTY!
---AND I GOT ORDERS TO LET NO ONE IN WHO ISN'T ON THIS GUEST LIST!
2

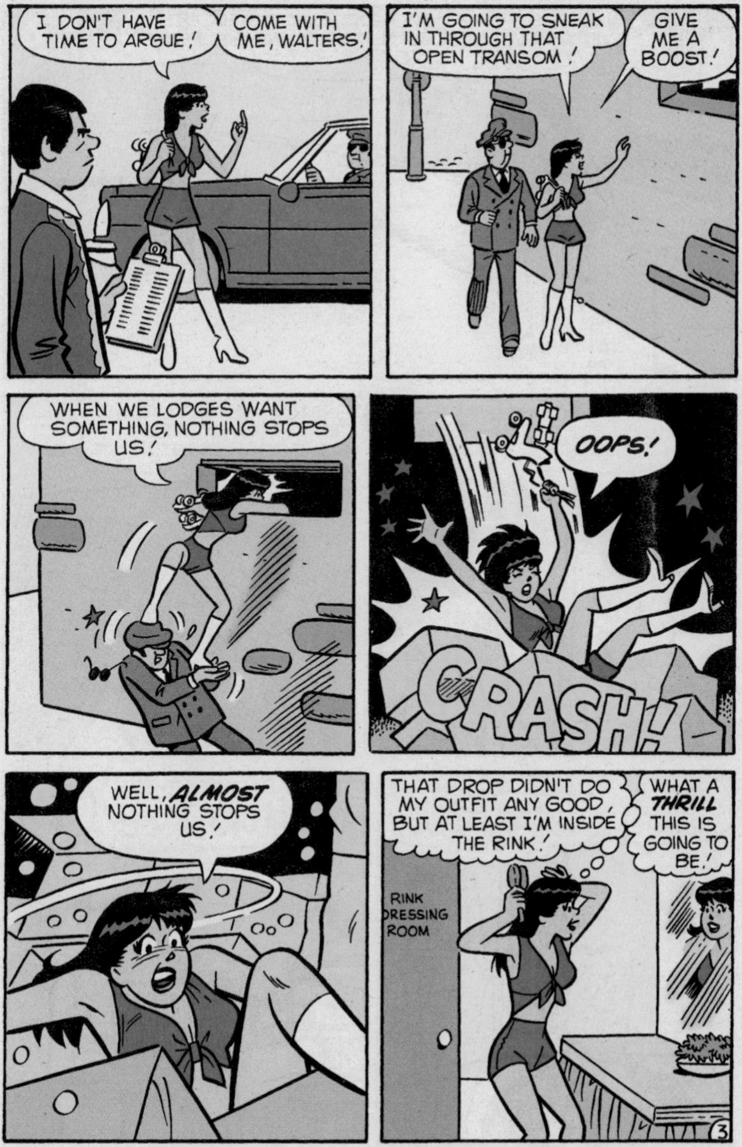

I DON'T HAVE TIME TO ARGUE!
COME WITH ME, WALTERS!
I'M GOING TO SNEAK IN THROUGH THAT OPEN TRANSOM!
GIVE ME A BOOST!
WHEN WE LODGES WANT SOMETHING, NOTHING STOPS US!
OOPS!
CRASH!
WELL, ALMOST NOTHING STOPS US!
THAT DROP DIDN'T DO MY OUTFIT ANY GOOD, BUT AT LEAST I'M INSIDE THE RINK!
WHAT A THRILL THIS IS GOING TO BE!
RINK DRESSING ROOM
3

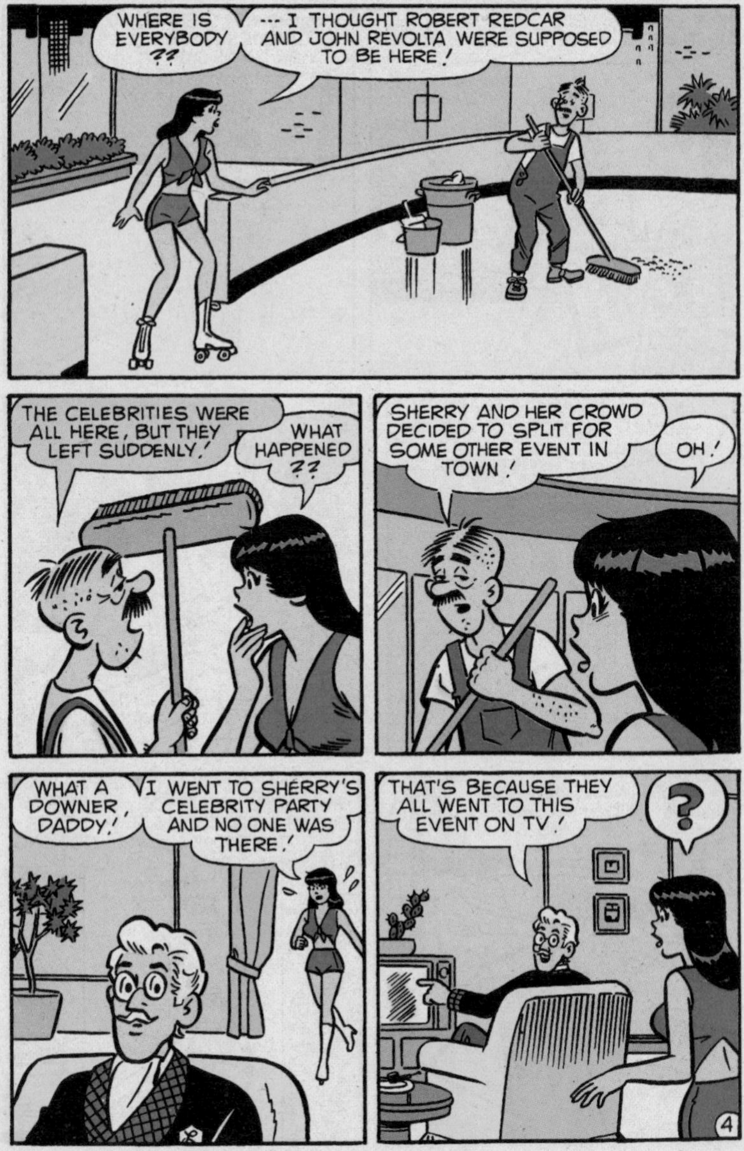
WHERE IS EVERYBODY ??
--- I THOUGHT ROBERT REDCAR AND JOHN REVOLTA WERE SUPPOSED TO BE HERE!
THE CELEBRITIES WERE ALL HERE, BUT THEY LEFT SUDDENLY!
WHAT HAPPENED ??
SHERRY AND HER CROWD DECIDED TO SPLIT FOR SOME OTHER EVENT IN TOWN!
OH!
WHAT A DOWNER, DADDY!
I WENT TO SHERRY'S CELEBRITY PARTY AND NO ONE WAS THERE!
THAT'S BECAUSE THEY ALL WENT TO THIS EVENT ON TV!
?
4

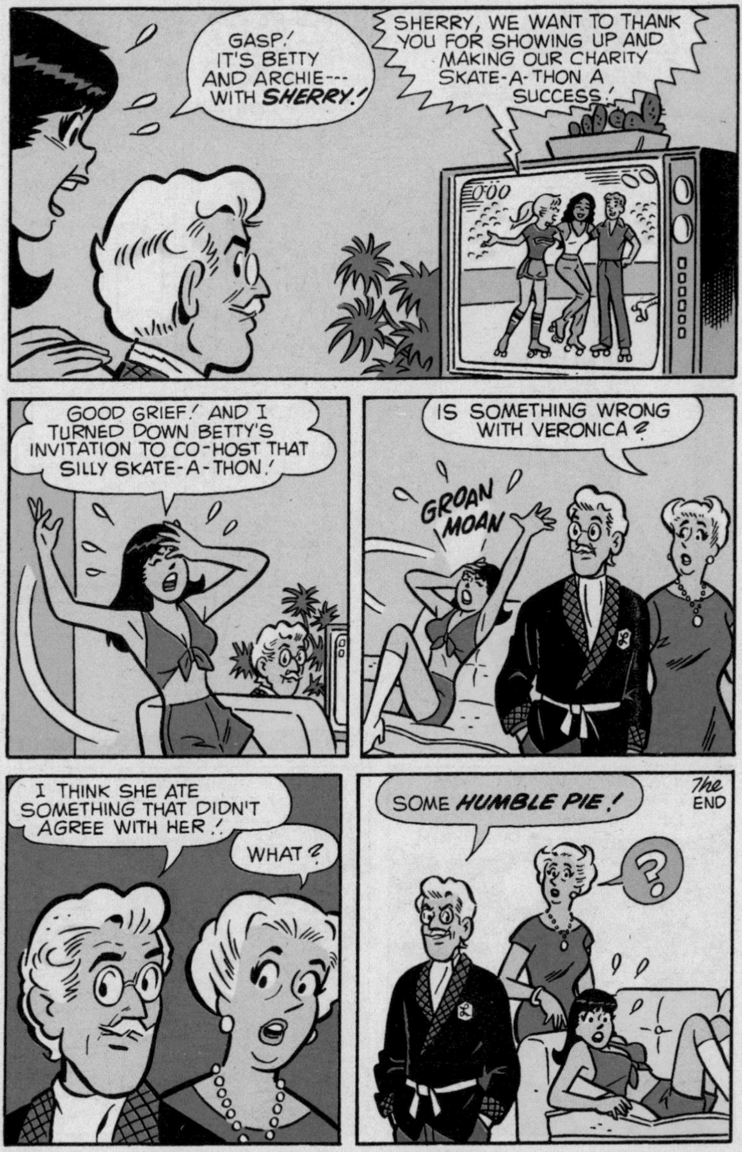
GASP! IT'S BETTY AND ARCHIE--- WITH *SHERRY*!
SHERRY, WE WANT TO THANK YOU FOR SHOWING UP AND MAKING OUR CHARITY SKATE-A-THON A SUCCESS!
GOOD GRIEF! AND I TURNED DOWN BETTY'S INVITATION TO CO-HOST THAT SILLY SKATE-A-THON!
IS SOMETHING WRONG WITH VERONICA?
GROAN
MOAN
I THINK SHE ATE SOMETHING THAT DIDN'T AGREE WITH HER!
WHAT?
SOME *HUMBLE PIE*!
?
The END

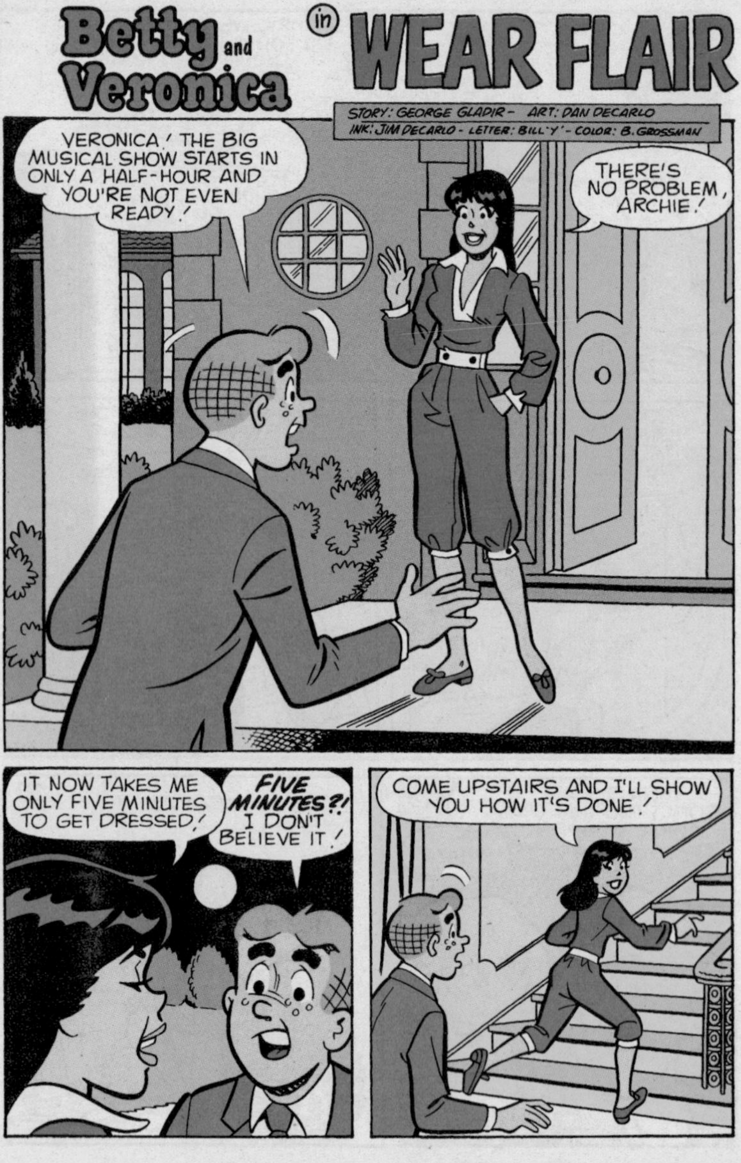

Betty and Veronica
in
WEAR FLAIR
STORY: GEORGE GLADIR - ART: DAN DECARLO
INK: JIM DECARLO - LETTER: BILL "Y" - COLOR: B. GROSSMAN
VERONICA! THE BIG MUSICAL SHOW STARTS IN ONLY A HALF-HOUR AND YOU'RE NOT EVEN READY!
THERE'S NO PROBLEM, ARCHIE!
IT NOW TAKES ME ONLY FIVE MINUTES TO GET DRESSED!
FIVE MINUTES?! I DON'T BELIEVE IT!
COME UPSTAIRS AND I'LL SHOW YOU HOW IT'S DONE!

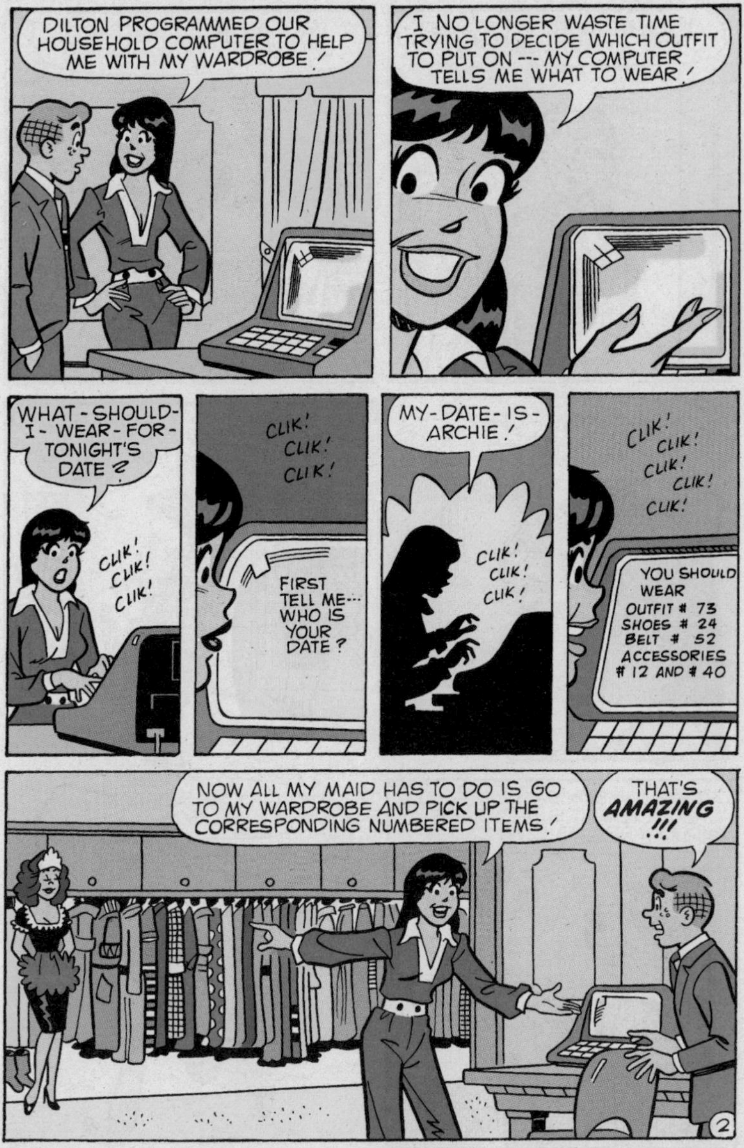
DILTON PROGRAMMED OUR HOUSEHOLD COMPUTER TO HELP ME WITH MY WARDROBE!
I NO LONGER WASTE TIME TRYING TO DECIDE WHICH OUTFIT TO PUT ON --- MY COMPUTER TELLS ME WHAT TO WEAR!
WHAT-SHOULD-I-WEAR-FOR-TONIGHT'S DATE?
CLIK! CLIK! CLIK!
CLIK! CLIK! CLIK!
FIRST TELL ME... WHO IS YOUR DATE?
MY-DATE-IS-ARCHIE!
CLIK! CLIK! CLIK!
CLIK! CLIK! CLIK! CLIK! CLIK!
YOU SHOULD WEAR OUTFIT # 73 SHOES # 24 BELT # 52 ACCESSORIES # 12 AND # 40
NOW ALL MY MAID HAS TO DO IS GO TO MY WARDROBE AND PICK UP THE CORRESPONDING NUMBERED ITEMS!
THAT'S AMAZING!!!
2

OKAY, BUTTERCUP! I'LL WAIT FOR YOU DOWNSTAIRS!

I HAVE ALL THE ITEMS EXCEPT BELT #52! IT'S MISSING!

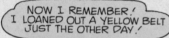

NOW I REMEMBER! I LOANED OUT A YELLOW BELT JUST THE OTHER DAY!

DID I LOAN IT TO BETTY FOR SUE'S PARTY?

--- OR DID I LOAN IT TO SUE FOR BETTY'S PARTY?

ARCHIE! VERONICA WANTS YOU TO GO TO BETTY'S AND SUE'S AND PICK UP A YELLOW BELT!

BUT WE SHOULD BE LEAVING RIGHT NOW!

OH, ALL RIGHT! I'LL GO!

③

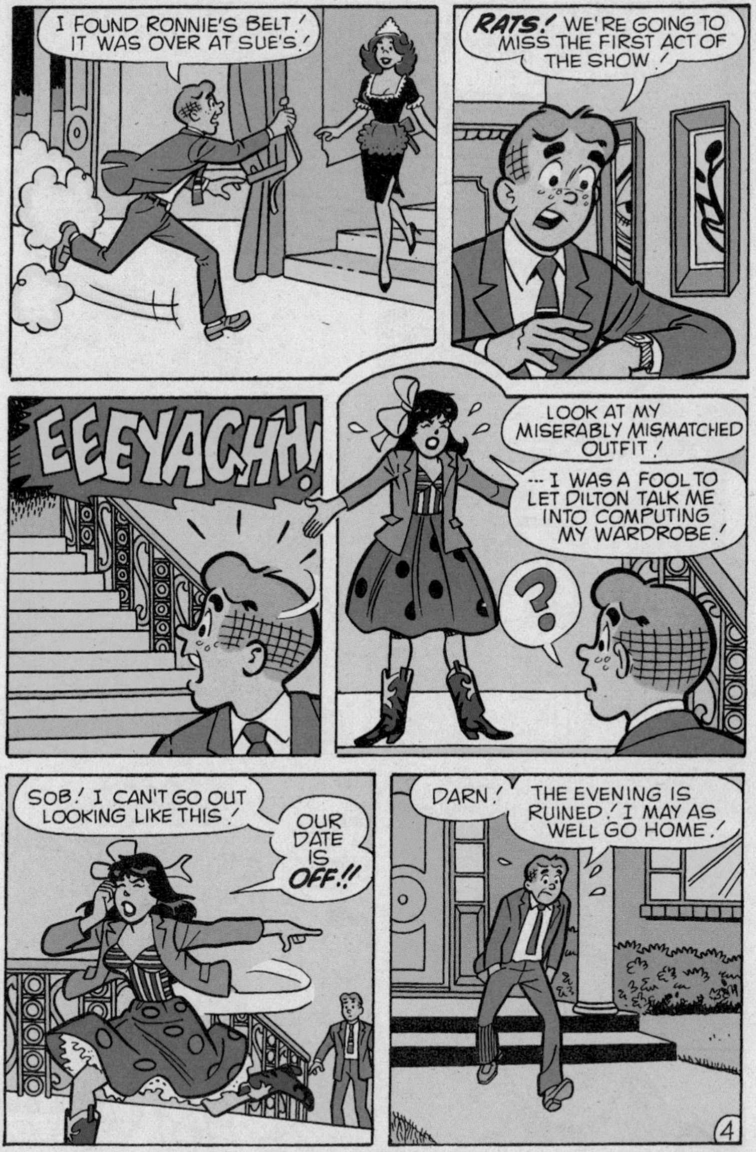

I FOUND RONNIE'S BELT! IT WAS OVER AT SUE'S!
RATS! WE'RE GOING TO MISS THE FIRST ACT OF THE SHOW!
EEEYACHH!
LOOK AT MY MISERABLY MISMATCHED OUTFIT!
--- I WAS A FOOL TO LET DILTON TALK ME INTO COMPUTING MY WARDROBE!
?
SOB! I CAN'T GO OUT LOOKING LIKE THIS!
OUR DATE IS OFF!!
DARN!
THE EVENING IS RUINED! I MAY AS WELL GO HOME!

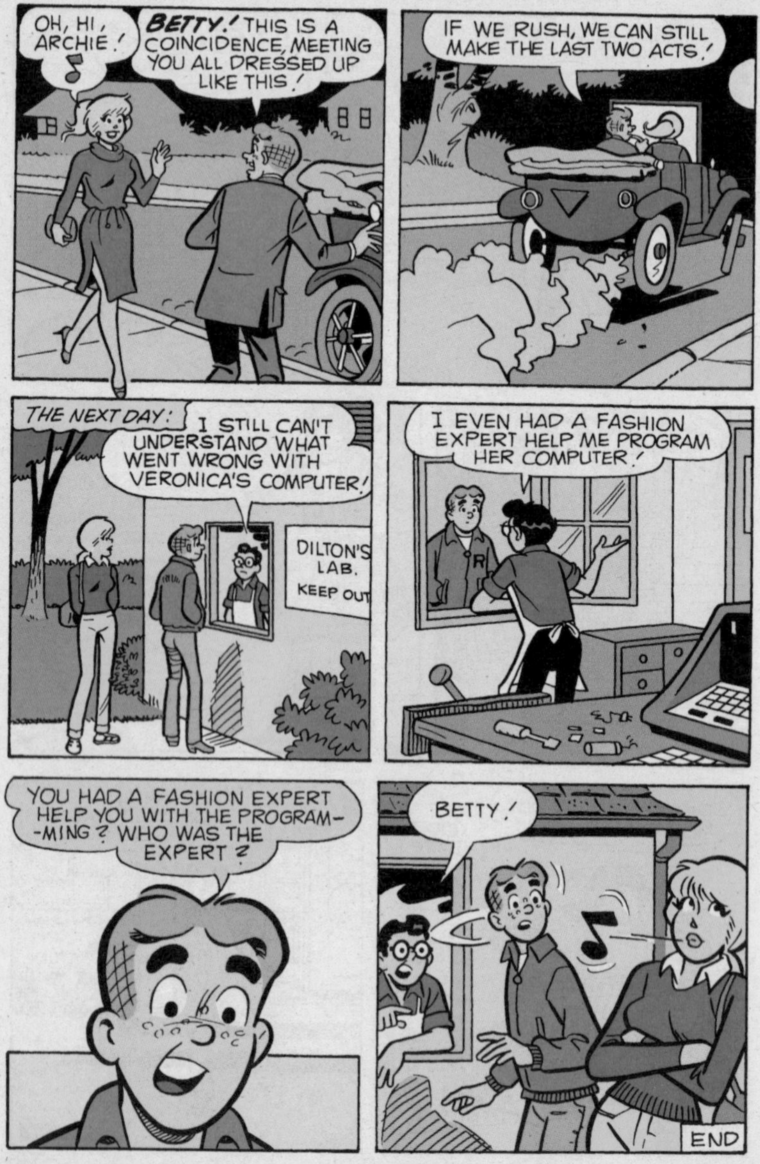
OH, HI, ARCHIE!
BETTY! THIS IS A COINCIDENCE, MEETING YOU ALL DRESSED UP LIKE THIS!
IF WE RUSH, WE CAN STILL MAKE THE LAST TWO ACTS!
THE NEXT DAY:
I STILL CAN'T UNDERSTAND WHAT WENT WRONG WITH VERONICA'S COMPUTER!
DILTON'S LAB. KEEP OUT
I EVEN HAD A FASHION EXPERT HELP ME PROGRAM HER COMPUTER!
YOU HAD A FASHION EXPERT HELP YOU WITH THE PROGRAM--MING? WHO WAS THE EXPERT?
BETTY!
END

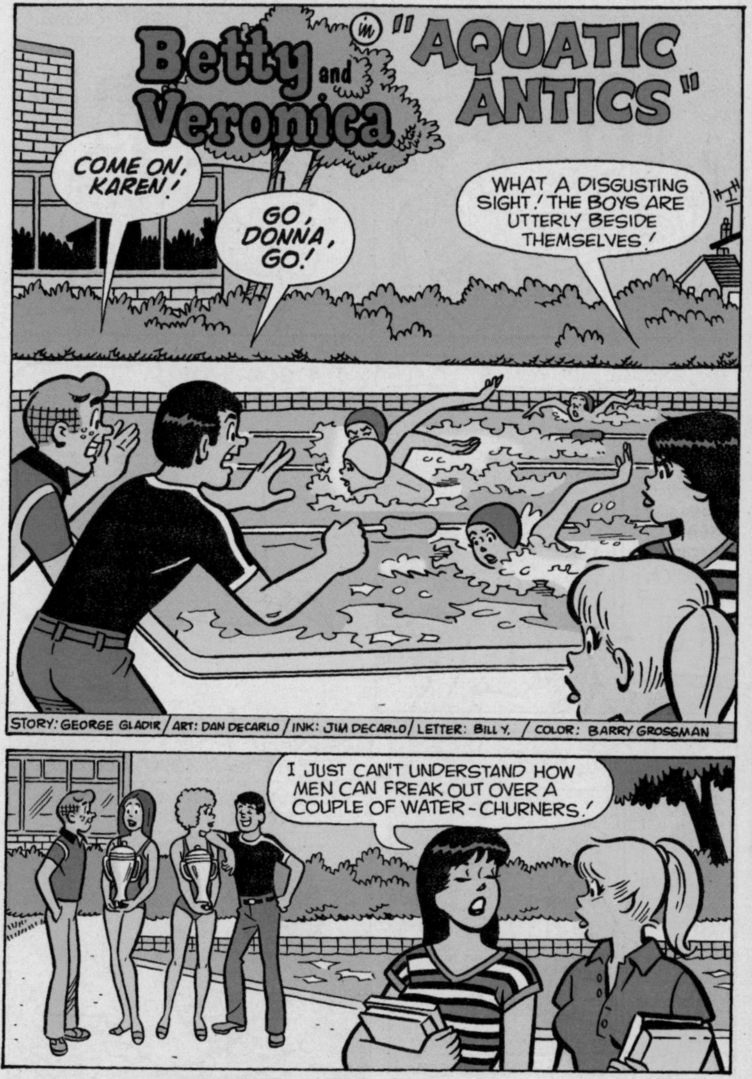
Betty and Veronica in "AQUATIC ANTICS"
COME ON, KAREN!
GO, DONNA, GO!
WHAT A DISGUSTING SIGHT! THE BOYS ARE UTTERLY BESIDE THEMSELVES!
STORY: GEORGE GLADIR / ART: DAN DECARLO / INK: JIM DECARLO / LETTER: BILL Y. / COLOR: BARRY GROSSMAN
I JUST CAN'T UNDERSTAND HOW MEN CAN FREAK OUT OVER A COUPLE OF WATER-CHURNERS!

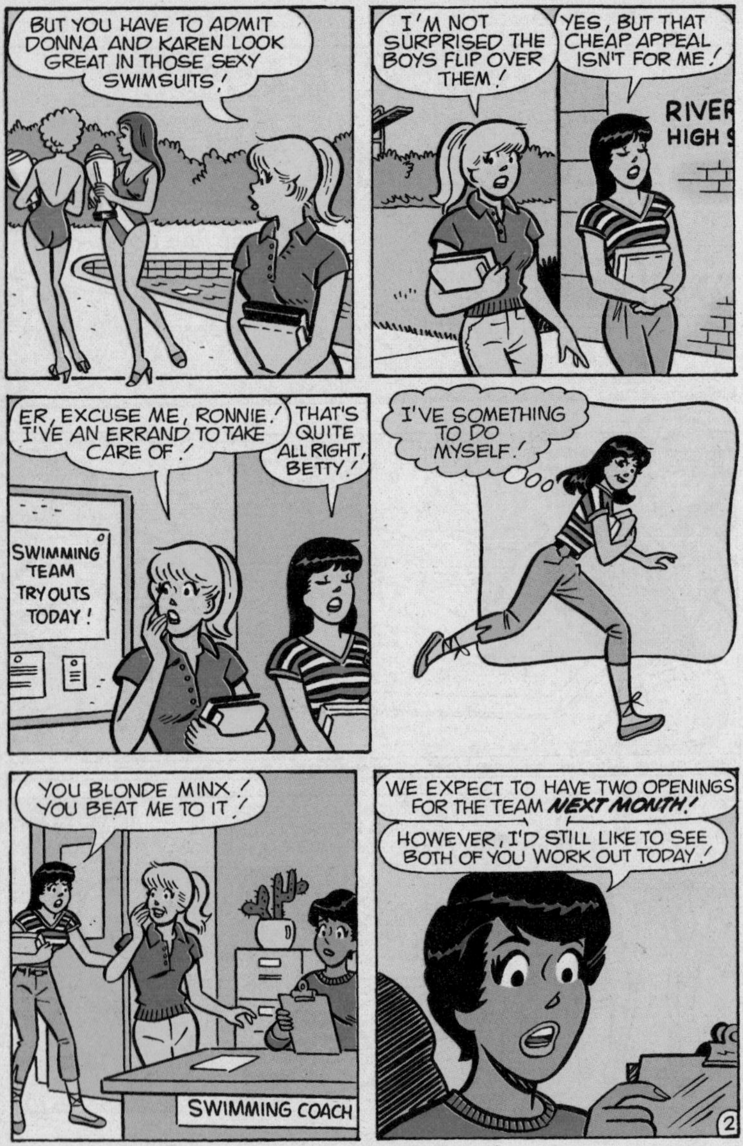
BUT YOU HAVE TO ADMIT DONNA AND KAREN LOOK GREAT IN THOSE SEXY SWIMSUITS!
I'M NOT SURPRISED THE BOYS FLIP OVER THEM!
YES, BUT THAT CHEAP APPEAL ISN'T FOR ME!
RIVER HIGH
ER, EXCUSE ME, RONNIE! I'VE AN ERRAND TO TAKE CARE OF!
THAT'S QUITE ALL RIGHT, BETTY!
SWIMMING TEAM TRY OUTS TODAY!
I'VE SOMETHING TO DO MYSELF!
YOU BLONDE MINX! YOU BEAT ME TO IT!
SWIMMING COACH
WE EXPECT TO HAVE TWO OPENINGS FOR THE TEAM NEXT MONTH!
HOWEVER, I'D STILL LIKE TO SEE BOTH OF YOU WORK OUT TODAY!
2

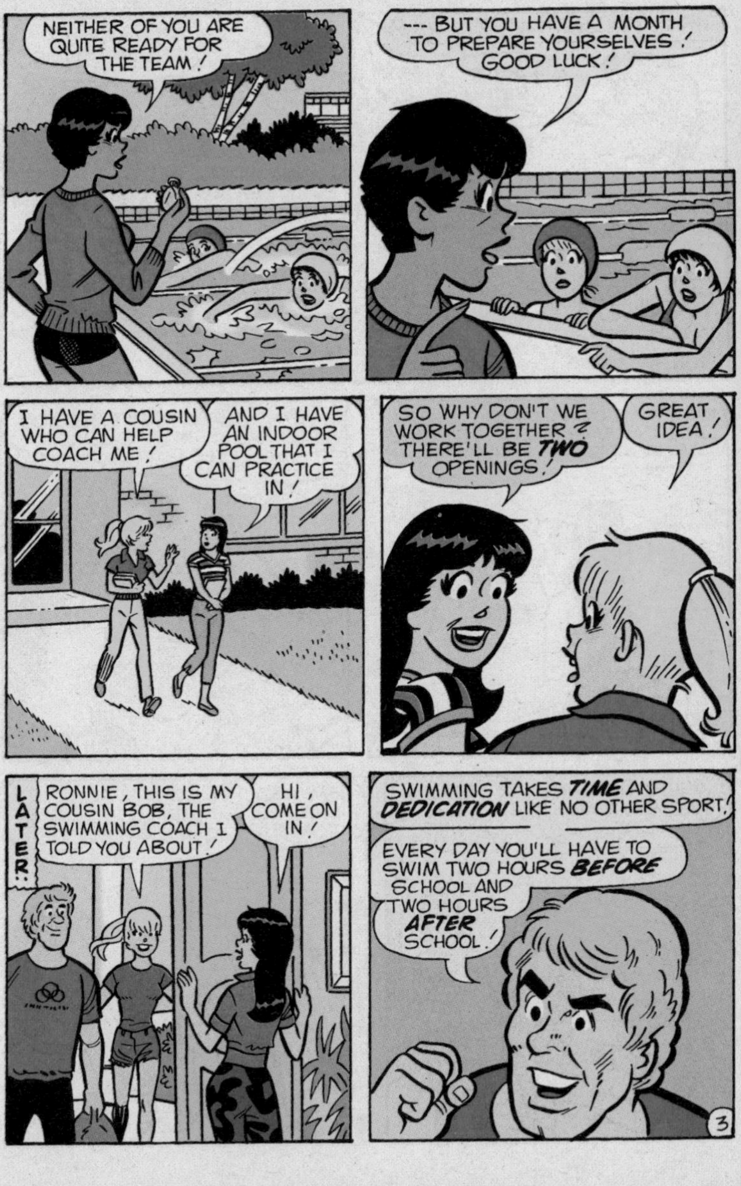
NEITHER OF YOU ARE QUITE READY FOR THE TEAM!
--- BUT YOU HAVE A MONTH TO PREPARE YOURSELVES! GOOD LUCK!
I HAVE A COUSIN WHO CAN HELP COACH ME!
AND I HAVE AN INDOOR POOL THAT I CAN PRACTICE IN!
SO WHY DON'T WE WORK TOGETHER? THERE'LL BE TWO OPENINGS!
GREAT IDEA!
LATER:
RONNIE, THIS IS MY COUSIN BOB, THE SWIMMING COACH I TOLD YOU ABOUT!
HI, COME ON IN!
SWIMMING TAKES TIME AND DEDICATION LIKE NO OTHER SPORT!
EVERY DAY YOU'LL HAVE TO SWIM TWO HOURS BEFORE SCHOOL AND TWO HOURS AFTER SCHOOL!
3

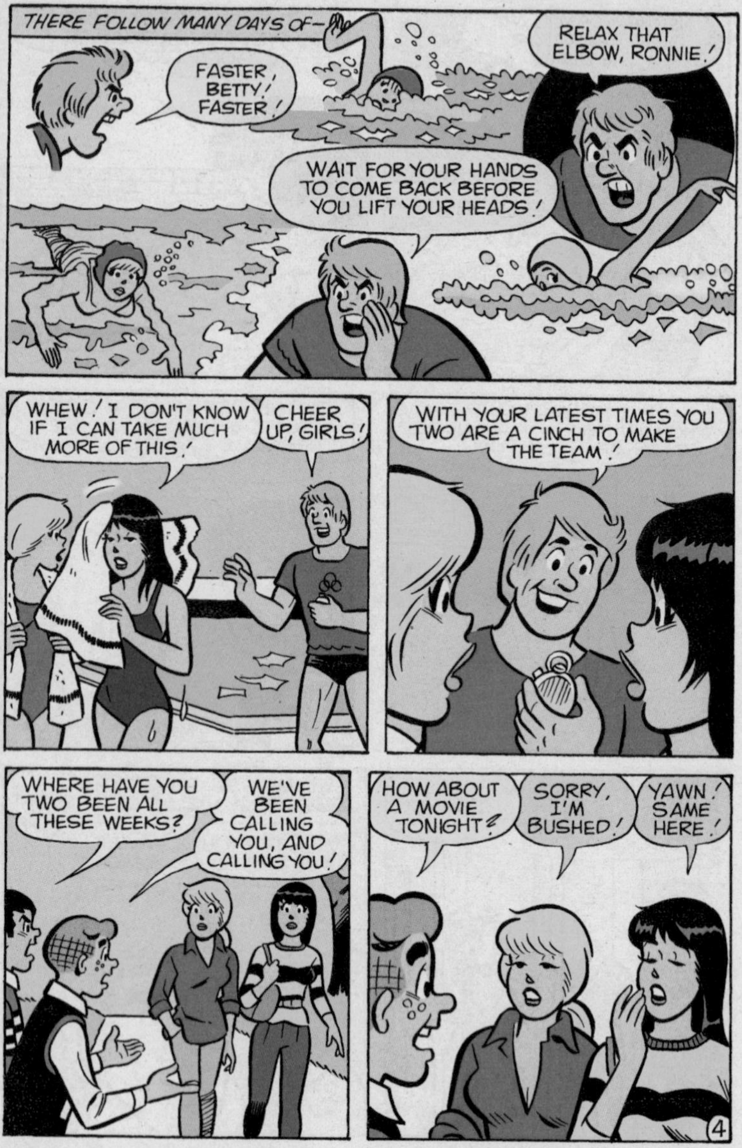
THERE FOLLOW MANY DAYS OF—
FASTER, BETTY! FASTER!
RELAX THAT ELBOW, RONNIE!
WAIT FOR YOUR HANDS TO COME BACK BEFORE YOU LIFT YOUR HEADS!
WHEW! I DON'T KNOW IF I CAN TAKE MUCH MORE OF THIS!
CHEER UP, GIRLS!
WITH YOUR LATEST TIMES YOU TWO ARE A CINCH TO MAKE THE TEAM!
WHERE HAVE YOU TWO BEEN ALL THESE WEEKS?
WE'VE BEEN CALLING YOU, AND CALLING YOU!
HOW ABOUT A MOVIE TONIGHT?
SORRY, I'M BUSHED!
YAWN! SAME HERE!
4

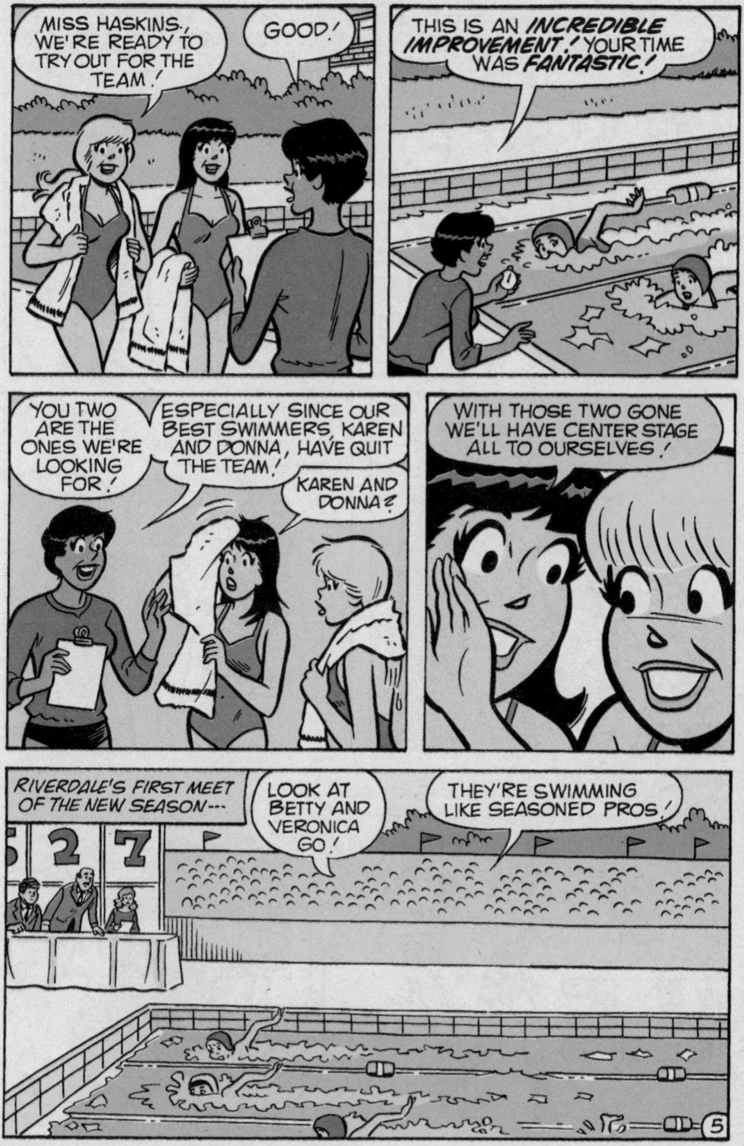
MISS HASKINS., WE'RE READY TO TRY OUT FOR THE TEAM!
GOOD!
THIS IS AN INCREDIBLE IMPROVEMENT! YOUR TIME WAS FANTASTIC!
YOU TWO ARE THE ONES WE'RE LOOKING FOR!
ESPECIALLY SINCE OUR BEST SWIMMERS, KAREN AND DONNA, HAVE QUIT THE TEAM!
KAREN AND DONNA?
WITH THOSE TWO GONE WE'LL HAVE CENTER STAGE ALL TO OURSELVES!
RIVERDALE'S FIRST MEET OF THE NEW SEASON---
LOOK AT BETTY AND VERONICA GO!
THEY'RE SWIMMING LIKE SEASONED PROS!
527
5

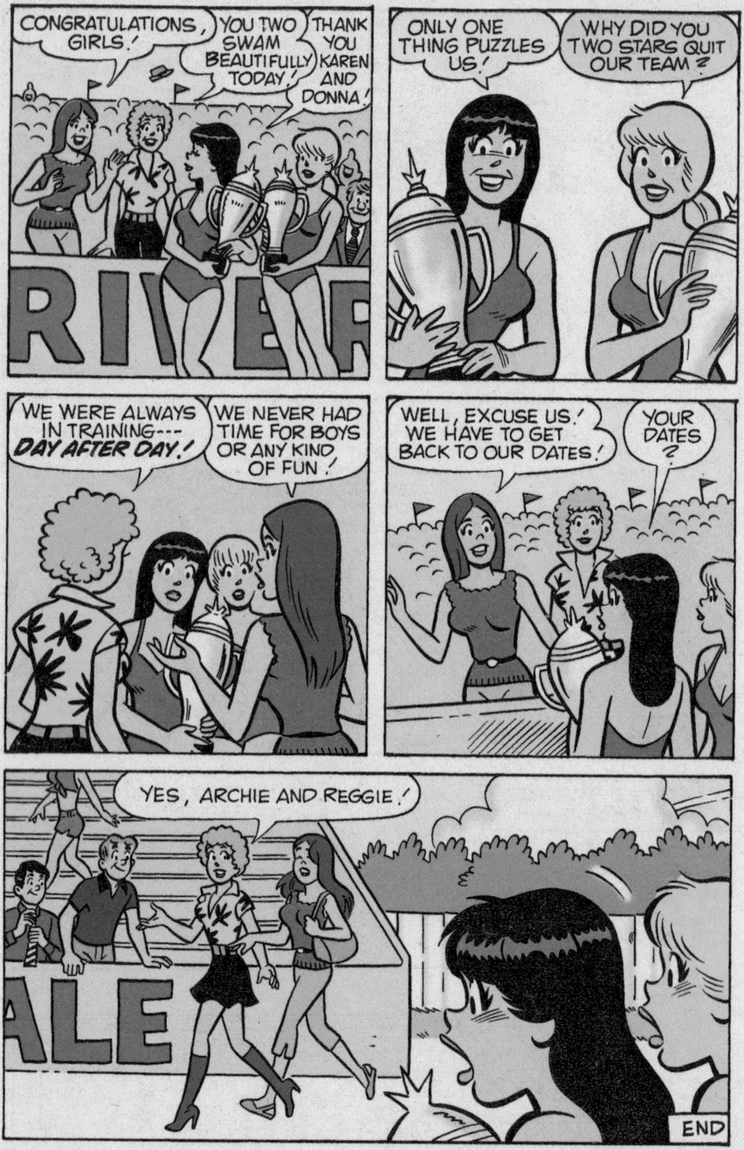
CONGRATULATIONS, GIRLS!
YOU TWO SWAM BEAUTIFULLY TODAY!
THANK YOU KAREN AND DONNA!
RIVER
ONLY ONE THING PUZZLES US!
WHY DID YOU TWO STARS QUIT OUR TEAM?
WE WERE ALWAYS IN TRAINING--- DAY AFTER DAY!
WE NEVER HAD TIME FOR BOYS OR ANY KIND OF FUN!
WELL, EXCUSE US! WE HAVE TO GET BACK TO OUR DATES!
YOUR DATES?
YES, ARCHIE AND REGGIE!
ALE
END

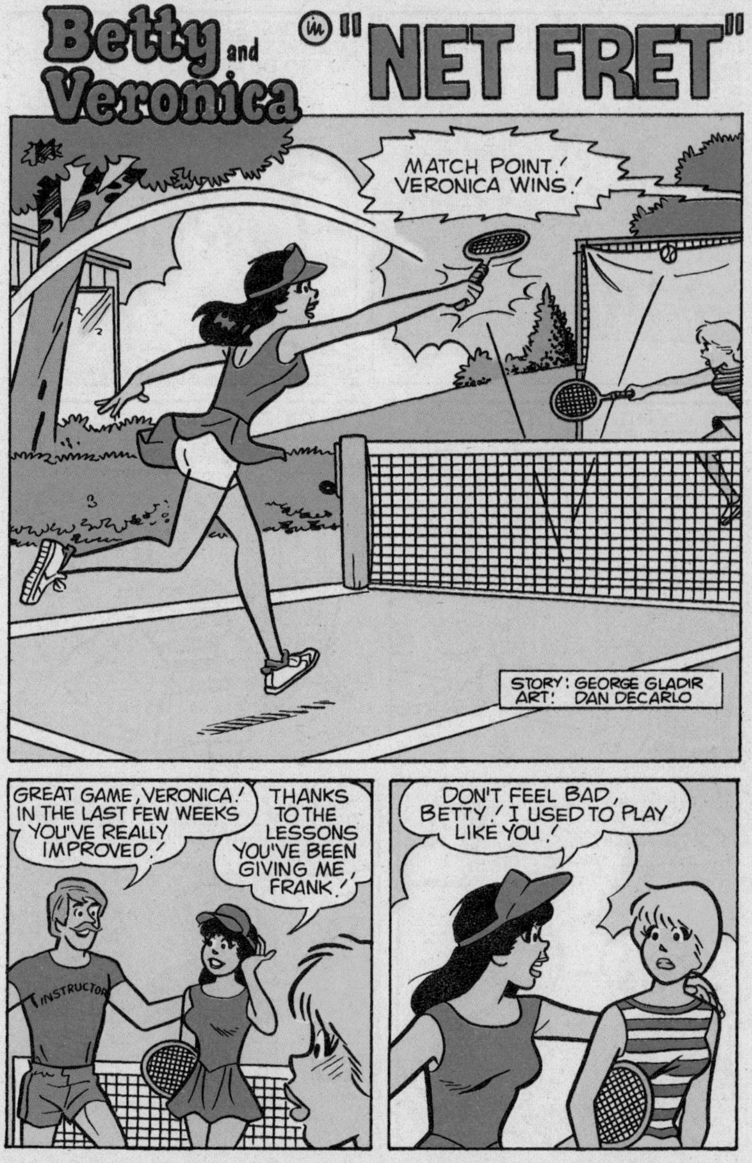

Betty and Veronica
in "NET FRET"
MATCH POINT! VERONICA WINS!
STORY: GEORGE GLADIR
ART: DAN DECARLO
GREAT GAME, VERONICA! IN THE LAST FEW WEEKS YOU'VE REALLY IMPROVED!
THANKS TO THE LESSONS YOU'VE BEEN GIVING ME, FRANK!
INSTRUCTOR
DON'T FEEL BAD, BETTY! I USED TO PLAY LIKE YOU!

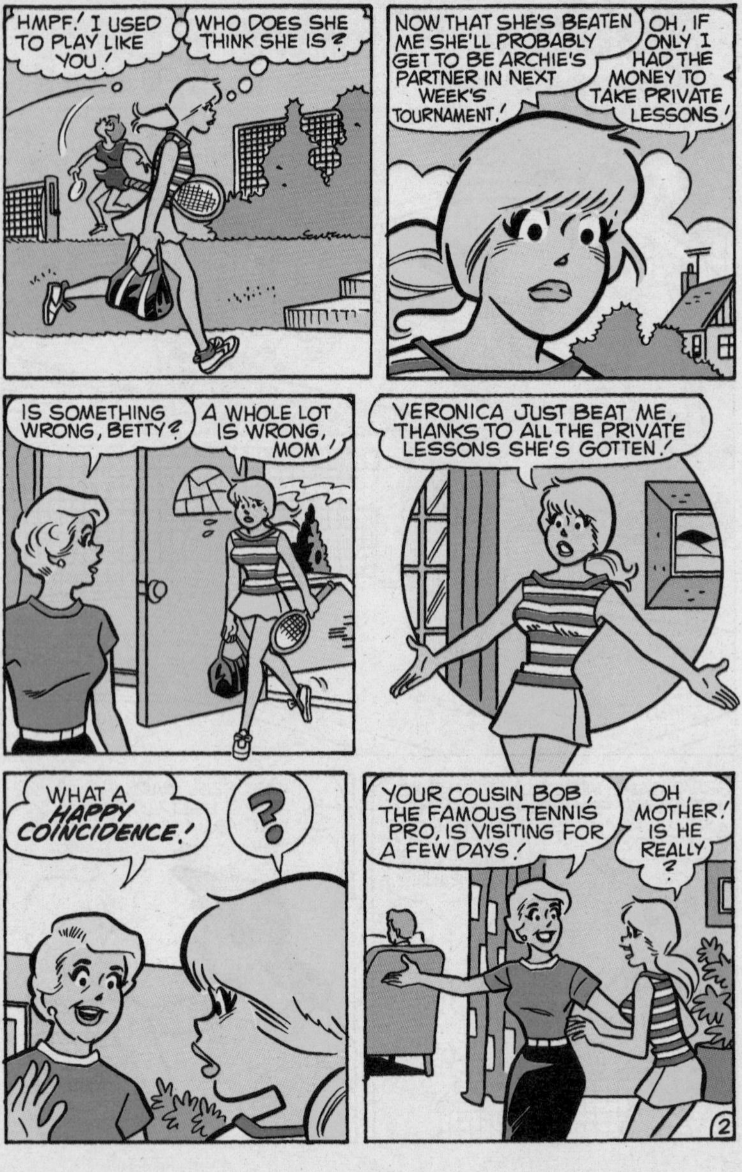
HMPF! I USED TO PLAY LIKE YOU!
WHO DOES SHE THINK SHE IS?
NOW THAT SHE'S BEATEN ME SHE'LL PROBABLY GET TO BE ARCHIE'S PARTNER IN NEXT WEEK'S TOURNAMENT!
OH, IF ONLY I HAD THE MONEY TO TAKE PRIVATE LESSONS!
IS SOMETHING WRONG, BETTY?
A WHOLE LOT IS WRONG, MOM!
VERONICA JUST BEAT ME, THANKS TO ALL THE PRIVATE LESSONS SHE'S GOTTEN!
WHAT A HAPPY COINCIDENCE!
?
YOUR COUSIN BOB, THE FAMOUS TENNIS PRO, IS VISITING FOR A FEW DAYS!
OH MOTHER! IS HE REALLY?
2

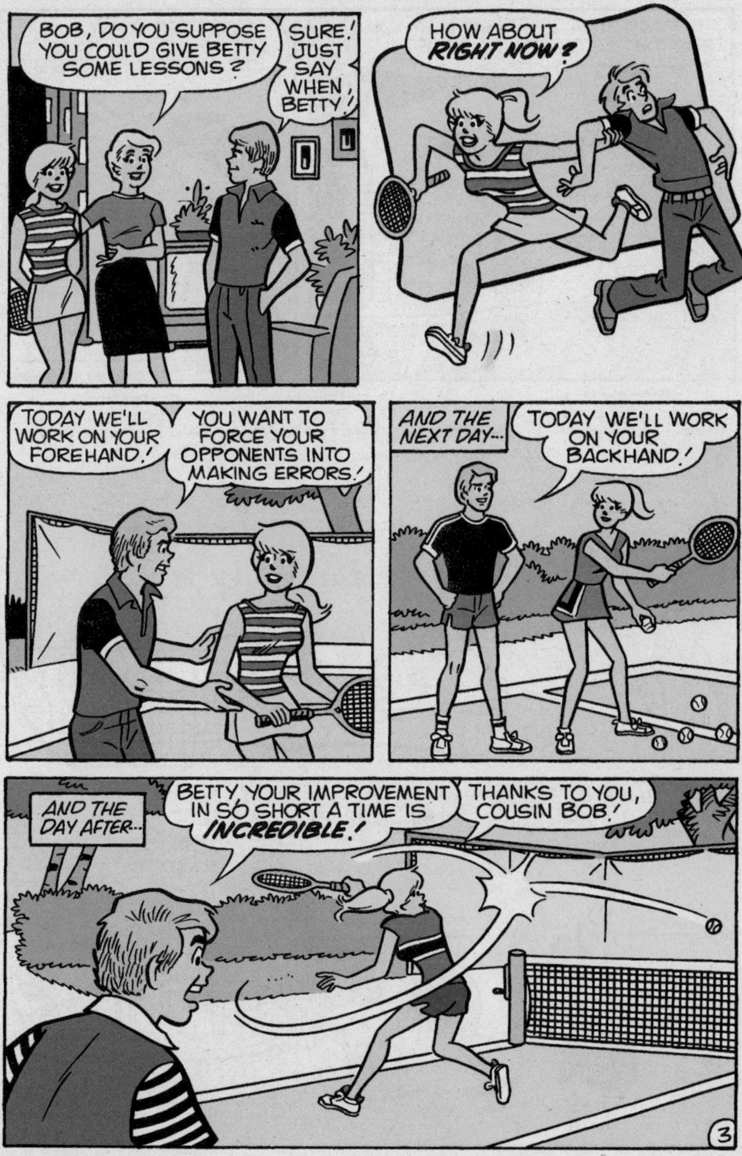
BOB, DO YOU SUPPOSE YOU COULD GIVE BETTY SOME LESSONS?
SURE! JUST SAY WHEN, BETTY!
HOW ABOUT RIGHT NOW?
TODAY WE'LL WORK ON YOUR FOREHAND!
YOU WANT TO FORCE YOUR OPPONENTS INTO MAKING ERRORS!
AND THE NEXT DAY...
TODAY WE'LL WORK ON YOUR BACKHAND!
AND THE DAY AFTER...
BETTY, YOUR IMPROVEMENT IN SO SHORT A TIME IS INCREDIBLE!
THANKS TO YOU, COUSIN BOB!
3

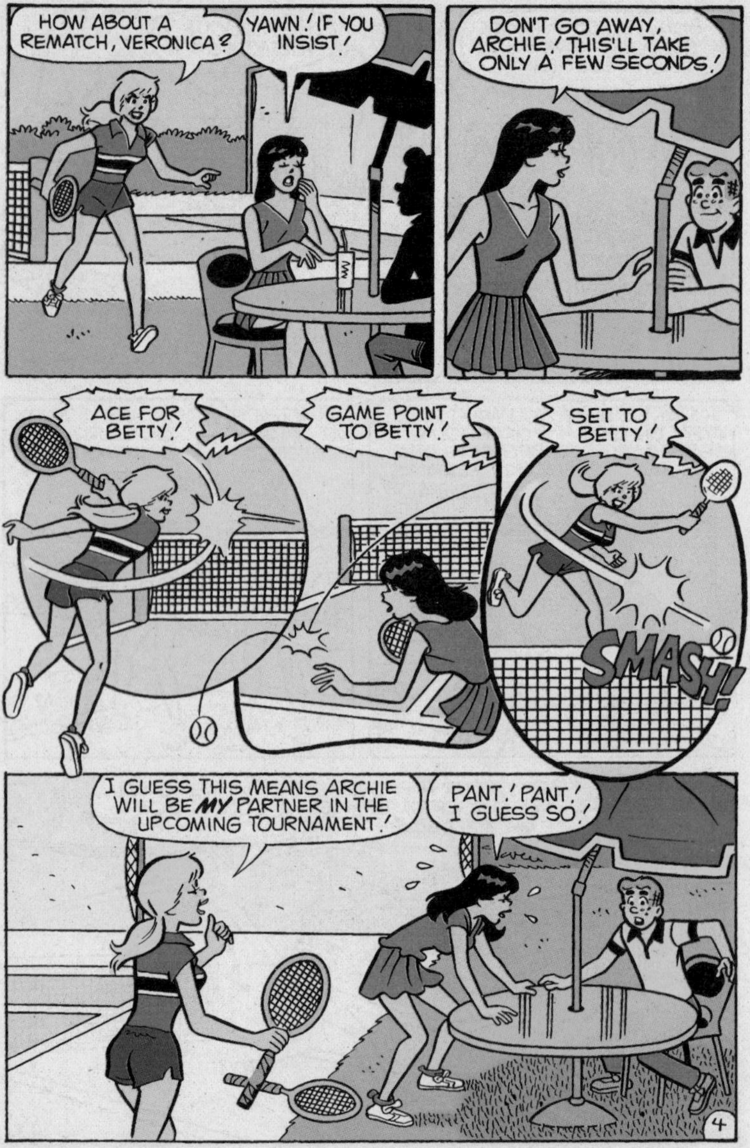
HOW ABOUT A REMATCH, VERONICA?
YAWN! IF YOU INSIST!
DON'T GO AWAY, ARCHIE! THIS'LL TAKE ONLY A FEW SECONDS!
ACE FOR BETTY!
GAME POINT TO BETTY!
SET TO BETTY!
SMASH!
I GUESS THIS MEANS ARCHIE WILL BE *MY* PARTNER IN THE UPCOMING TOURNAMENT!
PANT! PANT! I GUESS SO!
4

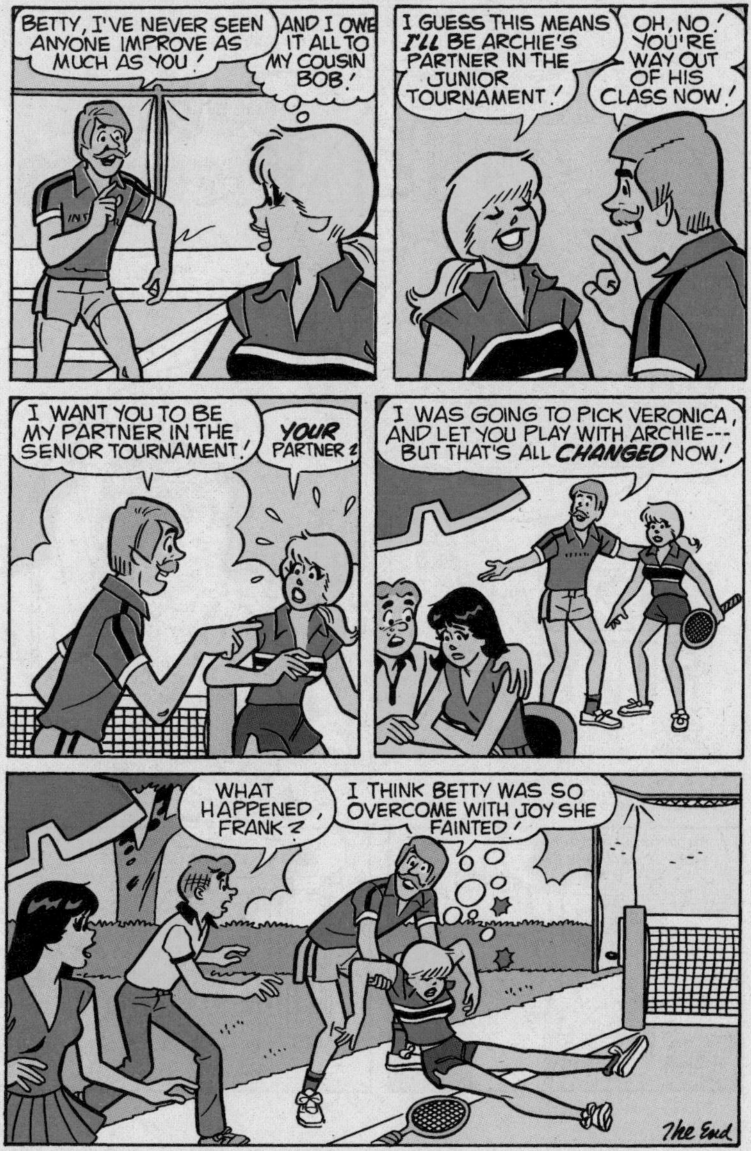

BETTY, I'VE NEVER SEEN ANYONE IMPROVE AS MUCH AS YOU!
AND I OWE IT ALL TO MY COUSIN BOB!
I GUESS THIS MEANS *I'LL* BE ARCHIE'S PARTNER IN THE JUNIOR TOURNAMENT!
OH, NO! YOU'RE WAY OUT OF HIS CLASS NOW!
I WANT YOU TO BE MY PARTNER IN THE SENIOR TOURNAMENT!
YOUR PARTNER?
I WAS GOING TO PICK VERONICA, AND LET YOU PLAY WITH ARCHIE--- BUT THAT'S ALL *CHANGED* NOW!
WHAT HAPPENED, FRANK?
I THINK BETTY WAS SO OVERCOME WITH JOY SHE FAINTED!
The End

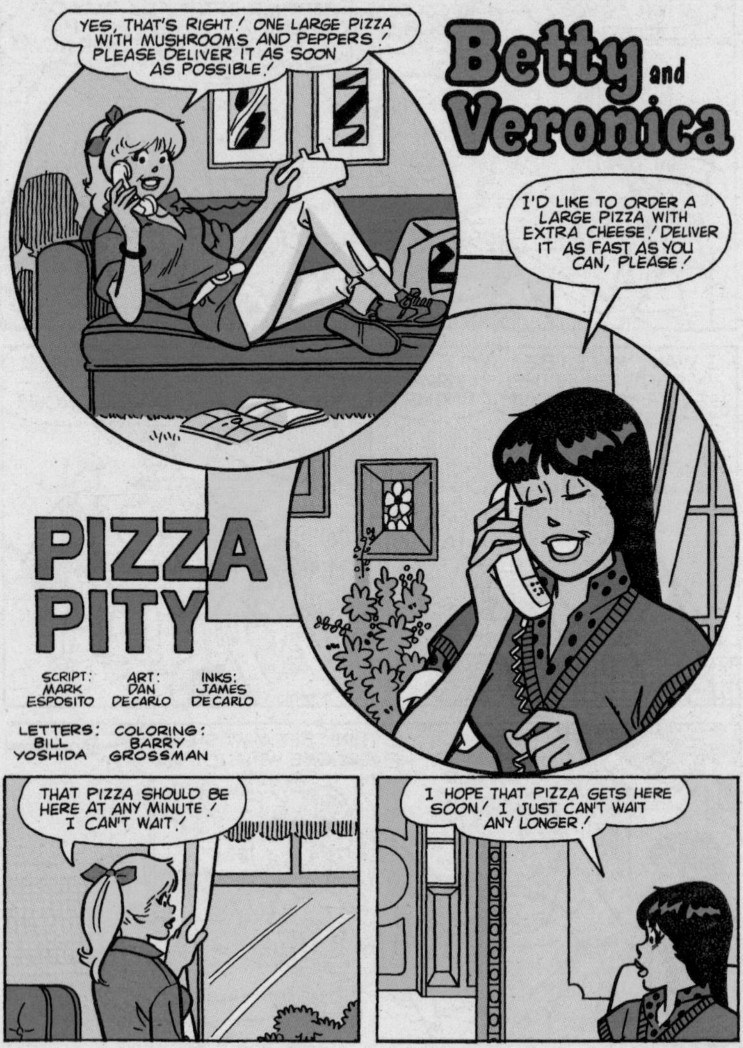

YES, THAT'S RIGHT! ONE LARGE PIZZA WITH MUSHROOMS AND PEPPERS! PLEASE DELIVER IT AS SOON AS POSSIBLE!
Betty and Veronica
I'D LIKE TO ORDER A LARGE PIZZA WITH EXTRA CHEESE! DELIVER IT AS FAST AS YOU CAN, PLEASE!
PIZZA PITY
SCRIPT: MARK ESPOSITO
ART: DAN DECARLO
INKS: JAMES DECARLO
LETTERS: BILL YOSHIDA
COLORING: BARRY GROSSMAN
THAT PIZZA SHOULD BE HERE AT ANY MINUTE! I CAN'T WAIT!
I HOPE THAT PIZZA GETS HERE SOON! I JUST CAN'T WAIT ANY LONGER!

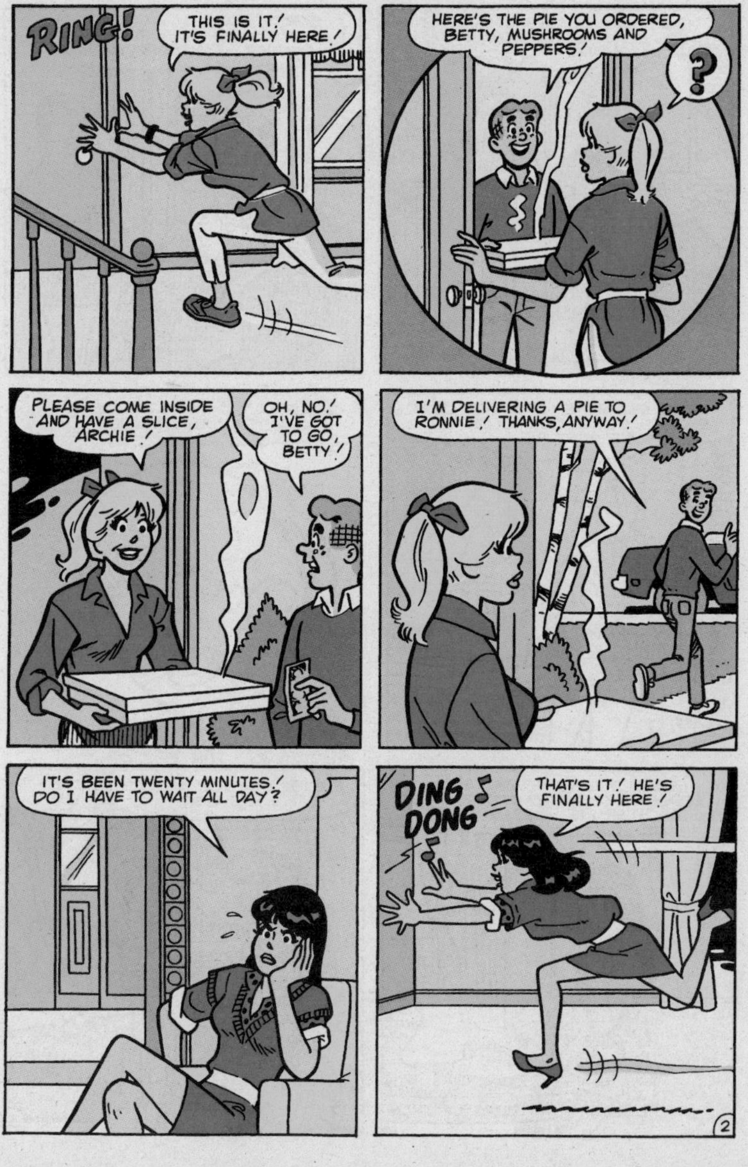
RING!
THIS IS IT! IT'S FINALLY HERE!
HERE'S THE PIE YOU ORDERED, BETTY, MUSHROOMS AND PEPPERS!
?
PLEASE COME INSIDE AND HAVE A SLICE, ARCHIE!
OH, NO! I'VE GOT TO GO, BETTY!
I'M DELIVERING A PIE TO RONNIE! THANKS, ANYWAY!
IT'S BEEN TWENTY MINUTES! DO I HAVE TO WAIT ALL DAY?
DING DONG
THAT'S IT! HE'S FINALLY HERE!
2

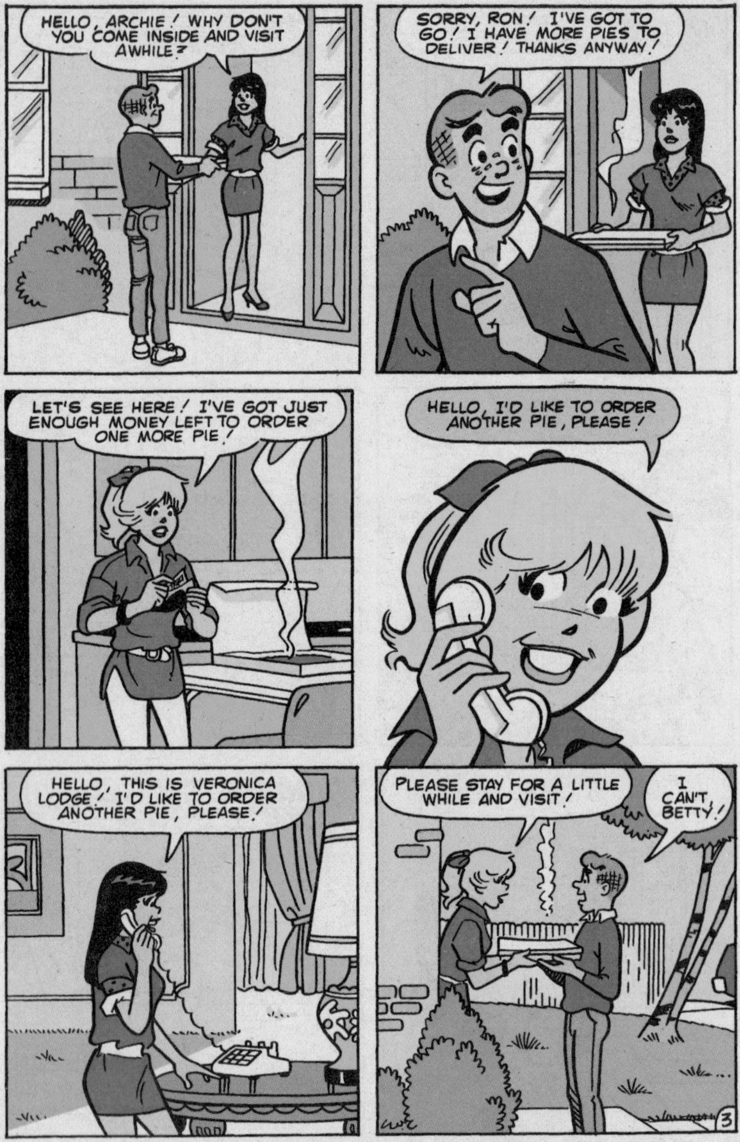
HELLO, ARCHIE! WHY DON'T YOU COME INSIDE AND VISIT AWHILE?
SORRY, RON! I'VE GOT TO GO! I HAVE MORE PIES TO DELIVER! THANKS ANYWAY!
LET'S SEE HERE! I'VE GOT JUST ENOUGH MONEY LEFT TO ORDER ONE MORE PIE!
HELLO, I'D LIKE TO ORDER ANOTHER PIE, PLEASE!
HELLO, THIS IS VERONICA LODGE! I'D LIKE TO ORDER ANOTHER PIE, PLEASE!
PLEASE STAY FOR A LITTLE WHILE AND VISIT!
I CAN'T, BETTY!
3

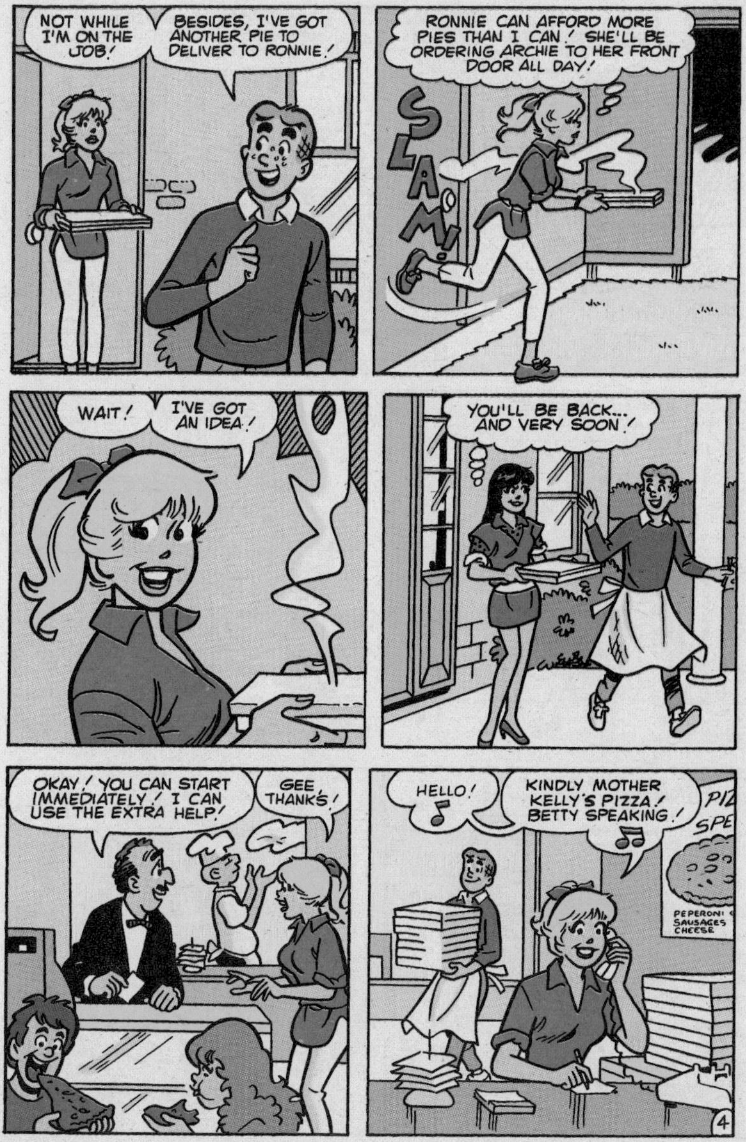
NOT WHILE I'M ON THE JOB!
BESIDES, I'VE GOT ANOTHER PIE TO DELIVER TO RONNIE!
RONNIE CAN AFFORD MORE PIES THAN I CAN! SHE'LL BE ORDERING ARCHIE TO HER FRONT DOOR ALL DAY!
SLAM!
WAIT!
I'VE GOT AN IDEA!
YOU'LL BE BACK... AND VERY SOON!
OKAY! YOU CAN START IMMEDIATELY! I CAN USE THE EXTRA HELP!
GEE, THANKS!
HELLO!
KINDLY MOTHER KELLY'S PIZZA! BETTY SPEAKING!
PEPERONI
SAUSAGES
CHEESE

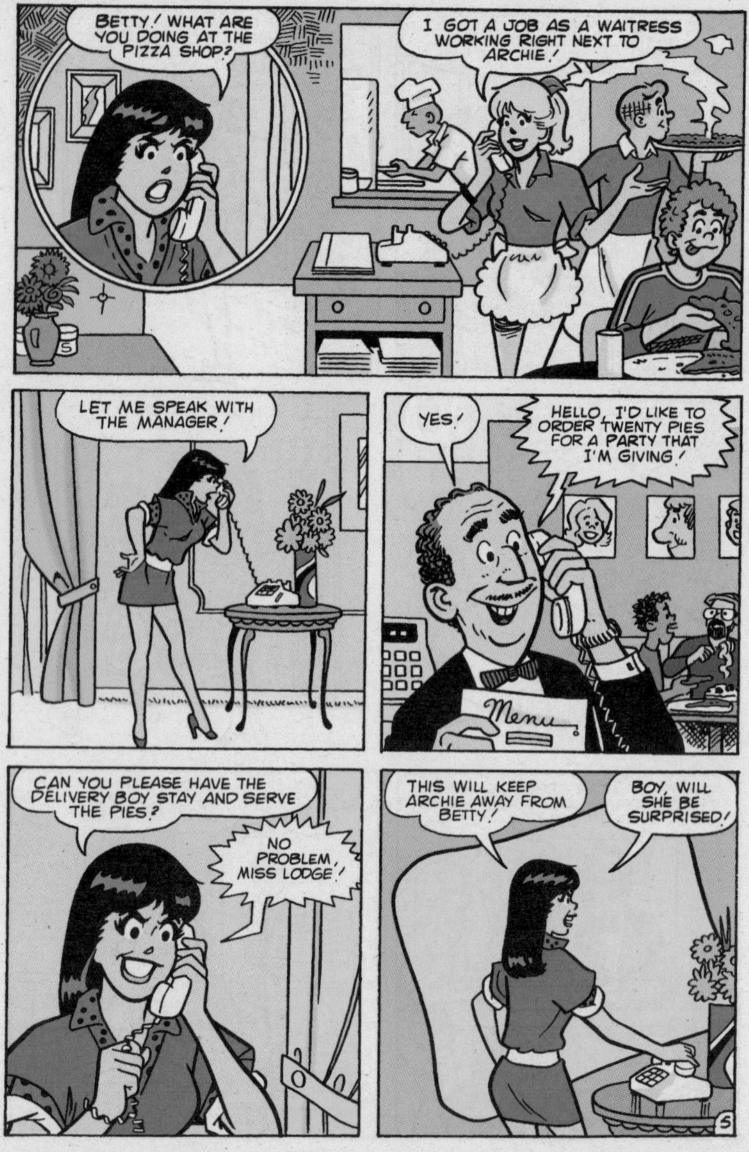
BETTY! WHAT ARE YOU DOING AT THE PIZZA SHOP?
I GOT A JOB AS A WAITRESS WORKING RIGHT NEXT TO ARCHIE!
LET ME SPEAK WITH THE MANAGER!
YES!
HELLO, I'D LIKE TO ORDER TWENTY PIES FOR A PARTY THAT I'M GIVING!
Menu
CAN YOU PLEASE HAVE THE DELIVERY BOY STAY AND SERVE THE PIES?
NO PROBLEM, MISS LODGE!
THIS WILL KEEP ARCHIE AWAY FROM BETTY!
BOY, WILL SHE BE SURPRISED!
5

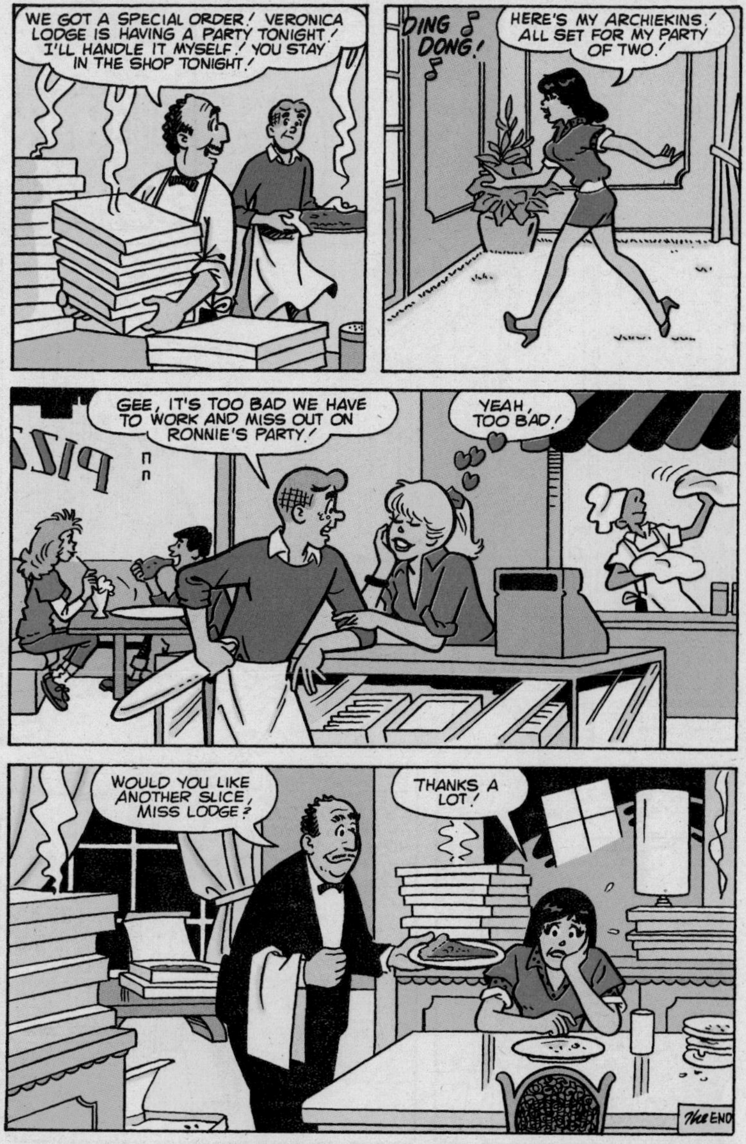
WE GOT A SPECIAL ORDER! VERONICA LODGE IS HAVING A PARTY TONIGHT! I'LL HANDLE IT MYSELF! YOU STAY IN THE SHOP TONIGHT!
DING DONG!
HERE'S MY ARCHIEKINS! ALL SET FOR MY PARTY OF TWO!
GEE, IT'S TOO BAD WE HAVE TO WORK AND MISS OUT ON RONNIE'S PARTY!
YEAH, TOO BAD!
WOULD YOU LIKE ANOTHER SLICE, MISS LODGE?
THANKS A LOT!
END

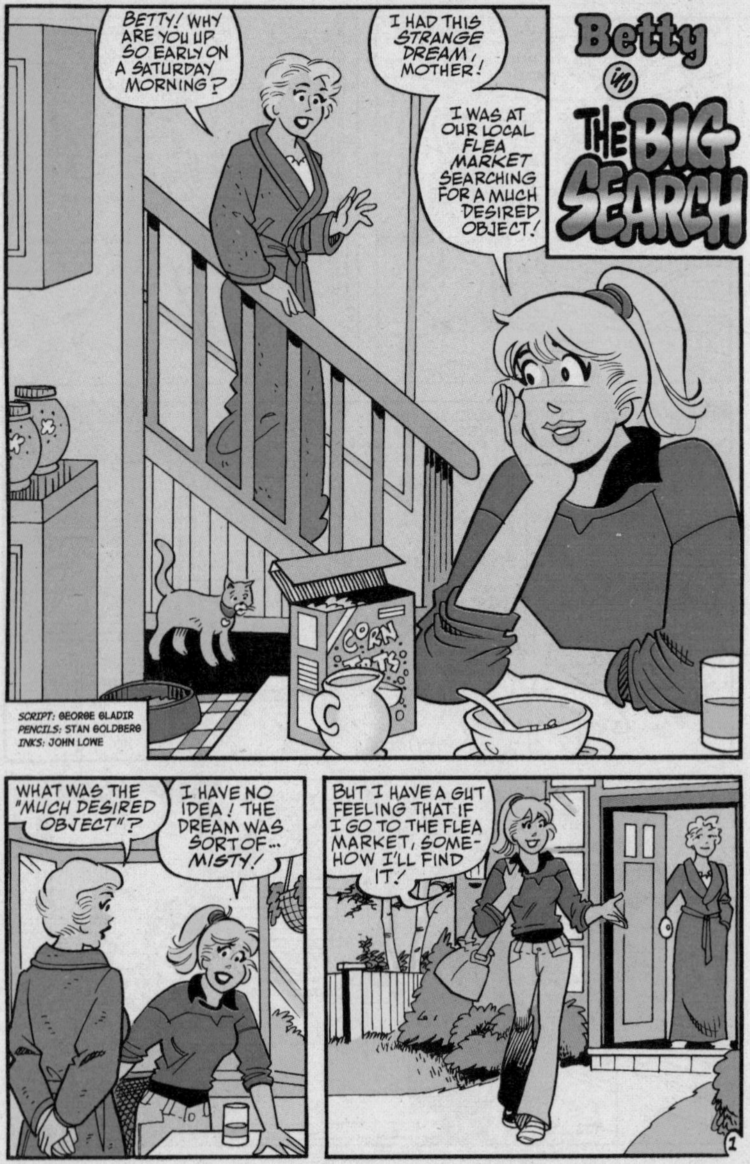
Betty in THE BIG SEARCH
BETTY! WHY ARE YOU UP SO EARLY ON A SATURDAY MORNING?
I HAD THIS STRANGE DREAM, MOTHER!
I WAS AT OUR LOCAL FLEA MARKET SEARCHING FOR A MUCH DESIRED OBJECT!
CORN TOTS
SCRIPT: GEORGE GLADIR
PENCILS: STAN GOLDBERG
INKS: JOHN LOWE
WHAT WAS THE "MUCH DESIRED OBJECT"?
I HAVE NO IDEA! THE DREAM WAS SORT OF... MISTY!
BUT I HAVE A GUT FEELING THAT IF I GO TO THE FLEA MARKET, SOME-HOW I'LL FIND IT!

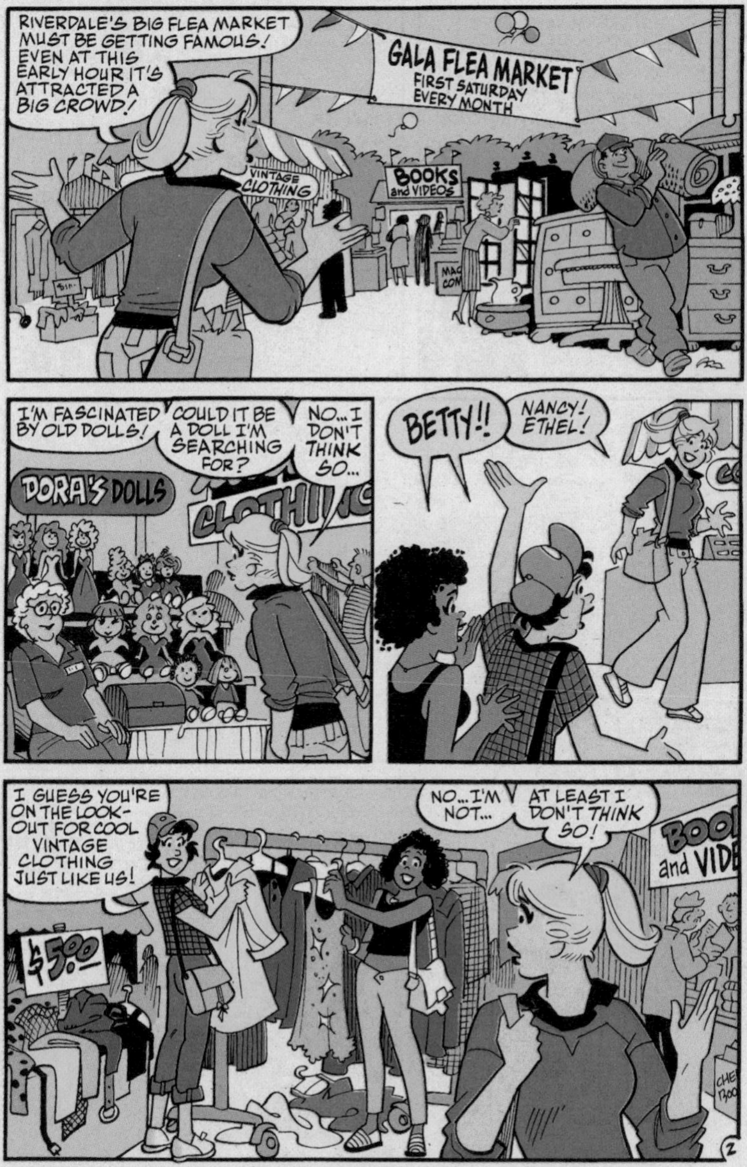

RIVERDALE'S BIG FLEA MARKET MUST BE GETTING FAMOUS! EVEN AT THIS EARLY HOUR IT'S ATTRACTED A BIG CROWD!
GALA FLEA MARKET
FIRST SATURDAY EVERY MONTH
VINTAGE CLOTHING
BOOKS and VIDEOS
I'M FASCINATED BY OLD DOLLS!
COULD IT BE A DOLL I'M SEARCHING FOR?
NO...I DON'T THINK SO...
DORA'S DOLLS
BETTY!!
NANCY! ETHEL!
I GUESS YOU'RE ON THE LOOK-OUT FOR COOL VINTAGE CLOTHING JUST LIKE US!
NO...I'M NOT...
AT LEAST I DON'T THINK SO!
$5.00

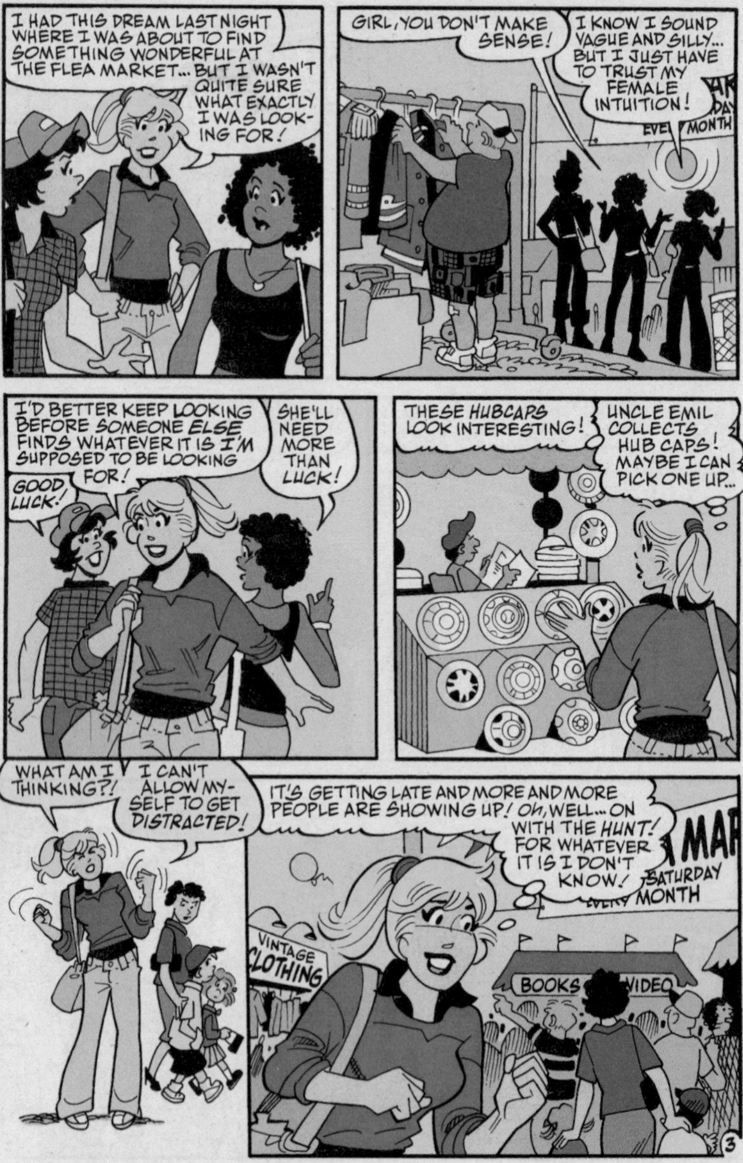

I HAD THIS DREAM LAST NIGHT WHERE I WAS ABOUT TO FIND SOMETHING WONDERFUL AT THE FLEA MARKET... BUT I WASN'T QUITE SURE WHAT EXACTLY I WAS LOOKING FOR!
GIRL, YOU DON'T MAKE SENSE!
I KNOW I SOUND VAGUE AND SILLY... BUT I JUST HAVE TO TRUST MY FEMALE INTUITION!
I'D BETTER KEEP LOOKING BEFORE SOMEONE ELSE FINDS WHATEVER IT IS I'M SUPPOSED TO BE LOOKING FOR!
GOOD LUCK!
SHE'LL NEED MORE THAN LUCK!
THESE HUBCAPS LOOK INTERESTING!
UNCLE EMIL COLLECTS HUB CAPS! MAYBE I CAN PICK ONE UP...
WHAT AM I THINKING?!
I CAN'T ALLOW MYSELF TO GET DISTRACTED!
IT'S GETTING LATE AND MORE AND MORE PEOPLE ARE SHOWING UP! Oh, WELL... ON WITH THE HUNT! FOR WHATEVER IT IS I DON'T KNOW!
VINTAGE CLOTHING
BOOKS
VIDEO
SATURDAY
MONTH

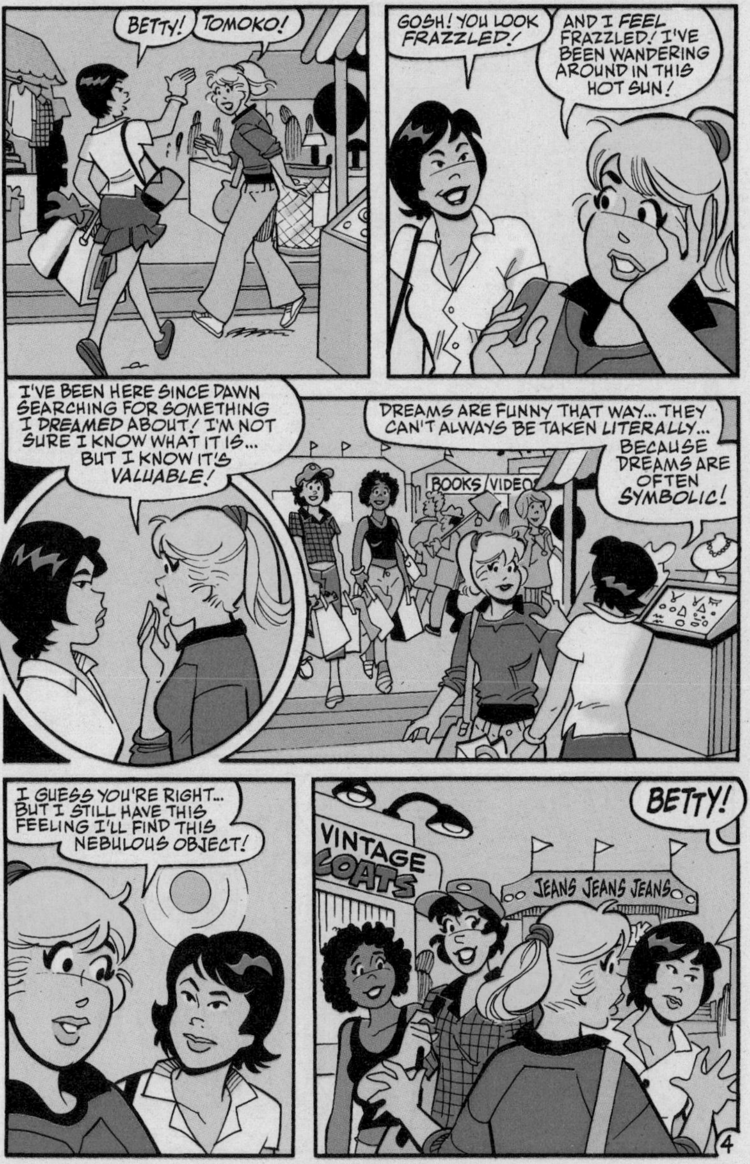

BETTY!
TOMOKO!
GOSH! YOU LOOK FRAZZLED!
AND I FEEL FRAZZLED! I'VE BEEN WANDERING AROUND IN THIS HOT SUN!
I'VE BEEN HERE SINCE DAWN SEARCHING FOR SOMETHING I DREAMED ABOUT! I'M NOT SURE I KNOW WHAT IT IS... BUT I KNOW IT'S VALUABLE!
DREAMS ARE FUNNY THAT WAY... THEY CAN'T ALWAYS BE TAKEN LITERALLY... BECAUSE DREAMS ARE OFTEN SYMBOLIC!
BOOKS
VIDEOS
I GUESS YOU'RE RIGHT... BUT I STILL HAVE THIS FEELING I'LL FIND THIS NEBULOUS OBJECT!
BETTY!
VINTAGE COATS
JEANS JEANS JEANS

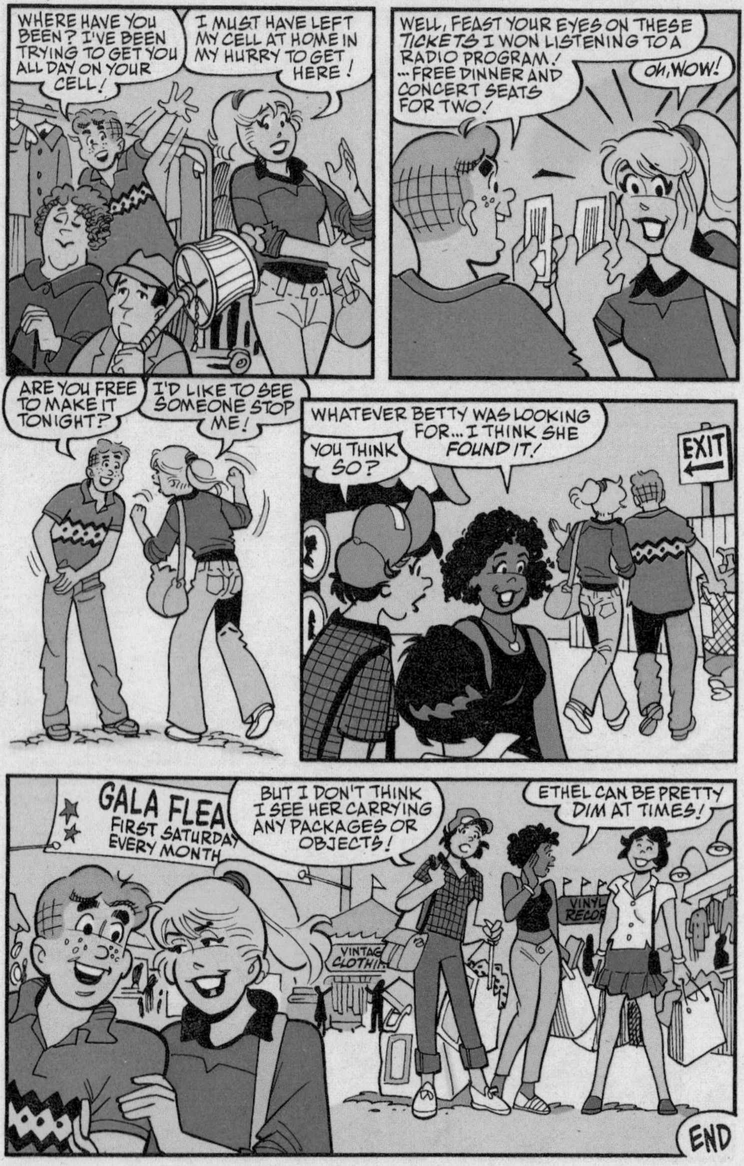
WHERE HAVE YOU BEEN? I'VE BEEN TRYING TO GET YOU ALL DAY ON YOUR CELL!
I MUST HAVE LEFT MY CELL AT HOME IN MY HURRY TO GET HERE!
WELL, FEAST YOUR EYES ON THESE TICKETS I WON LISTENING TO A RADIO PROGRAM! ...FREE DINNER AND CONCERT SEATS FOR TWO!
OH, WOW!
ARE YOU FREE TO MAKE IT TONIGHT?
I'D LIKE TO SEE SOMEONE STOP ME!
WHATEVER BETTY WAS LOOKING FOR... I THINK SHE FOUND IT!
YOU THINK SO?
EXIT
GALA FLEA
FIRST SATURDAY EVERY MONTH
BUT I DON'T THINK I SEE HER CARRYING ANY PACKAGES OR OBJECTS!
ETHEL CAN BE PRETTY DIM AT TIMES!
END

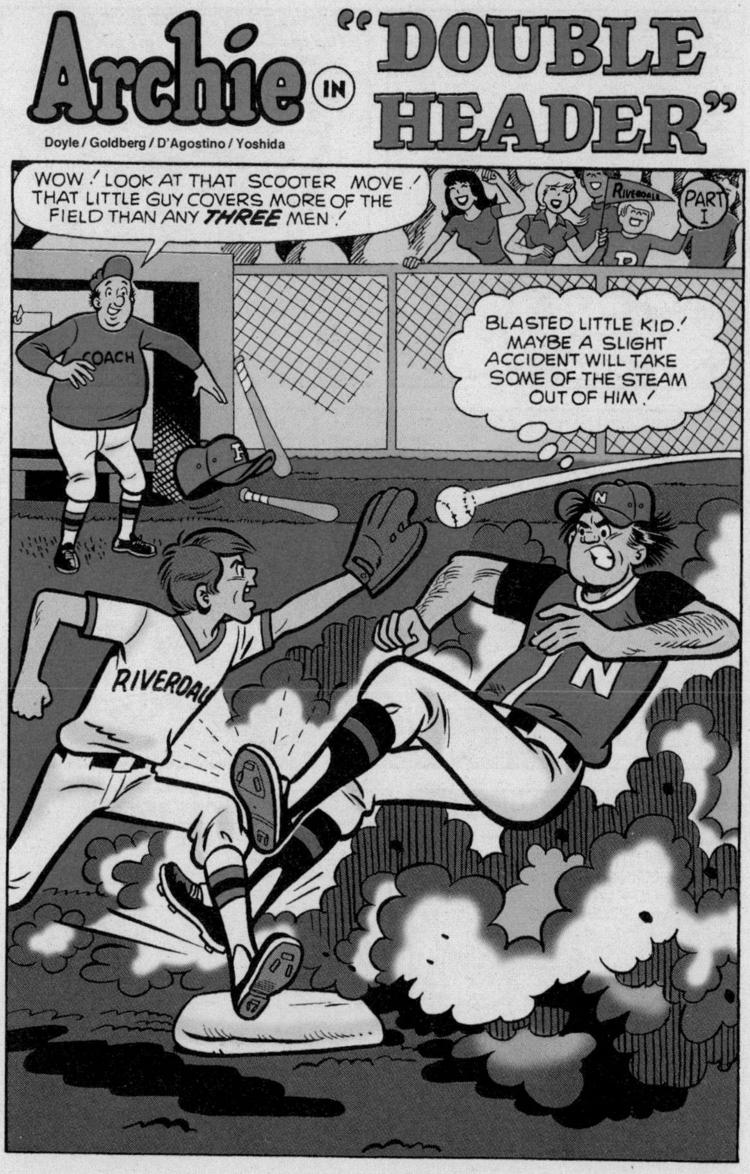
Archie IN "DOUBLE HEADER"
Doyle / Goldberg / D'Agostino / Yoshida
WOW! LOOK AT THAT SCOOTER MOVE! THAT LITTLE GUY COVERS MORE OF THE FIELD THAN ANY THREE MEN!
PART I
RIVERDALE
COACH
BLASTED LITTLE KID! MAYBE A SLIGHT ACCIDENT WILL TAKE SOME OF THE STEAM OUT OF HIM!
RIVERDALE
N

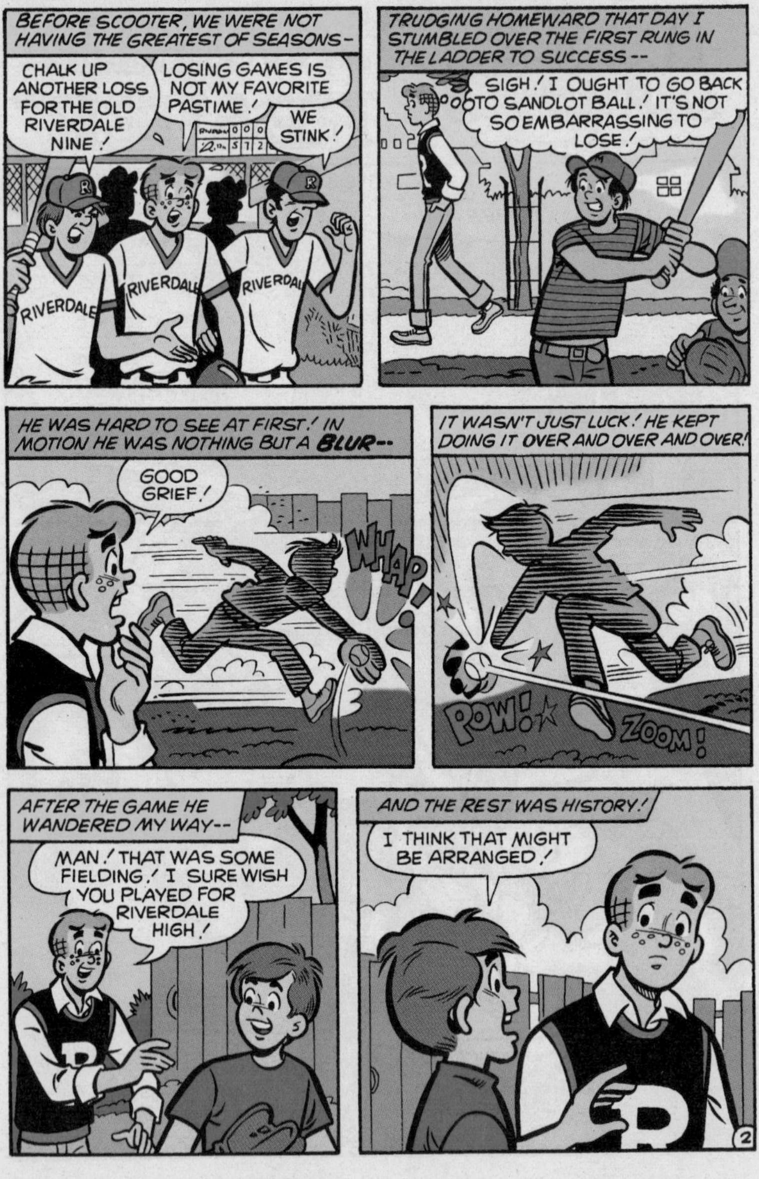

BEFORE SCOOTER, WE WERE NOT HAVING THE GREATEST OF SEASONS-
CHALK UP ANOTHER LOSS FOR THE OLD RIVERDALE NINE!
LOSING GAMES IS NOT MY FAVORITE PASTIME!
WE STINK!
RIVERDALE
RIVERDALE
RIVERDALE
TRUDGING HOMEWARD THAT DAY I STUMBLED OVER THE FIRST RUNG IN THE LADDER TO SUCCESS--
SIGH! I OUGHT TO GO BACK TO SANDLOT BALL! IT'S NOT SO EMBARRASSING TO LOSE!
HE WAS HARD TO SEE AT FIRST! IN MOTION HE WAS NOTHING BUT A BLUR--
GOOD GRIEF!
WHAP!
IT WASN'T JUST LUCK! HE KEPT DOING IT OVER AND OVER AND OVER!
POW!
ZOOM!
AFTER THE GAME HE WANDERED MY WAY--
MAN! THAT WAS SOME FIELDING! I SURE WISH YOU PLAYED FOR RIVERDALE HIGH!
AND THE REST WAS HISTORY!
I THINK THAT MIGHT BE ARRANGED!
2

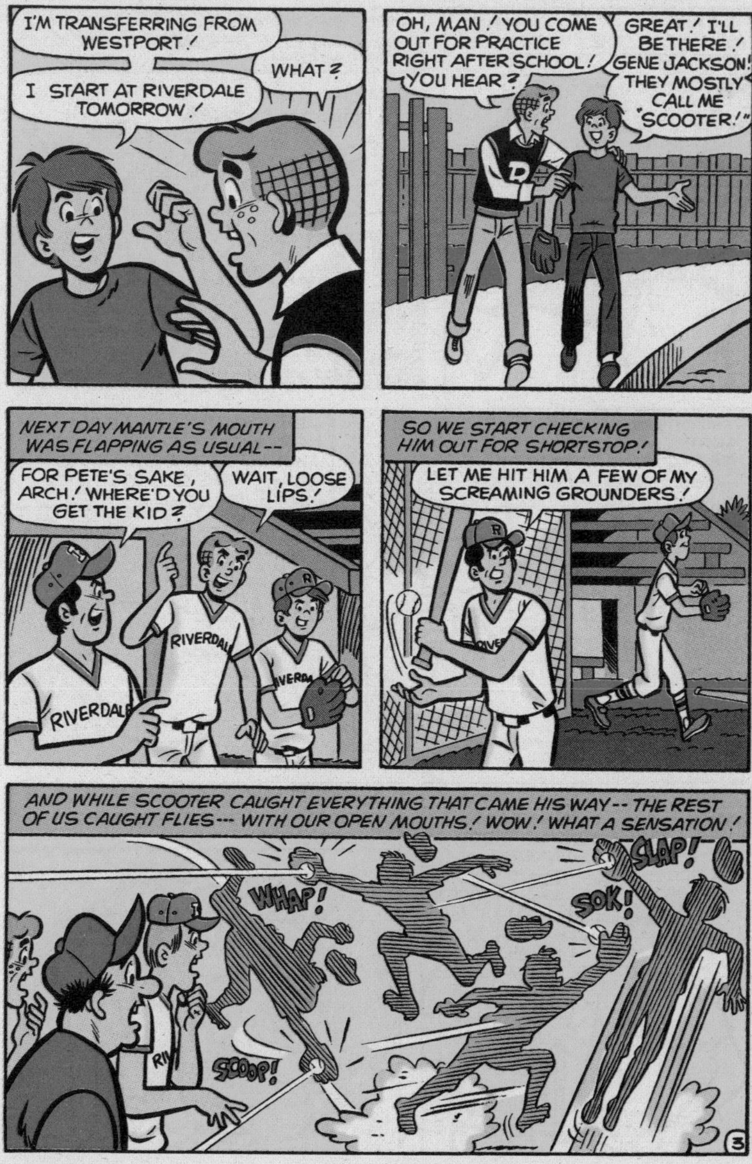
I'M TRANSFERRING FROM WESTPORT!
I START AT RIVERDALE TOMORROW!
WHAT?
OH, MAN! YOU COME OUT FOR PRACTICE RIGHT AFTER SCHOOL! YOU HEAR?
GREAT! I'LL BE THERE! GENE JACKSON! THEY MOSTLY CALL ME "SCOOTER!"
NEXT DAY MANTLE'S MOUTH WAS FLAPPING AS USUAL--
FOR PETE'S SAKE, ARCH! WHERE'D YOU GET THE KID?
WAIT, LOOSE LIPS!
RIVERDALE
SO WE START CHECKING HIM OUT FOR SHORTSTOP!
LET ME HIT HIM A FEW OF MY SCREAMING GROUNDERS!
AND WHILE SCOOTER CAUGHT EVERYTHING THAT CAME HIS WAY -- THE REST OF US CAUGHT FLIES --- WITH OUR OPEN MOUTHS! WOW! WHAT A SENSATION!
WHAP!
SLAP!
SOK!
SCOOP!
3

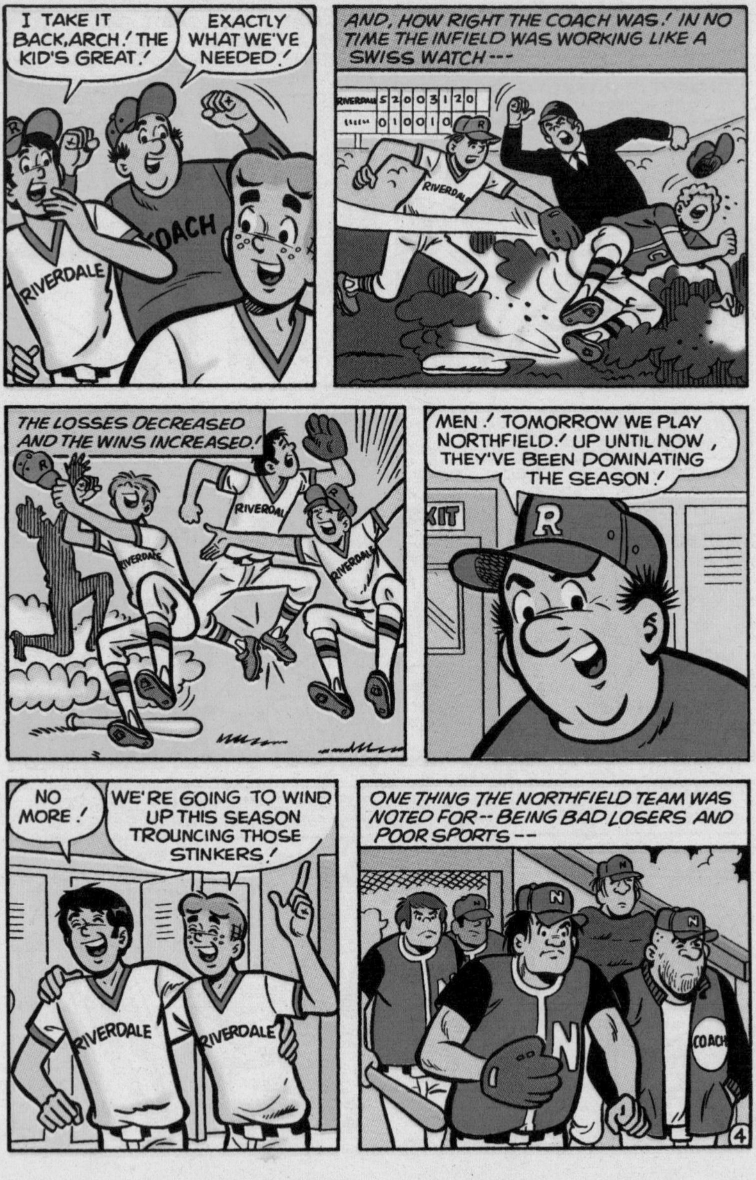
I TAKE IT BACK, ARCH! THE KID'S GREAT!
EXACTLY WHAT WE'VE NEEDED!
COACH
RIVERDALE
AND, HOW RIGHT THE COACH WAS! IN NO TIME THE INFIELD WAS WORKING LIKE A SWISS WATCH---
RIVERDALE 5 2 0 0 3 1 2 0
0 1 0 0 1 0
RIVERDALE
THE LOSSES DECREASED AND THE WINS INCREASED!
RIVERDALE
RIVERDALE
RIVERDALE
MEN! TOMORROW WE PLAY NORTHFIELD! UP UNTIL NOW, THEY'VE BEEN DOMINATING THE SEASON!
NO MORE!
WE'RE GOING TO WIND UP THIS SEASON TROUNCING THOSE STINKERS!
RIVERDALE
RIVERDALE
ONE THING THE NORTHFIELD TEAM WAS NOTED FOR -- BEING BAD LOSERS AND POOR SPORTS --
COACH
4

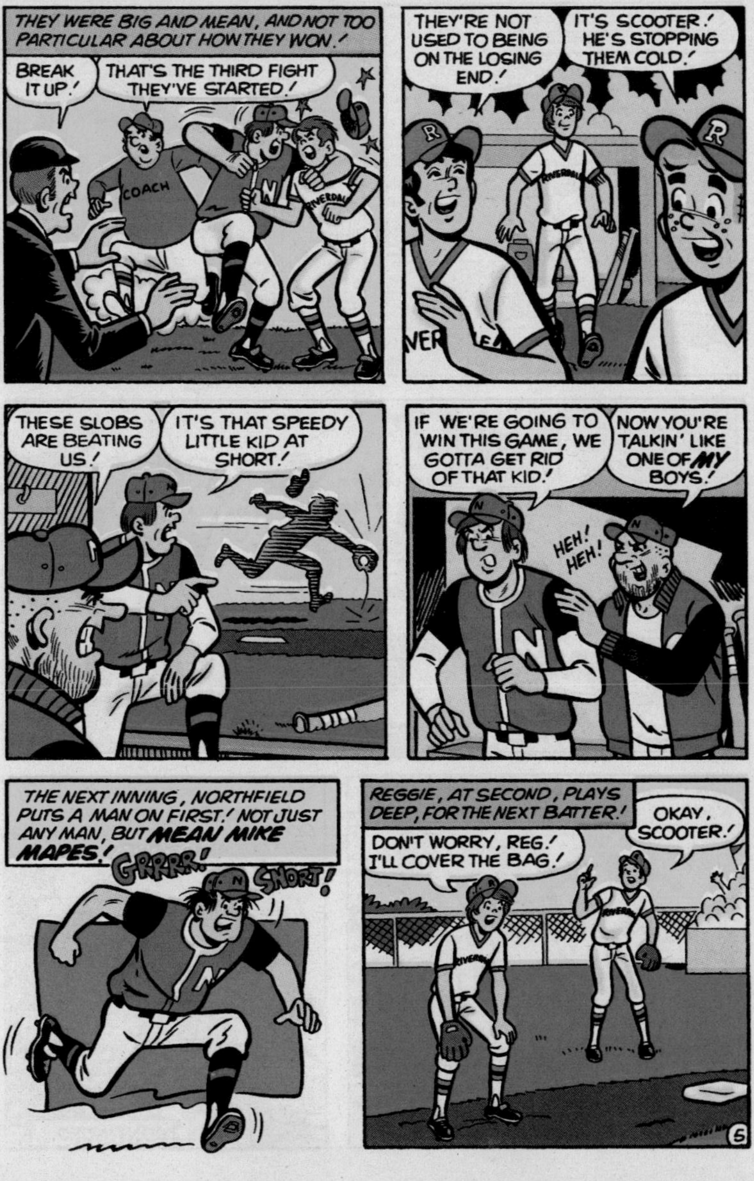
THEY WERE BIG AND MEAN, AND NOT TOO PARTICULAR ABOUT HOW THEY WON!
BREAK IT UP!
THAT'S THE THIRD FIGHT THEY'VE STARTED!
COACH
THEY'RE NOT USED TO BEING ON THE LOSING END!
IT'S SCOOTER! HE'S STOPPING THEM COLD!
THESE SLOBS ARE BEATING US!
IT'S THAT SPEEDY LITTLE KID AT SHORT!
IF WE'RE GOING TO WIN THIS GAME, WE GOTTA GET RID OF THAT KID!
NOW YOU'RE TALKIN' LIKE ONE OF MY BOYS!
HEH! HEH!
THE NEXT INNING, NORTHFIELD PUTS A MAN ON FIRST! NOT JUST ANY MAN, BUT MEAN MIKE MAPES!
GRRRR! SHORT!
REGGIE, AT SECOND, PLAYS DEEP, FOR THE NEXT BATTER!
DON'T WORRY, REG! I'LL COVER THE BAG!
OKAY, SCOOTER!

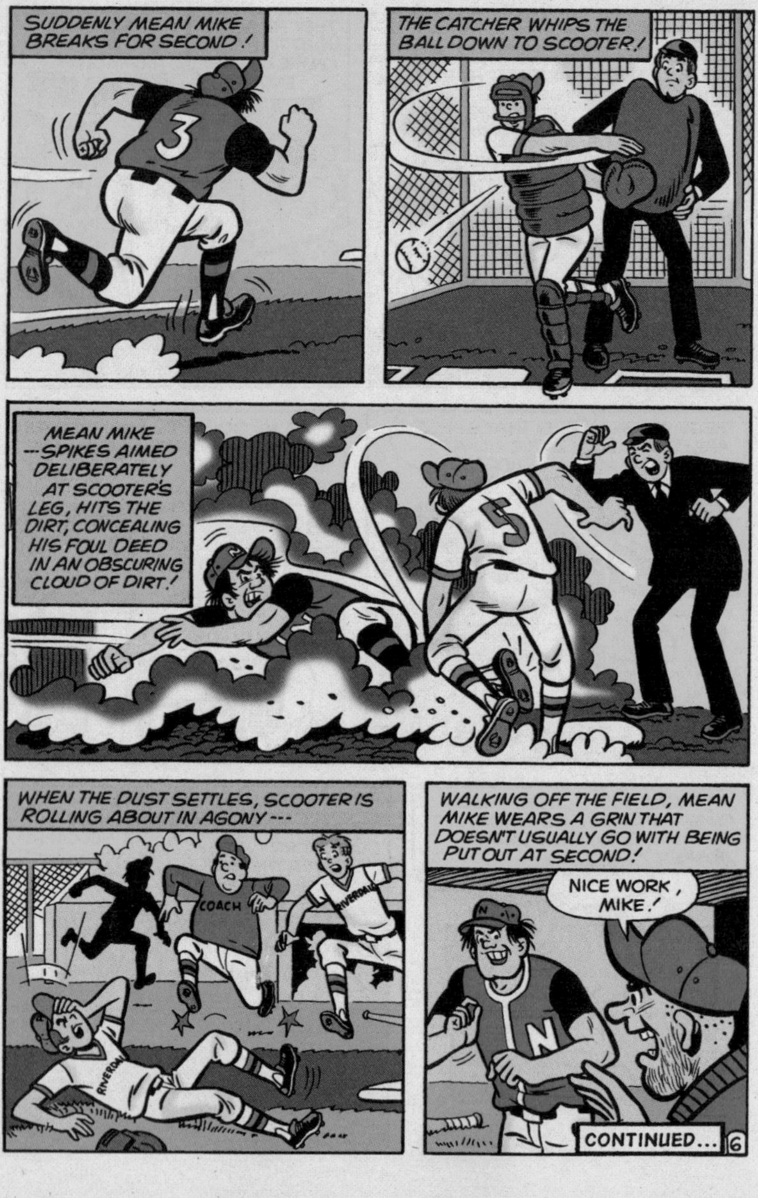
SUDDENLY MEAN MIKE BREAKS FOR SECOND!
THE CATCHER WHIPS THE BALL DOWN TO SCOOTER!
MEAN MIKE --SPIKES AIMED DELIBERATELY AT SCOOTER'S LEG, HITS THE DIRT, CONCEALING HIS FOUL DEED IN AN OBSCURING CLOUD OF DIRT!
WHEN THE DUST SETTLES, SCOOTER IS ROLLING ABOUT IN AGONY---
COACH
RIVERDALE
RIVERDALE
WALKING OFF THE FIELD, MEAN MIKE WEARS A GRIN THAT DOESN'T USUALLY GO WITH BEING PUT OUT AT SECOND!
NICE WORK, MIKE!
CONTINUED...
6

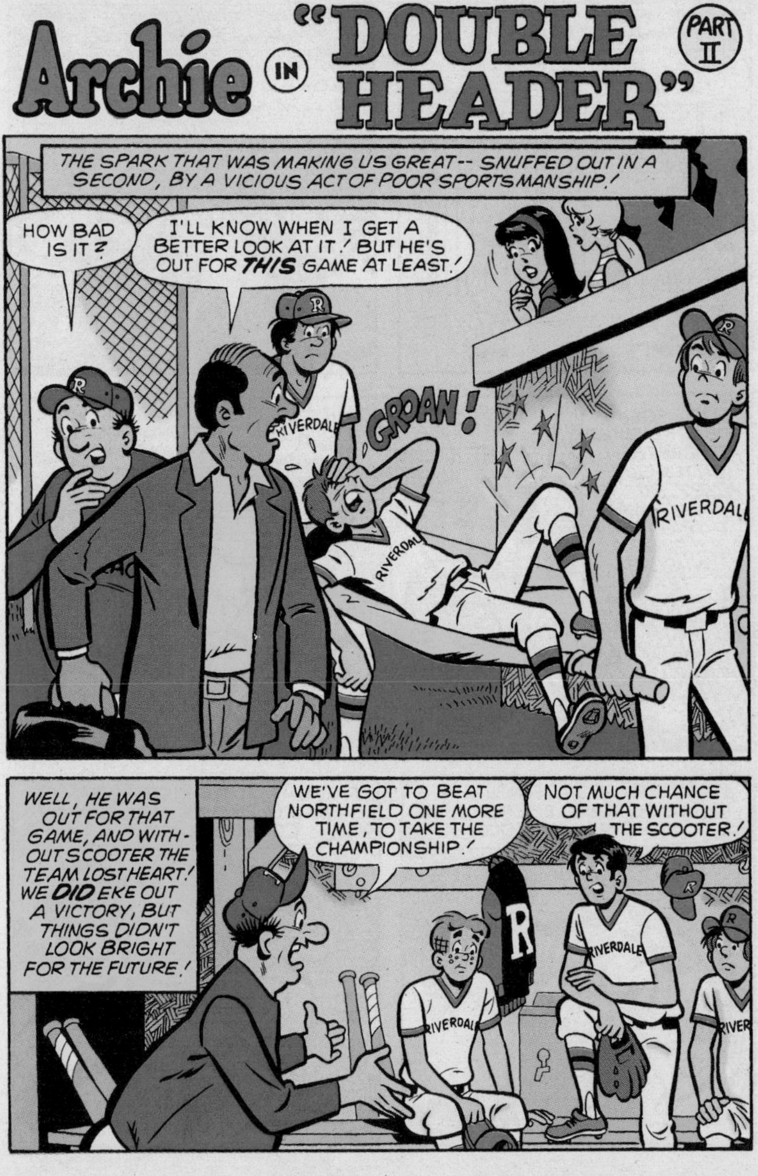
Archie in "DOUBLE HEADER" PART II
THE SPARK THAT WAS MAKING US GREAT-- SNUFFED OUT IN A SECOND, BY A VICIOUS ACT OF POOR SPORTSMANSHIP!
HOW BAD IS IT?
I'LL KNOW WHEN I GET A BETTER LOOK AT IT! BUT HE'S OUT FOR THIS GAME AT LEAST!
GROAN!
RIVERDALE
WELL, HE WAS OUT FOR THAT GAME, AND WITHOUT SCOOTER THE TEAM LOST HEART! WE DID EKE OUT A VICTORY, BUT THINGS DIDN'T LOOK BRIGHT FOR THE FUTURE!
WE'VE GOT TO BEAT NORTHFIELD ONE MORE TIME, TO TAKE THE CHAMPIONSHIP!
NOT MUCH CHANCE OF THAT WITHOUT THE SCOOTER!

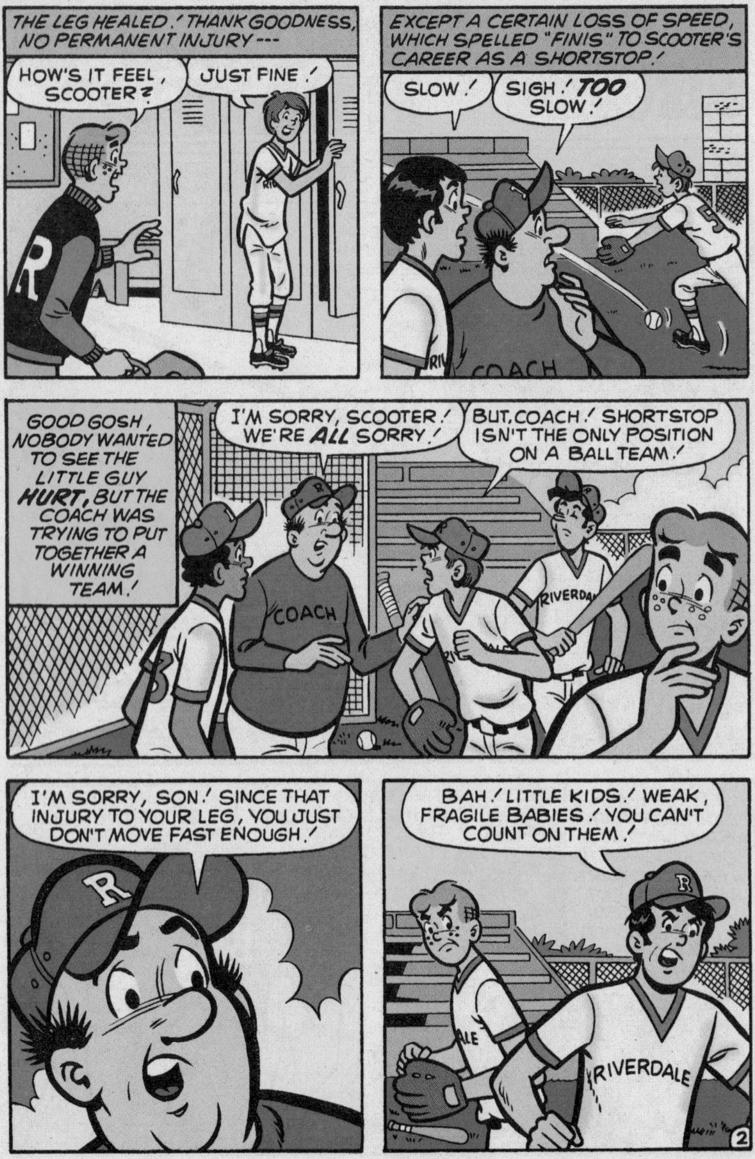

THE LEG HEALED! THANK GOODNESS, NO PERMANENT INJURY---
HOW'S IT FEEL, SCOOTER?
JUST FINE!
EXCEPT A CERTAIN LOSS OF SPEED, WHICH SPELLED "FINIS" TO SCOOTER'S CAREER AS A SHORTSTOP!
SLOW!
SIGH! TOO SLOW!
COACH
GOOD GOSH, NOBODY WANTED TO SEE THE LITTLE GUY HURT, BUT THE COACH WAS TRYING TO PUT TOGETHER A WINNING TEAM!
I'M SORRY, SCOOTER! WE'RE ALL SORRY!
BUT, COACH! SHORTSTOP ISN'T THE ONLY POSITION ON A BALL TEAM!
COACH
RIVERDALE
I'M SORRY, SON! SINCE THAT INJURY TO YOUR LEG, YOU JUST DON'T MOVE FAST ENOUGH!
BAH! LITTLE KIDS! WEAK, FRAGILE BABIES! YOU CAN'T COUNT ON THEM!
RIVERDALE

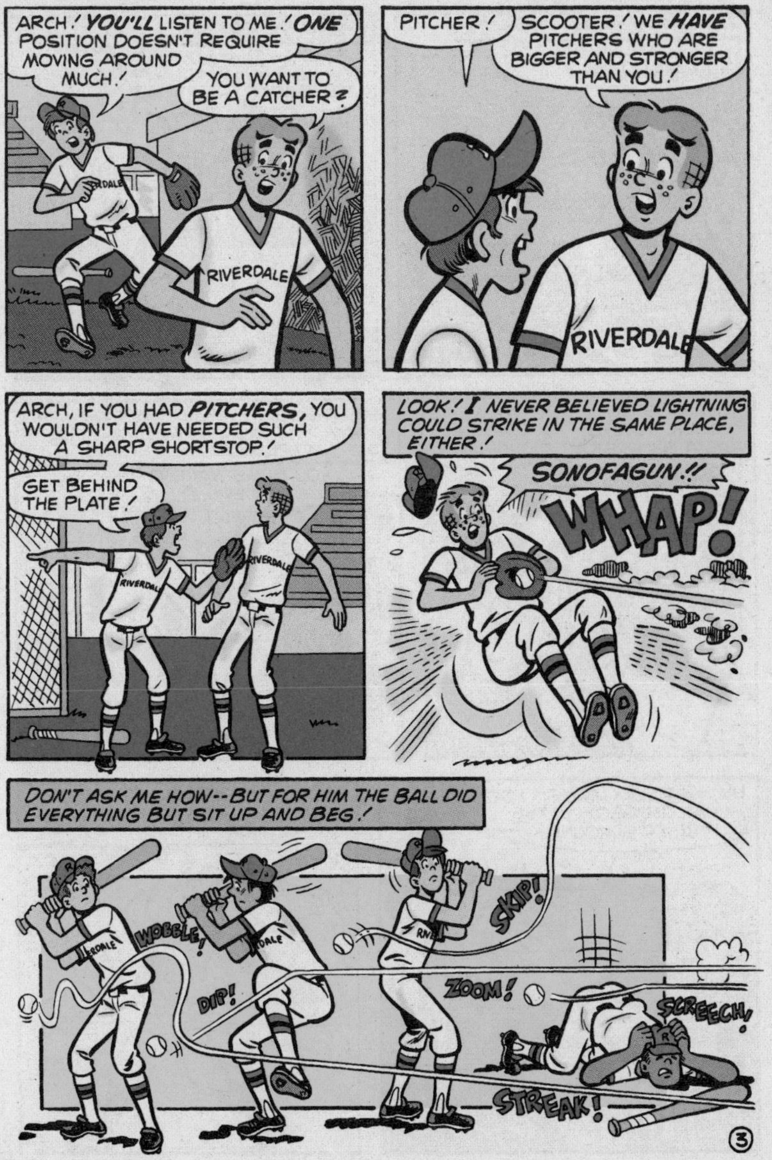
ARCH! YOU'LL LISTEN TO ME! ONE POSITION DOESN'T REQUIRE MOVING AROUND MUCH!
YOU WANT TO BE A CATCHER?
RIVERDALE
PITCHER!
SCOOTER! WE HAVE PITCHERS WHO ARE BIGGER AND STRONGER THAN YOU!
RIVERDALE
ARCH, IF YOU HAD PITCHERS, YOU WOULDN'T HAVE NEEDED SUCH A SHARP SHORTSTOP!
GET BEHIND THE PLATE!
RIVERDALE
RIVERDALE
LOOK! I NEVER BELIEVED LIGHTNING COULD STRIKE IN THE SAME PLACE, EITHER!
SONOFAGUN!!
WHAP!
DON'T ASK ME HOW--BUT FOR HIM THE BALL DID EVERYTHING BUT SIT UP AND BEG!
WOBBLE!
DIP!
SKIP!
ZOOM!
SCREECH!
STREAK!

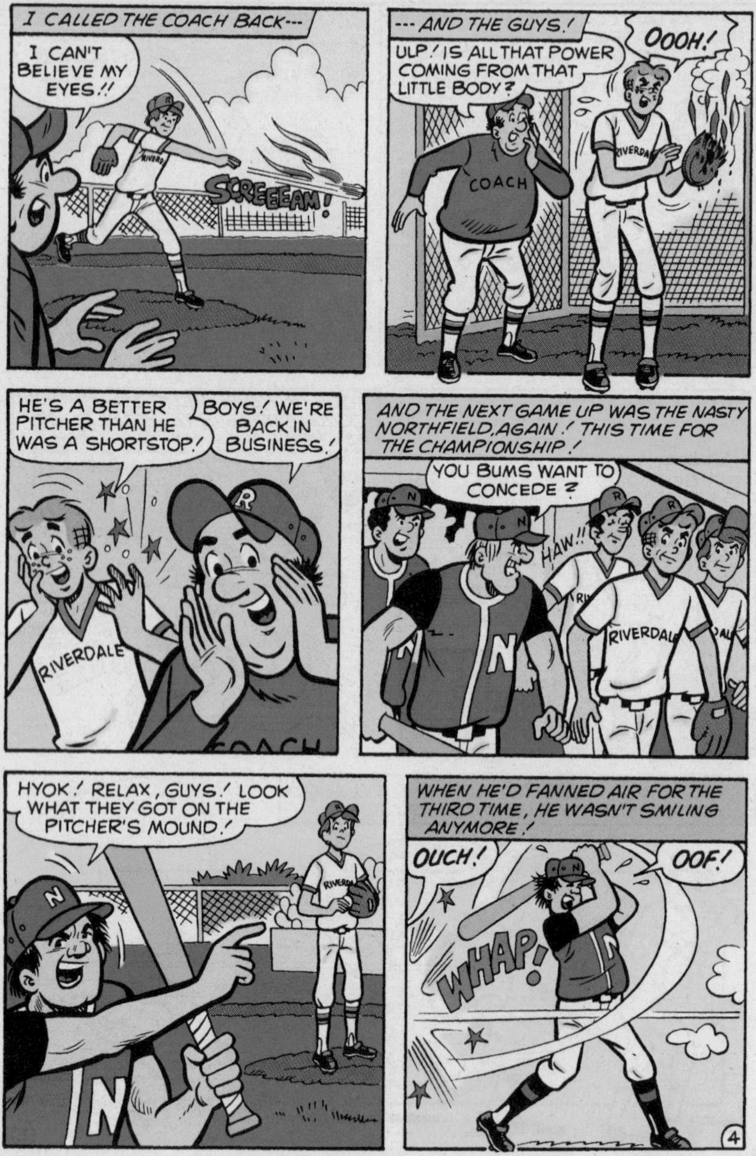
I CALLED THE COACH BACK---
I CAN'T BELIEVE MY EYES.!!
SCREEEAM!
--- AND THE GUYS.!
ULP.! IS ALL THAT POWER COMING FROM THAT LITTLE BODY?
OOOH!
COACH
RIVERDALE
HE'S A BETTER PITCHER THAN HE WAS A SHORTSTOP.!
BOYS.! WE'RE BACK IN BUSINESS.!
RIVERDALE
AND THE NEXT GAME UP WAS THE NASTY NORTHFIELD, AGAIN.! THIS TIME FOR THE CHAMPIONSHIP.!
YOU BUMS WANT TO CONCEDE?
HAW!!
RIVERDALE
HYOK.! RELAX, GUYS.! LOOK WHAT THEY GOT ON THE PITCHER'S MOUND.!
WHEN HE'D FANNED AIR FOR THE THIRD TIME, HE WASN'T SMILING ANYMORE.!
OUCH!
OOF!
WHAP!
4

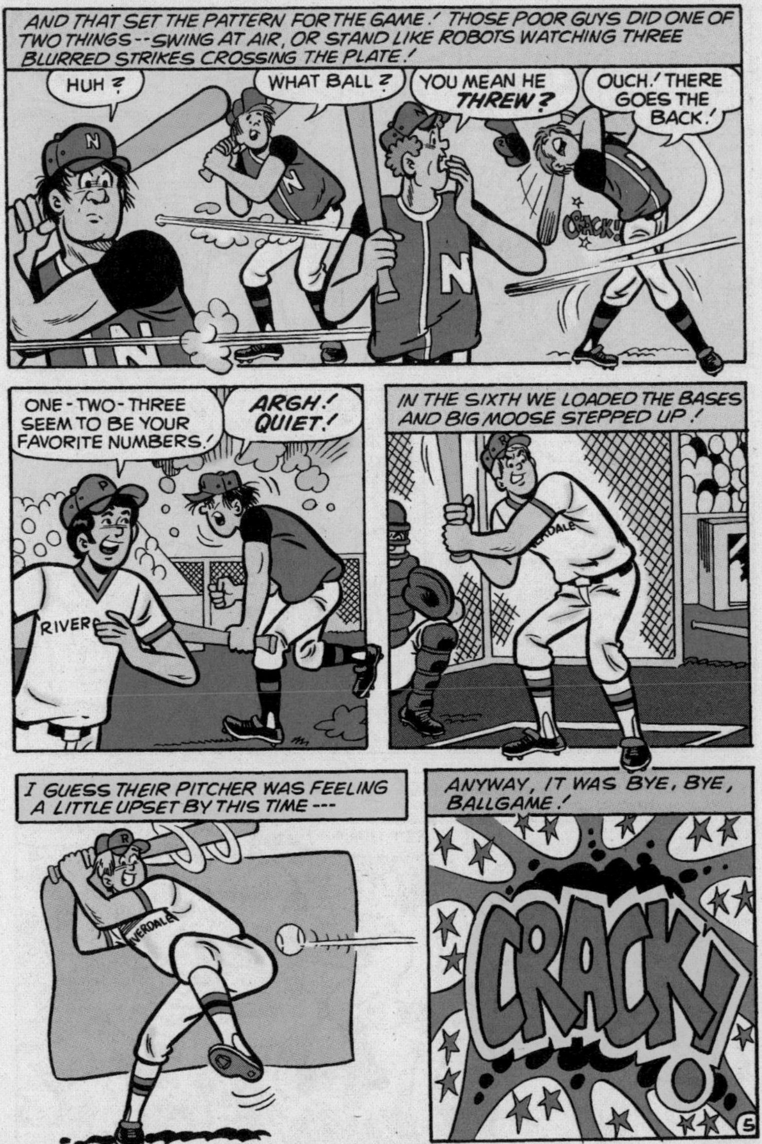
AND THAT SET THE PATTERN FOR THE GAME! THOSE POOR GUYS DID ONE OF TWO THINGS--SWING AT AIR, OR STAND LIKE ROBOTS WATCHING THREE BLURRED STRIKES CROSSING THE PLATE!
HUH?
WHAT BALL?
YOU MEAN HE THREW?
OUCH! THERE GOES THE BACK!
CRACK!
ONE-TWO-THREE SEEM TO BE YOUR FAVORITE NUMBERS!
ARGH! QUIET!
RIVER
IN THE SIXTH WE LOADED THE BASES AND BIG MOOSE STEPPED UP!
I GUESS THEIR PITCHER WAS FEELING A LITTLE UPSET BY THIS TIME---
ANYWAY, IT WAS BYE, BYE, BALLGAME!
CRACK!
5

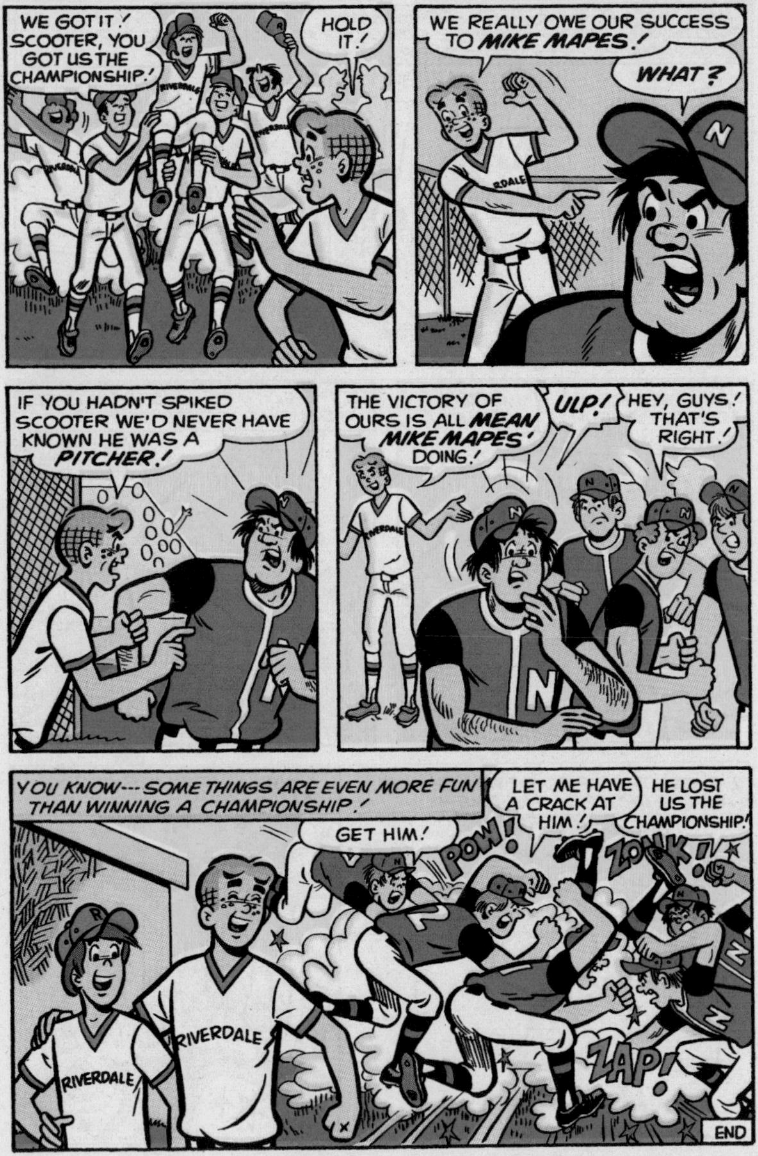

WE GOT IT! SCOOTER, YOU GOT US THE CHAMPIONSHIP!
HOLD IT!
WE REALLY OWE OUR SUCCESS TO MIKE MAPES!
WHAT?
IF YOU HADN'T SPIKED SCOOTER WE'D NEVER HAVE KNOWN HE WAS A PITCHER!
THE VICTORY OF OURS IS ALL MEAN MIKE MAPES' DOING!
ULP!
HEY, GUYS! THAT'S RIGHT!
YOU KNOW--- SOME THINGS ARE EVEN MORE FUN THAN WINNING A CHAMPIONSHIP!
GET HIM!
POW!
LET ME HAVE A CRACK AT HIM!
HE LOST US THE CHAMPIONSHIP!
ZONK!
ZAP!
END

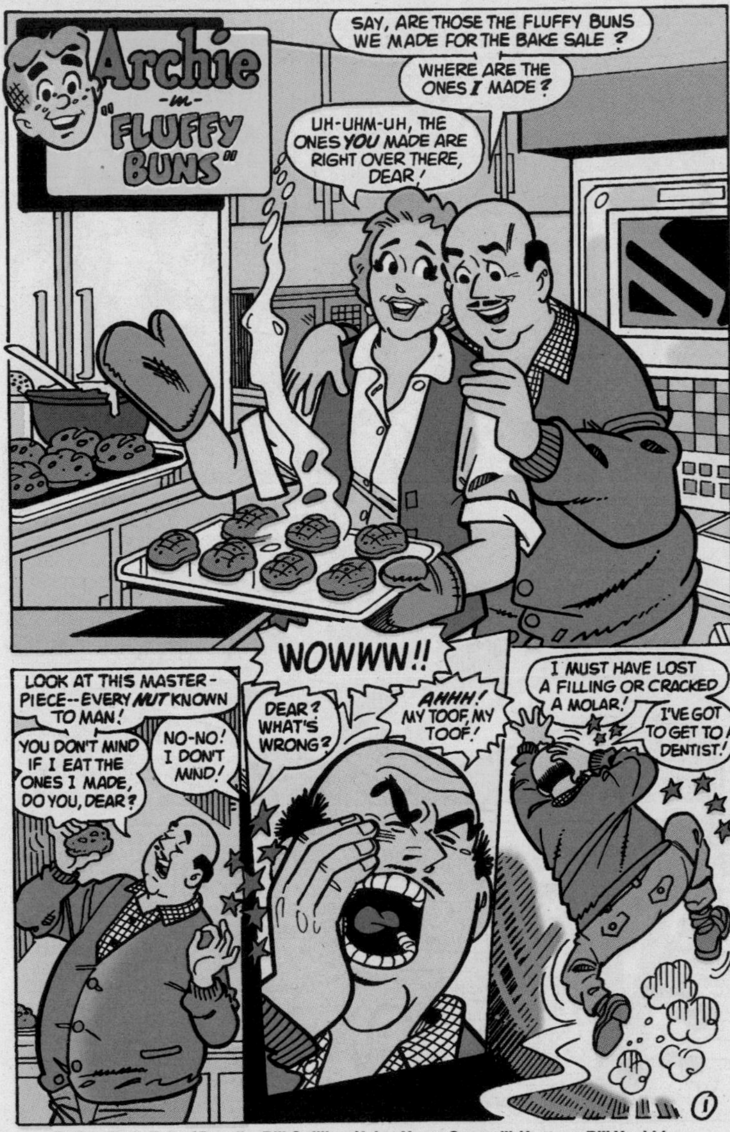
Archie
-in-
"FLUFFY BUNS"
SAY, ARE THOSE THE FLUFFY BUNS WE MADE FOR THE BAKE SALE ?
WHERE ARE THE ONES I MADE ?
UH-UHM-UH, THE ONES YOU MADE ARE RIGHT OVER THERE, DEAR!
LOOK AT THIS MASTER-PIECE--EVERY NUT KNOWN TO MAN!
YOU DON'T MIND IF I EAT THE ONES I MADE, DO YOU, DEAR?
NO-NO! I DON'T MIND!
WOWWW!!
DEAR? WHAT'S WRONG?
AHHH! MY TOOF, MY TOOF!
I MUST HAVE LOST A FILLING OR CRACKED A MOLAR!
I'VE GOT TO GET TO A DENTIST!
1

Script: Rurik Tyler / Pencils: Bill Golliher / Inks: Henry Scarpelli / Letters: Bill Yoshida

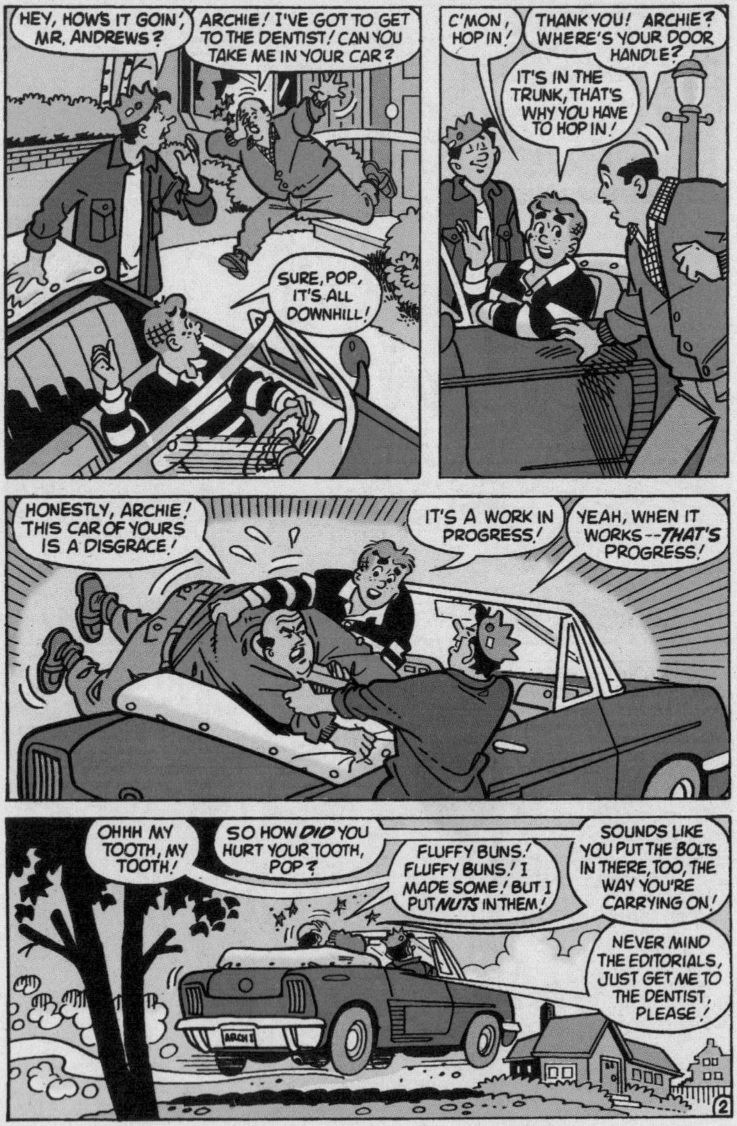
HEY, HOW'S IT GOIN', MR. ANDREWS?
ARCHIE! I'VE GOT TO GET TO THE DENTIST! CAN YOU TAKE ME IN YOUR CAR?
SURE, POP, IT'S ALL DOWNHILL!
C'MON, HOP IN!
THANK YOU! ARCHIE? WHERE'S YOUR DOOR HANDLE?
IT'S IN THE TRUNK, THAT'S WHY YOU HAVE TO HOP IN!
HONESTLY, ARCHIE! THIS CAR OF YOURS IS A DISGRACE!
IT'S A WORK IN PROGRESS!
YEAH, WHEN IT WORKS--THAT'S PROGRESS!
OHHH MY TOOTH, MY TOOTH!
SO HOW DID YOU HURT YOUR TOOTH, POP?
FLUFFY BUNS! FLUFFY BUNS! I MADE SOME! BUT I PUT NUTS IN THEM!
SOUNDS LIKE YOU PUT THE BOLTS IN THERE, TOO, THE WAY YOU'RE CARRYING ON!
NEVER MIND THE EDITORIALS, JUST GET ME TO THE DENTIST, PLEASE!
ARCH I
2

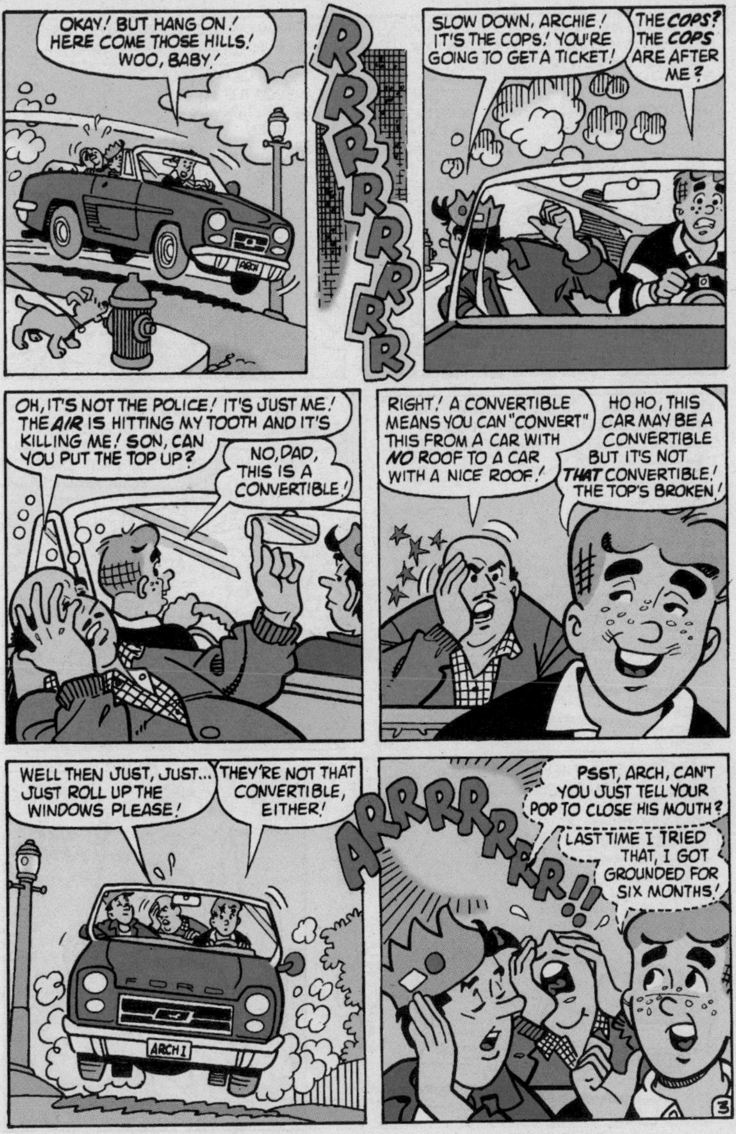

OKAY! BUT HANG ON! HERE COME THOSE HILLS! WOO, BABY!
RRRRRRRR
SLOW DOWN, ARCHIE! IT'S THE COPS! YOU'RE GOING TO GET A TICKET!
THE COPS? THE COPS ARE AFTER ME?
OH, IT'S NOT THE POLICE! IT'S JUST ME! THE AIR IS HITTING MY TOOTH AND IT'S KILLING ME! SON, CAN YOU PUT THE TOP UP?
NO, DAD, THIS IS A CONVERTIBLE!
RIGHT! A CONVERTIBLE MEANS YOU CAN "CONVERT" THIS FROM A CAR WITH NO ROOF TO A CAR WITH A NICE ROOF!
HO HO, THIS CAR MAY BE A CONVERTIBLE BUT IT'S NOT THAT CONVERTIBLE! THE TOP'S BROKEN!
WELL THEN JUST, JUST... JUST ROLL UP THE WINDOWS PLEASE!
THEY'RE NOT THAT CONVERTIBLE, EITHER!
ARCHI
ARRRRRRRR!!
PSST, ARCH, CAN'T YOU JUST TELL YOUR POP TO CLOSE HIS MOUTH?
LAST TIME I TRIED THAT, I GOT GROUNDED FOR SIX MONTHS!
3

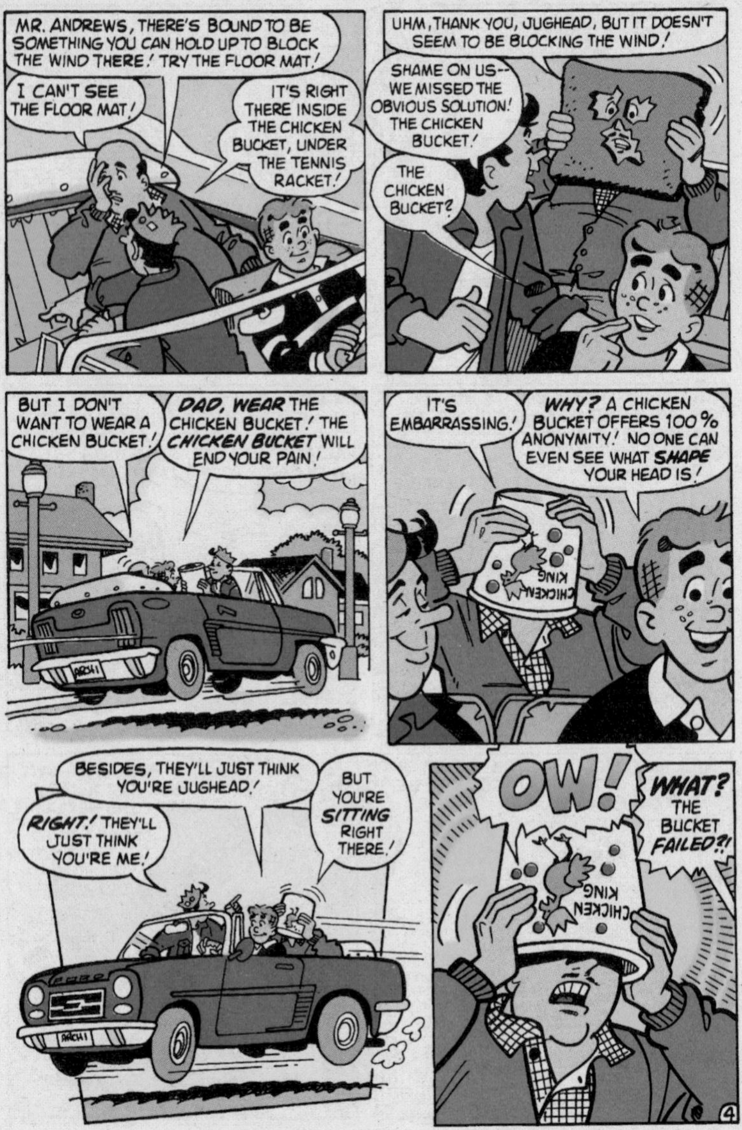
MR. ANDREWS, THERE'S BOUND TO BE SOMETHING YOU CAN HOLD UP TO BLOCK THE WIND THERE! TRY THE FLOOR MAT!
I CAN'T SEE THE FLOOR MAT!
IT'S RIGHT THERE INSIDE THE CHICKEN BUCKET, UNDER THE TENNIS RACKET!
UHM, THANK YOU, JUGHEAD, BUT IT DOESN'T SEEM TO BE BLOCKING THE WIND!
SHAME ON US-- WE MISSED THE OBVIOUS SOLUTION! THE CHICKEN BUCKET!
THE CHICKEN BUCKET?
BUT I DON'T WANT TO WEAR A CHICKEN BUCKET!
DAD, WEAR THE CHICKEN BUCKET! THE CHICKEN BUCKET WILL END YOUR PAIN!
ARCH 1
IT'S EMBARRASSING!
WHY? A CHICKEN BUCKET OFFERS 100% ANONYMITY! NO ONE CAN EVEN SEE WHAT SHAPE YOUR HEAD IS!
CHICKEN KING
BESIDES, THEY'LL JUST THINK YOU'RE JUGHEAD!
RIGHT! THEY'LL JUST THINK YOU'RE ME!
BUT YOU'RE SITTING RIGHT THERE!
ARCH 1
OW!
WHAT? THE BUCKET FAILED?!
CHICKEN KING
4

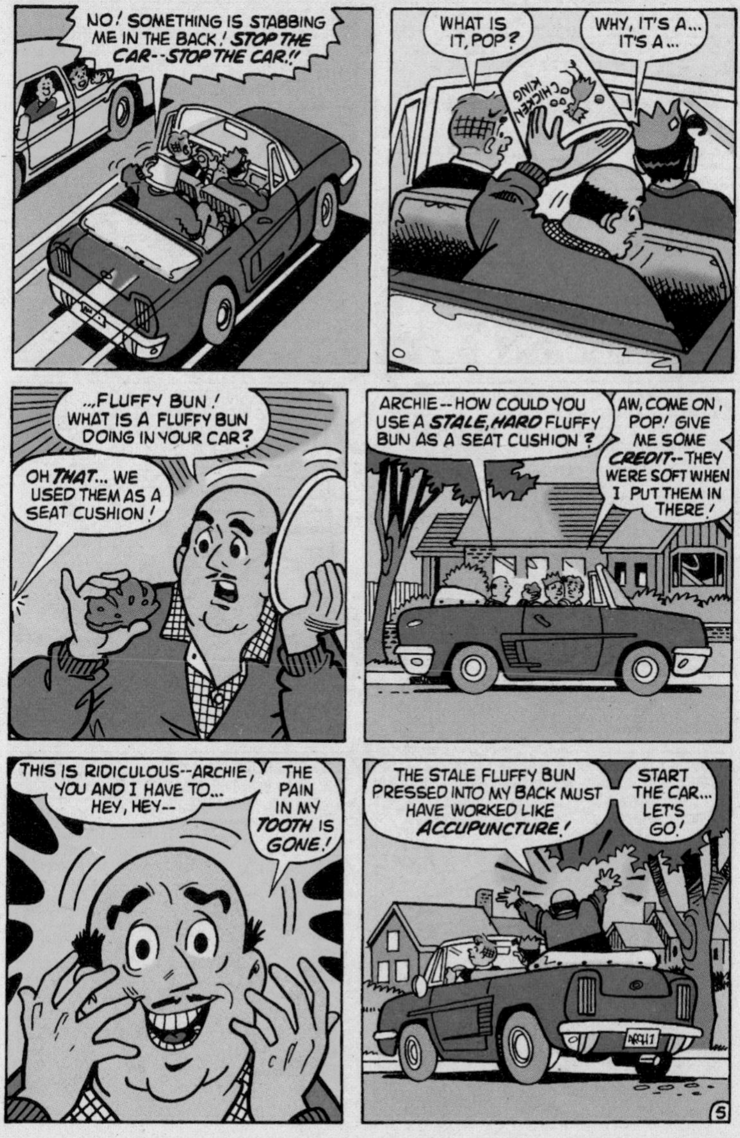
NO! SOMETHING IS STABBING ME IN THE BACK! STOP THE CAR--STOP THE CAR!!
WHAT IS IT, POP?
WHY, IT'S A... IT'S A...
CHICKEN KING
...FLUFFY BUN! WHAT IS A FLUFFY BUN DOING IN YOUR CAR?
OH THAT... WE USED THEM AS A SEAT CUSHION!
ARCHIE--HOW COULD YOU USE A STALE, HARD FLUFFY BUN AS A SEAT CUSHION?
AW, COME ON, POP! GIVE ME SOME CREDIT--THEY WERE SOFT WHEN I PUT THEM IN THERE!
THIS IS RIDICULOUS--ARCHIE, YOU AND I HAVE TO... HEY, HEY--
THE PAIN IN MY TOOTH IS GONE!
THE STALE FLUFFY BUN PRESSED INTO MY BACK MUST HAVE WORKED LIKE ACCUPUNCTURE!
START THE CAR... LET'S GO!
ARCH 1

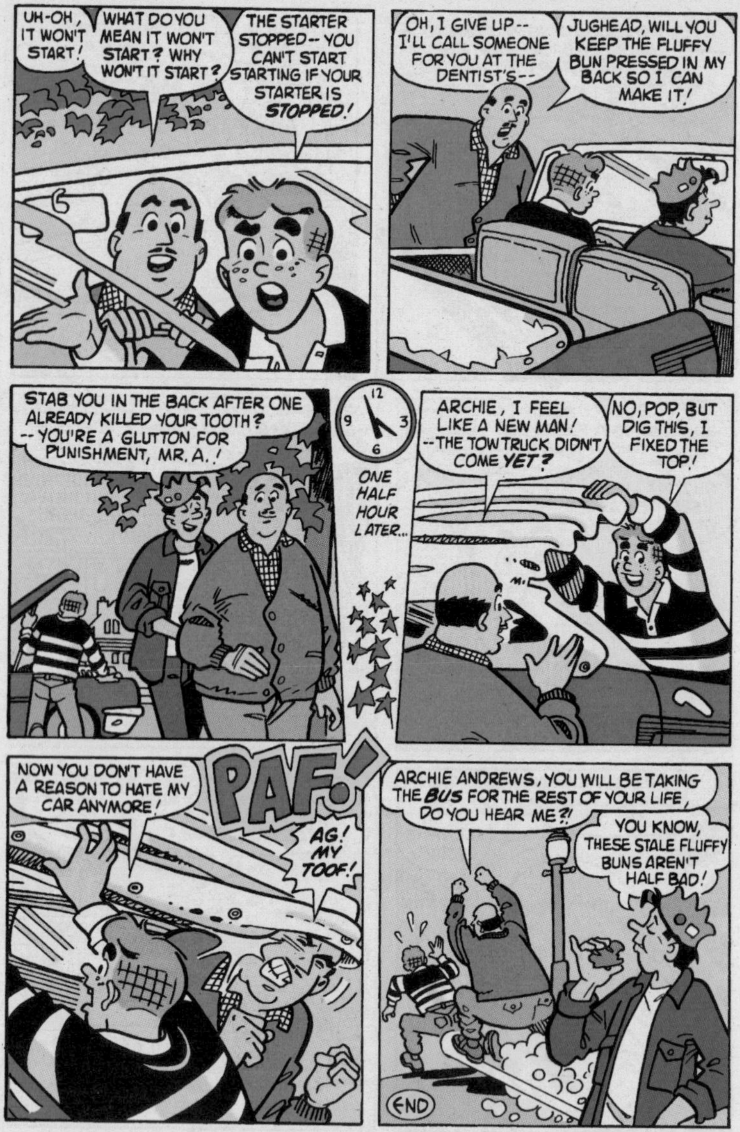

UH-OH, IT WON'T START!
WHAT DO YOU MEAN IT WON'T START? WHY WON'T IT START?
THE STARTER STOPPED-- YOU CAN'T START STARTING IF YOUR STARTER IS STOPPED!
OH, I GIVE UP-- I'LL CALL SOMEONE FOR YOU AT THE DENTIST'S--
JUGHEAD, WILL YOU KEEP THE FLUFFY BUN PRESSED IN MY BACK SO I CAN MAKE IT!
STAB YOU IN THE BACK AFTER ONE ALREADY KILLED YOUR TOOTH? -- YOU'RE A GLUTTON FOR PUNISHMENT, MR. A.!
12 3 6 9
ONE HALF HOUR LATER...
ARCHIE, I FEEL LIKE A NEW MAN! --THE TOW TRUCK DIDN'T COME YET?
NO, POP, BUT DIG THIS, I FIXED THE TOP!
NOW YOU DON'T HAVE A REASON TO HATE MY CAR ANYMORE!
PAF!
AG! MY TOOF!
ARCHIE ANDREWS, YOU WILL BE TAKING THE BUS FOR THE REST OF YOUR LIFE, DO YOU HEAR ME?!
YOU KNOW, THESE STALE FLUFFY BUNS AREN'T HALF BAD!
END

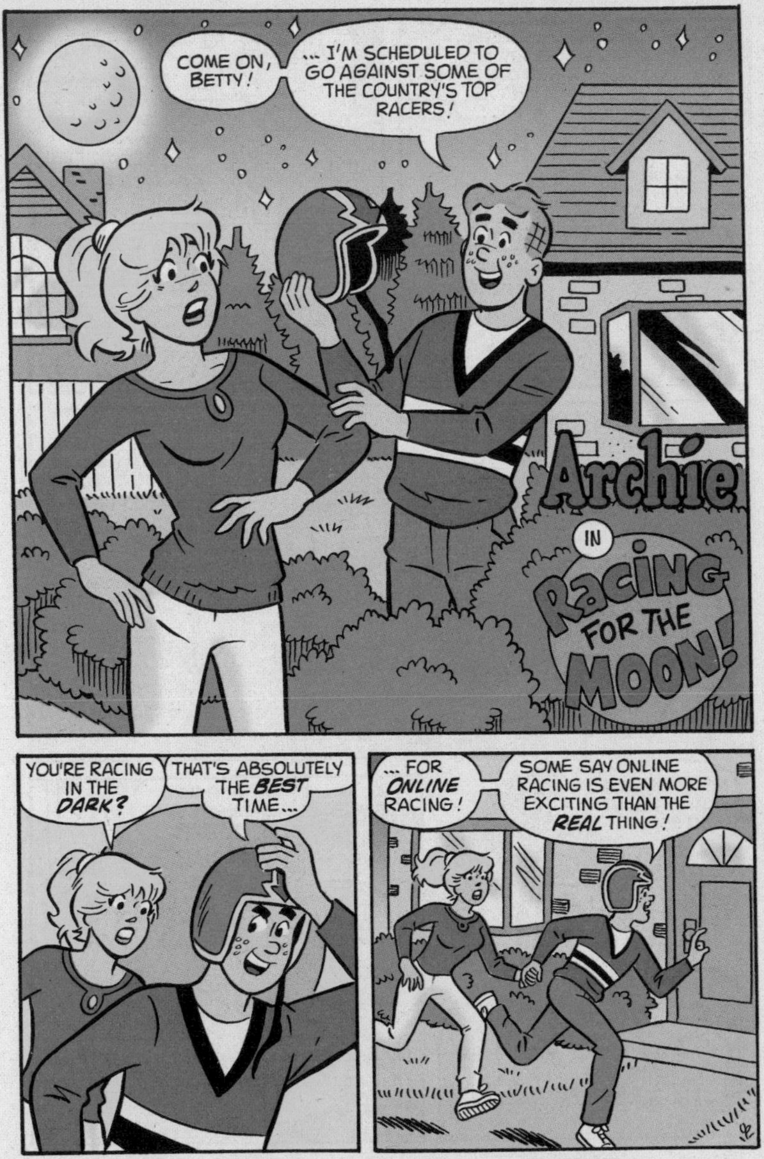
COME ON, BETTY!
... I'M SCHEDULED TO GO AGAINST SOME OF THE COUNTRY'S TOP RACERS!
Archie
IN
RACING FOR THE MOON!
YOU'RE RACING IN THE DARK?
THAT'S ABSOLUTELY THE BEST TIME...
... FOR ONLINE RACING!
SOME SAY ONLINE RACING IS EVEN MORE EXCITING THAN THE REAL THING!

Script & Pencils: Bill Golliher / Inks: Rudy Lapick / Letters: Bill Yoshida

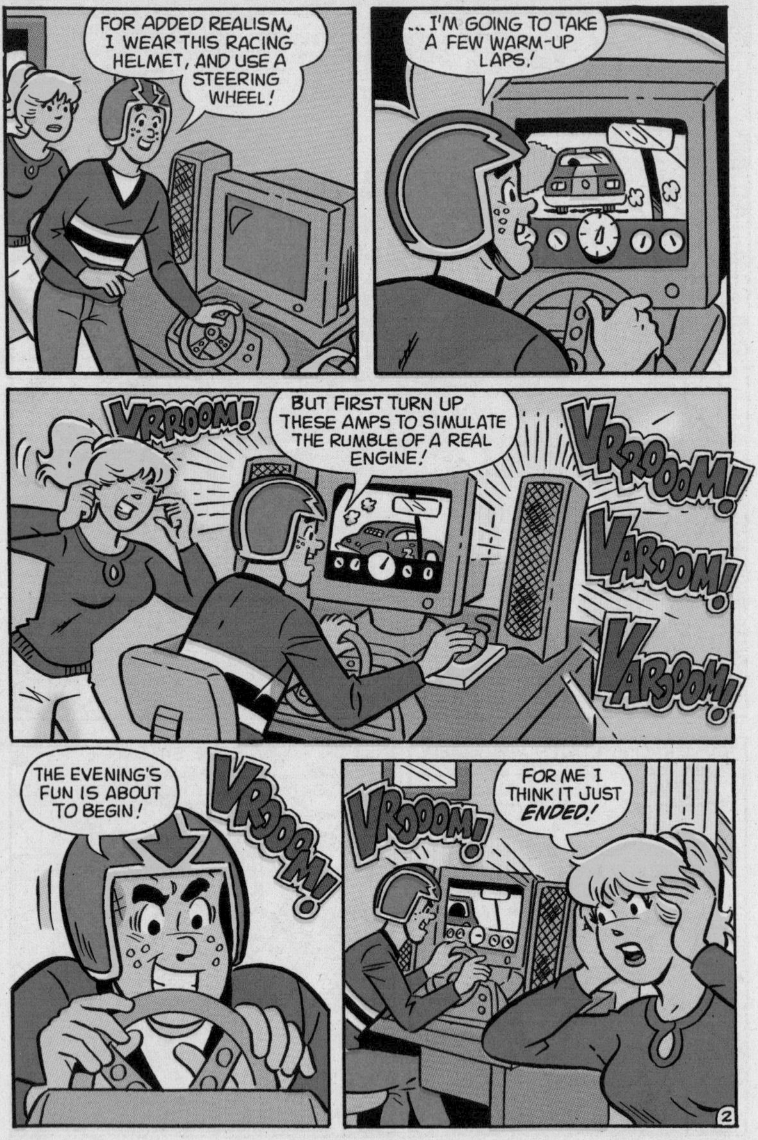
FOR ADDED REALISM, I WEAR THIS RACING HELMET, AND USE A STEERING WHEEL!
...I'M GOING TO TAKE A FEW WARM-UP LAPS!
VRROOM!
BUT FIRST TURN UP THESE AMPS TO SIMULATE THE RUMBLE OF A REAL ENGINE!
VRROOOM!
VAROOM!
VAROOM!
THE EVENING'S FUN IS ABOUT TO BEGIN!
VROOOOM!
VROOOM!
FOR ME I THINK IT JUST *ENDED!*

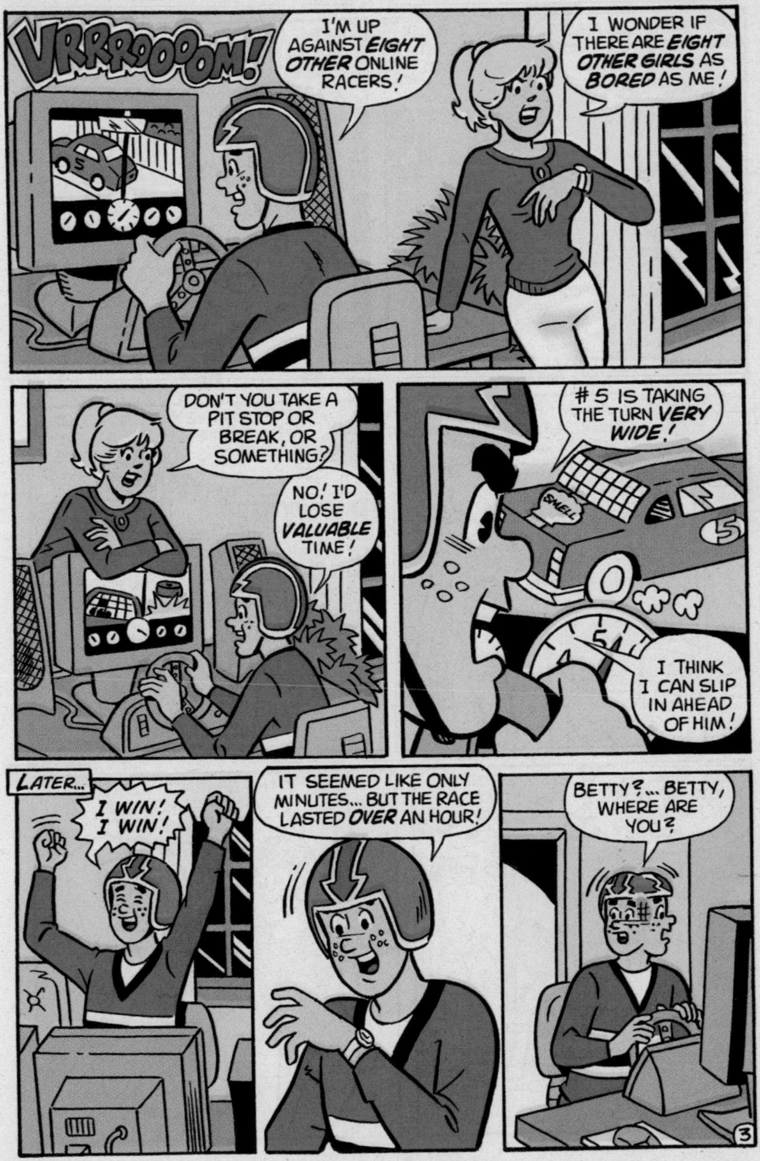

VRRR9OOOOM!
I'M UP AGAINST EIGHT OTHER ONLINE RACERS!
I WONDER IF THERE ARE EIGHT OTHER GIRLS AS BORED AS ME!
DON'T YOU TAKE A PIT STOP OR BREAK, OR SOMETHING?
NO! I'D LOSE VALUABLE TIME!
5 IS TAKING THE TURN VERY WIDE!
SHELL
I THINK I CAN SLIP IN AHEAD OF HIM!
LATER...
I WIN! I WIN!
IT SEEMED LIKE ONLY MINUTES... BUT THE RACE LASTED OVER AN HOUR!
BETTY?... BETTY, WHERE ARE YOU?
3

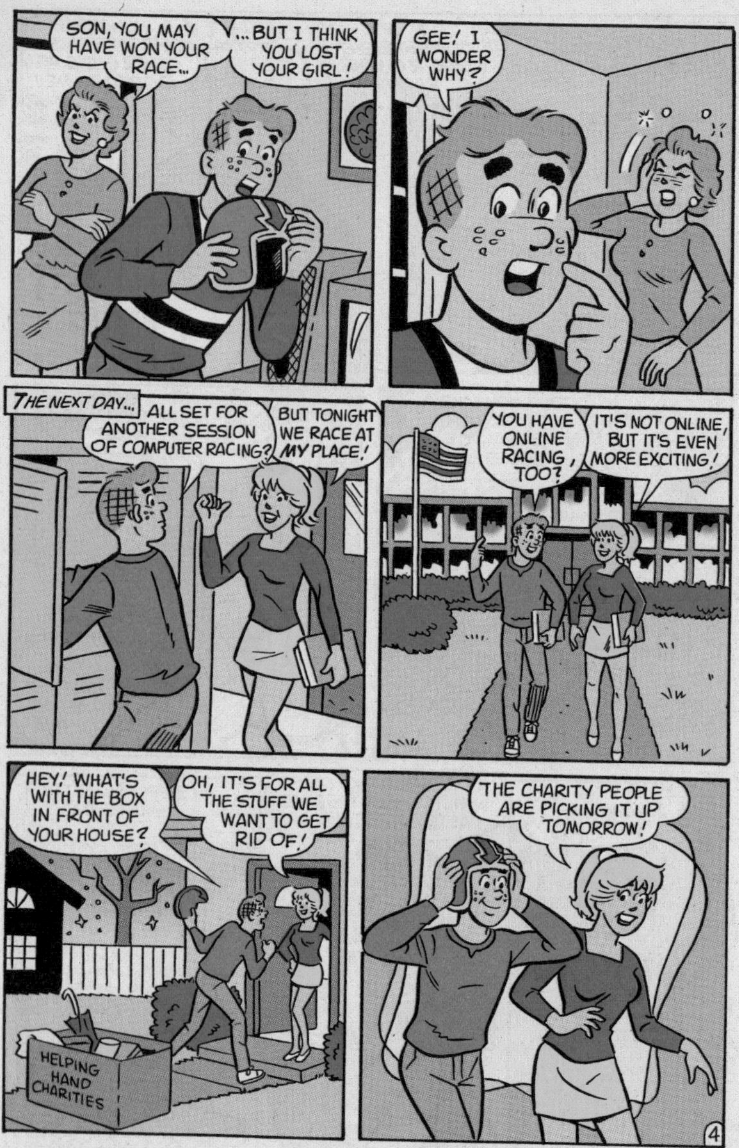
SON, YOU MAY HAVE WON YOUR RACE...
...BUT I THINK YOU LOST YOUR GIRL!
GEE! I WONDER WHY?
THE NEXT DAY...
ALL SET FOR ANOTHER SESSION OF COMPUTER RACING?
BUT TONIGHT WE RACE AT MY PLACE!
YOU HAVE ONLINE RACING, TOO?
IT'S NOT ONLINE, BUT IT'S EVEN MORE EXCITING!
HEY! WHAT'S WITH THE BOX IN FRONT OF YOUR HOUSE?
OH, IT'S FOR ALL THE STUFF WE WANT TO GET RID OF!
HELPING HAND CHARITIES
THE CHARITY PEOPLE ARE PICKING IT UP TOMORROW!
4

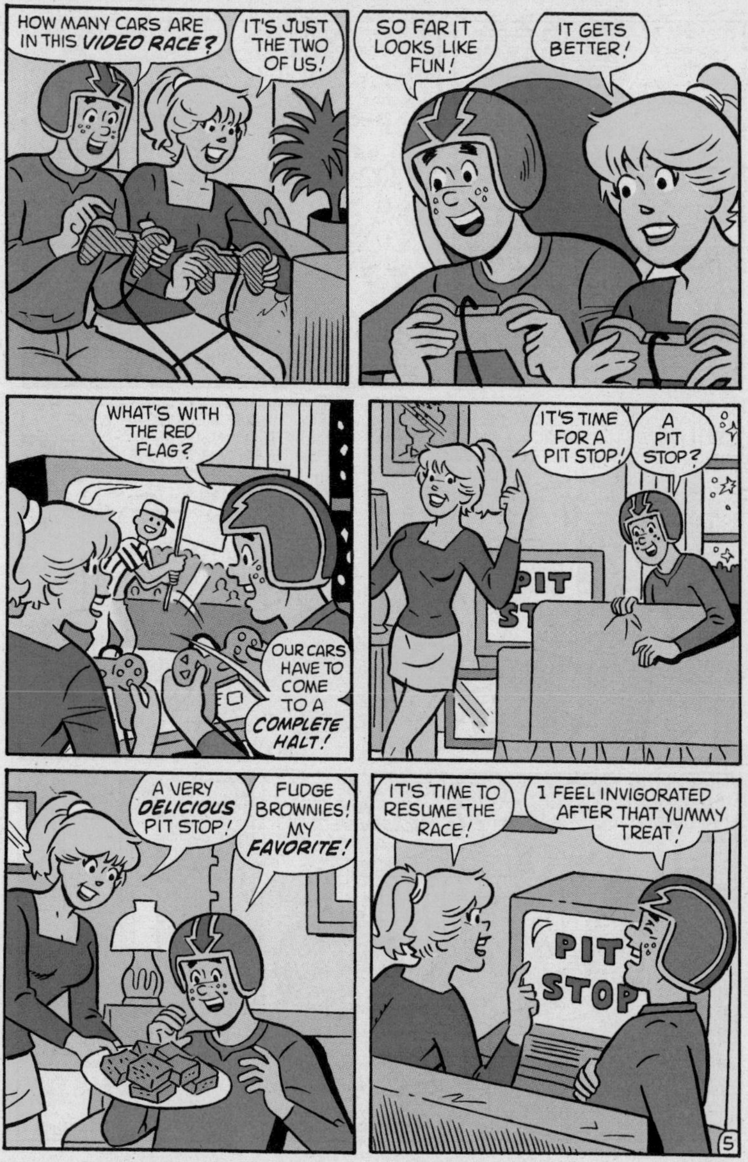
HOW MANY CARS ARE IN THIS VIDEO RACE?
IT'S JUST THE TWO OF US!
SO FAR IT LOOKS LIKE FUN!
IT GETS BETTER!
WHAT'S WITH THE RED FLAG?
OUR CARS HAVE TO COME TO A COMPLETE HALT!
IT'S TIME FOR A PIT STOP!
A PIT STOP?
PIT STOP
A VERY DELICIOUS PIT STOP!
FUDGE BROWNIES! MY FAVORITE!
IT'S TIME TO RESUME THE RACE!
I FEEL INVIGORATED AFTER THAT YUMMY TREAT!
PIT STOP
5

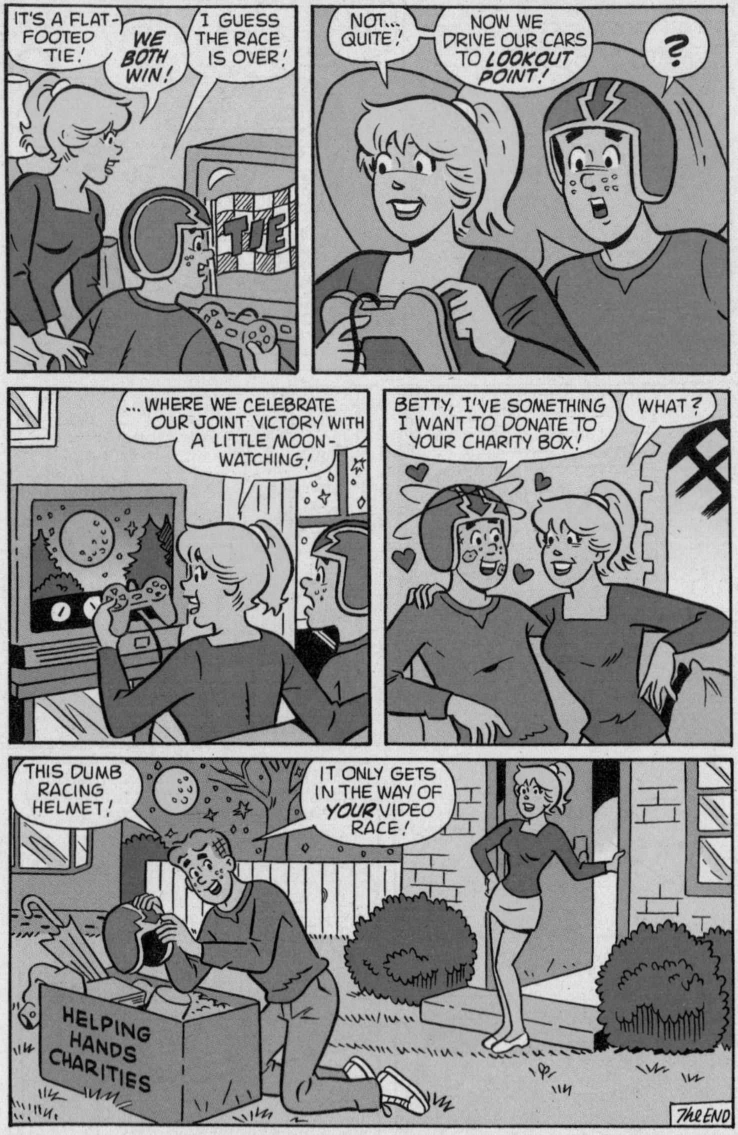
IT'S A FLAT-FOOTED TIE!
WE BOTH WIN!
I GUESS THE RACE IS OVER!
TIE
NOT... QUITE!
NOW WE DRIVE OUR CARS TO LOOKOUT POINT!
?
...WHERE WE CELEBRATE OUR JOINT VICTORY WITH A LITTLE MOON-WATCHING!
BETTY, I'VE SOMETHING I WANT TO DONATE TO YOUR CHARITY BOX!
WHAT?
THIS DUMB RACING HELMET!
IT ONLY GETS IN THE WAY OF YOUR VIDEO RACE!
HELPING HANDS CHARITIES
The END

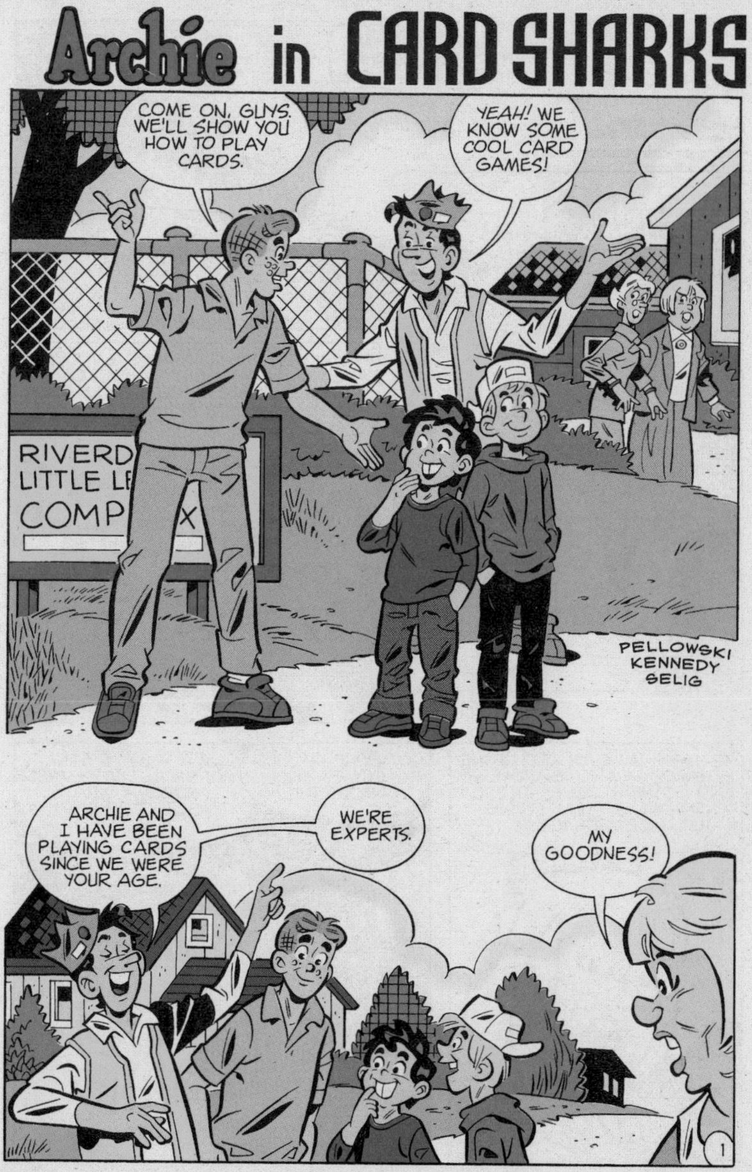
Archie in CARD SHARKS
COME ON, GUYS. WE'LL SHOW YOU HOW TO PLAY CARDS.
YEAH! WE KNOW SOME COOL CARD GAMES!
RIVERD
LITTLE LE
COMP
X
PELLOWSKI
KENNEDY
SELIG
ARCHIE AND I HAVE BEEN PLAYING CARDS SINCE WE WERE YOUR AGE.
WE'RE EXPERTS.
MY GOODNESS!
1

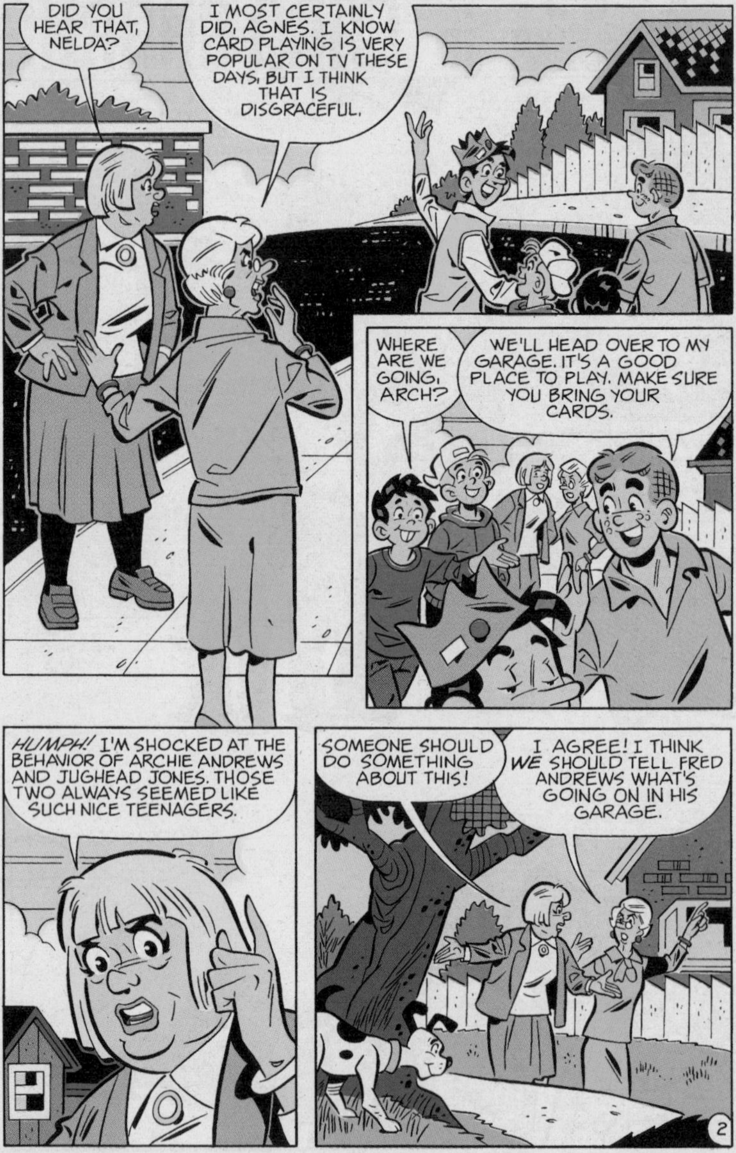
DID YOU HEAR THAT, NELDA?
I MOST CERTAINLY DID, AGNES. I KNOW CARD PLAYING IS VERY POPULAR ON TV THESE DAYS, BUT I THINK THAT IS DISGRACEFUL.
WHERE ARE WE GOING, ARCH?
WE'LL HEAD OVER TO MY GARAGE. IT'S A GOOD PLACE TO PLAY. MAKE SURE YOU BRING YOUR CARDS.
HUMPH! I'M SHOCKED AT THE BEHAVIOR OF ARCHIE ANDREWS AND JUGHEAD JONES. THOSE TWO ALWAYS SEEMED LIKE SUCH NICE TEENAGERS.
SOMEONE SHOULD DO SOMETHING ABOUT THIS!
I AGREE! I THINK *WE* SHOULD TELL FRED ANDREWS WHAT'S GOING ON IN HIS GARAGE.

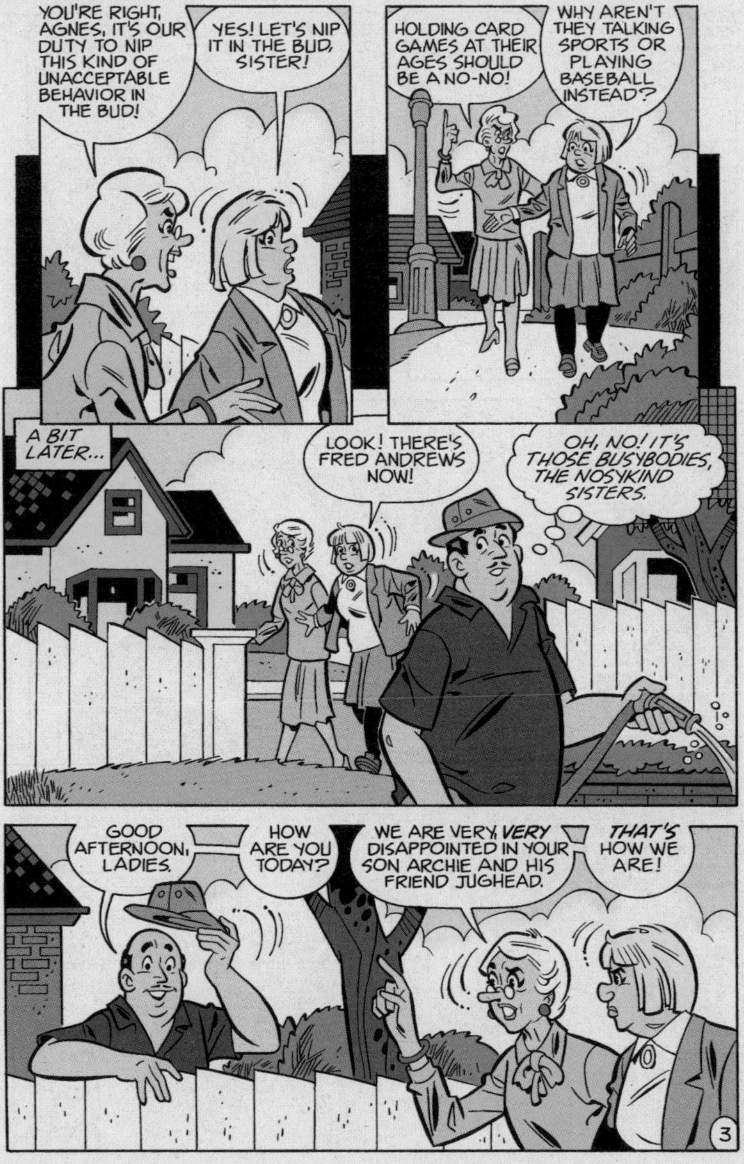
YOU'RE RIGHT, AGNES, IT'S OUR DUTY TO NIP THIS KIND OF UNACCEPTABLE BEHAVIOR IN THE BUD!
YES! LET'S NIP IT IN THE BUD, SISTER!
HOLDING CARD GAMES AT THEIR AGES SHOULD BE A NO-NO!
WHY AREN'T THEY TALKING SPORTS OR PLAYING BASEBALL INSTEAD?
A BIT LATER...
LOOK! THERE'S FRED ANDREWS NOW!
OH, NO! IT'S THOSE BUSYBODIES, THE NOSYKIND SISTERS.
GOOD AFTERNOON, LADIES.
HOW ARE YOU TODAY?
WE ARE VERY, *VERY* DISAPPOINTED IN YOUR SON ARCHIE AND HIS FRIEND JUGHEAD.
THAT'S HOW WE ARE!
3

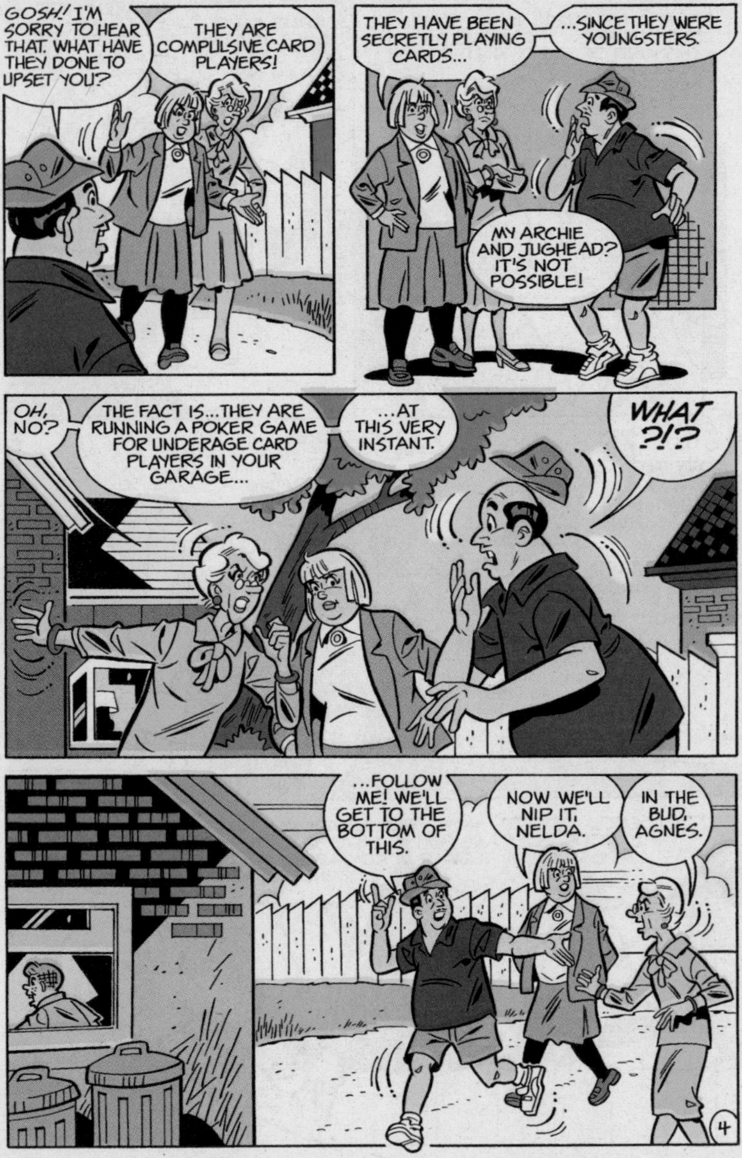

GOSH! I'M SORRY TO HEAR THAT. WHAT HAVE THEY DONE TO UPSET YOU?
THEY ARE COMPULSIVE CARD PLAYERS!
THEY HAVE BEEN SECRETLY PLAYING CARDS...
...SINCE THEY WERE YOUNGSTERS.
MY ARCHIE AND JUGHEAD? IT'S NOT POSSIBLE!
OH, NO?
THE FACT IS...THEY ARE RUNNING A POKER GAME FOR UNDERAGE CARD PLAYERS IN YOUR GARAGE...
...AT THIS VERY INSTANT.
WHAT ?!?
...FOLLOW ME! WE'LL GET TO THE BOTTOM OF THIS.
NOW WE'LL NIP IT, NELDA.
IN THE BUD, AGNES.
4

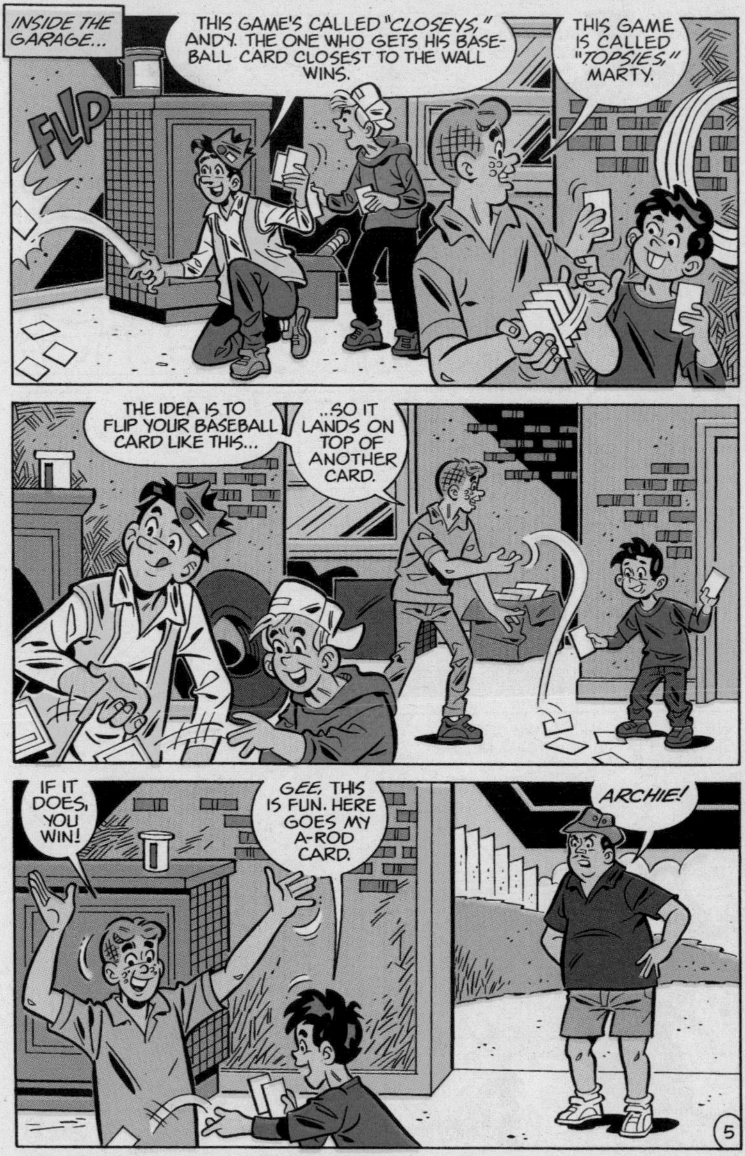
INSIDE THE GARAGE...
THIS GAME'S CALLED "CLOSEYS," ANDY. THE ONE WHO GETS HIS BASE-BALL CARD CLOSEST TO THE WALL WINS.
THIS GAME IS CALLED "TOPSIES," MARTY.
FLIP
THE IDEA IS TO FLIP YOUR BASEBALL CARD LIKE THIS...
...SO IT LANDS ON TOP OF ANOTHER CARD.
IF IT DOES, YOU WIN!
GEE, THIS IS FUN. HERE GOES MY A-ROD CARD.
ARCHIE!
5

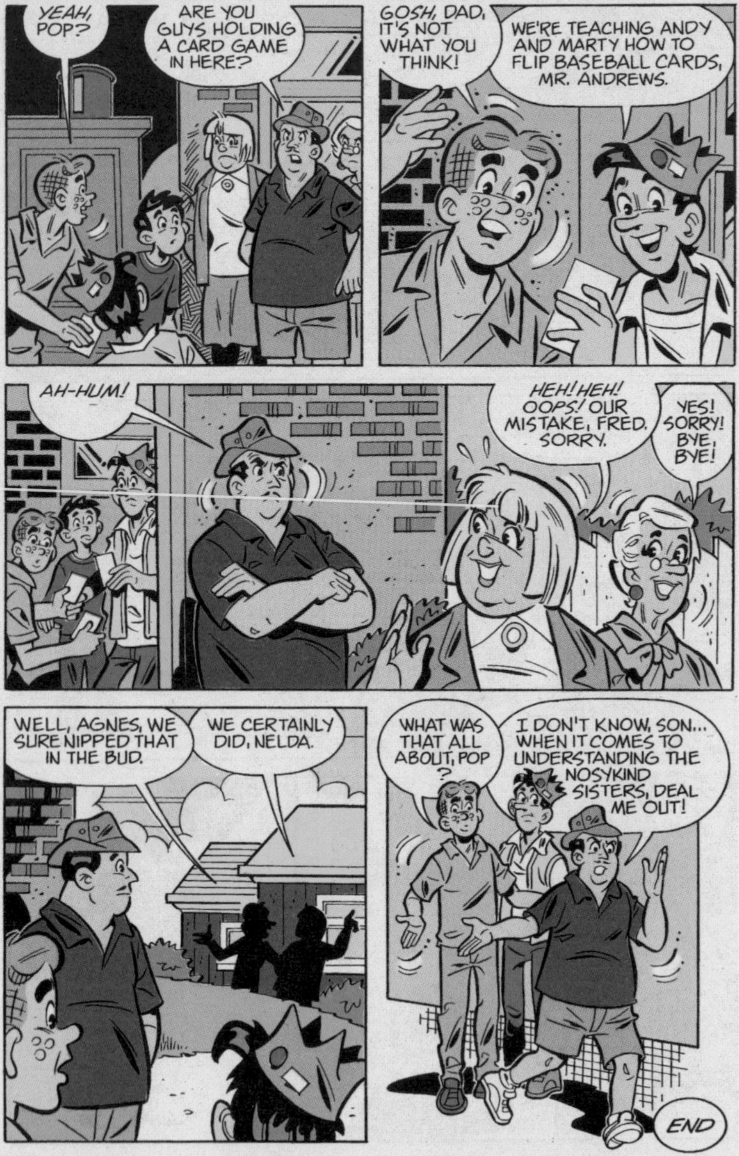
YEAH, POP?
ARE YOU GUYS HOLDING A CARD GAME IN HERE?
GOSH, DAD, IT'S NOT WHAT YOU THINK!
WE'RE TEACHING ANDY AND MARTY HOW TO FLIP BASEBALL CARDS, MR. ANDREWS.
AH-HUM!
HEH! HEH! OOPS! OUR MISTAKE, FRED. SORRY.
YES! SORRY! BYE, BYE!
WELL, AGNES, WE SURE NIPPED THAT IN THE BUD.
WE CERTAINLY DID, NELDA.
WHAT WAS THAT ALL ABOUT, POP?
I DON'T KNOW, SON... WHEN IT COMES TO UNDERSTANDING THE NOSYKIND SISTERS, DEAL ME OUT!
END

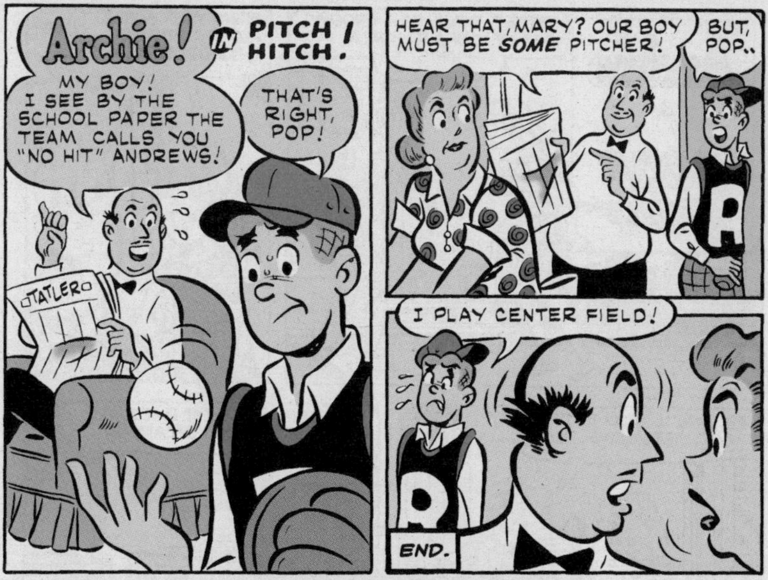

Archie! IN PITCH HITCH!
MY BOY! I SEE BY THE SCHOOL PAPER THE TEAM CALLS YOU "NO HIT" ANDREWS!
THAT'S RIGHT, POP!
TATLER
HEAR THAT, MARY? OUR BOY MUST BE *SOME* PITCHER!
BUT, POP..
I PLAY CENTER FIELD!
END.

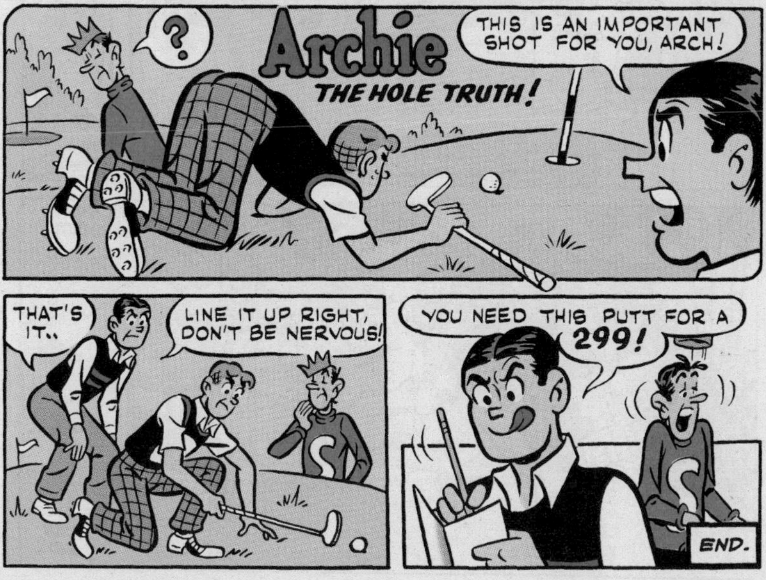

?
Archie
THE HOLE TRUTH!
THIS IS AN IMPORTANT SHOT FOR YOU, ARCH!
THAT'S IT..
LINE IT UP RIGHT, DON'T BE NERVOUS!
YOU NEED THIS PUTT FOR A 299!
END.

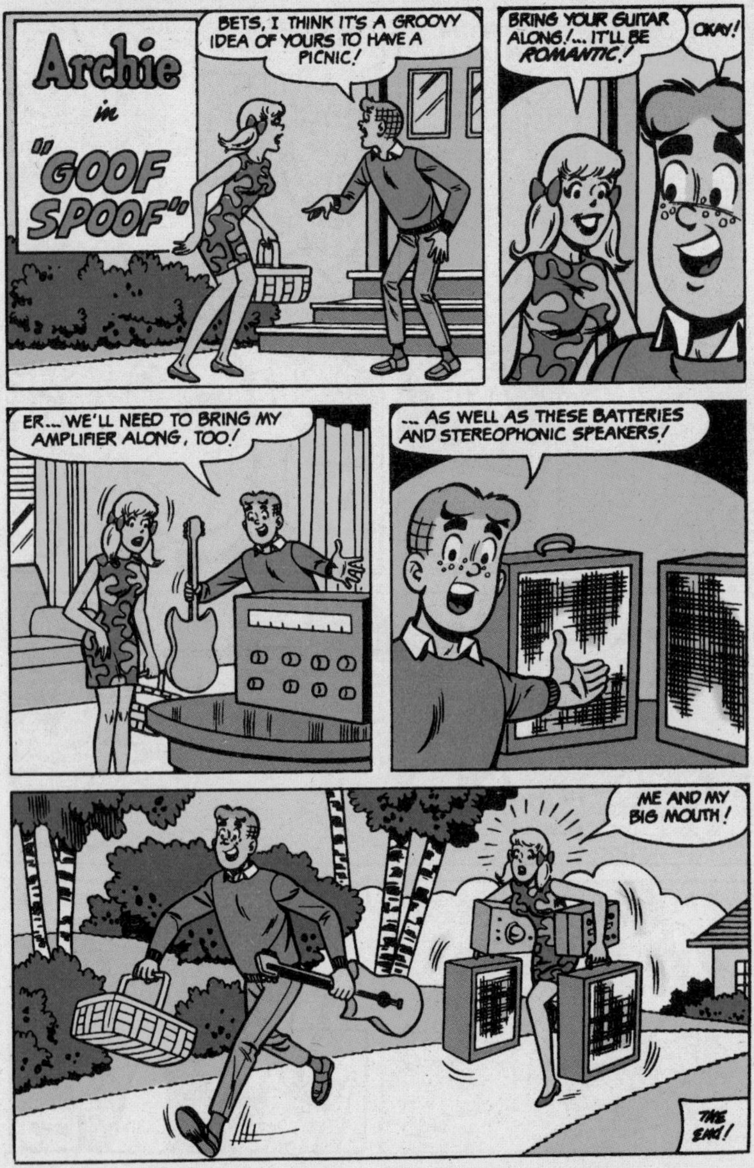
Archie
in
"GOOF SPOOF"
BETS, I THINK IT'S A GROOVY IDEA OF YOURS TO HAVE A PICNIC!
BRING YOUR GUITAR ALONG!... IT'LL BE ROMANTIC!
OKAY!
ER... WE'LL NEED TO BRING MY AMPLIFIER ALONG, TOO!
... AS WELL AS THESE BATTERIES AND STEREOPHONIC SPEAKERS!
ME AND MY BIG MOUTH!
THE END!

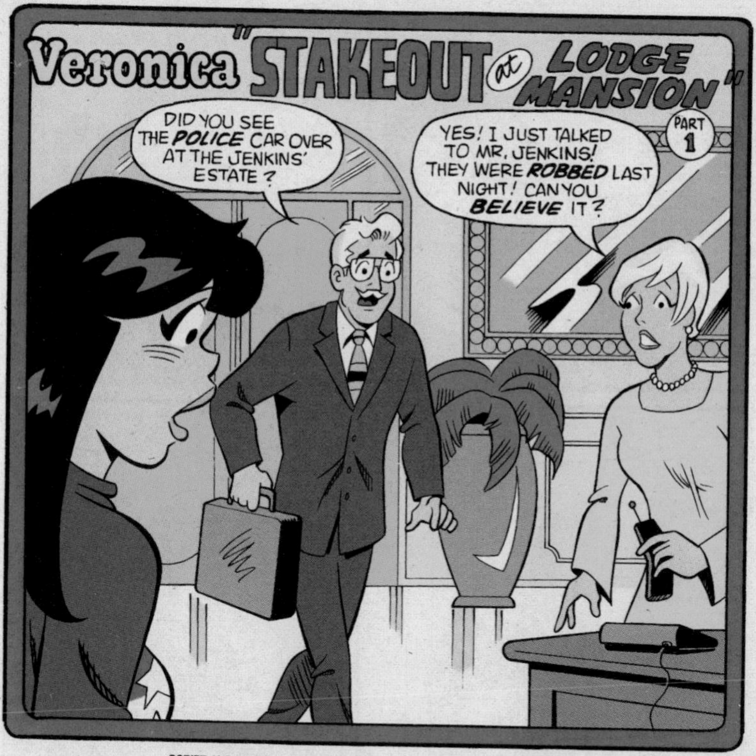
Veronica "STAKEOUT at LODGE MANSION"
PART 1
DID YOU SEE THE POLICE CAR OVER AT THE JENKINS' ESTATE?
YES! I JUST TALKED TO MR. JENKINS! THEY WERE ROBBED LAST NIGHT! CAN YOU BELIEVE IT?

SCRIPT AND PENCILS: DAN PARENT INKING: JIM AMASH LETTERING: BILL YOSHIDA COLORING: BARRY GROSSMAN

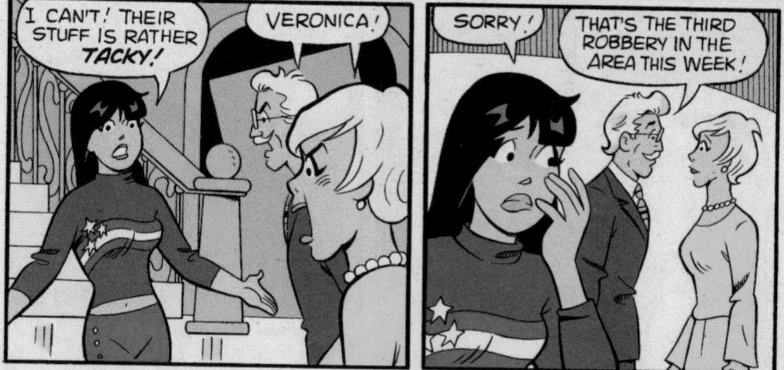
I CAN'T! THEIR STUFF IS RATHER TACKY!
VERONICA!
SORRY!
THAT'S THE THIRD ROBBERY IN THE AREA THIS WEEK!

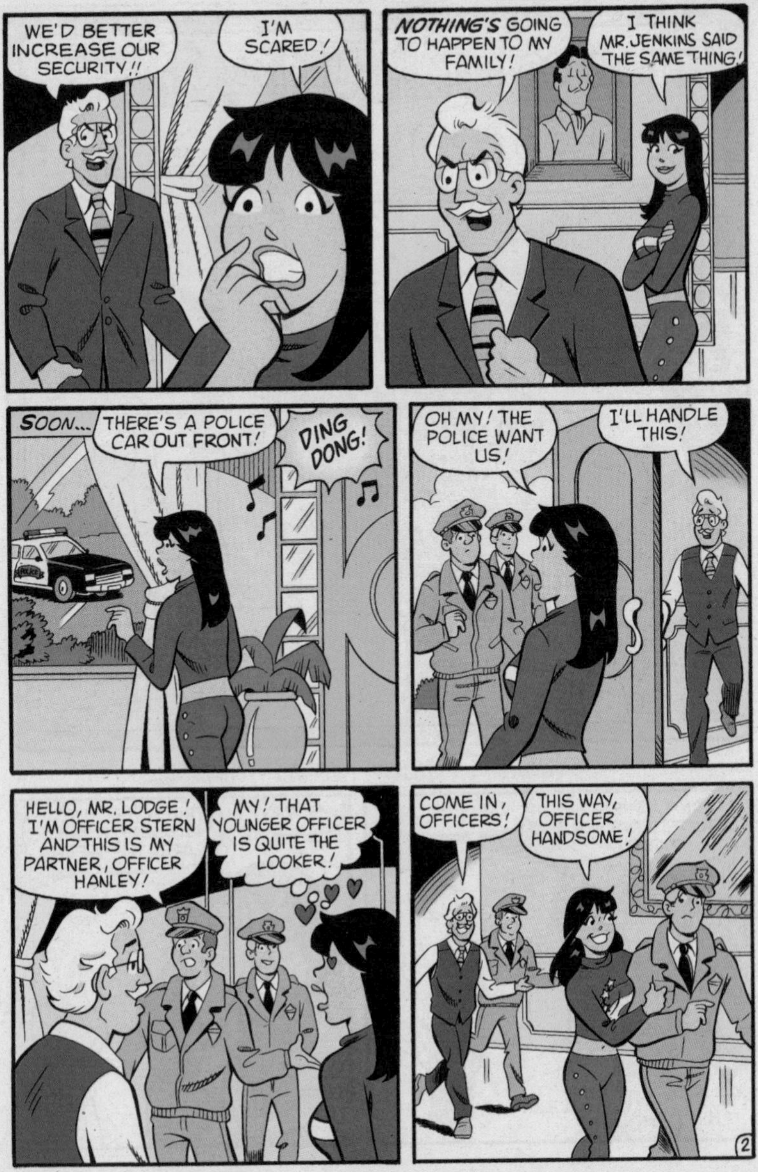
WE'D BETTER INCREASE OUR SECURITY!!
I'M SCARED!
NOTHING'S GOING TO HAPPEN TO MY FAMILY!
I THINK MR. JENKINS SAID THE SAME THING!
SOON...
THERE'S A POLICE CAR OUT FRONT!
DING DONG!
POLICE
OH MY! THE POLICE WANT US!
I'LL HANDLE THIS!
HELLO, MR. LODGE! I'M OFFICER STERN AND THIS IS MY PARTNER, OFFICER HANLEY!
MY! THAT YOUNGER OFFICER IS QUITE THE LOOKER!
COME IN, OFFICERS!
THIS WAY, OFFICER HANDSOME!
2

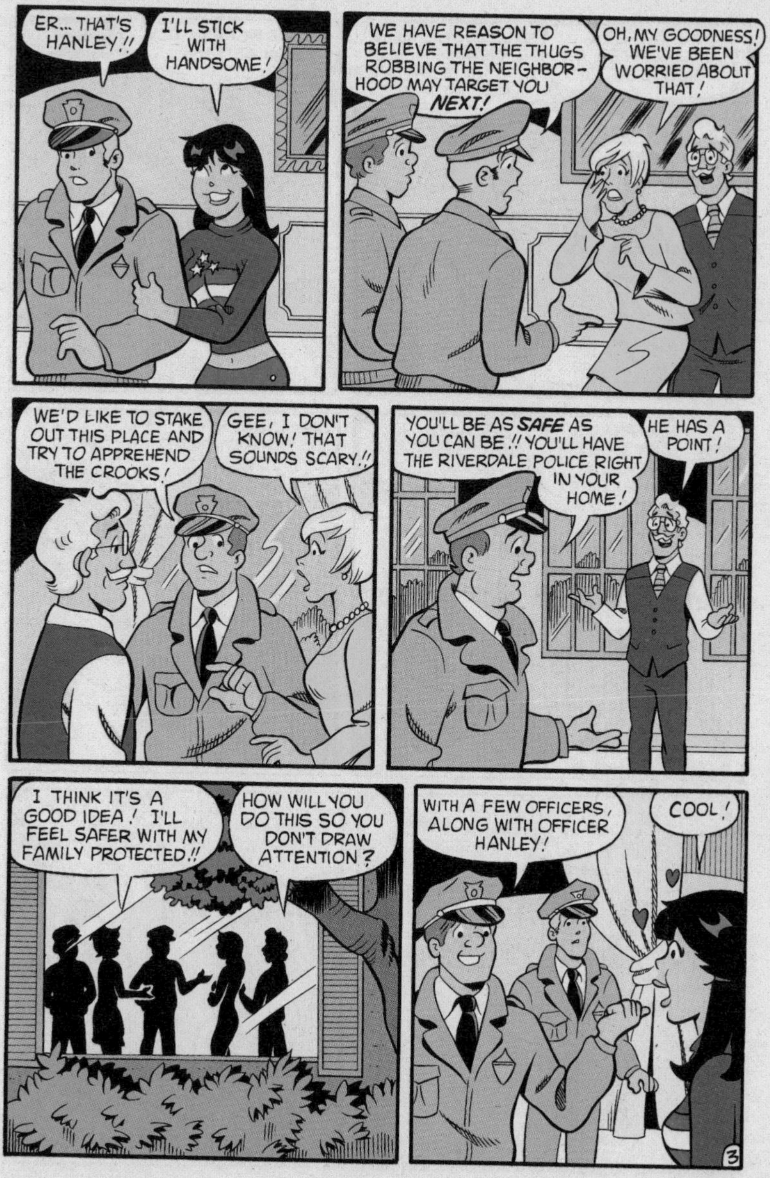
ER... THAT'S HANLEY!!
I'LL STICK WITH HANDSOME!
WE HAVE REASON TO BELIEVE THAT THE THUGS ROBBING THE NEIGHBORHOOD MAY TARGET YOU NEXT!
OH, MY GOODNESS! WE'VE BEEN WORRIED ABOUT THAT!
WE'D LIKE TO STAKE OUT THIS PLACE AND TRY TO APPREHEND THE CROOKS!
GEE, I DON'T KNOW! THAT SOUNDS SCARY!!
YOU'LL BE AS SAFE AS YOU CAN BE!! YOU'LL HAVE THE RIVERDALE POLICE RIGHT IN YOUR HOME!
HE HAS A POINT!
I THINK IT'S A GOOD IDEA! I'LL FEEL SAFER WITH MY FAMILY PROTECTED!!
HOW WILL YOU DO THIS SO YOU DON'T DRAW ATTENTION?
WITH A FEW OFFICERS, ALONG WITH OFFICER HANLEY!
COOL!
3

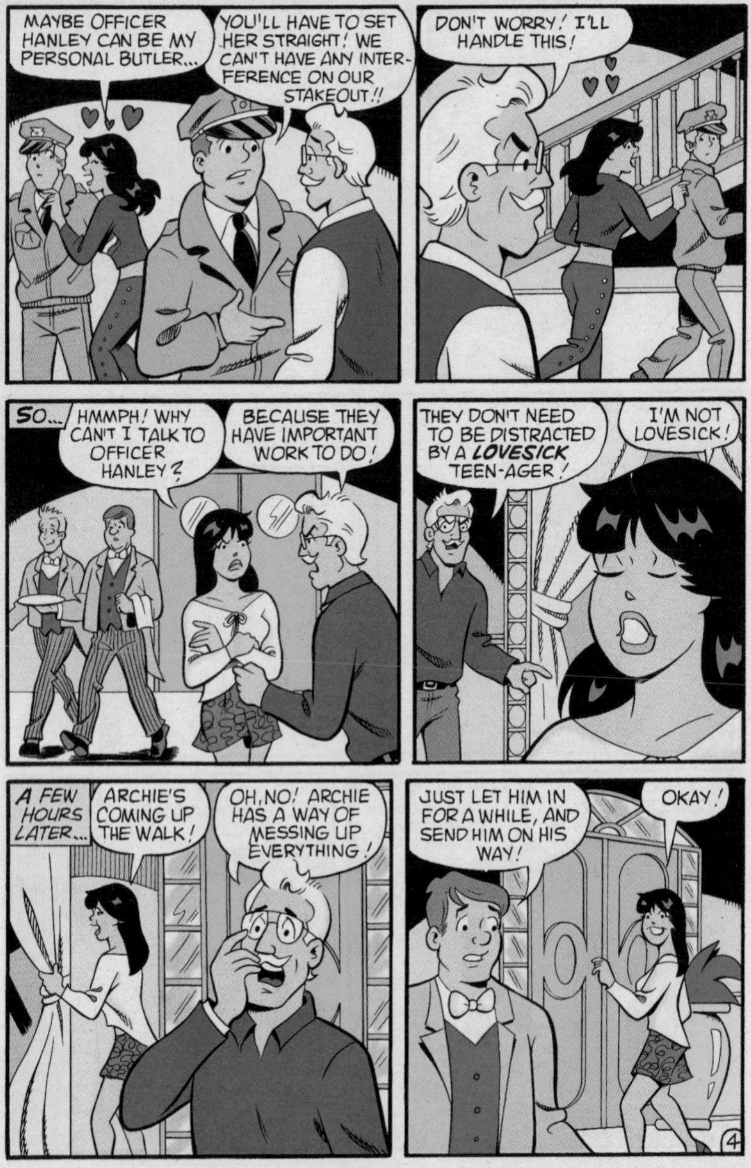
MAYBE OFFICER HANLEY CAN BE MY PERSONAL BUTLER...
YOU'LL HAVE TO SET HER STRAIGHT! WE CAN'T HAVE ANY INTERFERENCE ON OUR STAKEOUT!!
DON'T WORRY! I'LL HANDLE THIS!
SO...
HMMPH! WHY CAN'T I TALK TO OFFICER HANLEY?
BECAUSE THEY HAVE IMPORTANT WORK TO DO!
THEY DON'T NEED TO BE DISTRACTED BY A LOVESICK TEEN-AGER!
I'M NOT LOVESICK!
A FEW HOURS LATER...
ARCHIE'S COMING UP THE WALK!
OH, NO! ARCHIE HAS A WAY OF MESSING UP EVERYTHING!
JUST LET HIM IN FOR A WHILE, AND SEND HIM ON HIS WAY!
OKAY!
4

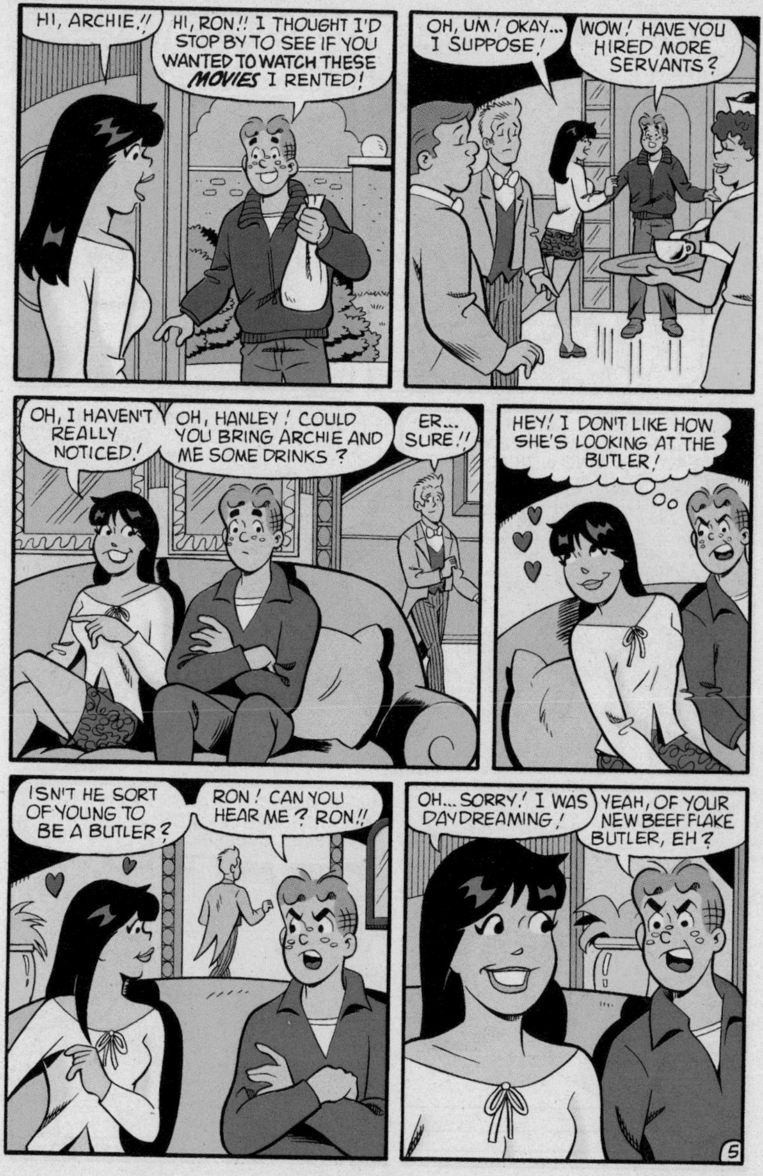
HI, ARCHIE!!
HI, RON!! I THOUGHT I'D STOP BY TO SEE IF YOU WANTED TO WATCH THESE MOVIES I RENTED!
OH, UM! OKAY... I SUPPOSE!
WOW! HAVE YOU HIRED MORE SERVANTS?
OH, I HAVEN'T REALLY NOTICED!
OH, HANLEY! COULD YOU BRING ARCHIE AND ME SOME DRINKS?
ER... SURE!!
HEY! I DON'T LIKE HOW SHE'S LOOKING AT THE BUTLER!
ISN'T HE SORT OF YOUNG TO BE A BUTLER?
RON! CAN YOU HEAR ME? RON!!
OH... SORRY! I WAS DAYDREAMING!
YEAH, OF YOUR NEW BEEFFLAKE BUTLER, EH?
5

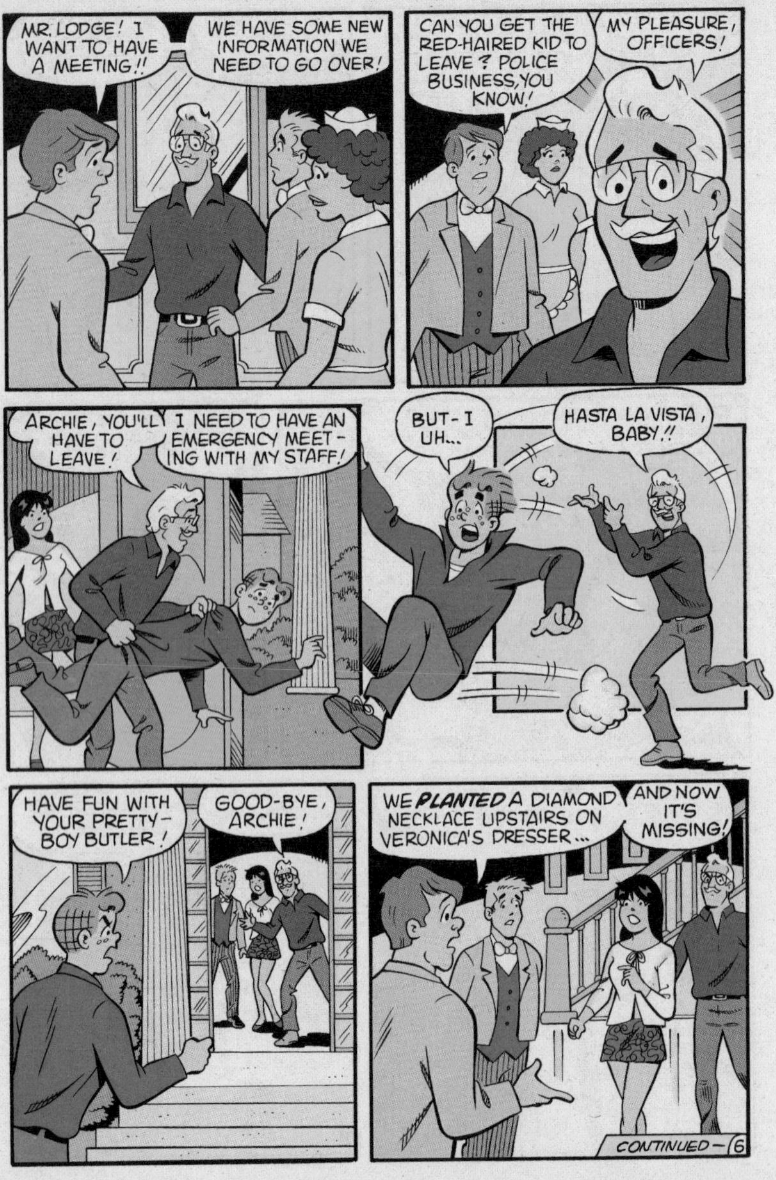
MR. LODGE! I WANT TO HAVE A MEETING!!
WE HAVE SOME NEW INFORMATION WE NEED TO GO OVER!
CAN YOU GET THE RED-HAIRED KID TO LEAVE? POLICE BUSINESS, YOU KNOW!
MY PLEASURE, OFFICERS!
ARCHIE, YOU'LL HAVE TO LEAVE!
I NEED TO HAVE AN EMERGENCY MEETING WITH MY STAFF!
BUT- I UH...
HASTA LA VISTA, BABY!!
HAVE FUN WITH YOUR PRETTY-BOY BUTLER!
GOOD-BYE, ARCHIE!
WE *PLANTED* A DIAMOND NECKLACE UPSTAIRS ON VERONICA'S DRESSER...
AND NOW IT'S MISSING!
CONTINUED- 6

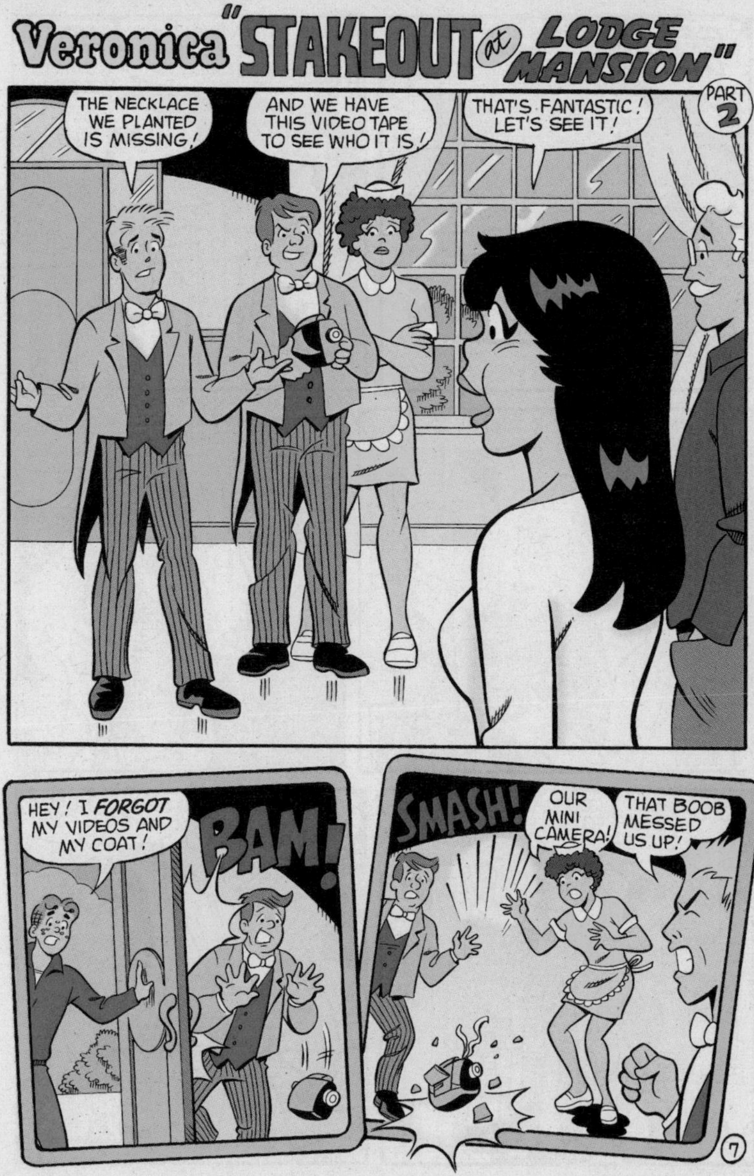
Veronica "STAKEOUT at LODGE MANSION"
PART 2
THE NECKLACE WE PLANTED IS MISSING!
AND WE HAVE THIS VIDEO TAPE TO SEE WHO IT IS!
THAT'S FANTASTIC! LET'S SEE IT!
HEY! I FORGOT MY VIDEOS AND MY COAT!
BAM!
SMASH!
OUR MINI CAMERA!
THAT BOOB MESSED US UP!

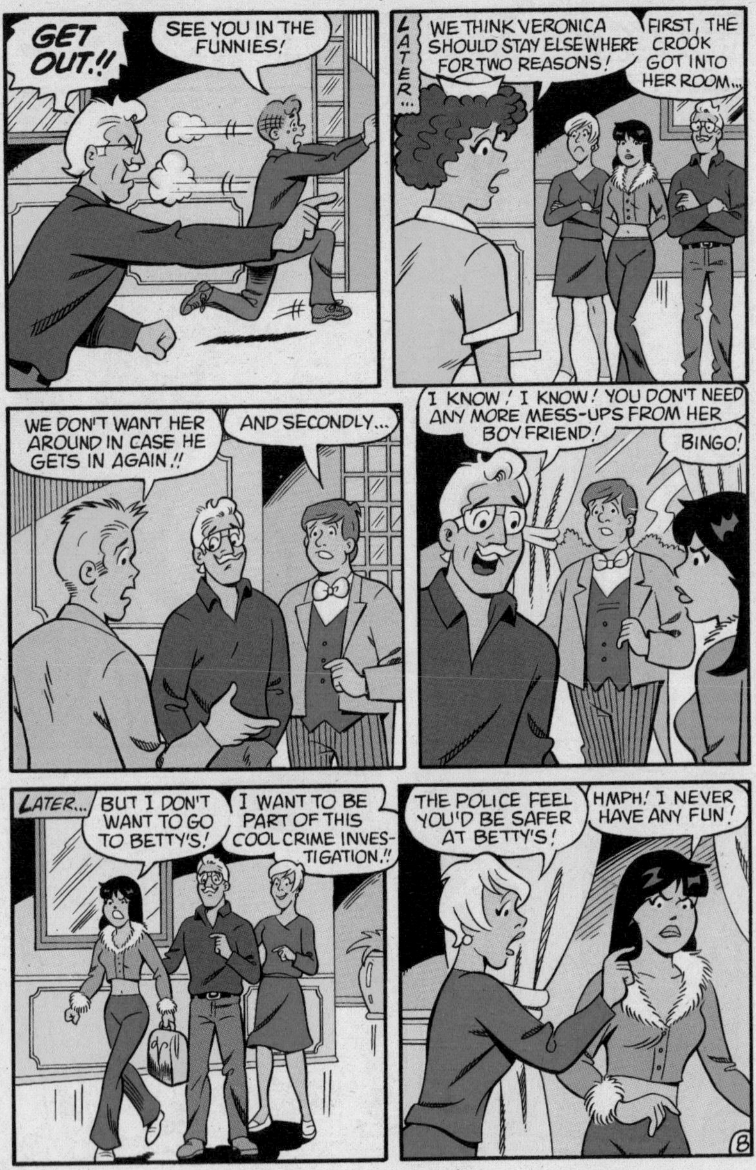
GET OUT.!!
SEE YOU IN THE FUNNIES!
LATER...
WE THINK VERONICA SHOULD STAY ELSEWHERE FOR TWO REASONS!
FIRST, THE CROOK GOT INTO HER ROOM...
WE DON'T WANT HER AROUND IN CASE HE GETS IN AGAIN.!!
AND SECONDLY...
I KNOW! I KNOW! YOU DON'T NEED ANY MORE MESS-UPS FROM HER BOY FRIEND!
BINGO!
LATER...
BUT I DON'T WANT TO GO TO BETTY'S!
I WANT TO BE PART OF THIS COOL CRIME INVES-TIGATION.!!
THE POLICE FEEL YOU'D BE SAFER AT BETTY'S!
HMPH! I NEVER HAVE ANY FUN!
8

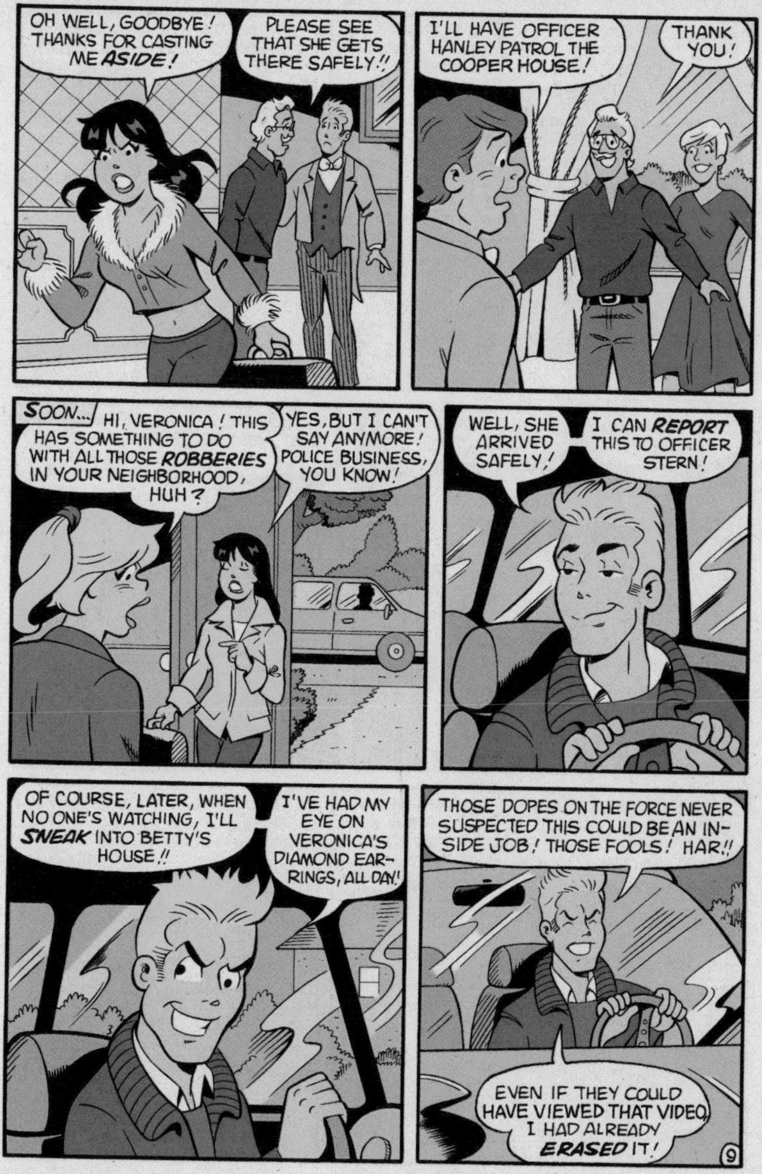

OH WELL, GOODBYE! THANKS FOR CASTING ME ASIDE!
PLEASE SEE THAT SHE GETS THERE SAFELY!!
I'LL HAVE OFFICER HANLEY PATROL THE COOPER HOUSE!
THANK YOU!
SOON...
HI, VERONICA! THIS HAS SOMETHING TO DO WITH ALL THOSE ROBBERIES IN YOUR NEIGHBORHOOD, HUH?
YES, BUT I CAN'T SAY ANYMORE! POLICE BUSINESS, YOU KNOW!
WELL, SHE ARRIVED SAFELY!
I CAN REPORT THIS TO OFFICER STERN!
OF COURSE, LATER, WHEN NO ONE'S WATCHING, I'LL SNEAK INTO BETTY'S HOUSE!!
I'VE HAD MY EYE ON VERONICA'S DIAMOND EAR-RINGS, ALL DAY!
THOSE DOPES ON THE FORCE NEVER SUSPECTED THIS COULD BE AN IN-SIDE JOB! THOSE FOOLS! HAR!!
EVEN IF THEY COULD HAVE VIEWED THAT VIDEO, I HAD ALREADY ERASED IT!

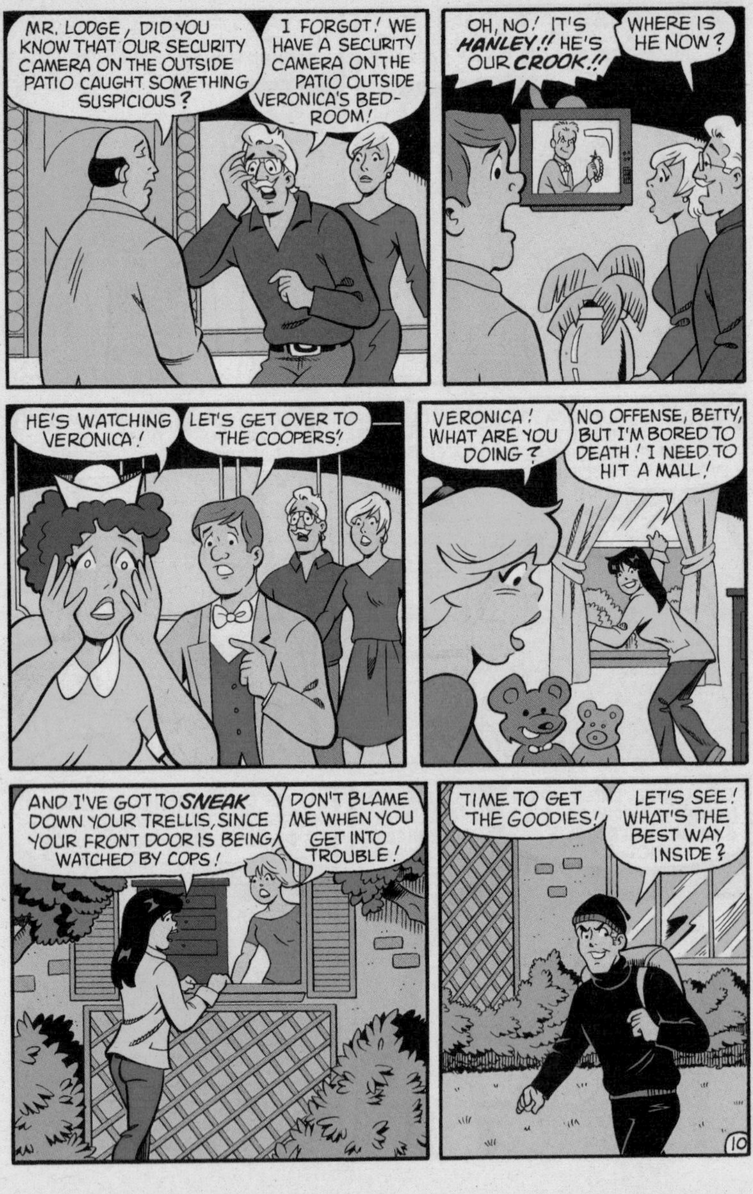
MR. LODGE, DID YOU KNOW THAT OUR SECURITY CAMERA ON THE OUTSIDE PATIO CAUGHT SOMETHING SUSPICIOUS?
I FORGOT! WE HAVE A SECURITY CAMERA ON THE PATIO OUTSIDE VERONICA'S BED-ROOM!
OH, NO! IT'S HANLEY!! HE'S OUR CROOK!!
WHERE IS HE NOW?
HE'S WATCHING VERONICA!
LET'S GET OVER TO THE COOPERS'!
VERONICA! WHAT ARE YOU DOING?
NO OFFENSE, BETTY, BUT I'M BORED TO DEATH! I NEED TO HIT A MALL!
AND I'VE GOT TO SNEAK DOWN YOUR TRELLIS, SINCE YOUR FRONT DOOR IS BEING WATCHED BY COPS!
DON'T BLAME ME WHEN YOU GET INTO TROUBLE!
TIME TO GET THE GOODIES!
LET'S SEE! WHAT'S THE BEST WAY INSIDE?
10

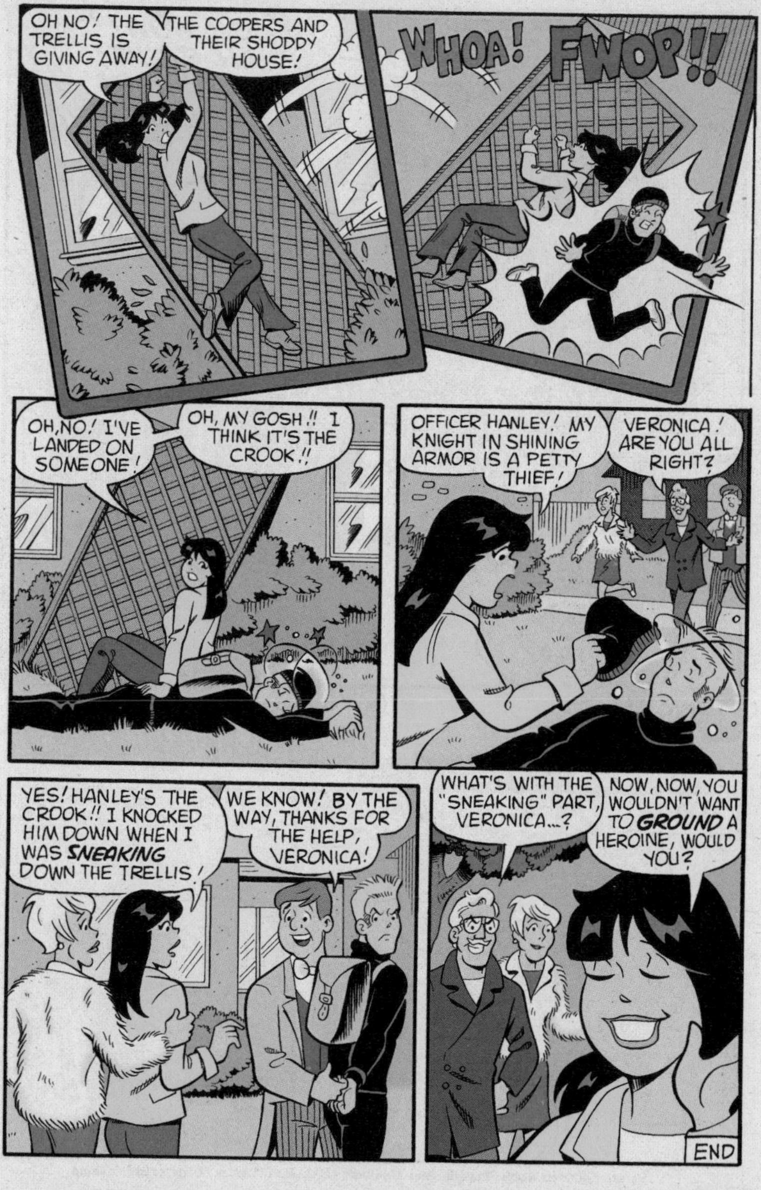
OH NO! THE TRELLIS IS GIVING AWAY!
THE COOPERS AND THEIR SHODDY HOUSE!
WHOA!
FWOP!!
OH, NO! I'VE LANDED ON SOMEONE!
OH, MY GOSH!! I THINK IT'S THE CROOK!!
OFFICER HANLEY! MY KNIGHT IN SHINING ARMOR IS A PETTY THIEF!
VERONICA! ARE YOU ALL RIGHT?
YES! HANLEY'S THE CROOK!! I KNOCKED HIM DOWN WHEN I WAS SNEAKING DOWN THE TRELLIS!
WE KNOW! BY THE WAY, THANKS FOR THE HELP, VERONICA!
WHAT'S WITH THE "SNEAKING" PART, VERONICA...?
NOW, NOW, YOU WOULDN'T WANT TO GROUND A HEROINE, WOULD YOU?
END

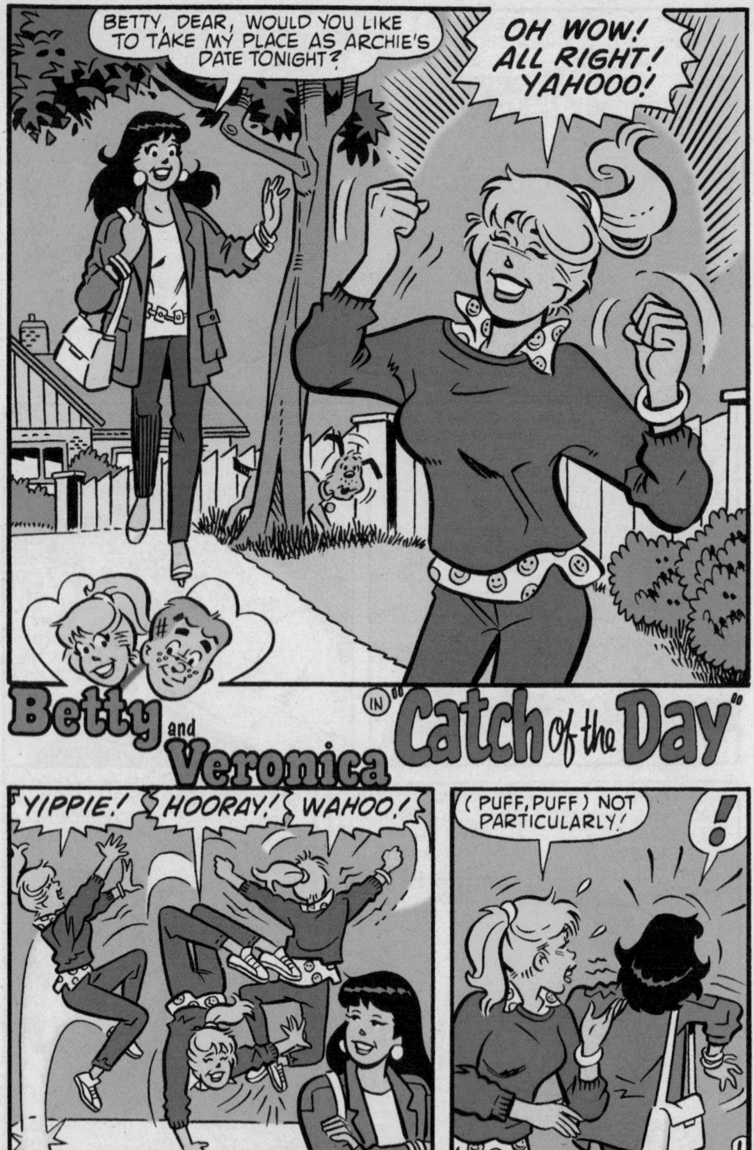
BETTY, DEAR, WOULD YOU LIKE TO TAKE MY PLACE AS ARCHIE'S DATE TONIGHT?
OH WOW! ALL RIGHT! YAHOOO!
Betty and Veronica IN "Catch of the Day"
YIPPIE!
HOORAY!
WAHOO!
(PUFF, PUFF) NOT PARTICULARLY!
!
1

Script: Kathleen Webb / Pencils: Stan Goldberg / Inks: Rudy Lapick / Letters: Bill Yoshida

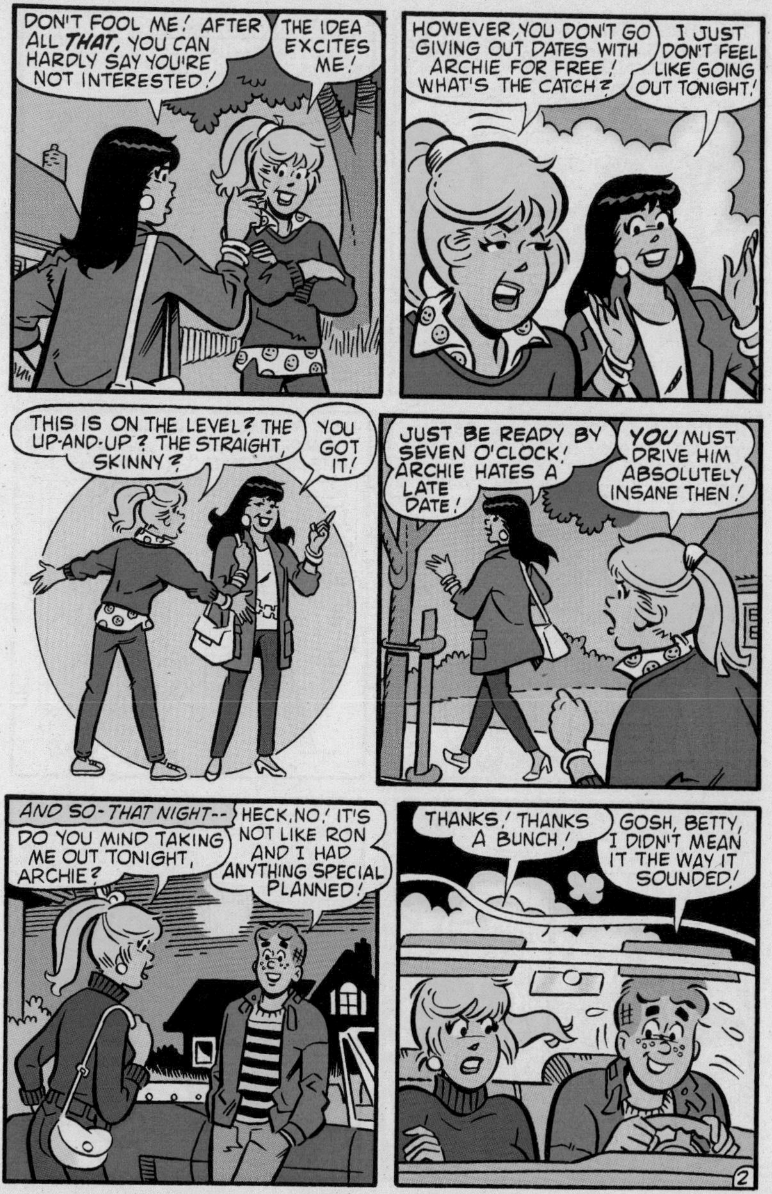
DON'T FOOL ME! AFTER ALL *THAT,* YOU CAN HARDLY SAY YOU'RE NOT INTERESTED!
THE IDEA EXCITES ME!
HOWEVER, YOU DON'T GO GIVING OUT DATES WITH ARCHIE FOR FREE! WHAT'S THE CATCH?
I JUST DON'T FEEL LIKE GOING OUT TONIGHT!
THIS IS ON THE LEVEL? THE UP-AND-UP? THE STRAIGHT SKINNY?
YOU GOT IT!
JUST BE READY BY SEVEN O'CLOCK! ARCHIE HATES A LATE DATE!
YOU MUST DRIVE HIM ABSOLUTELY INSANE THEN!
AND SO-THAT NIGHT--
DO YOU MIND TAKING ME OUT TONIGHT, ARCHIE?
HECK, NO! IT'S NOT LIKE RON AND I HAD ANYTHING SPECIAL PLANNED!
THANKS! THANKS A BUNCH!
GOSH, BETTY, I DIDN'T MEAN IT THE WAY IT SOUNDED!
2

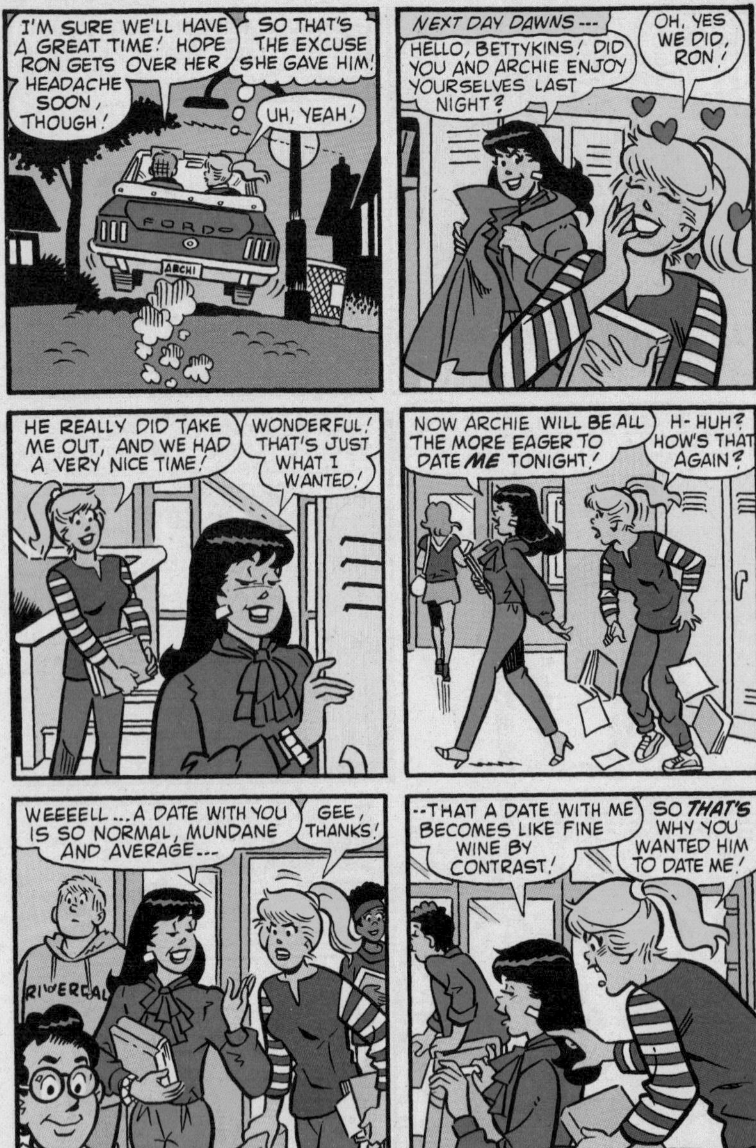
I'M SURE WE'LL HAVE A GREAT TIME! HOPE RON GETS OVER HER HEADACHE SOON, THOUGH!
SO THAT'S THE EXCUSE SHE GAVE HIM!
UH, YEAH!
FORDO
ARCHI
NEXT DAY DAWNS ---
HELLO, BETTYKINS! DID YOU AND ARCHIE ENJOY YOURSELVES LAST NIGHT?
OH, YES WE DID, RON!
HE REALLY DID TAKE ME OUT, AND WE HAD A VERY NICE TIME!
WONDERFUL! THAT'S JUST WHAT I WANTED!
NOW ARCHIE WILL BE ALL THE MORE EAGER TO DATE ME TONIGHT!
H-HUH? HOW'S THAT AGAIN?
WEEEELL ... A DATE WITH YOU IS SO NORMAL, MUNDANE AND AVERAGE ---
GEE, THANKS!
RIVERDAL
--THAT A DATE WITH ME BECOMES LIKE FINE WINE BY CONTRAST!
SO THAT'S WHY YOU WANTED HIM TO DATE ME!
3

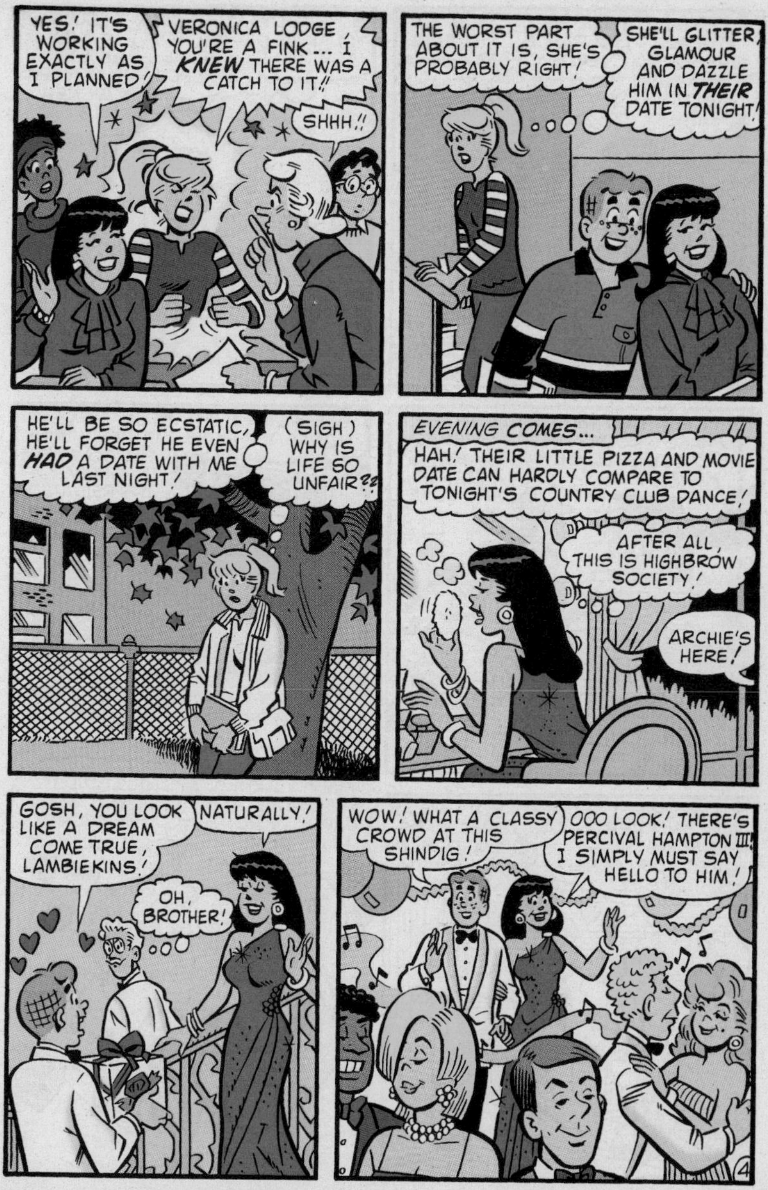
YES! IT'S WORKING EXACTLY AS I PLANNED!
VERONICA LODGE, YOU'RE A FINK... I KNEW THERE WAS A CATCH TO IT!!
SHHH!!
THE WORST PART ABOUT IT IS, SHE'S PROBABLY RIGHT!
SHE'LL GLITTER, GLAMOUR AND DAZZLE HIM IN THEIR DATE TONIGHT!
HE'LL BE SO ECSTATIC, HE'LL FORGET HE EVEN HAD A DATE WITH ME LAST NIGHT!
(SIGH) WHY IS LIFE SO UNFAIR??
EVENING COMES...
HAH! THEIR LITTLE PIZZA AND MOVIE DATE CAN HARDLY COMPARE TO TONIGHT'S COUNTRY CLUB DANCE!
AFTER ALL, THIS IS HIGHBROW SOCIETY!
ARCHIE'S HERE!
GOSH, YOU LOOK LIKE A DREAM COME TRUE, LAMBIEKINS!
NATURALLY!
OH, BROTHER!
WOW! WHAT A CLASSY CROWD AT THIS SHINDIG!
OOO LOOK! THERE'S PERCIVAL HAMPTON III! I SIMPLY MUST SAY HELLO TO HIM!
4

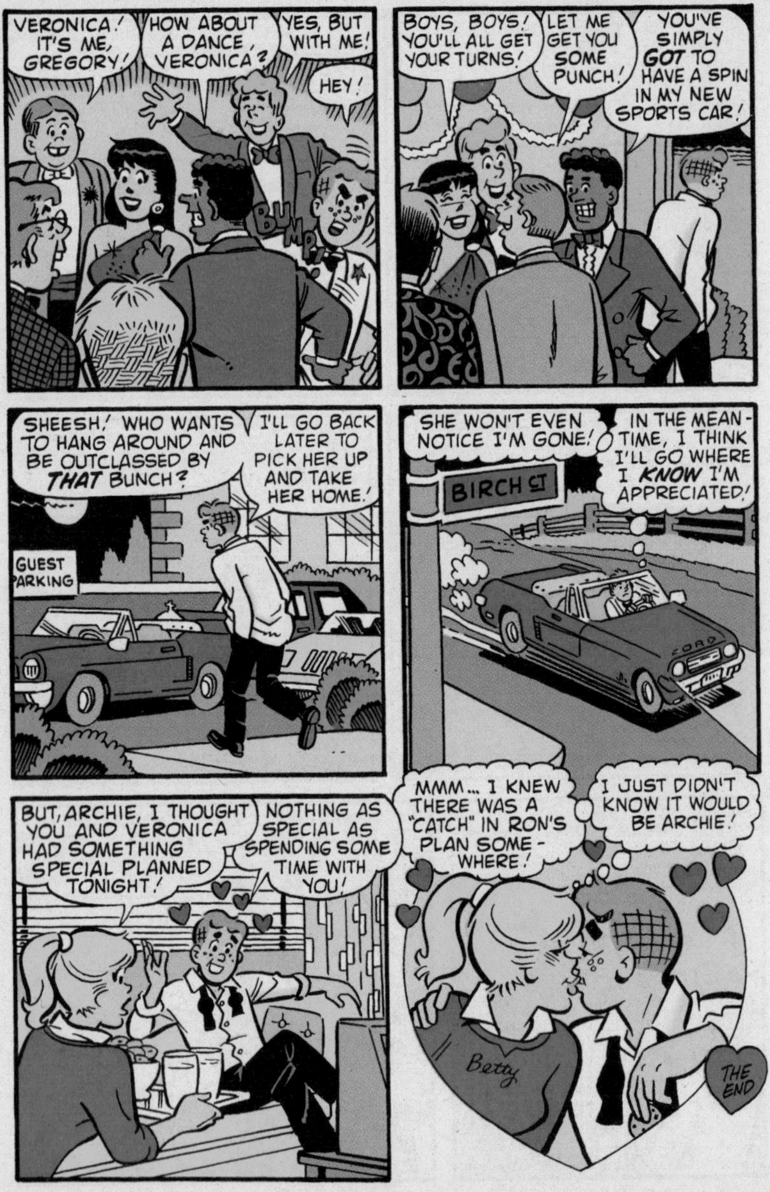

VERONICA! IT'S ME, GREGORY!
HOW ABOUT A DANCE, VERONICA?
YES, BUT WITH ME!
HEY!
BUMP!
BOYS, BOYS! YOU'LL ALL GET YOUR TURNS!
LET ME GET YOU SOME PUNCH!
YOU'VE SIMPLY GOT TO HAVE A SPIN IN MY NEW SPORTS CAR!
SHEESH! WHO WANTS TO HANG AROUND AND BE OUTCLASSED BY THAT BUNCH?
I'LL GO BACK LATER TO PICK HER UP AND TAKE HER HOME!
GUEST PARKING
SHE WON'T EVEN NOTICE I'M GONE!
IN THE MEAN-TIME, I THINK I'LL GO WHERE I KNOW I'M APPRECIATED!
BIRCH CT
FORD
BUT, ARCHIE, I THOUGHT YOU AND VERONICA HAD SOMETHING SPECIAL PLANNED TONIGHT!
NOTHING AS SPECIAL AS SPENDING SOME TIME WITH YOU!
MMM... I KNEW THERE WAS A "CATCH" IN RON'S PLAN SOME-WHERE!
I JUST DIDN'T KNOW IT WOULD BE ARCHIE!
Betty
THE END

Betty and Veronica in "HOW TO MEET BOYS!"

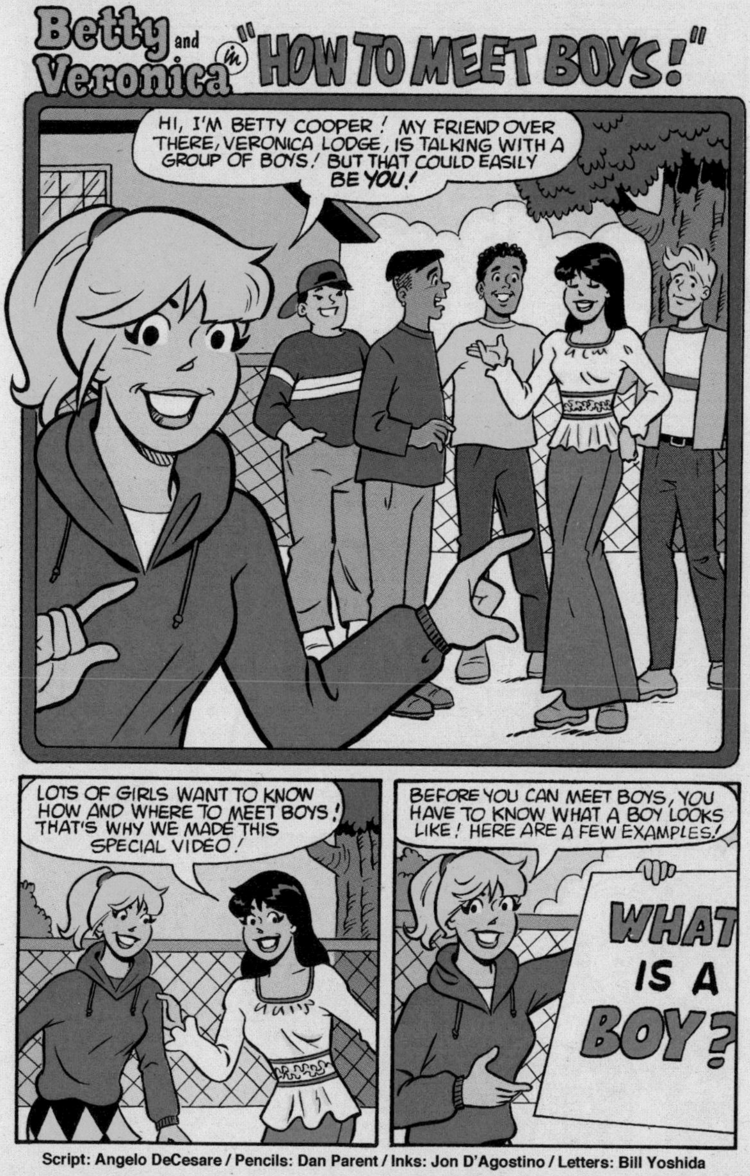

HI, I'M BETTY COOPER! MY FRIEND OVER THERE, VERONICA LODGE, IS TALKING WITH A GROUP OF BOYS! BUT THAT COULD EASILY BE YOU!
LOTS OF GIRLS WANT TO KNOW HOW AND WHERE TO MEET BOYS! THAT'S WHY WE MADE THIS SPECIAL VIDEO!
BEFORE YOU CAN MEET BOYS, YOU HAVE TO KNOW WHAT A BOY LOOKS LIKE! HERE ARE A FEW EXAMPLES!
WHAT IS A BOY?

Script: Angelo DeCesare / Pencils: Dan Parent / Inks: Jon D'Agostino / Letters: Bill Yoshida

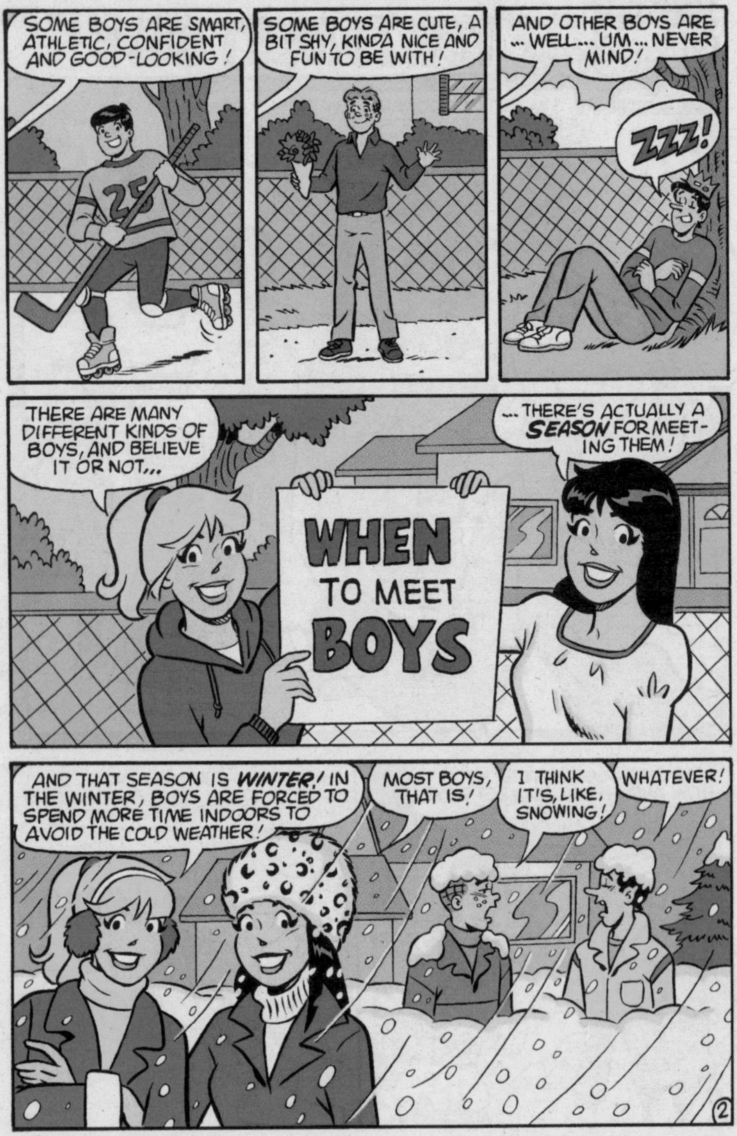
SOME BOYS ARE SMART, ATHLETIC, CONFIDENT AND GOOD-LOOKING!
SOME BOYS ARE CUTE, A BIT SHY, KINDA NICE AND FUN TO BE WITH!
AND OTHER BOYS ARE ... WELL... UM... NEVER MIND!
ZZZ!
THERE ARE MANY DIFFERENT KINDS OF BOYS, AND BELIEVE IT OR NOT...
...THERE'S ACTUALLY A SEASON FOR MEETING THEM!
WHEN TO MEET BOYS
AND THAT SEASON IS WINTER! IN THE WINTER, BOYS ARE FORCED TO SPEND MORE TIME INDOORS TO AVOID THE COLD WEATHER!
MOST BOYS, THAT IS!
I THINK IT'S, LIKE, SNOWING!
WHATEVER!
2

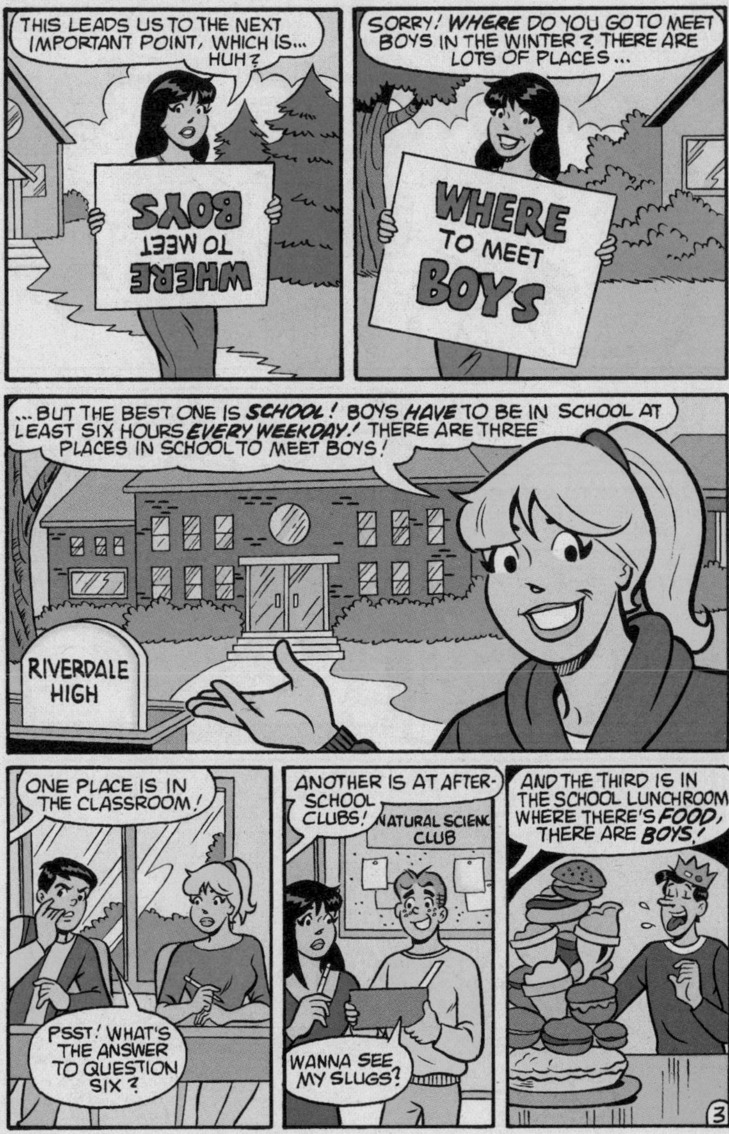
THIS LEADS US TO THE NEXT IMPORTANT POINT, WHICH IS... HUH?
WHERE TO MEET BOYS
SORRY! WHERE DO YOU GO TO MEET BOYS IN THE WINTER? THERE ARE LOTS OF PLACES...
WHERE TO MEET BOYS
...BUT THE BEST ONE IS SCHOOL! BOYS HAVE TO BE IN SCHOOL AT LEAST SIX HOURS EVERY WEEKDAY! THERE ARE THREE PLACES IN SCHOOL TO MEET BOYS!
RIVERDALE HIGH
ONE PLACE IS IN THE CLASSROOM!
PSST! WHAT'S THE ANSWER TO QUESTION SIX?
ANOTHER IS AT AFTER-SCHOOL CLUBS!
NATURAL SCIENC CLUB
WANNA SEE MY SLUGS?
AND THE THIRD IS IN THE SCHOOL LUNCHROOM! WHERE THERE'S FOOD, THERE ARE BOYS!
3

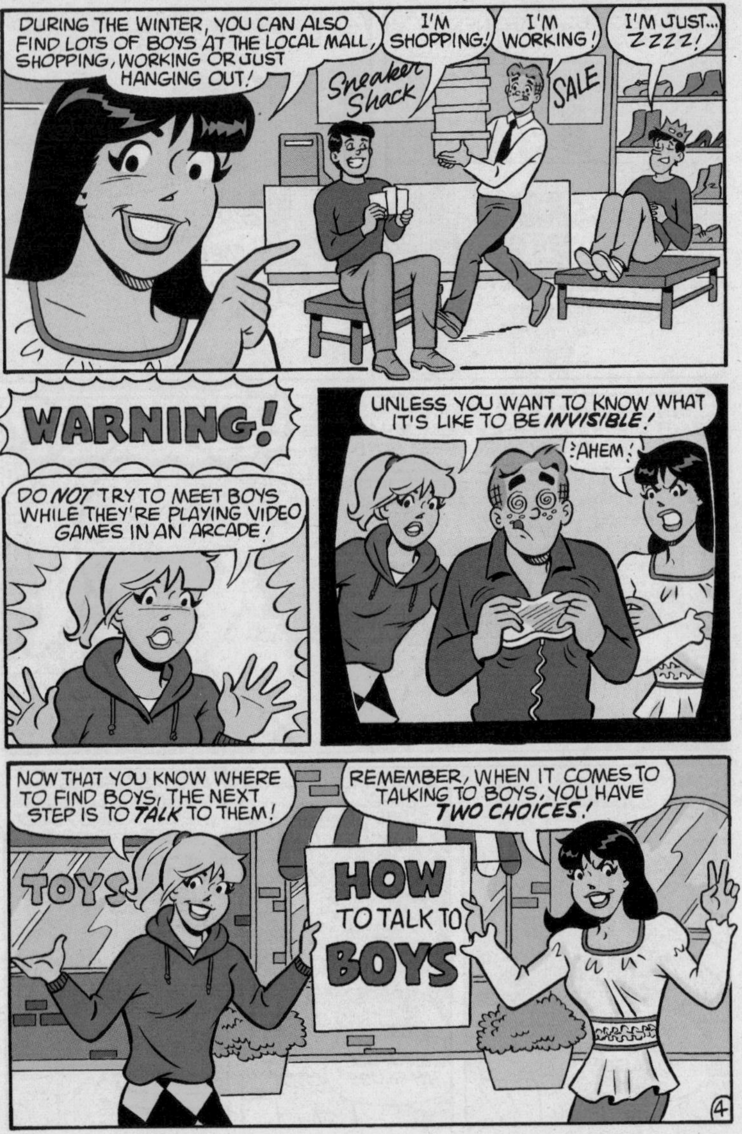
DURING THE WINTER, YOU CAN ALSO FIND LOTS OF BOYS AT THE LOCAL MALL, SHOPPING, WORKING OR JUST HANGING OUT!
I'M SHOPPING!
I'M WORKING!
I'M JUST... ZZZZ!
Sneaker Shack
SALE
WARNING!
DO NOT TRY TO MEET BOYS WHILE THEY'RE PLAYING VIDEO GAMES IN AN ARCADE!
UNLESS YOU WANT TO KNOW WHAT IT'S LIKE TO BE INVISIBLE!
AHEM!
NOW THAT YOU KNOW WHERE TO FIND BOYS, THE NEXT STEP IS TO TALK TO THEM!
REMEMBER, WHEN IT COMES TO TALKING TO BOYS, YOU HAVE TWO CHOICES!
TOYS
HOW TO TALK TO BOYS
4

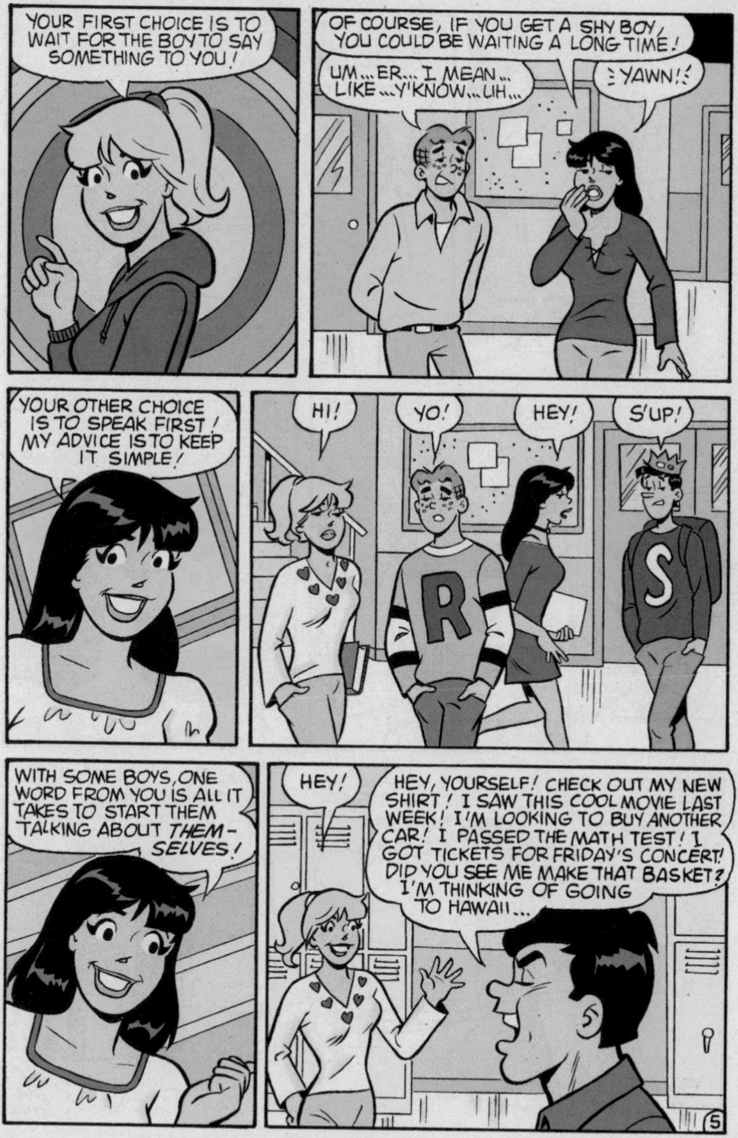
YOUR FIRST CHOICE IS TO WAIT FOR THE BOY TO SAY SOMETHING TO YOU!
OF COURSE, IF YOU GET A SHY BOY, YOU COULD BE WAITING A LONG TIME!
UM... ER... I MEAN... LIKE... Y'KNOW... UH...
YAWN!
YOUR OTHER CHOICE IS TO SPEAK FIRST! MY ADVICE IS TO KEEP IT SIMPLE!
HI!
YO!
HEY!
S'UP!
WITH SOME BOYS, ONE WORD FROM YOU IS ALL IT TAKES TO START THEM TALKING ABOUT THEMSELVES!
HEY!
HEY, YOURSELF! CHECK OUT MY NEW SHIRT! I SAW THIS COOL MOVIE LAST WEEK! I'M LOOKING TO BUY ANOTHER CAR! I PASSED THE MATH TEST! I GOT TICKETS FOR FRIDAY'S CONCERT! DID YOU SEE ME MAKE THAT BASKET? I'M THINKING OF GOING TO HAWAII...
5

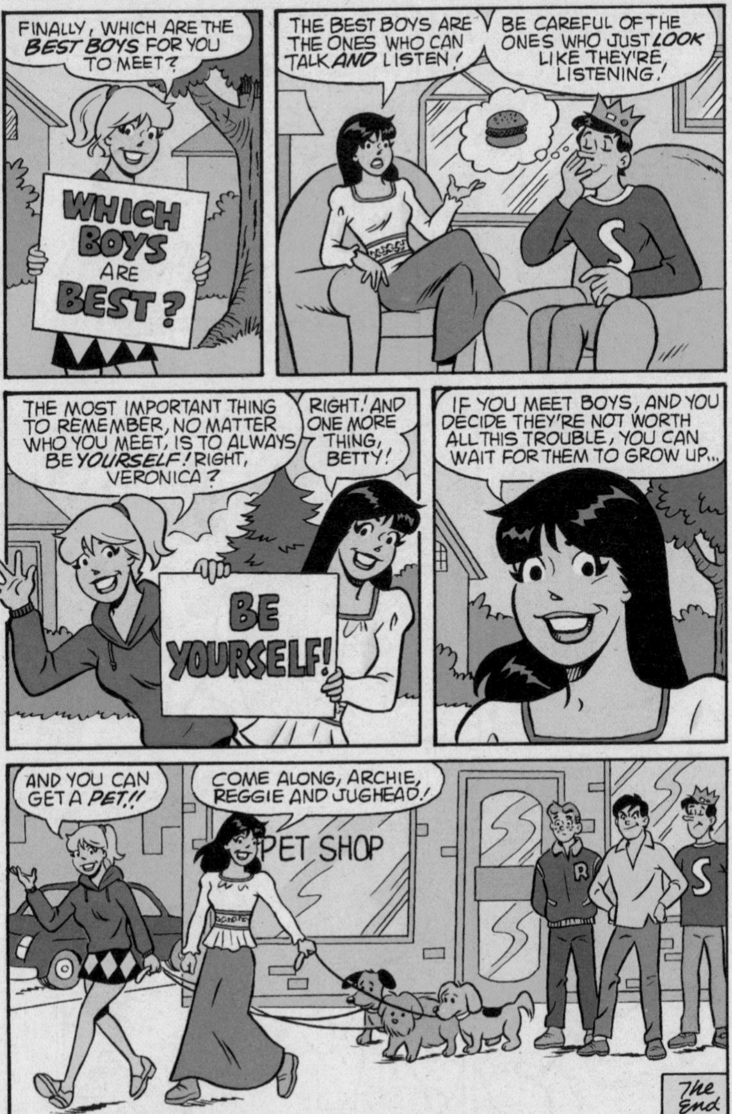
FINALLY, WHICH ARE THE BEST BOYS FOR YOU TO MEET?
WHICH BOYS ARE BEST?
THE BEST BOYS ARE THE ONES WHO CAN TALK AND LISTEN!
BE CAREFUL OF THE ONES WHO JUST LOOK LIKE THEY'RE LISTENING!
THE MOST IMPORTANT THING TO REMEMBER, NO MATTER WHO YOU MEET, IS TO ALWAYS BE YOURSELF! RIGHT, VERONICA?
RIGHT! AND ONE MORE THING, BETTY!
BE YOURSELF!
IF YOU MEET BOYS, AND YOU DECIDE THEY'RE NOT WORTH ALL THIS TROUBLE, YOU CAN WAIT FOR THEM TO GROW UP...
AND YOU CAN GET A PET!!
COME ALONG, ARCHIE, REGGIE AND JUGHEAD!
PET SHOP
The End

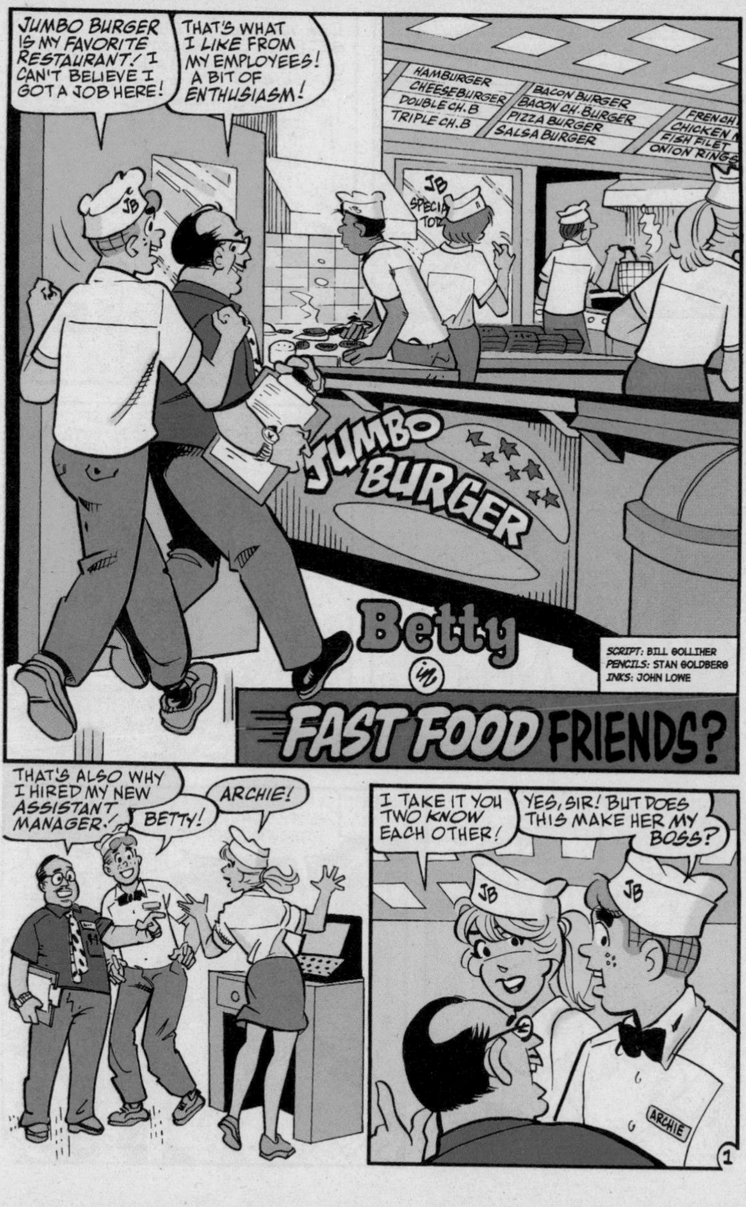
JUMBO BURGER IS MY FAVORITE RESTAURANT! I CAN'T BELIEVE I GOT A JOB HERE!
THAT'S WHAT I LIKE FROM MY EMPLOYEES! A BIT OF ENTHUSIASM!
HAMBURGER
CHEESEBURGER
DOUBLE CH.B
TRIPLE CH.B
BACON BURGER
BACON CH.BURGER
PIZZA BURGER
SALSA BURGER
JUMBO BURGER
Betty in
FAST FOOD FRIENDS?
SCRIPT: BILL GOLLIHER
PENCILS: STAN GOLDBERG
INKS: JOHN LOWE
THAT'S ALSO WHY I HIRED MY NEW ASSISTANT MANAGER!
BETTY!
ARCHIE!
I TAKE IT YOU TWO KNOW EACH OTHER!
YES, SIR! BUT DOES THIS MAKE HER MY BOSS?
ARCHIE

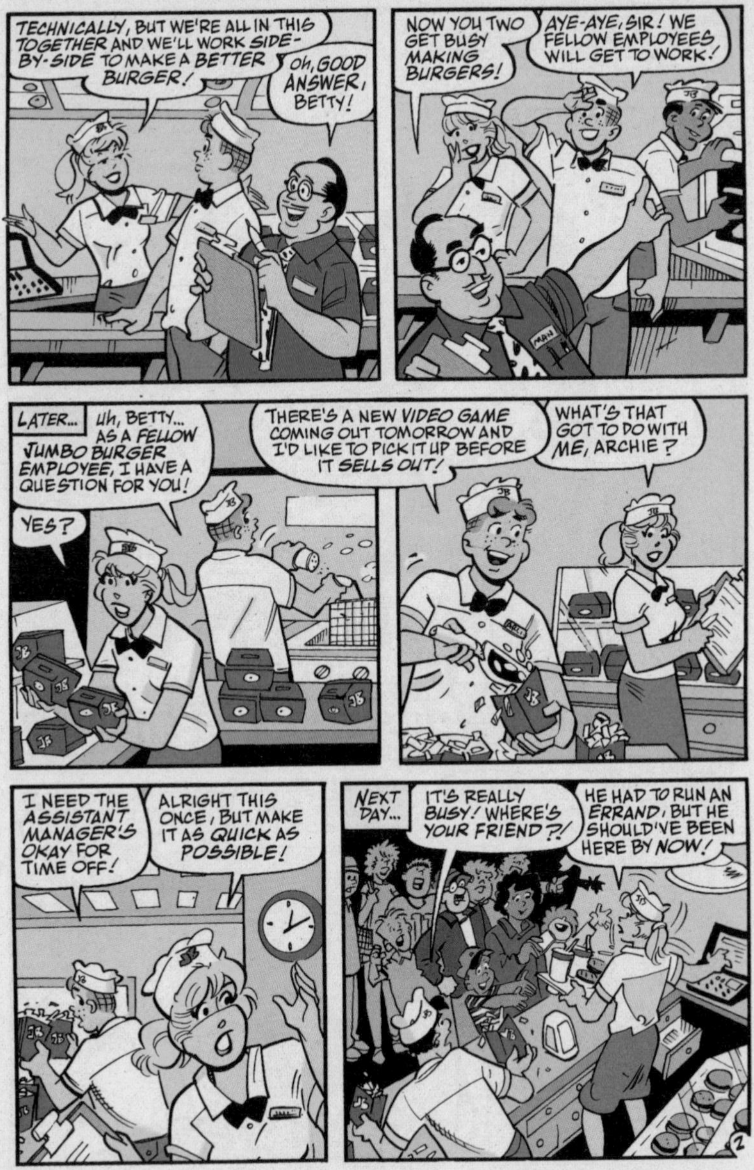

TECHNICALLY, BUT WE'RE ALL IN THIS TOGETHER AND WE'LL WORK SIDE-BY-SIDE TO MAKE A BETTER BURGER!
OH, GOOD ANSWER, BETTY!
NOW YOU TWO GET BUSY MAKING BURGERS!
AYE-AYE, SIR! WE FELLOW EMPLOYEES WILL GET TO WORK!
MAN
LATER...
UH, BETTY... AS A FELLOW JUMBO BURGER EMPLOYEE, I HAVE A QUESTION FOR YOU!
YES?
THERE'S A NEW VIDEO GAME COMING OUT TOMORROW AND I'D LIKE TO PICK IT UP BEFORE IT SELLS OUT!
WHAT'S THAT GOT TO DO WITH ME, ARCHIE?
I NEED THE ASSISTANT MANAGER'S OKAY FOR TIME OFF!
ALRIGHT THIS ONCE, BUT MAKE IT AS QUICK AS POSSIBLE!
NEXT DAY...
IT'S REALLY BUSY! WHERE'S YOUR FRIEND?!
HE HAD TO RUN AN ERRAND, BUT HE SHOULD'VE BEEN HERE BY NOW!

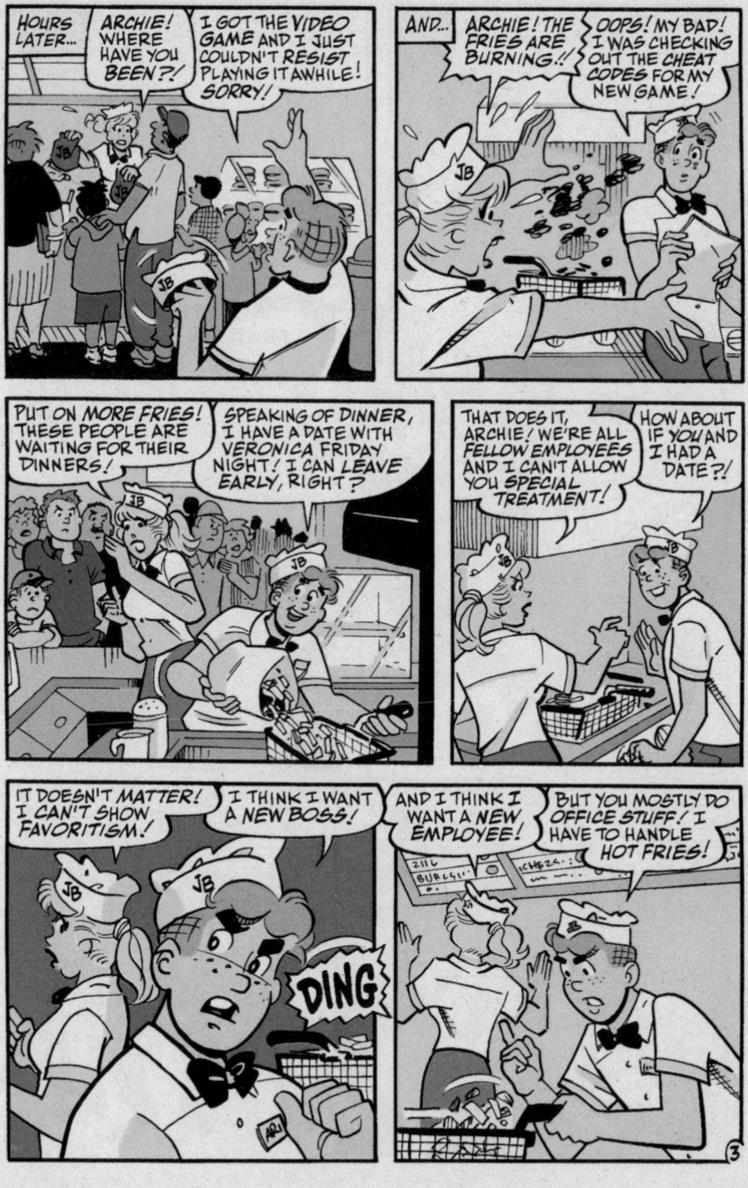
HOURS LATER...
ARCHIE! WHERE HAVE YOU BEEN?!
I GOT THE VIDEO GAME AND I JUST COULDN'T RESIST PLAYING IT AWHILE! SORRY!
AND...
ARCHIE! THE FRIES ARE BURNING!!
OOPS! MY BAD! I WAS CHECKING OUT THE CHEAT CODES FOR MY NEW GAME!
PUT ON MORE FRIES! THESE PEOPLE ARE WAITING FOR THEIR DINNERS!
SPEAKING OF DINNER, I HAVE A DATE WITH VERONICA FRIDAY NIGHT! I CAN LEAVE EARLY, RIGHT?
THAT DOES IT, ARCHIE! WE'RE ALL FELLOW EMPLOYEES AND I CAN'T ALLOW YOU SPECIAL TREATMENT!
HOW ABOUT IF YOU AND I HAD A DATE?!
IT DOESN'T MATTER! I CAN'T SHOW FAVORITISM!
I THINK I WANT A NEW BOSS!
DING
AND I THINK I WANT A NEW EMPLOYEE!
BUT YOU MOSTLY DO OFFICE STUFF! I HAVE TO HANDLE HOT FRIES!

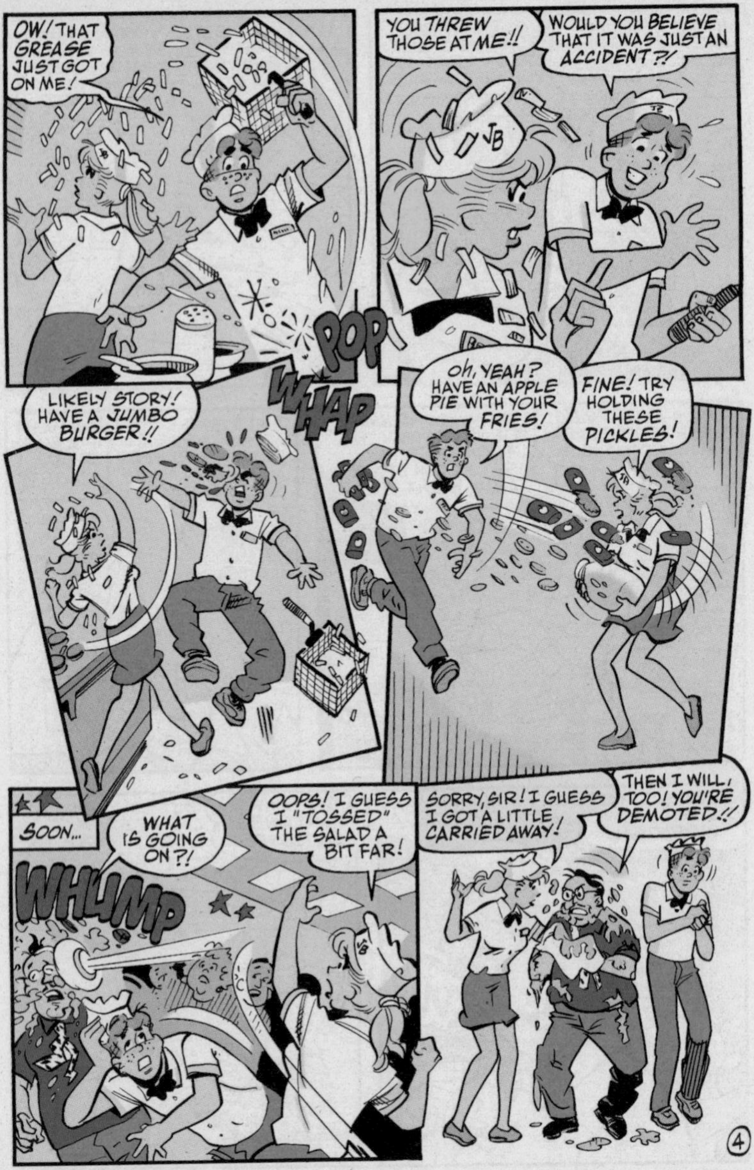

OW! THAT GREASE JUST GOT ON ME!
POP
YOU THREW THOSE AT ME!!
WOULD YOU BELIEVE THAT IT WAS JUST AN ACCIDENT?!
WHAP
LIKELY STORY! HAVE A JUMBO BURGER!!
oh, YEAH? HAVE AN APPLE PIE WITH YOUR FRIES!
FINE! TRY HOLDING THESE PICKLES!
SOON...
WHAT IS GOING ON?!
WHUMP
OOPS! I GUESS I "TOSSED" THE SALAD A BIT FAR!
SORRY, SIR! I GUESS I GOT A LITTLE CARRIED AWAY!
THEN I WILL, TOO! YOU'RE DEMOTED!!

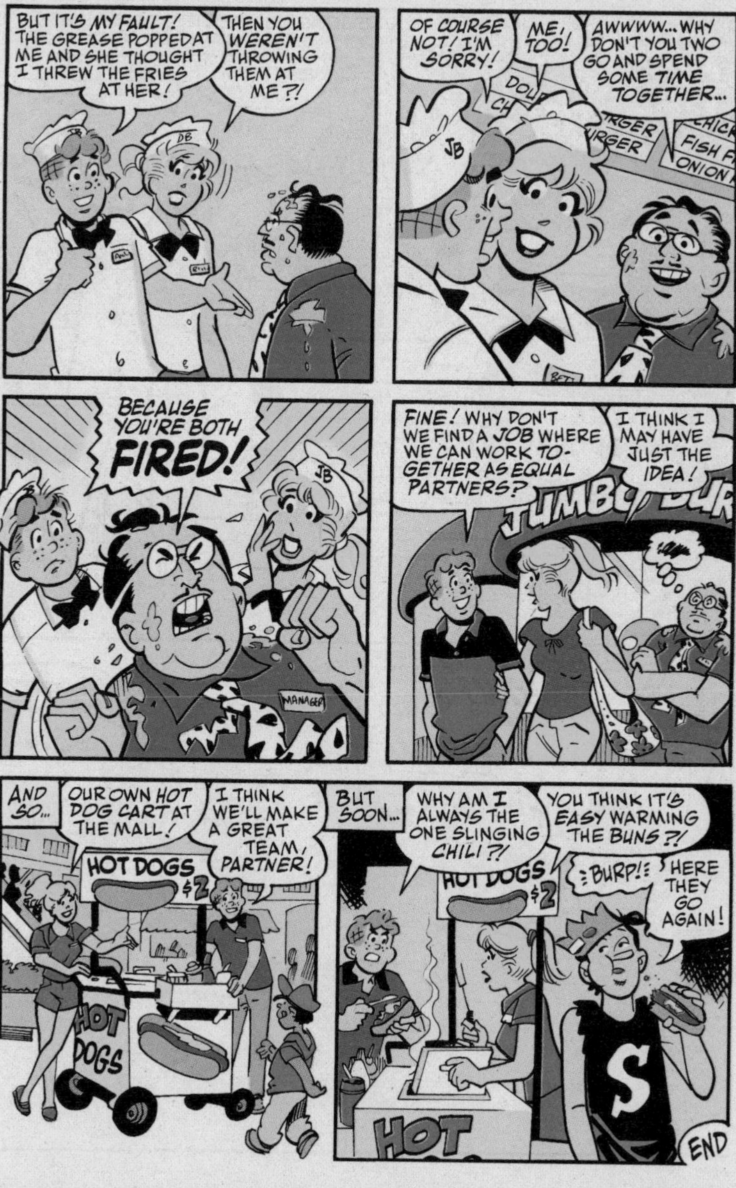
BUT IT'S MY FAULT! THE GREASE POPPED AT ME AND SHE THOUGHT I THREW THE FRIES AT HER!
THEN YOU WEREN'T THROWING THEM AT ME?!
OF COURSE NOT! I'M SORRY!
ME, TOO!
AWWWW... WHY DON'T YOU TWO GO AND SPEND SOME TIME TOGETHER...
BECAUSE YOU'RE BOTH FIRED!
MANAGER
FINE! WHY DON'T WE FIND A JOB WHERE WE CAN WORK TO-GETHER AS EQUAL PARTNERS?
I THINK I MAY HAVE JUST THE IDEA!
AND SO...
OUR OWN HOT DOG CART AT THE MALL!
I THINK WE'LL MAKE A GREAT TEAM, PARTNER!
HOT DOGS $2
HOT DOGS
BUT SOON...
WHY AM I ALWAYS THE ONE SLINGING CHILI?!
YOU THINK IT'S EASY WARMING THE BUNS?!
HOT DOGS $2
BURP!
HERE THEY GO AGAIN!
HOT
END

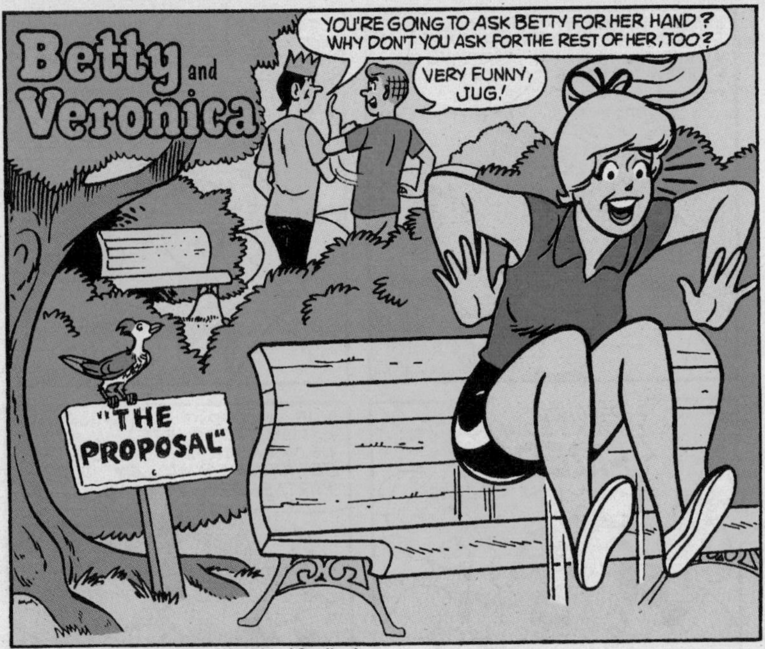
Betty and Veronica
YOU'RE GOING TO ASK BETTY FOR HER HAND? WHY DON'T YOU ASK FOR THE REST OF HER, TOO?
VERY FUNNY, JUG!
"THE PROPOSAL"

Webb / Bolling / Costanza / Yoshida / Gagliardo

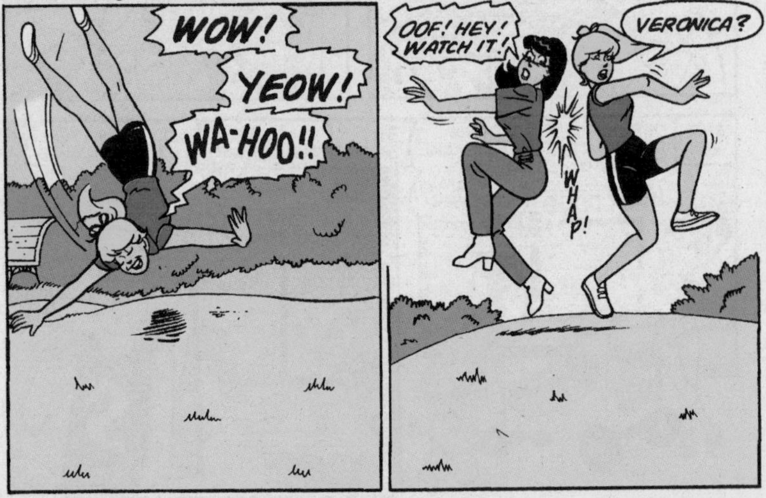
WOW!
YEOW!
WA-HOO!!
OOF! HEY! WATCH IT!
VERONICA?
WHAP!

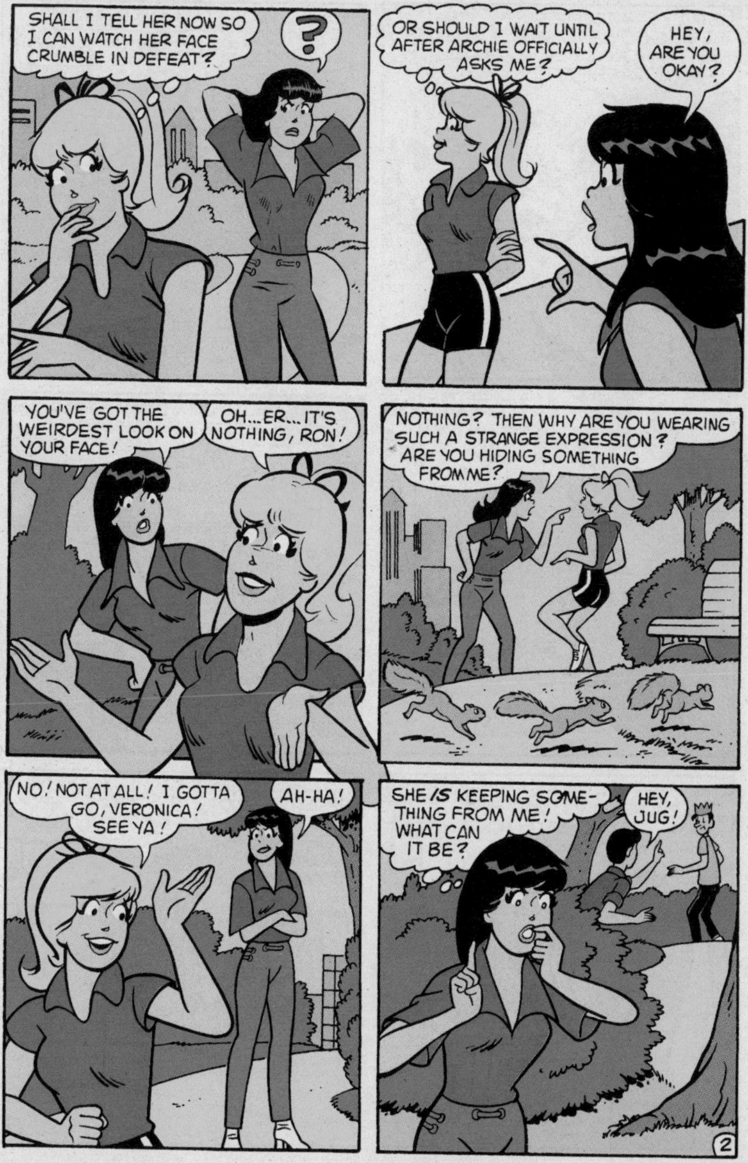
SHALL I TELL HER NOW SO I CAN WATCH HER FACE CRUMBLE IN DEFEAT?
?
OR SHOULD I WAIT UNTIL AFTER ARCHIE OFFICIALLY ASKS ME?
HEY, ARE YOU OKAY?
YOU'VE GOT THE WEIRDEST LOOK ON YOUR FACE!
OH...ER...IT'S NOTHING, RON!
NOTHING? THEN WHY ARE YOU WEARING SUCH A STRANGE EXPRESSION? ARE YOU HIDING SOMETHING FROM ME?
NO! NOT AT ALL! I GOTTA GO, VERONICA! SEE YA!
AH-HA!
SHE IS KEEPING SOME-THING FROM ME! WHAT CAN IT BE?
HEY, JUG!
2

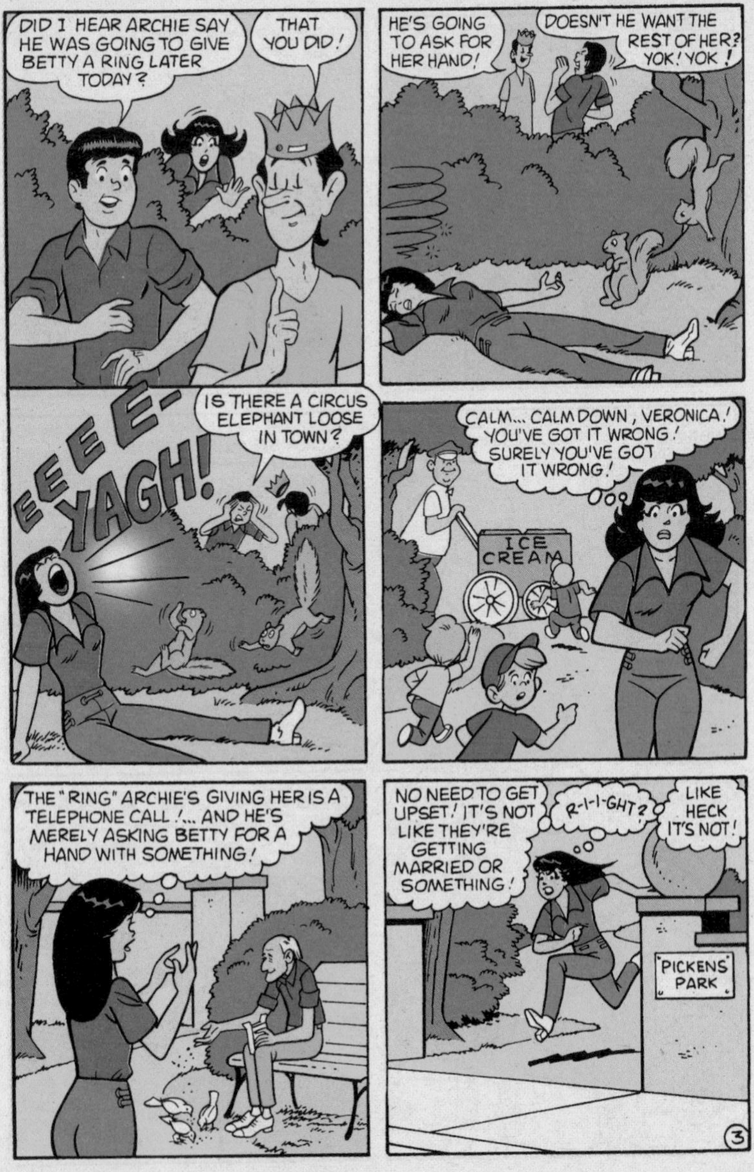

DID I HEAR ARCHIE SAY HE WAS GOING TO GIVE BETTY A RING LATER TODAY?
THAT YOU DID!
HE'S GOING TO ASK FOR HER HAND!
DOESN'T HE WANT THE REST OF HER? YOK! YOK!
IS THERE A CIRCUS ELEPHANT LOOSE IN TOWN?
EEEEE-YAGH!
CALM... CALM DOWN, VERONICA! YOU'VE GOT IT WRONG! SURELY YOU'VE GOT IT WRONG!
ICE CREAM
THE "RING" ARCHIE'S GIVING HER IS A TELEPHONE CALL!... AND HE'S MERELY ASKING BETTY FOR A HAND WITH SOMETHING!
NO NEED TO GET UPSET! IT'S NOT LIKE THEY'RE GETTING MARRIED OR SOMETHING!
R-I-I-GHT?
LIKE HECK IT'S NOT!
PICKENS PARK
3

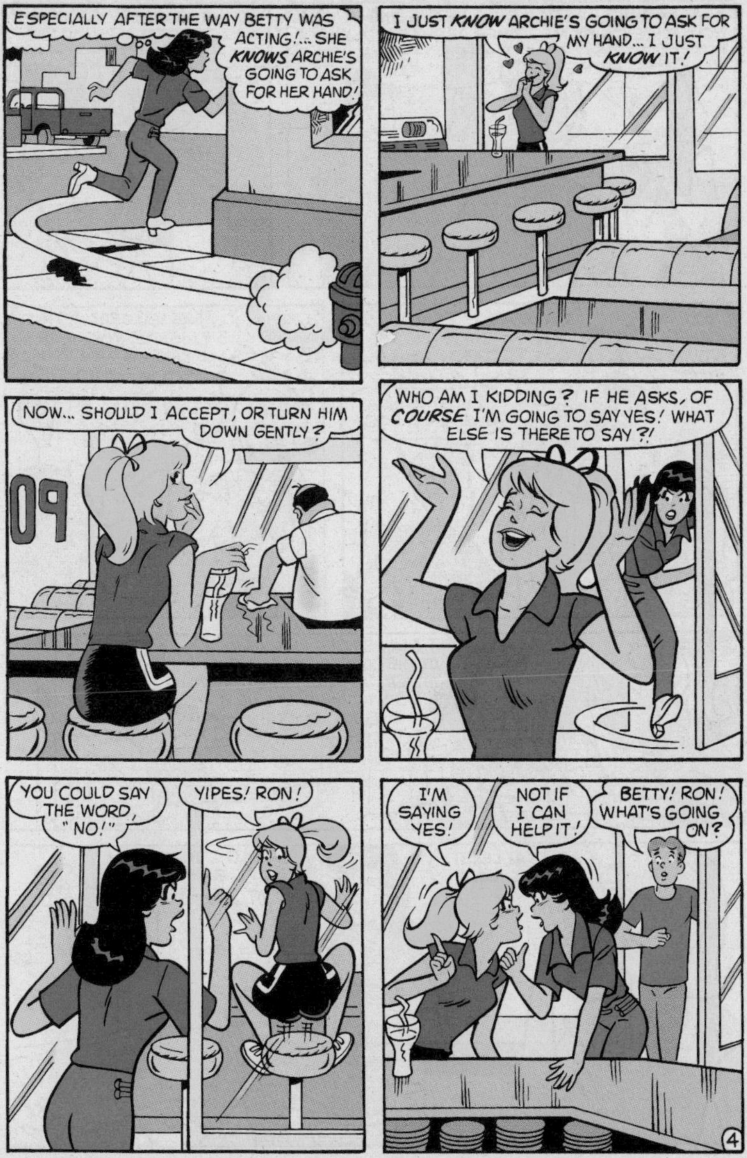

ESPECIALLY AFTER THE WAY BETTY WAS ACTING!... SHE KNOWS ARCHIE'S GOING TO ASK FOR HER HAND!
I JUST KNOW ARCHIE'S GOING TO ASK FOR MY HAND... I JUST KNOW IT!
NOW... SHOULD I ACCEPT, OR TURN HIM DOWN GENTLY?
WHO AM I KIDDING? IF HE ASKS, OF COURSE I'M GOING TO SAY YES! WHAT ELSE IS THERE TO SAY?!
YOU COULD SAY THE WORD, "NO!"
YIPES! RON!
I'M SAYING YES!
NOT IF I CAN HELP IT!
BETTY! RON! WHAT'S GOING ON?
4

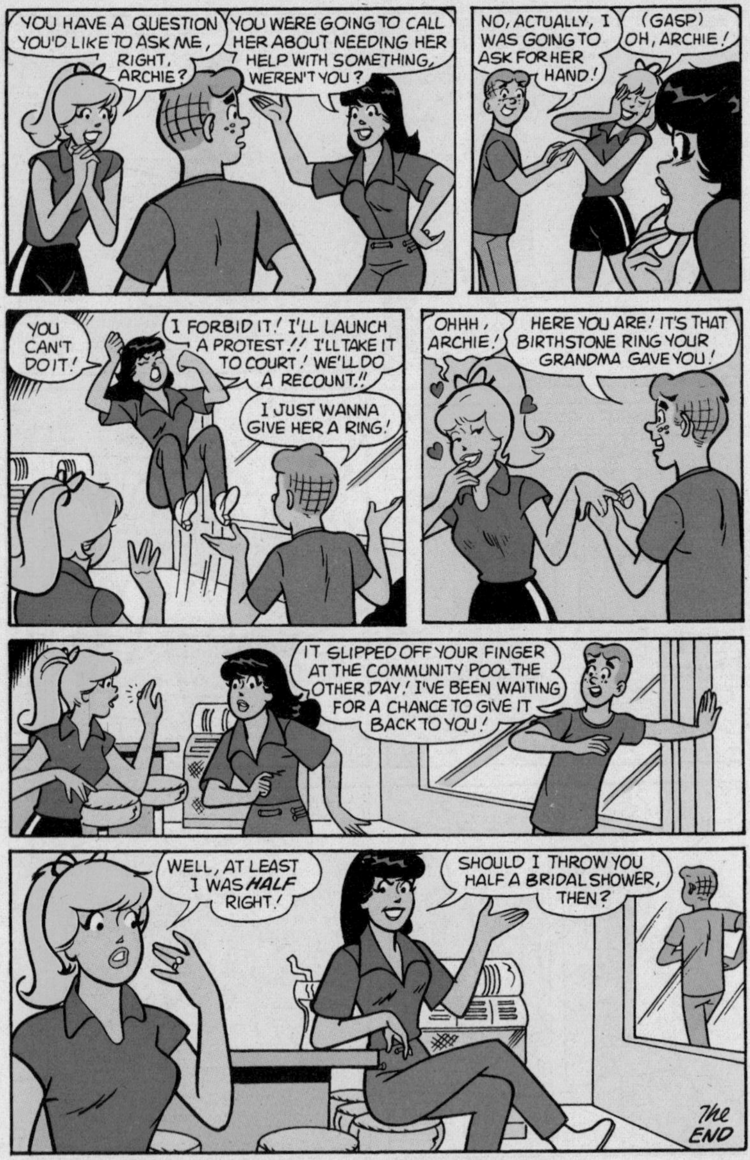
YOU HAVE A QUESTION YOU'D LIKE TO ASK ME, RIGHT, ARCHIE?
YOU WERE GOING TO CALL HER ABOUT NEEDING HER HELP WITH SOMETHING, WEREN'T YOU?
NO, ACTUALLY, I WAS GOING TO ASK FOR HER HAND!
(GASP) OH, ARCHIE!
YOU CAN'T DO IT!
I FORBID IT! I'LL LAUNCH A PROTEST!! I'LL TAKE IT TO COURT! WE'LL DO A RECOUNT!!
I JUST WANNA GIVE HER A RING!
OHHH, ARCHIE!
HERE YOU ARE! IT'S THAT BIRTHSTONE RING YOUR GRANDMA GAVE YOU!
IT SLIPPED OFF YOUR FINGER AT THE COMMUNITY POOL THE OTHER DAY! I'VE BEEN WAITING FOR A CHANCE TO GIVE IT BACK TO YOU!
WELL, AT LEAST I WAS HALF RIGHT!
SHOULD I THROW YOU HALF A BRIDAL SHOWER, THEN?
The END

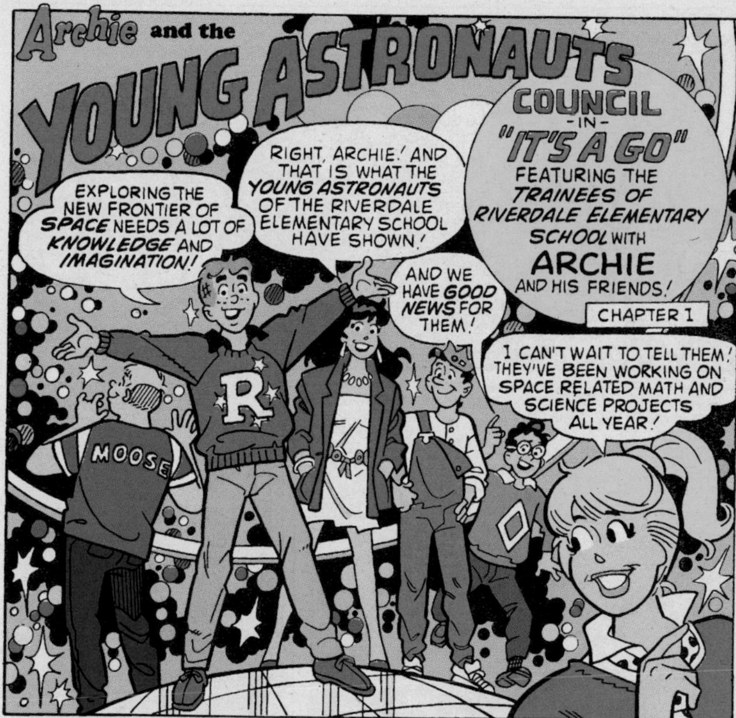
Archie and the
YOUNG ASTRONAUTS COUNCIL
-IN-
"IT'S A GO"
FEATURING THE TRAINEES OF RIVERDALE ELEMENTARY SCHOOL WITH ARCHIE AND HIS FRIENDS!
CHAPTER 1
EXPLORING THE NEW FRONTIER OF SPACE NEEDS A LOT OF KNOWLEDGE AND IMAGINATION!
RIGHT, ARCHIE! AND THAT IS WHAT THE YOUNG ASTRONAUTS OF THE RIVERDALE ELEMENTARY SCHOOL HAVE SHOWN!
AND WE HAVE GOOD NEWS FOR THEM!
I CAN'T WAIT TO TELL THEM! THEY'VE BEEN WORKING ON SPACE RELATED MATH AND SCIENCE PROJECTS ALL YEAR!
MOOSE
R

Script: Joe Edwards / Pencils: Stan Goldberg / Inks: Henry Scarpelli / Letters: Bill Yoshida

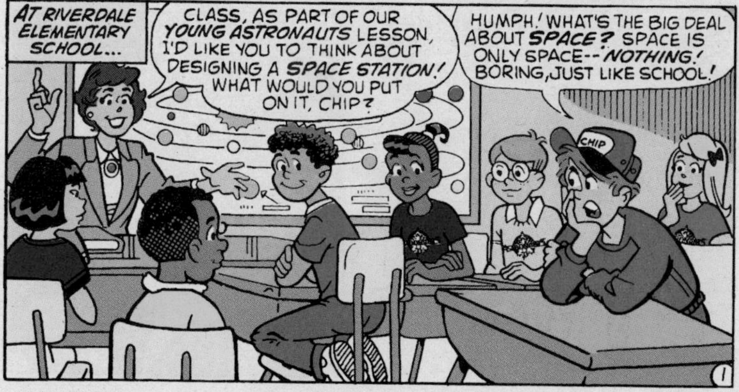
AT RIVERDALE ELEMENTARY SCHOOL...
CLASS, AS PART OF OUR YOUNG ASTRONAUTS LESSON, I'D LIKE YOU TO THINK ABOUT DESIGNING A SPACE STATION! WHAT WOULD YOU PUT ON IT, CHIP?
HUMPH! WHAT'S THE BIG DEAL ABOUT SPACE? SPACE IS ONLY SPACE--"NOTHING!" BORING, JUST LIKE SCHOOL!
CHIP

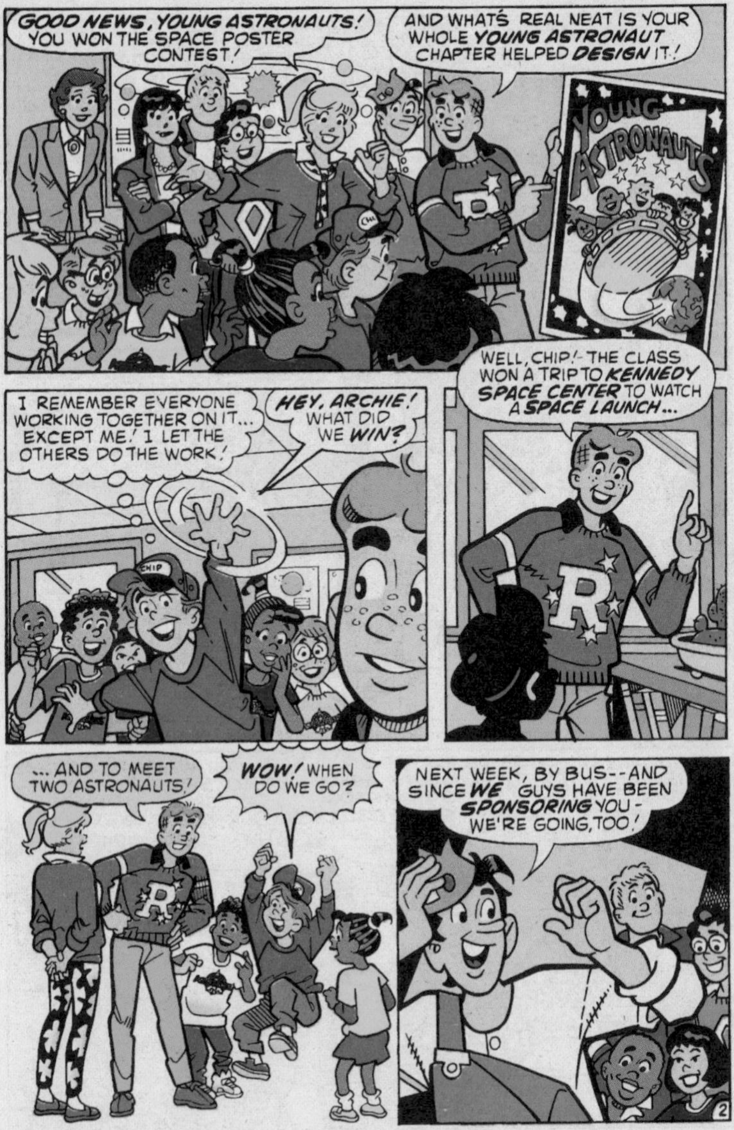
GOOD NEWS, YOUNG ASTRONAUTS! YOU WON THE SPACE POSTER CONTEST!
AND WHAT'S REAL NEAT IS YOUR WHOLE YOUNG ASTRONAUT CHAPTER HELPED DESIGN IT!
YOUNG ASTRONAUTS
I REMEMBER EVERYONE WORKING TOGETHER ON IT... EXCEPT ME! I LET THE OTHERS DO THE WORK!
HEY, ARCHIE! WHAT DID WE WIN?
WELL, CHIP!- THE CLASS WON A TRIP TO KENNEDY SPACE CENTER TO WATCH A SPACE LAUNCH...
... AND TO MEET TWO ASTRONAUTS!
WOW! WHEN DO WE GO?
NEXT WEEK, BY BUS--AND SINCE WE GUYS HAVE BEEN SPONSORING YOU - WE'RE GOING, TOO!
2

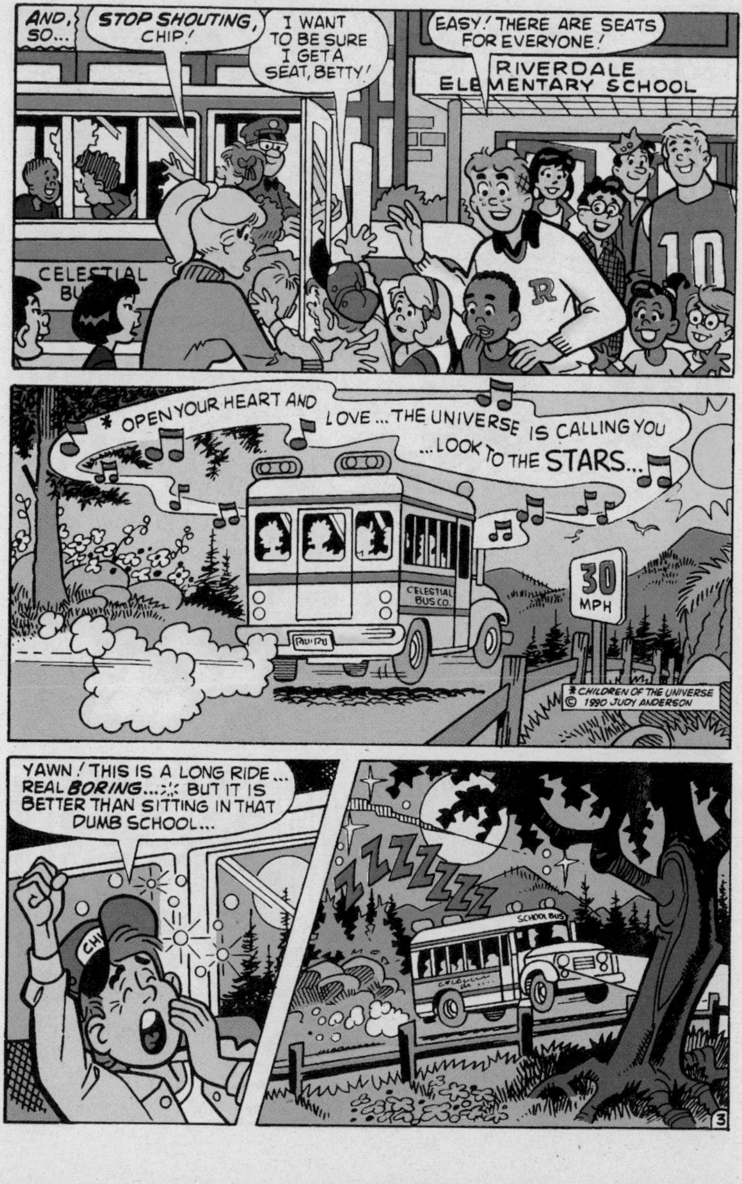

AND, SO...
STOP SHOUTING, CHIP!
I WANT TO BE SURE I GET A SEAT, BETTY!
EASY! THERE ARE SEATS FOR EVERYONE!
RIVERDALE ELEMENTARY SCHOOL
CELESTIAL BUS
R
10
* OPEN YOUR HEART AND LOVE ... THE UNIVERSE IS CALLING YOU ...LOOK TO THE STARS...
CELESTIAL BUS CO.
30 MPH
* CHILDREN OF THE UNIVERSE © 1990 JUDY ANDERSON
YAWN! THIS IS A LONG RIDE... REAL BORING... BUT IT IS BETTER THAN SITTING IN THAT DUMB SCHOOL...
ZZZZZZZZ
SCHOOL BUS

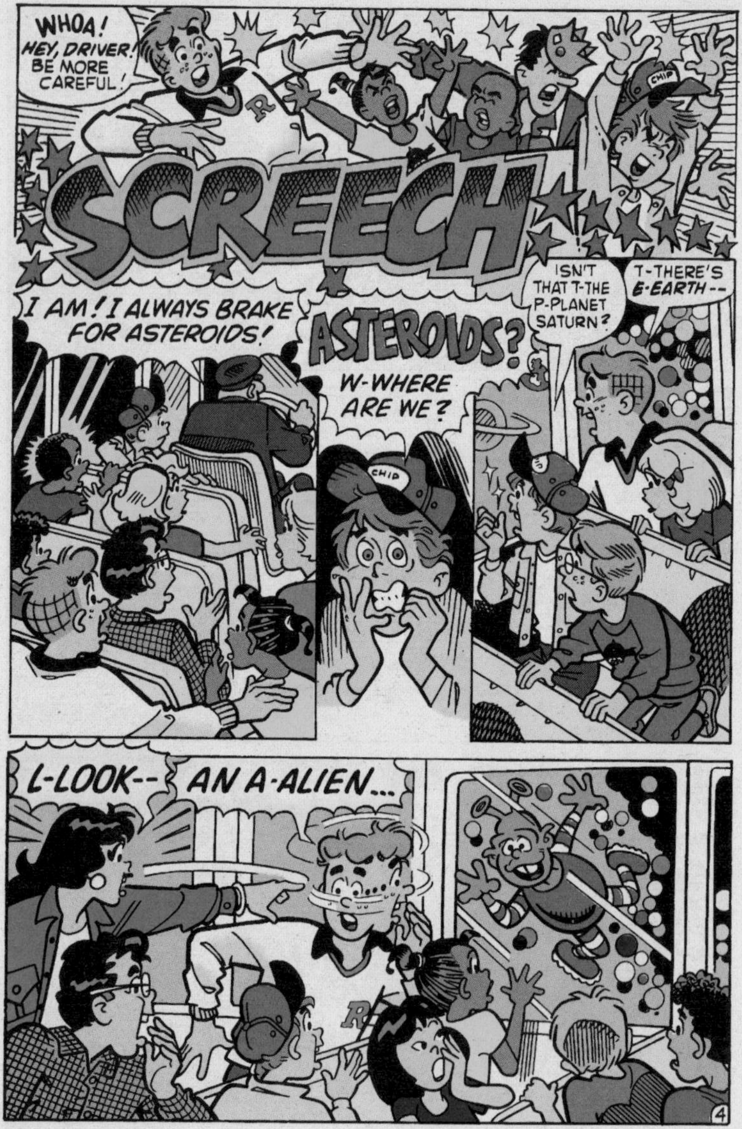

WHOA! HEY, DRIVER! BE MORE CAREFUL!
SCREECH
I AM! I ALWAYS BRAKE FOR ASTEROIDS!
ASTEROIDS?
W-WHERE ARE WE?
ISN'T THAT T-THE P-PLANET SATURN?
T-THERE'S E-EARTH--
CHIP
L-LOOK--
AN A-ALIEN...

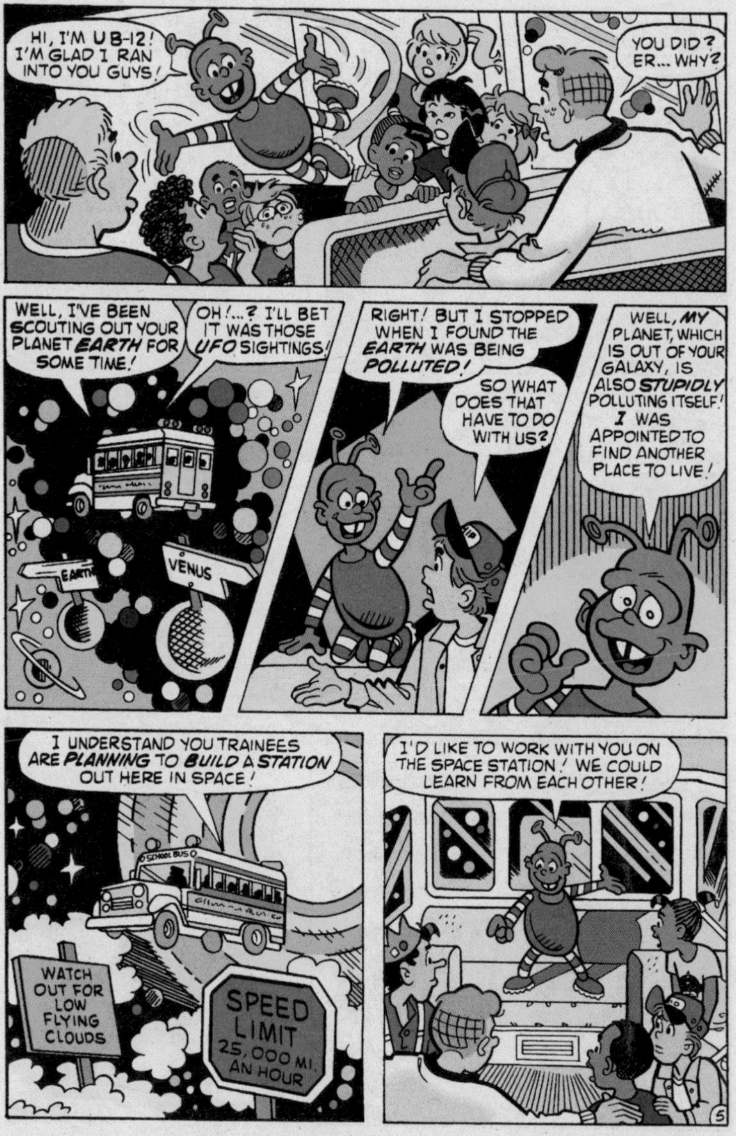
HI, I'M UB-12! I'M GLAD I RAN INTO YOU GUYS!
YOU DID? ER... WHY?
WELL, I'VE BEEN SCOUTING OUT YOUR PLANET EARTH FOR SOME TIME!
OH!...? I'LL BET IT WAS THOSE UFO SIGHTINGS!
EARTH
VENUS
RIGHT! BUT I STOPPED WHEN I FOUND THE EARTH WAS BEING POLLUTED!
SO WHAT DOES THAT HAVE TO DO WITH US?
WELL, MY PLANET, WHICH IS OUT OF YOUR GALAXY, IS ALSO STUPIDLY POLLUTING ITSELF! I WAS APPOINTED TO FIND ANOTHER PLACE TO LIVE!
I UNDERSTAND YOU TRAINEES ARE PLANNING TO BUILD A STATION OUT HERE IN SPACE!
SCHOOL BUS
WATCH OUT FOR LOW FLYING CLOUDS
SPEED LIMIT 25,000 MI. AN HOUR
I'D LIKE TO WORK WITH YOU ON THE SPACE STATION! WE COULD LEARN FROM EACH OTHER!

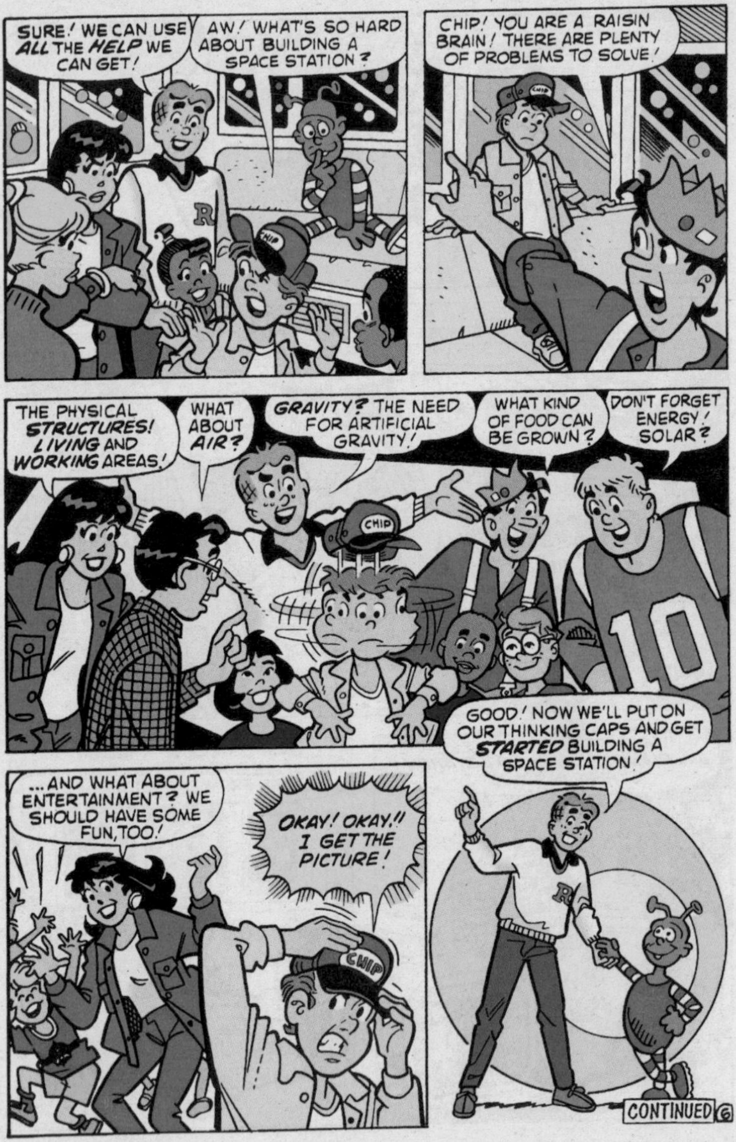
SURE! WE CAN USE ALL THE HELP WE CAN GET!
AW! WHAT'S SO HARD ABOUT BUILDING A SPACE STATION?
CHIP
CHIP! YOU ARE A RAISIN BRAIN! THERE ARE PLENTY OF PROBLEMS TO SOLVE!
CHIP
R
THE PHYSICAL STRUCTURES! LIVING AND WORKING AREAS!
WHAT ABOUT AIR?
GRAVITY? THE NEED FOR ARTIFICIAL GRAVITY!
WHAT KIND OF FOOD CAN BE GROWN?
DON'T FORGET ENERGY! SOLAR?
CHIP
10
...AND WHAT ABOUT ENTERTAINMENT? WE SHOULD HAVE SOME FUN, TOO!
OKAY! OKAY!! I GET THE PICTURE!
CHIP
GOOD! NOW WE'LL PUT ON OUR THINKING CAPS AND GET STARTED BUILDING A SPACE STATION!
R
CONTINUED

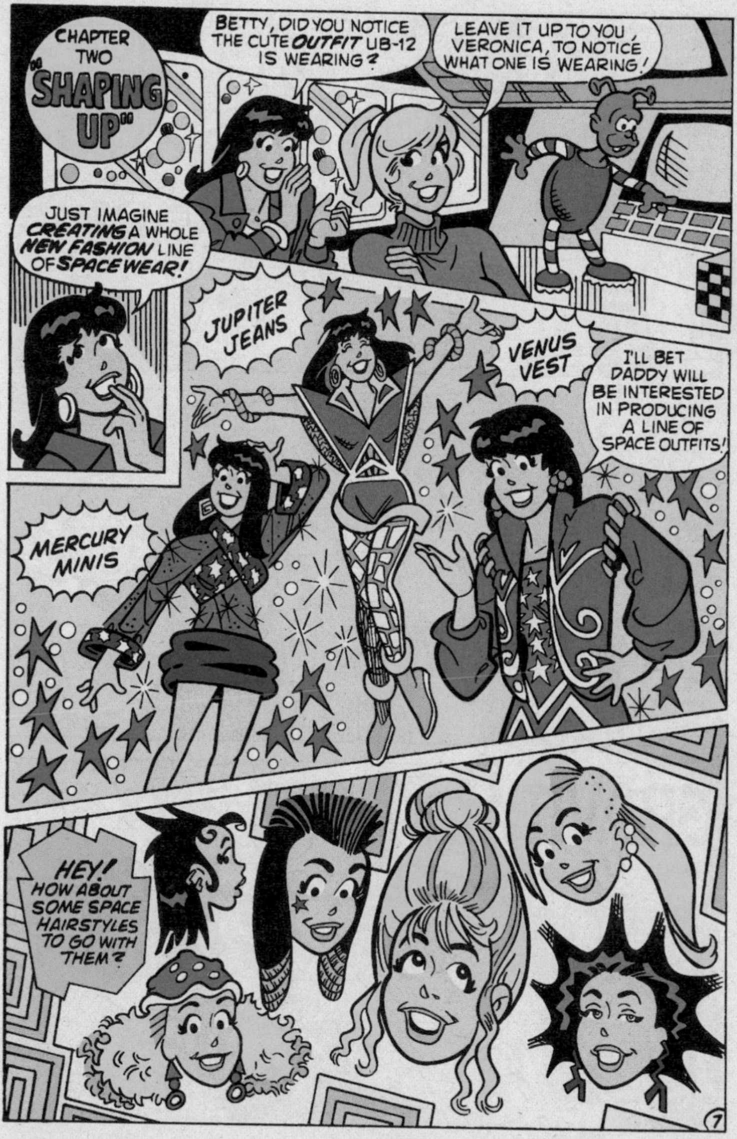
CHAPTER TWO "SHAPING UP"
BETTY, DID YOU NOTICE THE CUTE OUTFIT UB-12 IS WEARING?
LEAVE IT UP TO YOU, VERONICA, TO NOTICE WHAT ONE IS WEARING!
JUST IMAGINE CREATING A WHOLE NEW FASHION LINE OF SPACE WEAR!
JUPITER JEANS
VENUS VEST
I'LL BET DADDY WILL BE INTERESTED IN PRODUCING A LINE OF SPACE OUTFITS!
MERCURY MINIS
HEY! HOW ABOUT SOME SPACE HAIRSTYLES TO GO WITH THEM?
7

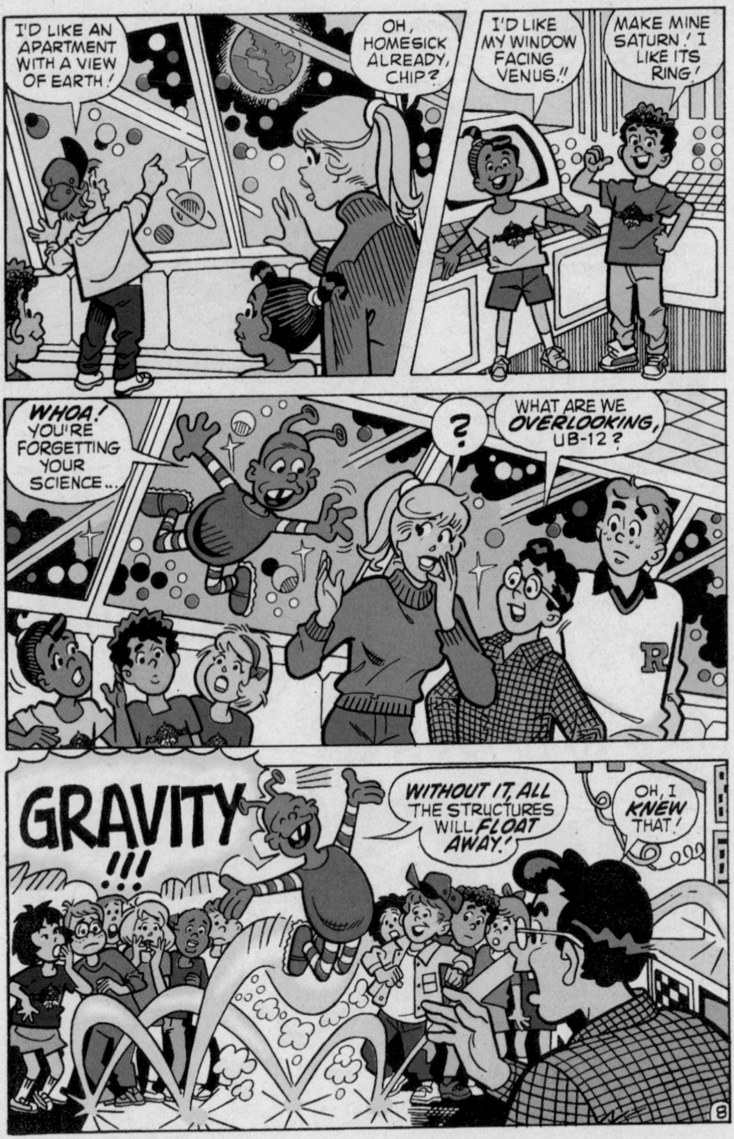
I'D LIKE AN APARTMENT WITH A VIEW OF EARTH!
OH, HOMESICK ALREADY, CHIP?
I'D LIKE MY WINDOW FACING VENUS!!
MAKE MINE SATURN! I LIKE ITS RING!
WHOA! YOU'RE FORGETTING YOUR SCIENCE...
?
WHAT ARE WE OVERLOOKING, UB-12?
GRAVITY!!!
WITHOUT IT, ALL THE STRUCTURES WILL FLOAT AWAY!
OH, I KNEW THAT!
8

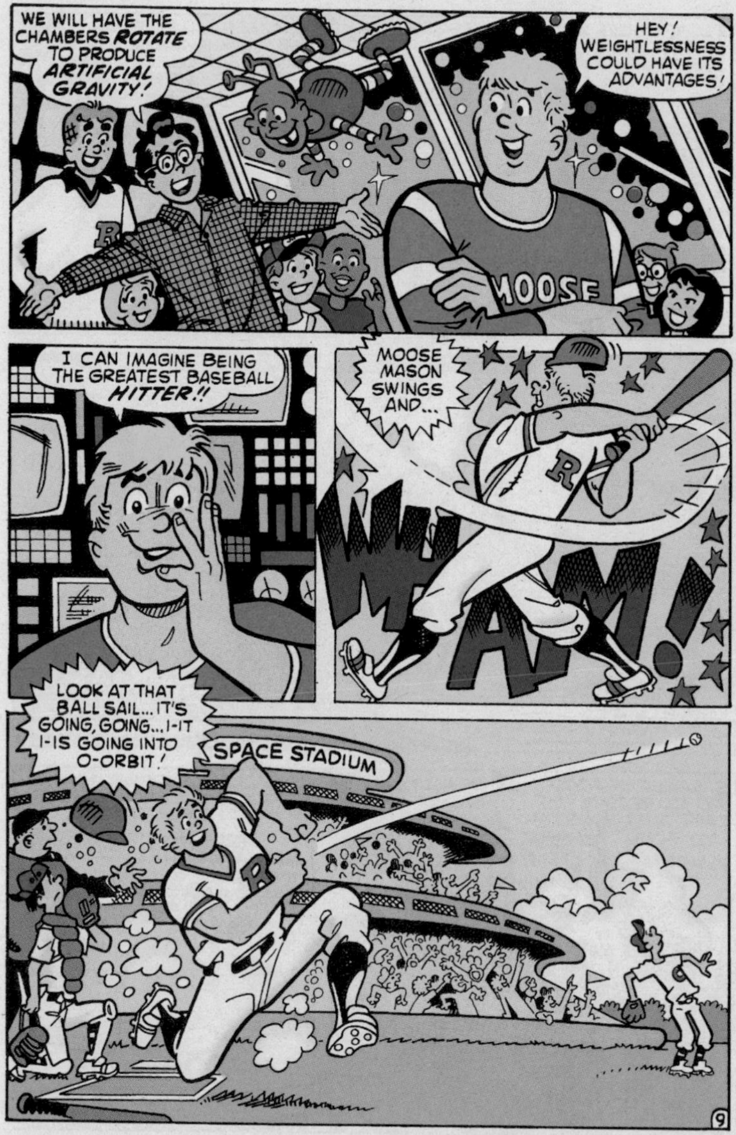
WE WILL HAVE THE CHAMBERS ROTATE TO PRODUCE ARTIFICIAL GRAVITY!
HEY! WEIGHTLESSNESS COULD HAVE ITS ADVANTAGES!
MOOSE
I CAN IMAGINE BEING THE GREATEST BASEBALL HITTER!!
MOOSE MASON SWINGS AND...
WHAM!
LOOK AT THAT BALL SAIL... IT'S GOING, GOING... I-IT I-IS GOING INTO O-ORBIT!
SPACE STADIUM

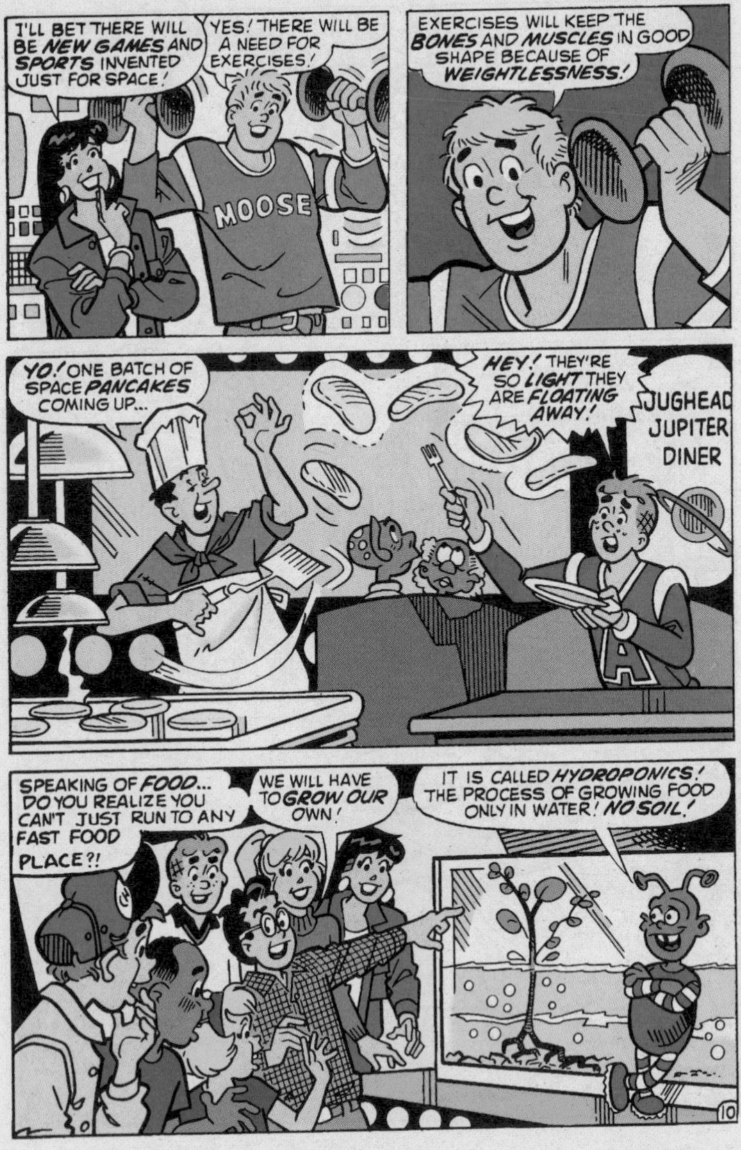
I'LL BET THERE WILL BE NEW GAMES AND SPORTS INVENTED JUST FOR SPACE!
YES! THERE WILL BE A NEED FOR EXERCISES!
MOOSE
EXERCISES WILL KEEP THE BONES AND MUSCLES IN GOOD SHAPE BECAUSE OF WEIGHTLESSNESS!
YO! ONE BATCH OF SPACE PANCAKES COMING UP...
HEY! THEY'RE SO LIGHT THEY ARE FLOATING AWAY!
JUGHEAD JUPITER DINER
SPEAKING OF FOOD... DO YOU REALIZE YOU CAN'T JUST RUN TO ANY FAST FOOD PLACE?!
WE WILL HAVE TO GROW OUR OWN!
IT IS CALLED HYDROPONICS! THE PROCESS OF GROWING FOOD ONLY IN WATER! NO SOIL!
10

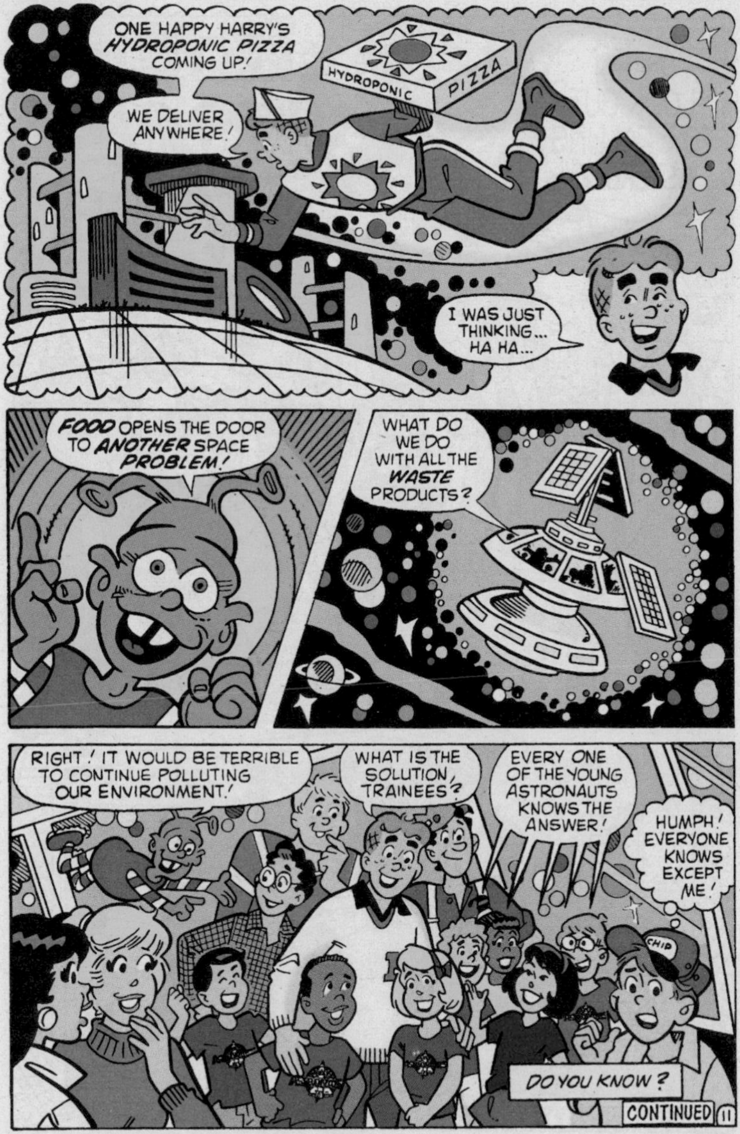

ONE HAPPY HARRY'S *HYDROPONIC PIZZA* COMING UP!
HYDROPONIC PIZZA
WE DELIVER ANYWHERE!
I WAS JUST THINKING... HA HA...
FOOD OPENS THE DOOR TO *ANOTHER* SPACE *PROBLEM!*
WHAT DO WE DO WITH ALL THE *WASTE* PRODUCTS?
RIGHT! IT WOULD BE TERRIBLE TO CONTINUE POLLUTING OUR ENVIRONMENT!
WHAT IS THE SOLUTION, TRAINEES?
EVERY ONE OF THE YOUNG ASTRONAUTS KNOWS THE ANSWER!
HUMPH! EVERYONE KNOWS EXCEPT ME!
CHIP
DO YOU KNOW?
CONTINUED

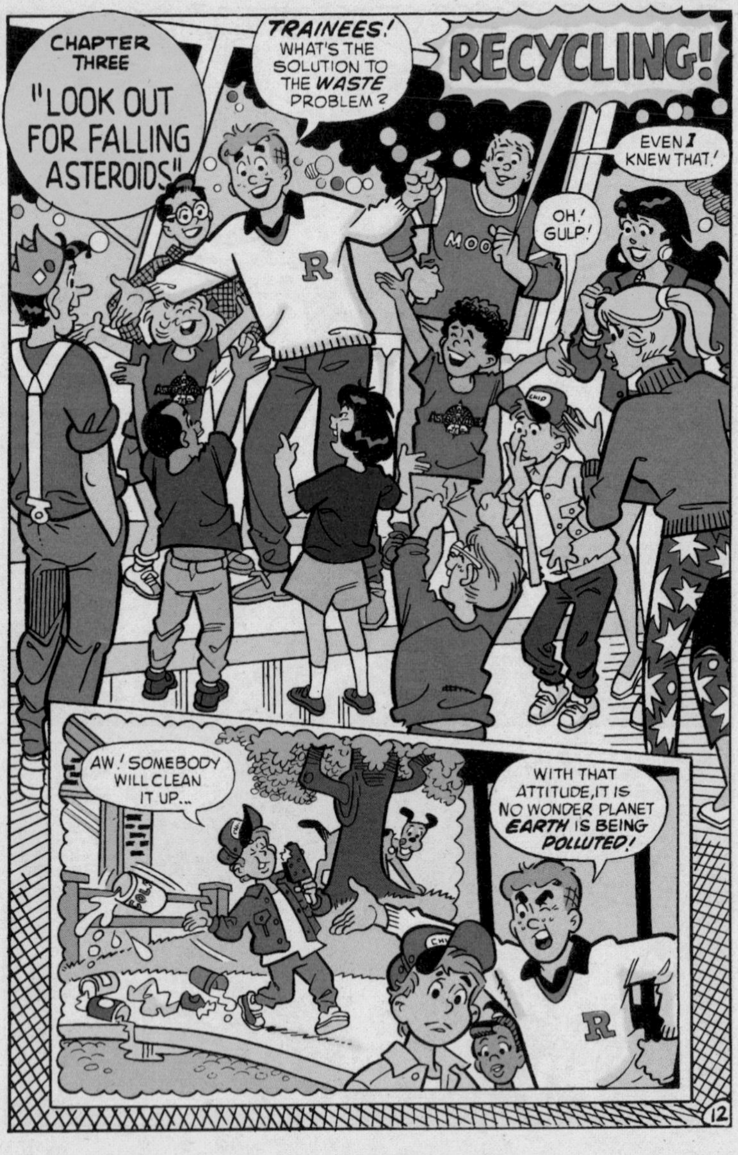

CHAPTER THREE
"LOOK OUT FOR FALLING ASTEROIDS"
TRAINEES! WHAT'S THE SOLUTION TO THE WASTE PROBLEM?
RECYCLING!
EVEN I KNEW THAT!
OH! GULP!
AW! SOMEBODY WILL CLEAN IT UP...
WITH THAT ATTITUDE, IT IS NO WONDER PLANET EARTH IS BEING POLLUTED!

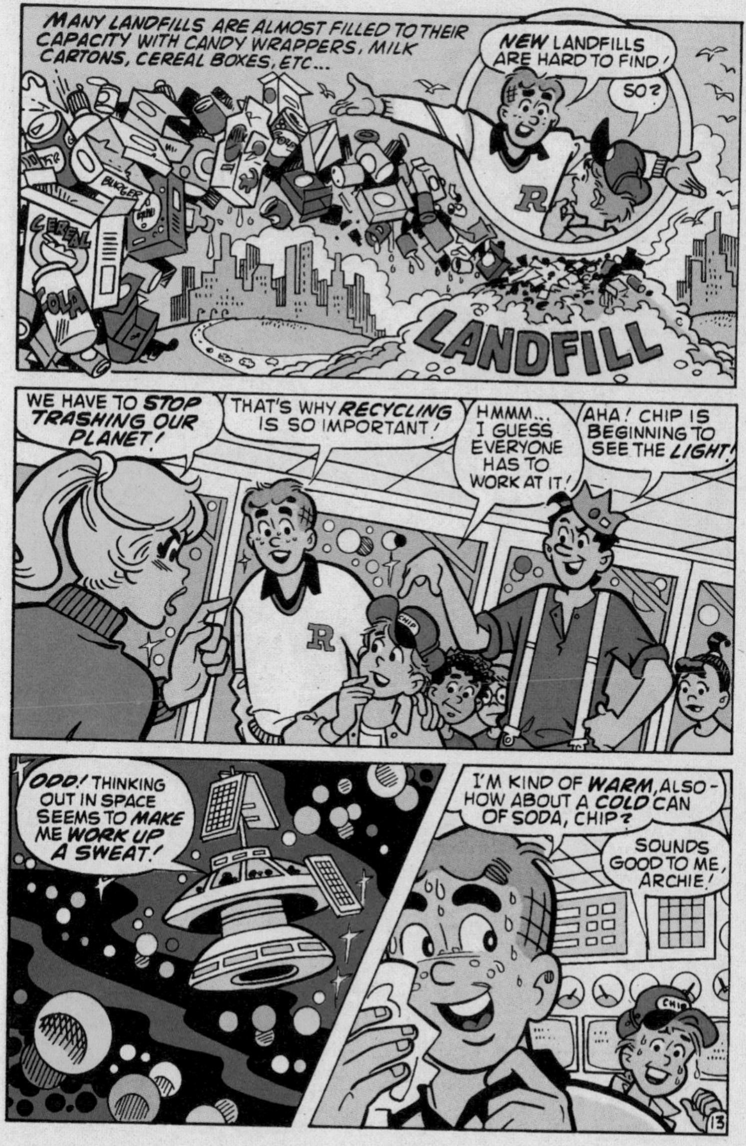
MANY LANDFILLS ARE ALMOST FILLED TO THEIR CAPACITY WITH CANDY WRAPPERS, MILK CARTONS, CEREAL BOXES, ETC...
NEW LANDFILLS ARE HARD TO FIND!
SO?
CEREAL
BURGER
COLA
LANDFILL
WE HAVE TO STOP TRASHING OUR PLANET!
THAT'S WHY RECYCLING IS SO IMPORTANT!
HMMM... I GUESS EVERYONE HAS TO WORK AT IT!
AHA! CHIP IS BEGINNING TO SEE THE LIGHT!
CHIP
ODD! THINKING OUT IN SPACE SEEMS TO MAKE ME WORK UP A SWEAT!
I'M KIND OF WARM, ALSO- HOW ABOUT A COLD CAN OF SODA, CHIP?
SOUNDS GOOD TO ME, ARCHIE!
CHIP

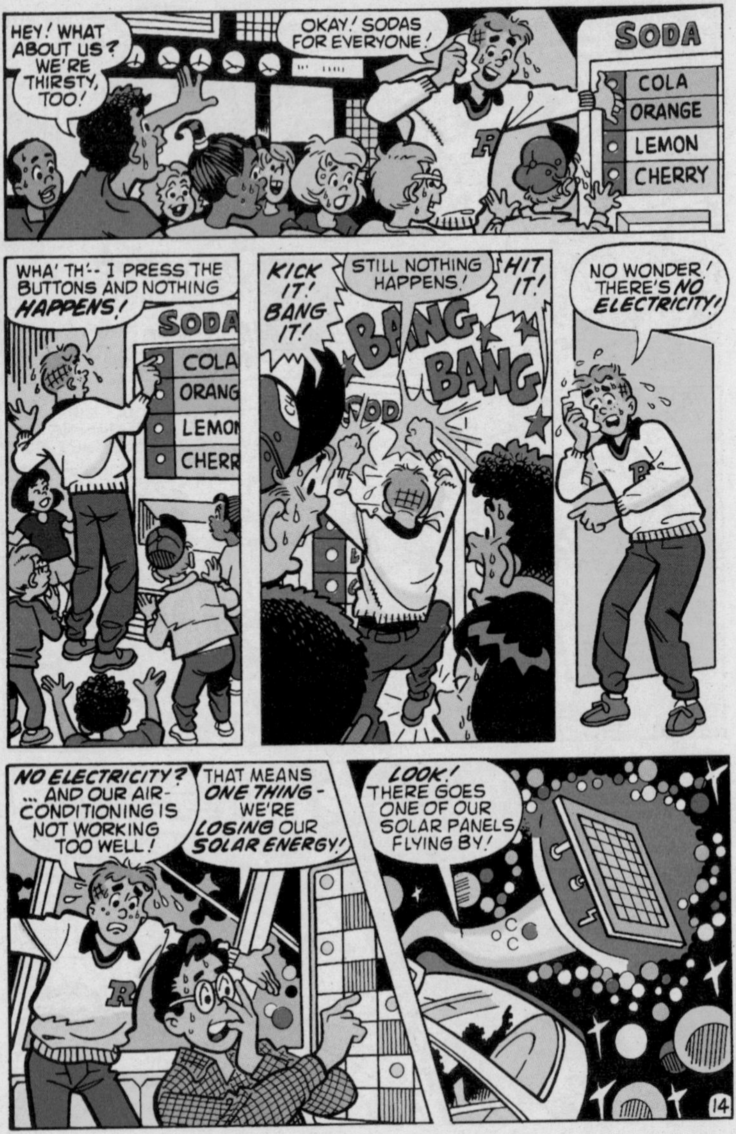
HEY! WHAT ABOUT US? WE'RE THIRSTY, TOO!
OKAY! SODAS FOR EVERYONE!
SODA
COLA
ORANGE
LEMON
CHERRY
WHA' TH'-- I PRESS THE BUTTONS AND NOTHING HAPPENS!
SODA
KICK IT! BANG IT!
STILL NOTHING HAPPENS!
HIT IT!
BANG
BANG
NO WONDER! THERE'S NO ELECTRICITY!
NO ELECTRICITY? ... AND OUR AIR-CONDITIONING IS NOT WORKING TOO WELL!
THAT MEANS ONE THING - WE'RE LOSING OUR SOLAR ENERGY!
LOOK! THERE GOES ONE OF OUR SOLAR PANELS FLYING BY!

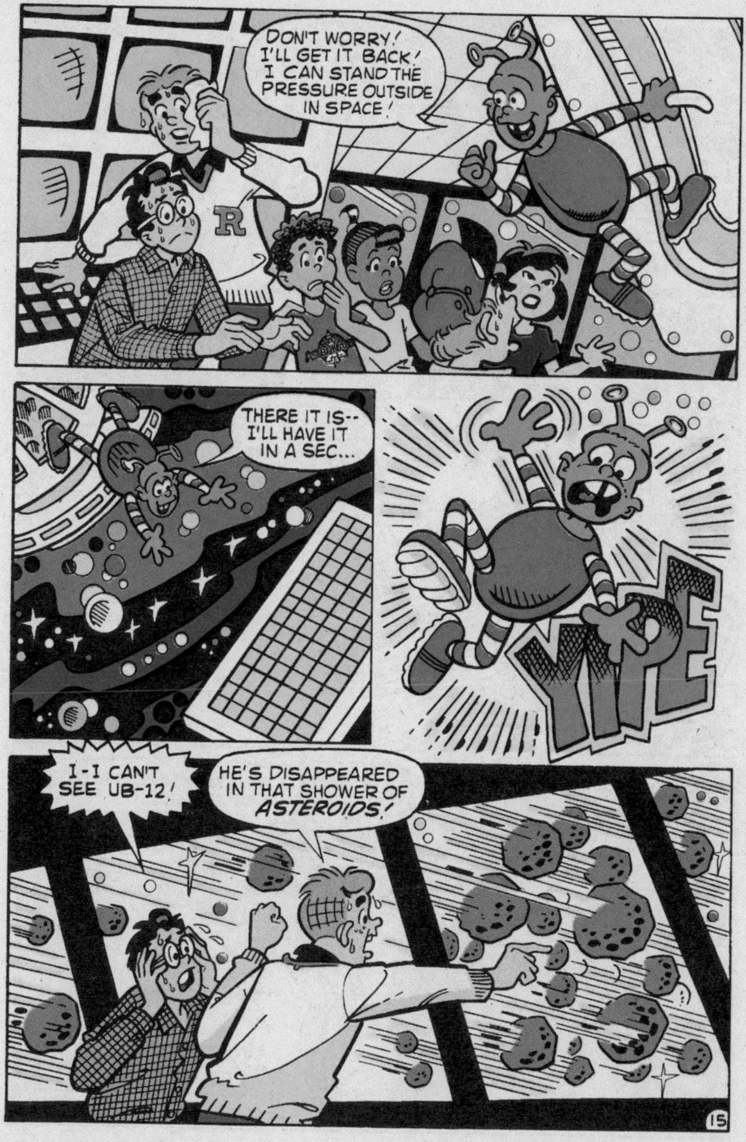
DON'T WORRY! I'LL GET IT BACK! I CAN STAND THE PRESSURE OUTSIDE IN SPACE!
THERE IT IS-- I'LL HAVE IT IN A SEC...
YIPE
I-I CAN'T SEE UB-12!
HE'S DISAPPEARED IN THAT SHOWER OF ASTEROIDS!

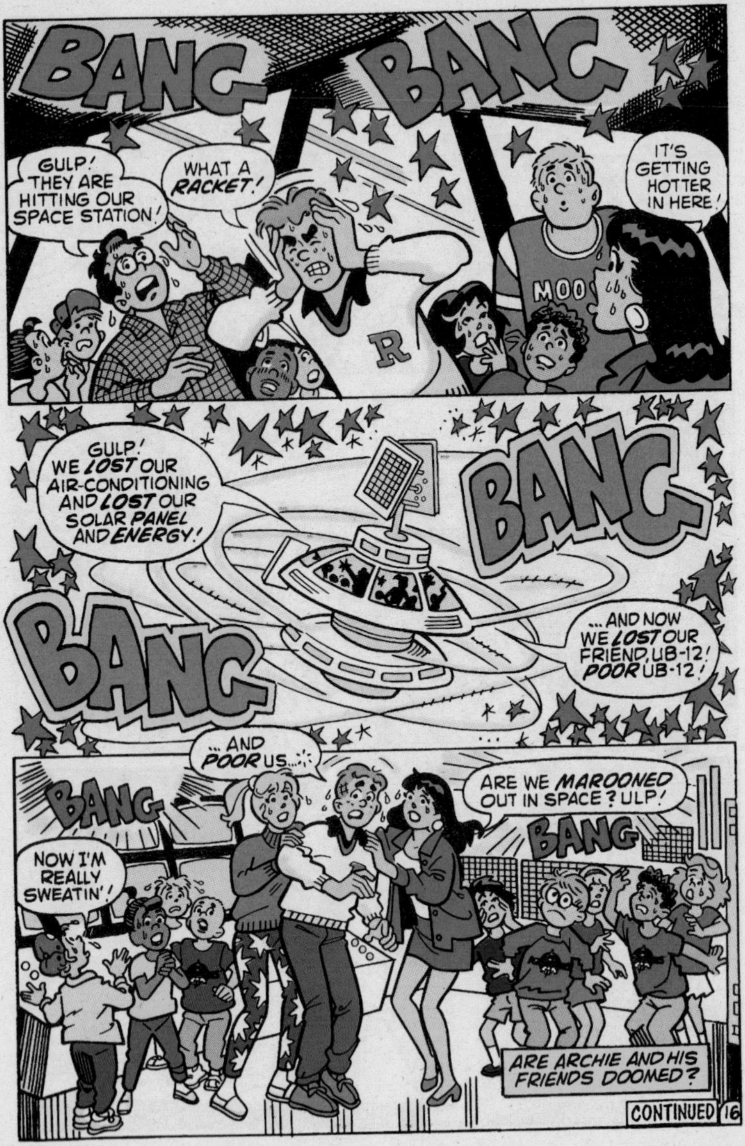
BANG BANG
GULP! THEY ARE HITTING OUR SPACE STATION!
WHAT A RACKET!
IT'S GETTING HOTTER IN HERE!
MOO
GULP! WE LOST OUR AIR-CONDITIONING AND LOST OUR SOLAR PANEL AND ENERGY!
BANG
BANG
...AND NOW WE LOST OUR FRIEND, UB-12! POOR UB-12!
...AND POOR US...
BANG
ARE WE MAROONED OUT IN SPACE? ULP!
BANG
NOW I'M REALLY SWEATIN'!
ARE ARCHIE AND HIS FRIENDS DOOMED?
CONTINUED 16

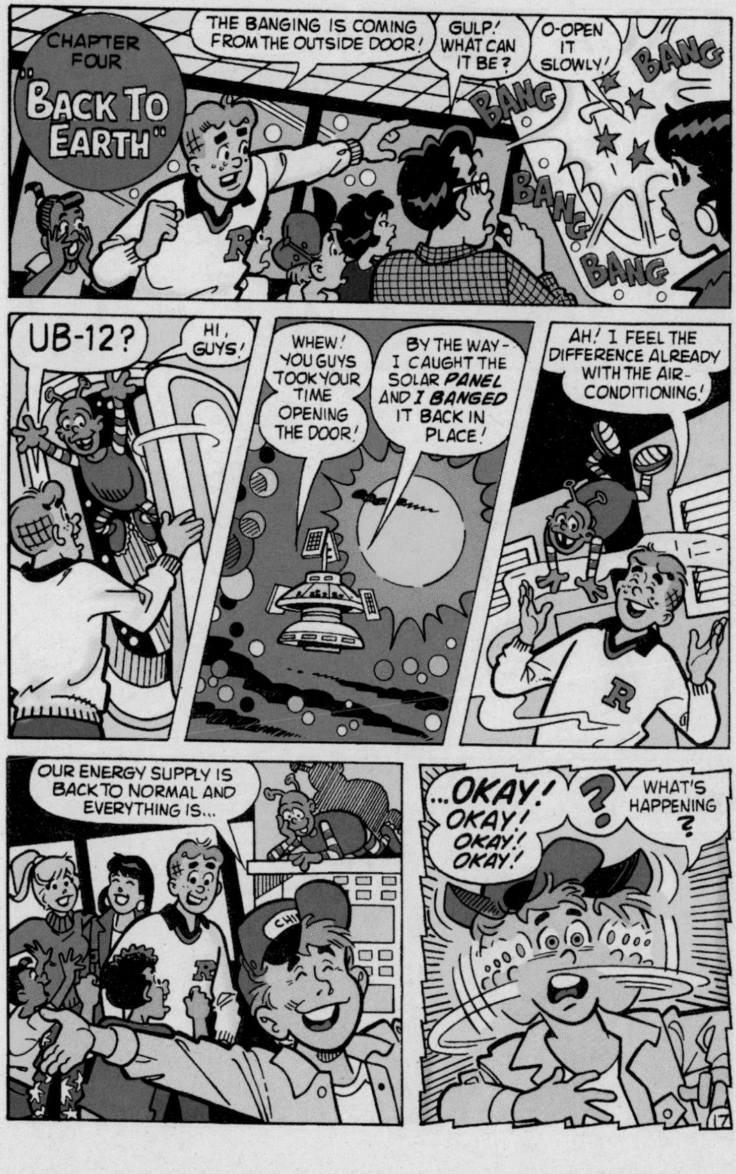
CHAPTER FOUR
"BACK TO EARTH"
THE BANGING IS COMING FROM THE OUTSIDE DOOR!
GULP! WHAT CAN IT BE?
O-OPEN IT SLOWLY!
BANG
BANG
BANG
BANG
UB-12?
HI, GUYS!
WHEW! YOU GUYS TOOK YOUR TIME OPENING THE DOOR!
BY THE WAY- I CAUGHT THE SOLAR PANEL AND I BANGED IT BACK IN PLACE!
AH! I FEEL THE DIFFERENCE ALREADY WITH THE AIR-CONDITIONING!
OUR ENERGY SUPPLY IS BACK TO NORMAL AND EVERYTHING IS...
...OKAY! OKAY! OKAY! OKAY!
?
WHAT'S HAPPENING ?
17

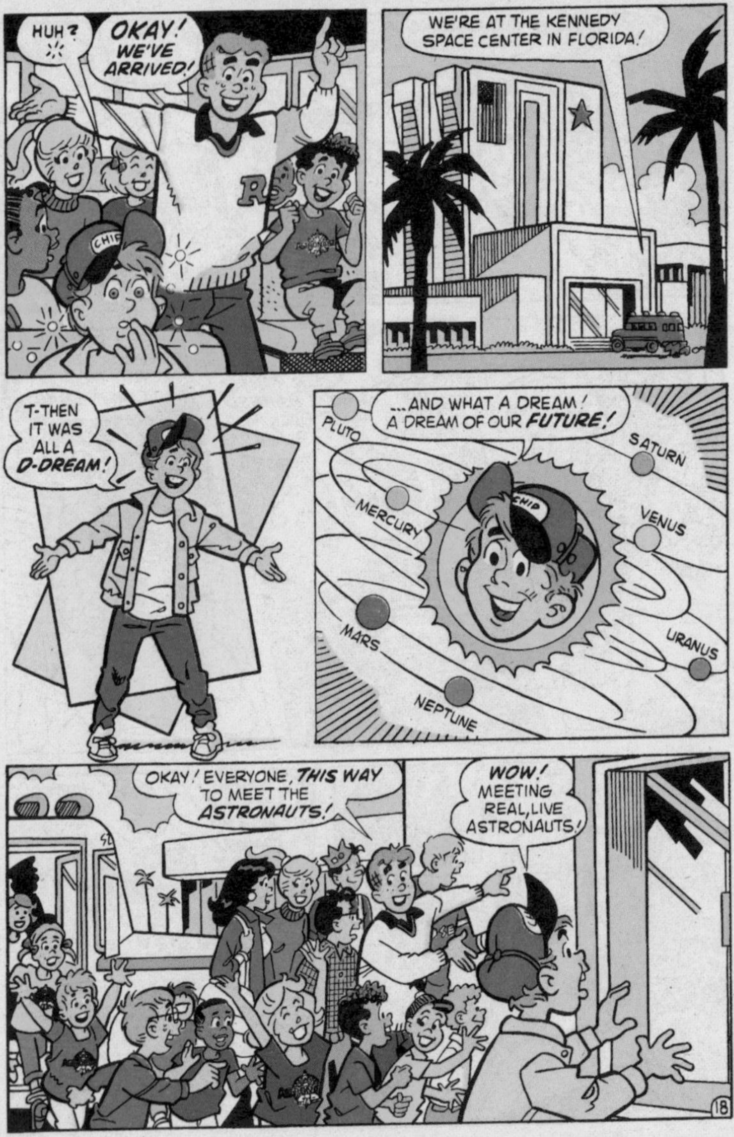
HUH?
OKAY! WE'VE ARRIVED!
CHIP
R
WE'RE AT THE KENNEDY SPACE CENTER IN FLORIDA!
T-THEN IT WAS ALL A D-DREAM!
...AND WHAT A DREAM! A DREAM OF OUR FUTURE!
PLUTO
SATURN
MERCURY
CHIP
VENUS
MARS
URANUS
NEPTUNE
OKAY! EVERYONE, THIS WAY TO MEET THE ASTRONAUTS!
WOW! MEETING REAL, LIVE ASTRONAUTS!

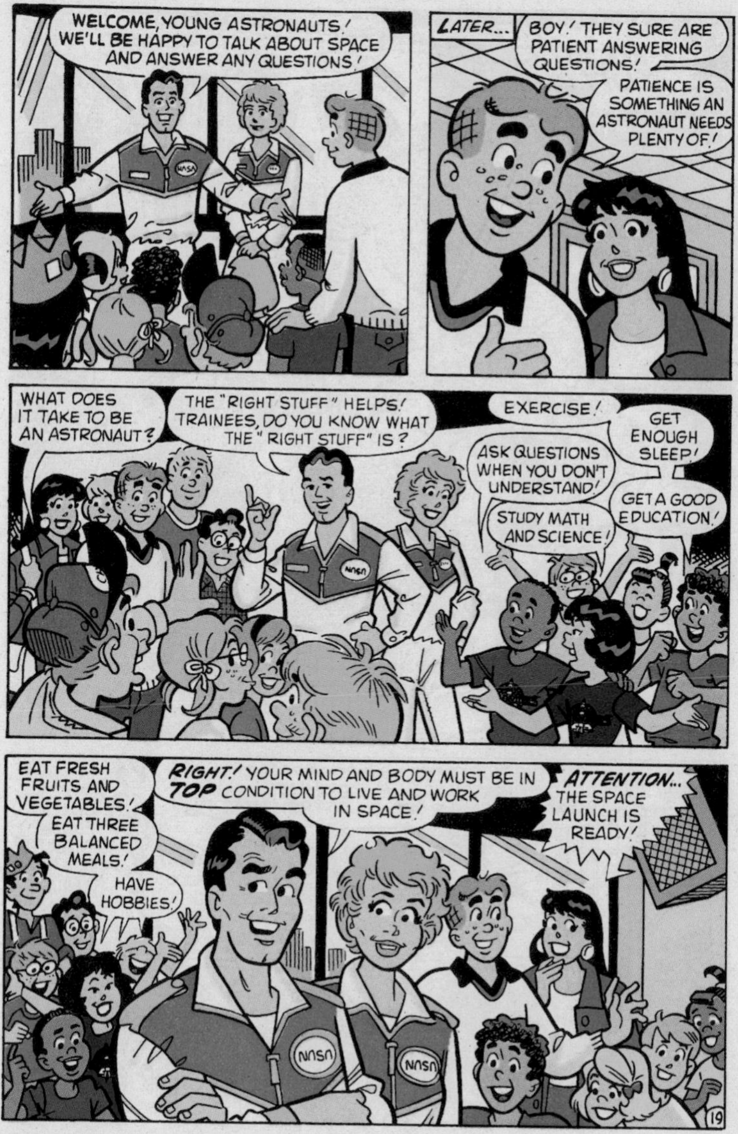

WELCOME, YOUNG ASTRONAUTS! WE'LL BE HAPPY TO TALK ABOUT SPACE AND ANSWER ANY QUESTIONS!
LATER...
BOY! THEY SURE ARE PATIENT ANSWERING QUESTIONS!
PATIENCE IS SOMETHING AN ASTRONAUT NEEDS PLENTY OF!
WHAT DOES IT TAKE TO BE AN ASTRONAUT?
THE "RIGHT STUFF" HELPS! TRAINEES, DO YOU KNOW WHAT THE "RIGHT STUFF" IS?
EXERCISE!
GET ENOUGH SLEEP!
ASK QUESTIONS WHEN YOU DON'T UNDERSTAND!
GET A GOOD EDUCATION!
STUDY MATH AND SCIENCE!
EAT FRESH FRUITS AND VEGETABLES!
EAT THREE BALANCED MEALS!
HAVE HOBBIES!
RIGHT! YOUR MIND AND BODY MUST BE IN TOP CONDITION TO LIVE AND WORK IN SPACE!
ATTENTION... THE SPACE LAUNCH IS READY!

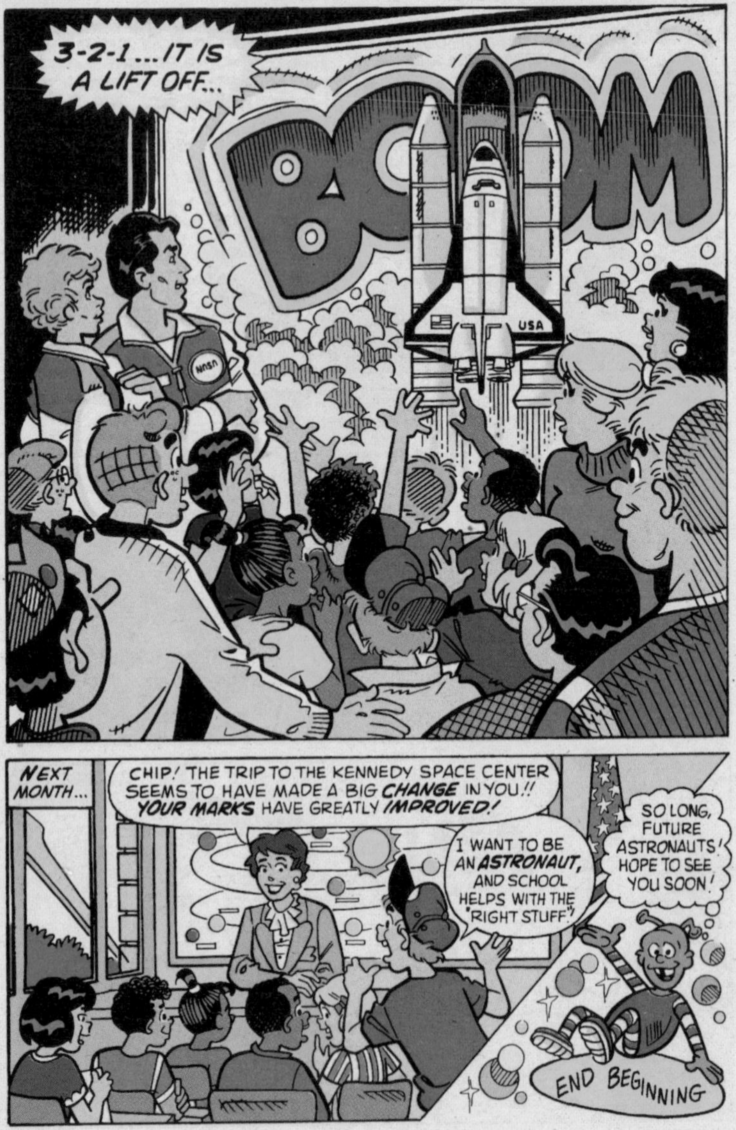
3-2-1 ... IT IS A LIFT OFF...
BOOM
NASA
USA
NEXT MONTH...
CHIP! THE TRIP TO THE KENNEDY SPACE CENTER SEEMS TO HAVE MADE A BIG CHANGE IN YOU!! YOUR MARKS HAVE GREATLY IMPROVED!
I WANT TO BE AN ASTRONAUT, AND SCHOOL HELPS WITH THE "RIGHT STUFF."
SO LONG, FUTURE ASTRONAUTS! HOPE TO SEE YOU SOON!
END BEGINNING

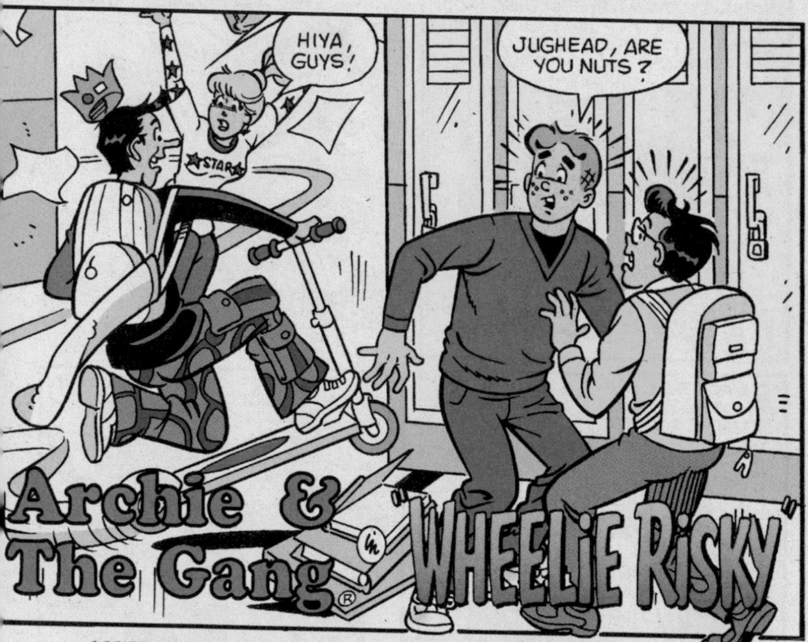
HIYA, GUYS!
JUGHEAD, ARE YOU NUTS?
Archie & The Gang®
WHEELIE RISKY

SCRIPT: MIKE PELLOWSKI PENCILS: HOWARD BENDER INKS: BOB SMITH
COLORS: BARRY GROSSMAN LETTERS: BILL YOSHIDA

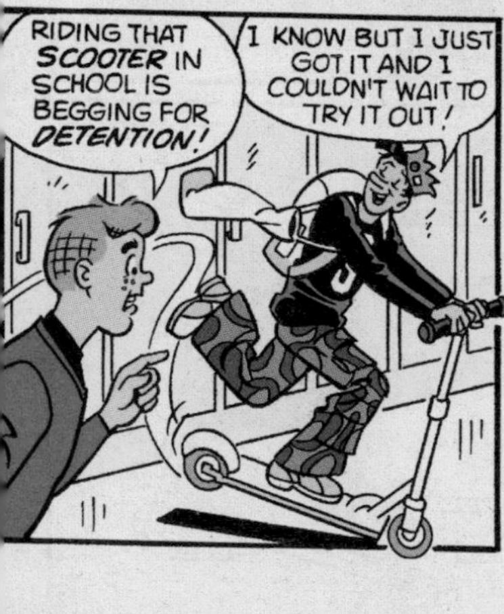
RIDING THAT SCOOTER IN SCHOOL IS BEGGING FOR DETENTION!
I KNOW BUT I JUST GOT IT AND I COULDN'T WAIT TO TRY IT OUT!

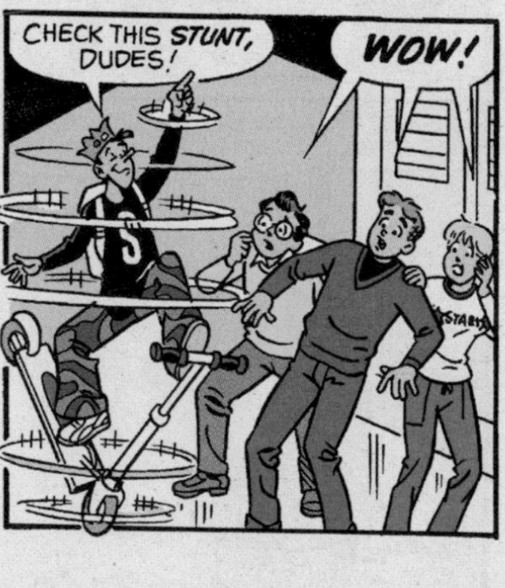
CHECK THIS STUNT, DUDES!
WOW!

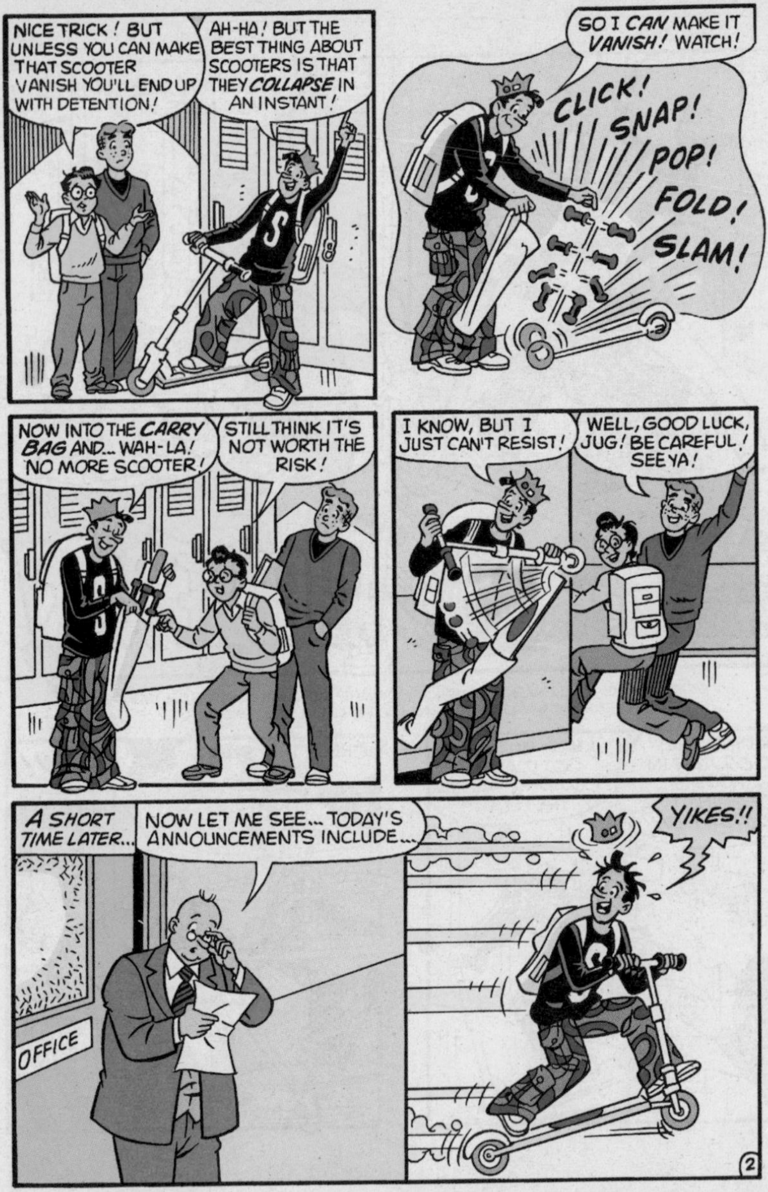

NICE TRICK! BUT UNLESS YOU CAN MAKE THAT SCOOTER VANISH YOU'LL END UP WITH DETENTION!
AH-HA! BUT THE BEST THING ABOUT SCOOTERS IS THAT THEY COLLAPSE IN AN INSTANT!
SO I CAN MAKE IT VANISH! WATCH!
CLICK!
SNAP!
POP!
FOLD!
SLAM!
NOW INTO THE CARRY BAG AND... WAH-LA! NO MORE SCOOTER!
STILL THINK IT'S NOT WORTH THE RISK!
I KNOW, BUT I JUST CAN'T RESIST!
WELL, GOOD LUCK, JUG! BE CAREFUL! SEE YA!
A SHORT TIME LATER...
NOW LET ME SEE... TODAY'S ANNOUNCEMENTS INCLUDE...
OFFICE
YIKES!!

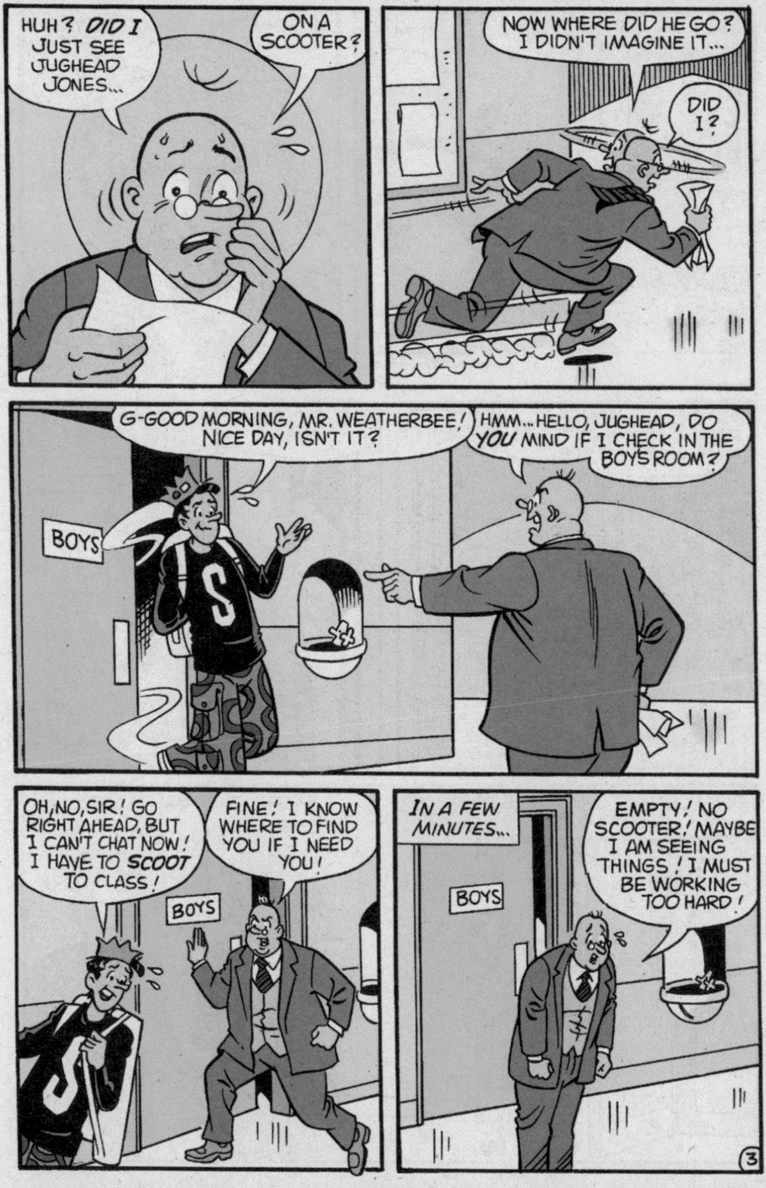
HUH? DID I JUST SEE JUGHEAD JONES...
ON A SCOOTER?
NOW WHERE DID HE GO? I DIDN'T IMAGINE IT...
DID I?
G-GOOD MORNING, MR. WEATHERBEE! NICE DAY, ISN'T IT?
HMM... HELLO, JUGHEAD, DO YOU MIND IF I CHECK IN THE BOY'S ROOM?
BOYS
OH, NO, SIR! GO RIGHT AHEAD, BUT I CAN'T CHAT NOW! I HAVE TO SCOOT TO CLASS!
FINE! I KNOW WHERE TO FIND YOU IF I NEED YOU!
BOYS
IN A FEW MINUTES...
EMPTY! NO SCOOTER! MAYBE I AM SEEING THINGS! I MUST BE WORKING TOO HARD!
BOYS
3

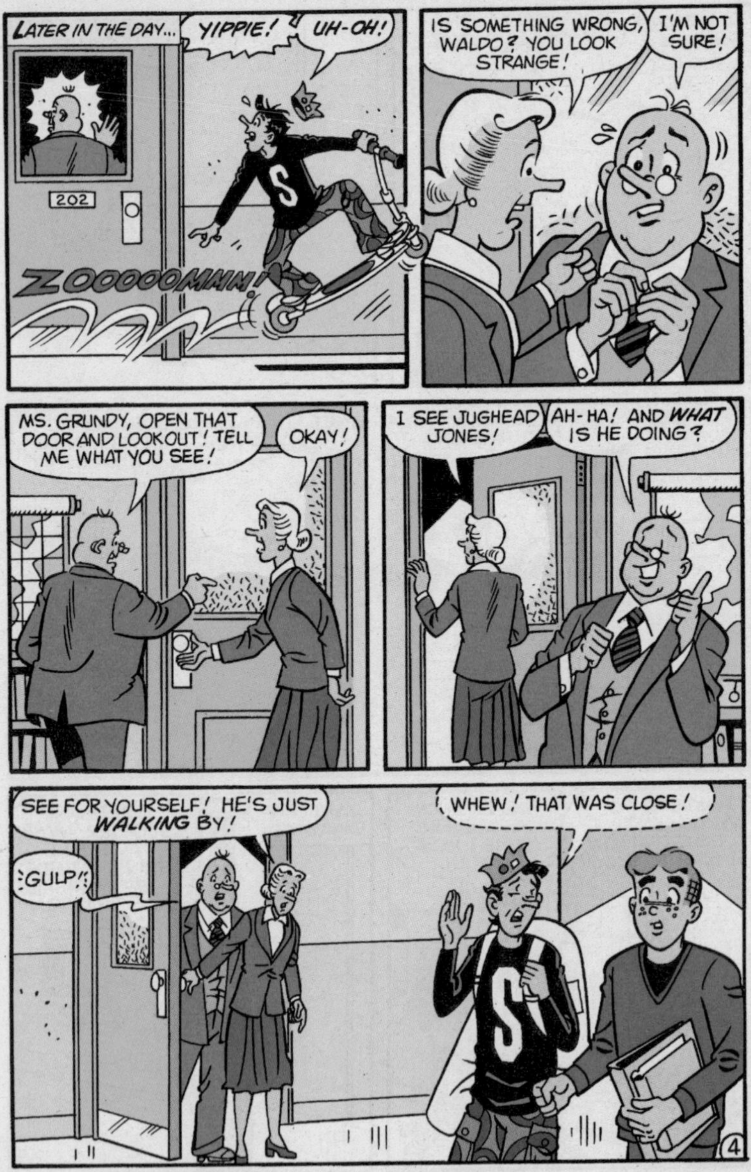

LATER IN THE DAY...
YIPPIE!
UH-OH!
202
ZOOOOOOMMM!
IS SOMETHING WRONG, WALDO? YOU LOOK STRANGE!
I'M NOT SURE!
MS. GRUNDY, OPEN THAT DOOR AND LOOKOUT! TELL ME WHAT YOU SEE!
OKAY!
I SEE JUGHEAD JONES!
AH-HA! AND WHAT IS HE DOING?
SEE FOR YOURSELF! HE'S JUST WALKING BY!
GULP!
WHEW! THAT WAS CLOSE!
4

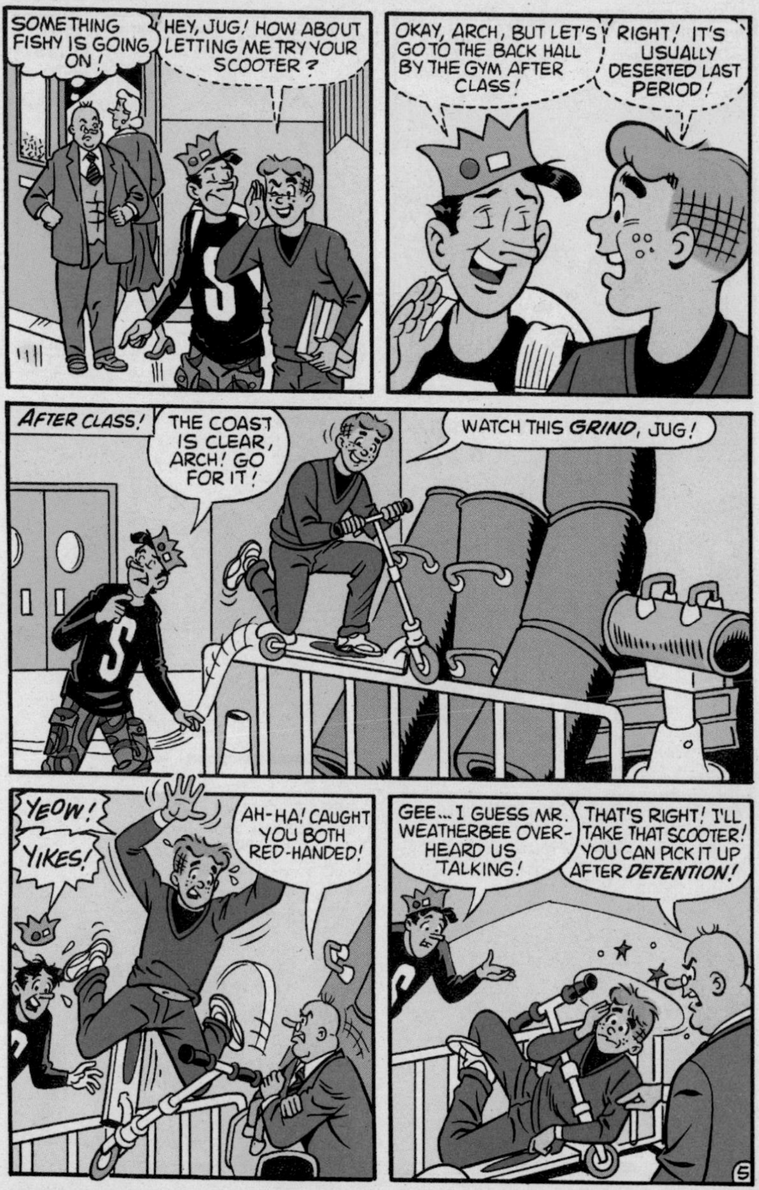
SOMETHING FISHY IS GOING ON!
HEY, JUG! HOW ABOUT LETTING ME TRY YOUR SCOOTER?
OKAY, ARCH, BUT LET'S GO TO THE BACK HALL BY THE GYM AFTER CLASS!
RIGHT! IT'S USUALLY DESERTED LAST PERIOD!
AFTER CLASS!
THE COAST IS CLEAR, ARCH! GO FOR IT!
WATCH THIS GRIND, JUG!
YEOW!
YIKES!
AH-HA! CAUGHT YOU BOTH RED-HANDED!
GEE... I GUESS MR. WEATHERBEE OVER-HEARD US TALKING!
THAT'S RIGHT! I'LL TAKE THAT SCOOTER! YOU CAN PICK IT UP AFTER DETENTION!
5

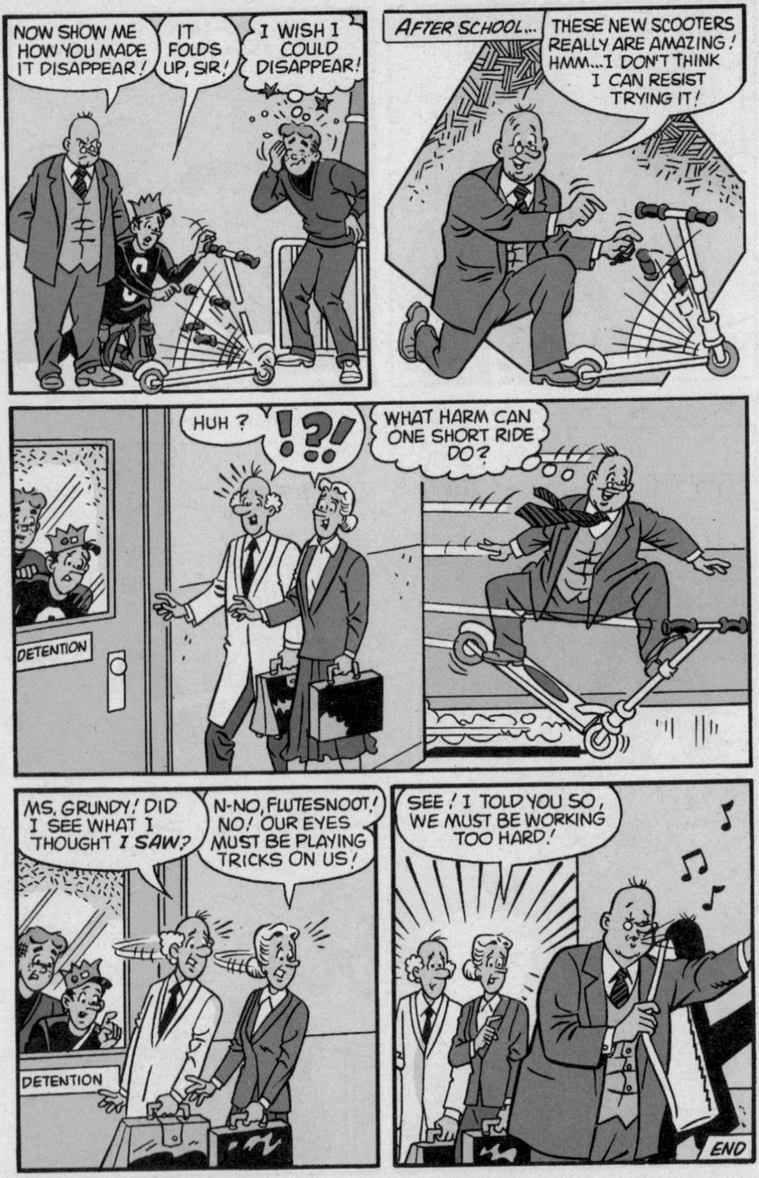
NOW SHOW ME HOW YOU MADE IT DISAPPEAR!
IT FOLDS UP, SIR!
I WISH I COULD DISAPPEAR!
AFTER SCHOOL...
THESE NEW SCOOTERS REALLY ARE AMAZING! HMM...I DON'T THINK I CAN RESIST TRYING IT!
DETENTION
HUH ?
!?!
WHAT HARM CAN ONE SHORT RIDE DO?
MS. GRUNDY! DID I SEE WHAT I THOUGHT I SAW?
N-NO, FLUTESNOOT! NO! OUR EYES MUST BE PLAYING TRICKS ON US!
DETENTION
SEE! I TOLD YOU SO, WE MUST BE WORKING TOO HARD!
END

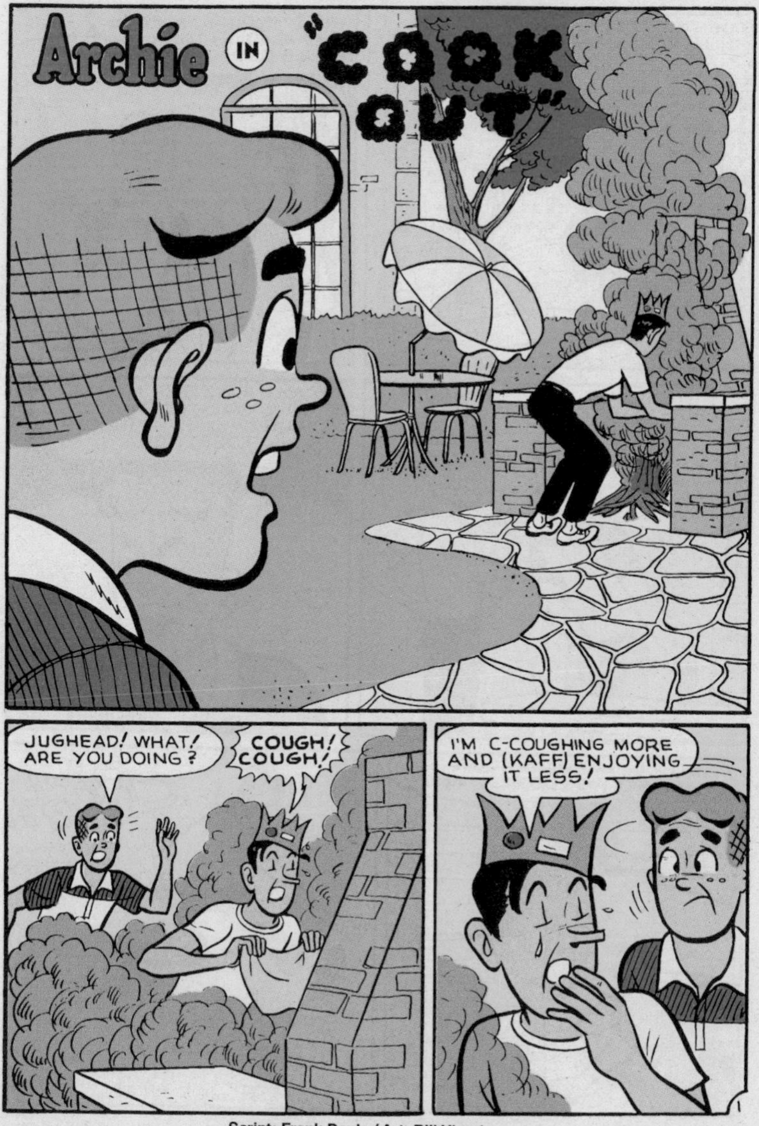
Archie
IN
"COOK OUT"
JUGHEAD! WHAT! ARE YOU DOING?
COUGH! COUGH!
I'M C-COUGHING MORE AND (KAFF) ENJOYING IT LESS!
1

Script: Frank Doyle / Art: Bill Vigoda

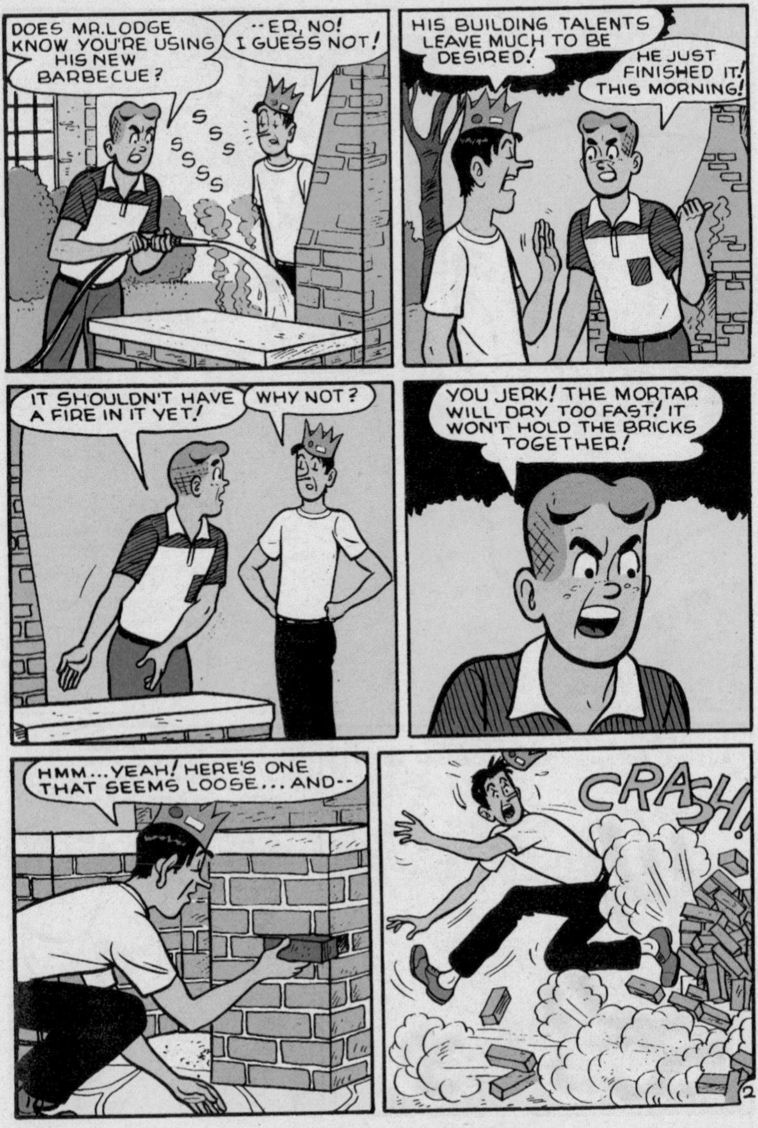

DOES MR.LODGE KNOW YOU'RE USING HIS NEW BARBECUE?
--ER, NO! I GUESS NOT!
S S S S S S S
HIS BUILDING TALENTS LEAVE MUCH TO BE DESIRED!
HE JUST FINISHED IT! THIS MORNING!
IT SHOULDN'T HAVE A FIRE IN IT YET!
WHY NOT?
YOU JERK! THE MORTAR WILL DRY TOO FAST! IT WON'T HOLD THE BRICKS TOGETHER!
HMM...YEAH! HERE'S ONE THAT SEEMS LOOSE... AND--
CRASH!

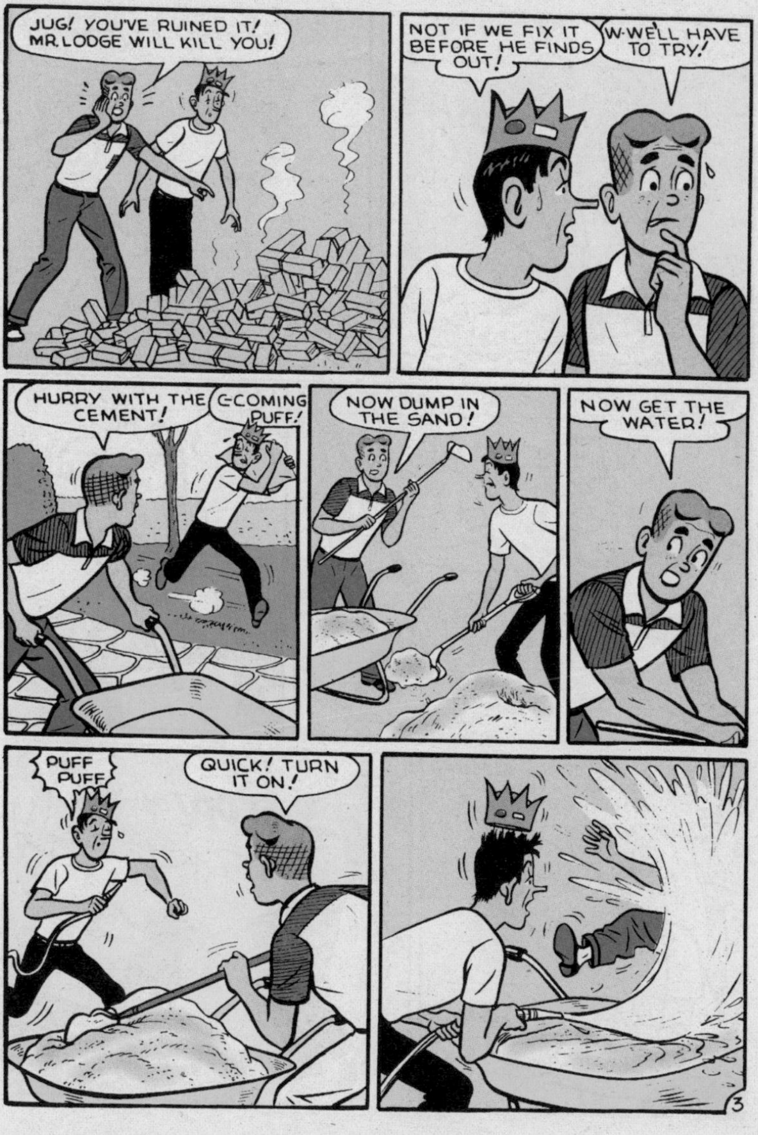
JUG! YOU'VE RUINED IT! MR. LODGE WILL KILL YOU!
NOT IF WE FIX IT BEFORE HE FINDS OUT!
W-WE'LL HAVE TO TRY!
HURRY WITH THE CEMENT!
C-COMING PUFF!
NOW DUMP IN THE SAND!
NOW GET THE WATER!
PUFF PUFF
QUICK! TURN IT ON!
3

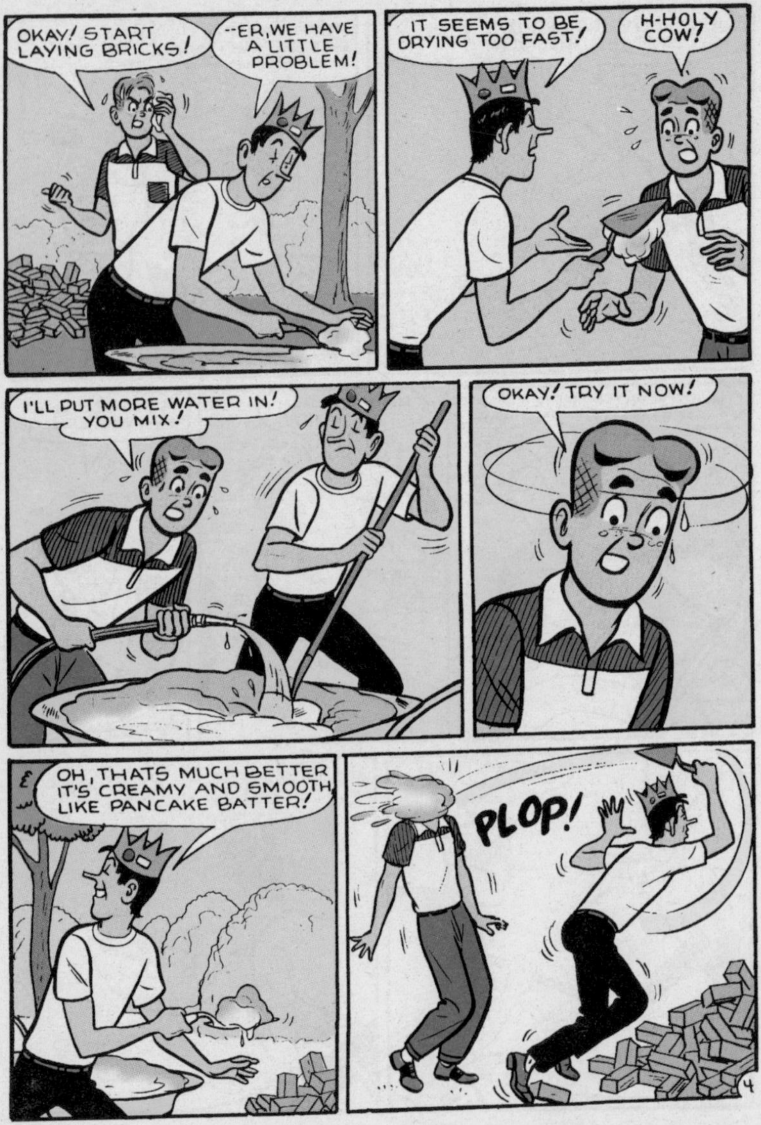
OKAY! START LAYING BRICKS!
--ER, WE HAVE A LITTLE PROBLEM!
IT SEEMS TO BE DRYING TOO FAST!
H-HOLY COW!
I'LL PUT MORE WATER IN! YOU MIX!
OKAY! TRY IT NOW!
OH, THATS MUCH BETTER IT'S CREAMY AND SMOOTH LIKE PANCAKE BATTER!
PLOP!
4

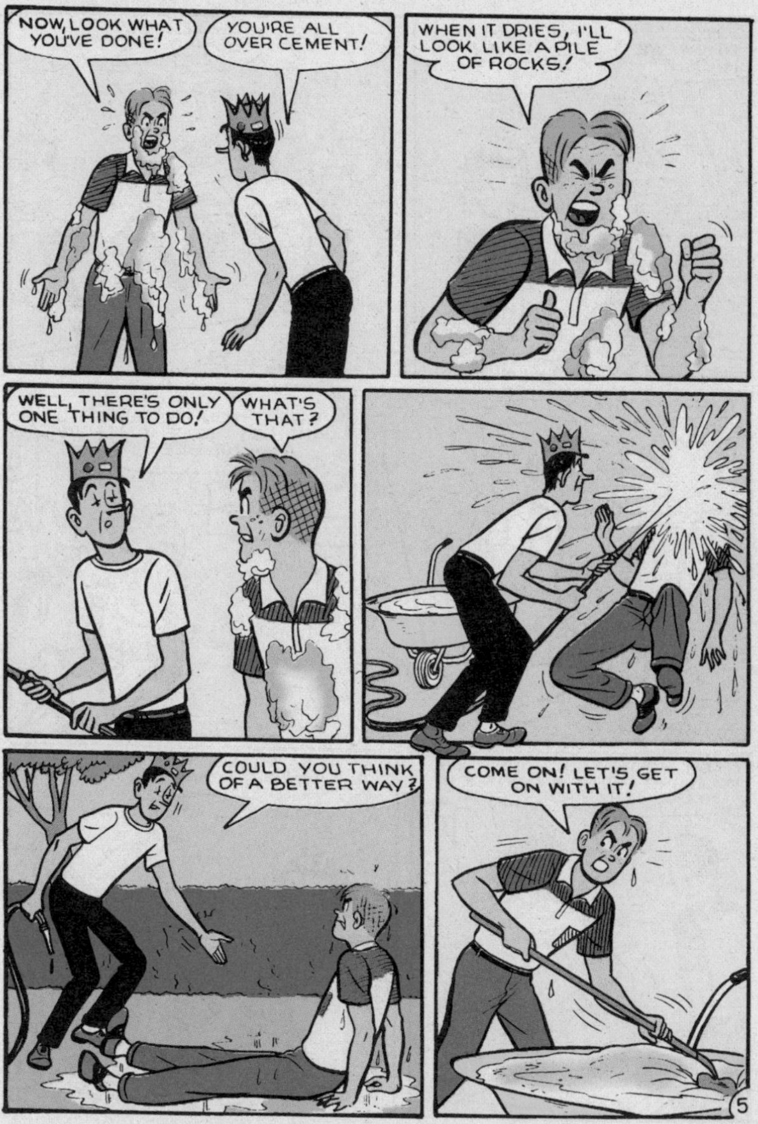
NOW, LOOK WHAT YOU'VE DONE!
YOU'RE ALL OVER CEMENT!
WHEN IT DRIES, I'LL LOOK LIKE A PILE OF ROCKS!
WELL, THERE'S ONLY ONE THING TO DO!
WHAT'S THAT?
COULD YOU THINK OF A BETTER WAY?
COME ON! LET'S GET ON WITH IT!

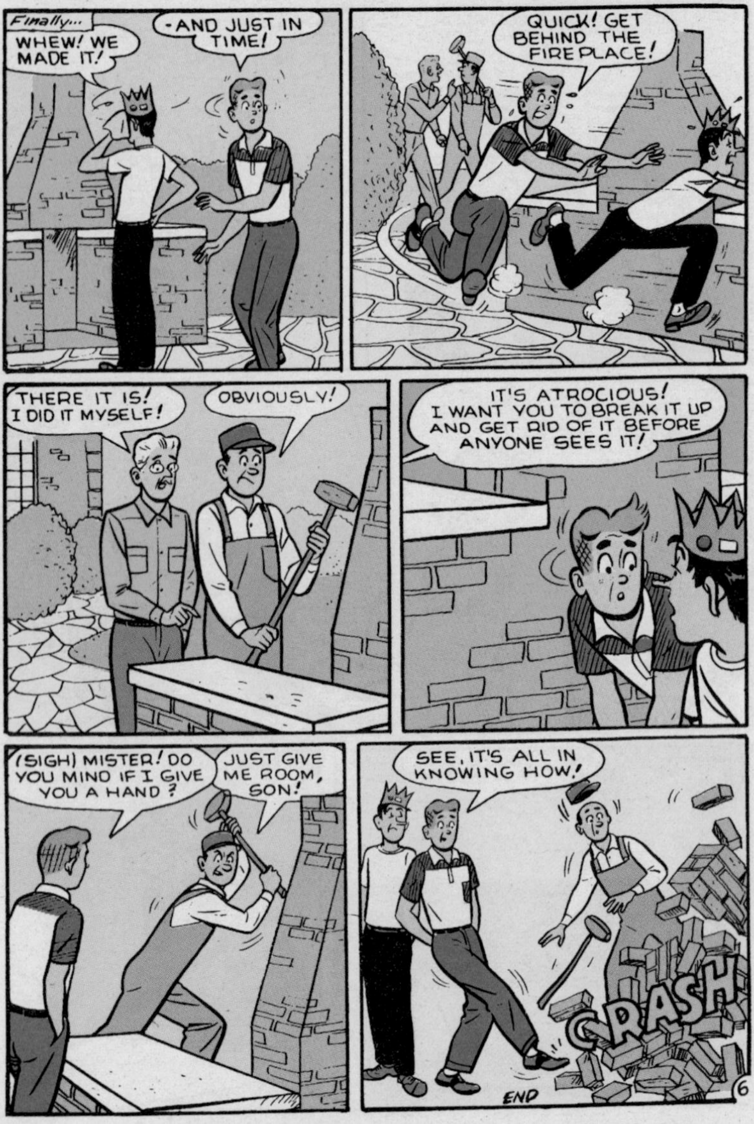
Finally...
WHEW! WE MADE IT!
-AND JUST IN TIME!
QUICK! GET BEHIND THE FIREPLACE!
THERE IT IS! I DID IT MYSELF!
OBVIOUSLY!
IT'S ATROCIOUS! I WANT YOU TO BREAK IT UP AND GET RID OF IT BEFORE ANYONE SEES IT!
(SIGH) MISTER! DO YOU MIND IF I GIVE YOU A HAND?
JUST GIVE ME ROOM, SON!
SEE, IT'S ALL IN KNOWING HOW!
CRASH
END

Nancy & Chuck in "TWO PLACES AT ONE TIME"

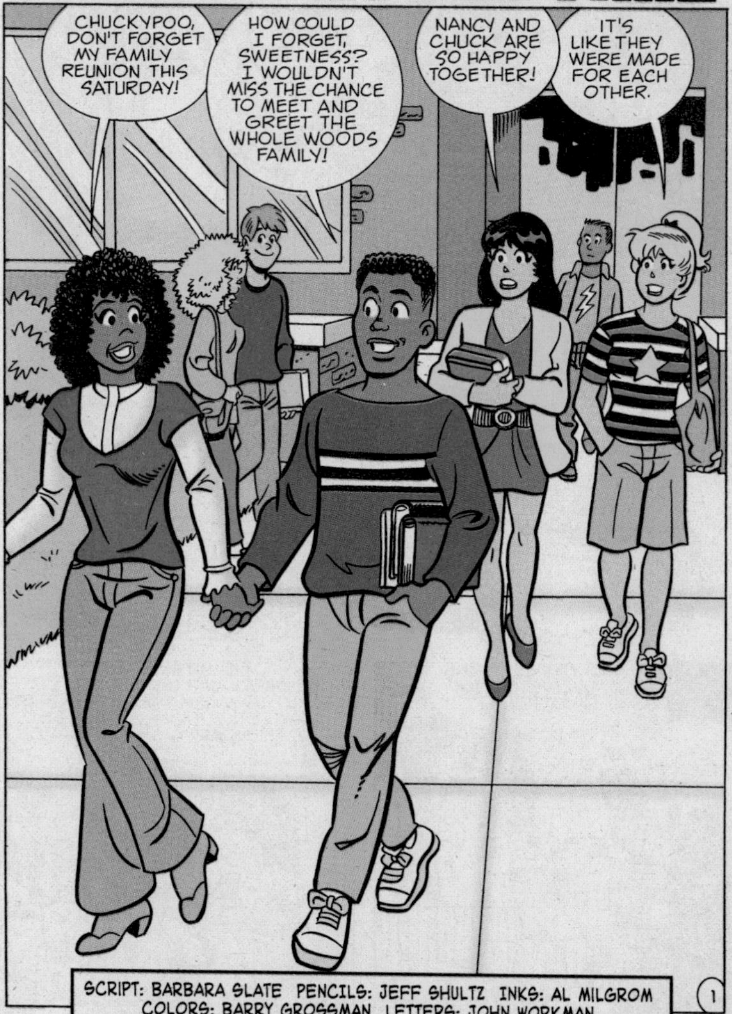
CHUCKYPOO, DON'T FORGET MY FAMILY REUNION THIS SATURDAY!
HOW COULD I FORGET, SWEETNESS? I WOULDN'T MISS THE CHANCE TO MEET AND GREET THE WHOLE WOODS FAMILY!
NANCY AND CHUCK ARE SO HAPPY TOGETHER!
IT'S LIKE THEY WERE MADE FOR EACH OTHER.
SCRIPT: BARBARA SLATE PENCILS: JEFF SHULTZ INKS: AL MILGROM
COLORS: BARRY GROSSMAN LETTERS: JOHN WORKMAN

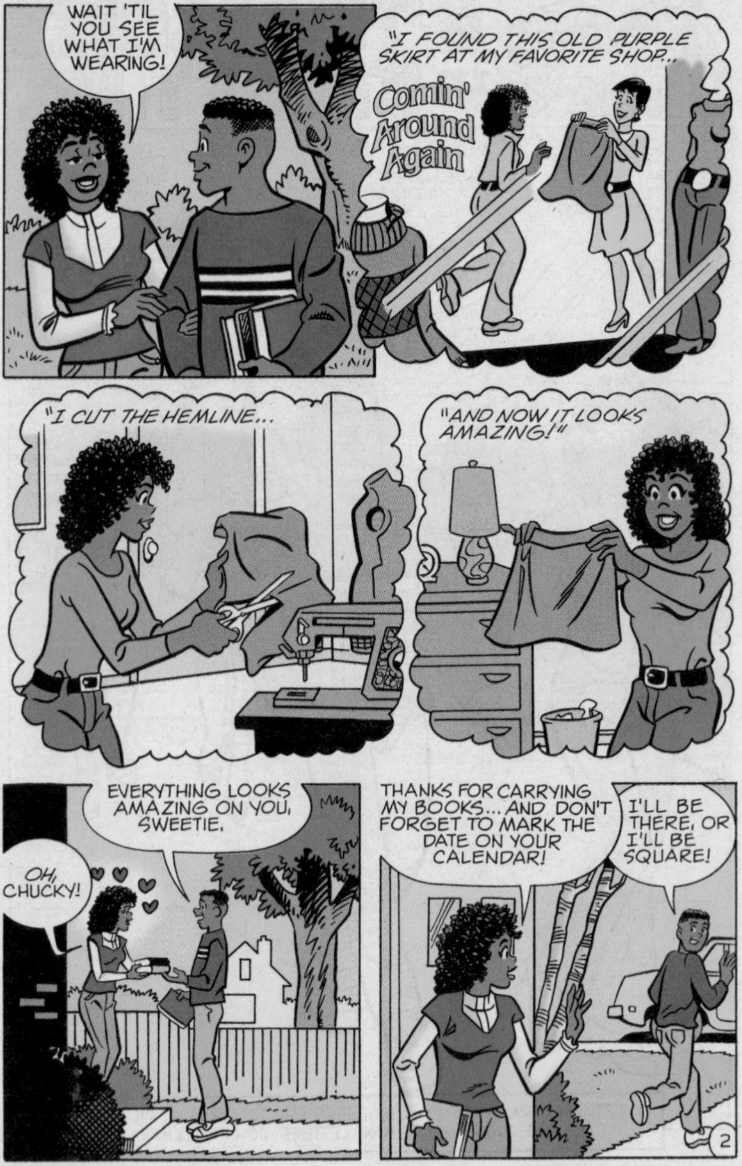

WAIT 'TIL YOU SEE WHAT I'M WEARING!
"I FOUND THIS OLD PURPLE SKIRT AT MY FAVORITE SHOP...
Comin' Around Again
"I CUT THE HEMLINE...
"AND NOW IT LOOKS AMAZING!"
EVERYTHING LOOKS AMAZING ON YOU, SWEETIE.
OH, CHUCKY!
THANKS FOR CARRYING MY BOOKS... AND DON'T FORGET TO MARK THE DATE ON YOUR CALENDAR!
I'LL BE THERE, OR I'LL BE SQUARE!
2

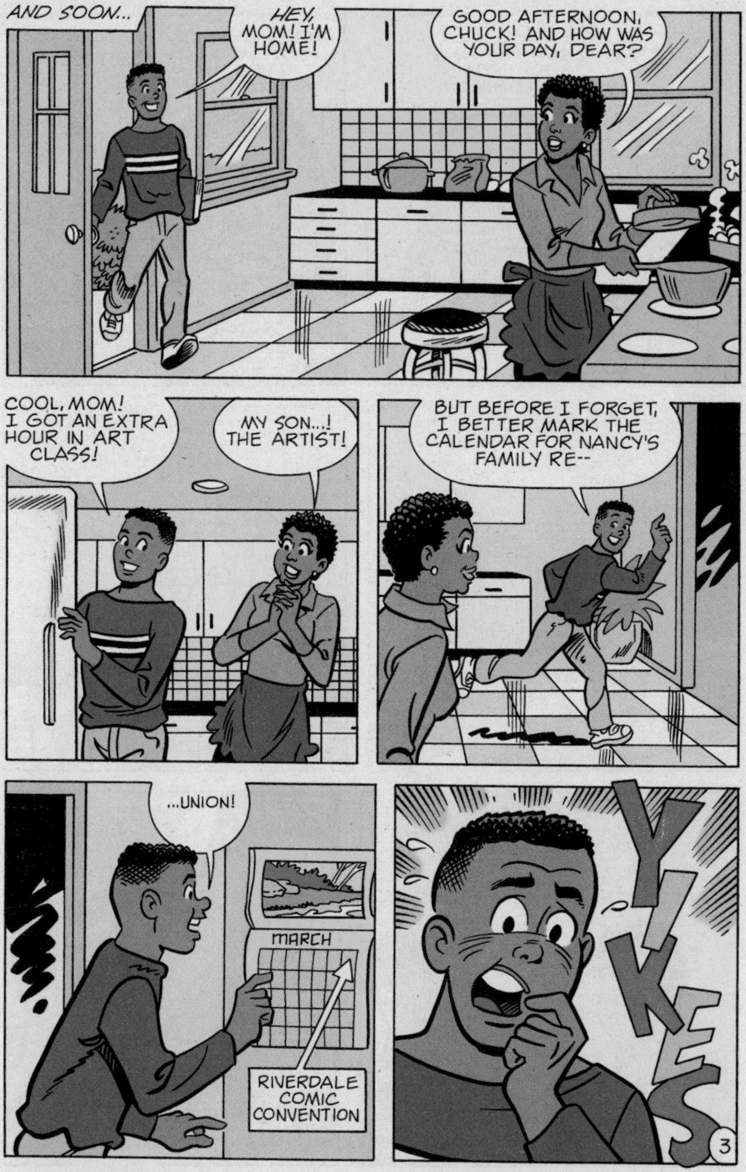
AND SOON...
HEY, MOM! I'M HOME!
GOOD AFTERNOON, CHUCK! AND HOW WAS YOUR DAY, DEAR?
COOL, MOM! I GOT AN EXTRA HOUR IN ART CLASS!
MY SON...! THE ARTIST!
BUT BEFORE I FORGET, I BETTER MARK THE CALENDAR FOR NANCY'S FAMILY RE--
...UNION!
MARCH
RIVERDALE COMIC CONVENTION
YIKES

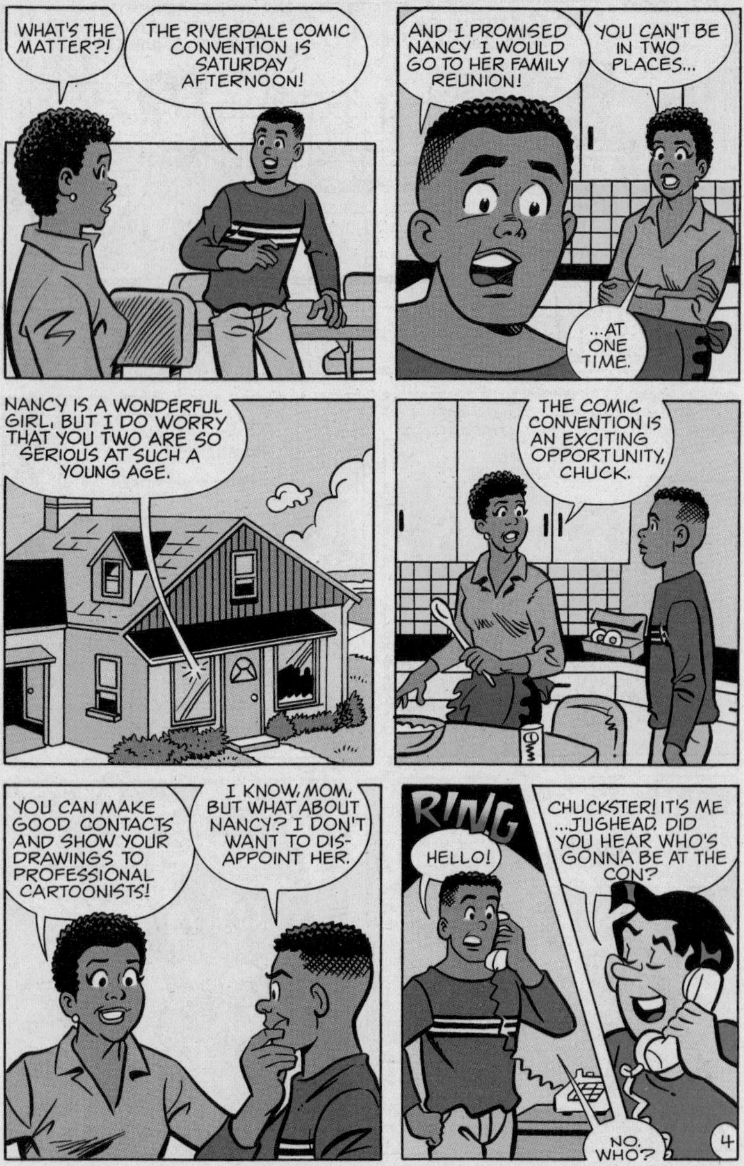
WHAT'S THE MATTER?!
THE RIVERDALE COMIC CONVENTION IS SATURDAY AFTERNOON!
AND I PROMISED NANCY I WOULD GO TO HER FAMILY REUNION!
YOU CAN'T BE IN TWO PLACES...
...AT ONE TIME.
NANCY IS A WONDERFUL GIRL, BUT I DO WORRY THAT YOU TWO ARE SO SERIOUS AT SUCH A YOUNG AGE.
THE COMIC CONVENTION IS AN EXCITING OPPORTUNITY, CHUCK.
YOU CAN MAKE GOOD CONTACTS AND SHOW YOUR DRAWINGS TO PROFESSIONAL CARTOONISTS!
I KNOW, MOM, BUT WHAT ABOUT NANCY? I DON'T WANT TO DIS-APPOINT HER.
RING
HELLO!
CHUCKSTER! IT'S ME ...JUGHEAD. DID YOU HEAR WHO'S GONNA BE AT THE CON?
NO. WHO?
4

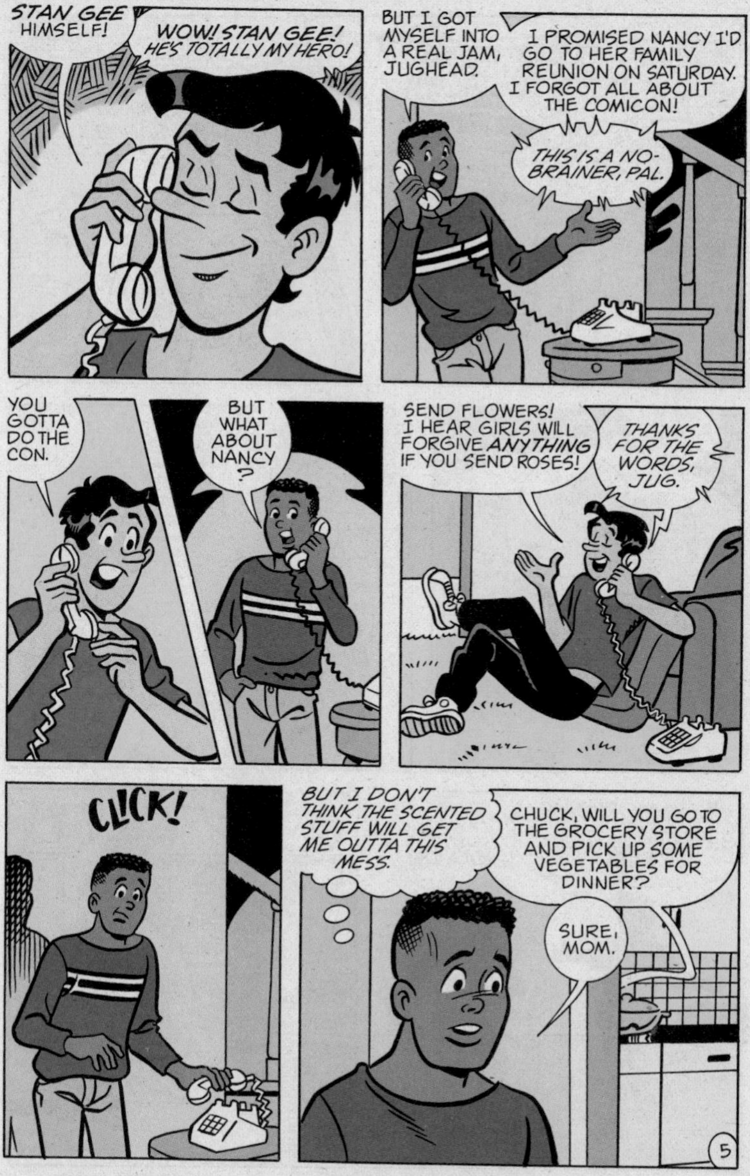
STAN GEE HIMSELF!
WOW! STAN GEE! HE'S TOTALLY MY HERO!
BUT I GOT MYSELF INTO A REAL JAM, JUGHEAD.
I PROMISED NANCY I'D GO TO HER FAMILY REUNION ON SATURDAY. I FORGOT ALL ABOUT THE COMICON!
THIS IS A NO-BRAINER, PAL.
YOU GOTTA DO THE CON.
BUT WHAT ABOUT NANCY?
SEND FLOWERS! I HEAR GIRLS WILL FORGIVE ANYTHING IF YOU SEND ROSES!
THANKS FOR THE WORDS, JUG.
CLICK!
BUT I DON'T THINK THE SCENTED STUFF WILL GET ME OUTTA THIS MESS.
CHUCK, WILL YOU GO TO THE GROCERY STORE AND PICK UP SOME VEGETABLES FOR DINNER?
SURE, MOM.
5

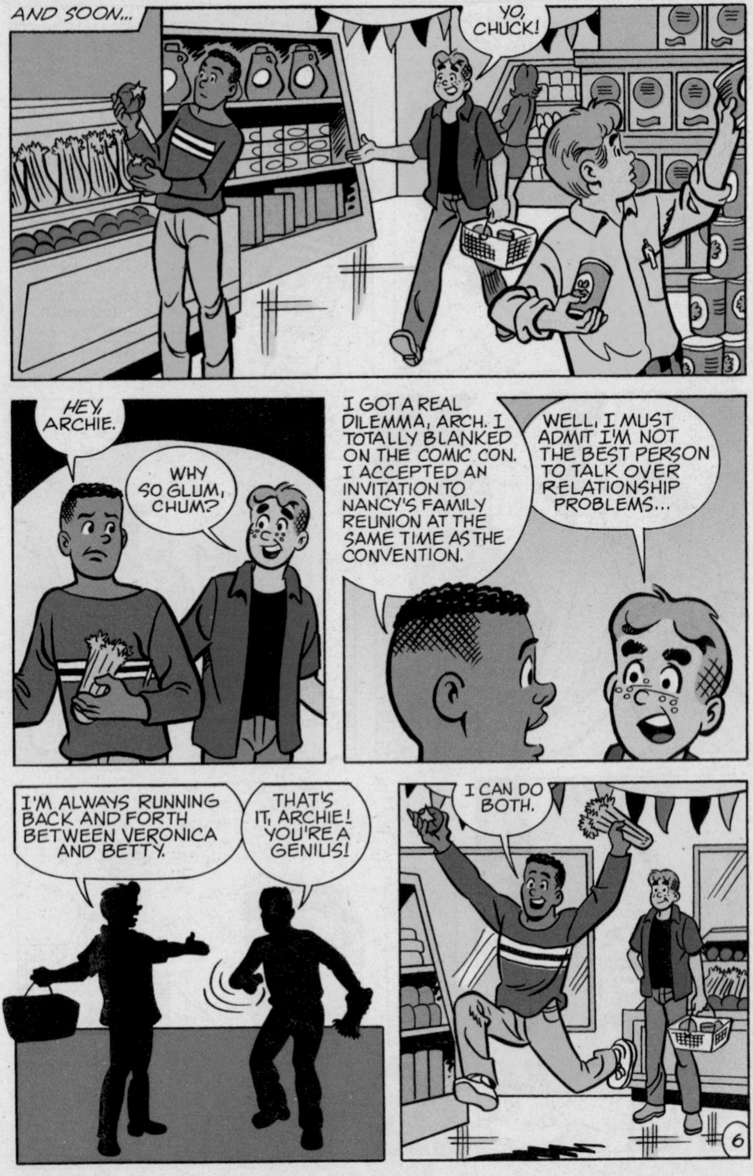
AND SOON...
YO, CHUCK!
HEY, ARCHIE.
WHY SO GLUM, CHUM?
I GOT A REAL DILEMMA, ARCH. I TOTALLY BLANKED ON THE COMIC CON. I ACCEPTED AN INVITATION TO NANCY'S FAMILY REUNION AT THE SAME TIME AS THE CONVENTION.
WELL, I MUST ADMIT I'M NOT THE BEST PERSON TO TALK OVER RELATIONSHIP PROBLEMS...
I'M ALWAYS RUNNING BACK AND FORTH BETWEEN VERONICA AND BETTY.
THAT'S IT, ARCHIE! YOU'RE A GENIUS!
I CAN DO BOTH.
6

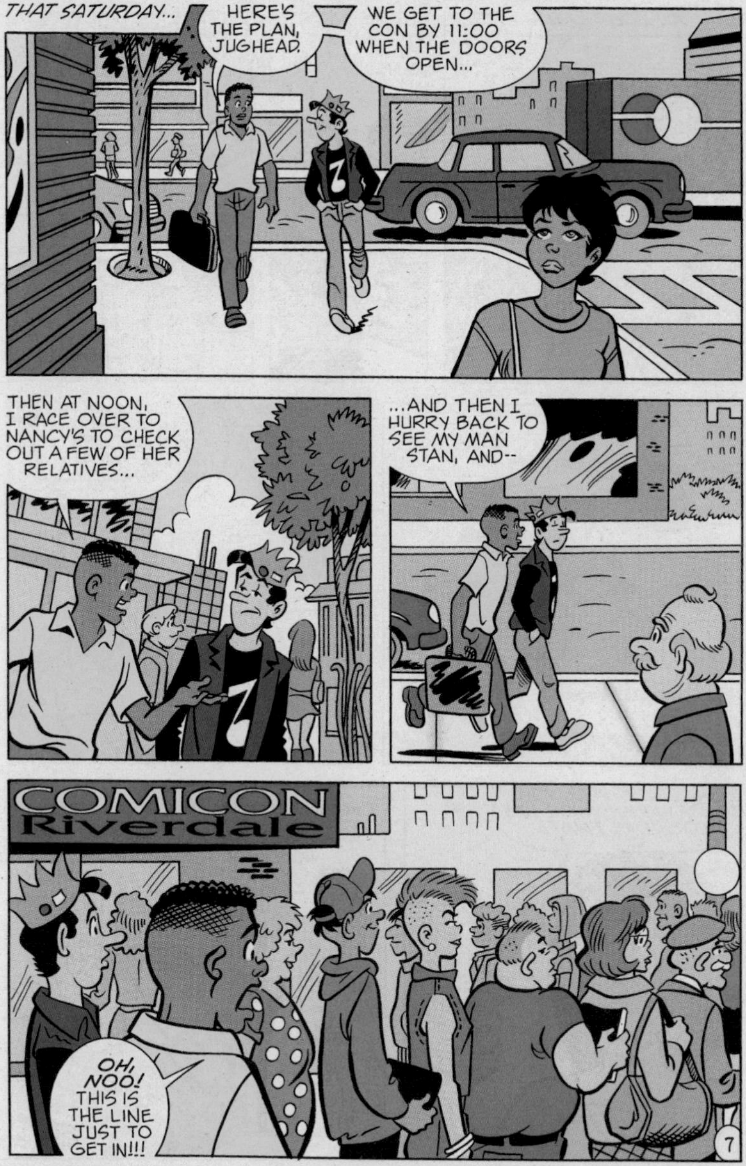
THAT SATURDAY...
HERE'S THE PLAN, JUGHEAD.
WE GET TO THE CON BY 11:00 WHEN THE DOORS OPEN...
THEN AT NOON, I RACE OVER TO NANCY'S TO CHECK OUT A FEW OF HER RELATIVES...
...AND THEN I HURRY BACK TO SEE MY MAN STAN, AND--
COMICON
Riverdale
OH, NOO! THIS IS THE LINE JUST TO GET IN!!!
7

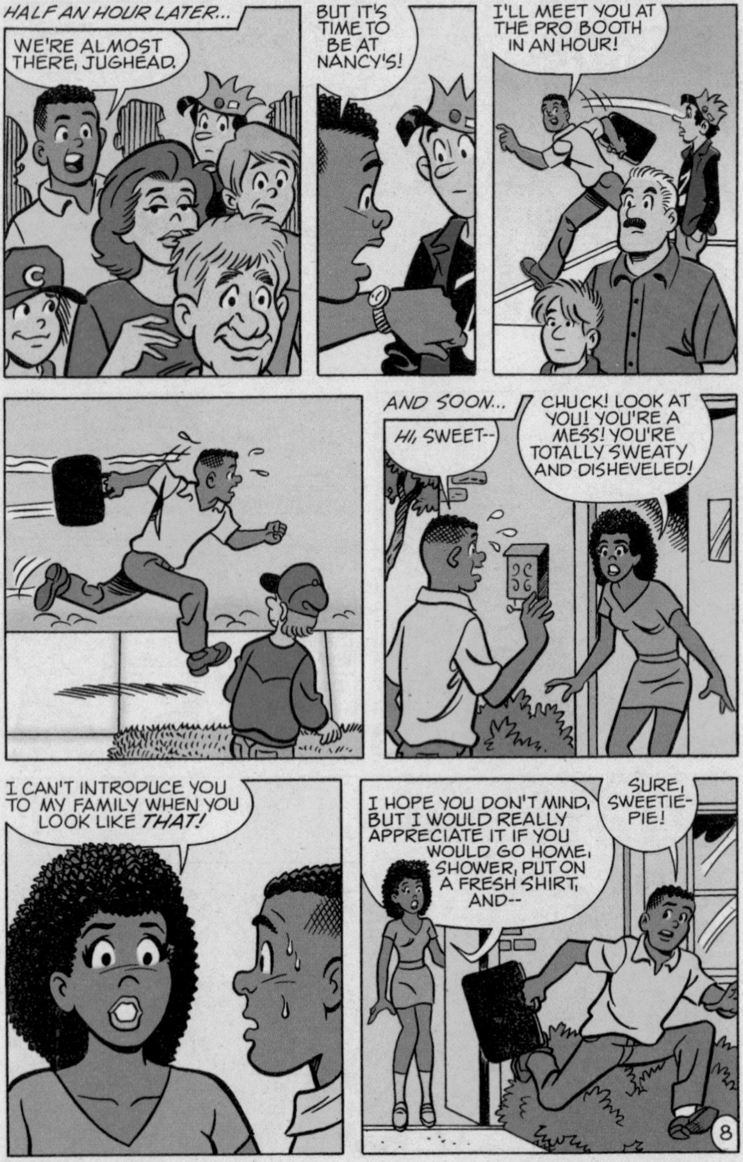

HALF AN HOUR LATER...
WE'RE ALMOST THERE, JUGHEAD.
BUT IT'S TIME TO BE AT NANCY'S!
I'LL MEET YOU AT THE PRO BOOTH IN AN HOUR!
AND SOON...
HI, SWEET--
CHUCK! LOOK AT YOU! YOU'RE A MESS! YOU'RE TOTALLY SWEATY AND DISHEVELED!
I CAN'T INTRODUCE YOU TO MY FAMILY WHEN YOU LOOK LIKE *THAT!*
I HOPE YOU DON'T MIND, BUT I WOULD REALLY APPRECIATE IT IF YOU WOULD GO HOME, SHOWER, PUT ON A FRESH SHIRT, AND--
SURE, SWEETIE-PIE!
8

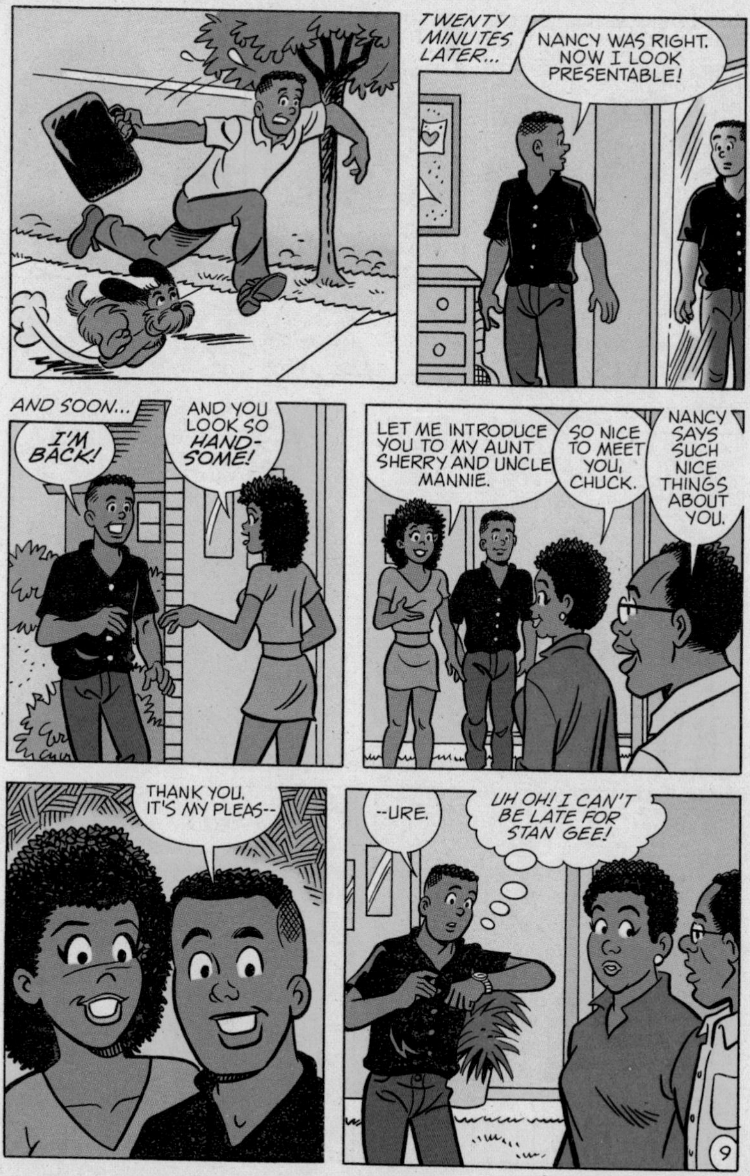

TWENTY MINUTES LATER...
NANCY WAS RIGHT. NOW I LOOK PRESENTABLE!
AND SOON...
I'M BACK!
AND YOU LOOK SO HANDSOME!
LET ME INTRODUCE YOU TO MY AUNT SHERRY AND UNCLE MANNIE.
SO NICE TO MEET YOU, CHUCK.
NANCY SAYS SUCH NICE THINGS ABOUT YOU.
THANK YOU. IT'S MY PLEAS--
--URE.
UH OH! I CAN'T BE LATE FOR STAN GEE!

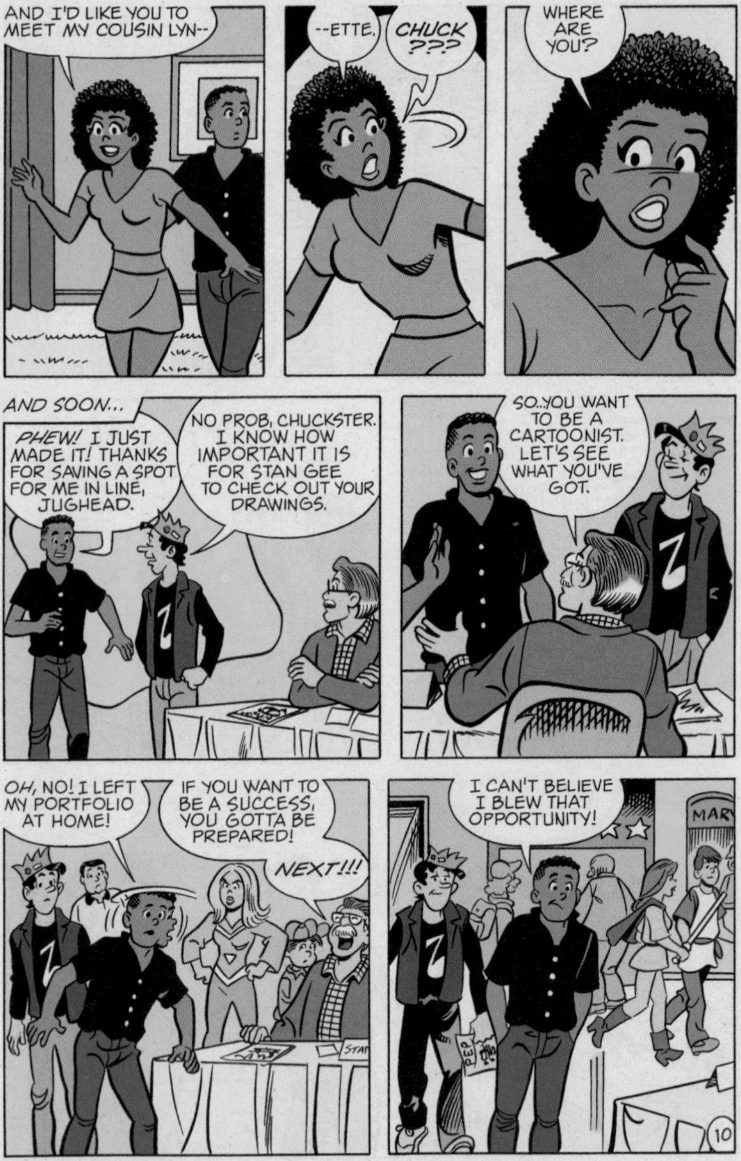
AND I'D LIKE YOU TO MEET MY COUSIN LYN--
--ETTE.
CHUCK ???
WHERE ARE YOU?
AND SOON...
PHEW! I JUST MADE IT! THANKS FOR SAVING A SPOT FOR ME IN LINE, JUGHEAD.
NO PROB, CHUCKSTER. I KNOW HOW IMPORTANT IT IS FOR STAN GEE TO CHECK OUT YOUR DRAWINGS.
SO...YOU WANT TO BE A CARTOONIST. LET'S SEE WHAT YOU'VE GOT.
OH, NO! I LEFT MY PORTFOLIO AT HOME!
IF YOU WANT TO BE A SUCCESS, YOU GOTTA BE PREPARED!
NEXT!!!
I CAN'T BELIEVE I BLEW THAT OPPORTUNITY!
10

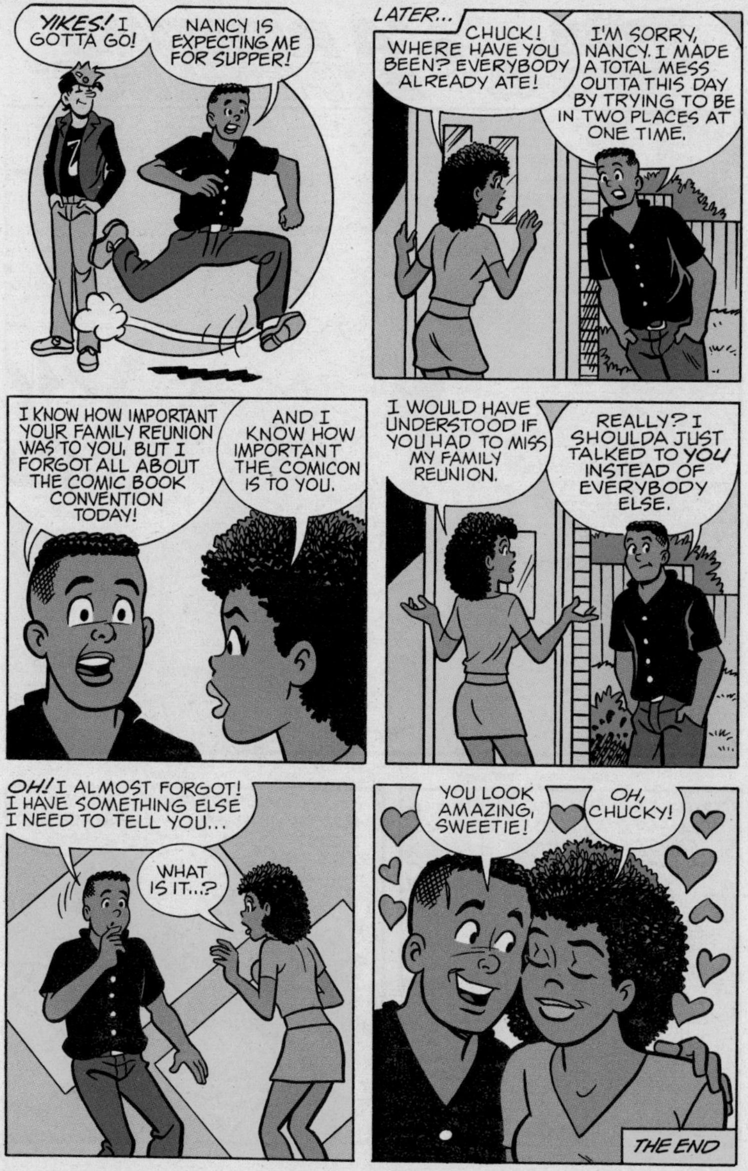
YIKES! I GOTTA GO!
NANCY IS EXPECTING ME FOR SUPPER!
LATER...
CHUCK! WHERE HAVE YOU BEEN? EVERYBODY ALREADY ATE!
I'M SORRY, NANCY. I MADE A TOTAL MESS OUTTA THIS DAY BY TRYING TO BE IN TWO PLACES AT ONE TIME.
I KNOW HOW IMPORTANT YOUR FAMILY REUNION WAS TO YOU, BUT I FORGOT ALL ABOUT THE COMIC BOOK CONVENTION TODAY!
AND I KNOW HOW IMPORTANT THE COMICON IS TO YOU.
I WOULD HAVE UNDERSTOOD IF YOU HAD TO MISS MY FAMILY REUNION.
REALLY? I SHOULDA JUST TALKED TO YOU INSTEAD OF EVERYBODY ELSE.
OH! I ALMOST FORGOT! I HAVE SOMETHING ELSE I NEED TO TELL YOU...
WHAT IS IT...?
YOU LOOK AMAZING, SWEETIE!
OH, CHUCKY!
THE END

Betty and Veronica in "A RIBITING EXPERIENCE"

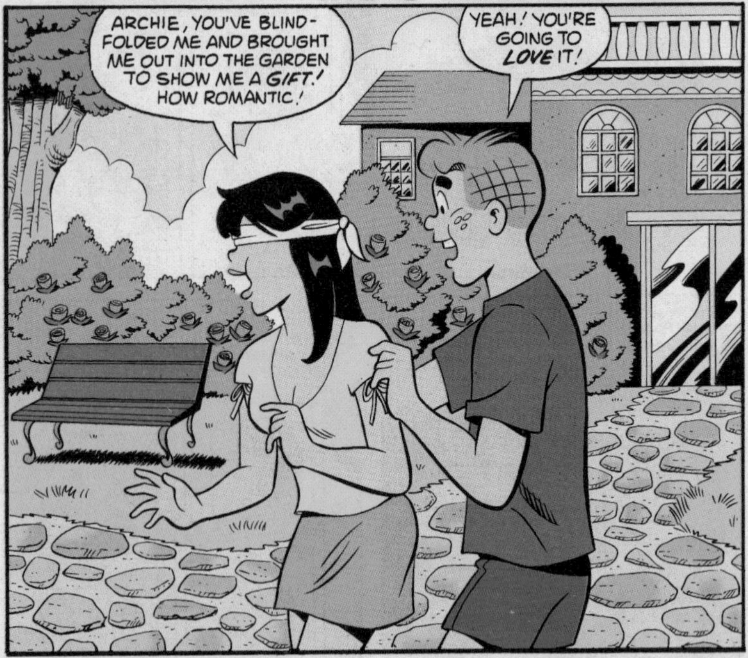
ARCHIE, YOU'VE BLIND-FOLDED ME AND BROUGHT ME OUT INTO THE GARDEN TO SHOW ME A *GIFT*! HOW ROMANTIC!
YEAH! YOU'RE GOING TO *LOVE* IT!

SCRIPT: BILL GOLLIHER PENCILS: DAN PARENT INKING: JIM AMASH LETTERING: BILL YOSHIDA COLORING: BARRY GROSSMAN

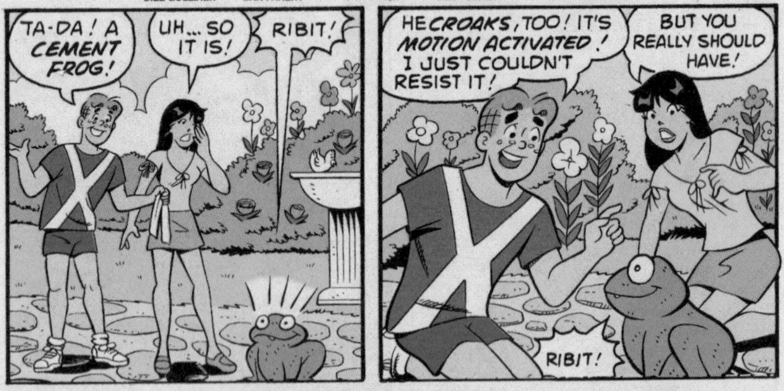
TA-DA! A *CEMENT FROG*!
UH... SO IT IS!
RIBIT!
HE *CROAKS*, TOO! IT'S *MOTION ACTIVATED*! I JUST COULDN'T RESIST IT!
BUT YOU REALLY SHOULD HAVE!
RIBIT!

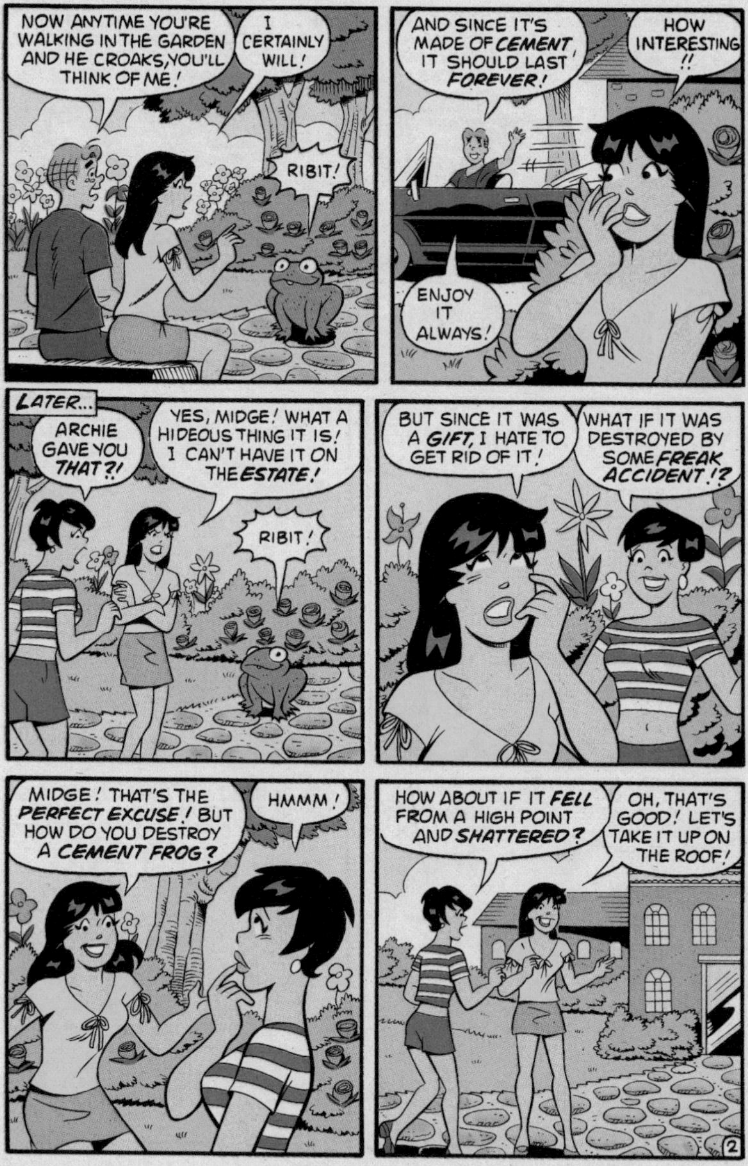
NOW ANYTIME YOU'RE WALKING IN THE GARDEN AND HE CROAKS, YOU'LL THINK OF ME!
I CERTAINLY WILL!
RIBIT!
AND SINCE IT'S MADE OF CEMENT, IT SHOULD LAST FOREVER!
HOW INTERESTING!!
ENJOY IT ALWAYS!
LATER...
ARCHIE GAVE YOU THAT?!
YES, MIDGE! WHAT A HIDEOUS THING IT IS! I CAN'T HAVE IT ON THE ESTATE!
RIBIT!
BUT SINCE IT WAS A GIFT, I HATE TO GET RID OF IT!
WHAT IF IT WAS DESTROYED BY SOME FREAK ACCIDENT!?
MIDGE! THAT'S THE PERFECT EXCUSE! BUT HOW DO YOU DESTROY A CEMENT FROG?
HMMM!
HOW ABOUT IF IT FELL FROM A HIGH POINT AND SHATTERED?
OH, THAT'S GOOD! LET'S TAKE IT UP ON THE ROOF!
2

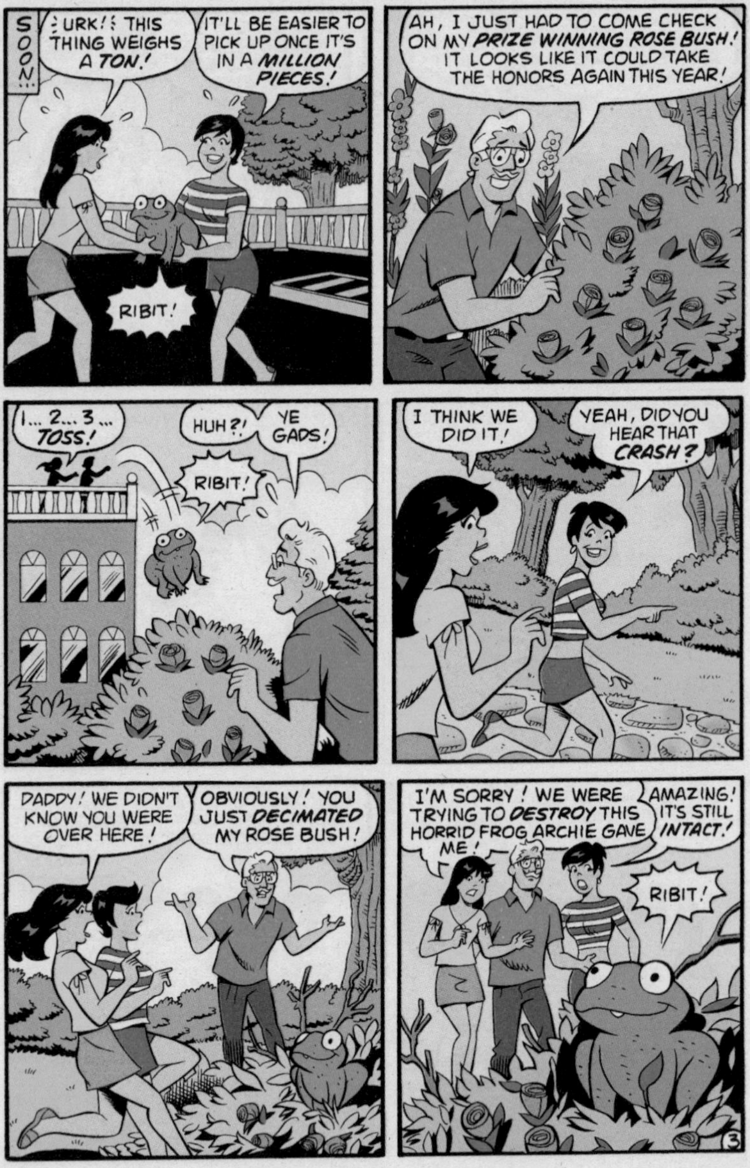
SOON...
URK! THIS THING WEIGHS A TON!
IT'LL BE EASIER TO PICK UP ONCE IT'S IN A MILLION PIECES!
RIBIT!
AH, I JUST HAD TO COME CHECK ON MY PRIZE WINNING ROSE BUSH! IT LOOKS LIKE IT COULD TAKE THE HONORS AGAIN THIS YEAR!
1... 2... 3... TOSS!
HUH?!
YE GADS!
RIBIT!
I THINK WE DID IT!
YEAH, DID YOU HEAR THAT CRASH?
DADDY! WE DIDN'T KNOW YOU WERE OVER HERE!
OBVIOUSLY! YOU JUST DECIMATED MY ROSE BUSH!
I'M SORRY! WE WERE TRYING TO DESTROY THIS HORRID FROG ARCHIE GAVE ME!
AMAZING! IT'S STILL INTACT!
RIBIT!
3

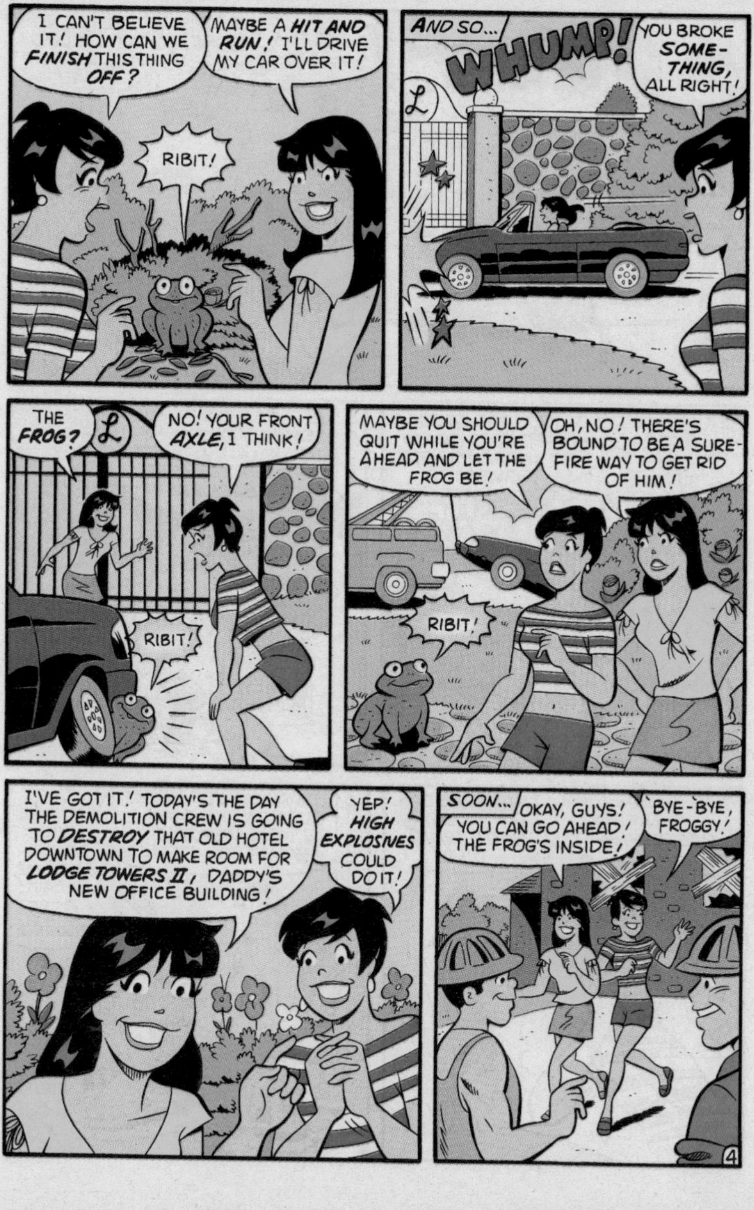
I CAN'T BELIEVE IT! HOW CAN WE FINISH THIS THING OFF?
MAYBE A HIT AND RUN! I'LL DRIVE MY CAR OVER IT!
RIBIT!
AND SO...
WHUMP!
YOU BROKE SOMETHING, ALL RIGHT!
THE FROG?
NO! YOUR FRONT AXLE, I THINK!
RIBIT!
MAYBE YOU SHOULD QUIT WHILE YOU'RE AHEAD AND LET THE FROG BE!
OH, NO! THERE'S BOUND TO BE A SURE-FIRE WAY TO GET RID OF HIM!
RIBIT!
I'VE GOT IT! TODAY'S THE DAY THE DEMOLITION CREW IS GOING TO DESTROY THAT OLD HOTEL DOWNTOWN TO MAKE ROOM FOR LODGE TOWERS II, DADDY'S NEW OFFICE BUILDING!
YEP! HIGH EXPLOSIVES COULD DO IT!
SOON...
OKAY, GUYS! YOU CAN GO AHEAD! THE FROG'S INSIDE!
BYE-BYE, FROGGY!
4

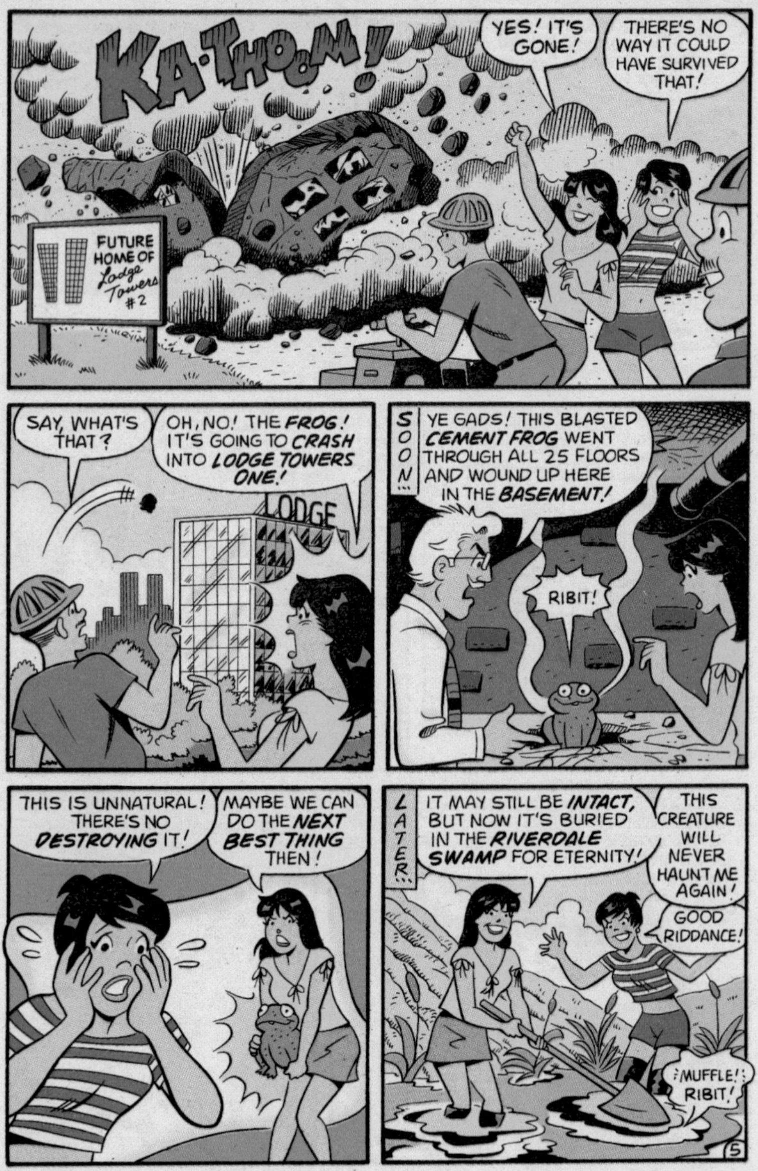
KA-THOOM!
FUTURE HOME OF Lodge Towers #2
YES! IT'S GONE!
THERE'S NO WAY IT COULD HAVE SURVIVED THAT!
SAY, WHAT'S THAT?
OH, NO! THE FROG! IT'S GOING TO CRASH INTO LODGE TOWERS ONE!
LODGE
SOON...
YE GADS! THIS BLASTED CEMENT FROG WENT THROUGH ALL 25 FLOORS AND WOUND UP HERE IN THE BASEMENT!
RIBIT!
THIS IS UNNATURAL! THERE'S NO DESTROYING IT!
MAYBE WE CAN DO THE NEXT BEST THING THEN!
LATER...
IT MAY STILL BE INTACT, BUT NOW IT'S BURIED IN THE RIVERDALE SWAMP FOR ETERNITY!
THIS CREATURE WILL NEVER HAUNT ME AGAIN!
GOOD RIDDANCE!
MUFFLE! RIBIT!
5

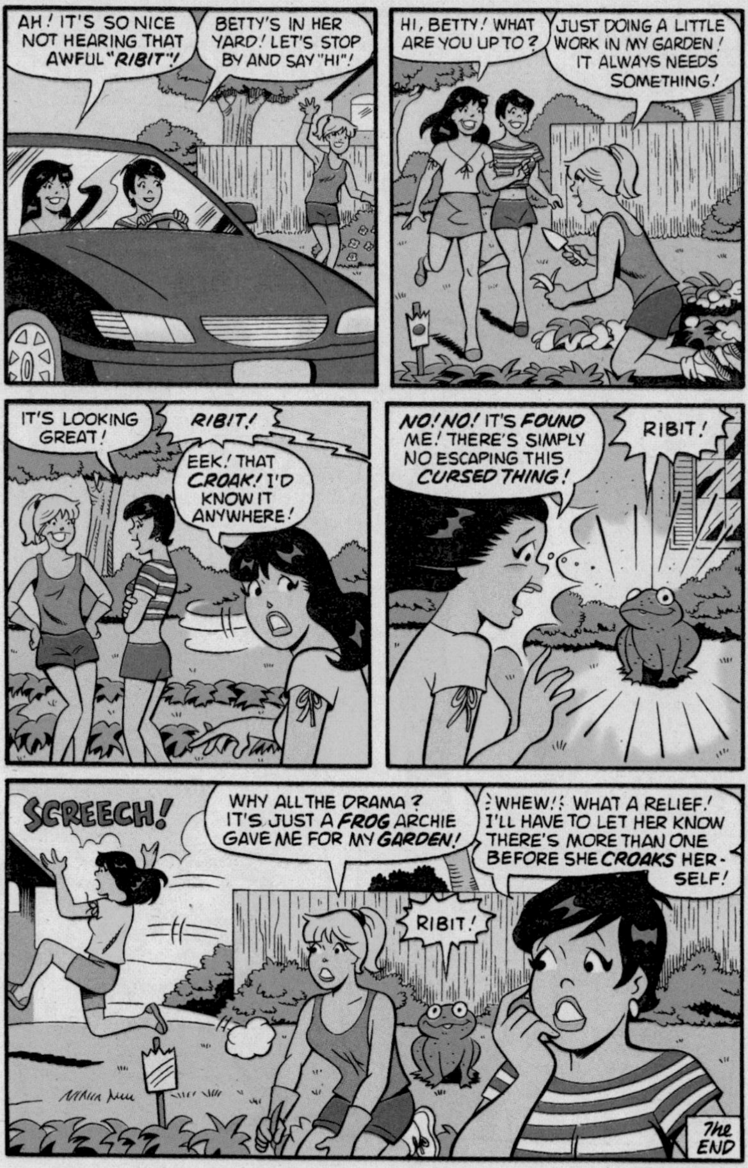
AH! IT'S SO NICE NOT HEARING THAT AWFUL "RIBIT"!
BETTY'S IN HER YARD! LET'S STOP BY AND SAY "HI"!
HI, BETTY! WHAT ARE YOU UP TO?
JUST DOING A LITTLE WORK IN MY GARDEN! IT ALWAYS NEEDS SOMETHING!
IT'S LOOKING GREAT!
RIBIT!
EEK! THAT CROAK! I'D KNOW IT ANYWHERE!
NO! NO! IT'S FOUND ME! THERE'S SIMPLY NO ESCAPING THIS CURSED THING!
RIBIT!
SCREECH!
WHY ALL THE DRAMA? IT'S JUST A FROG ARCHIE GAVE ME FOR MY GARDEN!
WHEW! WHAT A RELIEF! I'LL HAVE TO LET HER KNOW THERE'S MORE THAN ONE BEFORE SHE CROAKS HER-SELF!
RIBIT!
The END

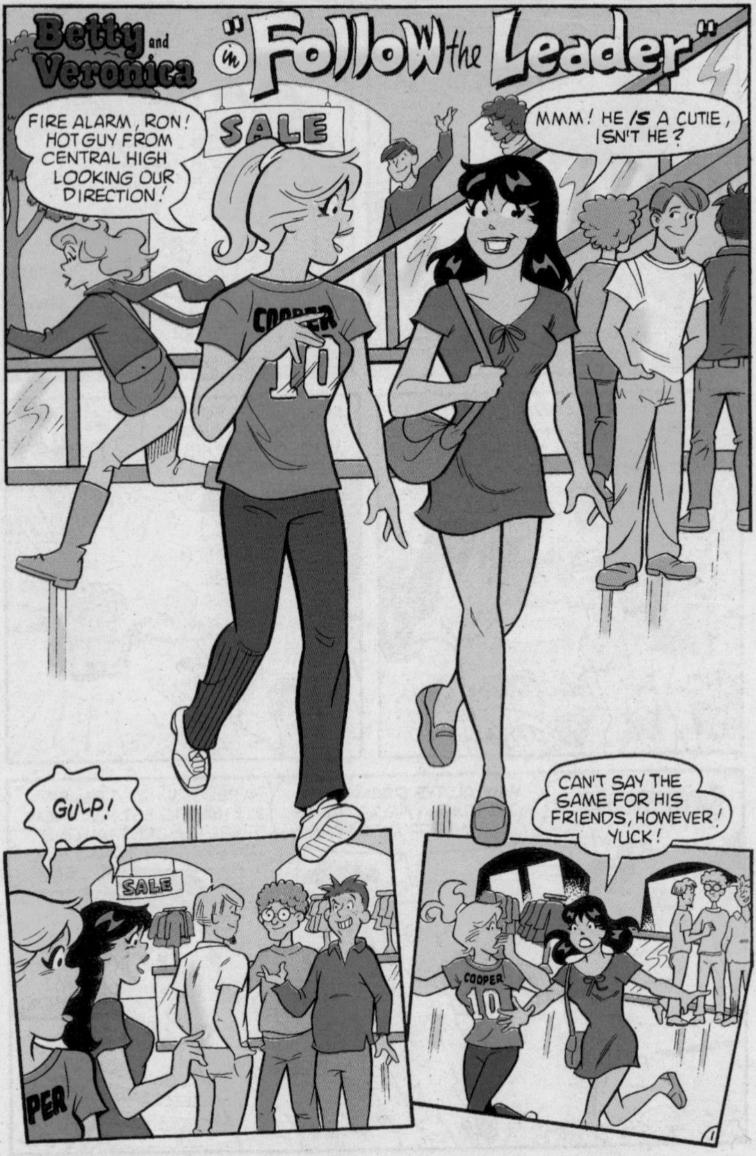
Betty and Veronica
in "Follow the Leader"
SALE
FIRE ALARM, RON! HOTGUY FROM CENTRAL HIGH LOOKING OUR DIRECTION!
MMM! HE IS A CUTIE, ISN'T HE?
COOPER 10
GULP!
SALE
CAN'T SAY THE SAME FOR HIS FRIENDS, HOWEVER! YUCK!
COOPER 10
1

Script: Kathleen Webb / Pencils: Dan Parent / Inks: Rich Koslowski / Letters: Bill Yoshida

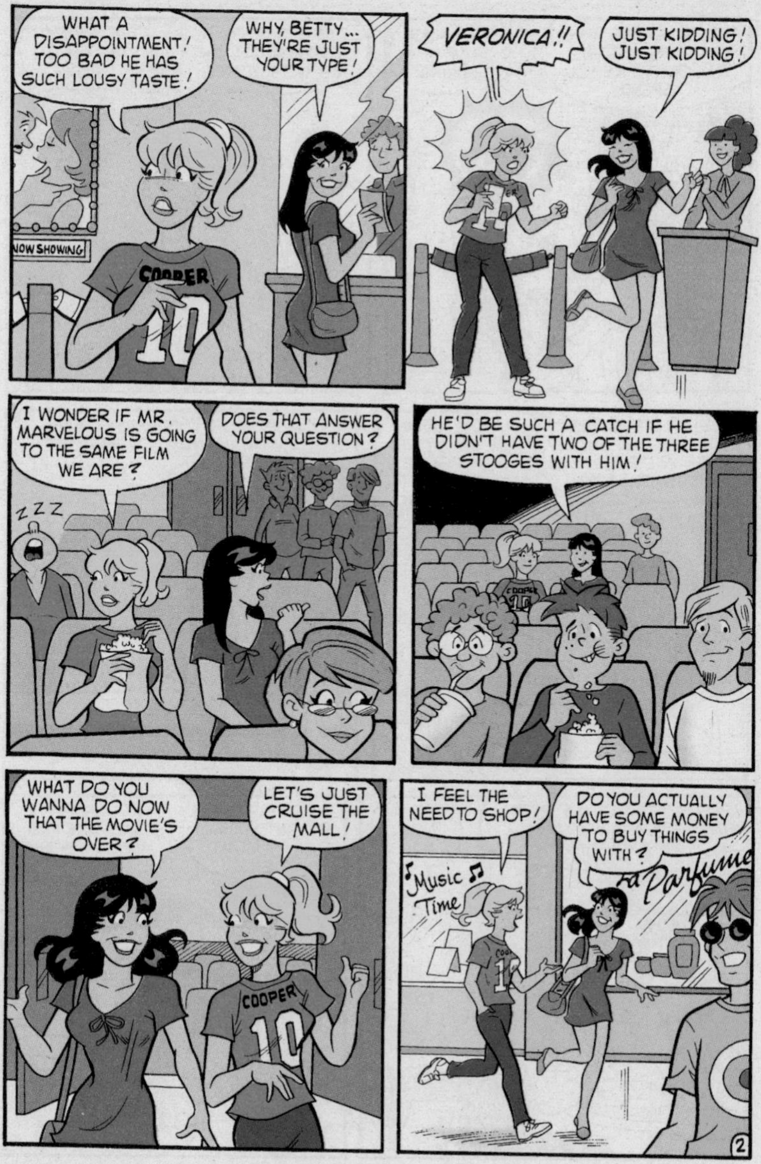
WHAT A DISAPPOINTMENT! TOO BAD HE HAS SUCH LOUSY TASTE!
WHY, BETTY... THEY'RE JUST YOUR TYPE!
NOW SHOWING
COOPER 10
VERONICA!!
JUST KIDDING! JUST KIDDING!
I WONDER IF MR. MARVELOUS IS GOING TO THE SAME FILM WE ARE?
DOES THAT ANSWER YOUR QUESTION?
ZZZ
HE'D BE SUCH A CATCH IF HE DIDN'T HAVE TWO OF THE THREE STOOGES WITH HIM!
WHAT DO YOU WANNA DO NOW THAT THE MOVIE'S OVER?
LET'S JUST CRUISE THE MALL!
COOPER 10
I FEEL THE NEED TO SHOP!
DO YOU ACTUALLY HAVE SOME MONEY TO BUY THINGS WITH?
Music Time
La Parfume
2

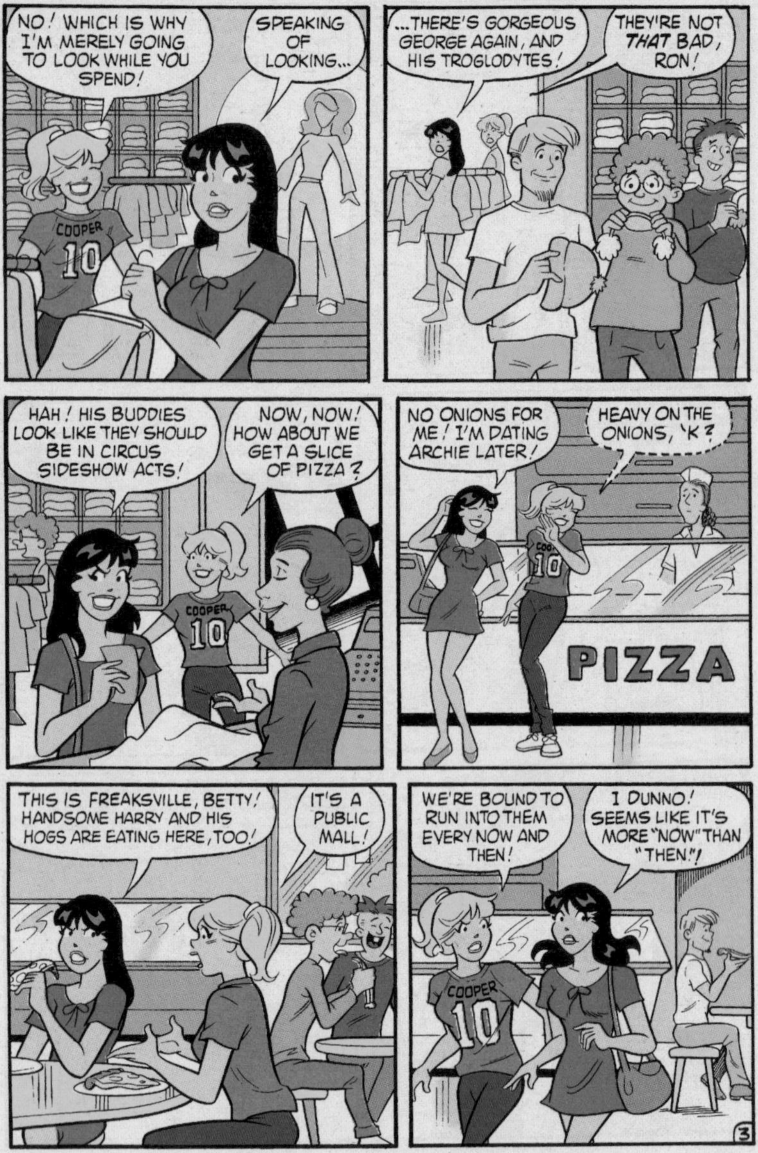
NO! WHICH IS WHY I'M MERELY GOING TO LOOK WHILE YOU SPEND!
SPEAKING OF LOOKING...
COOPER 10
...THERE'S GORGEOUS GEORGE AGAIN, AND HIS TROGLODYTES!
THEY'RE NOT THAT BAD, RON!
HAH! HIS BUDDIES LOOK LIKE THEY SHOULD BE IN CIRCUS SIDESHOW ACTS!
NOW, NOW! HOW ABOUT WE GET A SLICE OF PIZZA?
COOPER 10
NO ONIONS FOR ME! I'M DATING ARCHIE LATER!
HEAVY ON THE ONIONS, 'K?
PIZZA
THIS IS FREAKSVILLE, BETTY! HANDSOME HARRY AND HIS HOGS ARE EATING HERE, TOO!
IT'S A PUBLIC MALL!
WE'RE BOUND TO RUN INTO THEM EVERY NOW AND THEN!
I DUNNO! SEEMS LIKE IT'S MORE "NOW" THAN "THEN."!
COOPER 10
3

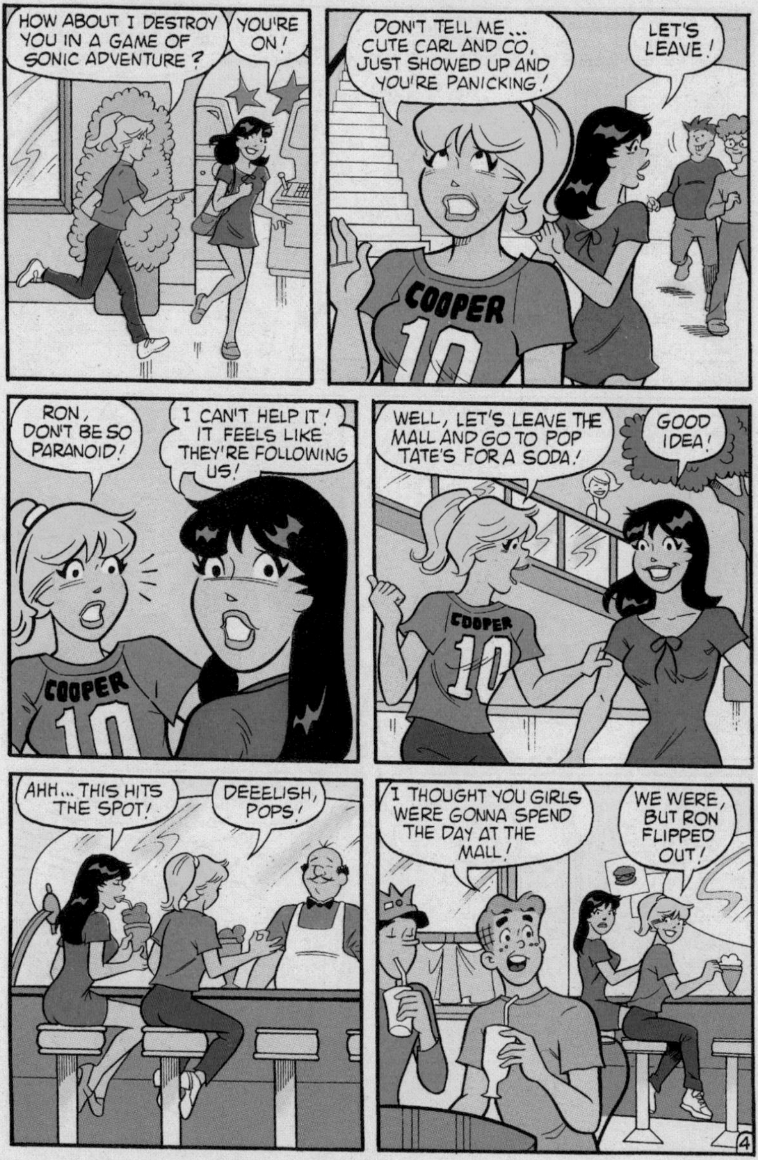
HOW ABOUT I DESTROY YOU IN A GAME OF SONIC ADVENTURE ?
YOU'RE ON!
DON'T TELL ME... CUTE CARL AND CO, JUST SHOWED UP AND YOU'RE PANICKING!
LET'S LEAVE!
COOPER 10
RON, DON'T BE SO PARANOID!
I CAN'T HELP IT! IT FEELS LIKE THEY'RE FOLLOWING US!
COOPER 10
WELL, LET'S LEAVE THE MALL AND GO TO POP TATE'S FOR A SODA!
GOOD IDEA!
COOPER 10
AHH... THIS HITS THE SPOT!
DEEELISH, POPS!
I THOUGHT YOU GIRLS WERE GONNA SPEND THE DAY AT THE MALL!
WE WERE, BUT RON FLIPPED OUT!
4

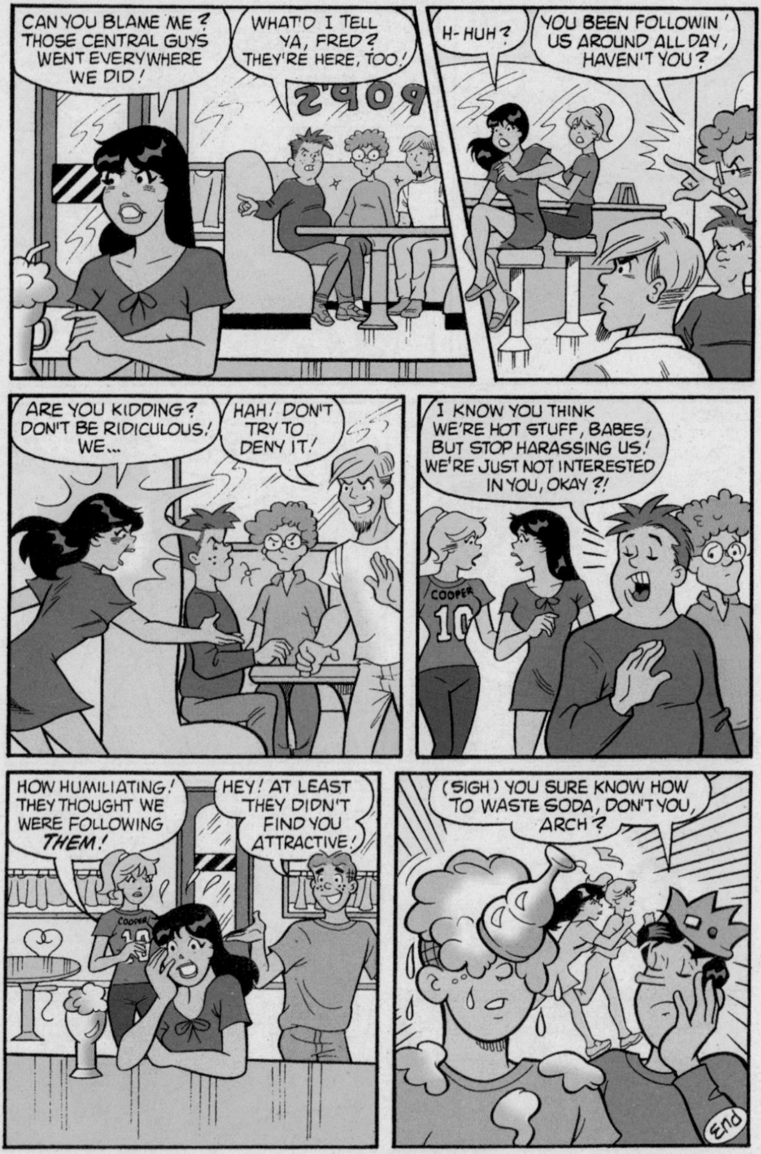
CAN YOU BLAME ME? THOSE CENTRAL GUYS WENT EVERYWHERE WE DID!
WHAT'D I TELL YA, FRED? THEY'RE HERE, TOO!
POP'S
H-HUH?
YOU BEEN FOLLOWIN' US AROUND ALL DAY, HAVEN'T YOU?
ARE YOU KIDDING? DON'T BE RIDICULOUS! WE...
HAH! DON'T TRY TO DENY IT!
I KNOW YOU THINK WE'RE HOT STUFF, BABES, BUT STOP HARASSING US! WE'RE JUST NOT INTERESTED IN YOU, OKAY?!
COOPER 10
HOW HUMILIATING! THEY THOUGHT WE WERE FOLLOWING *THEM*!
HEY! AT LEAST THEY DIDN'T FIND YOU ATTRACTIVE!
(SIGH) YOU SURE KNOW HOW TO WASTE SODA, DON'T YOU, ARCH?
End

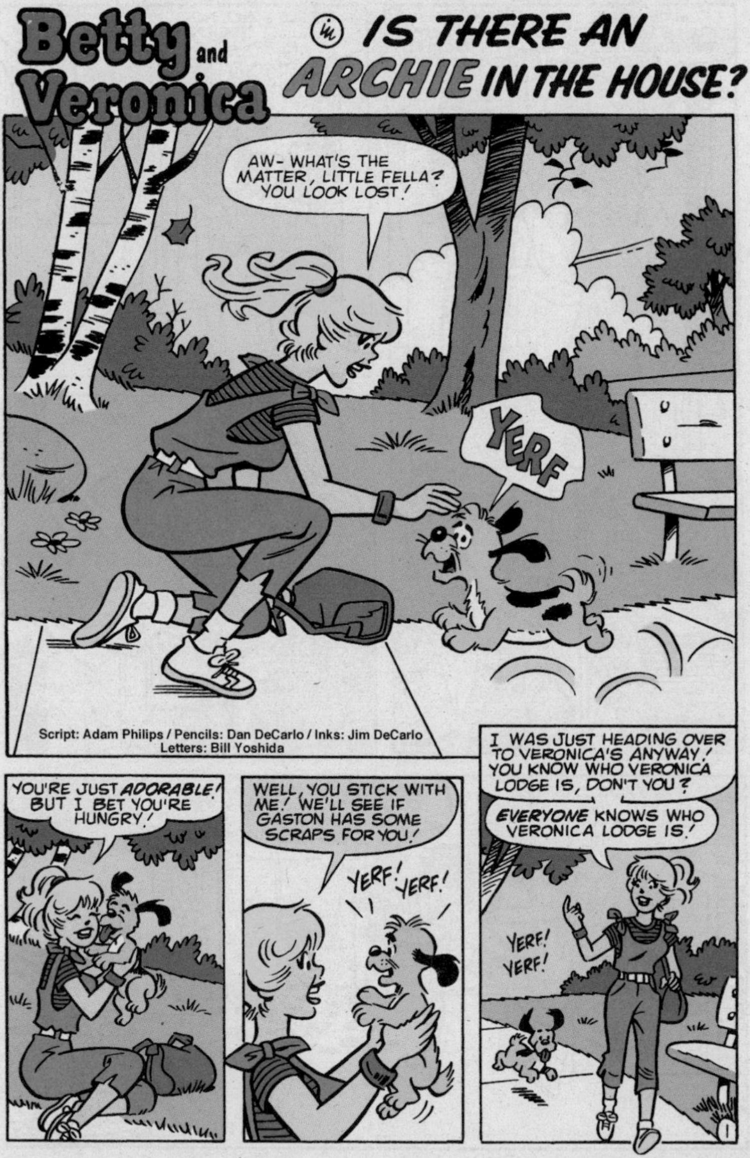
Betty and Veronica
IS THERE AN ARCHIE IN THE HOUSE?
AW- WHAT'S THE MATTER, LITTLE FELLA? YOU LOOK LOST!
YERF
Script: Adam Philips / Pencils: Dan DeCarlo / Inks: Jim DeCarlo
Letters: Bill Yoshida
YOU'RE JUST ADORABLE! BUT I BET YOU'RE HUNGRY!
WELL, YOU STICK WITH ME! WE'LL SEE IF GASTON HAS SOME SCRAPS FOR YOU!
YERF! YERF!
I WAS JUST HEADING OVER TO VERONICA'S ANYWAY! YOU KNOW WHO VERONICA LODGE IS, DON'T YOU?
EVERYONE KNOWS WHO VERONICA LODGE IS!
YERF! YERF!
1

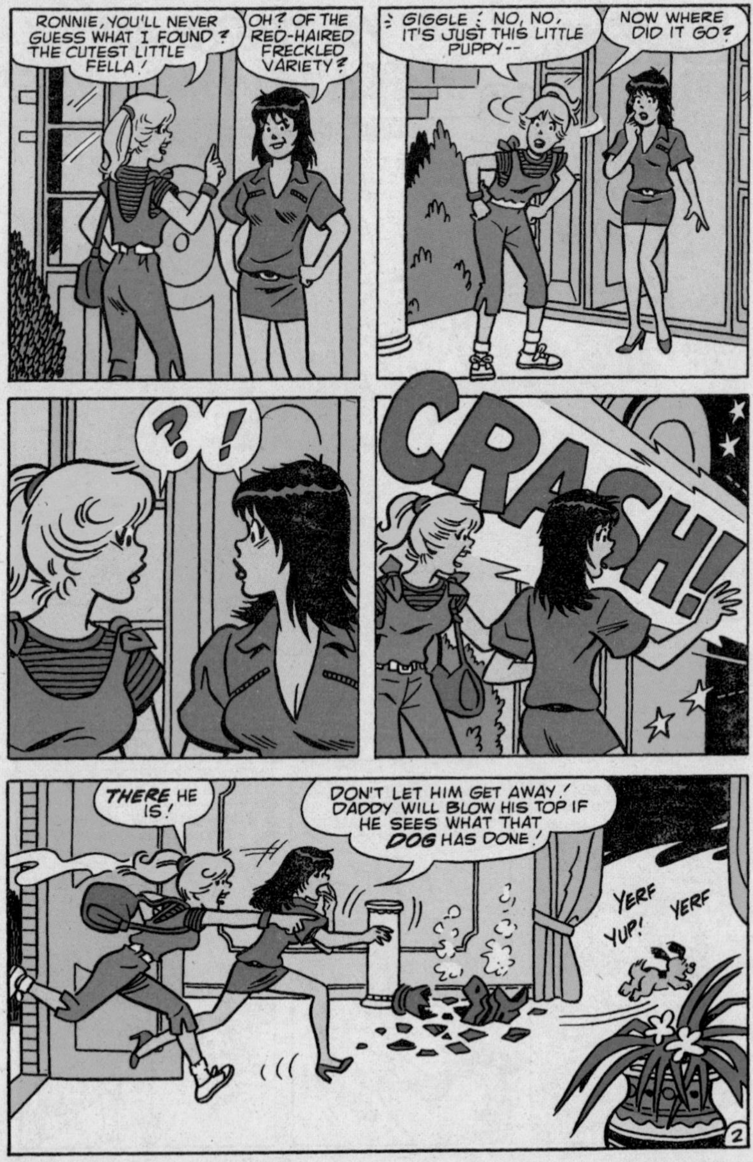
RONNIE, YOU'LL NEVER GUESS WHAT I FOUND! THE CUTEST LITTLE FELLA!
OH? OF THE RED-HAIRED FRECKLED VARIETY?
GIGGLE! NO, NO, IT'S JUST THIS LITTLE PUPPY--
NOW WHERE DID IT GO?
?!
CRASH!
THERE HE IS!
DON'T LET HIM GET AWAY! DADDY WILL BLOW HIS TOP IF HE SEES WHAT THAT DOG HAS DONE!
YERF
YERF
YUP!
2

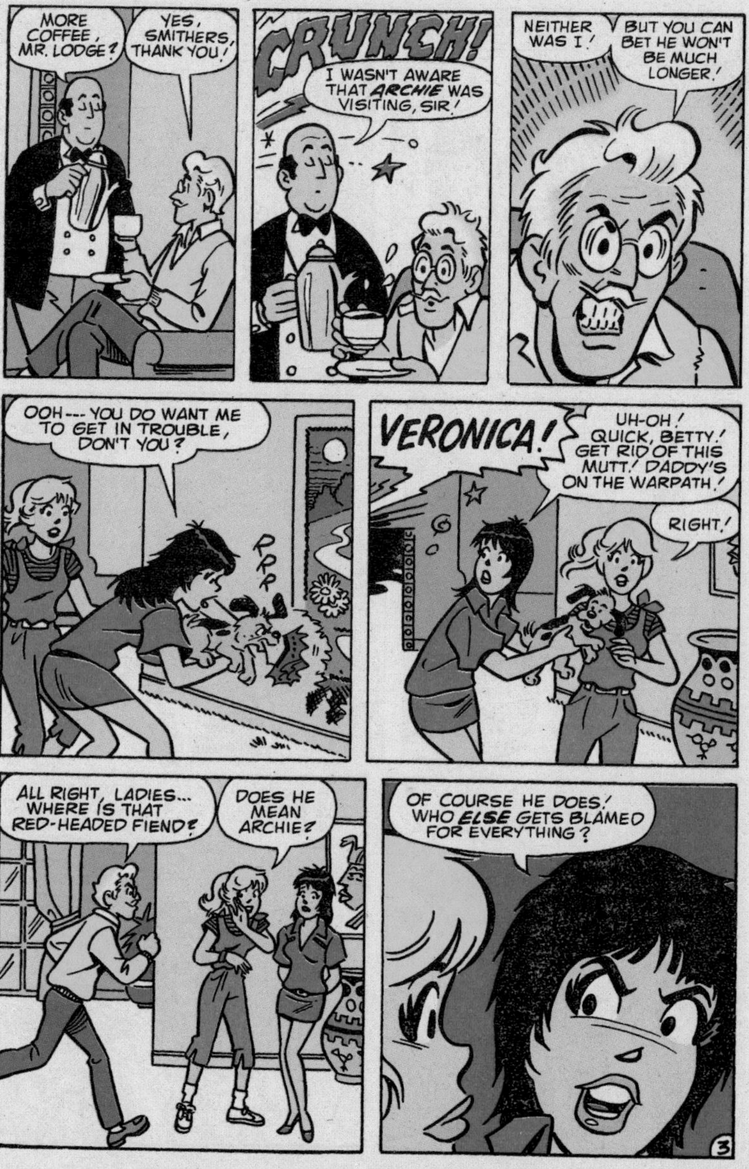
MORE COFFEE, MR. LODGE?
YES, SMITHERS, THANK YOU!
CRUNCH!
I WASN'T AWARE THAT ARCHIE WAS VISITING, SIR!
NEITHER WAS I!
BUT YOU CAN BET HE WON'T BE MUCH LONGER!
OOH--- YOU DO WANT ME TO GET IN TROUBLE, DON'T YOU?
RRR
VERONICA!
UH-OH! QUICK, BETTY! GET RID OF THIS MUTT! DADDY'S ON THE WARPATH!
RIGHT!
ALL RIGHT, LADIES... WHERE IS THAT RED-HEADED FIEND?
DOES HE MEAN ARCHIE?
OF COURSE HE DOES! WHO ELSE GETS BLAMED FOR EVERYTHING?
3

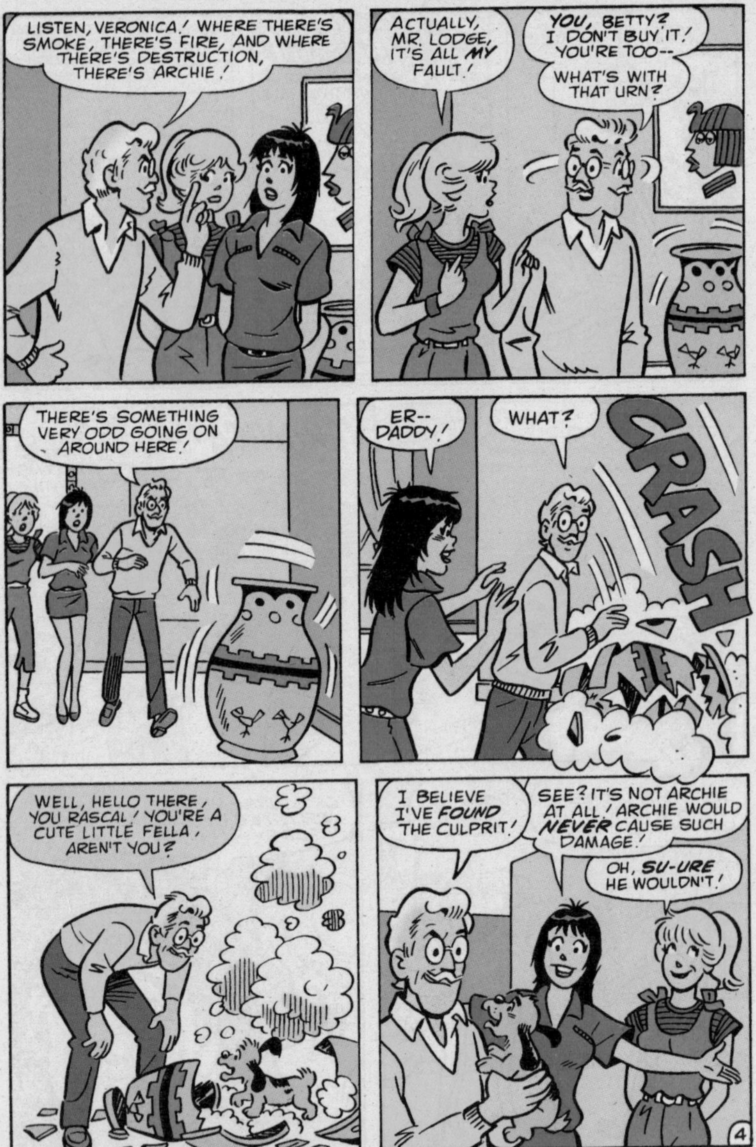

LISTEN, VERONICA! WHERE THERE'S SMOKE, THERE'S FIRE, AND WHERE THERE'S DESTRUCTION, THERE'S ARCHIE!
ACTUALLY, MR. LODGE, IT'S ALL MY FAULT!
YOU, BETTY? I DON'T BUY IT! YOU'RE TOO--
WHAT'S WITH THAT URN?
THERE'S SOMETHING VERY ODD GOING ON AROUND HERE!
ER-- DADDY!
WHAT?
CRASH
WELL, HELLO THERE, YOU RASCAL! YOU'RE A CUTE LITTLE FELLA, AREN'T YOU?
I BELIEVE I'VE FOUND THE CULPRIT!
SEE? IT'S NOT ARCHIE AT ALL! ARCHIE WOULD NEVER CAUSE SUCH DAMAGE!
OH, SU-URE HE WOULDN'T!
4

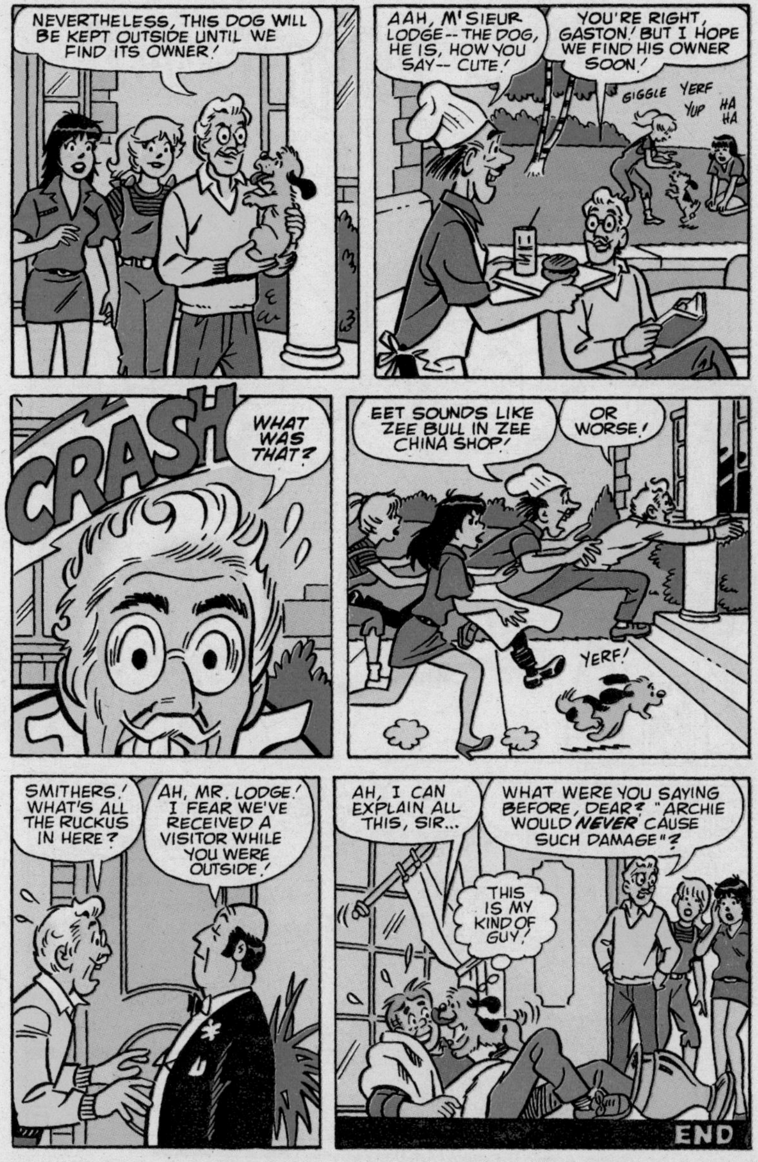
NEVERTHELESS, THIS DOG WILL BE KEPT OUTSIDE UNTIL WE FIND ITS OWNER!
AAH, M'SIEUR LODGE -- THE DOG, HE IS, HOW YOU SAY -- CUTE!
YOU'RE RIGHT, GASTON! BUT I HOPE WE FIND HIS OWNER SOON!
GIGGLE
YERF
YUP
HA HA
CRASH
WHAT WAS THAT?
EET SOUNDS LIKE ZEE BULL IN ZEE CHINA SHOP!
OR WORSE!
YERF!
SMITHERS! WHAT'S ALL THE RUCKUS IN HERE?
AH, MR. LODGE! I FEAR WE'VE RECEIVED A VISITOR WHILE YOU WERE OUTSIDE!
AH, I CAN EXPLAIN ALL THIS, SIR...
WHAT WERE YOU SAYING BEFORE, DEAR? "ARCHIE WOULD NEVER CAUSE SUCH DAMAGE"?
THIS IS MY KIND OF GUY!
END

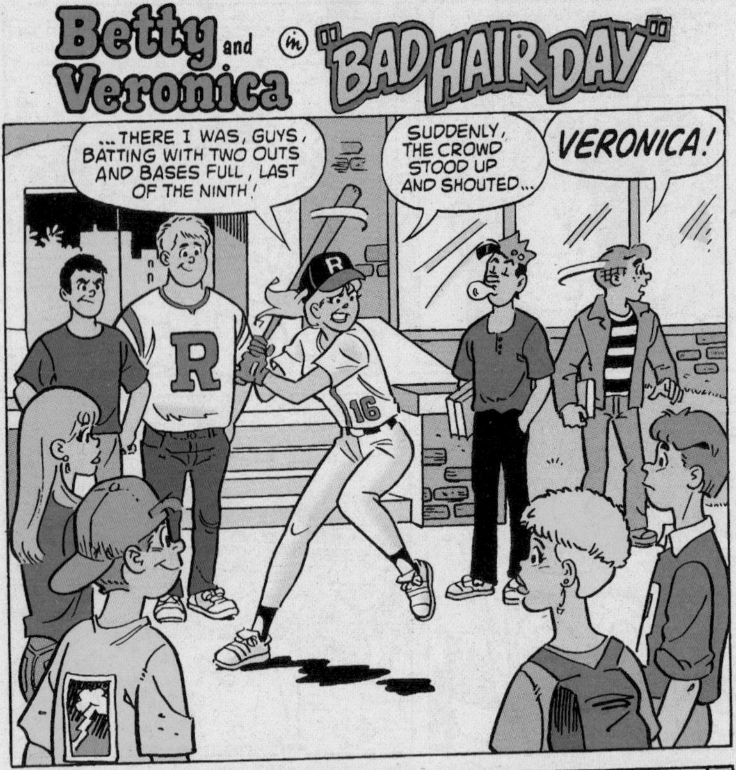
Betty and Veronica
in
"BAD HAIR DAY"
...THERE I WAS, GUYS, BATTING WITH TWO OUTS AND BASES FULL, LAST OF THE NINTH!
SUDDENLY, THE CROWD STOOD UP AND SHOUTED...
VERONICA!

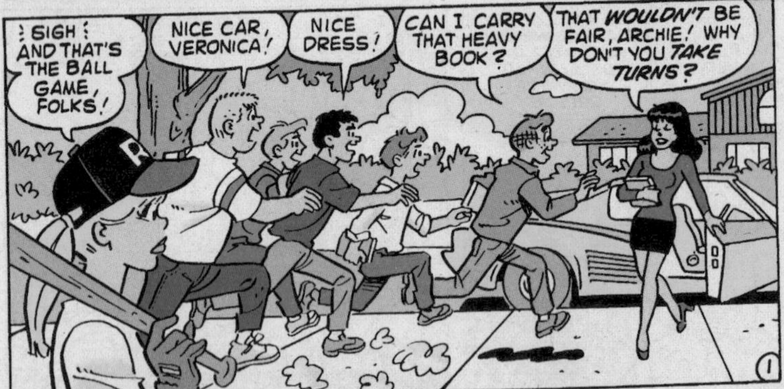
SIGH AND THAT'S THE BALL GAME, FOLKS!
NICE CAR, VERONICA!
NICE DRESS!
CAN I CARRY THAT HEAVY BOOK?
THAT WOULDN'T BE FAIR, ARCHIE! WHY DON'T YOU TAKE TURNS?
1

Script: Angelo DeCesare / Art: Dan DeCarlo / Letters: Bill Yoshida

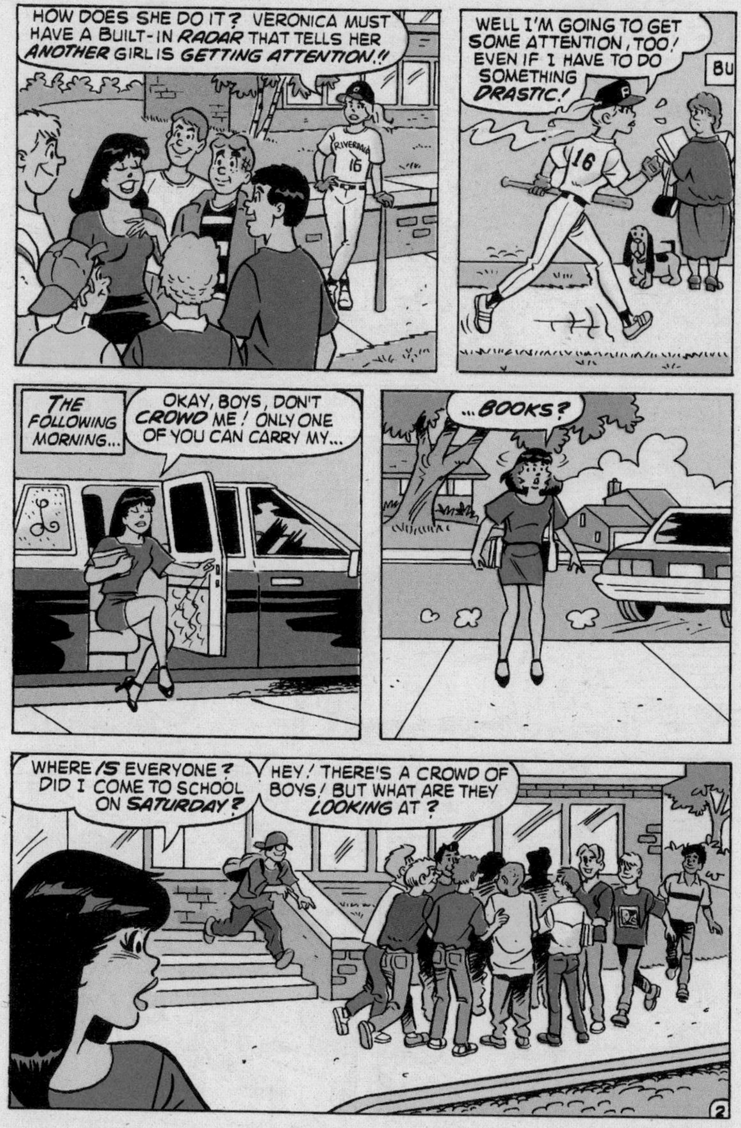
HOW DOES SHE DO IT? VERONICA MUST HAVE A BUILT-IN RADAR THAT TELLS HER ANOTHER GIRL IS GETTING ATTENTION!!
RIVERDALE 16
WELL I'M GOING TO GET SOME ATTENTION, TOO! EVEN IF I HAVE TO DO SOMETHING DRASTIC!
BU
16
THE FOLLOWING MORNING...
OKAY, BOYS, DON'T CROWD ME! ONLY ONE OF YOU CAN CARRY MY...
...BOOKS?
WHERE IS EVERYONE? DID I COME TO SCHOOL ON SATURDAY?
HEY! THERE'S A CROWD OF BOYS! BUT WHAT ARE THEY LOOKING AT?
2

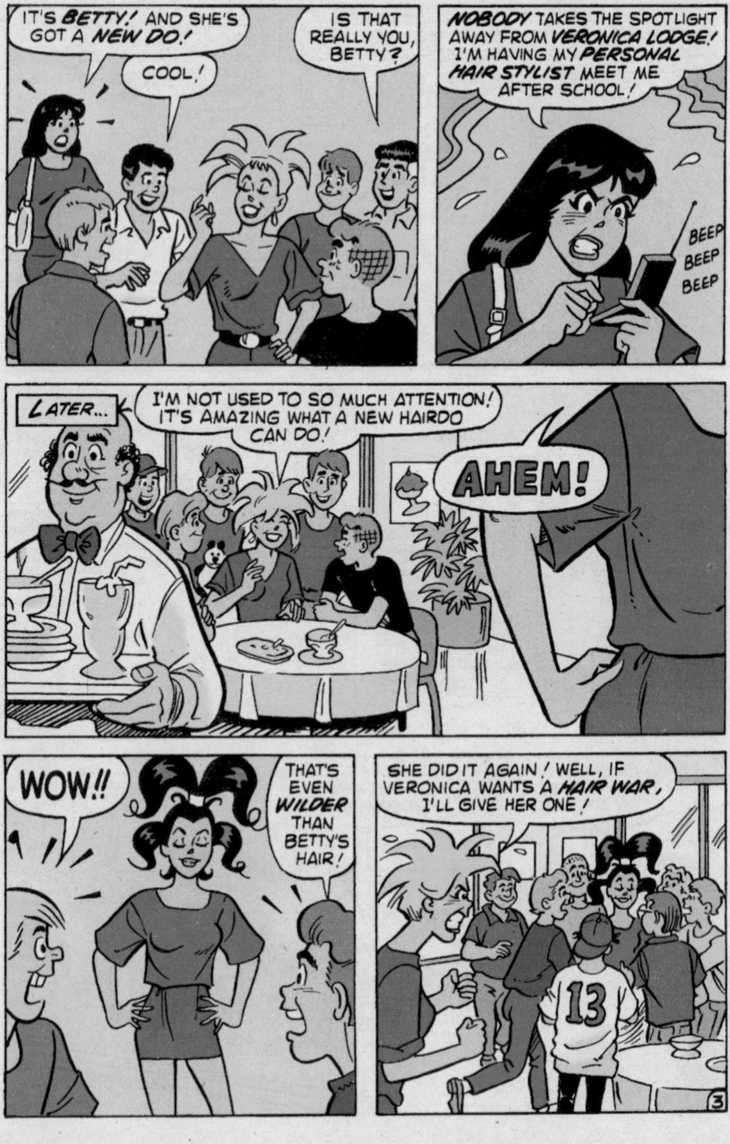
IT'S BETTY! AND SHE'S GOT A NEW DO!
COOL!
IS THAT REALLY YOU, BETTY?
NOBODY TAKES THE SPOTLIGHT AWAY FROM VERONICA LODGE! I'M HAVING MY PERSONAL HAIR STYLIST MEET ME AFTER SCHOOL!
BEEP BEEP BEEP
LATER...
I'M NOT USED TO SO MUCH ATTENTION! IT'S AMAZING WHAT A NEW HAIRDO CAN DO!
AHEM!
WOW!!
THAT'S EVEN WILDER THAN BETTY'S HAIR!
SHE DID IT AGAIN! WELL, IF VERONICA WANTS A HAIR WAR, I'LL GIVE HER ONE!
13
3

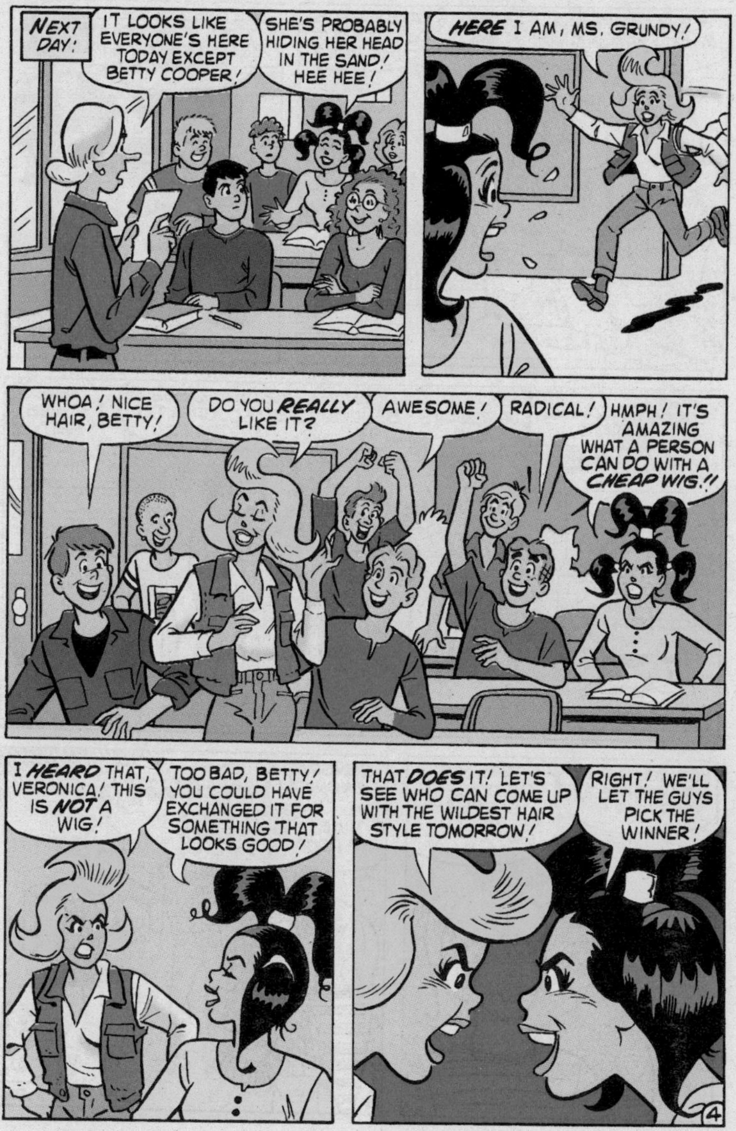
NEXT DAY:
IT LOOKS LIKE EVERYONE'S HERE TODAY EXCEPT BETTY COOPER!
SHE'S PROBABLY HIDING HER HEAD IN THE SAND! HEE HEE!
HERE I AM, MS. GRUNDY!
WHOA! NICE HAIR, BETTY!
DO YOU REALLY LIKE IT?
AWESOME!
RADICAL!
HMPH! IT'S AMAZING WHAT A PERSON CAN DO WITH A CHEAP WIG!!
I HEARD THAT, VERONICA! THIS IS NOT A WIG!
TOO BAD, BETTY! YOU COULD HAVE EXCHANGED IT FOR SOMETHING THAT LOOKS GOOD!
THAT DOES IT! LET'S SEE WHO CAN COME UP WITH THE WILDEST HAIR STYLE TOMORROW!
RIGHT! WE'LL LET THE GUYS PICK THE WINNER!
4

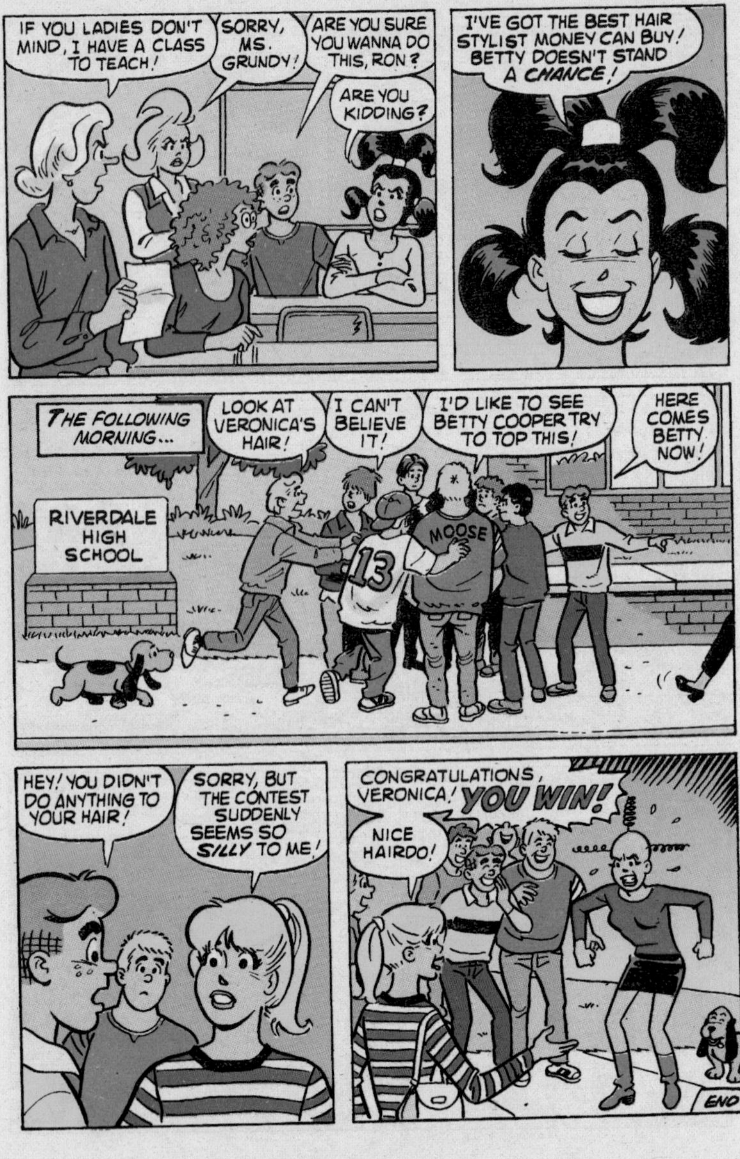
IF YOU LADIES DON'T MIND, I HAVE A CLASS TO TEACH!
SORRY, MS. GRUNDY!
ARE YOU SURE YOU WANNA DO THIS, RON?
ARE YOU KIDDING?
I'VE GOT THE BEST HAIR STYLIST MONEY CAN BUY! BETTY DOESN'T STAND A CHANCE!
THE FOLLOWING MORNING...
LOOK AT VERONICA'S HAIR!
I CAN'T BELIEVE IT!
I'D LIKE TO SEE BETTY COOPER TRY TO TOP THIS!
HERE COMES BETTY NOW!
RIVERDALE HIGH SCHOOL
MOOSE
13
HEY! YOU DIDN'T DO ANYTHING TO YOUR HAIR!
SORRY, BUT THE CONTEST SUDDENLY SEEMS SO SILLY TO ME!
CONGRATULATIONS, VERONICA! YOU WIN!
NICE HAIRDO!
END

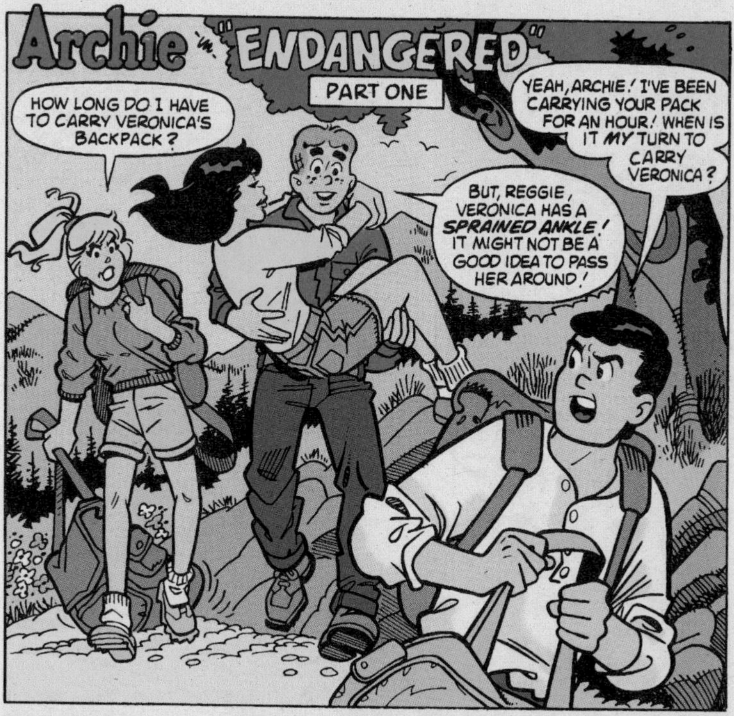
Archie "ENDANGERED"
PART ONE
HOW LONG DO I HAVE TO CARRY VERONICA'S BACKPACK?
YEAH, ARCHIE! I'VE BEEN CARRYING YOUR PACK FOR AN HOUR! WHEN IS IT MY TURN TO CARRY VERONICA?
BUT, REGGIE, VERONICA HAS A SPRAINED ANKLE! IT MIGHT NOT BE A GOOD IDEA TO PASS HER AROUND!

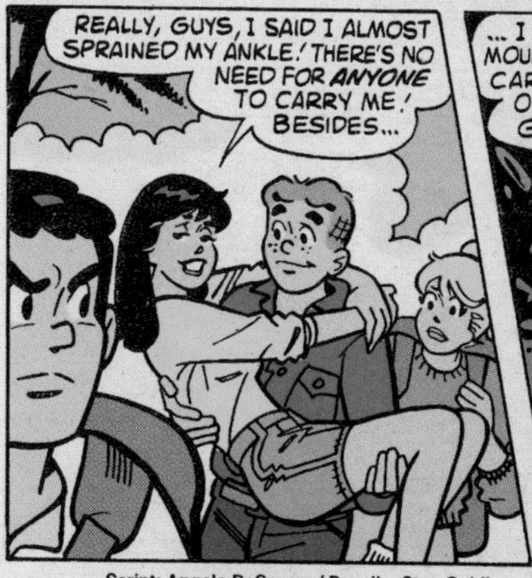
REALLY, GUYS, I SAID I ALMOST SPRAINED MY ANKLE! THERE'S NO NEED FOR ANYONE TO CARRY ME! BESIDES...

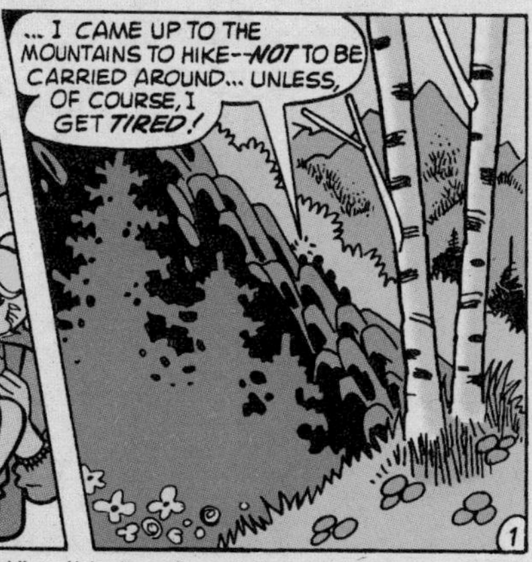
... I CAME UP TO THE MOUNTAINS TO HIKE--NOT TO BE CARRIED AROUND... UNLESS, OF COURSE, I GET TIRED!
1

Script: Angelo DeCesare / Pencils: Stan Goldberg / Inks: Henry Scarpelli / Letters: Bill Yoshida

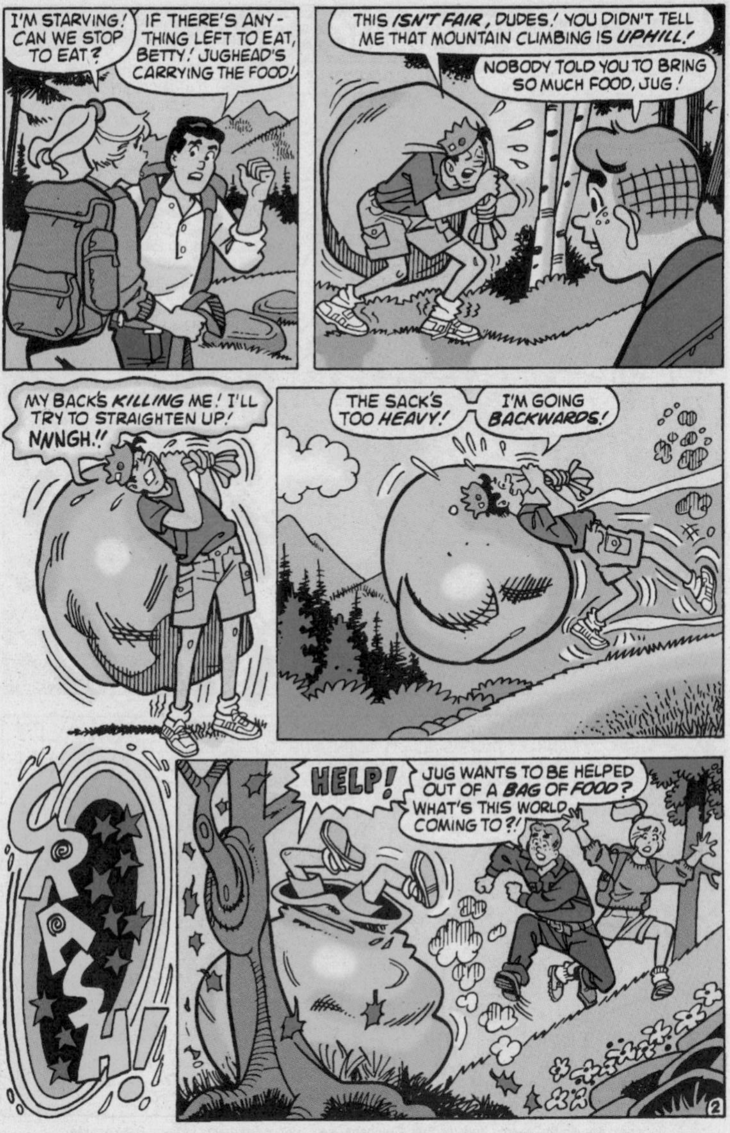
I'M STARVING! CAN WE STOP TO EAT?
IF THERE'S ANYTHING LEFT TO EAT, BETTY! JUGHEAD'S CARRYING THE FOOD!
THIS *ISN'T FAIR*, DUDES! YOU DIDN'T TELL ME THAT MOUNTAIN CLIMBING IS *UPHILL!*
NOBODY TOLD YOU TO BRING SO MUCH FOOD, JUG!
MY BACK'S *KILLING* ME! I'LL TRY TO STRAIGHTEN UP! NNNGH!!
THE SACK'S TOO *HEAVY!*
I'M GOING *BACKWARDS!*
CRASH!
HELP!
JUG WANTS TO BE HELPED OUT OF A *BAG* OF *FOOD?* WHAT'S THIS WORLD COMING TO?!
2

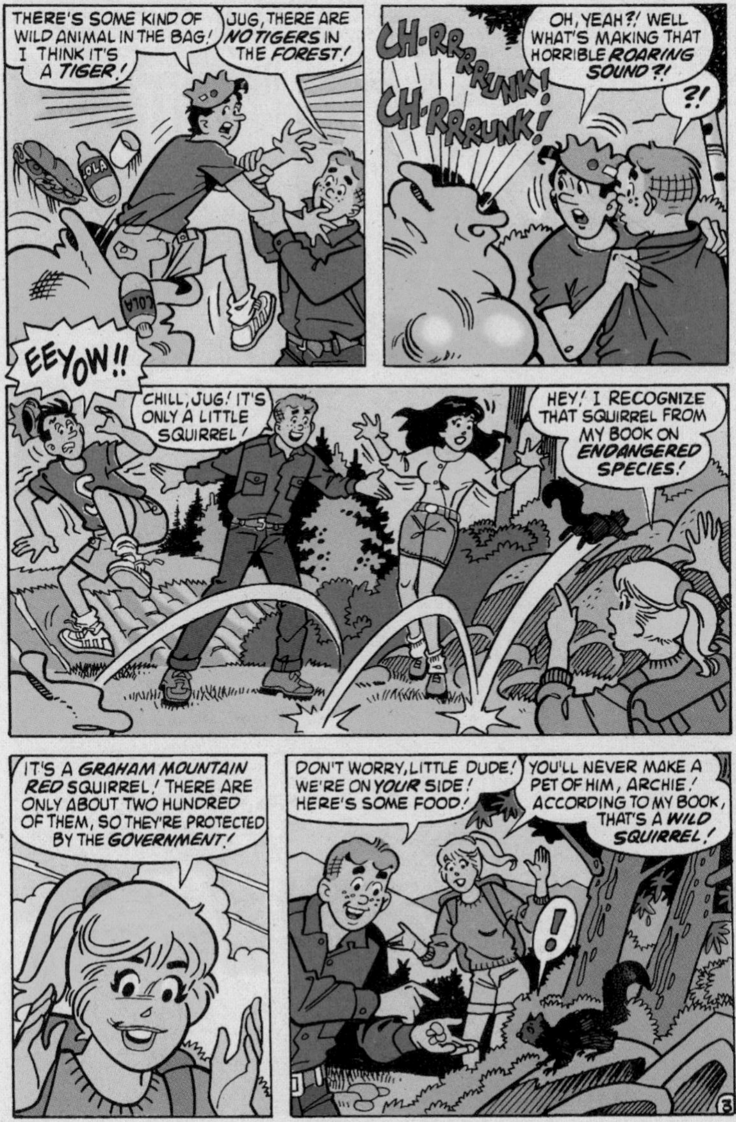

THERE'S SOME KIND OF WILD ANIMAL IN THE BAG! I THINK IT'S A TIGER!
JUG, THERE ARE NO TIGERS IN THE FOREST!
LOLA
LOLA
EEYOW!!
CH-RRRRRUNK!
CH-RRRRUNK!
OH, YEAH?! WELL WHAT'S MAKING THAT HORRIBLE ROARING SOUND?!
?!
CHILL, JUG! IT'S ONLY A LITTLE SQUIRREL!
HEY! I RECOGNIZE THAT SQUIRREL FROM MY BOOK ON ENDANGERED SPECIES!
IT'S A GRAHAM MOUNTAIN RED SQUIRREL! THERE ARE ONLY ABOUT TWO HUNDRED OF THEM, SO THEY'RE PROTECTED BY THE GOVERNMENT!
DON'T WORRY, LITTLE DUDE! WE'RE ON YOUR SIDE! HERE'S SOME FOOD!
YOU'LL NEVER MAKE A PET OF HIM, ARCHIE! ACCORDING TO MY BOOK, THAT'S A WILD SQUIRREL!
!
3

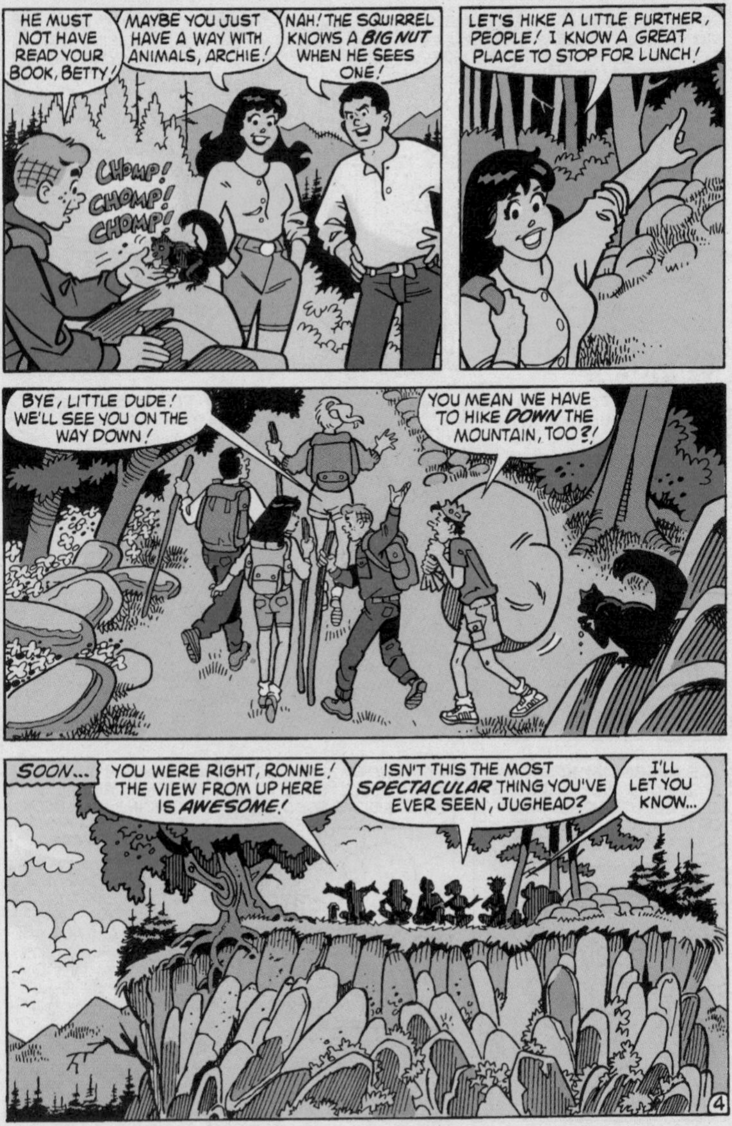
HE MUST NOT HAVE READ YOUR BOOK, BETTY!
MAYBE YOU JUST HAVE A WAY WITH ANIMALS, ARCHIE!
NAH! THE SQUIRREL KNOWS A BIG NUT WHEN HE SEES ONE!
CHOMP! CHOMP! CHOMP!
LET'S HIKE A LITTLE FURTHER, PEOPLE! I KNOW A GREAT PLACE TO STOP FOR LUNCH!
BYE, LITTLE DUDE! WE'LL SEE YOU ON THE WAY DOWN!
YOU MEAN WE HAVE TO HIKE DOWN THE MOUNTAIN, TOO?!
SOON...
YOU WERE RIGHT, RONNIE! THE VIEW FROM UP HERE IS AWESOME!
ISN'T THIS THE MOST SPECTACULAR THING YOU'VE EVER SEEN, JUGHEAD?
I'LL LET YOU KNOW...
4

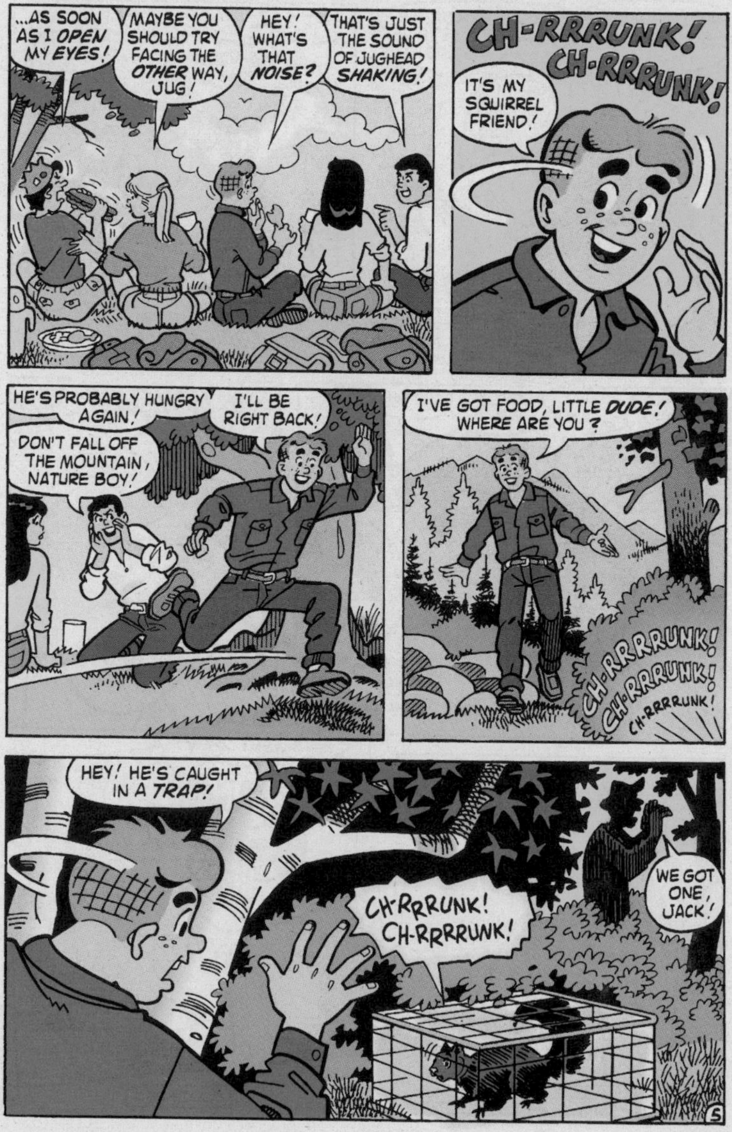
...AS SOON AS I OPEN MY EYES!
MAYBE YOU SHOULD TRY FACING THE OTHER WAY, JUG!
HEY! WHAT'S THAT NOISE?
THAT'S JUST THE SOUND OF JUGHEAD SHAKING!
CH-RRRUNK! CH-RRRUNK!
IT'S MY SQUIRREL FRIEND!
HE'S PROBABLY HUNGRY AGAIN!
I'LL BE RIGHT BACK!
DON'T FALL OFF THE MOUNTAIN, NATURE BOY!
I'VE GOT FOOD, LITTLE DUDE! WHERE ARE YOU?
CH-RRRRUNK! CH-RRRRUNK! CH-RRRRUNK!
HEY! HE'S CAUGHT IN A TRAP!
CH-RRRUNK! CH-RRRRUNK!
WE GOT ONE, JACK!
5

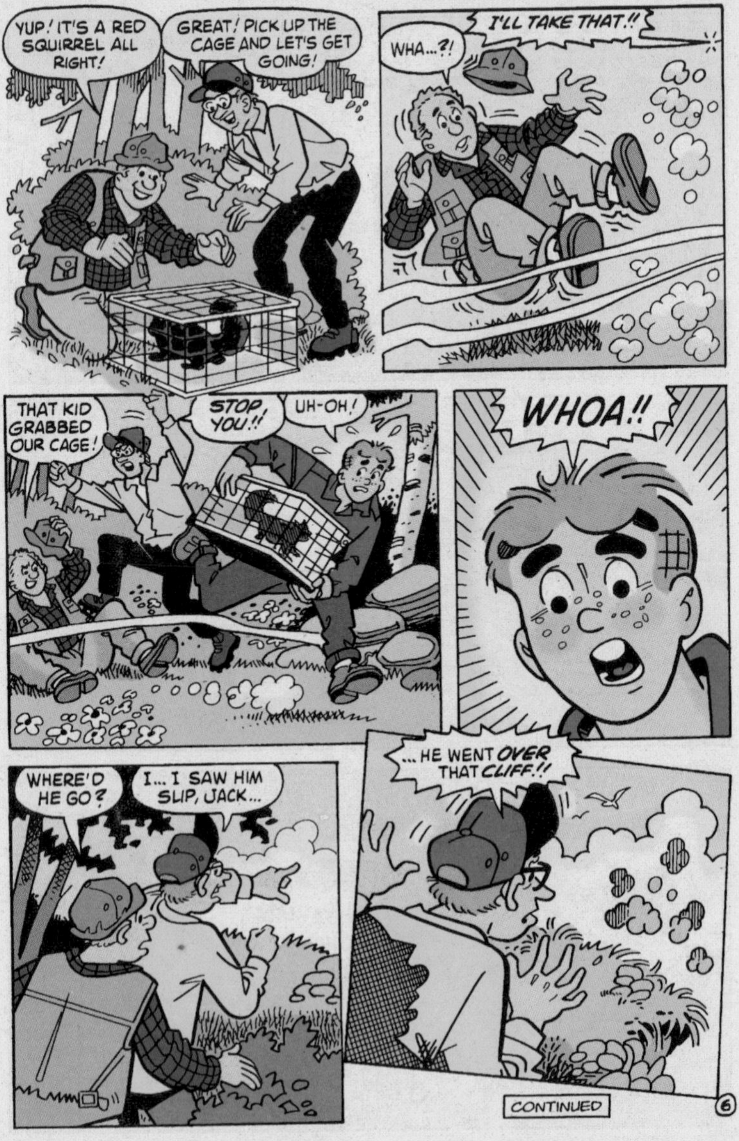
YUP! IT'S A RED SQUIRREL ALL RIGHT!
GREAT! PICK UP THE CAGE AND LET'S GET GOING!
I'LL TAKE THAT!!
WHA...?!
THAT KID GRABBED OUR CAGE!
STOP, YOU!!
UH-OH!
WHOA!!
WHERE'D HE GO?
I... I SAW HIM SLIP, JACK...
... HE WENT OVER THAT CLIFF!!
CONTINUED
6

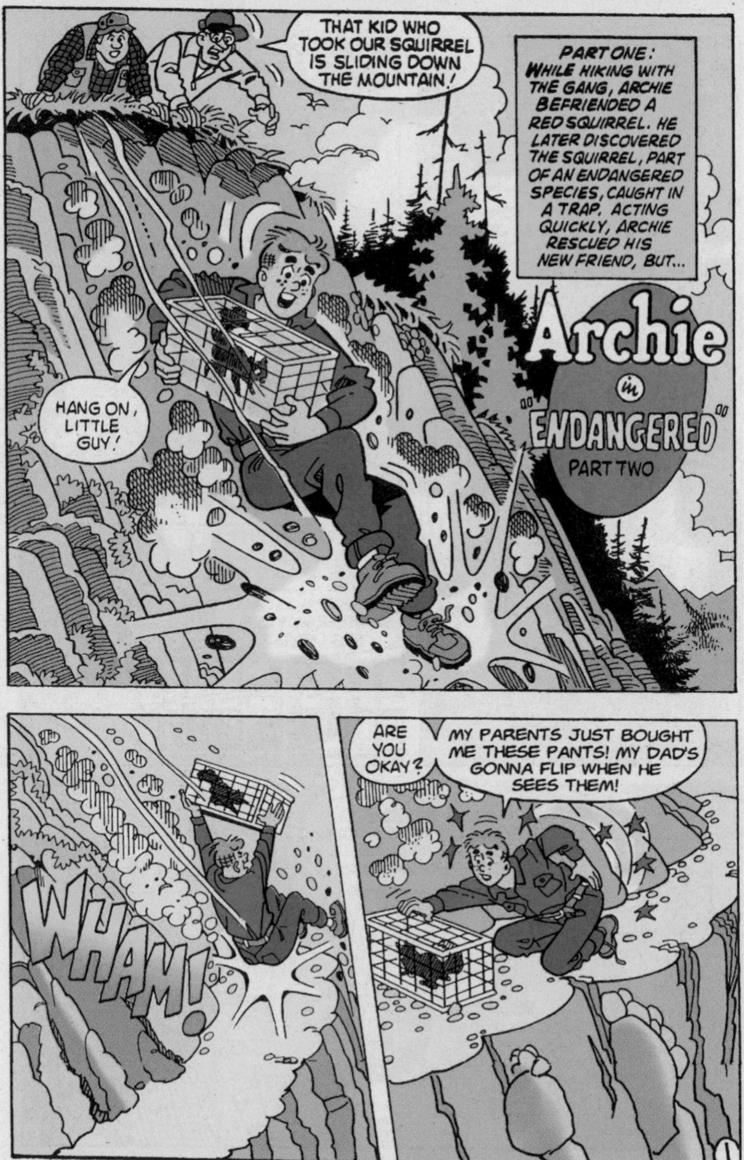
THAT KID WHO TOOK OUR SQUIRREL IS SLIDING DOWN THE MOUNTAIN!
PART ONE: WHILE HIKING WITH THE GANG, ARCHIE BEFRIENDED A RED SQUIRREL. HE LATER DISCOVERED THE SQUIRREL, PART OF AN ENDANGERED SPECIES, CAUGHT IN A TRAP. ACTING QUICKLY, ARCHIE RESCUED HIS NEW FRIEND, BUT...
Archie in "ENDANGERED" PART TWO
HANG ON, LITTLE GUY!
WHAM!
ARE YOU OKAY?
MY PARENTS JUST BOUGHT ME THESE PANTS! MY DAD'S GONNA FLIP WHEN HE SEES THEM!

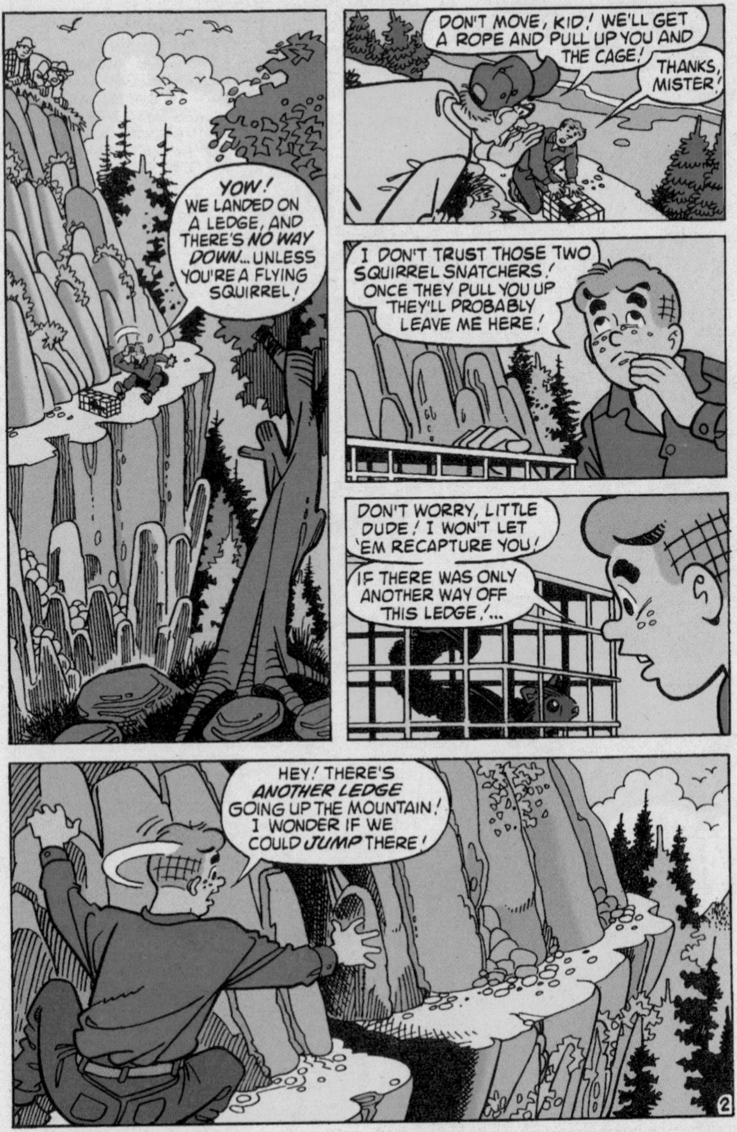

YOW! WE LANDED ON A LEDGE, AND THERE'S NO WAY DOWN... UNLESS YOU'RE A FLYING SQUIRREL!
DON'T MOVE, KID! WE'LL GET A ROPE AND PULL UP YOU AND THE CAGE!
THANKS, MISTER!
I DON'T TRUST THOSE TWO SQUIRREL SNATCHERS! ONCE THEY PULL YOU UP THEY'LL PROBABLY LEAVE ME HERE!
DON'T WORRY, LITTLE DUDE! I WON'T LET 'EM RECAPTURE YOU!
IF THERE WAS ONLY ANOTHER WAY OFF THIS LEDGE!...
HEY! THERE'S ANOTHER LEDGE GOING UP THE MOUNTAIN! I WONDER IF WE COULD JUMP THERE!
2

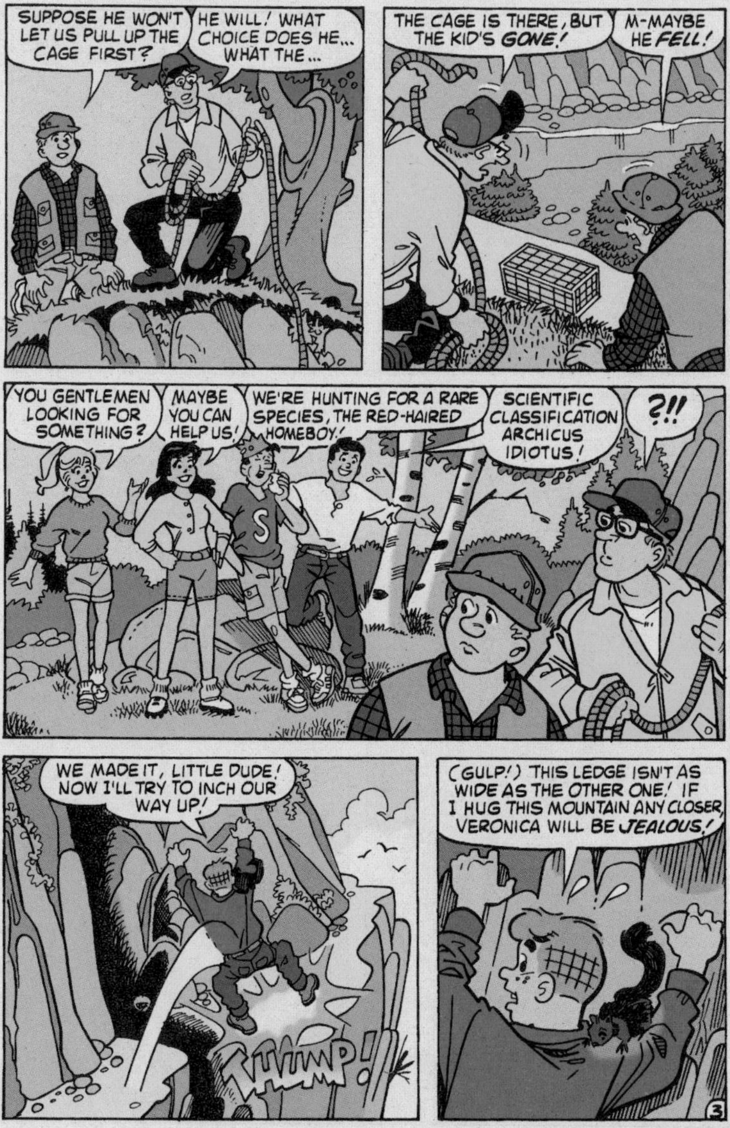

SUPPOSE HE WON'T LET US PULL UP THE CAGE FIRST?
HE WILL! WHAT CHOICE DOES HE... WHAT THE...
THE CAGE IS THERE, BUT THE KID'S GONE!
M-MAYBE HE FELL!
YOU GENTLEMEN LOOKING FOR SOMETHING?
MAYBE YOU CAN HELP US!
WE'RE HUNTING FOR A RARE SPECIES, THE RED-HAIRED HOMEBOY!
SCIENTIFIC CLASSIFICATION ARCHICUS IDIOTUS!
?!!
WE MADE IT, LITTLE DUDE! NOW I'LL TRY TO INCH OUR WAY UP!
THWMP!
(GULP!) THIS LEDGE ISN'T AS WIDE AS THE OTHER ONE! IF I HUG THIS MOUNTAIN ANY CLOSER, VERONICA WILL BE JEALOUS!
3

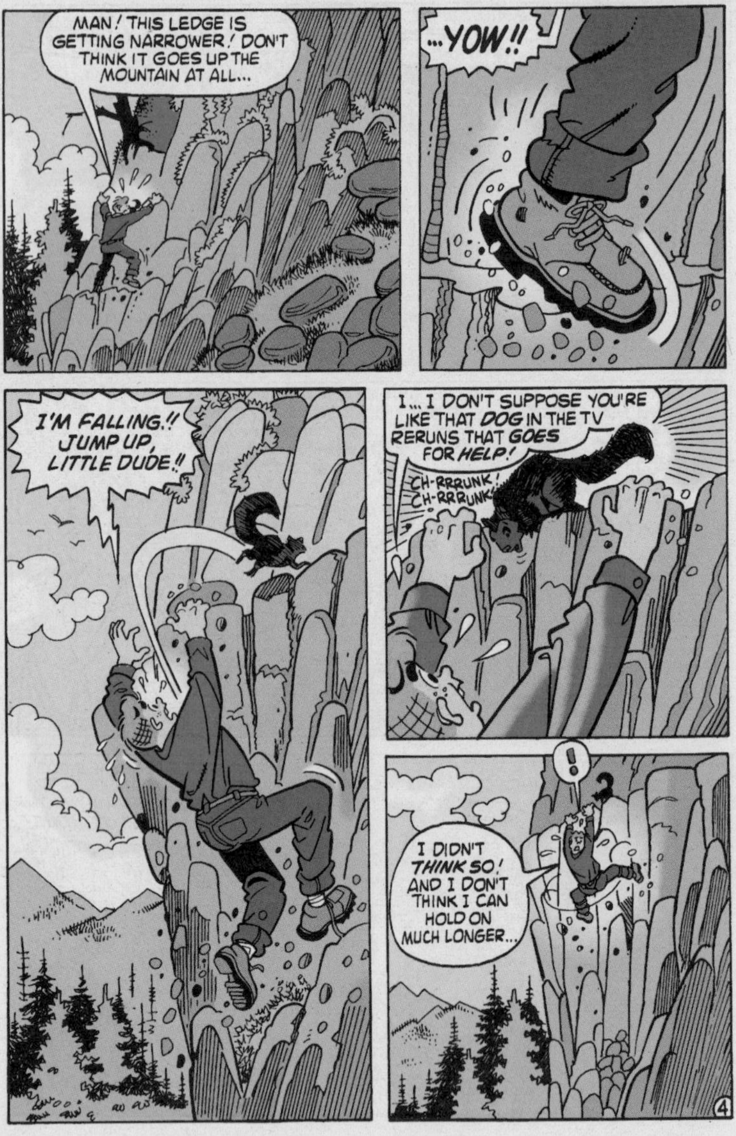
MAN! THIS LEDGE IS GETTING NARROWER! DON'T THINK IT GOES UP THE MOUNTAIN AT ALL...
...YOW!!
I'M FALLING!! JUMP UP, LITTLE DUDE!!
I... I DON'T SUPPOSE YOU'RE LIKE THAT DOG IN THE TV RERUNS THAT GOES FOR HELP!
CH-RRRUNK! CH-RRRUNK!
!
I DIDN'T THINK SO! AND I DON'T THINK I CAN HOLD ON MUCH LONGER...
4

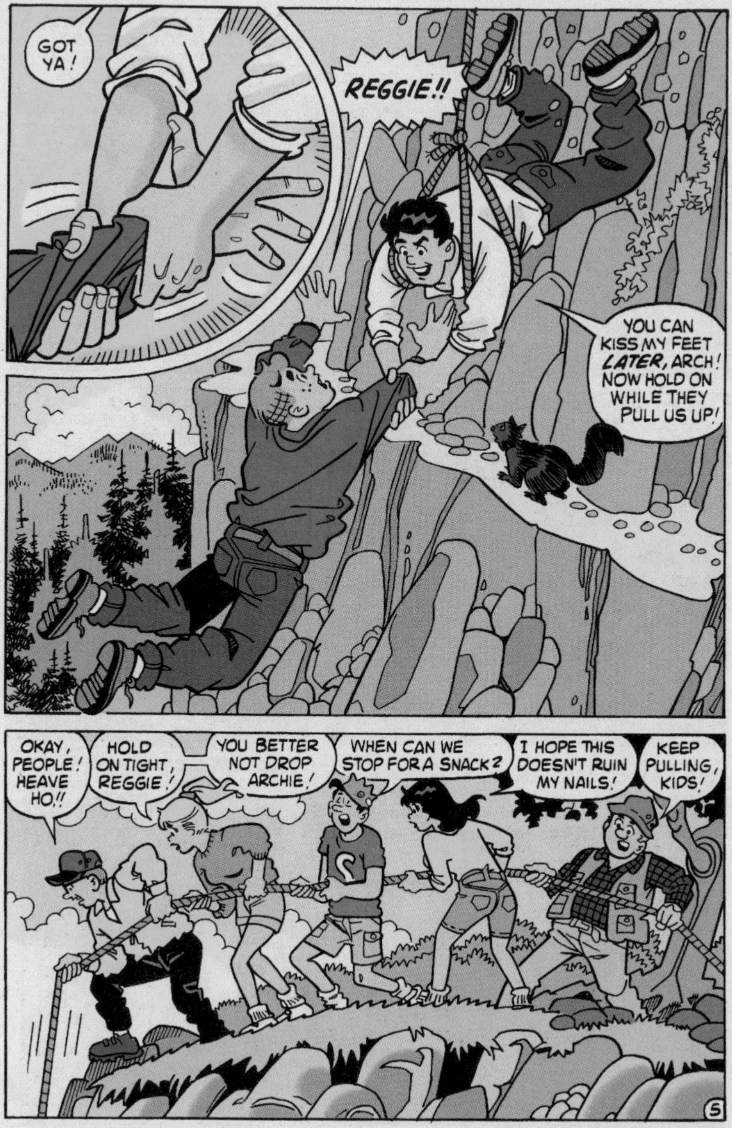
GOT YA!
REGGIE!!
YOU CAN KISS MY FEET LATER, ARCH! NOW HOLD ON WHILE THEY PULL US UP!
OKAY, PEOPLE! HEAVE HO!!
HOLD ON TIGHT, REGGIE!
YOU BETTER NOT DROP ARCHIE!
WHEN CAN WE STOP FOR A SNACK?
I HOPE THIS DOESN'T RUIN MY NAILS!
KEEP PULLING, KIDS!
5

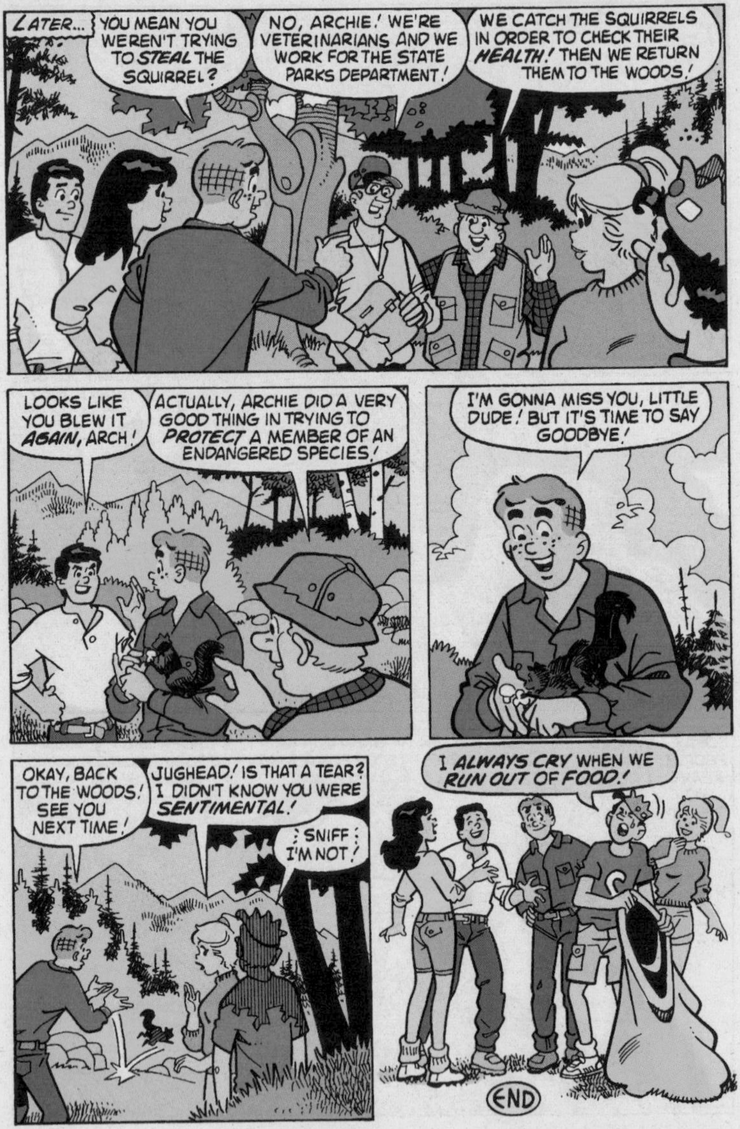
LATER...
YOU MEAN YOU WEREN'T TRYING TO STEAL THE SQUIRREL?
NO, ARCHIE! WE'RE VETERINARIANS AND WE WORK FOR THE STATE PARKS DEPARTMENT!
WE CATCH THE SQUIRRELS IN ORDER TO CHECK THEIR HEALTH! THEN WE RETURN THEM TO THE WOODS!
LOOKS LIKE YOU BLEW IT AGAIN, ARCH!
ACTUALLY, ARCHIE DID A VERY GOOD THING IN TRYING TO PROTECT A MEMBER OF AN ENDANGERED SPECIES!
I'M GONNA MISS YOU, LITTLE DUDE! BUT IT'S TIME TO SAY GOODBYE!
OKAY, BACK TO THE WOODS! SEE YOU NEXT TIME!
JUGHEAD! IS THAT A TEAR? I DIDN'T KNOW YOU WERE SENTIMENTAL!
SNIFF I'M NOT!
I ALWAYS CRY WHEN WE RUN OUT OF FOOD!
END

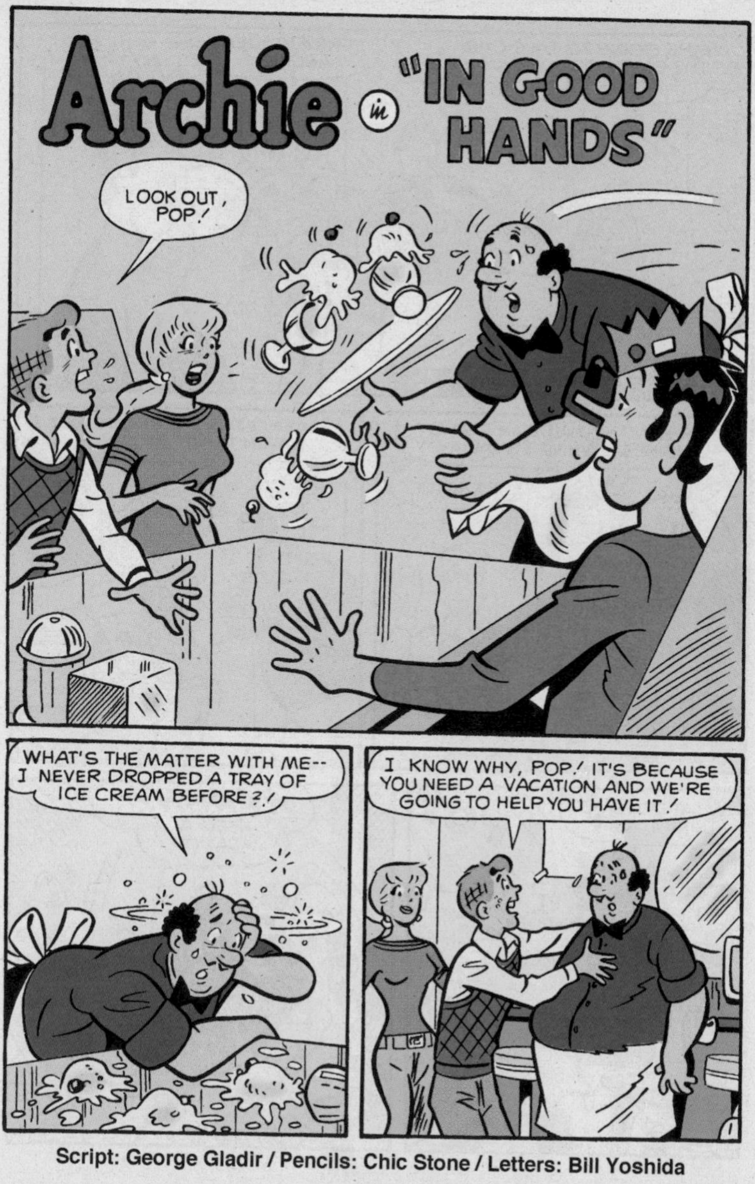
Archie in "IN GOOD HANDS"
LOOK OUT, POP!
WHAT'S THE MATTER WITH ME-- I NEVER DROPPED A TRAY OF ICE CREAM BEFORE?!
I KNOW WHY, POP! IT'S BECAUSE YOU NEED A VACATION AND WE'RE GOING TO HELP YOU HAVE IT!
1

Script: George Gladir / Pencils: Chic Stone / Letters: Bill Yoshida

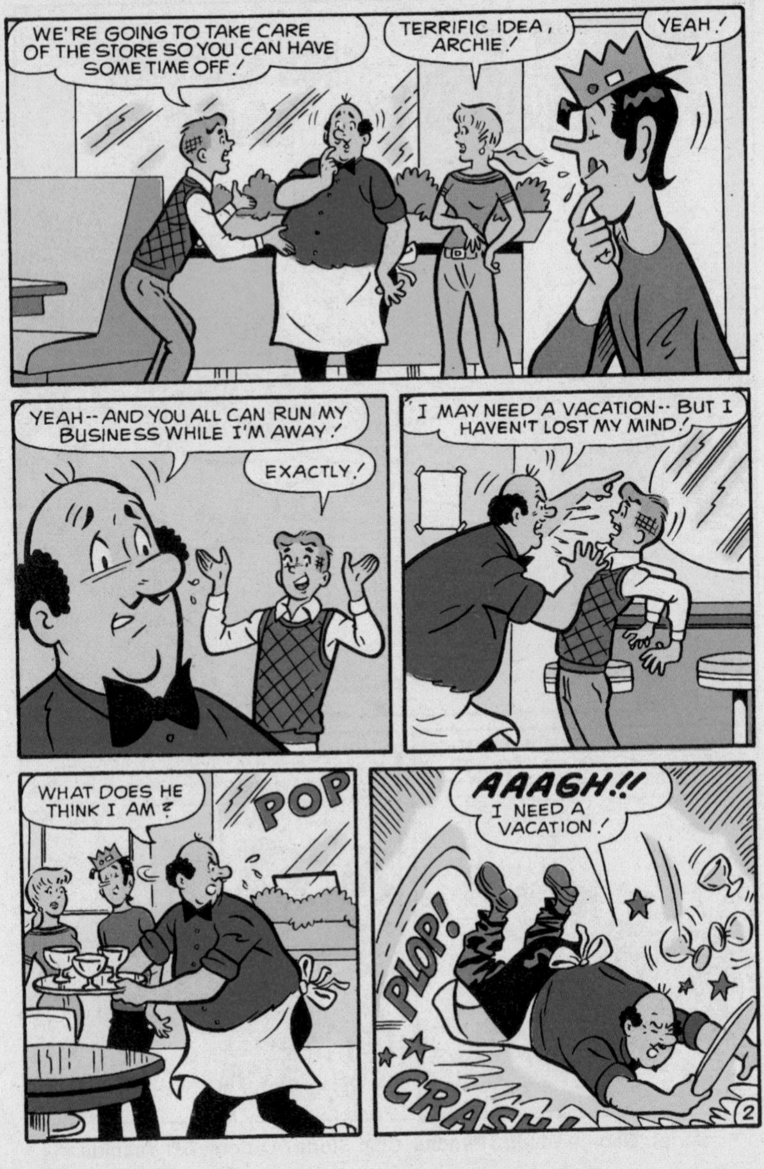
WE'RE GOING TO TAKE CARE OF THE STORE SO YOU CAN HAVE SOME TIME OFF!
TERRIFIC IDEA, ARCHIE!
YEAH!
YEAH-- AND YOU ALL CAN RUN MY BUSINESS WHILE I'M AWAY!
EXACTLY!
I MAY NEED A VACATION-- BUT I HAVEN'T LOST MY MIND!
WHAT DOES HE THINK I AM?
POP
AAAGH!! I NEED A VACATION!
PLOP!
2

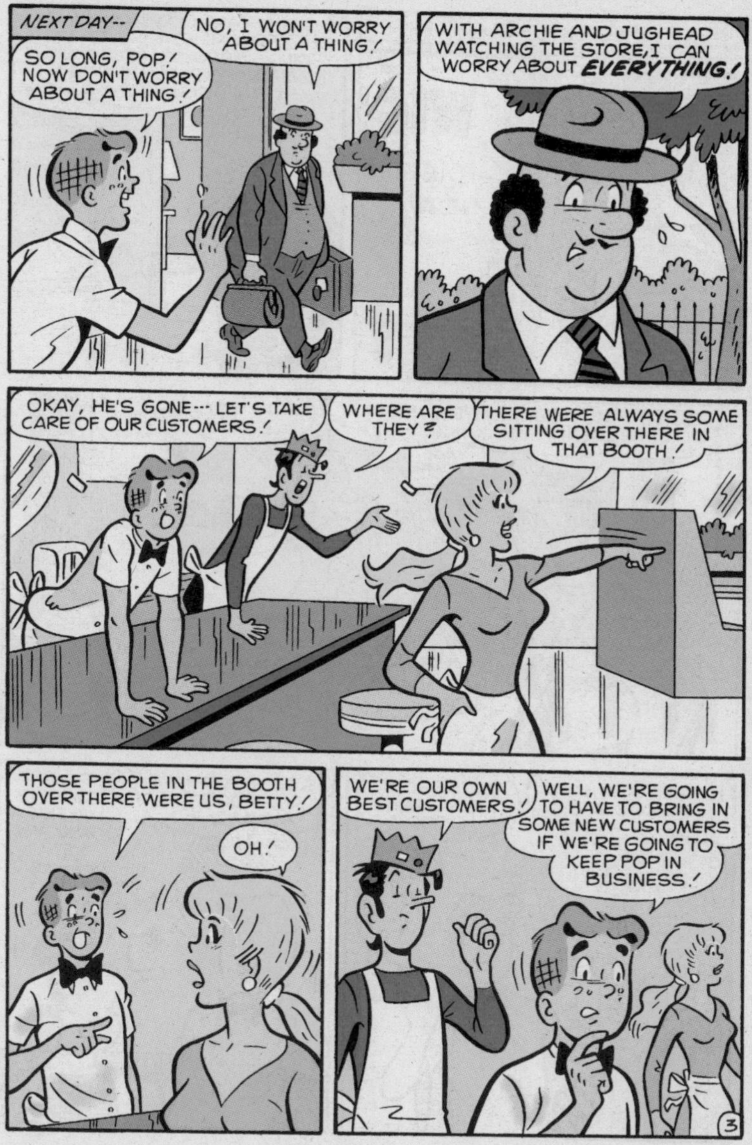
NEXT DAY--
SO LONG, POP! NOW DON'T WORRY ABOUT A THING!
NO, I WON'T WORRY ABOUT A THING!
WITH ARCHIE AND JUGHEAD WATCHING THE STORE, I CAN WORRY ABOUT EVERYTHING!
OKAY, HE'S GONE--- LET'S TAKE CARE OF OUR CUSTOMERS!
WHERE ARE THEY?
THERE WERE ALWAYS SOME SITTING OVER THERE IN THAT BOOTH!
THOSE PEOPLE IN THE BOOTH OVER THERE WERE US, BETTY!
OH!
WE'RE OUR OWN BEST CUSTOMERS!
WELL, WE'RE GOING TO HAVE TO BRING IN SOME NEW CUSTOMERS IF WE'RE GOING TO KEEP POP IN BUSINESS!
3

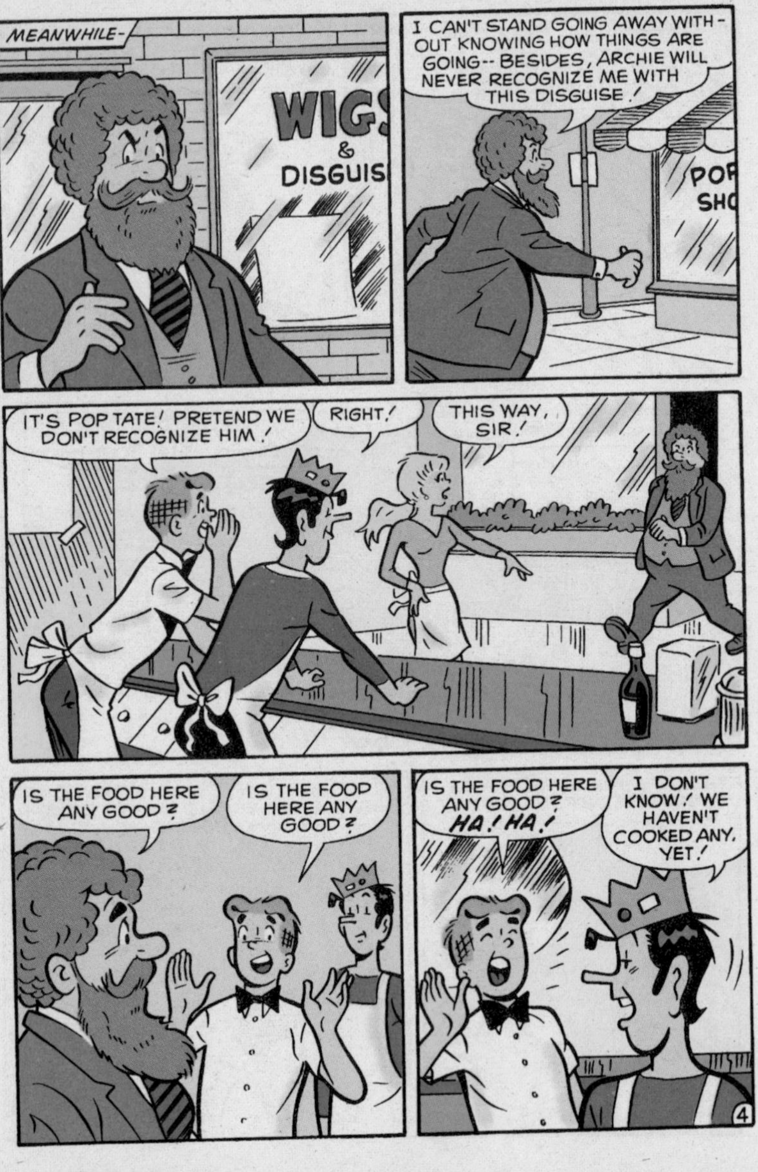
MEANWHILE-
WIGS & DISGUIS
I CAN'T STAND GOING AWAY WITH-OUT KNOWING HOW THINGS ARE GOING-- BESIDES, ARCHIE WILL NEVER RECOGNIZE ME WITH THIS DISGUISE!
POP SHO
IT'S POP TATE! PRETEND WE DON'T RECOGNIZE HIM!
RIGHT!
THIS WAY, SIR!
IS THE FOOD HERE ANY GOOD?
IS THE FOOD HERE ANY GOOD?
IS THE FOOD HERE ANY GOOD? HA! HA!
I DON'T KNOW! WE HAVEN'T COOKED ANY, YET!
4

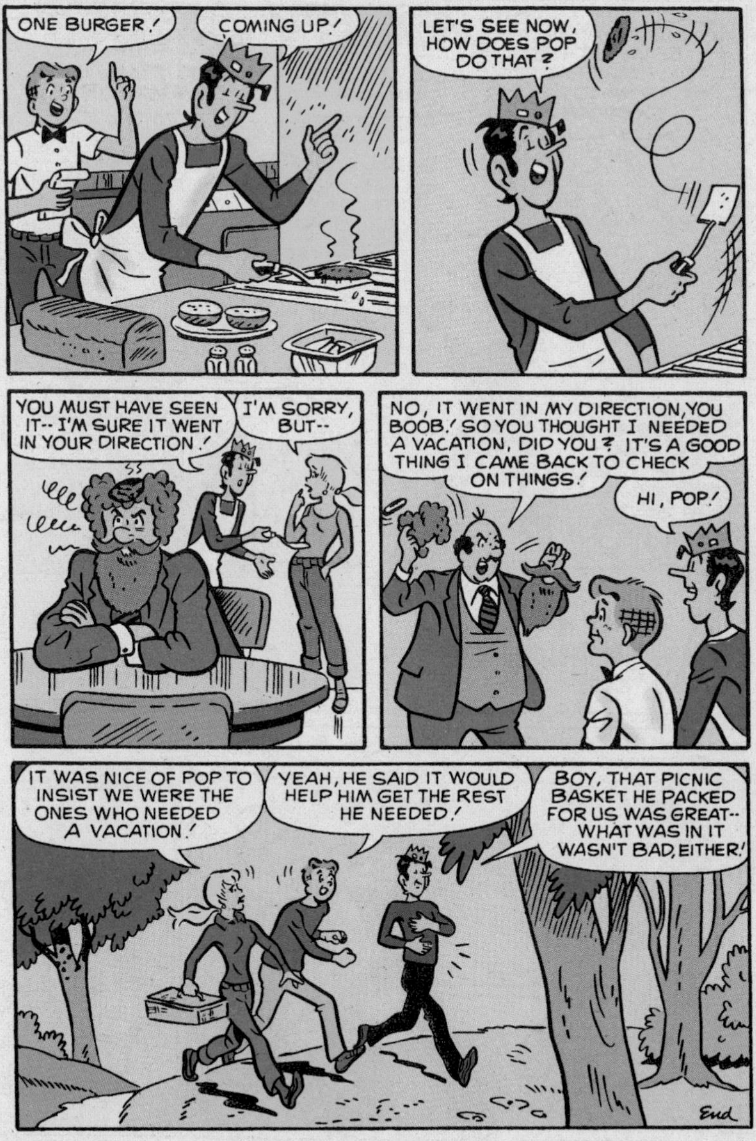
ONE BURGER!
COMING UP!
LET'S SEE NOW, HOW DOES POP DO THAT?
YOU MUST HAVE SEEN IT-- I'M SURE IT WENT IN YOUR DIRECTION!
I'M SORRY, BUT--
NO, IT WENT IN MY DIRECTION, YOU BOOB! SO YOU THOUGHT I NEEDED A VACATION, DID YOU? IT'S A GOOD THING I CAME BACK TO CHECK ON THINGS!
HI, POP!
IT WAS NICE OF POP TO INSIST WE WERE THE ONES WHO NEEDED A VACATION!
YEAH, HE SAID IT WOULD HELP HIM GET THE REST HE NEEDED!
BOY, THAT PICNIC BASKET HE PACKED FOR US WAS GREAT-- WHAT WAS IN IT WASN'T BAD, EITHER!
End

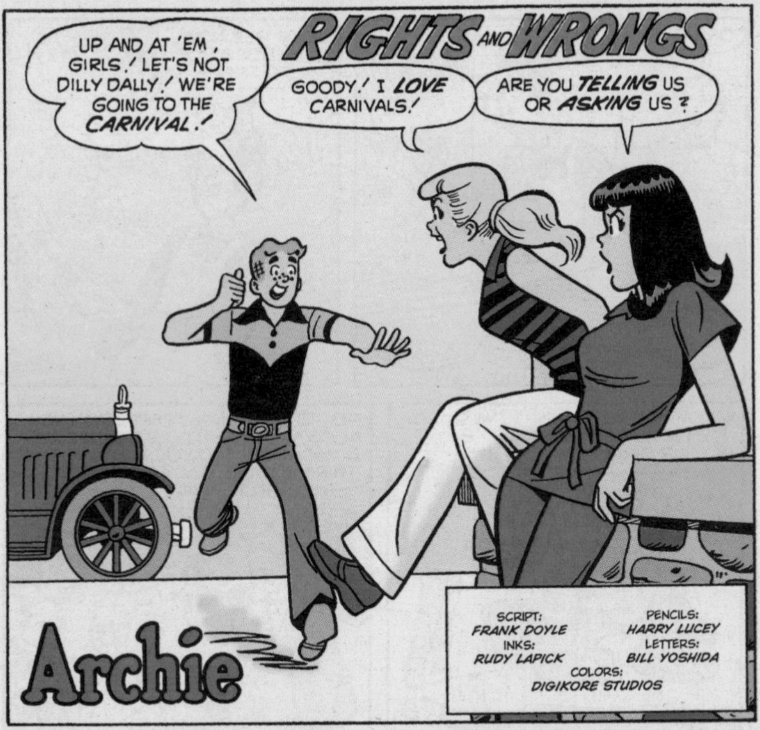
RIGHTS AND WRONGS
UP AND AT 'EM, GIRLS! LET'S NOT DILLY DALLY! WE'RE GOING TO THE CARNIVAL!
GOODY! I LOVE CARNIVALS!
ARE YOU TELLING US OR ASKING US?
Archie
SCRIPT: FRANK DOYLE
PENCILS: HARRY LUCEY
INKS: RUDY LAPICK
LETTERS: BILL YOSHIDA
COLORS: DIGIKORE STUDIOS

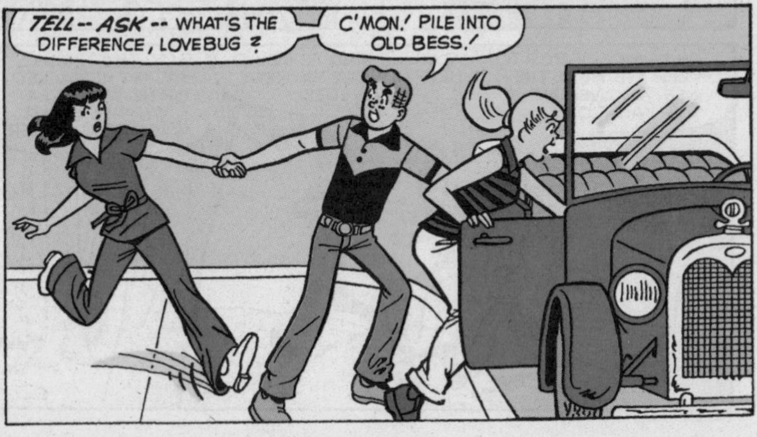
TELL -- ASK -- WHAT'S THE DIFFERENCE, LOVEBUG?
C'MON! PILE INTO OLD BESS!

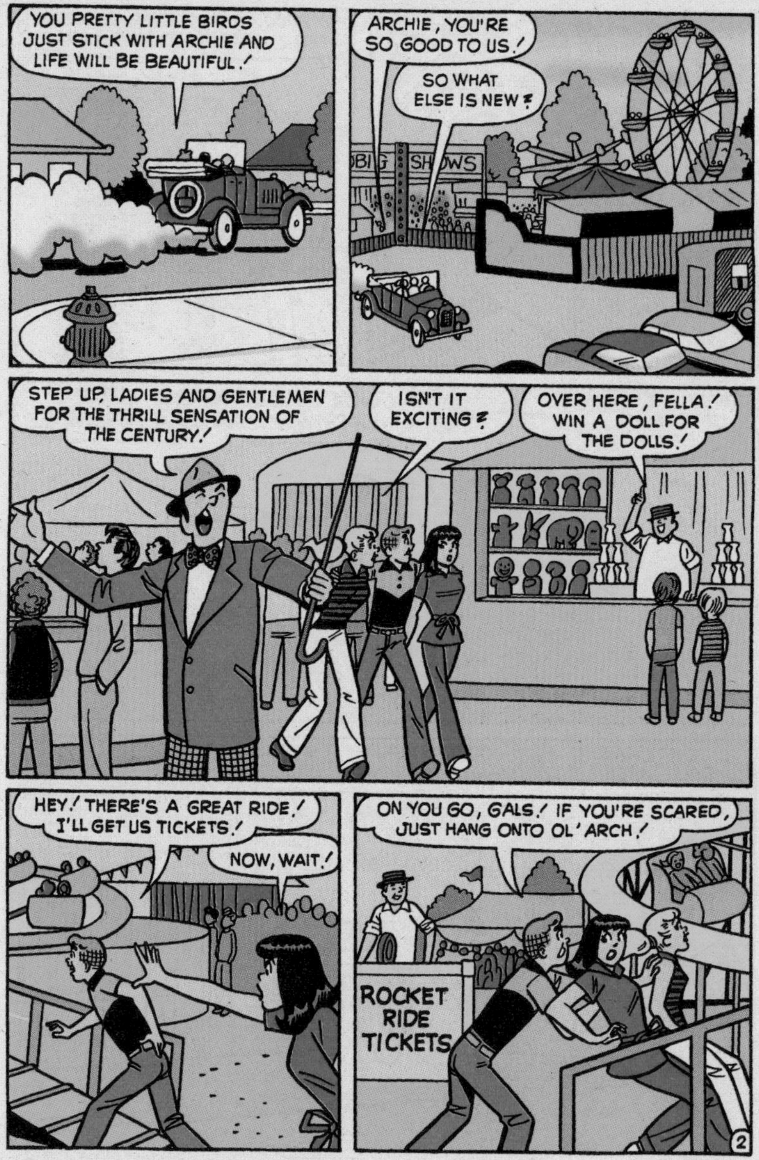
YOU PRETTY LITTLE BIRDS JUST STICK WITH ARCHIE AND LIFE WILL BE BEAUTIFUL!
ARCHIE, YOU'RE SO GOOD TO US!
SO WHAT ELSE IS NEW?
BIG SHOWS
STEP UP, LADIES AND GENTLEMEN FOR THE THRILL SENSATION OF THE CENTURY!
ISN'T IT EXCITING?
OVER HERE, FELLA! WIN A DOLL FOR THE DOLLS!
HEY! THERE'S A GREAT RIDE! I'LL GET US TICKETS!
NOW, WAIT!
ON YOU GO, GALS! IF YOU'RE SCARED, JUST HANG ONTO OL' ARCH!
ROCKET RIDE TICKETS
2

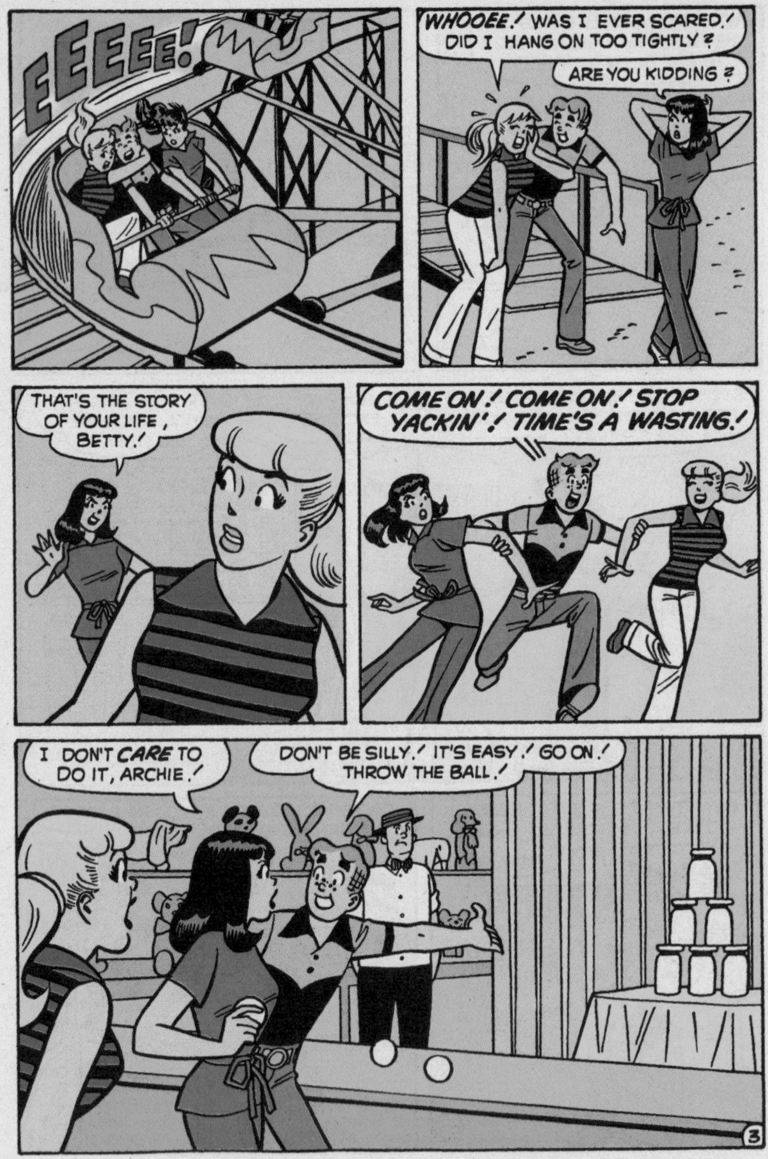
EEEEE!
WHOOEE! WAS I EVER SCARED! DID I HANG ON TOO TIGHTLY?
ARE YOU KIDDING?
THAT'S THE STORY OF YOUR LIFE, BETTY!
COME ON! COME ON! STOP YACKIN'! TIME'S A WASTING!
I DON'T CARE TO DO IT, ARCHIE!
DON'T BE SILLY! IT'S EASY! GO ON! THROW THE BALL!
3

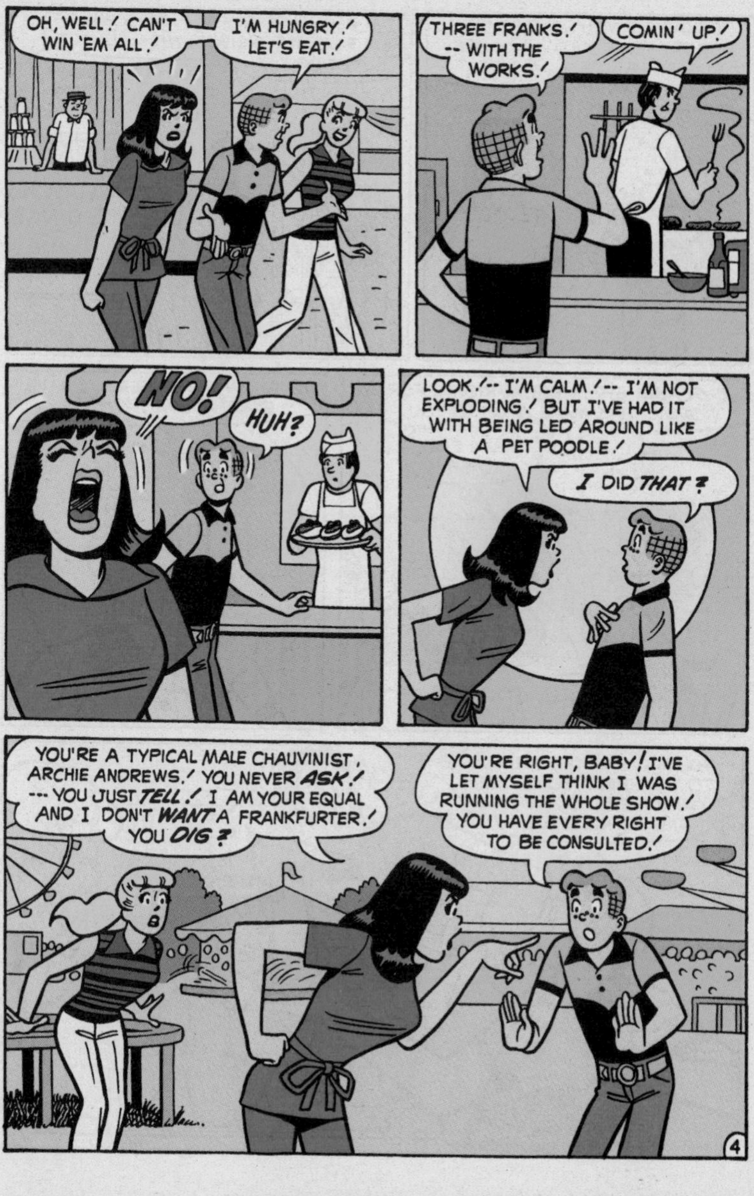
OH, WELL! CAN'T WIN 'EM ALL!
I'M HUNGRY! LET'S EAT!
THREE FRANKS! -- WITH THE WORKS!
COMIN' UP!
NO!
HUH?
LOOK!-- I'M CALM!-- I'M NOT EXPLODING! BUT I'VE HAD IT WITH BEING LED AROUND LIKE A PET POODLE!
I DID THAT?
YOU'RE A TYPICAL MALE CHAUVINIST, ARCHIE ANDREWS! YOU NEVER ASK! --- YOU JUST TELL! I AM YOUR EQUAL AND I DON'T WANT A FRANKFURTER! YOU DIG?
YOU'RE RIGHT, BABY! I'VE LET MYSELF THINK I WAS RUNNING THE WHOLE SHOW! YOU HAVE EVERY RIGHT TO BE CONSULTED!
4

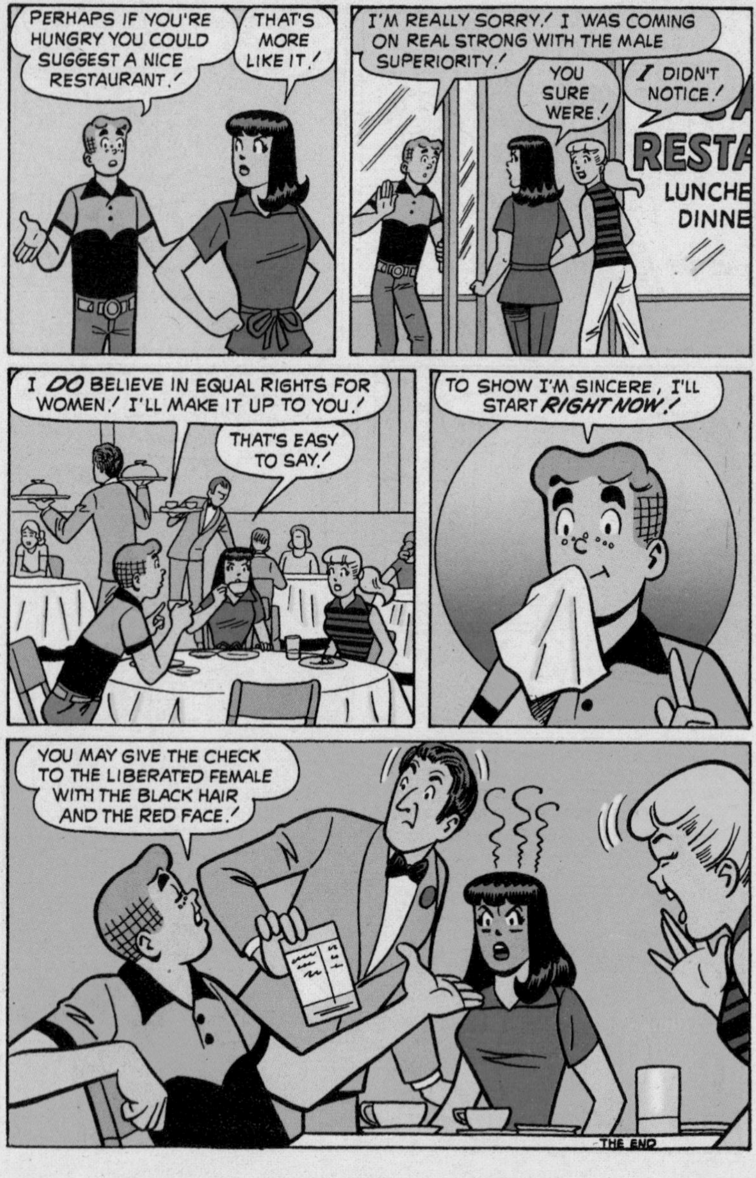
PERHAPS IF YOU'RE HUNGRY YOU COULD SUGGEST A NICE RESTAURANT!
THAT'S MORE LIKE IT!
I'M REALLY SORRY! I WAS COMING ON REAL STRONG WITH THE MALE SUPERIORITY!
YOU SURE WERE!
I DIDN'T NOTICE!
RESTA
LUNCHE
DINNE
I DO BELIEVE IN EQUAL RIGHTS FOR WOMEN! I'LL MAKE IT UP TO YOU!
THAT'S EASY TO SAY!
TO SHOW I'M SINCERE, I'LL START RIGHT NOW!
YOU MAY GIVE THE CHECK TO THE LIBERATED FEMALE WITH THE BLACK HAIR AND THE RED FACE!
THE END

Archie in "Going My Way"

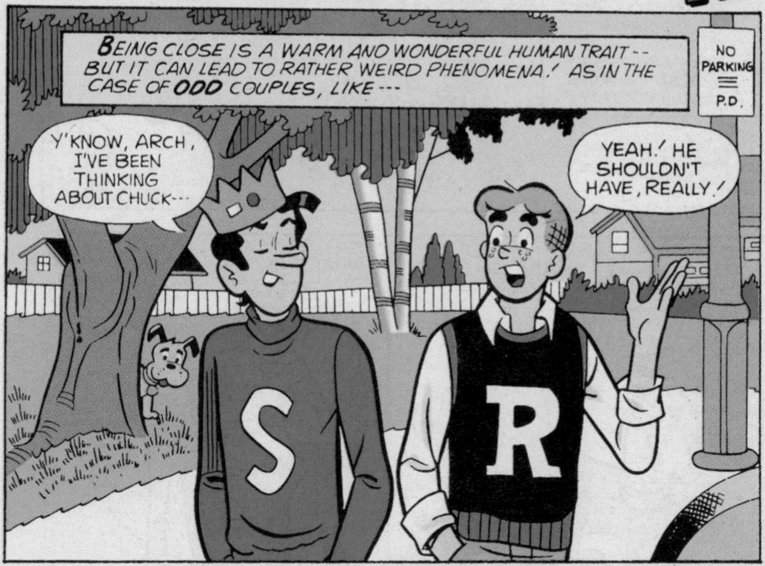

BEING CLOSE IS A WARM AND WONDERFUL HUMAN TRAIT -- BUT IT CAN LEAD TO RATHER WEIRD PHENOMENA! AS IN THE CASE OF ODD COUPLES, LIKE ---
NO PARKING P.D.
Y'KNOW, ARCH, I'VE BEEN THINKING ABOUT CHUCK---
YEAH! HE SHOULDN'T HAVE, REALLY!

Script: Frank Doyle / Pencils: Stan Goldberg / Inks: Jim DeCarlo / Letters: Bill Yoshida

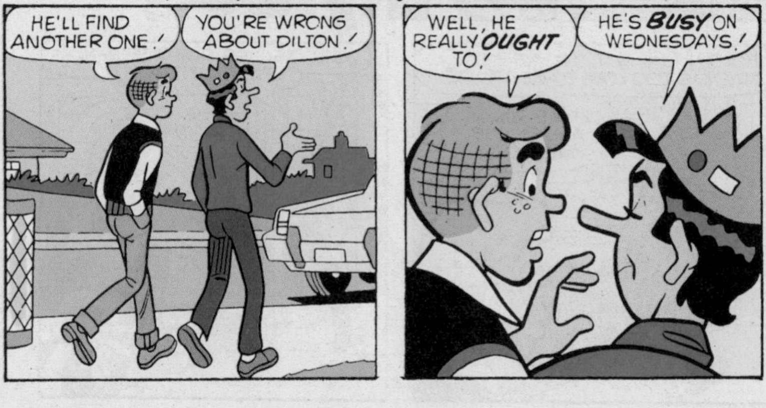

HE'LL FIND ANOTHER ONE!
YOU'RE WRONG ABOUT DILTON!
WELL, HE REALLY OUGHT TO!
HE'S BUSY ON WEDNESDAYS!

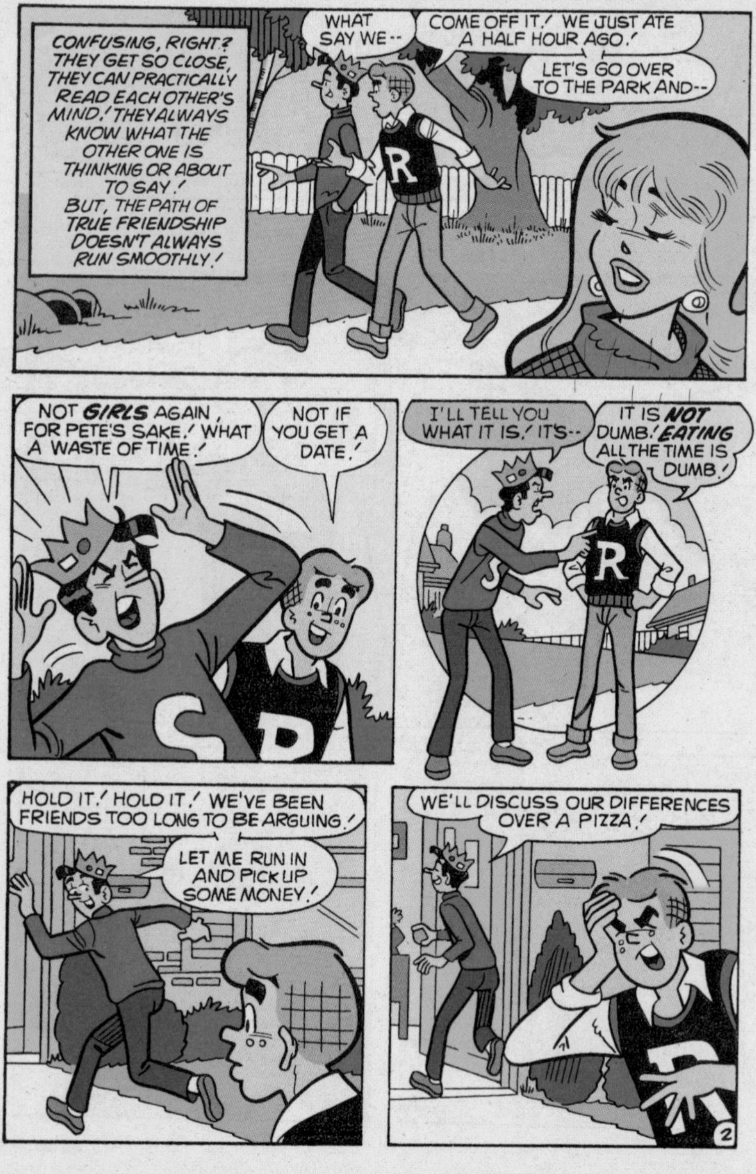

CONFUSING, RIGHT? THEY GET SO CLOSE, THEY CAN PRACTICALLY READ EACH OTHER'S MIND! THEY ALWAYS KNOW WHAT THE OTHER ONE IS THINKING OR ABOUT TO SAY! BUT, THE PATH OF TRUE FRIENDSHIP DOESN'T ALWAYS RUN SMOOTHLY!
WHAT SAY WE--
COME OFF IT! WE JUST ATE A HALF HOUR AGO!
LET'S GO OVER TO THE PARK AND--
NOT GIRLS AGAIN, FOR PETE'S SAKE! WHAT A WASTE OF TIME!
NOT IF YOU GET A DATE!
I'LL TELL YOU WHAT IT IS! IT'S--
IT IS NOT DUMB! EATING ALL THE TIME IS DUMB!
HOLD IT! HOLD IT! WE'VE BEEN FRIENDS TOO LONG TO BE ARGUING!
LET ME RUN IN AND PICK UP SOME MONEY!
WE'LL DISCUSS OUR DIFFERENCES OVER A PIZZA!
2

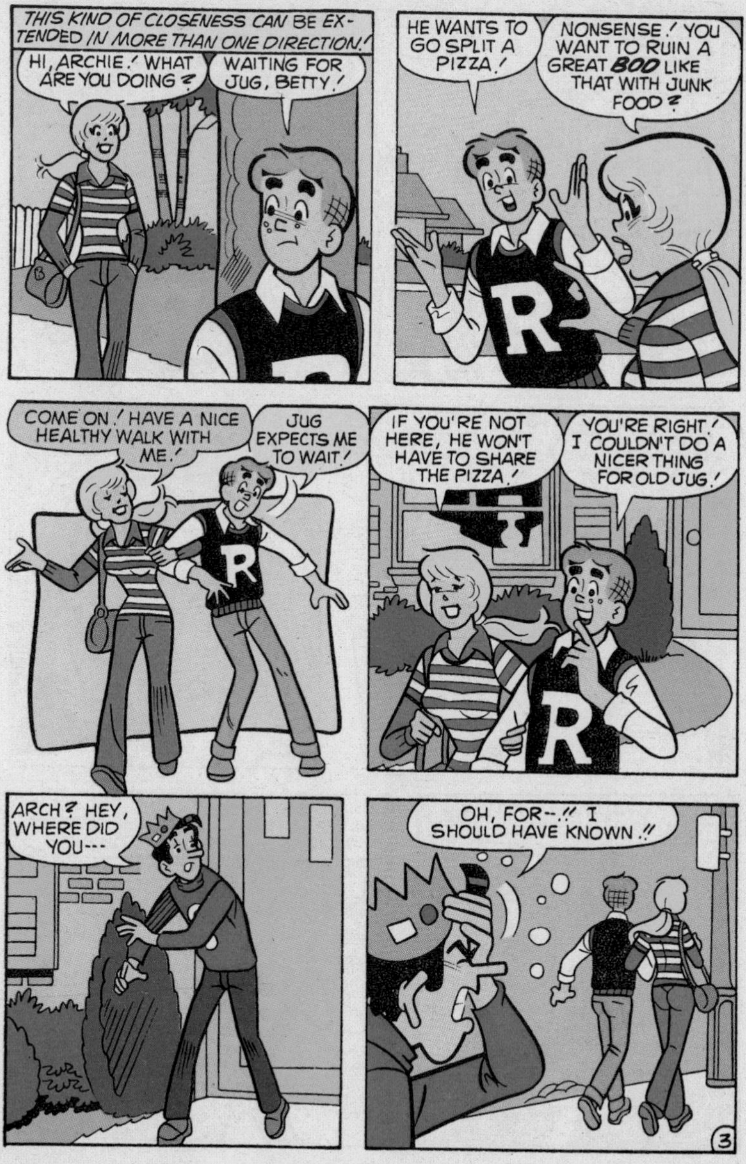
THIS KIND OF CLOSENESS CAN BE EXTENDED IN MORE THAN ONE DIRECTION!
HI, ARCHIE! WHAT ARE YOU DOING?
WAITING FOR JUG, BETTY!
HE WANTS TO GO SPLIT A PIZZA!
NONSENSE! YOU WANT TO RUIN A GREAT BOD LIKE THAT WITH JUNK FOOD?
COME ON! HAVE A NICE HEALTHY WALK WITH ME!
JUG EXPECTS ME TO WAIT!
IF YOU'RE NOT HERE, HE WON'T HAVE TO SHARE THE PIZZA!
YOU'RE RIGHT! I COULDN'T DO A NICER THING FOR OLD JUG!
ARCH? HEY, WHERE DID YOU---
OH, FOR--!! I SHOULD HAVE KNOWN!!
3

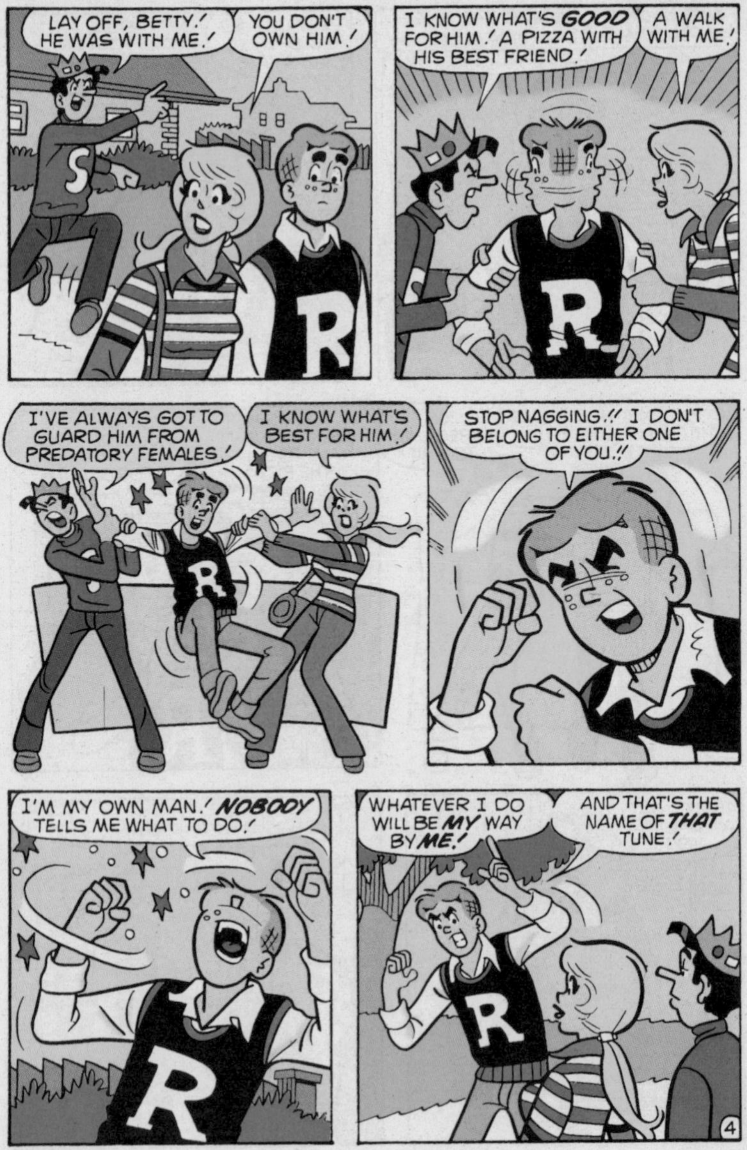
LAY OFF, BETTY.! HE WAS WITH ME.!
YOU DON'T OWN HIM.!
I KNOW WHAT'S GOOD FOR HIM.! A PIZZA WITH HIS BEST FRIEND.!
A WALK WITH ME.!
I'VE ALWAYS GOT TO GUARD HIM FROM PREDATORY FEMALES.!
I KNOW WHAT'S BEST FOR HIM.!
STOP NAGGING.!! I DON'T BELONG TO EITHER ONE OF YOU.!!
I'M MY OWN MAN.! NOBODY TELLS ME WHAT TO DO.!
WHATEVER I DO WILL BE MY WAY BY ME!
AND THAT'S THE NAME OF THAT TUNE.!
4

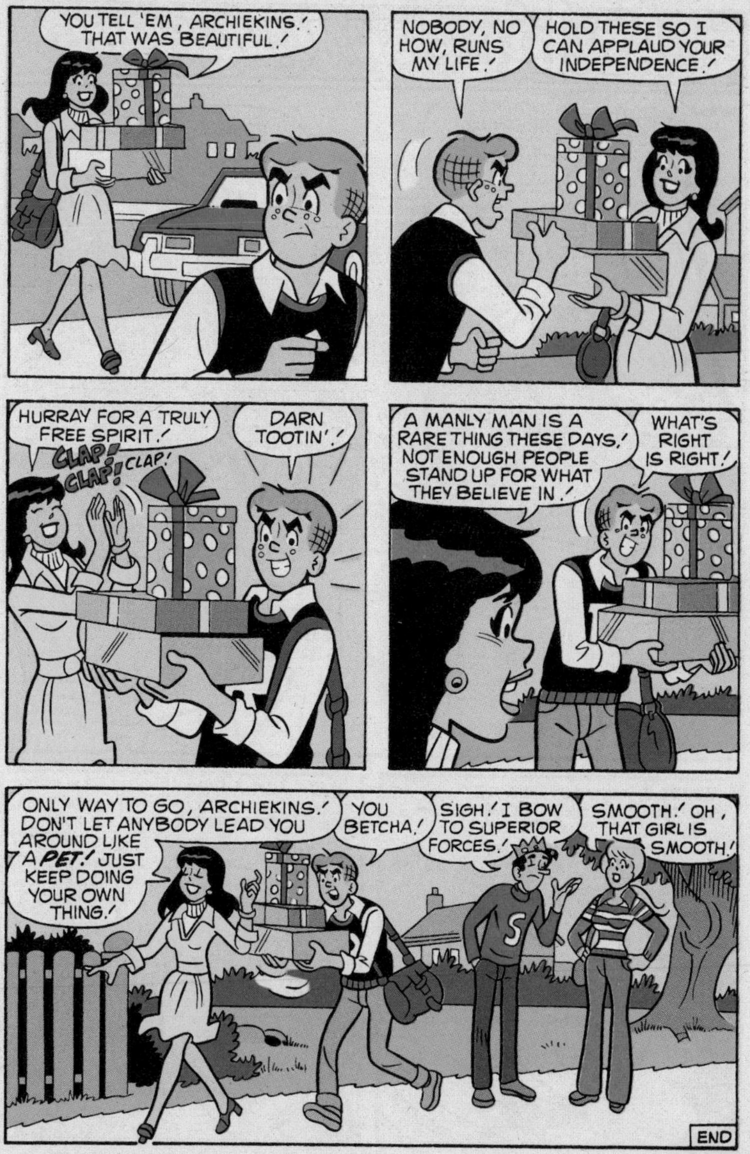
YOU TELL 'EM, ARCHIEKINS! THAT WAS BEAUTIFUL!
NOBODY, NO HOW, RUNS MY LIFE!
HOLD THESE SO I CAN APPLAUD YOUR INDEPENDENCE!
HURRAY FOR A TRULY FREE SPIRIT!
CLAP! CLAP! CLAP!
DARN TOOTIN'!
A MANLY MAN IS A RARE THING THESE DAYS! NOT ENOUGH PEOPLE STAND UP FOR WHAT THEY BELIEVE IN!
WHAT'S RIGHT IS RIGHT!
ONLY WAY TO GO, ARCHIEKINS! DON'T LET ANYBODY LEAD YOU AROUND LIKE A PET! JUST KEEP DOING YOUR OWN THING!
YOU BETCHA!
SIGH! I BOW TO SUPERIOR FORCES!
SMOOTH! OH, THAT GIRL IS SMOOTH!
END

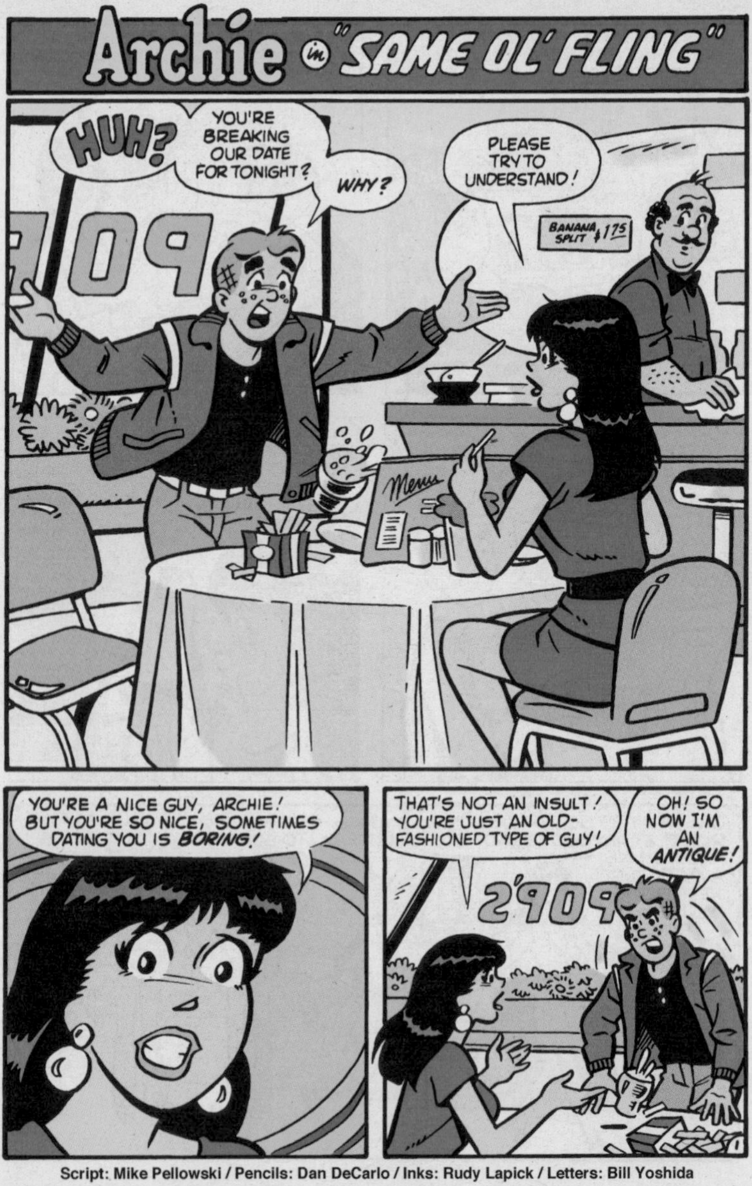
Archie in "SAME OL' FLING"
HUH?
YOU'RE BREAKING OUR DATE FOR TONIGHT? WHY?
PLEASE TRY TO UNDERSTAND!
BANANA SPLIT $1.75
POP'S
Menu
YOU'RE A NICE GUY, ARCHIE! BUT YOU'RE SO NICE, SOMETIMES DATING YOU IS BORING!
THAT'S NOT AN INSULT! YOU'RE JUST AN OLD-FASHIONED TYPE OF GUY!
OH! SO NOW I'M AN ANTIQUE!
POP'S

Script: Mike Pellowski / Pencils: Dan DeCarlo / Inks: Rudy Lapick / Letters: Bill Yoshida

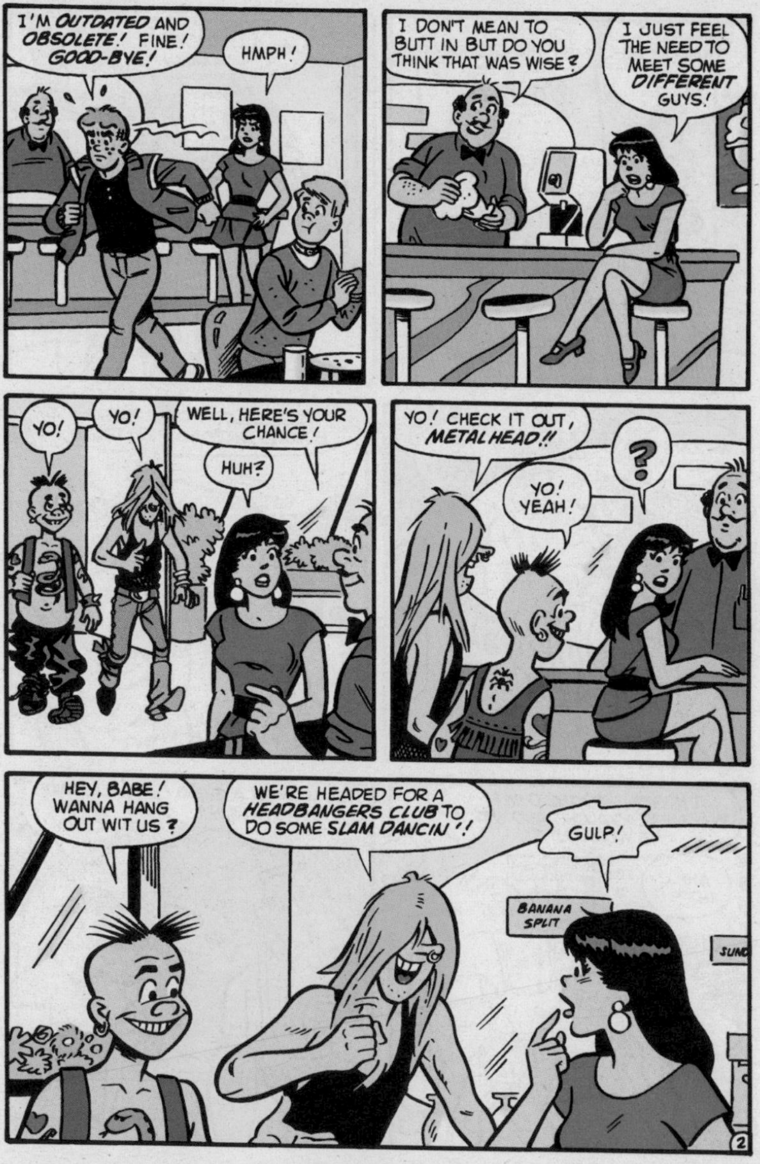
I'M OUTDATED AND OBSOLETE! FINE! GOOD-BYE!
HMPH!
I DON'T MEAN TO BUTT IN BUT DO YOU THINK THAT WAS WISE?
I JUST FEEL THE NEED TO MEET SOME DIFFERENT GUYS!
YO!
YO!
WELL, HERE'S YOUR CHANCE!
HUH?
YO! CHECK IT OUT, METALHEAD!!
?
YO! YEAH!
HEY, BABE! WANNA HANG OUT WIT US?
WE'RE HEADED FOR A HEADBANGERS CLUB TO DO SOME SLAM DANCIN'!
GULP!
BANANA SPLIT
2

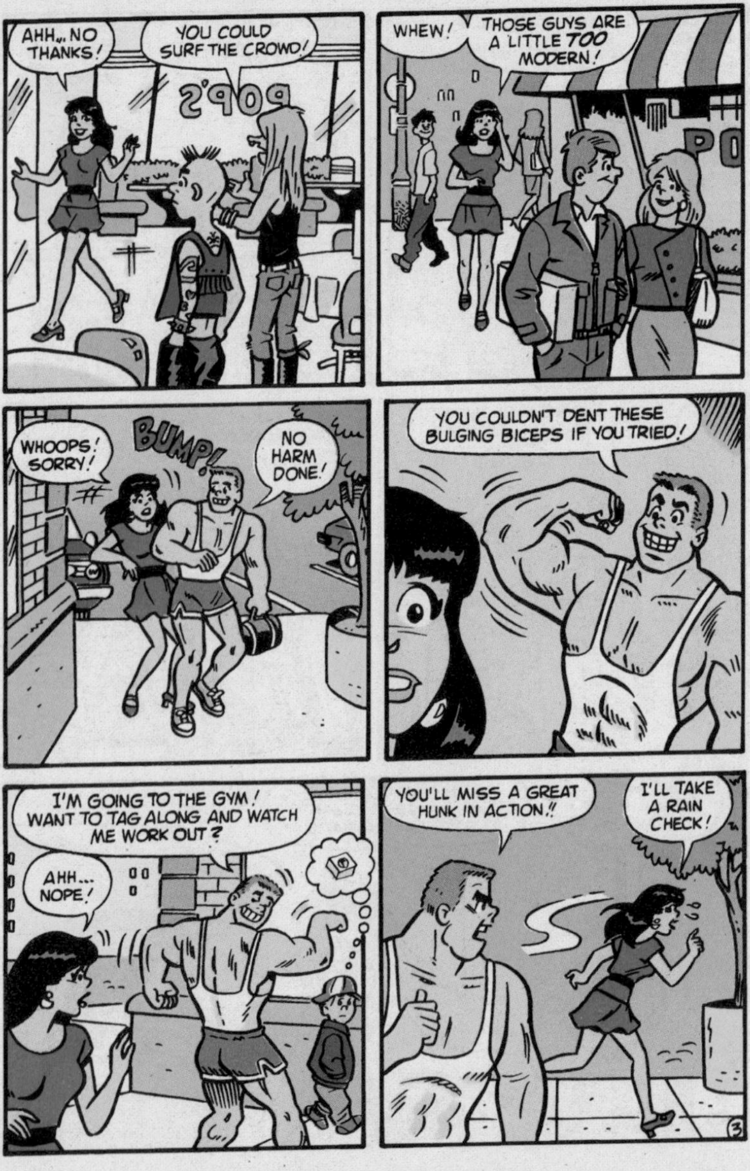

AHH... NO THANKS!
YOU COULD SURF THE CROWD!
POP'S
WHEW!
THOSE GUYS ARE A LITTLE TOO MODERN!
WHOOPS! SORRY!
BUMP!
NO HARM DONE!
YOU COULDN'T DENT THESE BULGING BICEPS IF YOU TRIED!
I'M GOING TO THE GYM! WANT TO TAG ALONG AND WATCH ME WORK OUT?
AHH... NOPE!
YOU'LL MISS A GREAT HUNK IN ACTION!!
I'LL TAKE A RAIN CHECK!
3

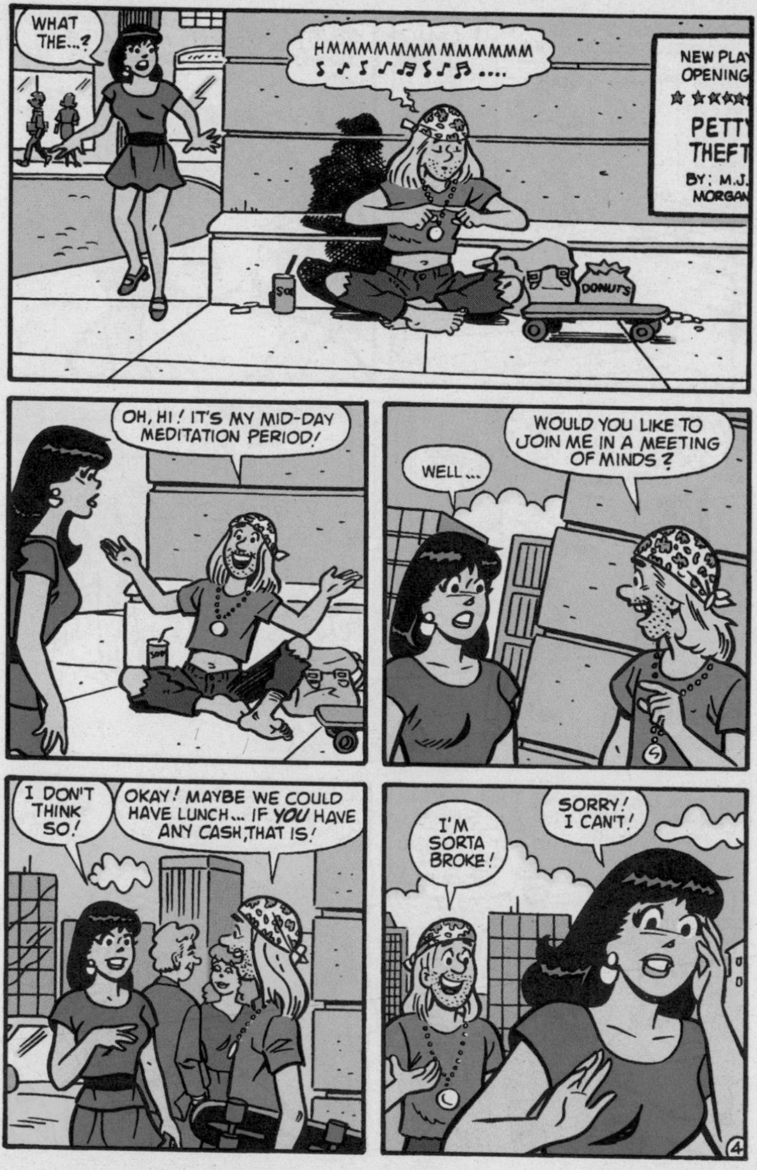
WHAT THE...?
HMMMMMMMM MMMMMMM ....
NEW PLAY OPENING
PETTY THEFT
BY: M.J. MORGAN
SO
DONUTS
OH, HI! IT'S MY MID-DAY MEDITATION PERIOD!
WOULD YOU LIKE TO JOIN ME IN A MEETING OF MINDS?
WELL...
I DON'T THINK SO!
OKAY! MAYBE WE COULD HAVE LUNCH... IF *YOU* HAVE ANY CASH, THAT IS!
SORRY! I CAN'T!
I'M SORTA BROKE!
4

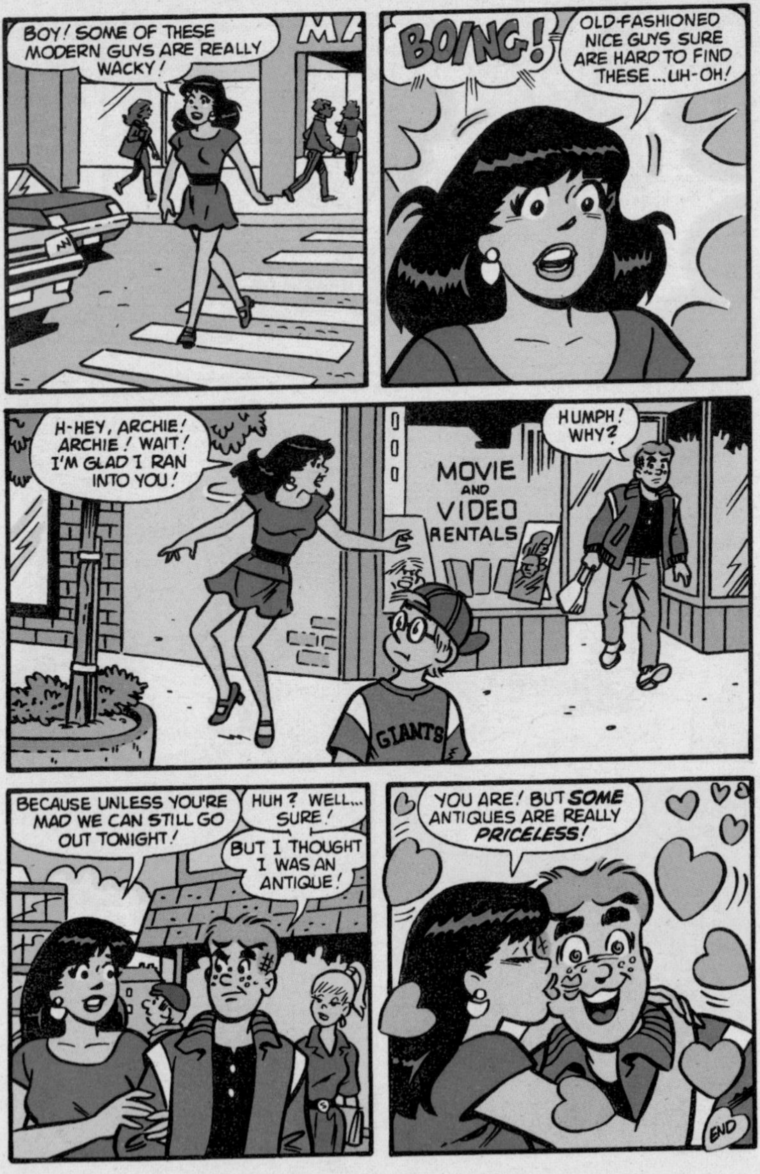
BOY! SOME OF THESE MODERN GUYS ARE REALLY WACKY!
BOING!
OLD-FASHIONED NICE GUYS SURE ARE HARD TO FIND THESE ... UH-OH!
H-HEY, ARCHIE! ARCHIE! WAIT! I'M GLAD I RAN INTO YOU!
HUMPH! WHY?
MOVIE AND VIDEO RENTALS
GIANTS
BECAUSE UNLESS YOU'RE MAD WE CAN STILL GO OUT TONIGHT!
HUH? WELL... SURE!
BUT I THOUGHT I WAS AN ANTIQUE!
YOU ARE! BUT SOME ANTIQUES ARE REALLY PRICELESS!
END

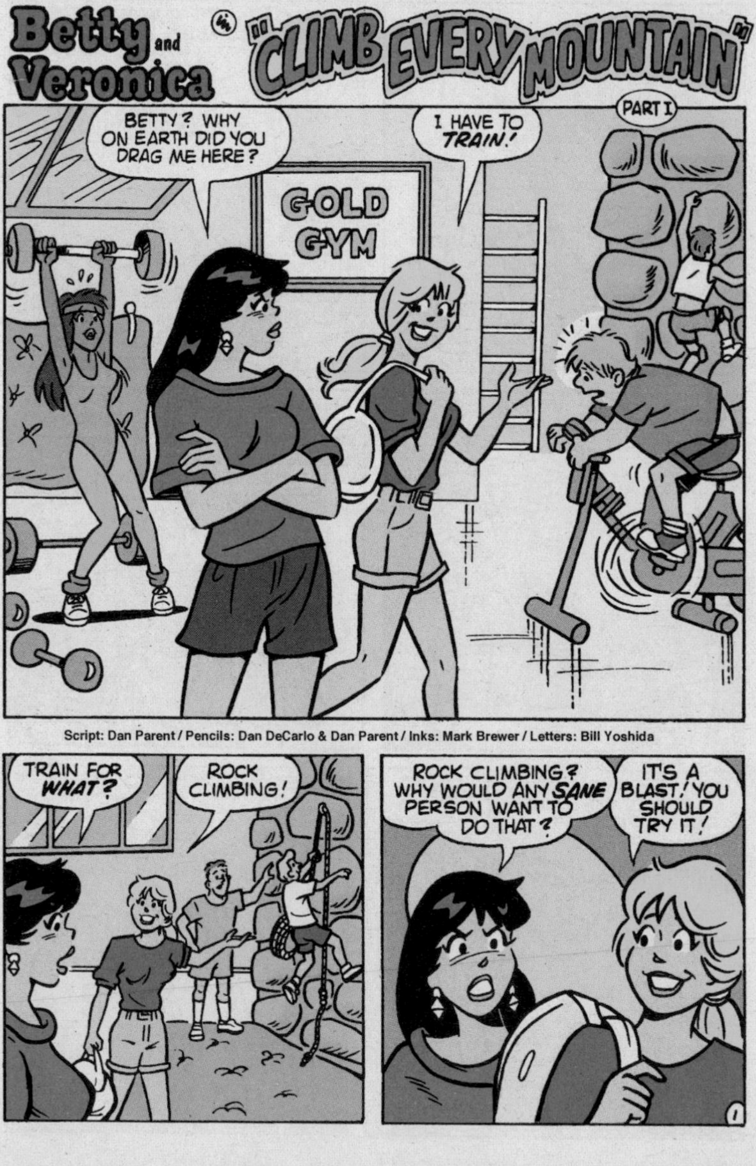
Betty and Veronica
"CLIMB EVERY MOUNTAIN"
PART I
BETTY? WHY ON EARTH DID YOU DRAG ME HERE?
I HAVE TO TRAIN!
GOLD GYM
Script: Dan Parent / Pencils: Dan DeCarlo & Dan Parent / Inks: Mark Brewer / Letters: Bill Yoshida
TRAIN FOR WHAT?
ROCK CLIMBING!
ROCK CLIMBING? WHY WOULD ANY SANE PERSON WANT TO DO THAT?
IT'S A BLAST! YOU SHOULD TRY IT!
1

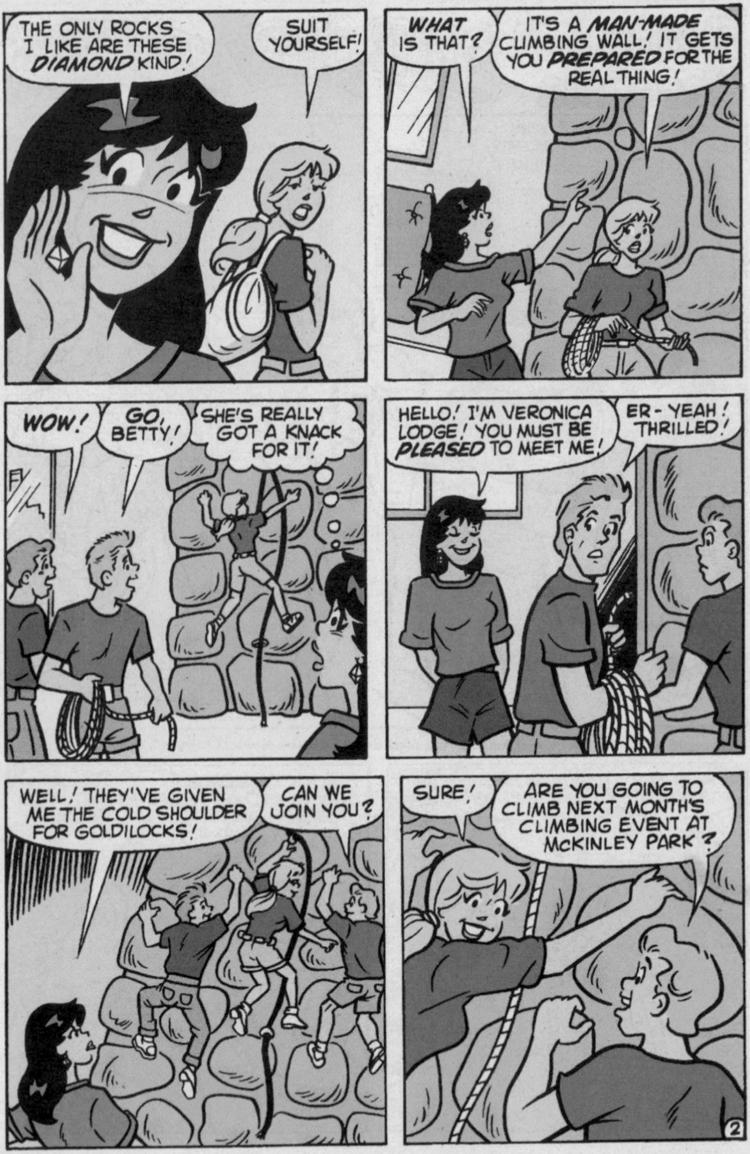
THE ONLY ROCKS I LIKE ARE THESE DIAMOND KIND!
SUIT YOURSELF!
WHAT IS THAT?
IT'S A MAN-MADE CLIMBING WALL! IT GETS YOU PREPARED FOR THE REAL THING!
WOW!
GO, BETTY!
SHE'S REALLY GOT A KNACK FOR IT!
HELLO! I'M VERONICA LODGE! YOU MUST BE PLEASED TO MEET ME!
ER- YEAH! THRILLED!
WELL! THEY'VE GIVEN ME THE COLD SHOULDER FOR GOLDILOCKS!
CAN WE JOIN YOU?
SURE!
ARE YOU GOING TO CLIMB NEXT MONTH'S CLIMBING EVENT AT McKINLEY PARK?
2

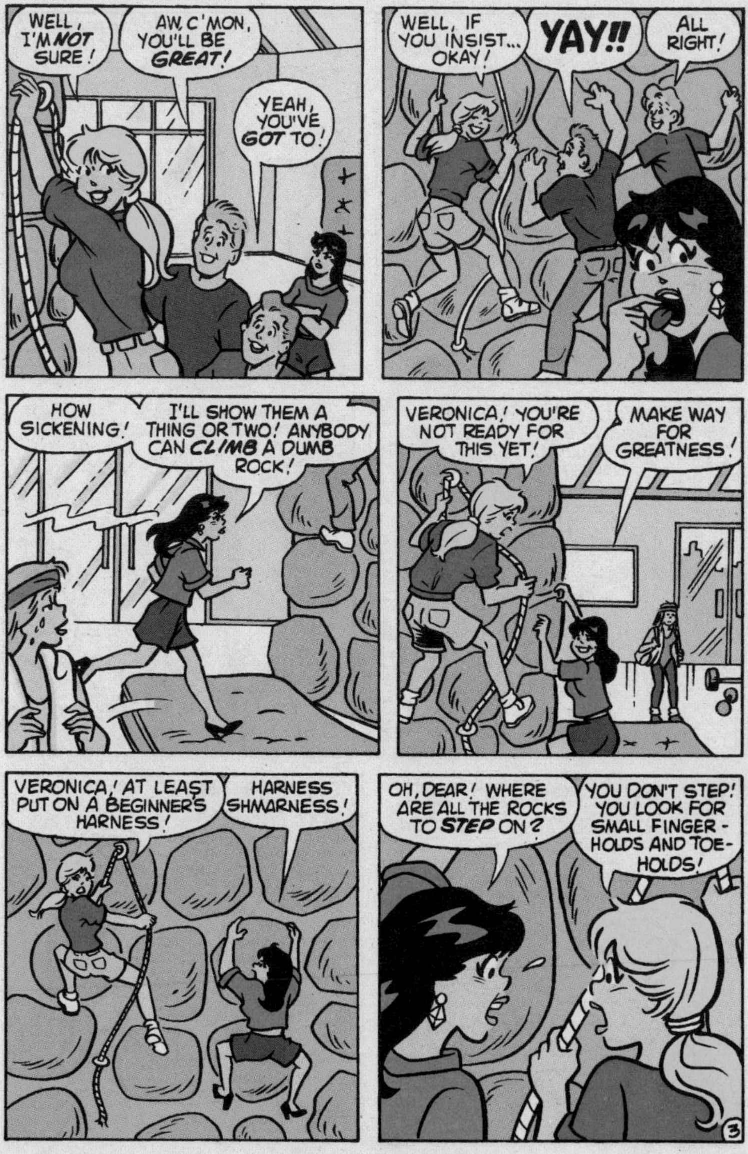
WELL, I'M NOT SURE!
AW, C'MON, YOU'LL BE GREAT!
YEAH, YOU'VE GOT TO!
WELL, IF YOU INSIST... OKAY!
YAY!!
ALL RIGHT!
HOW SICKENING!
I'LL SHOW THEM A THING OR TWO! ANYBODY CAN CLIMB A DUMB ROCK!
VERONICA! YOU'RE NOT READY FOR THIS YET!
MAKE WAY FOR GREATNESS!
VERONICA! AT LEAST PUT ON A BEGINNER'S HARNESS!
HARNESS SHMARNESS!
OH, DEAR! WHERE ARE ALL THE ROCKS TO STEP ON?
YOU DON'T STEP! YOU LOOK FOR SMALL FINGER-HOLDS AND TOE-HOLDS!
3

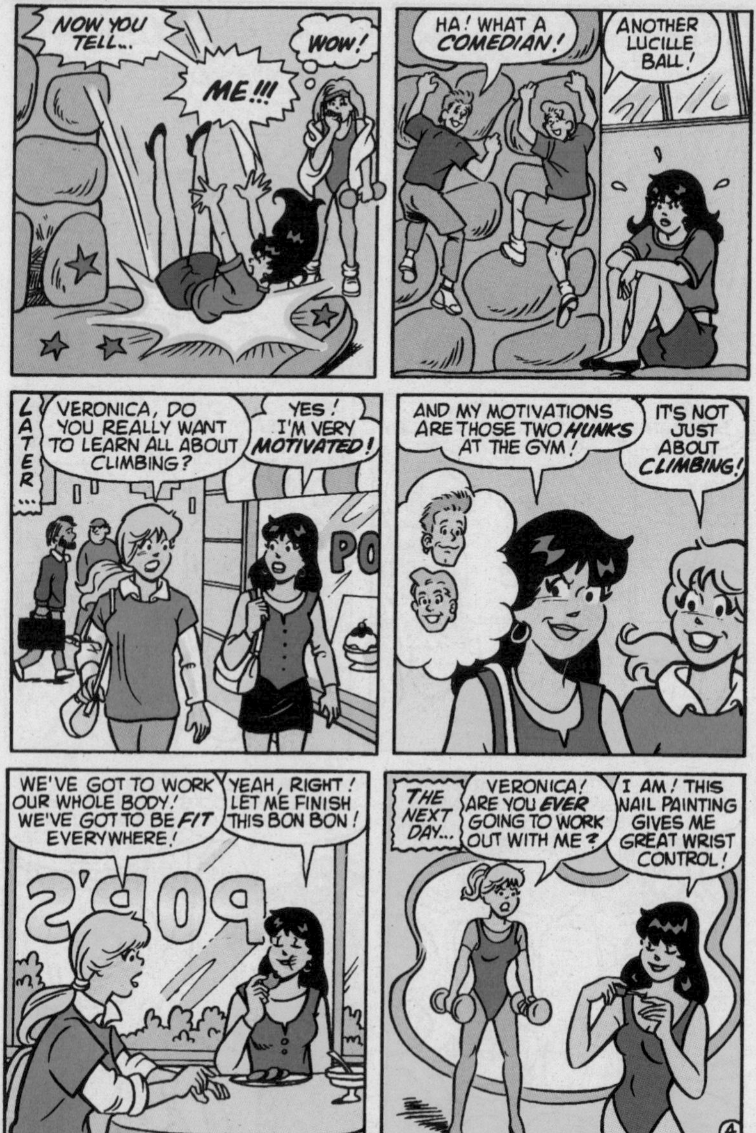
NOW YOU TELL...
ME!!!
WOW!
HA! WHAT A COMEDIAN!
ANOTHER LUCILLE BALL!
LATER...
VERONICA, DO YOU REALLY WANT TO LEARN ALL ABOUT CLIMBING?
YES! I'M VERY MOTIVATED!
PO
AND MY MOTIVATIONS ARE THOSE TWO HUNKS AT THE GYM!
IT'S NOT JUST ABOUT CLIMBING!
WE'VE GOT TO WORK OUR WHOLE BODY! WE'VE GOT TO BE FIT EVERYWHERE!
YEAH, RIGHT! LET ME FINISH THIS BON BON!
POP'S
THE NEXT DAY...
VERONICA! ARE YOU EVER GOING TO WORK OUT WITH ME?
I AM! THIS NAIL PAINTING GIVES ME GREAT WRIST CONTROL!
4

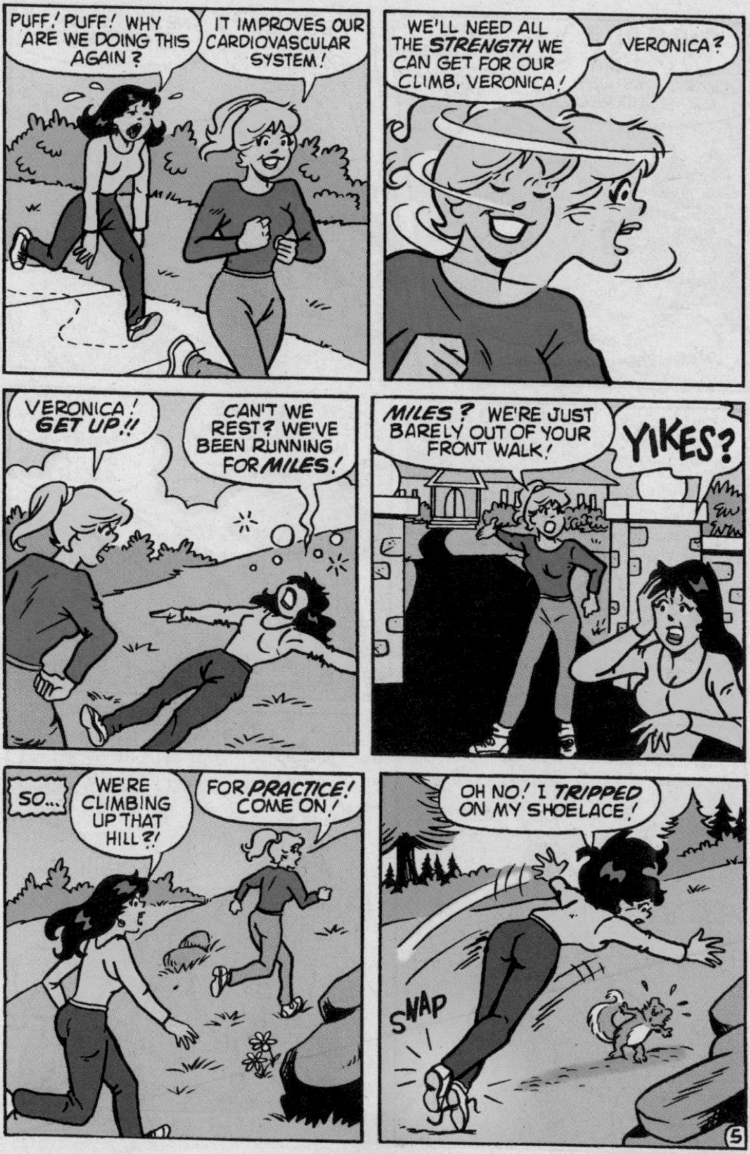
PUFF! PUFF! WHY ARE WE DOING THIS AGAIN?
IT IMPROVES OUR CARDIOVASCULAR SYSTEM!
WE'LL NEED ALL THE STRENGTH WE CAN GET FOR OUR CLIMB, VERONICA!
VERONICA?
VERONICA! GET UP!!
CAN'T WE REST? WE'VE BEEN RUNNING FOR MILES!
MILES? WE'RE JUST BARELY OUT OF YOUR FRONT WALK!
YIKES?
SO...
WE'RE CLIMBING UP THAT HILL?!
FOR PRACTICE! COME ON!
OH NO! I TRIPPED ON MY SHOELACE!
SNAP

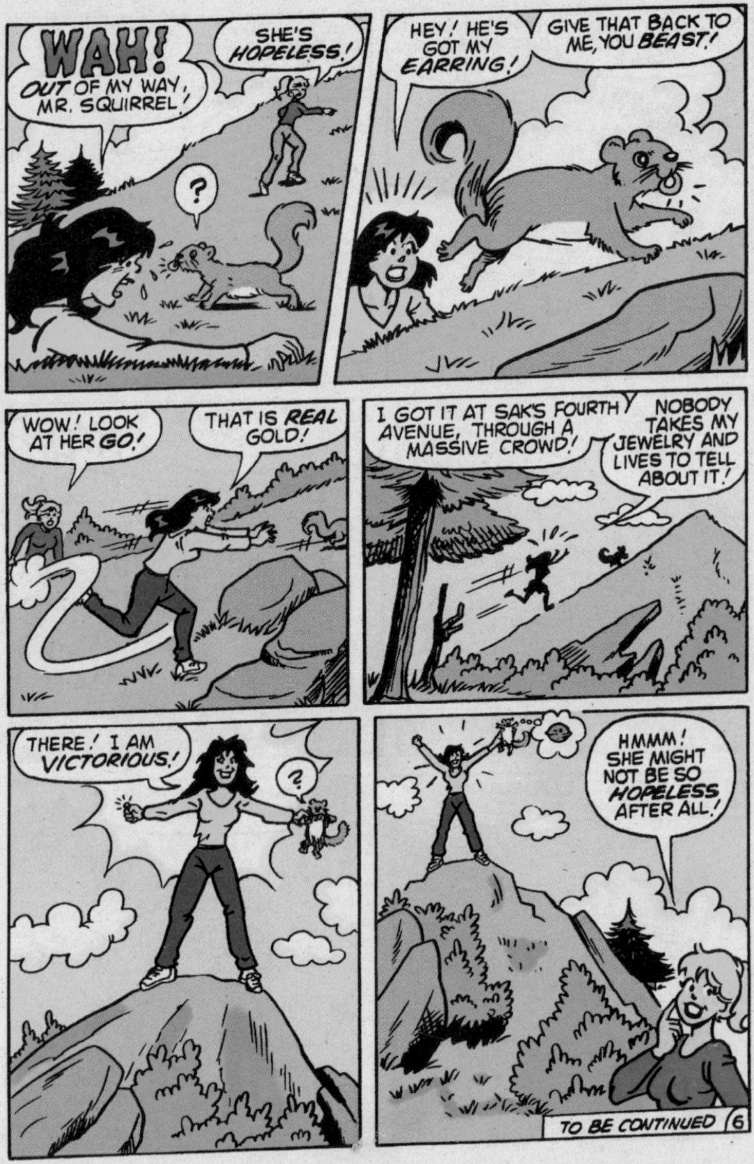
WAH! OUT OF MY WAY, MR. SQUIRREL!
SHE'S HOPELESS!
?
HEY! HE'S GOT MY EARRING!
GIVE THAT BACK TO ME, YOU BEAST!
WOW! LOOK AT HER GO!
THAT IS REAL GOLD!
I GOT IT AT SAK'S FOURTH AVENUE, THROUGH A MASSIVE CROWD!
NOBODY TAKES MY JEWELRY AND LIVES TO TELL ABOUT IT!
THERE! I AM VICTORIOUS!
?
HMMM! SHE MIGHT NOT BE SO HOPELESS AFTER ALL!
TO BE CONTINUED 6

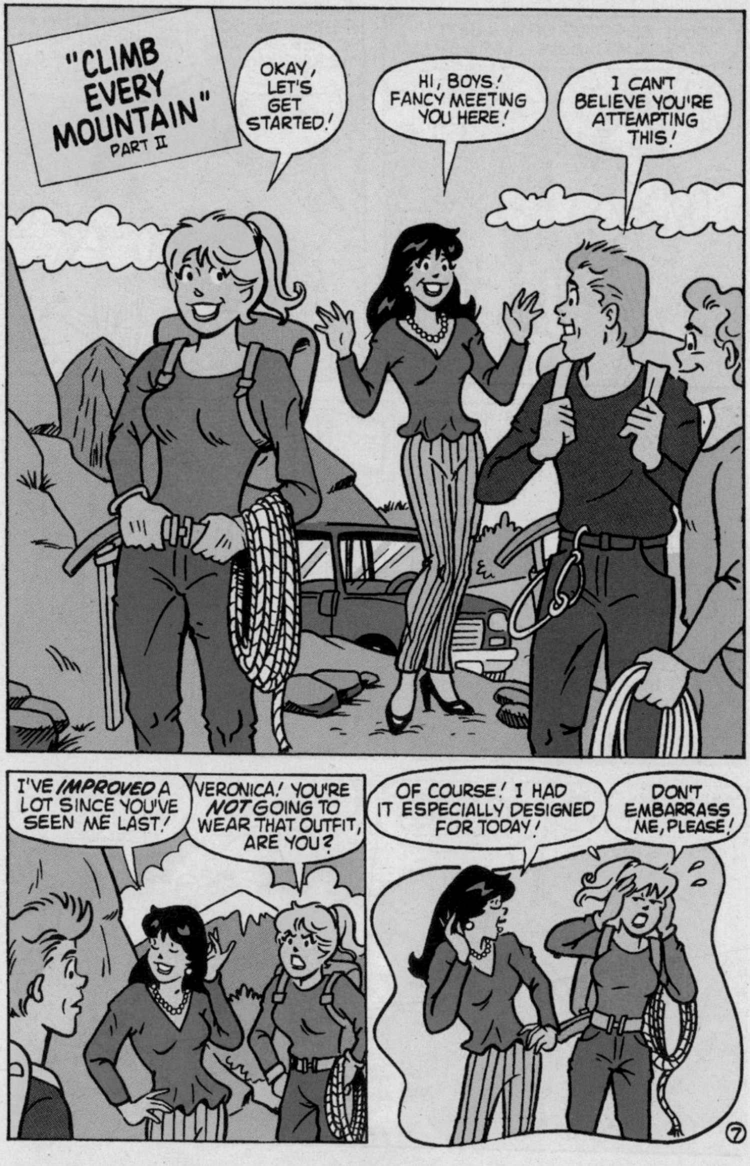

"CLIMB EVERY MOUNTAIN" PART II
OKAY, LET'S GET STARTED!
HI, BOYS! FANCY MEETING YOU HERE!
I CAN'T BELIEVE YOU'RE ATTEMPTING THIS!
I'VE *IMPROVED* A LOT SINCE YOU'VE SEEN ME LAST!
VERONICA! YOU'RE *NOT* GOING TO WEAR THAT OUTFIT, ARE YOU?
OF COURSE! I HAD IT ESPECIALLY DESIGNED FOR TODAY!
DON'T EMBARRASS ME, PLEASE!
7

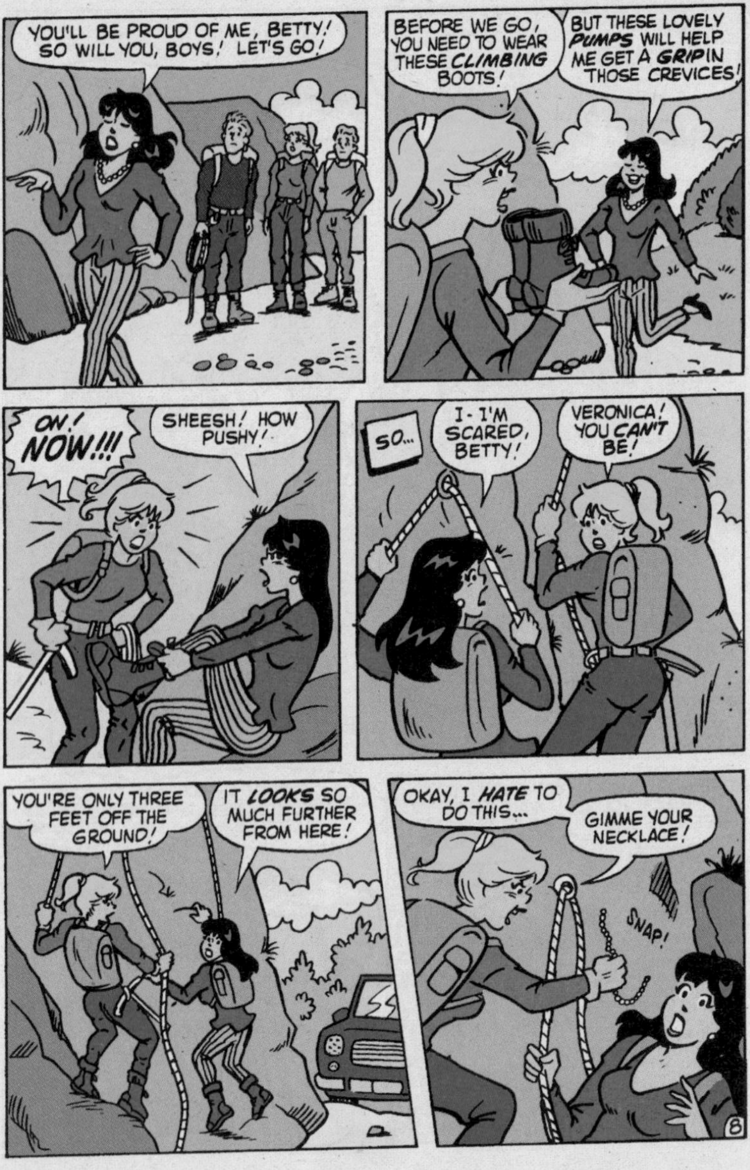
YOU'LL BE PROUD OF ME, BETTY! SO WILL YOU, BOYS! LET'S GO!
BEFORE WE GO, YOU NEED TO WEAR THESE CLIMBING BOOTS!
BUT THESE LOVELY PUMPS WILL HELP ME GET A GRIP IN THOSE CREVICES!
ON! NOW!!!
SHEESH! HOW PUSHY!
SO...
I-I'M SCARED, BETTY!
VERONICA! YOU CAN'T BE!
YOU'RE ONLY THREE FEET OFF THE GROUND!
IT LOOKS SO MUCH FURTHER FROM HERE!
OKAY, I HATE TO DO THIS...
GIMME YOUR NECKLACE!
SNAP!
8

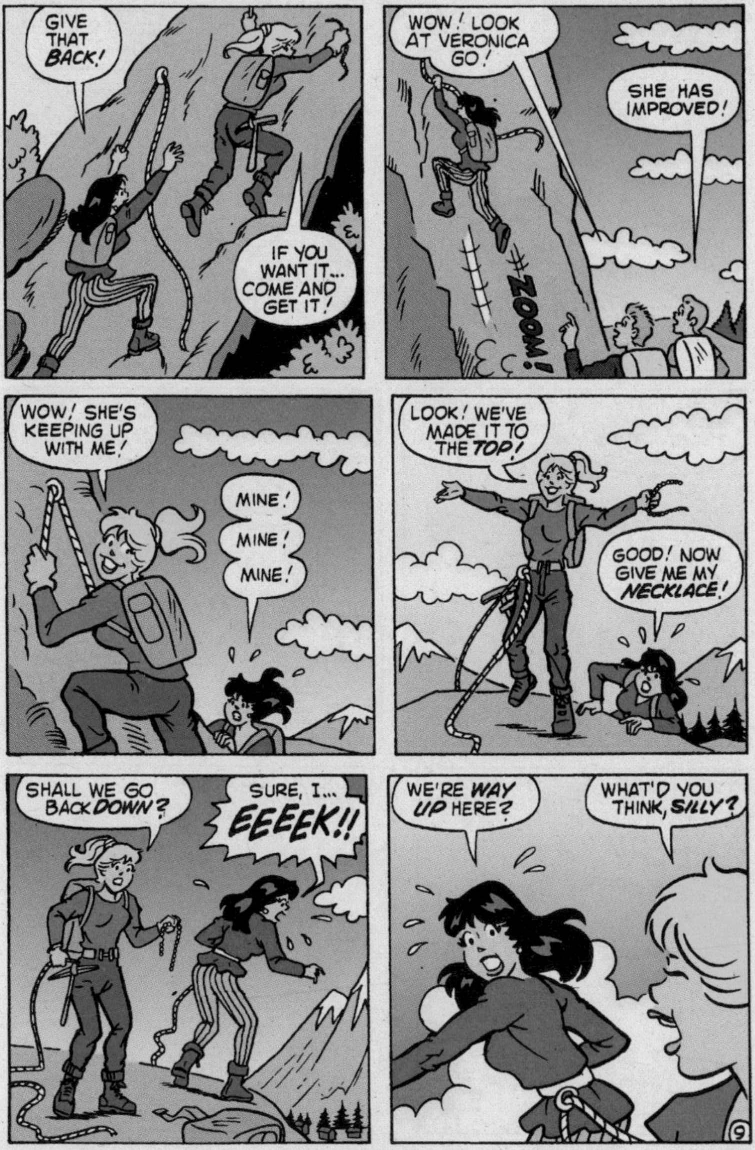
GIVE THAT BACK!
IF YOU WANT IT... COME AND GET IT!
WOW! LOOK AT VERONICA GO!
SHE HAS IMPROVED!
ZOOM!
WOW! SHE'S KEEPING UP WITH ME!
MINE!
MINE!
MINE!
LOOK! WE'VE MADE IT TO THE TOP!
GOOD! NOW GIVE ME MY NECKLACE!
SHALL WE GO BACK DOWN?
SURE, I... EEEEK!!
WE'RE WAY UP HERE?
WHAT'D YOU THINK, SILLY?
9

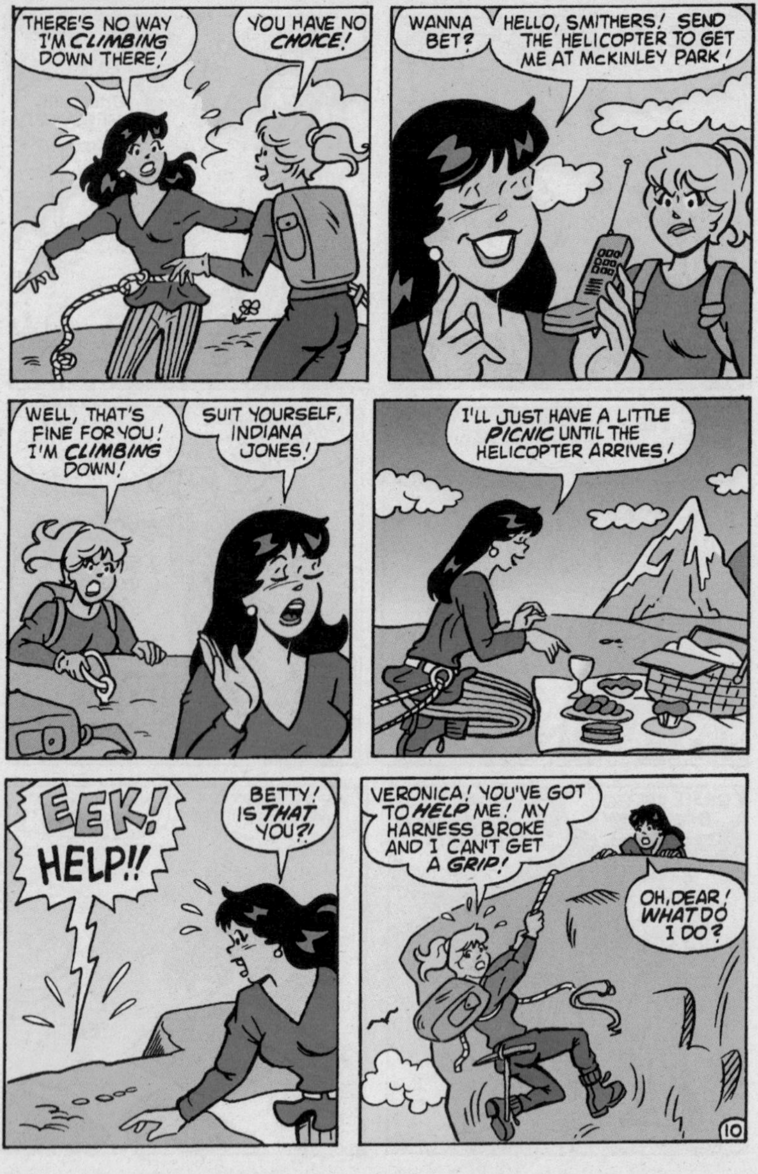

THERE'S NO WAY I'M CLIMBING DOWN THERE!
YOU HAVE NO CHOICE!
WANNA BET?
HELLO, SMITHERS! SEND THE HELICOPTER TO GET ME AT McKINLEY PARK!
WELL, THAT'S FINE FOR YOU! I'M CLIMBING DOWN!
SUIT YOURSELF, INDIANA JONES!
I'LL JUST HAVE A LITTLE PICNIC UNTIL THE HELICOPTER ARRIVES!
EEK! HELP!!
BETTY! IS THAT YOU?!
VERONICA! YOU'VE GOT TO HELP ME! MY HARNESS BROKE AND I CAN'T GET A GRIP!
OH, DEAR! WHAT DO I DO?
10

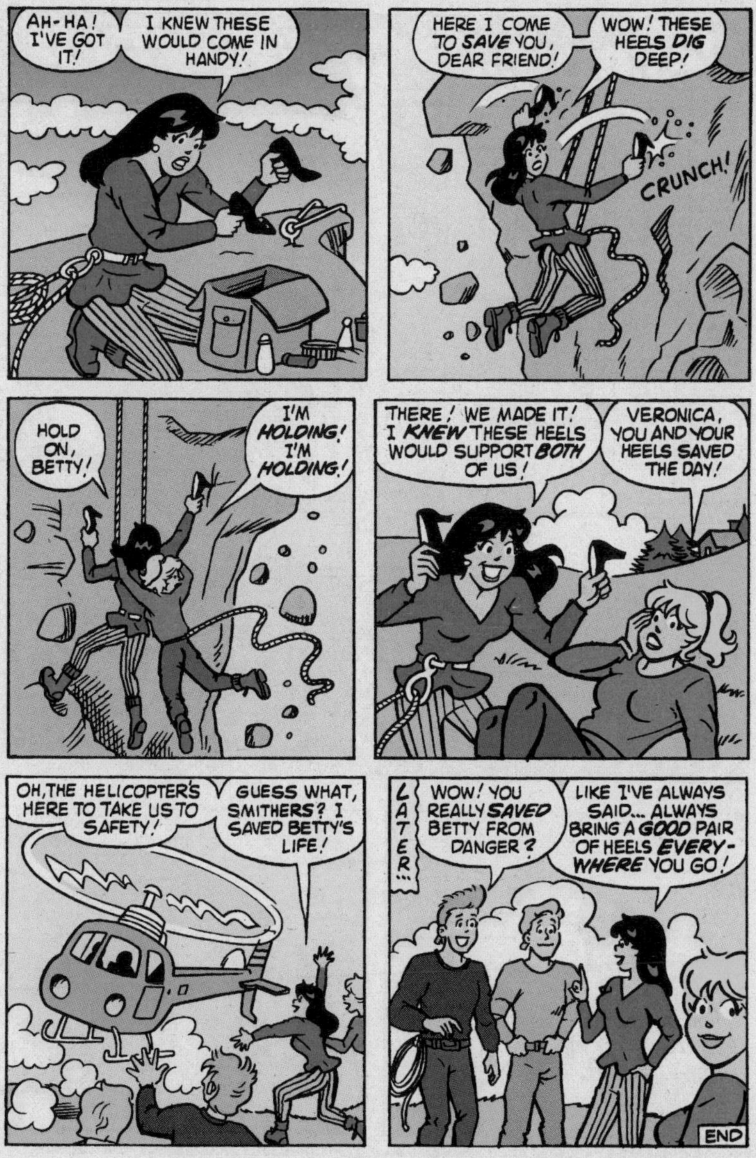
AH-HA! I'VE GOT IT!
I KNEW THESE WOULD COME IN HANDY!
HERE I COME TO SAVE YOU, DEAR FRIEND!
WOW! THESE HEELS DIG DEEP!
CRUNCH!
HOLD ON, BETTY!
I'M HOLDING! I'M HOLDING!
THERE! WE MADE IT! I KNEW THESE HEELS WOULD SUPPORT BOTH OF US!
VERONICA, YOU AND YOUR HEELS SAVED THE DAY!
OH, THE HELICOPTER'S HERE TO TAKE US TO SAFETY!
GUESS WHAT, SMITHERS? I SAVED BETTY'S LIFE!
LATER...
WOW! YOU REALLY SAVED BETTY FROM DANGER?
LIKE I'VE ALWAYS SAID... ALWAYS BRING A GOOD PAIR OF HEELS EVERY-WHERE YOU GO!
END

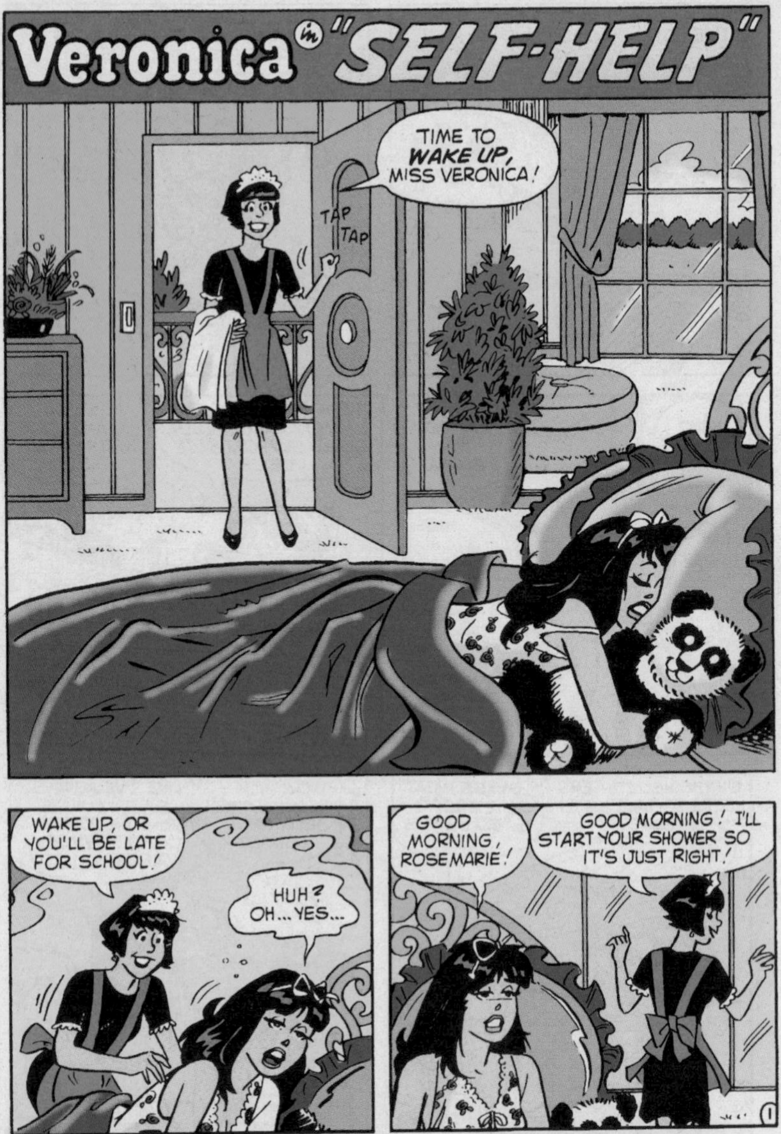
Veronica in "SELF-HELP"
TIME TO WAKE UP, MISS VERONICA!
TAP TAP
WAKE UP, OR YOU'LL BE LATE FOR SCHOOL!
HUH? OH... YES...
GOOD MORNING, ROSEMARIE!
GOOD MORNING! I'LL START YOUR SHOWER SO IT'S JUST RIGHT!
1

Script: Mike Pellowski / Pencils: Dan DeCarlo / Inks: Alison Flood / Letters: Bill Yoshida

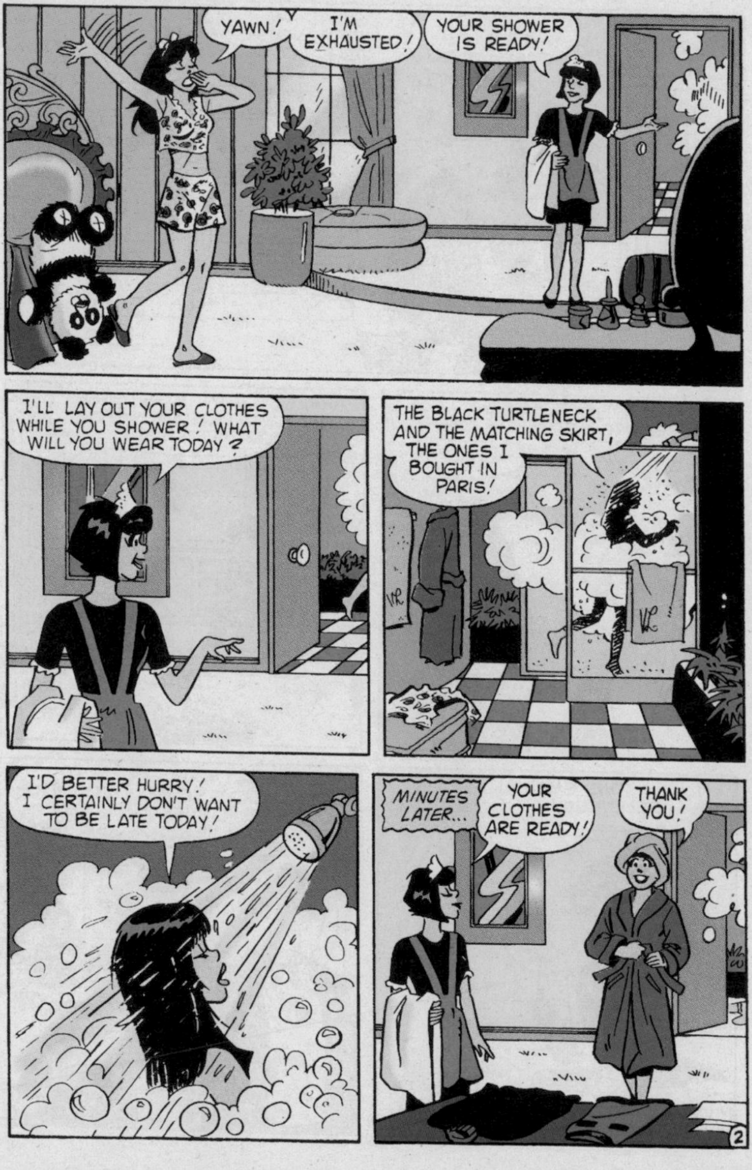
YAWN!
I'M EXHAUSTED!
YOUR SHOWER IS READY!
I'LL LAY OUT YOUR CLOTHES WHILE YOU SHOWER! WHAT WILL YOU WEAR TODAY?
THE BLACK TURTLENECK AND THE MATCHING SKIRT, THE ONES I BOUGHT IN PARIS!
I'D BETTER HURRY! I CERTAINLY DON'T WANT TO BE LATE TODAY!
MINUTES LATER...
YOUR CLOTHES ARE READY!
THANK YOU!
2

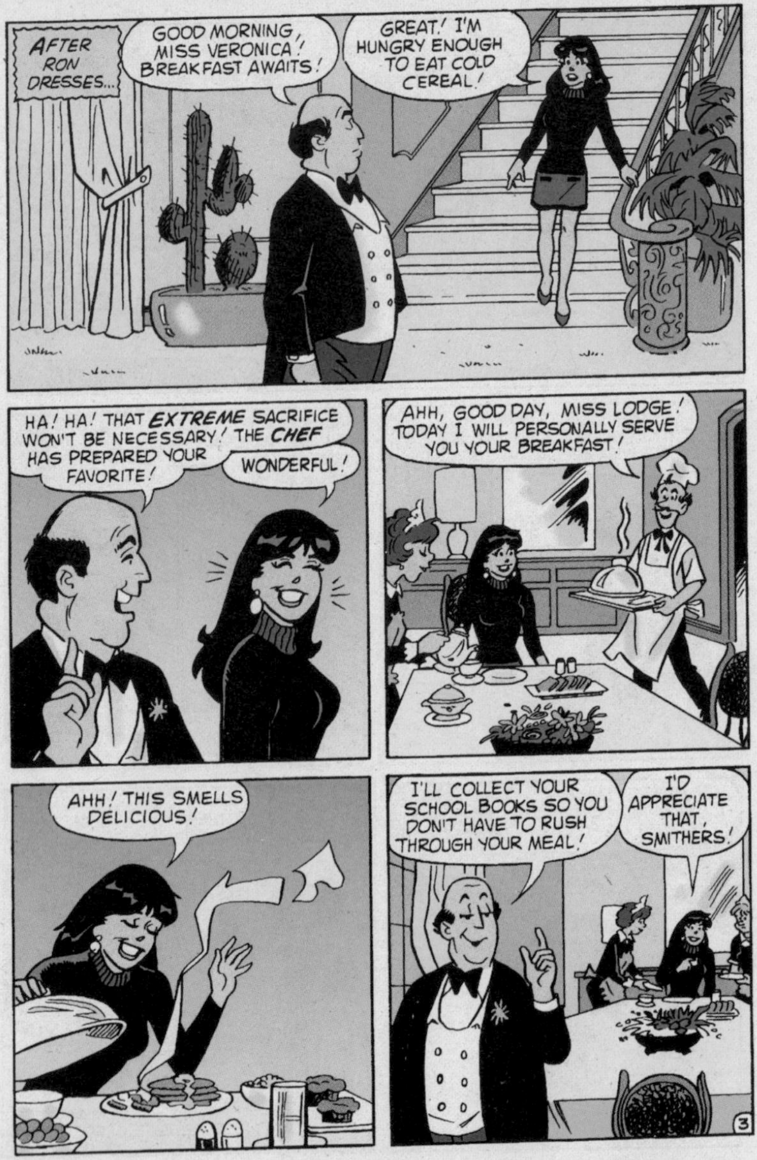
AFTER RON DRESSES...
GOOD MORNING, MISS VERONICA! BREAKFAST AWAITS!
GREAT! I'M HUNGRY ENOUGH TO EAT COLD CEREAL!
HA! HA! THAT EXTREME SACRIFICE WON'T BE NECESSARY! THE CHEF HAS PREPARED YOUR FAVORITE!
WONDERFUL!
AHH, GOOD DAY, MISS LODGE! TODAY I WILL PERSONALLY SERVE YOU YOUR BREAKFAST!
AHH! THIS SMELLS DELICIOUS!
I'LL COLLECT YOUR SCHOOL BOOKS SO YOU DON'T HAVE TO RUSH THROUGH YOUR MEAL!
I'D APPRECIATE THAT, SMITHERS!
3

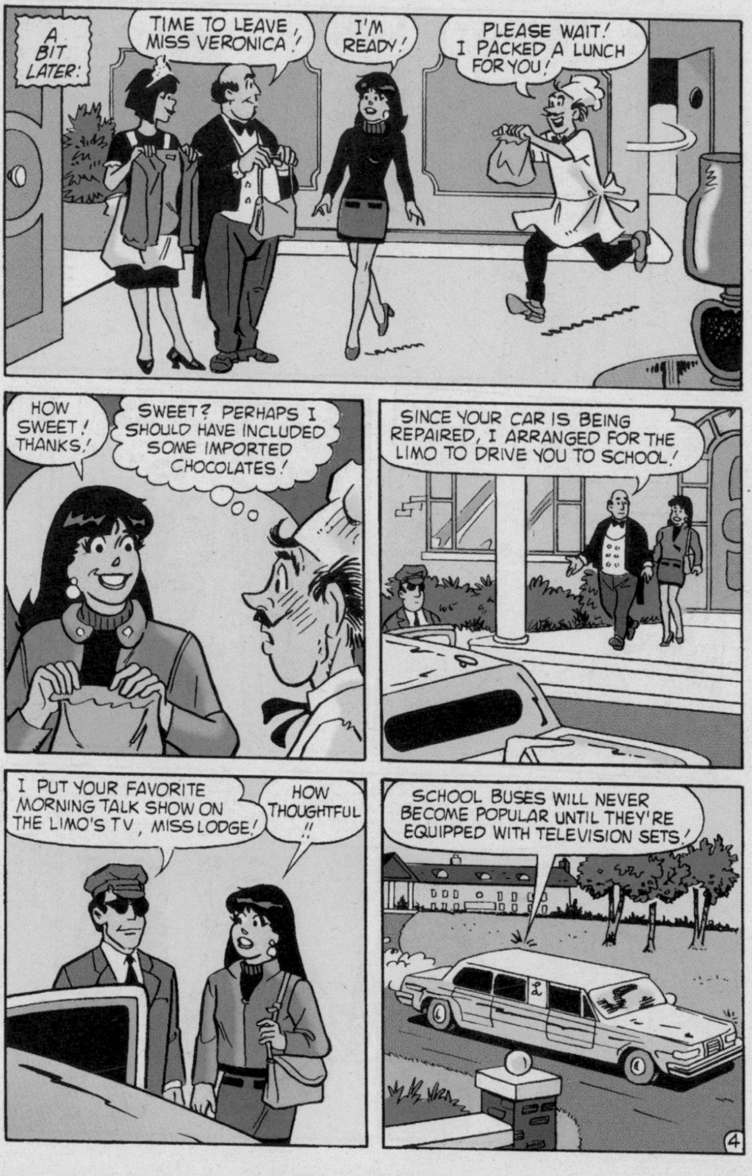
A BIT LATER:
TIME TO LEAVE, MISS VERONICA!
I'M READY!
PLEASE WAIT! I PACKED A LUNCH FOR YOU!
HOW SWEET! THANKS!
SWEET? PERHAPS I SHOULD HAVE INCLUDED SOME IMPORTED CHOCOLATES!
SINCE YOUR CAR IS BEING REPAIRED, I ARRANGED FOR THE LIMO TO DRIVE YOU TO SCHOOL!
I PUT YOUR FAVORITE MORNING TALK SHOW ON THE LIMO'S TV, MISS LODGE!
HOW THOUGHTFUL!!
SCHOOL BUSES WILL NEVER BECOME POPULAR UNTIL THEY'RE EQUIPPED WITH TELEVISION SETS!
4

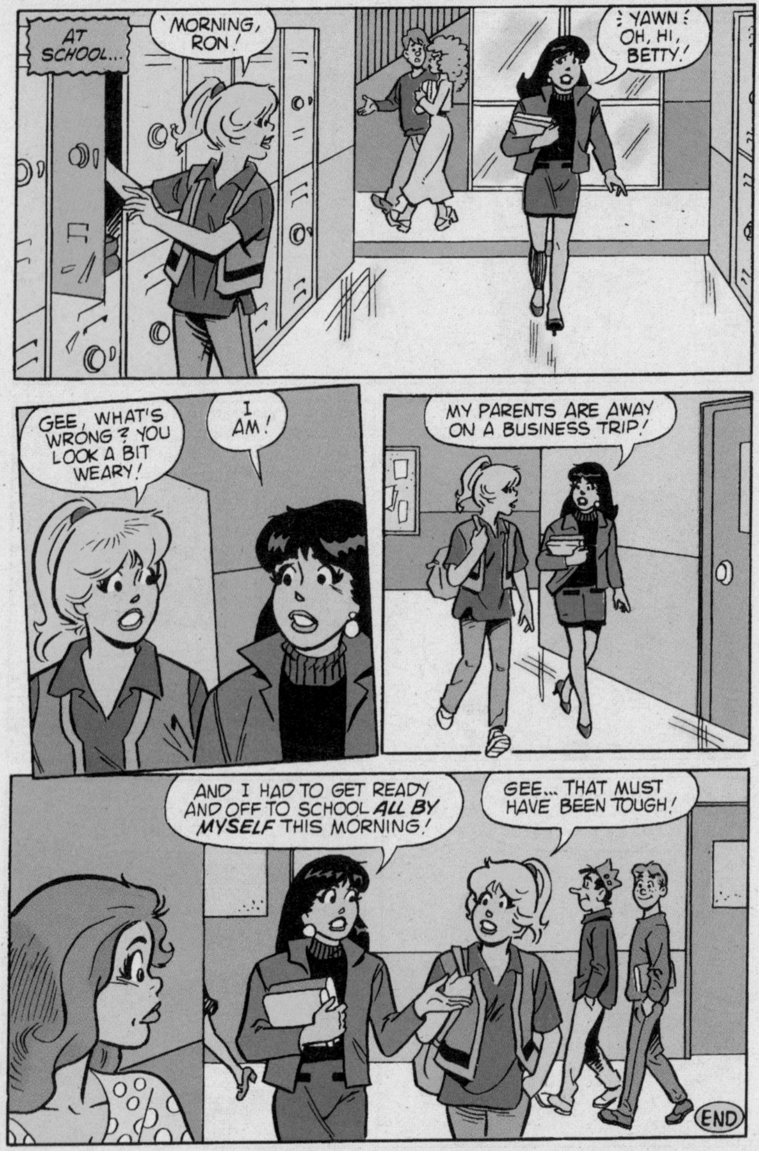
AT SCHOOL...
`MORNING, RON!
YAWN OH, HI, BETTY!
GEE, WHAT'S WRONG? YOU LOOK A BIT WEARY!
I AM!
MY PARENTS ARE AWAY ON A BUSINESS TRIP!
AND I HAD TO GET READY AND OFF TO SCHOOL ALL BY MYSELF THIS MORNING!
GEE... THAT MUST HAVE BEEN TOUGH!
END

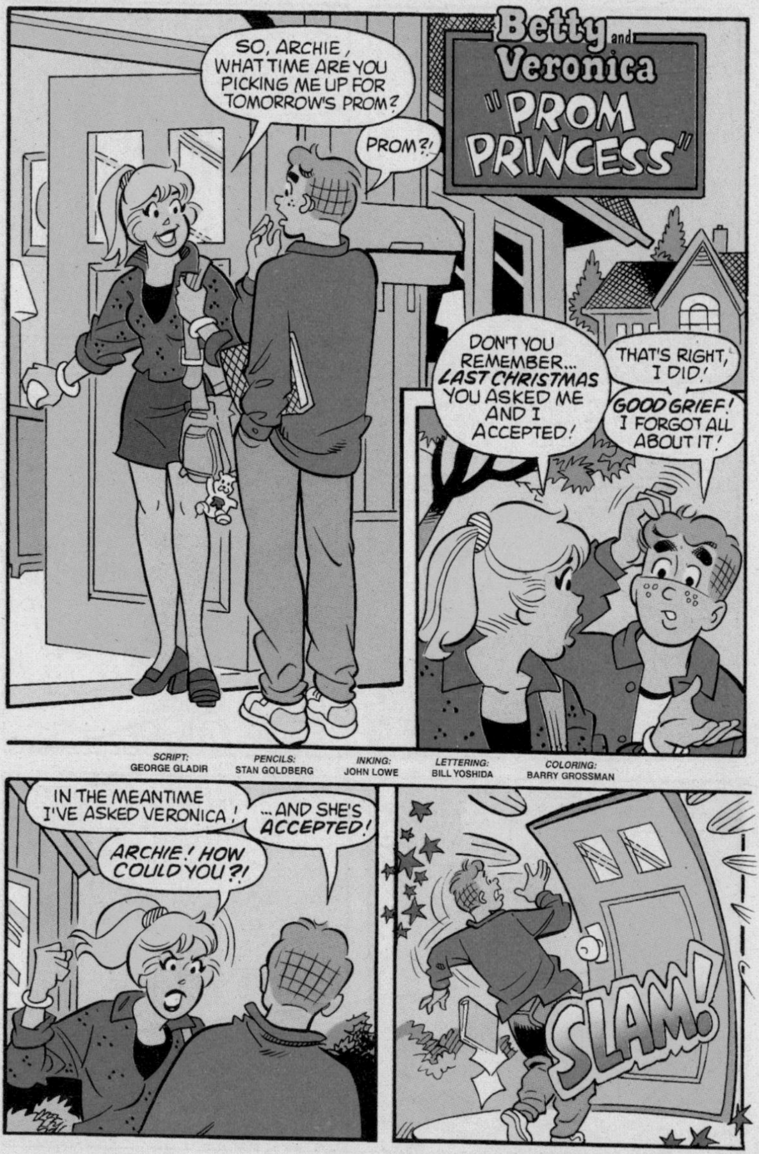
Betty and Veronica
"PROM PRINCESS"
SO, ARCHIE, WHAT TIME ARE YOU PICKING ME UP FOR TOMORROW'S PROM?
PROM?!
DON'T YOU REMEMBER... LAST CHRISTMAS YOU ASKED ME AND I ACCEPTED!
THAT'S RIGHT, I DID!
GOOD GRIEF! I FORGOT ALL ABOUT IT!
SCRIPT: GEORGE GLADIR
PENCILS: STAN GOLDBERG
INKING: JOHN LOWE
LETTERING: BILL YOSHIDA
COLORING: BARRY GROSSMAN
IN THE MEANTIME I'VE ASKED VERONICA!
...AND SHE'S ACCEPTED!
ARCHIE! HOW COULD YOU?!
SLAM!

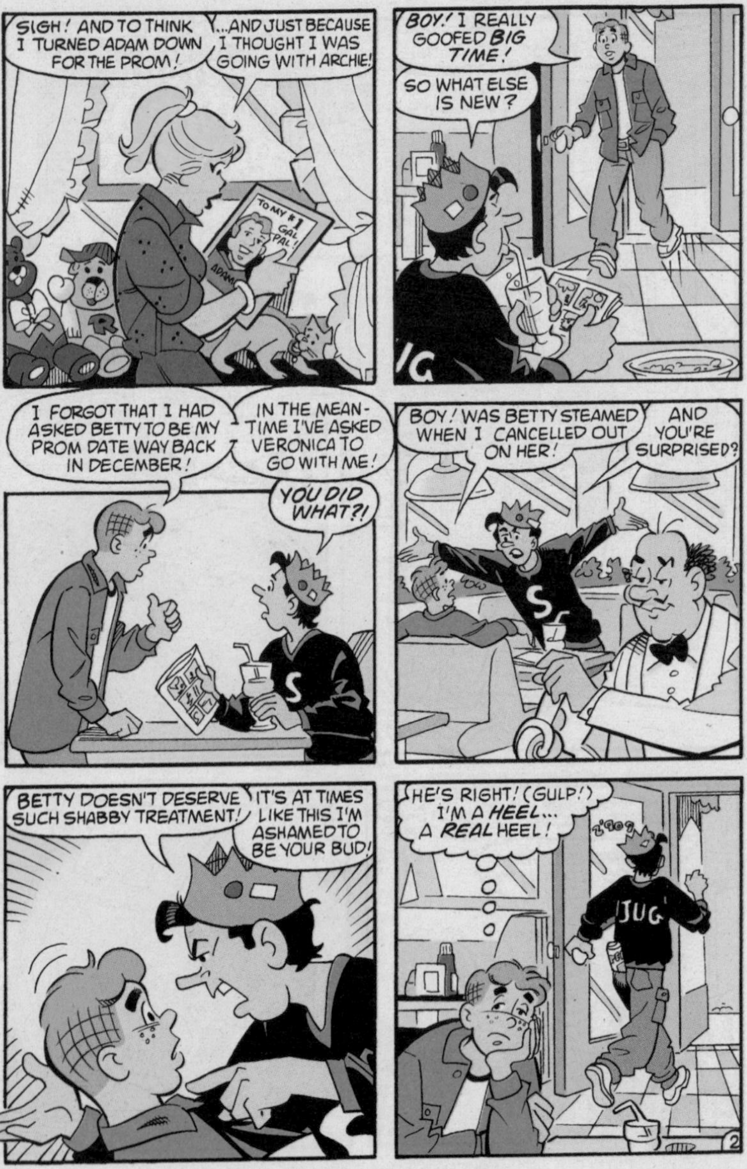
SIGH! AND TO THINK I TURNED ADAM DOWN FOR THE PROM!
...AND JUST BECAUSE I THOUGHT I WAS GOING WITH ARCHIE!
TO MY #1 GAL PAL!
ADAM
BOY! I REALLY GOOFED BIG TIME!
SO WHAT ELSE IS NEW?
I FORGOT THAT I HAD ASKED BETTY TO BE MY PROM DATE WAY BACK IN DECEMBER!
IN THE MEAN-TIME I'VE ASKED VERONICA TO GO WITH ME!
YOU DID WHAT?!
BOY! WAS BETTY STEAMED WHEN I CANCELLED OUT ON HER!
AND YOU'RE SURPRISED?
BETTY DOESN'T DESERVE SUCH SHABBY TREATMENT!
IT'S AT TIMES LIKE THIS I'M ASHAMED TO BE YOUR BUD!
HE'S RIGHT! (GULP!) I'M A HEEL... A REAL HEEL!
JUG
2

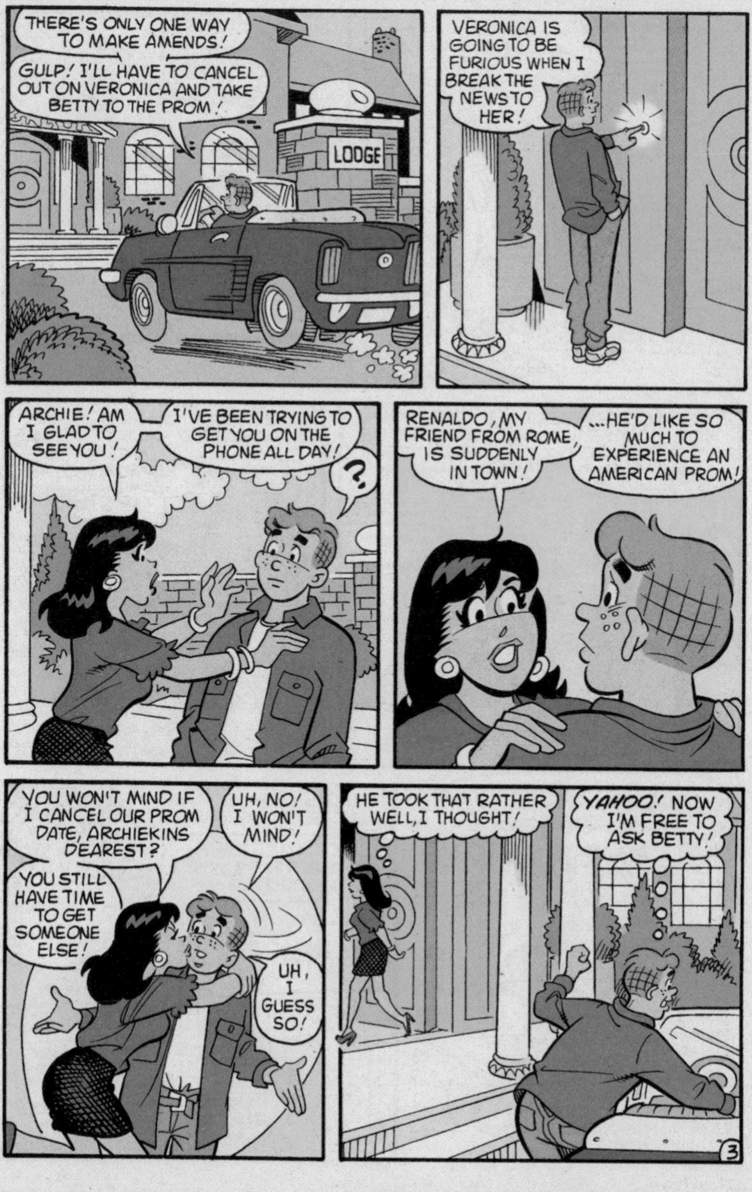
THERE'S ONLY ONE WAY TO MAKE AMENDS!
GULP! I'LL HAVE TO CANCEL OUT ON VERONICA AND TAKE BETTY TO THE PROM!
LODGE
VERONICA IS GOING TO BE FURIOUS WHEN I BREAK THE NEWS TO HER!
ARCHIE! AM I GLAD TO SEE YOU!
I'VE BEEN TRYING TO GET YOU ON THE PHONE ALL DAY!
?
RENALDO, MY FRIEND FROM ROME, IS SUDDENLY IN TOWN!
...HE'D LIKE SO MUCH TO EXPERIENCE AN AMERICAN PROM!
YOU WON'T MIND IF I CANCEL OUR PROM DATE, ARCHIEKINS DEAREST?
YOU STILL HAVE TIME TO GET SOMEONE ELSE!
UH, NO! I WON'T MIND!
UH, I GUESS SO!
HE TOOK THAT RATHER WELL, I THOUGHT!
YAHOO! NOW I'M FREE TO ASK BETTY!

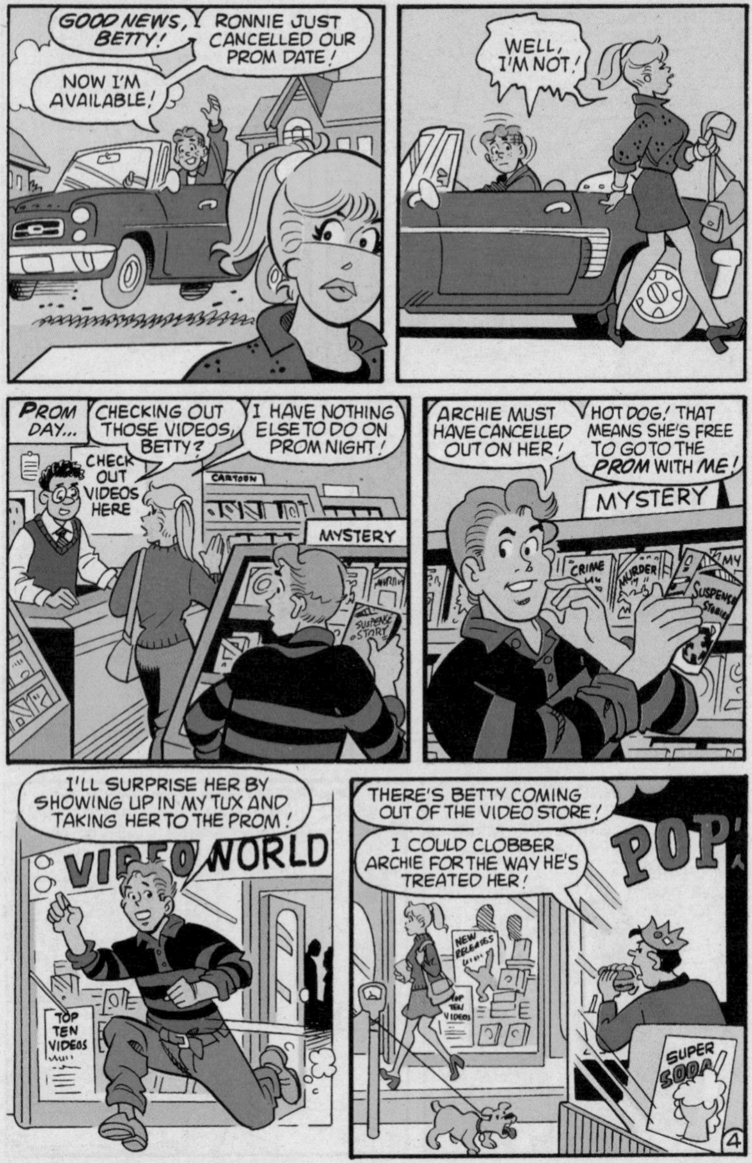
GOOD NEWS, BETTY!
RONNIE JUST CANCELLED OUR PROM DATE!
NOW I'M AVAILABLE!
WELL, I'M NOT!
PROM DAY...
CHECKING OUT THOSE VIDEOS, BETTY?
CHECK OUT VIDEOS HERE
I HAVE NOTHING ELSE TO DO ON PROM NIGHT!
CARTOON
MYSTERY
SUSPENSE STORY
ARCHIE MUST HAVE CANCELLED OUT ON HER!
HOT DOG! THAT MEANS SHE'S FREE TO GO TO THE PROM WITH ME!
MYSTERY
CRIME
MURDER
SUSPENSE STORIES
I'LL SURPRISE HER BY SHOWING UP IN MY TUX AND TAKING HER TO THE PROM!
VIDEO WORLD
TOP TEN VIDEOS
THERE'S BETTY COMING OUT OF THE VIDEO STORE!
I COULD CLOBBER ARCHIE FOR THE WAY HE'S TREATED HER!
POP'
NEW RELEASES
TOP TEN VIDEOS
SUPER SODA!
4

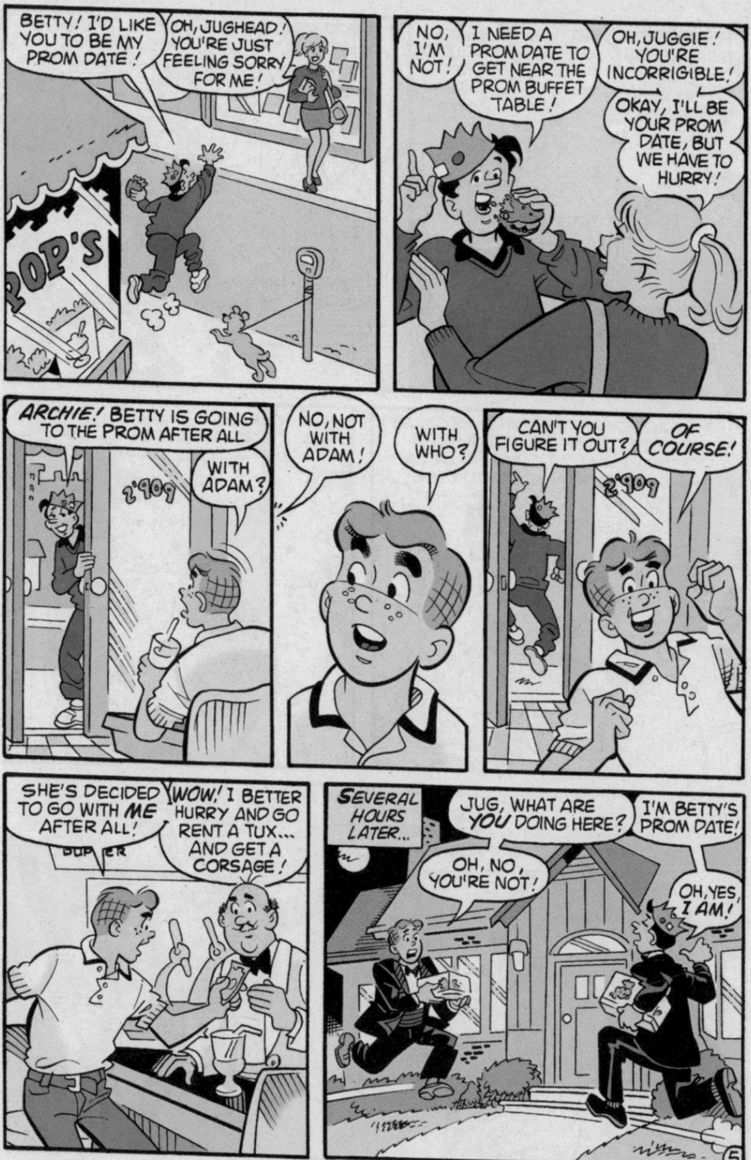
BETTY! I'D LIKE YOU TO BE MY PROM DATE!
OH, JUGHEAD! YOU'RE JUST FEELING SORRY FOR ME!
POP'S
NO, I'M NOT!
I NEED A PROM DATE TO GET NEAR THE PROM BUFFET TABLE!
OH, JUGGIE! YOU'RE INCORRIGIBLE!
OKAY, I'LL BE YOUR PROM DATE, BUT WE HAVE TO HURRY!
ARCHIE! BETTY IS GOING TO THE PROM AFTER ALL
WITH ADAM?
NO, NOT WITH ADAM!
WITH WHO?
CAN'T YOU FIGURE IT OUT?
OF COURSE!
SHE'S DECIDED TO GO WITH ME AFTER ALL!
WOW! I BETTER HURRY AND GO RENT A TUX... AND GET A CORSAGE!
SEVERAL HOURS LATER...
JUG, WHAT ARE YOU DOING HERE?
I'M BETTY'S PROM DATE!
OH, NO, YOU'RE NOT!
OH, YES, I AM!

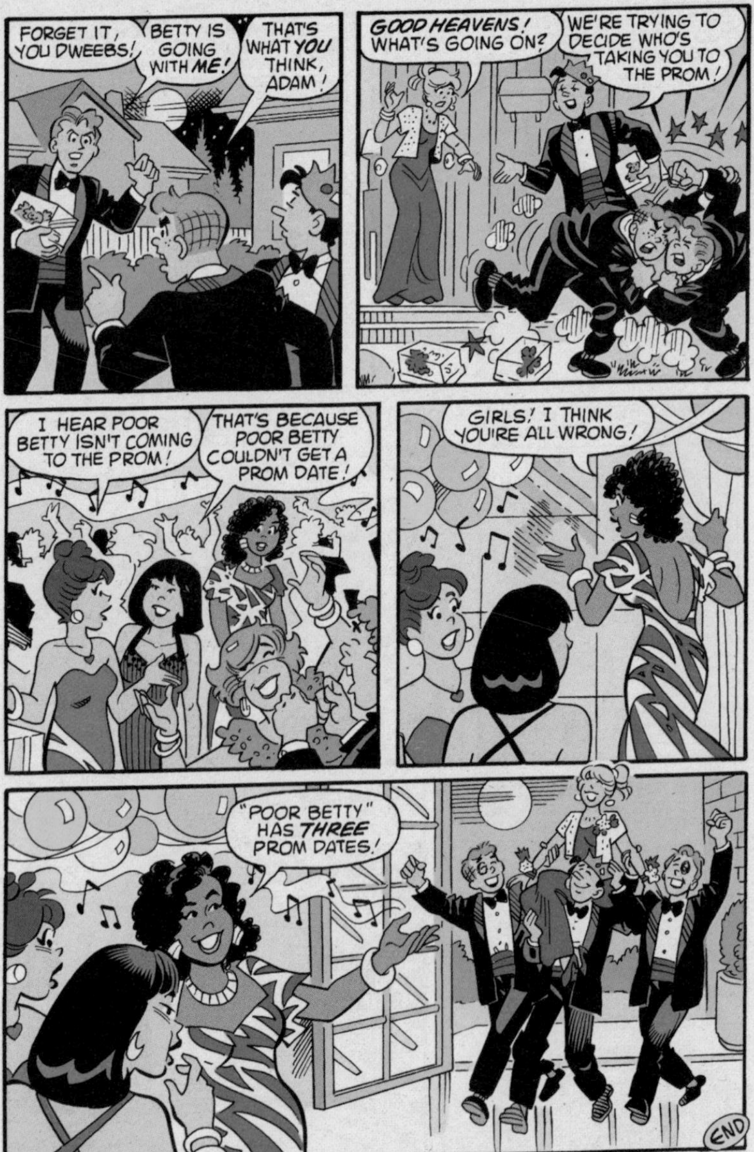

FORGET IT, YOU DWEEBS!
BETTY IS GOING WITH *ME*!
THAT'S WHAT *YOU* THINK, ADAM!
GOOD HEAVENS! WHAT'S GOING ON?
WE'RE TRYING TO DECIDE WHO'S TAKING YOU TO THE PROM!
I HEAR POOR BETTY ISN'T COMING TO THE PROM!
THAT'S BECAUSE POOR BETTY COULDN'T GET A PROM DATE!
GIRLS! I THINK YOU'RE ALL WRONG!
"POOR BETTY" HAS *THREE* PROM DATES!
END

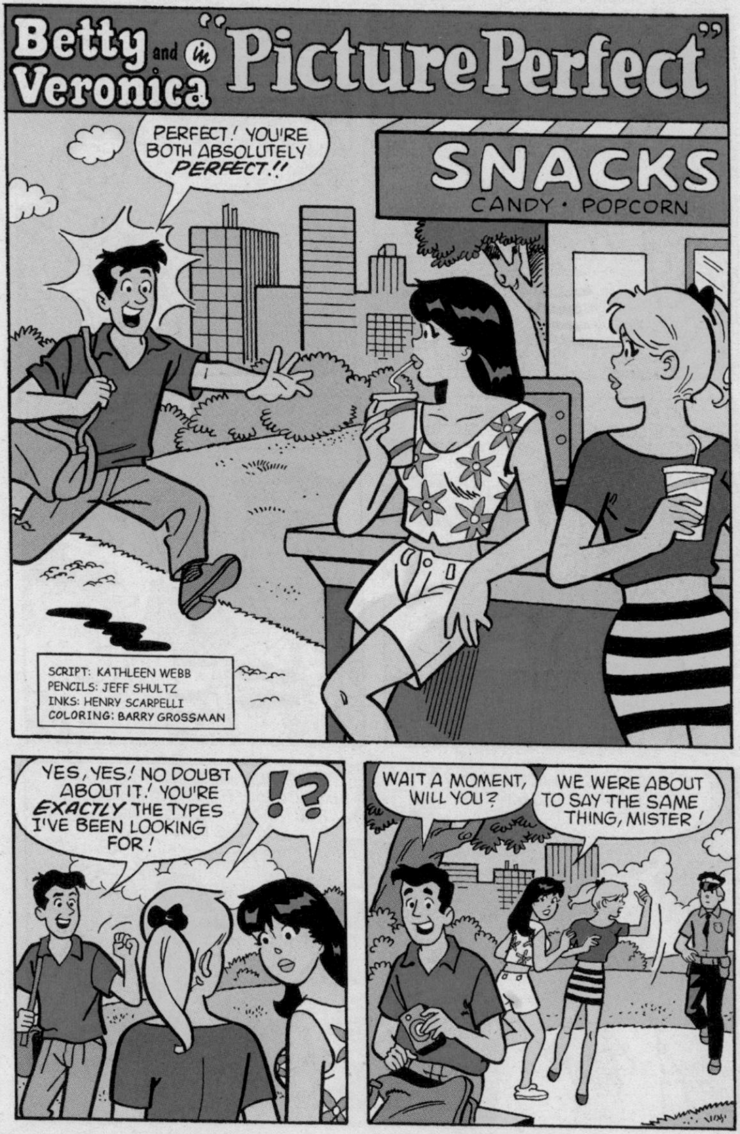
Betty and Veronica in "Picture Perfect"
PERFECT! YOU'RE BOTH ABSOLUTELY PERFECT!!
SNACKS
CANDY • POPCORN
SCRIPT: KATHLEEN WEBB
PENCILS: JEFF SHULTZ
INKS: HENRY SCARPELLI
COLORING: BARRY GROSSMAN
YES, YES! NO DOUBT ABOUT IT! YOU'RE EXACTLY THE TYPES I'VE BEEN LOOKING FOR!
!?
WAIT A MOMENT, WILL YOU?
WE WERE ABOUT TO SAY THE SAME THING, MISTER!

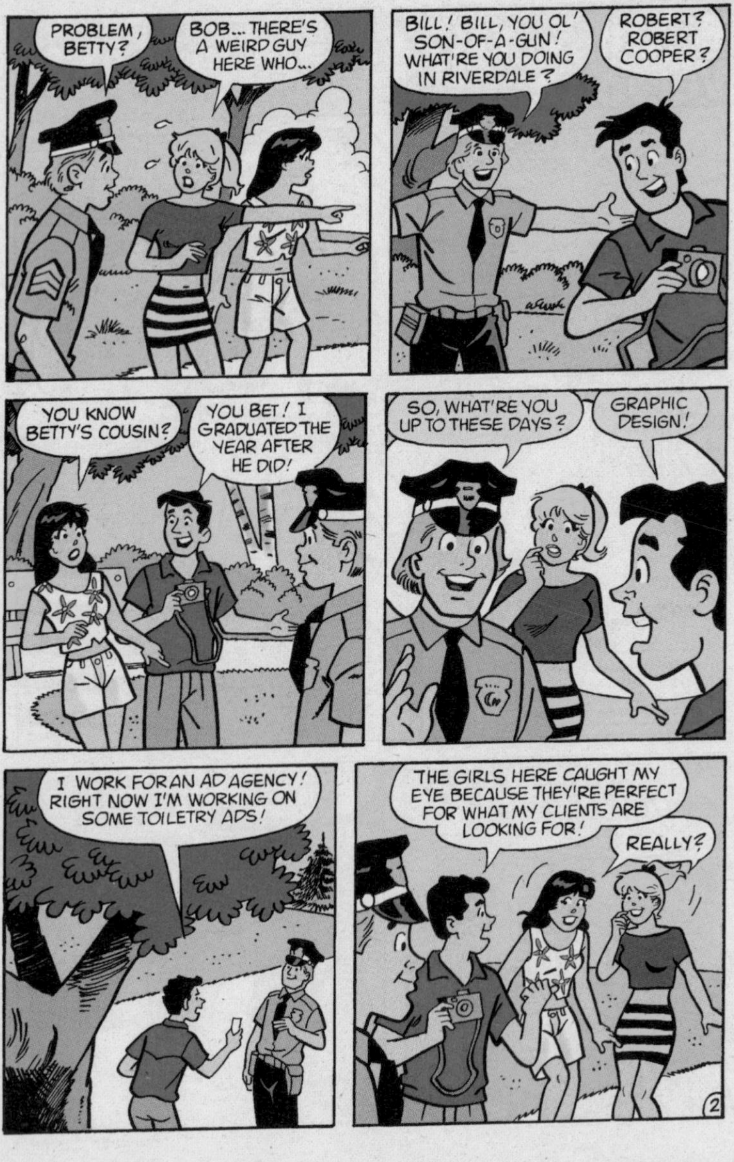
PROBLEM, BETTY?
BOB... THERE'S A WEIRD GUY HERE WHO...
BILL! BILL, YOU OL' SON-OF-A-GUN! WHAT'RE YOU DOING IN RIVERDALE?
ROBERT? ROBERT COOPER?
YOU KNOW BETTY'S COUSIN?
YOU BET! I GRADUATED THE YEAR AFTER HE DID!
SO, WHAT'RE YOU UP TO THESE DAYS?
GRAPHIC DESIGN!
I WORK FOR AN AD AGENCY! RIGHT NOW I'M WORKING ON SOME TOILETRY ADS!
THE GIRLS HERE CAUGHT MY EYE BECAUSE THEY'RE PERFECT FOR WHAT MY CLIENTS ARE LOOKING FOR!
REALLY?
2

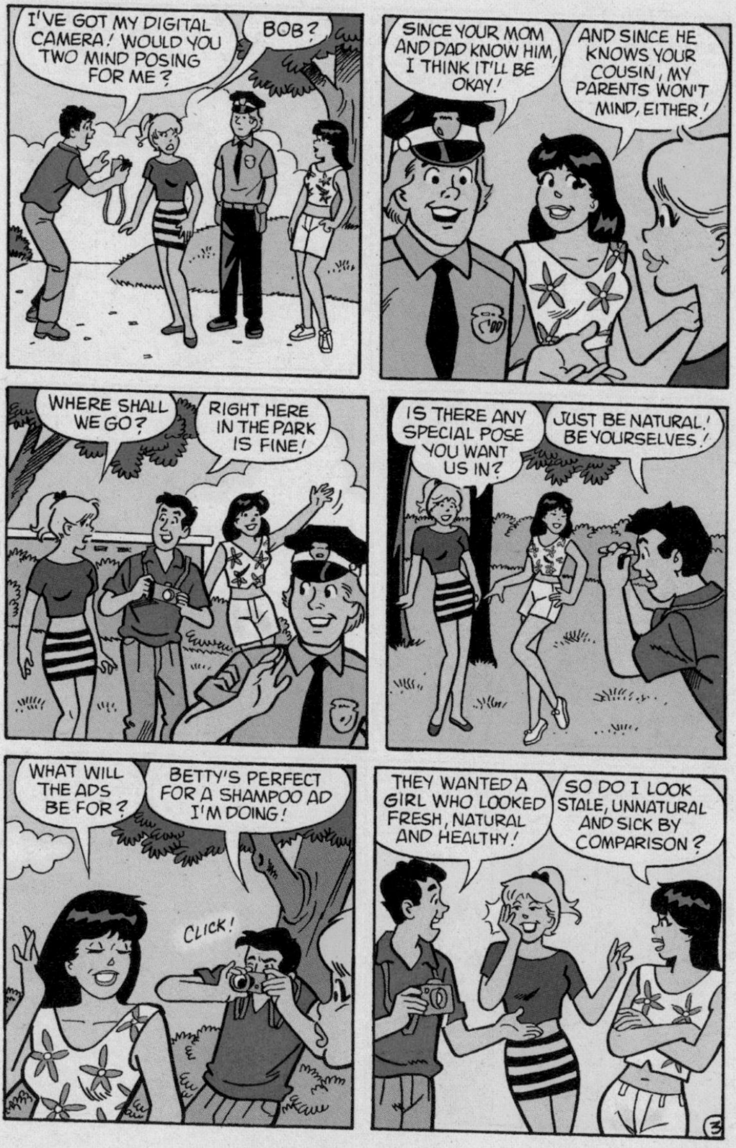
I'VE GOT MY DIGITAL CAMERA! WOULD YOU TWO MIND POSING FOR ME?
BOB?
SINCE YOUR MOM AND DAD KNOW HIM, I THINK IT'LL BE OKAY!
AND SINCE HE KNOWS YOUR COUSIN, MY PARENTS WON'T MIND, EITHER!
WHERE SHALL WE GO?
RIGHT HERE IN THE PARK IS FINE!
IS THERE ANY SPECIAL POSE YOU WANT US IN?
JUST BE NATURAL! BE YOURSELVES!
WHAT WILL THE ADS BE FOR?
BETTY'S PERFECT FOR A SHAMPOO AD I'M DOING!
CLICK!
THEY WANTED A GIRL WHO LOOKED FRESH, NATURAL AND HEALTHY!
SO DO I LOOK STALE, UNNATURAL AND SICK BY COMPARISON?
3

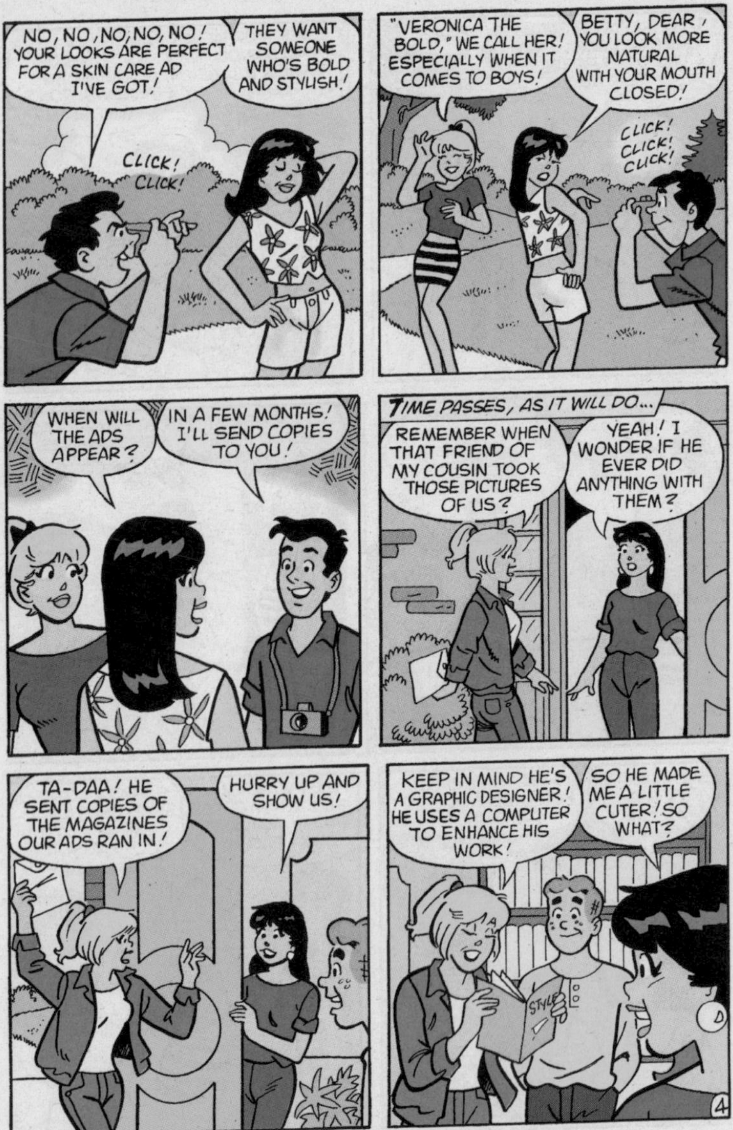
NO, NO, NO, NO, NO! YOUR LOOKS ARE PERFECT FOR A SKIN CARE AD I'VE GOT!
THEY WANT SOMEONE WHO'S BOLD AND STYLISH!
CLICK! CLICK!
"VERONICA THE BOLD," WE CALL HER! ESPECIALLY WHEN IT COMES TO BOYS!
BETTY, DEAR, YOU LOOK MORE NATURAL WITH YOUR MOUTH CLOSED!
CLICK! CLICK! CLICK!
WHEN WILL THE ADS APPEAR?
IN A FEW MONTHS! I'LL SEND COPIES TO YOU!
TIME PASSES, AS IT WILL DO...
REMEMBER WHEN THAT FRIEND OF MY COUSIN TOOK THOSE PICTURES OF US?
YEAH! I WONDER IF HE EVER DID ANYTHING WITH THEM?
TA-DAA! HE SENT COPIES OF THE MAGAZINES OUR ADS RAN IN!
HURRY UP AND SHOW US!
KEEP IN MIND HE'S A GRAPHIC DESIGNER! HE USES A COMPUTER TO ENHANCE HIS WORK!
SO HE MADE ME A LITTLE CUTER! SO WHAT?
STYLE
4

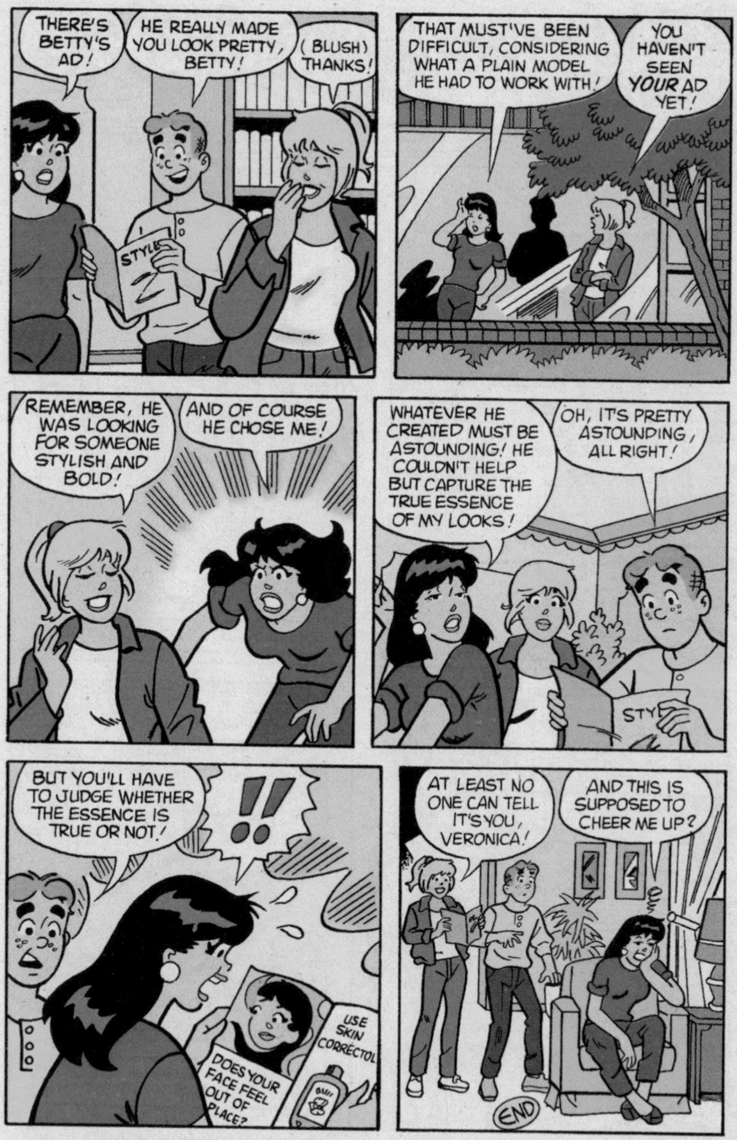
THERE'S BETTY'S AD!
HE REALLY MADE YOU LOOK PRETTY, BETTY!
(BLUSH) THANKS!
STYLE
THAT MUST'VE BEEN DIFFICULT, CONSIDERING WHAT A PLAIN MODEL HE HAD TO WORK WITH!
YOU HAVEN'T SEEN YOUR AD YET!
REMEMBER, HE WAS LOOKING FOR SOMEONE STYLISH AND BOLD!
AND OF COURSE HE CHOSE ME!
WHATEVER HE CREATED MUST BE ASTOUNDING! HE COULDN'T HELP BUT CAPTURE THE TRUE ESSENCE OF MY LOOKS!
OH, IT'S PRETTY ASTOUNDING, ALL RIGHT!
BUT YOU'LL HAVE TO JUDGE WHETHER THE ESSENCE IS TRUE OR NOT!
!!
USE SKIN CORRECTOL
DOES YOUR FACE FEEL OUT OF PLACE?
AT LEAST NO ONE CAN TELL IT'S YOU, VERONICA!
AND THIS IS SUPPOSED TO CHEER ME UP?
END

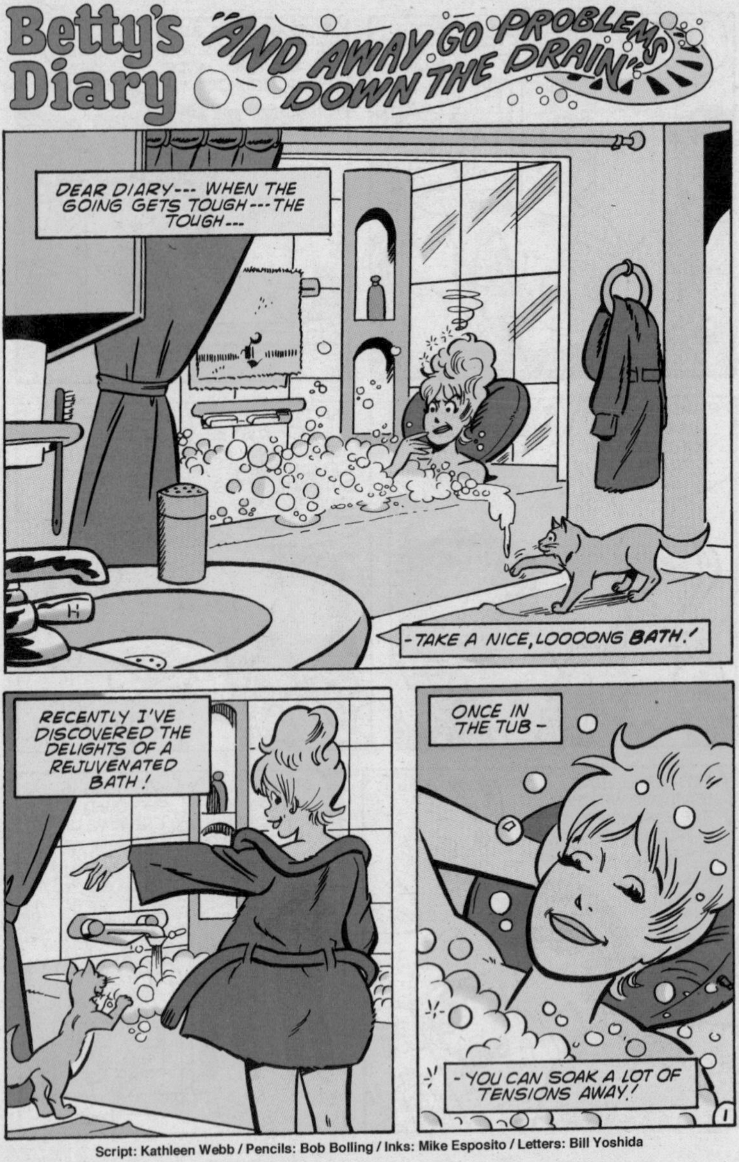
Betty's Diary
"AND AWAY GO PROBLEMS DOWN THE DRAIN"
DEAR DIARY--- WHEN THE GOING GETS TOUGH---THE TOUGH---
-TAKE A NICE, LOOOONG BATH!
RECENTLY I'VE DISCOVERED THE DELIGHTS OF A REJUVENATED BATH!
ONCE IN THE TUB-
-YOU CAN SOAK A LOT OF TENSIONS AWAY!
1

Script: Kathleen Webb / Pencils: Bob Bolling / Inks: Mike Esposito / Letters: Bill Yoshida

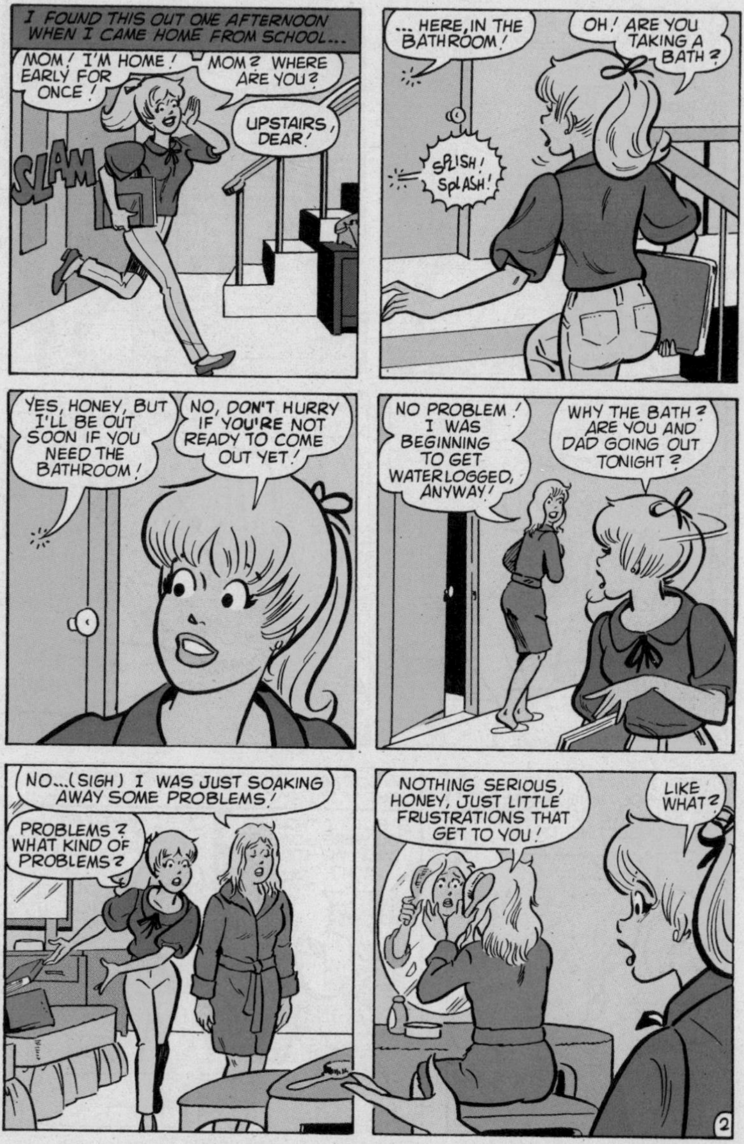
I FOUND THIS OUT ONE AFTERNOON WHEN I CAME HOME FROM SCHOOL...
MOM! I'M HOME! EARLY FOR ONCE!
MOM? WHERE ARE YOU?
SLAM
UPSTAIRS, DEAR!
... HERE, IN THE BATHROOM!
OH! ARE YOU TAKING A BATH?
SPLISH! SPLASH!
YES, HONEY, BUT I'LL BE OUT SOON IF YOU NEED THE BATHROOM!
NO, DON'T HURRY IF YOU'RE NOT READY TO COME OUT YET!
NO PROBLEM! I WAS BEGINNING TO GET WATERLOGGED, ANYWAY!
WHY THE BATH? ARE YOU AND DAD GOING OUT TONIGHT?
NO...(SIGH) I WAS JUST SOAKING AWAY SOME PROBLEMS!
PROBLEMS? WHAT KIND OF PROBLEMS?
NOTHING SERIOUS, HONEY, JUST LITTLE FRUSTRATIONS THAT GET TO YOU!
LIKE WHAT?
2

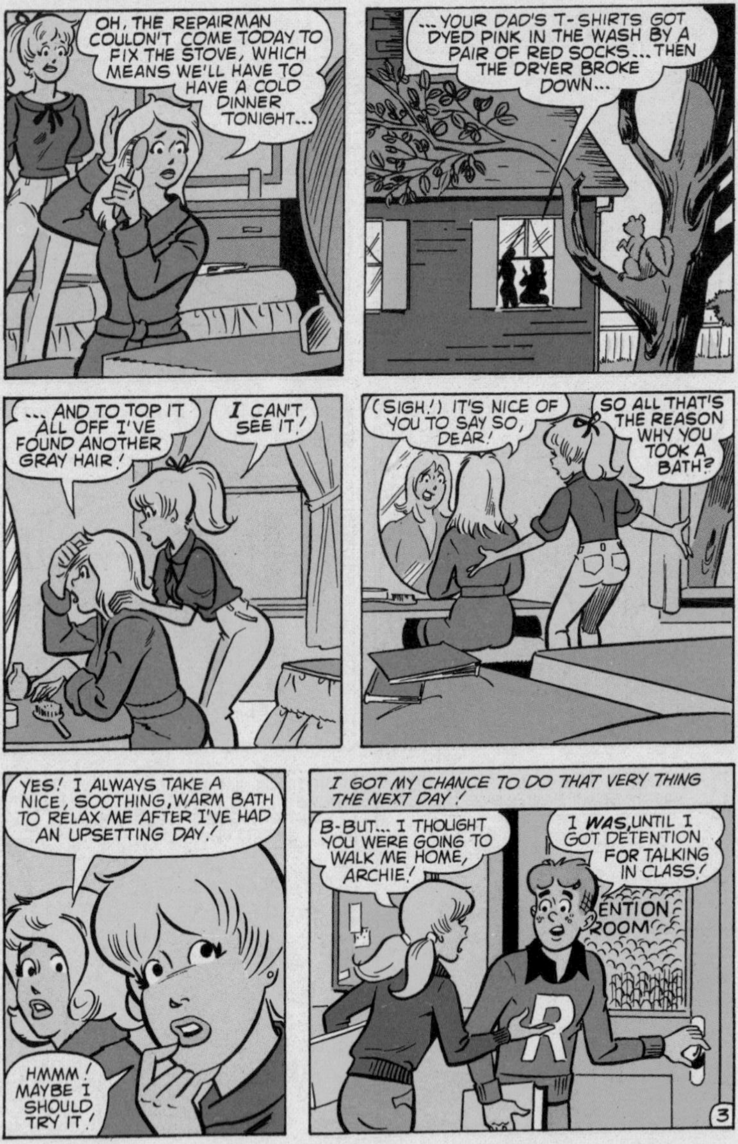
OH, THE REPAIRMAN COULDN'T COME TODAY TO FIX THE STOVE, WHICH MEANS WE'LL HAVE TO HAVE A COLD DINNER TONIGHT...
... YOUR DAD'S T-SHIRTS GOT DYED PINK IN THE WASH BY A PAIR OF RED SOCKS... THEN THE DRYER BROKE DOWN...
... AND TO TOP IT ALL OFF I'VE FOUND ANOTHER GRAY HAIR!
I CAN'T SEE IT!
(SIGH!) IT'S NICE OF YOU TO SAY SO, DEAR!
SO ALL THAT'S THE REASON WHY YOU TOOK A BATH?
YES! I ALWAYS TAKE A NICE, SOOTHING, WARM BATH TO RELAX ME AFTER I'VE HAD AN UPSETTING DAY!
HMMM! MAYBE I SHOULD TRY IT!
I GOT MY CHANCE TO DO THAT VERY THING THE NEXT DAY!
B-BUT... I THOUGHT YOU WERE GOING TO WALK ME HOME, ARCHIE!
I WAS, UNTIL I GOT DETENTION FOR TALKING IN CLASS!
ENTION ROOM
R
3

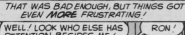

THAT WAS BAD ENOUGH, BUT THINGS GOT EVEN *MORE* FRUSTRATING!

WELL! LOOK WHO ELSE HAS DETENTION BESIDES ME! NOW I WON'T BE SO LONESOME!

RON!

DETENTION ROOM

GRRRRR!

ALL THE WAY HOME I KEPT PICTURING ARCHIE AND VERONICA'S "DETENTION"!

ONCE HOME, I RECEIVED SOME MORE BAD NEWS!

BETTY, REGGIE CALLED... HE SAYS HE'LL HAVE TO CANCEL TONIGHT'S DATE BECAUSE HIS RELATIVES CAME OVER!

THAT DOES IT!

I IMMEDIATELY RAN UPSTAIRS TO THE BATHROOM...

IF ANYBODY WANTS ME, MOM... YOU KNOW WHERE TO FIND ME!

I FILLED THE TUB WITH WARM WATER... ADDED BUBBLE BATH...

I WONDER IF PSYCHIATRISTS RECOMMEND THIS TREATMENT?

...TURNED ON MELLOW MUSIC AND STEPPED INTO THE TUB... AND...

AAAAHHHHHHHHH

4

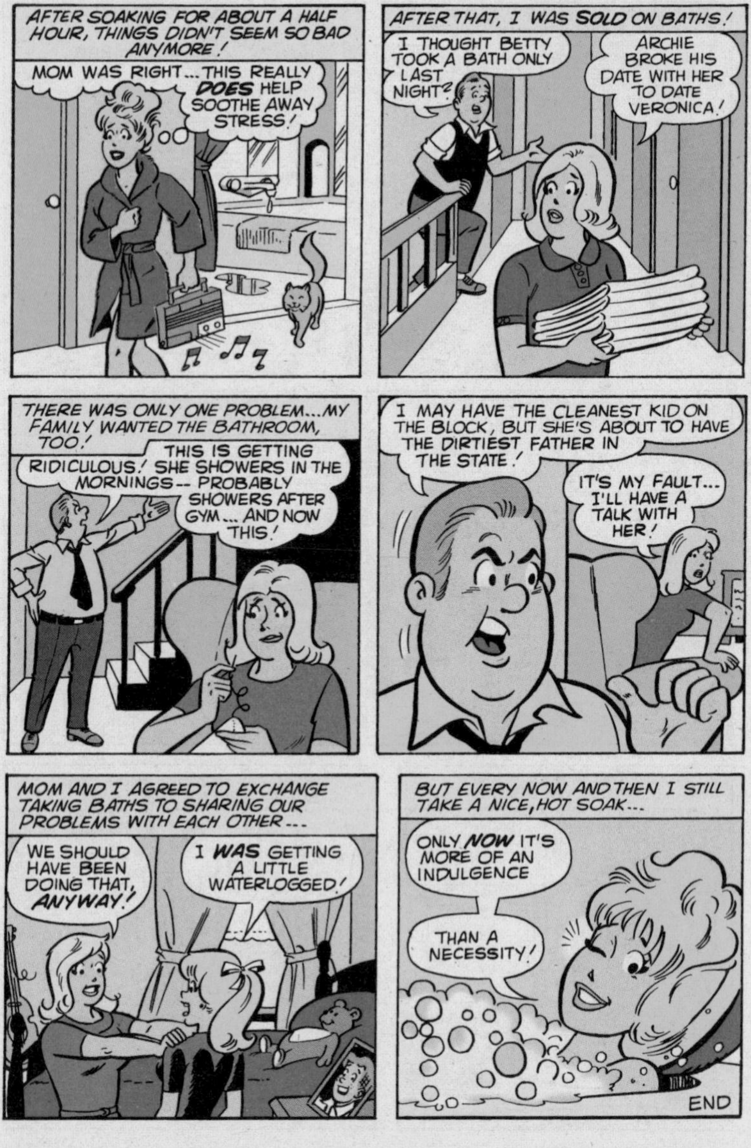

AFTER SOAKING FOR ABOUT A HALF HOUR, THINGS DIDN'T SEEM SO BAD ANYMORE!
MOM WAS RIGHT... THIS REALLY DOES HELP SOOTHE AWAY STRESS!
AFTER THAT, I WAS SOLD ON BATHS!
I THOUGHT BETTY TOOK A BATH ONLY LAST NIGHT?
ARCHIE BROKE HIS DATE WITH HER TO DATE VERONICA!
THERE WAS ONLY ONE PROBLEM... MY FAMILY WANTED THE BATHROOM, TOO!
THIS IS GETTING RIDICULOUS! SHE SHOWERS IN THE MORNINGS-- PROBABLY SHOWERS AFTER GYM... AND NOW THIS!
I MAY HAVE THE CLEANEST KID ON THE BLOCK, BUT SHE'S ABOUT TO HAVE THE DIRTIEST FATHER IN THE STATE!
IT'S MY FAULT... I'LL HAVE A TALK WITH HER!
MOM AND I AGREED TO EXCHANGE TAKING BATHS TO SHARING OUR PROBLEMS WITH EACH OTHER...
WE SHOULD HAVE BEEN DOING THAT, ANYWAY!
I WAS GETTING A LITTLE WATERLOGGED!
BUT EVERY NOW AND THEN I STILL TAKE A NICE, HOT SOAK...
ONLY NOW IT'S MORE OF AN INDULGENCE
THAN A NECESSITY!
END

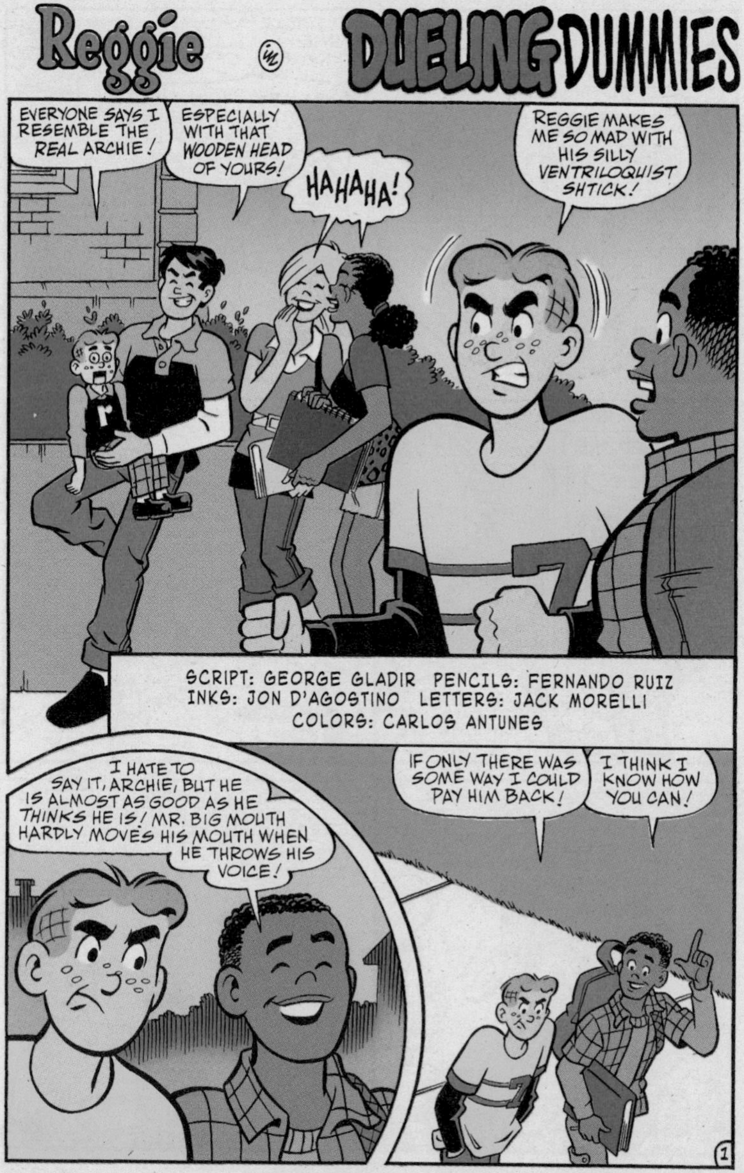
Reggie in DUELING DUMMIES
EVERYONE SAYS I RESEMBLE THE REAL ARCHIE!
ESPECIALLY WITH THAT WOODEN HEAD OF YOURS!
HAHAHA!
REGGIE MAKES ME SO MAD WITH HIS SILLY VENTRILOQUIST SHTICK!
SCRIPT: GEORGE GLADIR PENCILS: FERNANDO RUIZ
INKS: JON D'AGOSTINO LETTERS: JACK MORELLI
COLORS: CARLOS ANTUNES
I HATE TO SAY IT, ARCHIE, BUT HE IS ALMOST AS GOOD AS HE THINKS HE IS! MR. BIG MOUTH HARDLY MOVES HIS MOUTH WHEN HE THROWS HIS VOICE!
IF ONLY THERE WAS SOME WAY I COULD PAY HIM BACK!
I THINK I KNOW HOW YOU CAN!
1

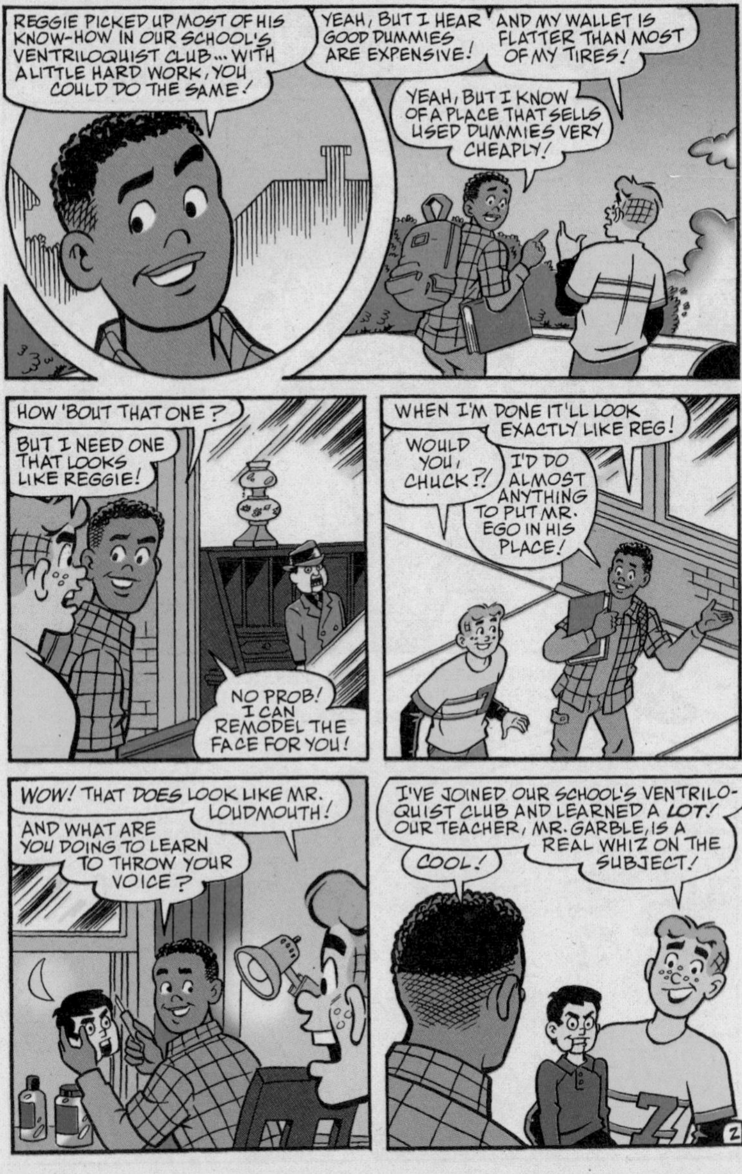
REGGIE PICKED UP MOST OF HIS KNOW-HOW IN OUR SCHOOL'S VENTRILOQUIST CLUB... WITH A LITTLE HARD WORK, YOU COULD DO THE SAME!
YEAH, BUT I HEAR GOOD DUMMIES ARE EXPENSIVE!
AND MY WALLET IS FLATTER THAN MOST OF MY TIRES!
YEAH, BUT I KNOW OF A PLACE THAT SELLS USED DUMMIES VERY CHEAPLY!
HOW 'BOUT THAT ONE?
BUT I NEED ONE THAT LOOKS LIKE REGGIE!
NO PROB! I CAN REMODEL THE FACE FOR YOU!
WHEN I'M DONE IT'LL LOOK EXACTLY LIKE REG!
WOULD YOU, CHUCK?!
I'D DO ALMOST ANYTHING TO PUT MR. EGO IN HIS PLACE!
WOW! THAT DOES LOOK LIKE MR. LOUDMOUTH!
AND WHAT ARE YOU DOING TO LEARN TO THROW YOUR VOICE?
I'VE JOINED OUR SCHOOL'S VENTRILOQUIST CLUB AND LEARNED A LOT! OUR TEACHER, MR. GARBLE, IS A REAL WHIZ ON THE SUBJECT!
COOL!
2

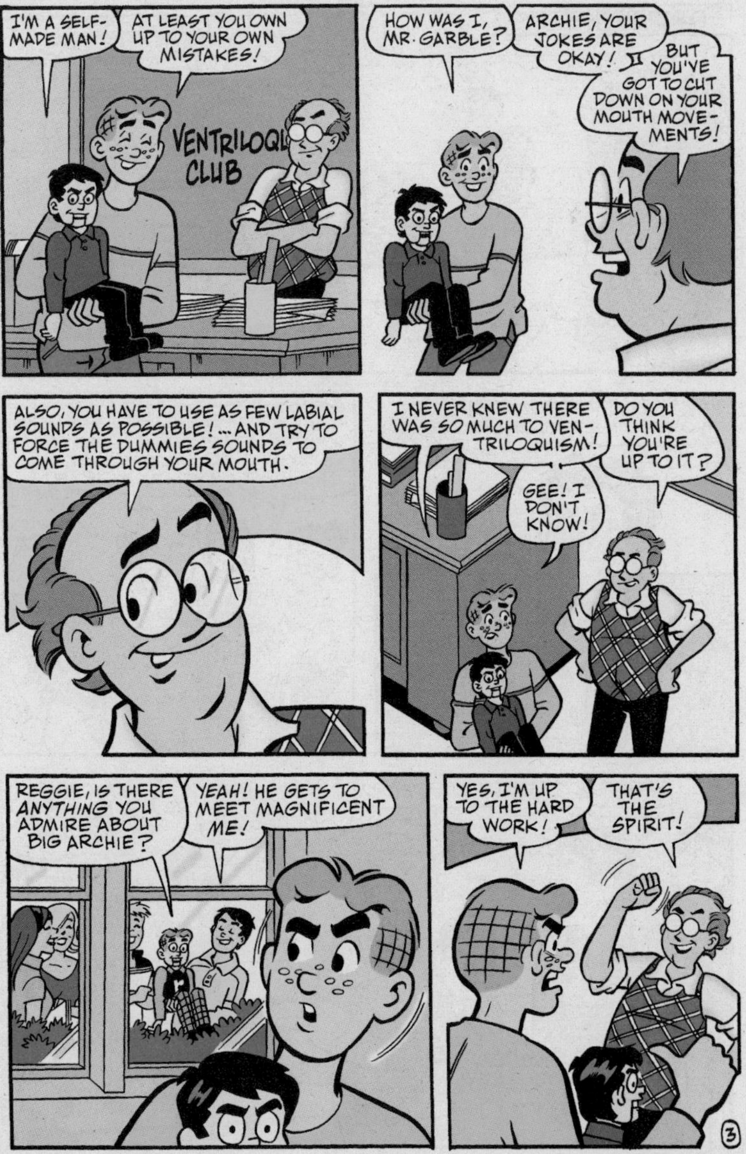
I'M A SELF-MADE MAN!
AT LEAST YOU OWN UP TO YOUR OWN MISTAKES!
VENTRILOQU CLUB
HOW WAS I, MR. GARBLE?
ARCHIE, YOUR JOKES ARE OKAY!
BUT YOU'VE GOT TO CUT DOWN ON YOUR MOUTH MOVE-MENTS!
ALSO, YOU HAVE TO USE AS FEW LABIAL SOUNDS AS POSSIBLE! ... AND TRY TO FORCE THE DUMMIES SOUNDS TO COME THROUGH YOUR MOUTH.
I NEVER KNEW THERE WAS SO MUCH TO VEN-TRILOQUISM!
DO YOU THINK YOU'RE UP TO IT?
GEE! I DON'T KNOW!
REGGIE, IS THERE ANYTHING YOU ADMIRE ABOUT BIG ARCHIE?
YEAH! HE GETS TO MEET MAGNIFICENT ME!
YES, I'M UP TO THE HARD WORK!
THAT'S THE SPIRIT!
3

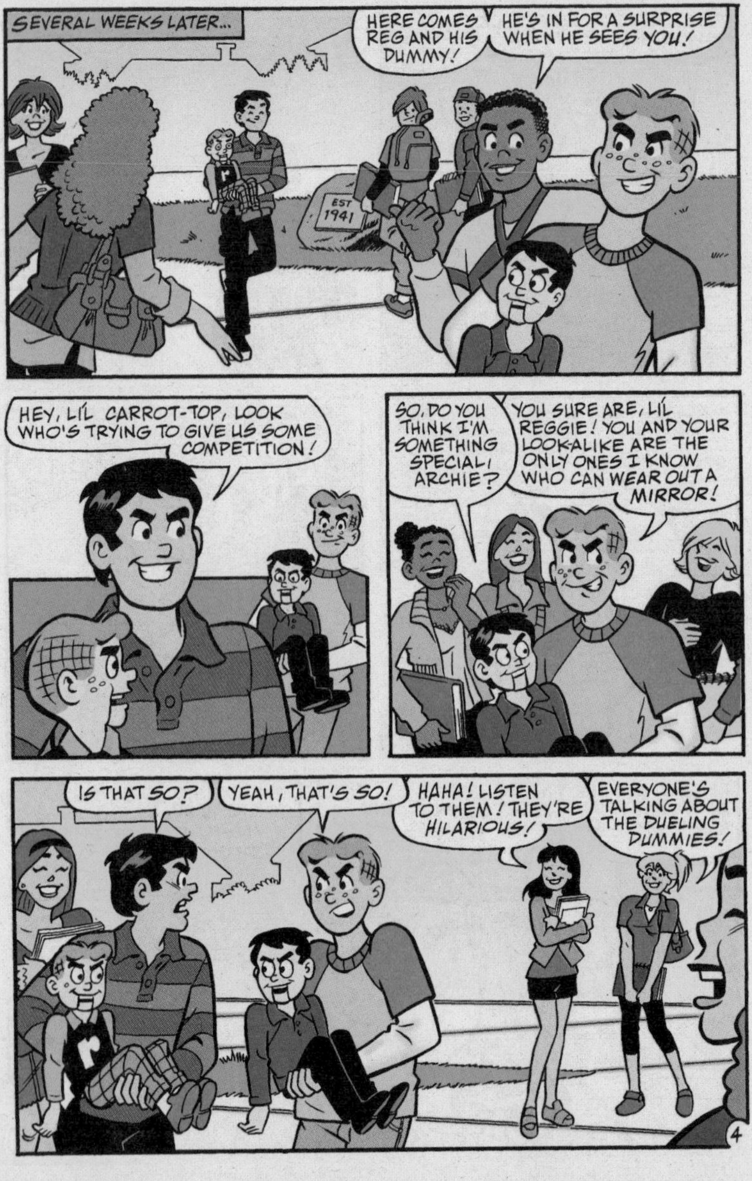

SEVERAL WEEKS LATER...
HERE COMES REG AND HIS DUMMY!
HE'S IN FOR A SURPRISE WHEN HE SEES YOU!
EST 1941
HEY, LI'L CARROT-TOP, LOOK WHO'S TRYING TO GIVE US SOME COMPETITION!
SO, DO YOU THINK I'M SOMETHING SPECIAL, ARCHIE?
YOU SURE ARE, LI'L REGGIE! YOU AND YOUR LOOK-ALIKE ARE THE ONLY ONES I KNOW WHO CAN WEAR OUT A MIRROR!
IS THAT SO?
YEAH, THAT'S SO!
HAHA! LISTEN TO THEM! THEY'RE HILARIOUS!
EVERYONE'S TALKING ABOUT THE DUELING DUMMIES!

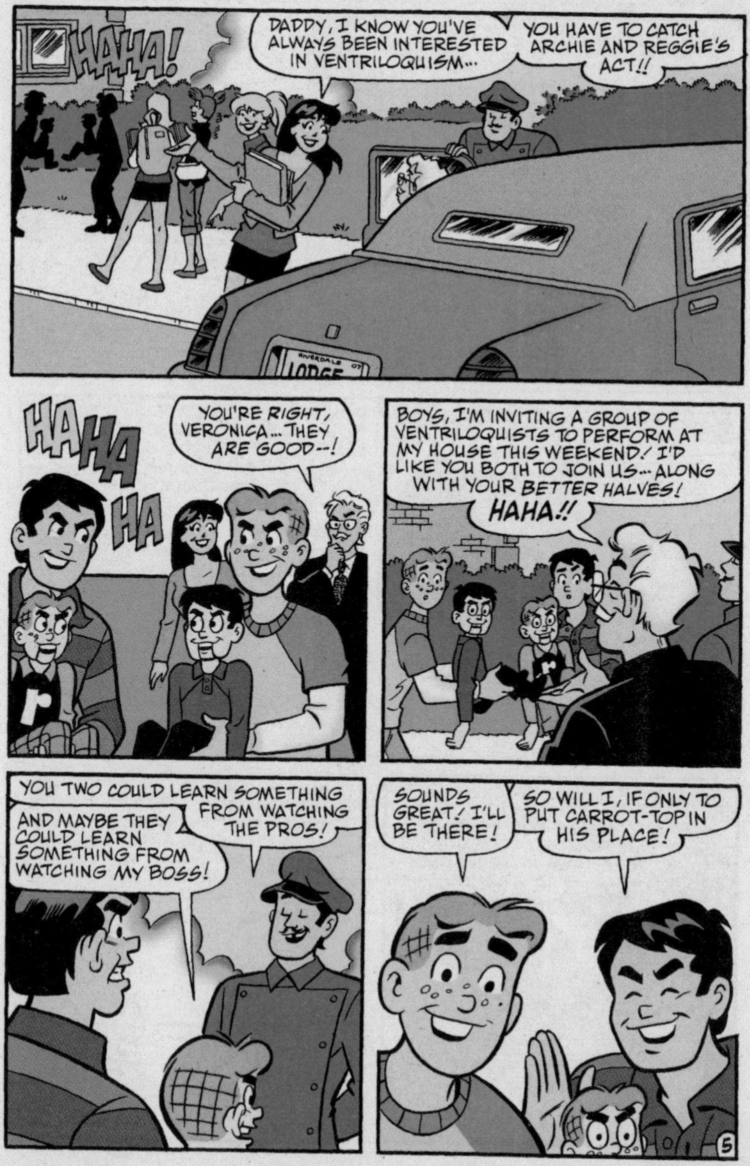
HAHA!
DADDY, I KNOW YOU'VE ALWAYS BEEN INTERESTED IN VENTRILOQUISM...
YOU HAVE TO CATCH ARCHIE AND REGGIE'S ACT!!
RIVERDALE 07
LODGE
HA HA HA
YOU'RE RIGHT, VERONICA... THEY ARE GOOD--!
BOYS, I'M INVITING A GROUP OF VENTRILOQUISTS TO PERFORM AT MY HOUSE THIS WEEKEND! I'D LIKE YOU BOTH TO JOIN US... ALONG WITH YOUR BETTER HALVES!
HAHA!!
YOU TWO COULD LEARN SOMETHING FROM WATCHING THE PROS!
AND MAYBE THEY COULD LEARN SOMETHING FROM WATCHING MY BOSS!
SOUNDS GREAT! I'LL BE THERE!
SO WILL I, IF ONLY TO PUT CARROT-TOP IN HIS PLACE!
5

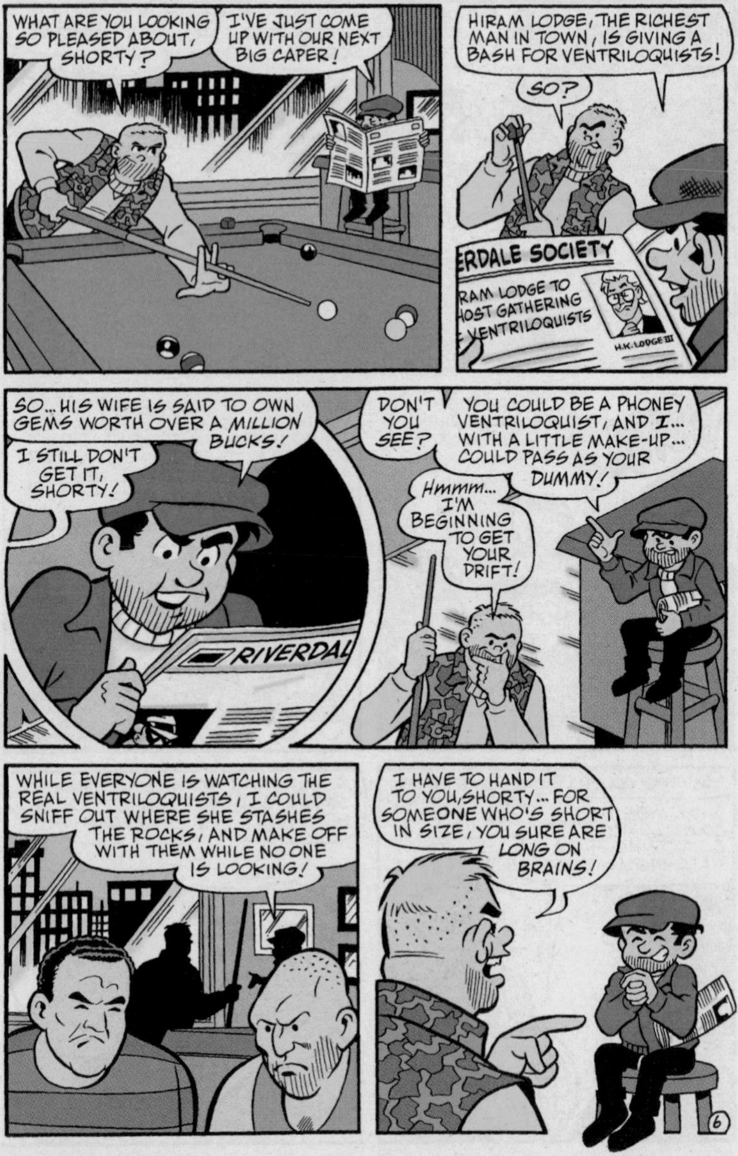
WHAT ARE YOU LOOKING SO PLEASED ABOUT, SHORTY?
I'VE JUST COME UP WITH OUR NEXT BIG CAPER!
HIRAM LODGE, THE RICHEST MAN IN TOWN, IS GIVING A BASH FOR VENTRILOQUISTS!
SO?
ERDALE SOCIETY
RAM LODGE TO HOST GATHERING VENTRILOQUISTS
H.K. LODGE III
SO... HIS WIFE IS SAID TO OWN GEMS WORTH OVER A MILLION BUCKS!
I STILL DON'T GET IT, SHORTY!
RIVERDAL
DON'T YOU SEE?
YOU COULD BE A PHONEY VENTRILOQUIST, AND I... WITH A LITTLE MAKE-UP... COULD PASS AS YOUR DUMMY!
Hmmm... I'M BEGINNING TO GET YOUR DRIFT!
WHILE EVERYONE IS WATCHING THE REAL VENTRILOQUISTS, I COULD SNIFF OUT WHERE SHE STASHES THE ROCKS, AND MAKE OFF WITH THEM WHILE NO ONE IS LOOKING!
I HAVE TO HAND IT TO YOU, SHORTY... FOR SOMEONE WHO'S SHORT IN SIZE, YOU SURE ARE LONG ON BRAINS!
6

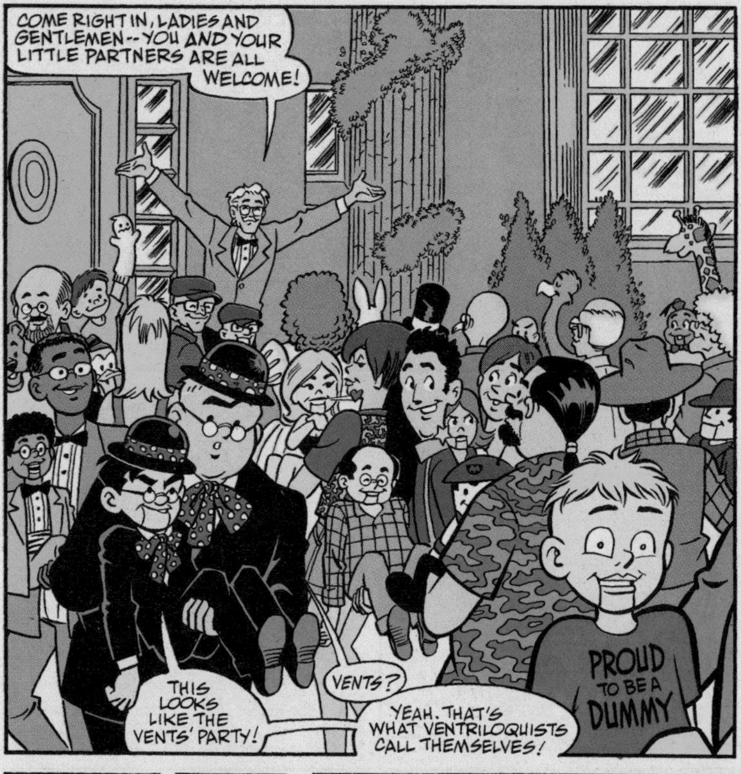
COME RIGHT IN, LADIES AND GENTLEMEN-- YOU AND YOUR LITTLE PARTNERS ARE ALL WELCOME!
THIS LOOKS LIKE THE VENTS' PARTY!
VENTS?
YEAH. THAT'S WHAT VENTRILOQUISTS CALL THEMSELVES!
PROUD TO BE A DUMMY

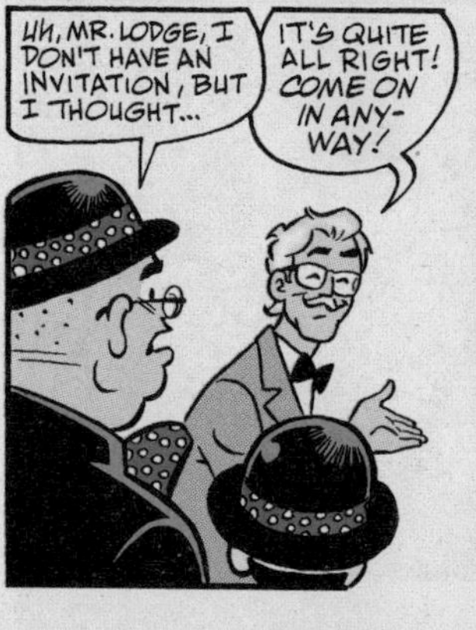
UH, MR. LODGE, I DON'T HAVE AN INVITATION, BUT I THOUGHT...
IT'S QUITE ALL RIGHT! COME ON IN ANY-WAY!

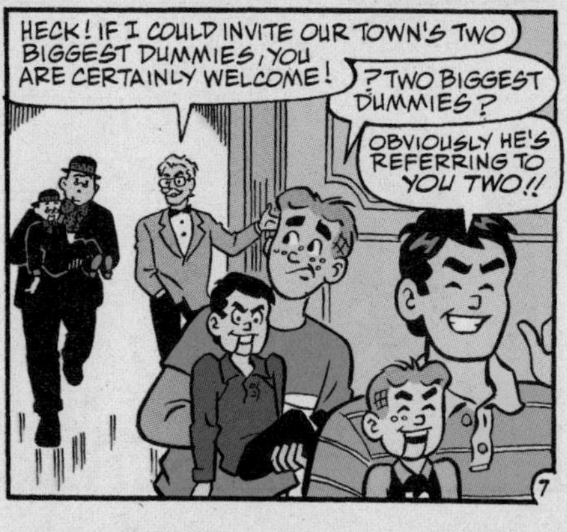
HECK! IF I COULD INVITE OUR TOWN'S TWO BIGGEST DUMMIES, YOU ARE CERTAINLY WELCOME!
?TWO BIGGEST DUMMIES?
OBVIOUSLY HE'S REFERRING TO YOU TWO!!

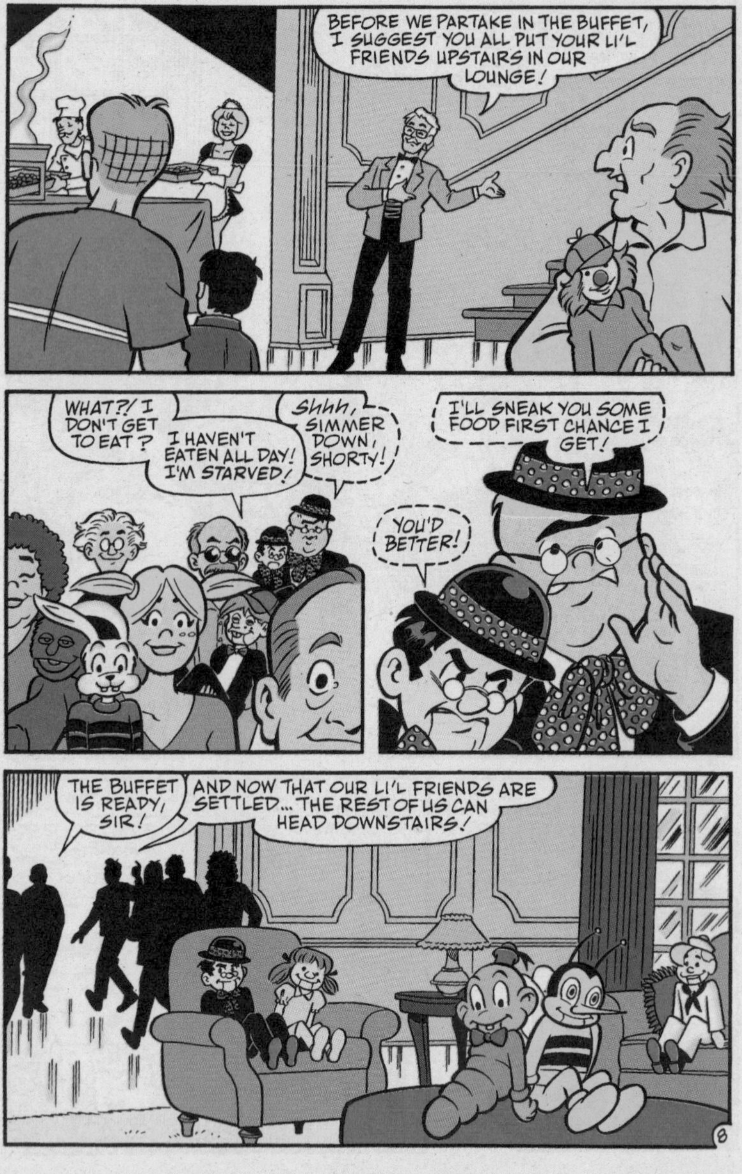
BEFORE WE PARTAKE IN THE BUFFET, I SUGGEST YOU ALL PUT YOUR LI'L FRIENDS UPSTAIRS IN OUR LOUNGE!
WHAT?! I DON'T GET TO EAT?
I HAVEN'T EATEN ALL DAY! I'M STARVED!
Shhh, SIMMER DOWN, SHORTY!
I'LL SNEAK YOU SOME FOOD FIRST CHANCE I GET!
YOU'D BETTER!
THE BUFFET IS READY, SIR!
AND NOW THAT OUR LI'L FRIENDS ARE SETTLED... THE REST OF US CAN HEAD DOWNSTAIRS!
8

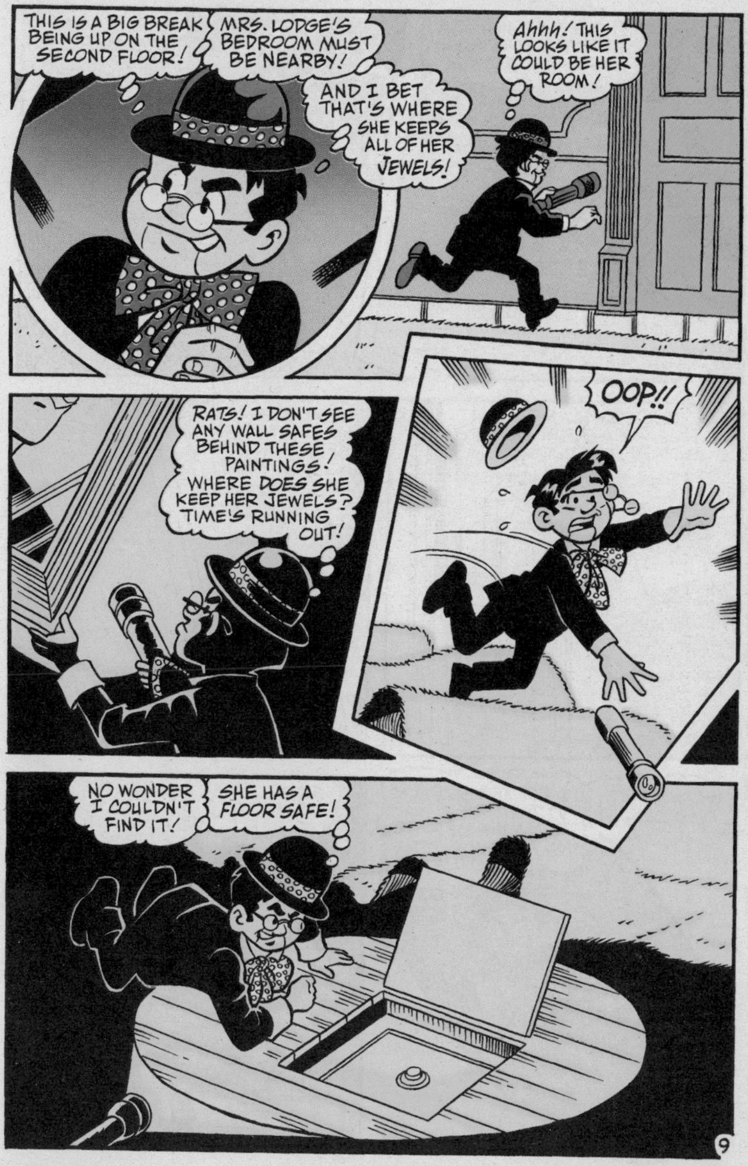
THIS IS A BIG BREAK BEING UP ON THE SECOND FLOOR!
MRS. LODGE'S BEDROOM MUST BE NEARBY!
AND I BET THAT'S WHERE SHE KEEPS ALL OF HER JEWELS!
Ahhh! THIS LOOKS LIKE IT COULD BE HER ROOM!
RATS! I DON'T SEE ANY WALL SAFES BEHIND THESE PAINTINGS! WHERE DOES SHE KEEP HER JEWELS? TIME'S RUNNING OUT!
OOP!!
NO WONDER I COULDN'T FIND IT!
SHE HAS A FLOOR SAFE!

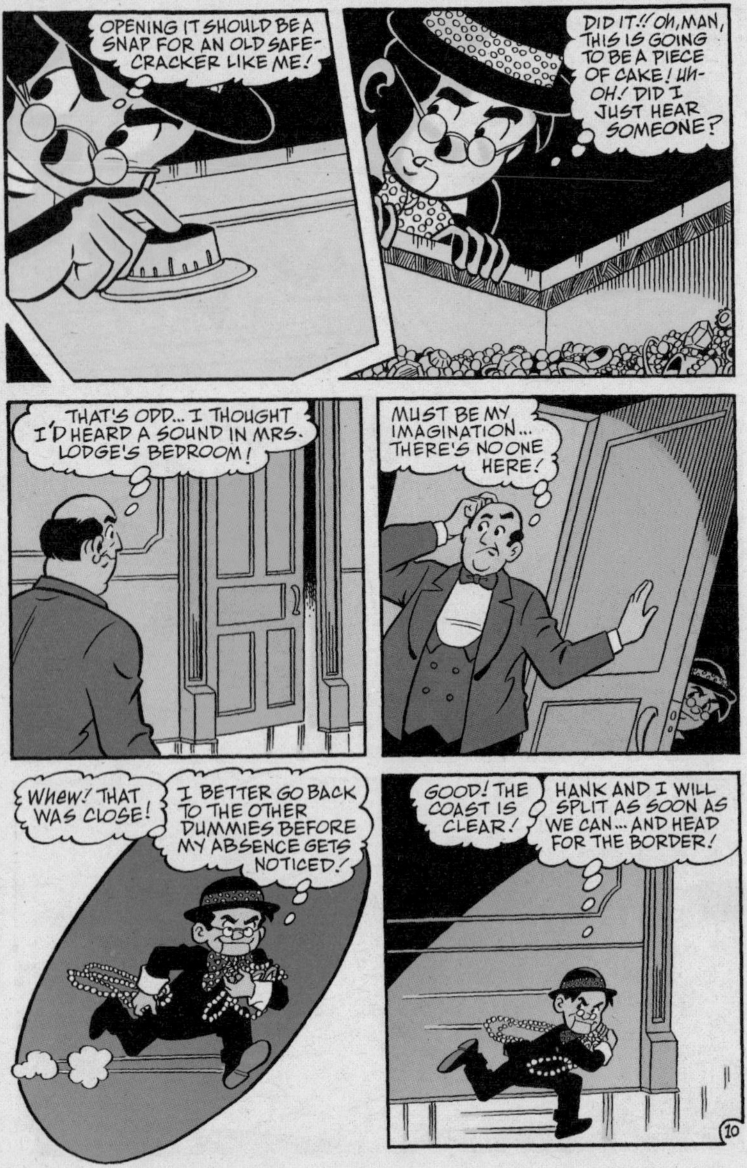
OPENING IT SHOULD BE A SNAP FOR AN OLD SAFE-CRACKER LIKE ME!
DID IT!! OH, MAN, THIS IS GOING TO BE A PIECE OF CAKE! UH-OH! DID I JUST HEAR SOMEONE?
THAT'S ODD... I THOUGHT I'D HEARD A SOUND IN MRS. LODGE'S BEDROOM!
MUST BE MY IMAGINATION... THERE'S NO ONE HERE!
WHEW! THAT WAS CLOSE!
I BETTER GO BACK TO THE OTHER DUMMIES BEFORE MY ABSENCE GETS NOTICED!
GOOD! THE COAST IS CLEAR!
HANK AND I WILL SPLIT AS SOON AS WE CAN... AND HEAD FOR THE BORDER!
10

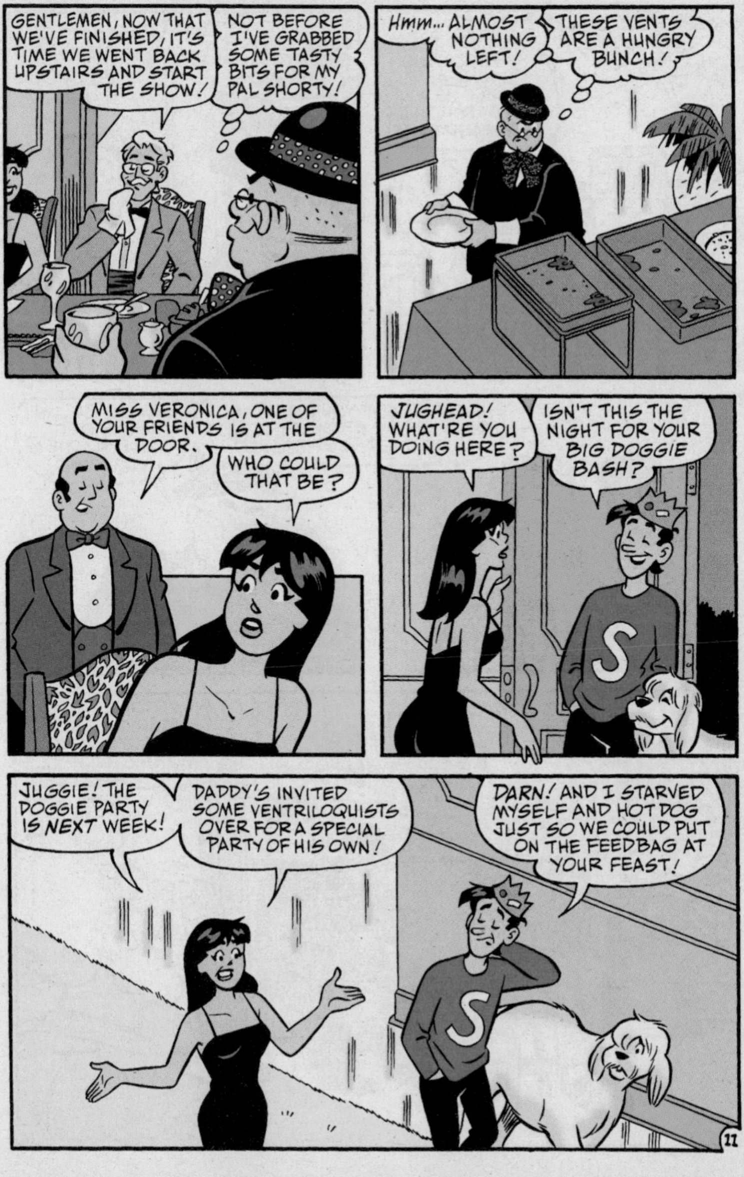
GENTLEMEN, NOW THAT WE'VE FINISHED, IT'S TIME WE WENT BACK UPSTAIRS AND START THE SHOW!
NOT BEFORE I'VE GRABBED SOME TASTY BITS FOR MY PAL SHORTY!
Hmm... ALMOST NOTHING LEFT!
THESE VENTS ARE A HUNGRY BUNCH!
MISS VERONICA, ONE OF YOUR FRIENDS IS AT THE DOOR.
WHO COULD THAT BE?
JUGHEAD! WHAT'RE YOU DOING HERE?
ISN'T THIS THE NIGHT FOR YOUR BIG DOGGIE BASH?
JUGGIE! THE DOGGIE PARTY IS NEXT WEEK!
DADDY'S INVITED SOME VENTRILOQUISTS OVER FOR A SPECIAL PARTY OF HIS OWN!
DARN! AND I STARVED MYSELF AND HOT DOG JUST SO WE COULD PUT ON THE FEEDBAG AT YOUR FEAST!

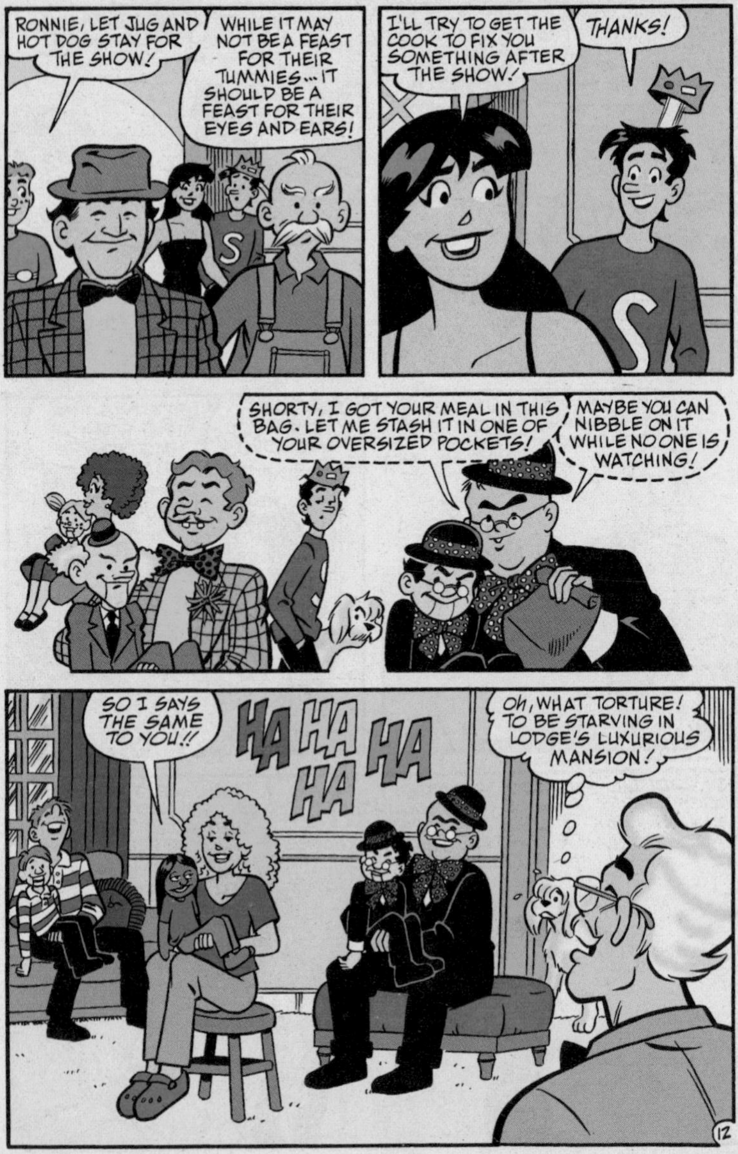

RONNIE, LET JUG AND HOT DOG STAY FOR THE SHOW!
WHILE IT MAY NOT BE A FEAST FOR THEIR TUMMIES... IT SHOULD BE A FEAST FOR THEIR EYES AND EARS!
I'LL TRY TO GET THE COOK TO FIX YOU SOMETHING AFTER THE SHOW!
THANKS!
SHORTY, I GOT YOUR MEAL IN THIS BAG. LET ME STASH IT IN ONE OF YOUR OVERSIZED POCKETS!
MAYBE YOU CAN NIBBLE ON IT WHILE NO ONE IS WATCHING!
SO I SAYS THE SAME TO YOU!!
HA HA HA HA HA
OH, WHAT TORTURE! TO BE STARVING IN LODGE'S LUXURIOUS MANSION!
12

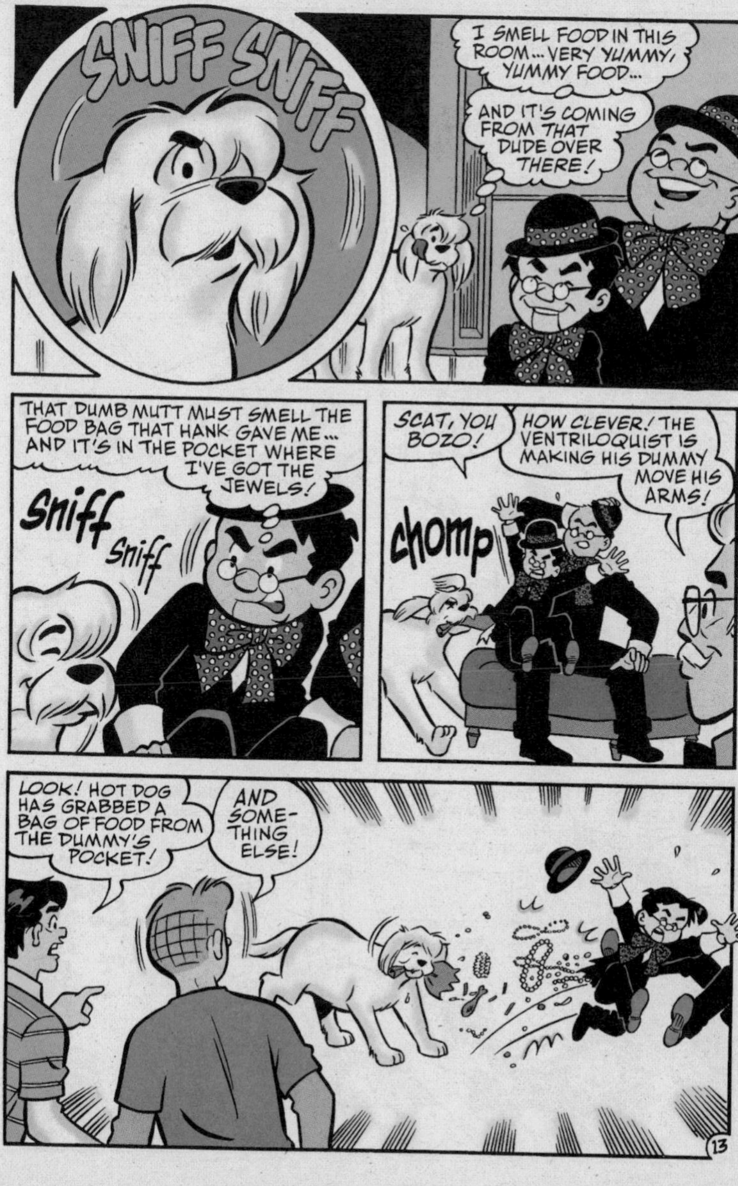
SNIFF SNIFF
I SMELL FOOD IN THIS ROOM... VERY YUMMY, YUMMY FOOD...
AND IT'S COMING FROM THAT DUDE OVER THERE!
THAT DUMB MUTT MUST SMELL THE FOOD BAG THAT HANK GAVE ME... AND IT'S IN THE POCKET WHERE I'VE GOT THE JEWELS!
Sniff Sniff
SCAT, YOU BOZO!
HOW CLEVER! THE VENTRILOQUIST IS MAKING HIS DUMMY MOVE HIS ARMS!
chomp
LOOK! HOT DOG HAS GRABBED A BAG OF FOOD FROM THE DUMMY'S POCKET!
AND SOMETHING ELSE!

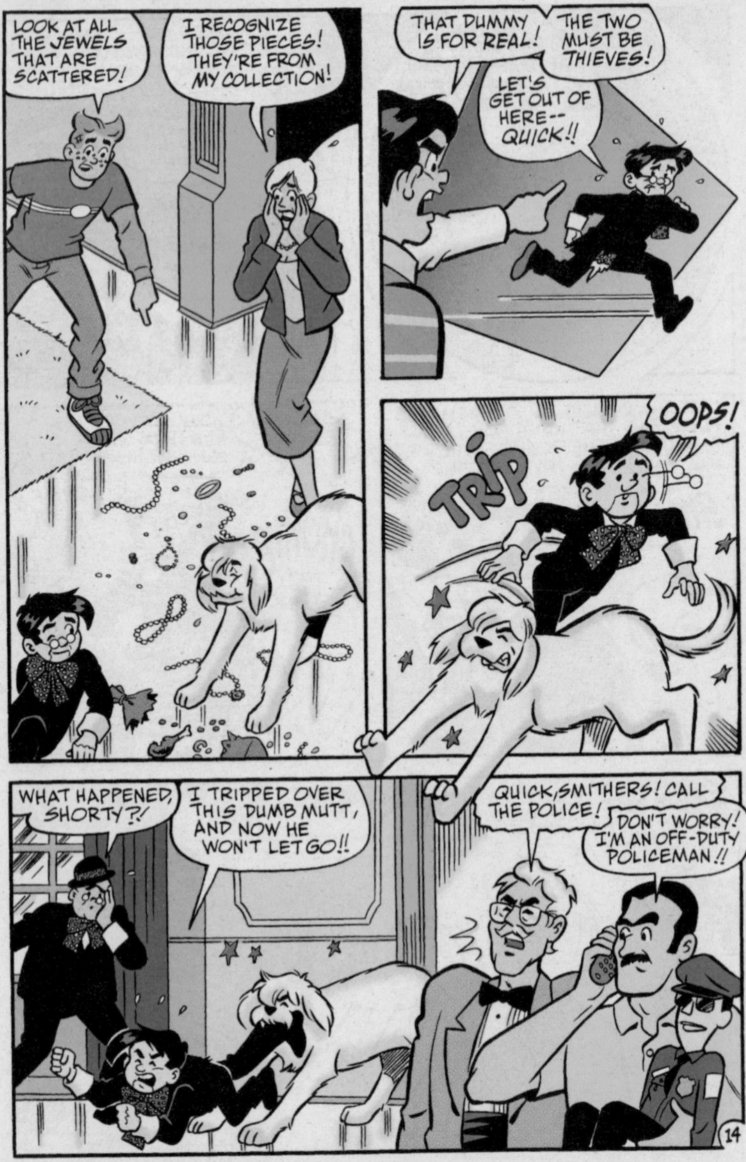
LOOK AT ALL THE JEWELS THAT ARE SCATTERED!
I RECOGNIZE THOSE PIECES! THEY'RE FROM MY COLLECTION!
THAT DUMMY IS FOR REAL!
THE TWO MUST BE THIEVES!
LET'S GET OUT OF HERE-- QUICK!!
TRIP
OOPS!
WHAT HAPPENED, SHORTY?!
I TRIPPED OVER THIS DUMB MUTT, AND NOW HE WON'T LET GO!!
QUICK, SMITHERS! CALL THE POLICE!
DON'T WORRY! I'M AN OFF-DUTY POLICEMAN!!

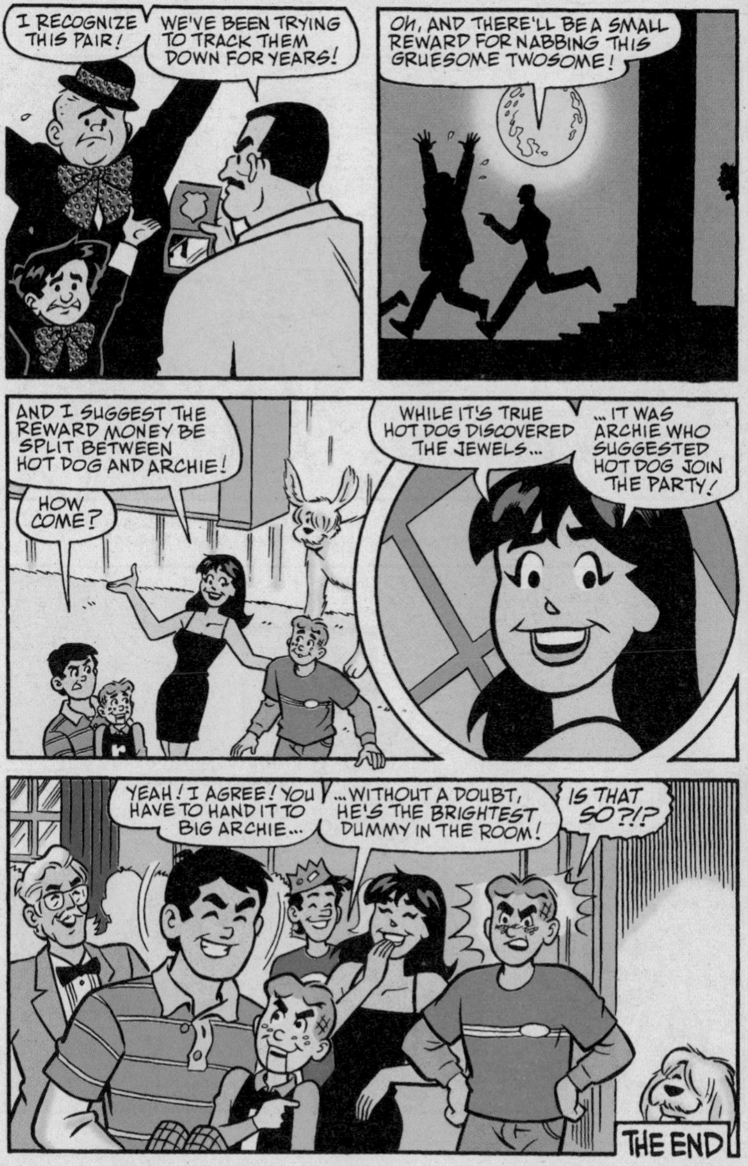
I RECOGNIZE THIS PAIR!
WE'VE BEEN TRYING TO TRACK THEM DOWN FOR YEARS!
OH, AND THERE'LL BE A SMALL REWARD FOR NABBING THIS GRUESOME TWOSOME!
AND I SUGGEST THE REWARD MONEY BE SPLIT BETWEEN HOT DOG AND ARCHIE!
HOW COME?
WHILE IT'S TRUE HOT DOG DISCOVERED THE JEWELS...
...IT WAS ARCHIE WHO SUGGESTED HOT DOG JOIN THE PARTY!
YEAH! I AGREE! YOU HAVE TO HAND IT TO BIG ARCHIE...
...WITHOUT A DOUBT, HE'S THE BRIGHTEST DUMMY IN THE ROOM!
IS THAT SO?!?
THE END

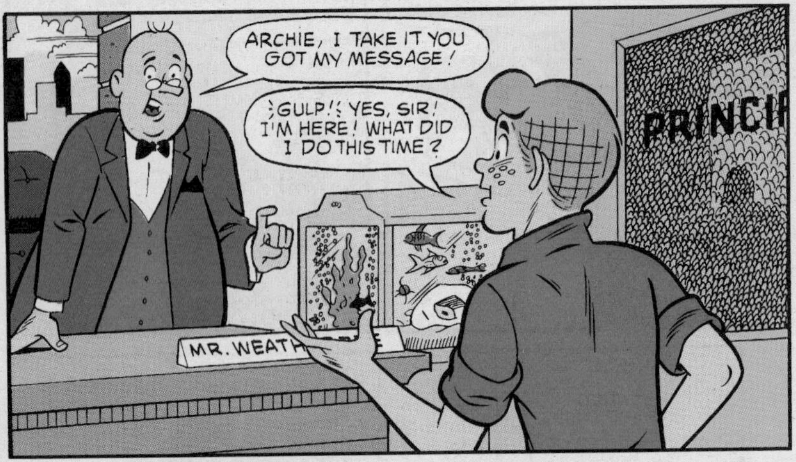
ARCHIE, I TAKE IT YOU GOT MY MESSAGE!
¡GULP!¡ YES, SIR! I'M HERE! WHAT DID I DO THIS TIME?
MR. WEATH
PRINCI

SCRIPT: BILL GOLLIHER PENCILS: BOB BOLLING INKS: BOB SMITH
COLORS: BARRY GROSSMAN LETTERS: BILL YOSHIDA

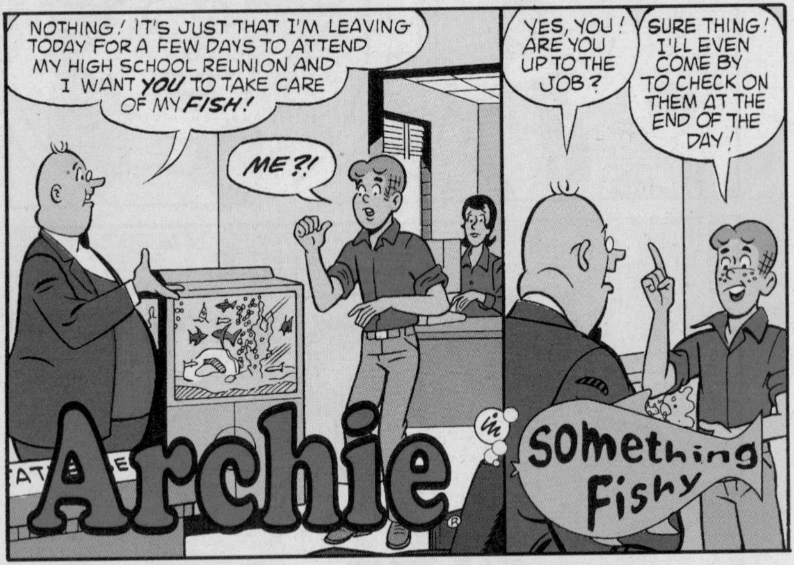
NOTHING! IT'S JUST THAT I'M LEAVING TODAY FOR A FEW DAYS TO ATTEND MY HIGH SCHOOL REUNION AND I WANT *YOU* TO TAKE CARE OF MY *FISH!*
ME?!
YES, YOU! ARE YOU UP TO THE JOB?
SURE THING! I'LL EVEN COME BY TO CHECK ON THEM AT THE END OF THE DAY!
Archie®
in
Something Fishy

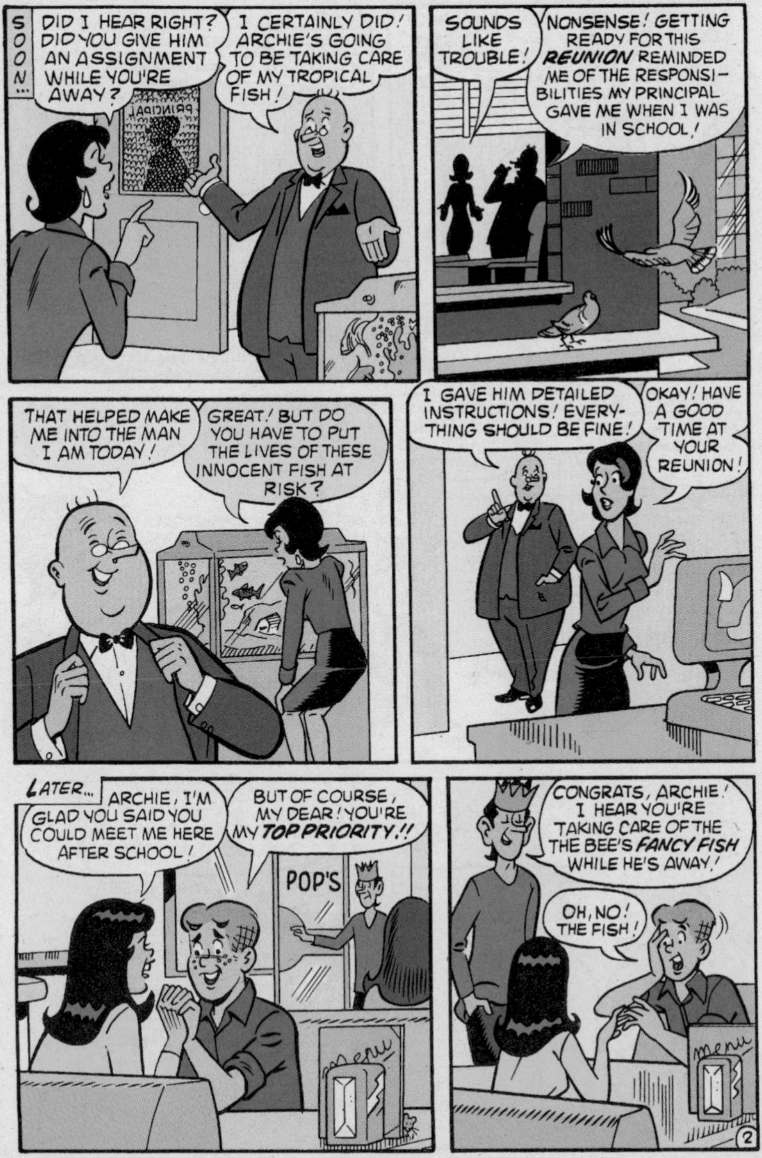
SOON...
DID I HEAR RIGHT? DID YOU GIVE HIM AN ASSIGNMENT WHILE YOU'RE AWAY?
PRINCIPAL
I CERTAINLY DID! ARCHIE'S GOING TO BE TAKING CARE OF MY TROPICAL FISH!
SOUNDS LIKE TROUBLE!
NONSENSE! GETTING READY FOR THIS REUNION REMINDED ME OF THE RESPONSIBILITIES MY PRINCIPAL GAVE ME WHEN I WAS IN SCHOOL!
THAT HELPED MAKE ME INTO THE MAN I AM TODAY!
GREAT! BUT DO YOU HAVE TO PUT THE LIVES OF THESE INNOCENT FISH AT RISK?
I GAVE HIM DETAILED INSTRUCTIONS! EVERYTHING SHOULD BE FINE!
OKAY! HAVE A GOOD TIME AT YOUR REUNION!
LATER...
ARCHIE, I'M GLAD YOU SAID YOU COULD MEET ME HERE AFTER SCHOOL!
BUT OF COURSE, MY DEAR! YOU'RE MY TOP PRIORITY!!
POP'S
Menu
CONGRATS, ARCHIE! I HEAR YOU'RE TAKING CARE OF THE THE BEE'S FANCY FISH WHILE HE'S AWAY!
OH, NO! THE FISH!
Menu

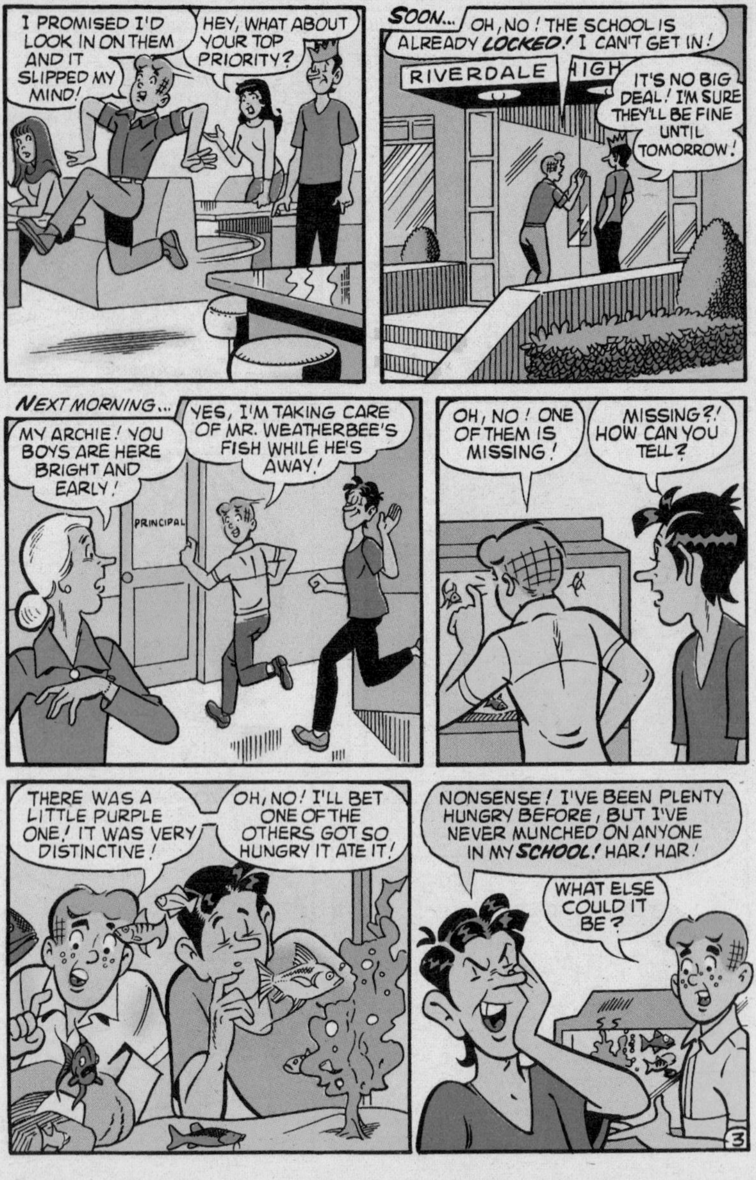
I PROMISED I'D LOOK IN ON THEM AND IT SLIPPED MY MIND!
HEY, WHAT ABOUT YOUR TOP PRIORITY?
SOON...
OH, NO! THE SCHOOL IS ALREADY LOCKED! I CAN'T GET IN!
RIVERDALE HIGH
IT'S NO BIG DEAL! I'M SURE THEY'LL BE FINE UNTIL TOMORROW!
NEXT MORNING...
MY ARCHIE! YOU BOYS ARE HERE BRIGHT AND EARLY!
YES, I'M TAKING CARE OF MR. WEATHERBEE'S FISH WHILE HE'S AWAY!
PRINCIPAL
OH, NO! ONE OF THEM IS MISSING!
MISSING?! HOW CAN YOU TELL?
THERE WAS A LITTLE PURPLE ONE! IT WAS VERY DISTINCTIVE!
OH, NO! I'LL BET ONE OF THE OTHERS GOT SO HUNGRY IT ATE IT!
NONSENSE! I'VE BEEN PLENTY HUNGRY BEFORE, BUT I'VE NEVER MUNCHED ON ANYONE IN MY SCHOOL! HAR! HAR!
WHAT ELSE COULD IT BE?
3

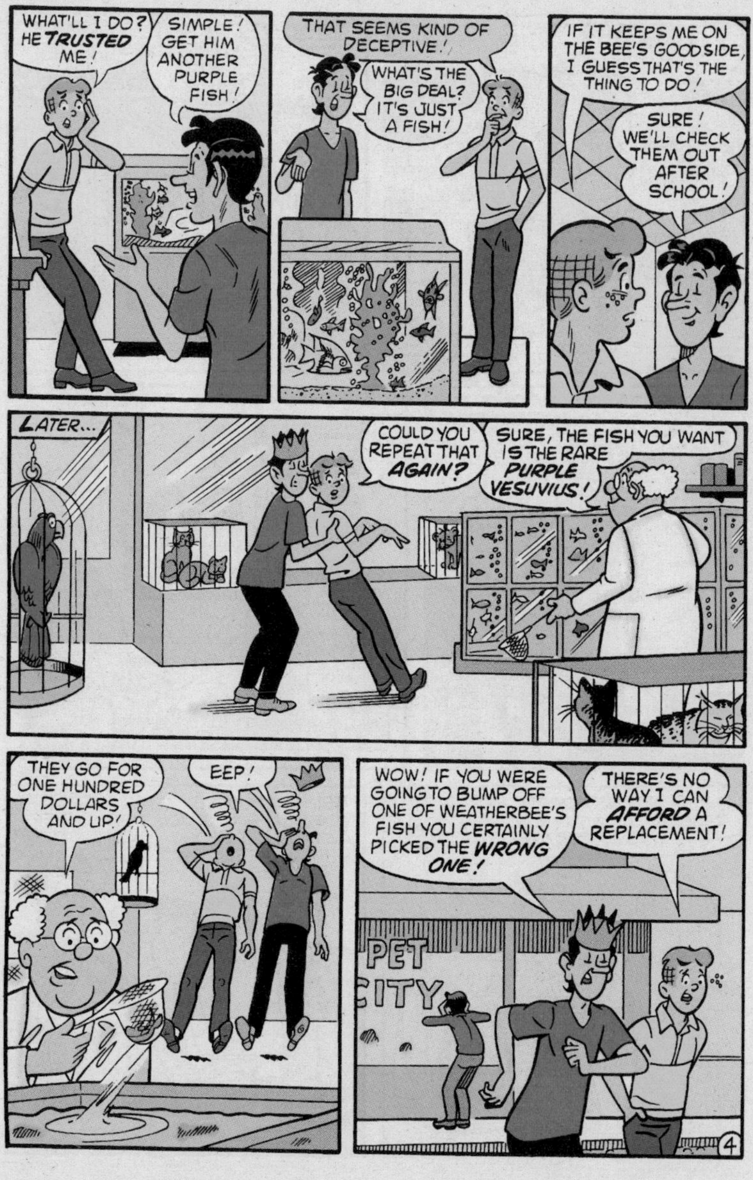
WHAT'LL I DO? HE TRUSTED ME!
SIMPLE! GET HIM ANOTHER PURPLE FISH!
THAT SEEMS KIND OF DECEPTIVE!
WHAT'S THE BIG DEAL? IT'S JUST A FISH!
IF IT KEEPS ME ON THE BEE'S GOOD SIDE, I GUESS THAT'S THE THING TO DO!
SURE! WE'LL CHECK THEM OUT AFTER SCHOOL!
LATER...
COULD YOU REPEAT THAT AGAIN?
SURE, THE FISH YOU WANT IS THE RARE PURPLE VESUVIUS!
THEY GO FOR ONE HUNDRED DOLLARS AND UP!
EEP!
WOW! IF YOU WERE GOING TO BUMP OFF ONE OF WEATHERBEE'S FISH YOU CERTAINLY PICKED THE WRONG ONE!
THERE'S NO WAY I CAN AFFORD A REPLACEMENT!
PET
CITY
4

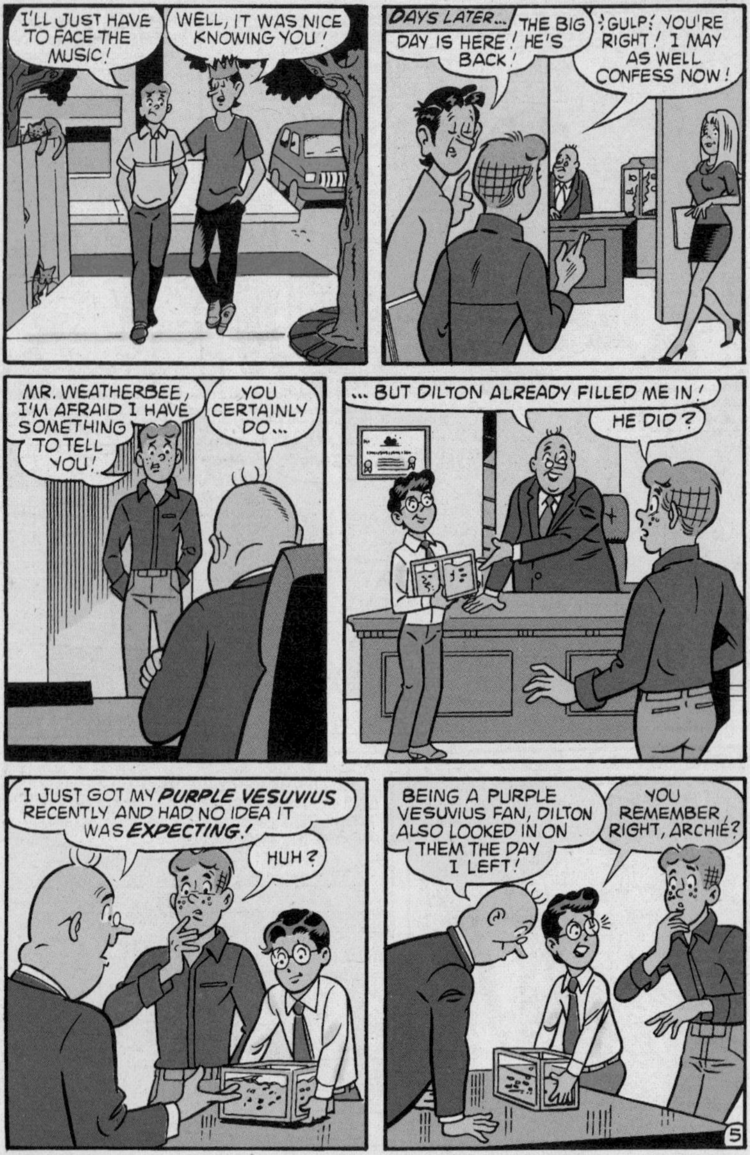

I'LL JUST HAVE TO FACE THE MUSIC!
WELL, IT WAS NICE KNOWING YOU!
DAYS LATER...
THE BIG DAY IS HERE! HE'S BACK!
GULP! YOU'RE RIGHT! I MAY AS WELL CONFESS NOW!
MR. WEATHERBEE, I'M AFRAID I HAVE SOMETHING TO TELL YOU!
YOU CERTAINLY DO...
... BUT DILTON ALREADY FILLED ME IN!
HE DID?
I JUST GOT MY PURPLE VESUVIUS RECENTLY AND HAD NO IDEA IT WAS EXPECTING!
HUH?
BEING A PURPLE VESUVIUS FAN, DILTON ALSO LOOKED IN ON THEM THE DAY I LEFT!
YOU REMEMBER, RIGHT, ARCHIE?
5

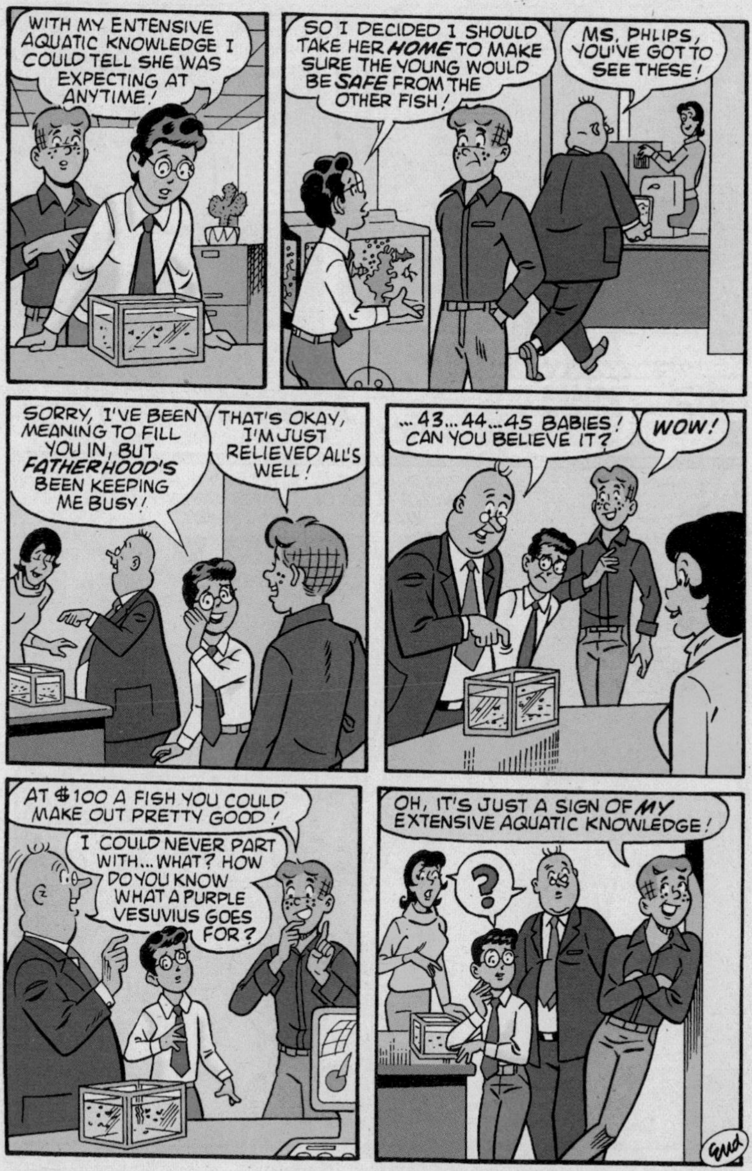
WITH MY ENTENSIVE AQUATIC KNOWLEDGE I COULD TELL SHE WAS EXPECTING AT ANYTIME!
SO I DECIDED I SHOULD TAKE HER HOME TO MAKE SURE THE YOUNG WOULD BE SAFE FROM THE OTHER FISH!
MS. PHLIPS, YOU'VE GOT TO SEE THESE!
SORRY, I'VE BEEN MEANING TO FILL YOU IN, BUT FATHERHOOD'S BEEN KEEPING ME BUSY!
THAT'S OKAY, I'M JUST RELIEVED ALL'S WELL!
...43...44...45 BABIES! CAN YOU BELIEVE IT?
WOW!
AT $100 A FISH YOU COULD MAKE OUT PRETTY GOOD!
I COULD NEVER PART WITH... WHAT? HOW DO YOU KNOW WHAT A PURPLE VESUVIUS GOES FOR?
OH, IT'S JUST A SIGN OF MY EXTENSIVE AQUATIC KNOWLEDGE!
?
END

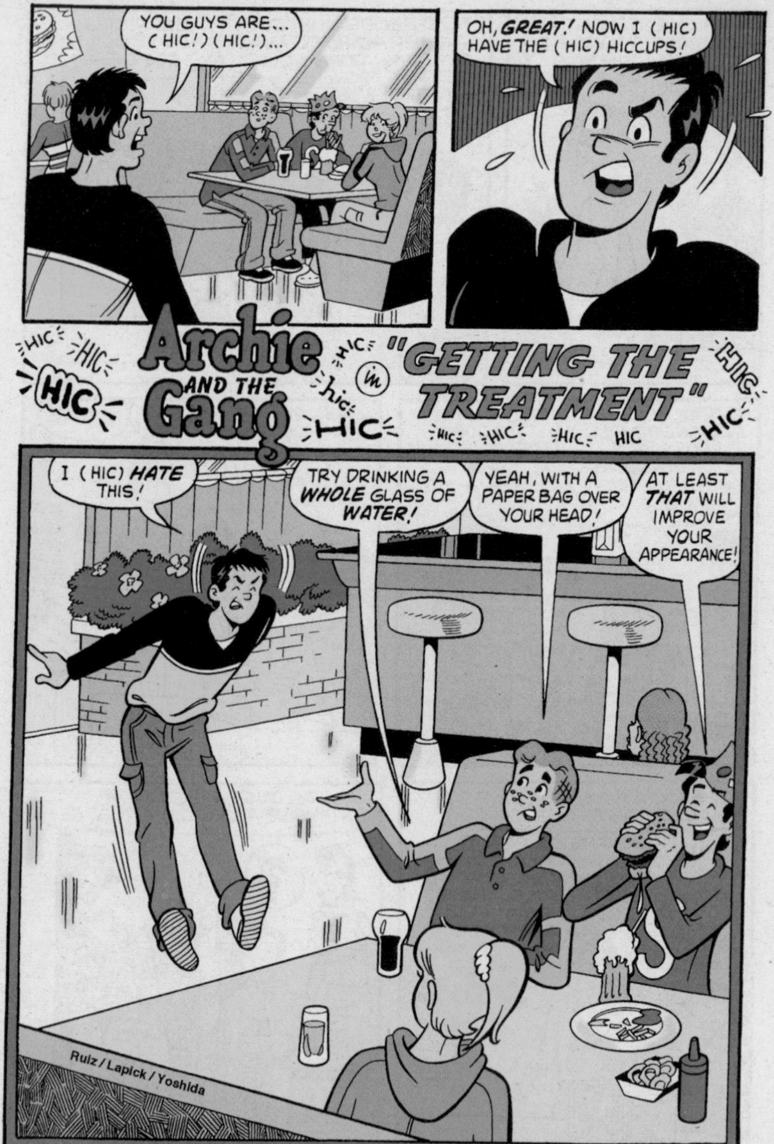

YOU GUYS ARE... (HIC!) (HIC!)...
OH, GREAT! NOW I (HIC) HAVE THE (HIC) HICCUPS!
HIC HIC HIC
Archie AND THE Gang
HIC hic HIC
in
"GETTING THE TREATMENT"
HIC HIC HIC HIC HIC HIC HIC
I (HIC) HATE THIS!
TRY DRINKING A WHOLE GLASS OF WATER!
YEAH, WITH A PAPER BAG OVER YOUR HEAD!
AT LEAST THAT WILL IMPROVE YOUR APPEARANCE!
Ruiz / Lapick / Yoshida

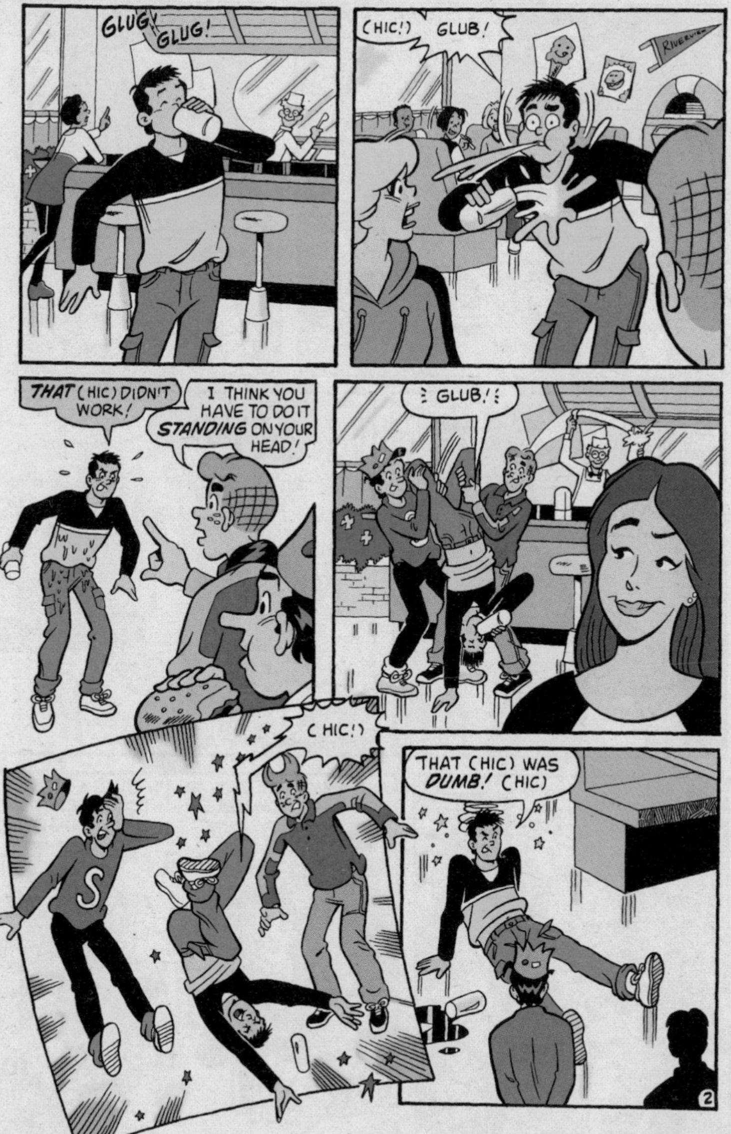
GLUG! GLUG!
(HIC!) GLUB!
RIVERVIEW
THAT (HIC) DIDN'T WORK!
I THINK YOU HAVE TO DO IT STANDING ON YOUR HEAD!
GLUB!
(HIC!)
THAT (HIC) WAS DUMB! (HIC)

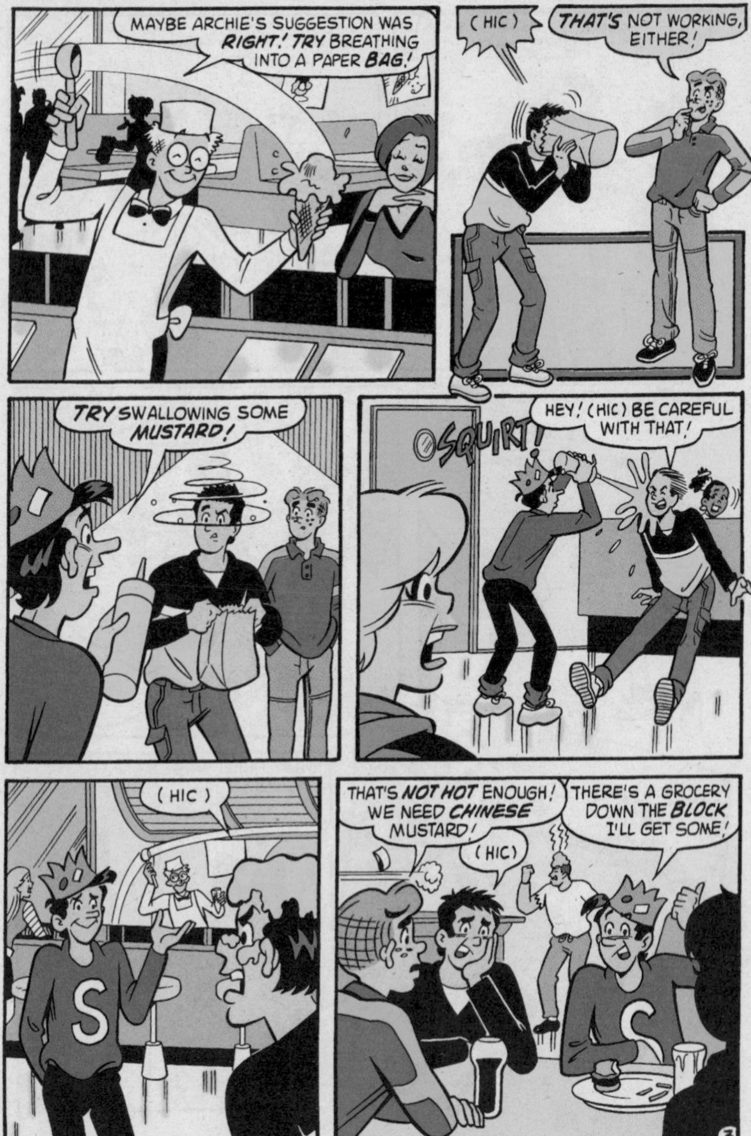
MAYBE ARCHIE'S SUGGESTION WAS RIGHT! TRY BREATHING INTO A PAPER BAG!
(HIC)
THAT'S NOT WORKING, EITHER!
TRY SWALLOWING SOME MUSTARD!
SQUIRT!
HEY! (HIC) BE CAREFUL WITH THAT!
(HIC)
THAT'S NOT HOT ENOUGH! WE NEED CHINESE MUSTARD!
(HIC)
THERE'S A GROCERY DOWN THE BLOCK I'LL GET SOME!
3

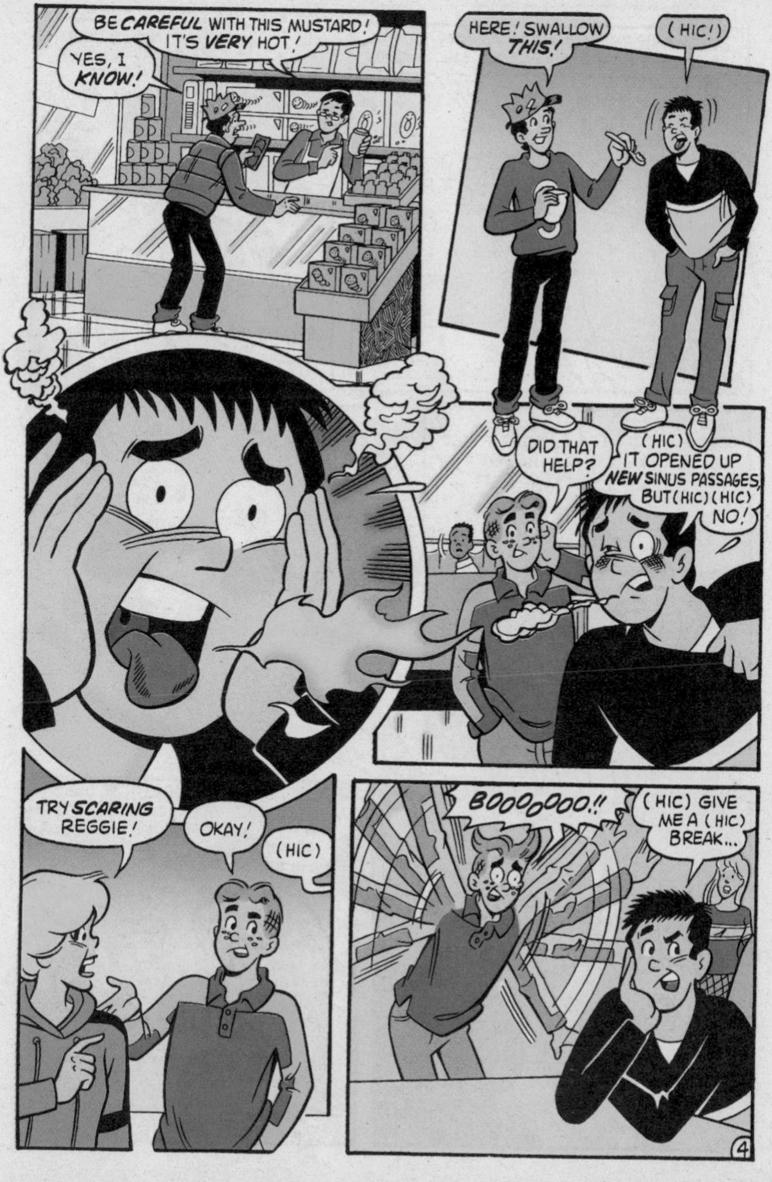
BE CAREFUL WITH THIS MUSTARD! IT'S VERY HOT!
YES, I KNOW!
HERE! SWALLOW THIS!
(HIC!)
DID THAT HELP?
(HIC) IT OPENED UP NEW SINUS PASSAGES, BUT (HIC) (HIC) NO!
TRY SCARING REGGIE!
OKAY!
(HIC)
BOOOOOOO!!
(HIC) GIVE ME A (HIC) BREAK...

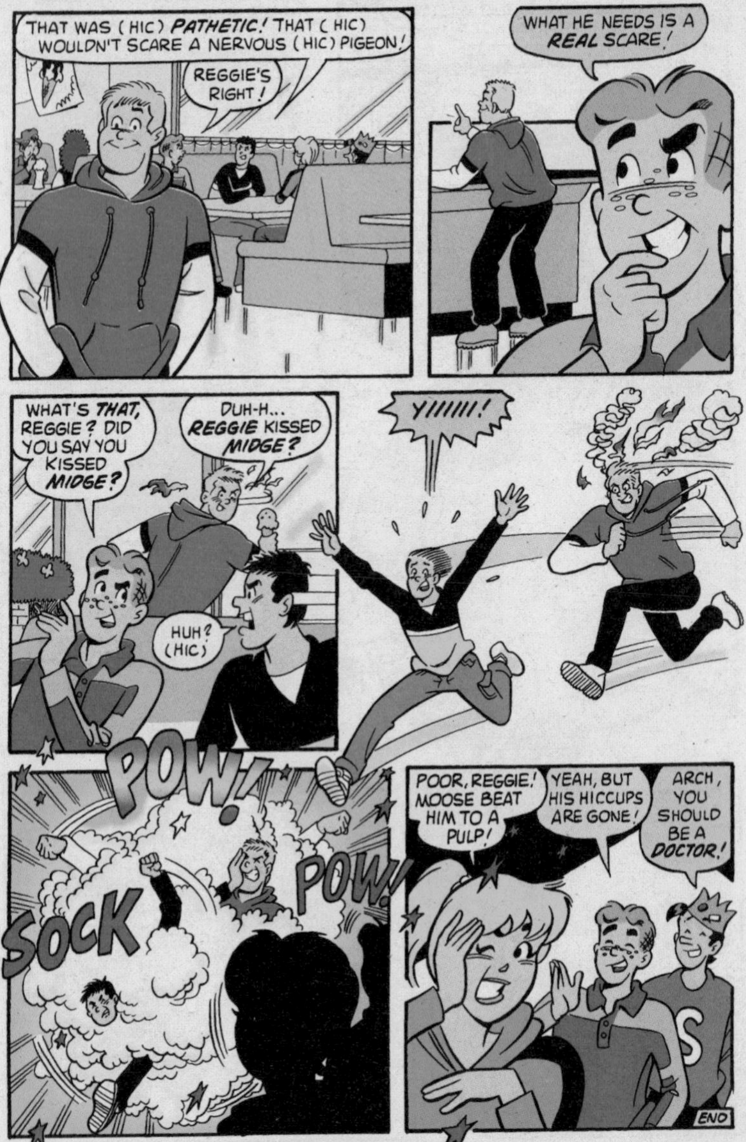

THAT WAS (HIC) PATHETIC! THAT (HIC) WOULDN'T SCARE A NERVOUS (HIC) PIGEON!
REGGIE'S RIGHT!
WHAT HE NEEDS IS A REAL SCARE!
WHAT'S THAT, REGGIE? DID YOU SAY YOU KISSED MIDGE?
DUH-H... REGGIE KISSED MIDGE?
HUH? (HIC)
YIIIIII!
POW!
SOCK
POW!
POOR, REGGIE! MOOSE BEAT HIM TO A PULP!
YEAH, BUT HIS HICCUPS ARE GONE!
ARCH, YOU SHOULD BE A DOCTOR!
END

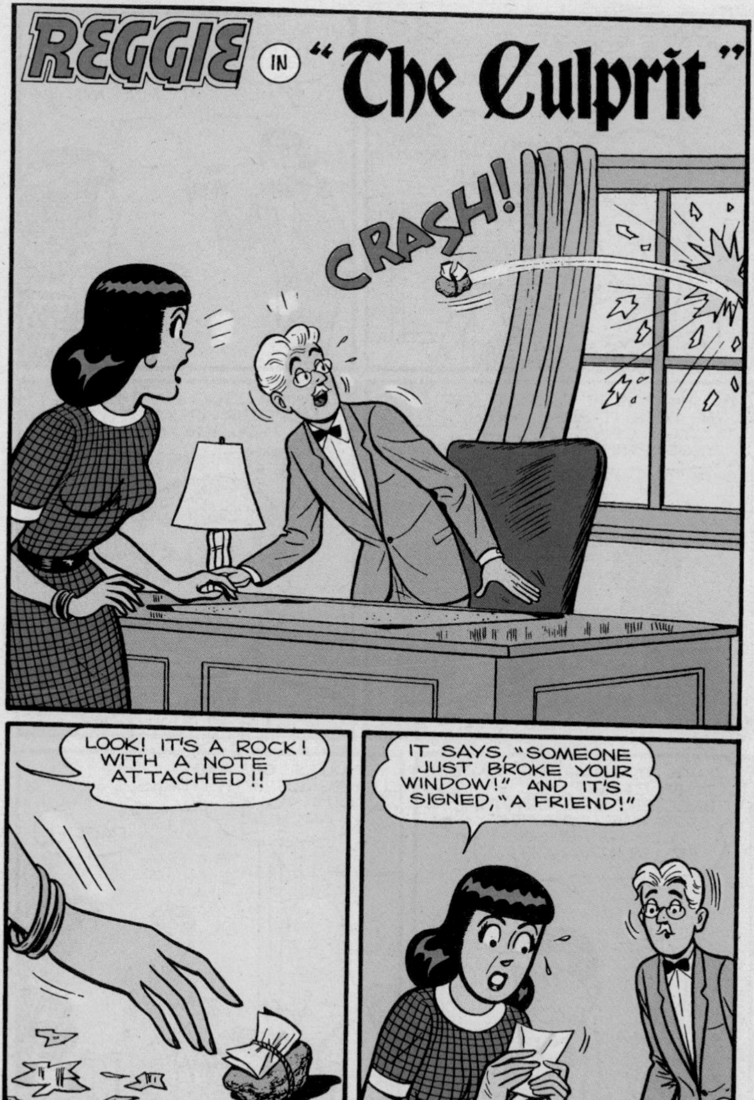
REGGIE IN "The Culprit"
CRASH!
LOOK! IT'S A ROCK! WITH A NOTE ATTACHED!!
IT SAYS, "SOMEONE JUST BROKE YOUR WINDOW!" AND IT'S SIGNED, "A FRIEND!"
1

Script: Frank Doyle / Art: Bill Vigoda

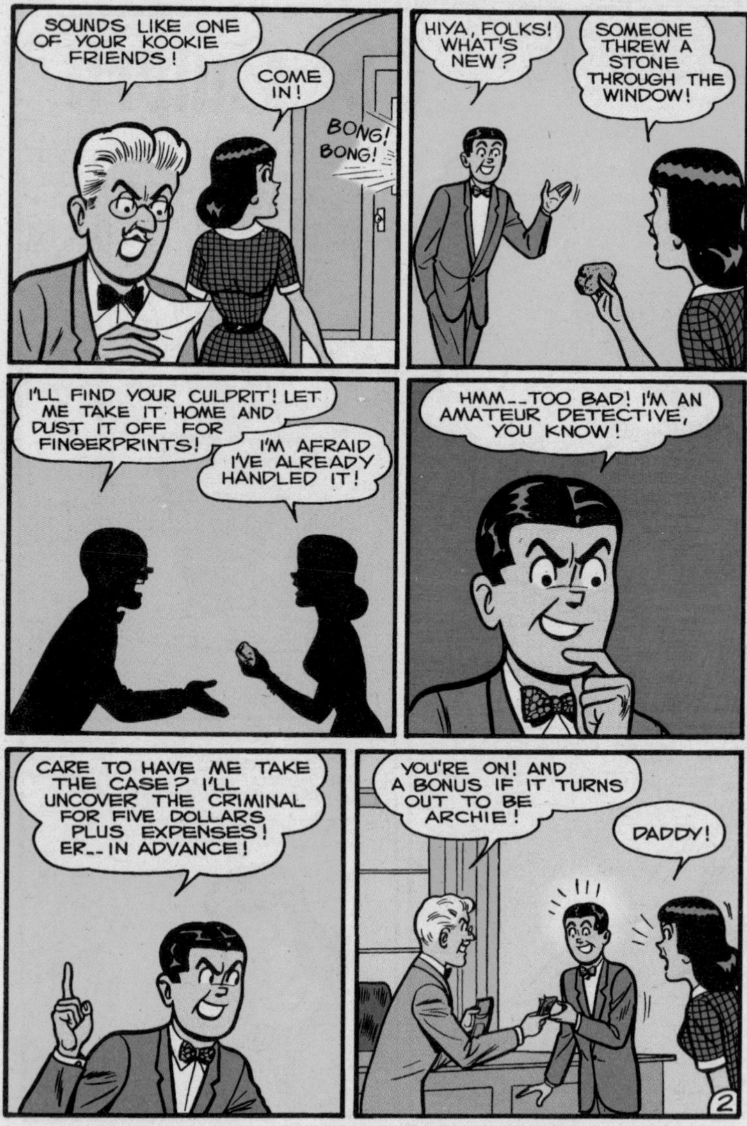
SOUNDS LIKE ONE OF YOUR KOOKIE FRIENDS!
COME IN!
BONG! BONG!
HIYA, FOLKS! WHAT'S NEW?
SOMEONE THREW A STONE THROUGH THE WINDOW!
I'LL FIND YOUR CULPRIT! LET ME TAKE IT HOME AND DUST IT OFF FOR FINGERPRINTS!
I'M AFRAID I'VE ALREADY HANDLED IT!
HMM--TOO BAD! I'M AN AMATEUR DETECTIVE, YOU KNOW!
CARE TO HAVE ME TAKE THE CASE? I'LL UNCOVER THE CRIMINAL FOR FIVE DOLLARS PLUS EXPENSES! ER-- IN ADVANCE!
YOU'RE ON! AND A BONUS IF IT TURNS OUT TO BE ARCHIE!
DADDY!
2

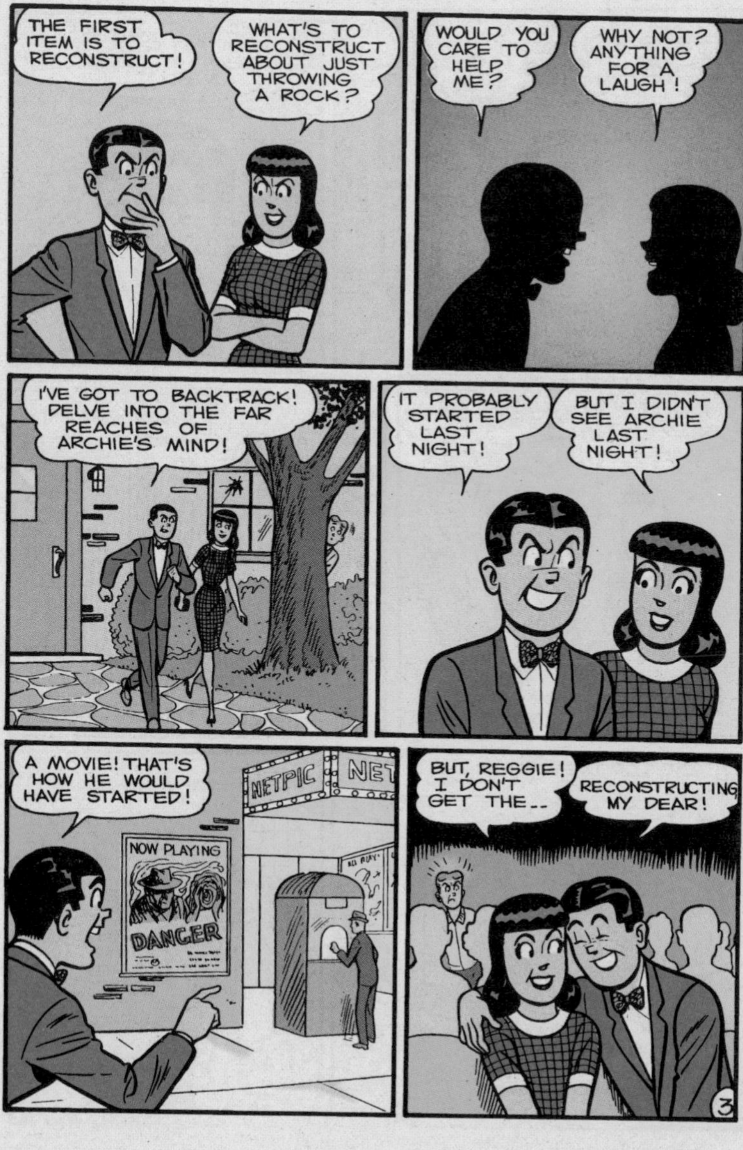
THE FIRST ITEM IS TO RECONSTRUCT!
WHAT'S TO RECONSTRUCT ABOUT JUST THROWING A ROCK?
WOULD YOU CARE TO HELP ME?
WHY NOT? ANYTHING FOR A LAUGH!
I'VE GOT TO BACKTRACK! DELVE INTO THE FAR REACHES OF ARCHIE'S MIND!
IT PROBABLY STARTED LAST NIGHT!
BUT I DIDN'T SEE ARCHIE LAST NIGHT!
A MOVIE! THAT'S HOW HE WOULD HAVE STARTED!
NETPIC
NET
NOW PLAYING
DANGER
BUT, REGGIE! I DON'T GET THE..
RECONSTRUCTING, MY DEAR!
3

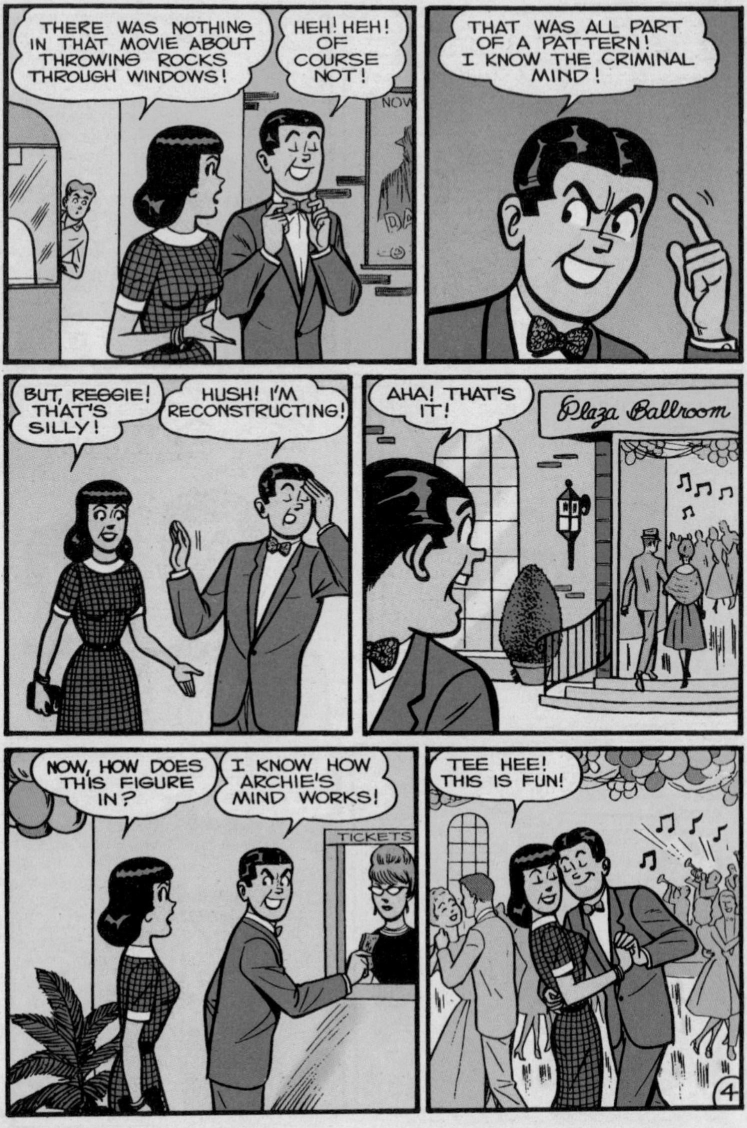
THERE WAS NOTHING IN THAT MOVIE ABOUT THROWING ROCKS THROUGH WINDOWS!
HEH! HEH! OF COURSE NOT!
NOW
THAT WAS ALL PART OF A PATTERN! I KNOW THE CRIMINAL MIND!
BUT, REGGIE! THAT'S SILLY!
HUSH! I'M RECONSTRUCTING!
AHA! THAT'S IT!
Plaza Ballroom
NOW, HOW DOES THIS FIGURE IN?
I KNOW HOW ARCHIE'S MIND WORKS!
TICKETS
TEE HEE! THIS IS FUN!
4

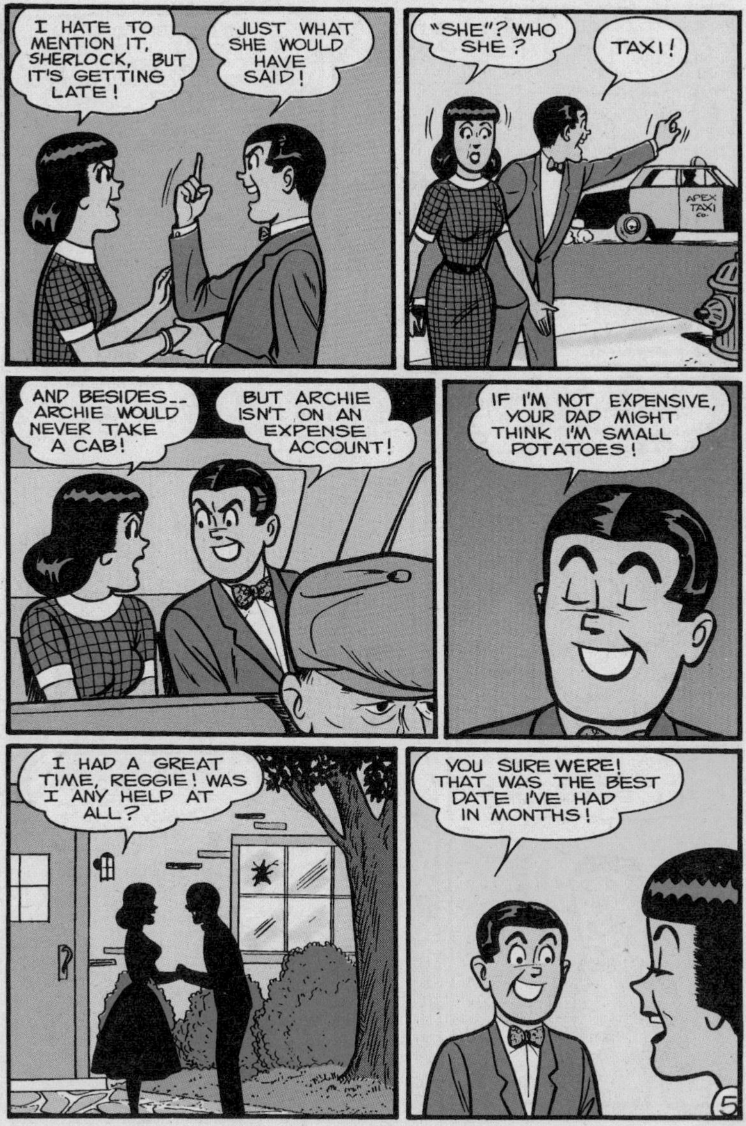
I HATE TO MENTION IT, SHERLOCK, BUT IT'S GETTING LATE!
JUST WHAT SHE WOULD HAVE SAID!
"SHE"? WHO SHE?
TAXI!
APEX TAXI CO.
AND BESIDES-- ARCHIE WOULD NEVER TAKE A CAB!
BUT ARCHIE ISN'T ON AN EXPENSE ACCOUNT!
IF I'M NOT EXPENSIVE, YOUR DAD MIGHT THINK I'M SMALL POTATOES!
I HAD A GREAT TIME, REGGIE! WAS I ANY HELP AT ALL?
YOU SURE WERE! THAT WAS THE BEST DATE I'VE HAD IN MONTHS!
5

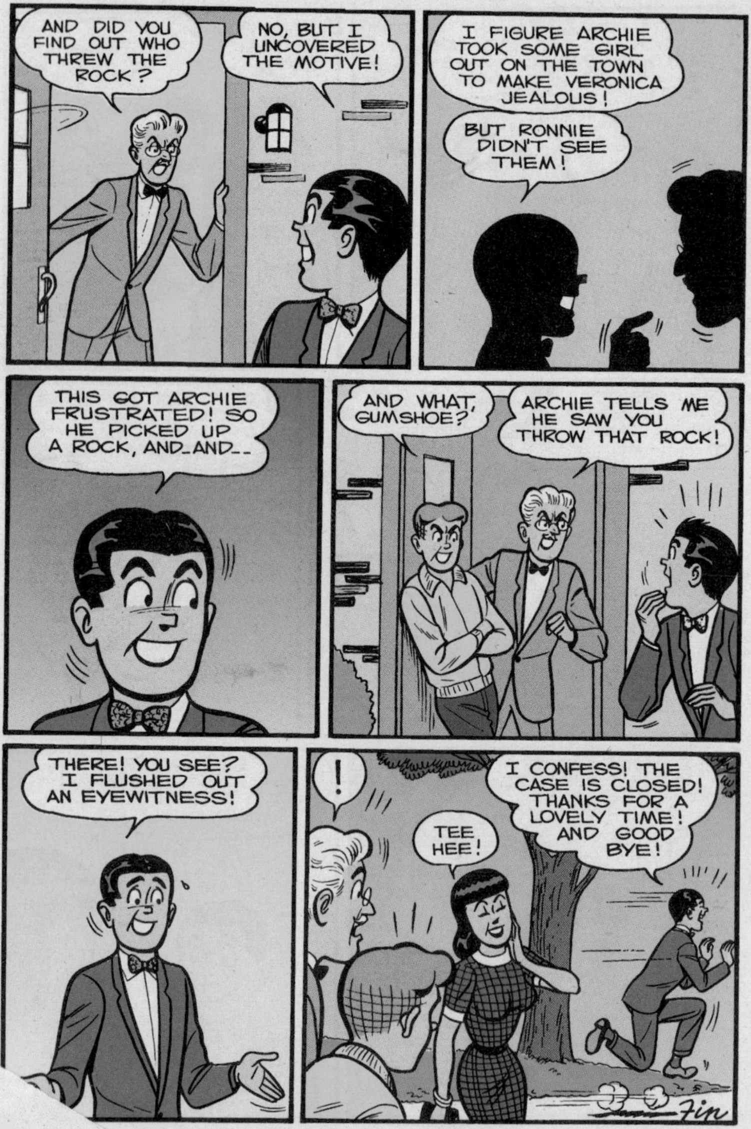

AND DID YOU FIND OUT WHO THREW THE ROCK?
NO, BUT I UNCOVERED THE MOTIVE!
I FIGURE ARCHIE TOOK SOME GIRL OUT ON THE TOWN TO MAKE VERONICA JEALOUS!
BUT RONNIE DIDN'T SEE THEM!
THIS GOT ARCHIE FRUSTRATED! SO HE PICKED UP A ROCK, AND-AND--
AND WHAT, GUMSHOE?
ARCHIE TELLS ME HE SAW YOU THROW THAT ROCK!
THERE! YOU SEE? I FLUSHED OUT AN EYEWITNESS!
!
TEE HEE!
I CONFESS! THE CASE IS CLOSED! THANKS FOR A LOVELY TIME! AND GOOD BYE!
Fin